Praise for the *Chronicles of the Cheysuli:*

"With every book, the magic of Jennifer Roberson waxes stronger and stronger. Wrought with an epic mysticism and power, the continuing strands of the Cheysuli saga glimmer with the sheen of excellence as they weave their way into a landmark collection of fantasy literature."   —*Rave Reviews*

"Roberson writes in a beautifully lyrical style, with a perceptive sense of drama that enthralls the reader."
—*Romantic Times*

"Roberson is one of the very best writers working in this kind of fantasy, and the Cheysuli series stands out from the crowd of similar novels."
—*Science Fiction Chronicle*

"Roberson is a master at character building. . . . very good reading, indeed."   —*Kliatt*

Jennifer Roberson

CHILDREN OF THE LION

THE CHRONICLES OF THE CHEYSULI
OMNIBUS THREE

Book Five
A PRIDE OF PRINCES

Book Six
DAUGHTER OF THE LION

DAW BOOKS, INC.
DONALD A. WOLLHEIM, FOUNDER
375 Hudson Street, New York, NY 10014

ELIZABETH R. WOLLHEIM
SHEILA E. GILBERT
PUBLISHERS
www.dawbooks.com

First Paperback Printing, August 2001
1 2 3 4 5 6 7 8 9

CHILDREN OF
THE LION

the Tuble Ocean

Valgaar

Atvia

Andemir

Homana

Rondule

Kilore

Mujhara

Erinn

Lestra

the Idrian Ocean

Solinde

Hondarth

the
Crystal Isle

Danjorith 1984

A Pride of Princes

Prologue

The cavern was dense with smoke. The woman stepped through and dutifully it followed, purling in her wake. It gathered along the hem of her skirts like puppies on a bitch, suckling at her feet.

She walked from shadow into glare, into the pure clean light of *godfire* as it leaped from a circular rent in the stone floor. A hole, like a wound in the earth itself, bleeding flame.

Sparks issued forth, fell, formed a glowing necklet on the nap of her velvet gown. But she did not flinch as they died; the fire—like the sparks—was cold.

Beyond the flame, she saw her brother. Standing as he stood so often, for hours on end, and days, at the rim of the netherworld. *Godfire* bathed his face in its lurid lavender glare, limning the magnificent planes of his bones. A beautiful man, her brother; she might have been jealous, once, but she knew she claimed more power.

He saw her. He smiled. In the light his eyes were mirrors.

Briefly the flame died back; was sucked down, withdrawn, like a tongue into a mouth. But the afterglow remained, shrouding him in light. A transcendent luminescence that made her want to squint.

Beneath her feet, the floor was hard and sharp. The entire cavern was formed of black, glassy basalt, faceted as a gemstone. There were no torches in deference to the *godfire*; there was no need for manmade light when the Seker lent them his.

All around her columns gleamed. Slow spirals mimicked blown glass, delicately fluted; twisted strands, oddly seductive, stretched from floor to ceiling. Light lost itself in endless glassy whorls. The world ran wet with fire.

She crossed, hearing the echoes of her steps and the chime of girdle, silver on black, nearly lost in the weight of velvet. As always, she smelled the breath of the god. But to her, it was not unpleasant. The promise of power was a heady scent that set her flesh to tingling.

She paused on the brink of the orifice. "How long has it been since you ate?"

He smiled. "Trust you to concern yourself with things such as food."

"How long, Strahan?"

He shrugged; smoke shrugged with him. "A day, two, three—what does it matter, Lillith? I will hardly waste away in the service of the god."

Briefly she glanced down. They stood but six feet apart; between them lay a world. The world of Asar-Suti.

They had only to open the Gate—

Not yet. There was time.

Time for the fruition of their plans.

"Come up," she said. "You should eat."

His hair, like hers, was black. And it flowed back from a brow as smooth and unlined as a girl's, though there was nothing girlish about him. It cloaked his shoulders and reached beyond, bound back by a silver fillet wrought with Ihlini runes. In the glare of the *godfire* his gray suede leathers were dyed an eerie lilac, glowing purple in the creases. The doublet hung open from throat and chest, and in the gap she saw the white edge of a linen tunic. Soft gray boots stretched to his thighs. His wide belt was clasped with a two-headed silver serpent.

Lillith sighed as he did not answer. She was his sister, not mother or father. But both parents were long dead, and so this fell to her. "Will you come up?"

"I am hungry," he admitted, "but for something more than food. And I am thirsty, also, but the wine I want is blood. The blood of Niall's sons."

His eyes were alight with something more than reflected glare. One brown, one blue; even *she* had difficulty looking past the mismatched pairing to the emotions in their depths. But she looked, and she saw, and knew his patience was nearly ended.

"A little longer," she said. "Surely you can wait."

"No. I *have* waited. I am *done* with waiting." He smiled his beautiful, beguiling smile. "Lillith—I am *hungry.*"

"Time," she said. "We have all the years of our lives."

"*They* do not. They are human, even if Cheysuli. They die. They live seventy, eighty years, and they die. While *we* are still but children."

"*You* are still a child." Lillith laughed, and the girdle chimed. "The last time I counted *mine*, my years were nearly two hundred."

He grunted, unimpressed; he was young in years, compared to her, but his power grew every day. "I have need of them, Lillith. The sons are no longer infants, no longer boys. They are men. Warriors. If we wait much longer—"

"But we will." Lillith shrugged naked shoulders. "We will wait as long as we must, and longer. Until the time is right."

"Twenty years, Lillith!" His shout reverberated in the hidden shadows of the cavern. "Twenty years since Niall thwarted me."

"Twenty years is but half a day to us." But she saw his frustration and felt a measure of her own. "I know. I know, Strahan . . . I weary of it, also. But we are close. The game begins—all of the pieces are in place. As you say, now they are of an age to make a difference."

"Of an age to serve me well." In the light, his mismatched eyes were eerie. "I want them. I want them here, within the walls of Valgaard, so I may make them mine. Mine to rule, as I will have *them* rule." He laughed suddenly, and their eyes locked in perfect accordance across the Gate of Asar-Suti. "When they are mine, Niall's sons, I will set them on their thrones, all three of them . . . I will take their *lir* and take their minds, *all three of them,* making them faithful Ihlini minions—" He broke off a moment, considering his words; continued in quiet, abiding contentment, "—and then *I* shall rule through their empty bodies in the name of Asar-Suti."

Lillith smiled, nodded, sketched an idle rune in the air between them that pulsed with purple *godfire*. It spun, whirled, twisted; tied itself in knots, was gone. "Of course. It is to be expected; we have laid our plans." She paused. "*Now* will you come up?"

"Up," he echoed. "Aye. In a moment. There is something I must do."

And in the eerie lurid light, Strahan the Ihlini knelt in deep obeisance to the god of the netherworld.

PART I

One

The sun hung low in the west, painting the city rose-red, ocher-gold, russet-brown. Sunlight, trapped and multiplied by mullioned glass, made mirrors of countless windows. Mujhara was ablaze with gilded glory.

The one-eyed man stood alone upon the curtain wall surrounding the massive palace of Homana-Mujhar. Spilling in all directions from the battlements was the royal city, home of kings and queens; home of the Mujhars of Homana. Home to countless others of lesser birth as well; he could not even begin to estimate Mujhara's population. He knew only that the number had increased one hundredfold, perhaps one *thousandfold*, over the past two weeks. The festival was even larger than his brother had predicted.

"Everyone will come," Ian had said, *"from everywhere, even the other realms. Scoff if you like, Niall, but it is past time the Homanans paid homage to their Mujhar. More than past time they showed their gratitude for twenty years of peaceful rule."*

Twenty years. It seemed longer than that. And then, at times, it seemed only days since he had assumed the Lion Throne from his Cheysuli father, Donal, who had given himself over to the death-ritual on the plague-born deaths of his *lir*. With Taj and Lorn gone, there had been nothing left for Donal, save madness. And no Cheysuli warrior willingly gave himself over to madness. Not when there was a choice. Not when there was the death-ritual, which was surely more merciful than madness.

Niall sighed deeply, frowning down at the street far below the curtain wall, and the smooth earthwork ridge that girded the lower portions of the thick wall. He could hear the distant sounds of celebration: faint ringing tambors of the street-dancers; cries of stall-merchants; shouts and screams of children in their finery, turned loose to play in crowded streets and alleys.

Dead so long, my jehan. He readily acknowledged the still familiar pain. There was grief. Regret. Even bitterness, that a man so strong and healthy as his father should throw his life away.

Homanan thinking, he told himself wryly, made aware yet again of the division in his attitudes; how pervasive that division could be. *Have you forgotten the oaths you made when you accepted the responsibilities of the* lir-*bond before Clan Council?*

No. Of course he had not forgotten. But it was difficult to be two men at once: one, born of a Homanan mother, who was the daughter of a king; the other born of a Cheysuli shapechanger, a warrior with a *lir,* and claiming all the magic the gods had given the race.

Automatically he looked for Serri, but the wolf was not with him. His lips tightened in annoyance. How could he have forgotten Serri was in the royal apartments?

Because, he told himself ironically, in a spasm of defensiveness, *with all the toasting going on, it is fortunate you can remember your own* name, *let alone Serri's whereabouts.*

Still, it displeased him that he could forget for even a moment. A sign of age, he wondered?

Niall abruptly laughed aloud. Perhaps. No doubt his children would agree he was aging, but *he* thought not. At forty, there were decades ahead of him still.

And then he recalled that his own father had not been so much older than forty when the loss of his *lir* had ended his life. His mother as well was gone; Aislinn, Queen of Homana, had died ten years after Donal. Some said of grief that grew too strong.

He stopped the laughter. Memories welled up. Most of them Niall had believed buried too deeply to trouble him. The gods knew he had *tried* to bury them; with drink, with daily council sessions lasting from dawn till midnight, with abrupt departures—*escapes*—into the woodlands with Serri, seeking respite in his *lir*-shape. But Deirdre had made him realize none of those things held the answers; that he would have to find a place for each memory and let it live there, where he could look at it from time to time and know what was lost, was gained, was learned.

Deirdre. The memories of her were fresh, beloved, cherished, and very near the surface. But there were other ones as well, buried more deeply: of guilt, of fear, of self-hatred, because once he had believed her murdered by his own unintended instigation. No matter how helpless, how unknowing he had been, trapped within the Ihlini web of madness, deceit, and sorcery, he could not think of that time in his life without experiencing a fresh burst of shame, guilt, pain.

"So." She approached from his right side, his blind side; he had not heard her, either. "With all your great palace in an uproar, you'll be coming out here to escape it." Deirdre smiled, glancing over the nearest crenel to look upon the crowded city. "Peace in turbulence, then?"

Though she had been with him twenty years in Homana, she had not lost the lilt of Erinn. He smiled. "Aye, escape, except there *is* no escape. Everywhere I turn there is a servant telling me I must go here, go there—even Ian. Even *you.*"

Deirdre laughed, green eyes alight, and moved in close to his side. His arm settled around her shoulders automatically. She wore green, as she so often did, to play up the color of her eyes. It suited her, as did the torque of braided gold and carved green jade he had given her the night before. "But 'tis for *you* all of this is being done," she reminded him tartly. "D'ye wish to disappoint so many people who have come here to pay their respects?"

He grimaced. "You make it sound like I am dead."

Deirdre leaned her head against his chest. She was neither tall nor short, but he was head and shoulders above most men, even the Cheysuli. "No, not dead," she said calmly. "Very much alive—or so you would have *me* thinking; I who share your bed."

Niall laughed and hugged her against his chest. "Aye, well, there is that." His fingers smoothed the weave of her braided hair. A year younger than he, she looked no more her thirty-nine years than his daughters. The hair was still thick and brassy gold; the skin still fair and smooth, with only a shallow threading of lines by her eyes; her hips and breasts, respectively, still slender and firm as a girl's.

"What were you thinking?" she asked.

"Remembering," he answered. "The night I stood atop the dragon's skull in Atvia, and lit the beacon-fire."

Deirdre stiffened. "Why?" she asked. She pulled away and faced him. "*Why*, Nial—why that? 'Twas more than twenty years ago."

"*That* is why," he told her. "Twenty years. The Homanans are even now celebrating twenty years of my rule, and all *I* can see are the memories of what I nearly did that many years ago." His voice was unsteady; he steadied it. "I killed your father, Deirdre. And nearly the rest of the eagles."

His pain was reflected in her face. "You fool," she said softly. "Oh, ye great silly fool. Liam would be taking his fist to you, he would. I *should*." She shook her head and sighed. "Aye, Shea died, but he took the assassin with him. Else we *would* all be dead, and you could be blaming yourself for that." Firmly, she shook her head. "You lit the fire, 'tis true, but 'twas Alaric's doing. Thanks to his addled daughter."

Addled daughter. Gisella of Atvia, half Cheysuli herself, and Niall's full cousin. Poor mad Gisella, who had married the Prince of Homana; Niall, now called Mujhar. The Queen of Homana, who now resided in Atvia in permanent exile from the land of her mother's birth.

He sighed. "Aye. 'Tis done, as *you* would say. But I cannot forget it."

"Then don't. Come in, instead, where a bath is being poured." She took his hand. "Are you forgetting? There is to be a feast for you in the Great Hall."

"Oh, gods, not again," he blurted. "Who is host tonight?"

"Prince Einar, heir to the King of Caledon," Deirdre answered, smiling. "The one you want to make a new trade alliance with."

He strolled with her along the sentry-walk. "Aye, I do. The old one is far out of date; there are more concessions to be won. Without them, we lose more money than we make, which serves Homana not at all. What I *want* to get—"

"No," Deirdre said firmly. "No, don't be filling my ears with that. I've been hearing too much of it these past two weeks, and I'll hear more of it over my food. *No*, Niall—not now."

He laughed. "Well enough, *meijha*—not now. I am sick of it myself."

The sentry-walk was not wide enough for two to walk abreast comfortably, not when one was as large as Niall. He moved Deirdre away from the edge, closer to the wall, and assumed the risk himself. Below them, in the other bailey, men-at-arms in new crimson livery practiced a close-order drill. The shouted orders from the captain carried easily to the sentry-walk, though Deirdre and Niall were still some distance away. It was easiest to stay on the wall and follow it around than to go down into the baileys, which were thronged with royal escorts and honor guards from other realms.

Niall sighed. "I think Homana-Mujhar will burst before the month is through. Certainly Mujhara will."

Deirdre frowned absently. "Einar," she said. " 'Twas him, was it not, so dissatisfied with his chambers?"

Niall snorted inelegantly. "*You* are chatelaine of this great sprawl of red stone, *meijha,* not I."

Deirdre's face cleared. "Aye, 'twas him. He demanded better quarters."

"Well, he *is* a king's son—and the heir to Caledon."

"And what of the heir to Ellas?" Deirdre demanded. "Am I to put Diarmuid out just because Einar wants his room?"

"What *did* you do?" Niall asked curiously.

Deirdre grinned. "Homana-Mujhar is filled to bursting, my lord Mujhar. I made them share."

Niall's shout of laughter erased the lines of tension that had etched themselves into his face as a result of trying to juggle multiple princes, envoys, cousins, and heirs without giving offense to any. Deirdre felt he needed no more lines at all, regardless of his responsibilities; Strahan's demon-hawk had already ruined enough of his face. A patch hid the empty right socket and most of the scarring, but the old talon weals still scored the bridge of his nose and much of his right cheek, as well as dividing one tawny eyebrow neatly in half.

She glanced up at his face. To her, it was familiar, beloved, unremarkable, save for the unmistakable stamp of

Cheysuli pride, even if he lacked the coloring. But to others, unaccustomed to the disfigurement, he was noteworthy only in that respect. *She* had first known him as a young man, at eighteen, when the handsome looks of his maternal grandsire, Carillon, had been fresh, boyish, as yet unformed by adversity. But the demon-born hawk of Asar-Suti had robbed him of his boyhood in addition to his looks.

For that, if for nothing else, Deirdre hated Strahan.

Through the casements of the palace came the dim glow of new-lit candles. The rose-red hue of the stone deepened as the sun dropped down behind the massive walls, from pink to dull, bloodied gray. Deirdre suppressed a shiver; there were times, she thought, Homana-Mujhar resembled a monument to war and death, rather than the home of Homanan kings.

Niall took her off the sentry-walk into one of the exterior corner towers, then down a coil of stairs to the interior of the palace. Deirdre had always felt Homana-Mujhar more confusing than Kilore, the clifftop fortress her brother Liam ruled from in Erinn. Kilore, known as the Aerie of Erinn, was plainer, more functional, lacking the multitudinous staircases and tower chambers of Homana-Mujhar. But then perhaps it was only time and distance that made it seem so; Deirdre had not been home in eighteen years.

"We should go," she said abruptly, as Niall took her into his chamber. Protocol required they keep separate apartments, and so they did—even had they wed, it would have been the same—but more often they spent the nights in his. "We should go to visit Liam before we are old and gray."

Niall bent to greet the black-masked silver wolf who got up from his place in the huge draperied tester bed to lean against one thigh-booted, royal leg. Their brief communion was intensely private, intensely singular, but Deirdre was used to it. No one came between a warrior and his *lir*, not even the woman he loved.

Serri, his greeting complete, went back to the bed. Niall smiled, brushed back a lock of hair from his brow and looked at Deirdre in amusement. "The gray begins already, *meijha*—perhaps we should leave for Erinn tomorrow."

"Ah, ye *skilfin*, you're no more gray than I am!" But she put a hand to her heavy braid as if to reassure herself she bore no tainted strands. " 'Tis serious I am, Niall—how many times must Liam invite us? And I his own sister?"

"And still a princess of Erinn." Niall stopped abruptly as he shut the heavy door behind her. "Ah, Deirdre, will you forgive me for that? You deserve to be a queen."

Astonished, she stared up at him. One slim hand was locked in his plain brown doublet. "Niall . . ." Slowly she shook her head. "Ah, no—d'ye think 'tis what I want? No, no, my love—'tis nothing to me, I swear, this thing of ti- tles." Her mouth flattened, then twisted scornfully. "Queen of Homana, indeed. Well, I say let Gisella keep it—'tis all she has. I have *you*."

"Not so much, I think," he said mildly, but bent his head to kiss her.

A knock at the door intruded. "My lord? My lord Mujhar? Taggart, my lord . . . are you there?"

Niall sighed. "A moment," he promised her, and went to open the door. "Aye, Taggart, I am. What is it?"

Taggart was a slim, wiry man of fifty, clad in Homanan colors: black tunic with a red rampant lion stitched over his left breast. His trews were also black, with a gilt-buckled red leather belt cinching his waist. Graying hair was trimmed neatly against his head. He bowed briefly. "My lord—it is the princes."

Niall looked past the man to the empty corridor. "Oh? Where?"

Taggart was clearly uncomfortable. "My lord—not *here*. That is why *I* am here." He paused. "Because they are *not*."

The Mujhar's tawny brows rose a trifle. "Taggart, what are you trying to tell me? And make haste—my bath is getting cold."

Taggart bowed again, eloquent apology. "My lord, I— well—" He paused. "They are missing."

"Missing?" Niall smiled indulgently. "For the moment, perhaps, but I am sure they are here somewhere. You might try the stables; Brennan has a new stallion. Or the guardroom, if Hart has coin enough left for a fortune- game." He shrugged negligently, patently unconcerned by the temporary disappearance of his three sons. "And only the *gods* know what Corin may have suggested as an after- noon's diversion."

"Or Keely," Deirdre added dryly.

"My lord, no," Taggart said plainly. "I have looked in all those places. They are not here. They are not in Homana-Mujhar."

Deirdre came up to Niall's left side, where he could see her clearly; it was a habit she encouraged in everyone so he would not be embarrassed unduly or caught off guard. "They knew about the banquet," she said, though it sounded more question than statement. "I know they did; Brennan remarked on it. He said he did not think much of Einar, or Einar's cousin, Reynald." She nodded, frowning a little. " 'Tis what he said, did Brennan about the Caledonese princes."

Niall heaved a weary sigh of distracted annoyance and scratched at the scars in his right cheek. "Well, if *Brennan* remarked on it, then it took Hart to persuade him to leave so soon before a banquet. And Hart, likely, was talked into it by Corin. Oh, gods—" he cast a long-suffering glance at the ceiling, "—when you saw fit to bless me with three sons, you might have given me proper ones. Ones who know how to respect their *jehan's* wishes." He shook his head. "How is it *I* have raised three rebels? I was never particularly rebellious, myself."

Deirdre laughed. "Were you not, my lord? But I think you *must* have been, because I'm seeing you in all of them. Though more, I'll own, in Brennan than in the others."

"He is the first-born," Niall said absently. "And he knows he will be Mujhar after me; it makes a difference."

"Keely probably knows where they are," Deirdre suggested, somewhat pointedly.

Niall cast her a disgusted glance. "For all we know, *Keely* might have encouraged their defection. She is as bad as any of them. There are times I think she is more a warrior than even myself."

"Shall I ask her, my lord?" Taggart inquired.

Niall waved the suggestion away. "No, no—Keely would never say. If Corin is involved, she'll say nothing simply to protect him, even if she had nothing to do with it. Even, I think, if *I* asked her." He shook his head, frowning again. "Brennan knows better. Hart and Corin may not, but *he* does."

"Aye," Deirdre said gently, "but he protects Hart and

Corin *now* just as he did when they were children. D'ye think he'd be stopping simply because they're grown?''

"Are they?" Niall's tone was sour. He did not wait for her answer, but turned to Taggart. "You may go. I attach no blame to you. It is not your fault if the Mujhar cannot control his own unruly sons."

Taggart, smiling, bowed and took his leave. Niall shut the door and turned back to face Deirdre once more. "Well, then, what is there to do? There will be three empty chairs where there are *supposed* to be princes, and Einar will undoubtedly consider it a snub."

"Oh, *Einar!*" Deirdre's tone clearly signified her opinion of the Caledonese heir. "I'll set Maeve next to him, and he'll not be noticing absent princes. And I'll put Keely on the *other* side." Her widening smile was suspiciously devious. "Caught between *those* two, he'll not be knowing what has become of him."

"Oh, gods," Niall begged, "save me from a woman who dearly loves intrigue." And then, abruptly, he began to smile. "Einar will never recover."

"No," Deirdre agreed contentedly. " 'Tis why I'll be doing it."

"Still—" Niall moved past her to the nearest chair and dropped into it, propping his booted feet up on a table that bore a decanter of wine and two goblets, "—they might have picked a better night to play truant. I *do* want that trade alliance. And I *did* want Brennan to handle as much of the negotiation as he could. He needs the practice."

"Brennan knows enough of negotiations." Deirdre poured him wine, passed him the goblet. "He is a mature, responsible man, Niall, not a boy. Save your disgust for Corin's bad tempers, or Hart's gambling debts, or Keely's waywardness—but give none of it to Brennan. He's not deserving of it."

"Come here." He sipped from his goblet as she came to perch on the arm of his wooden chair. "Tell me what *you* are deserving of."

"Your love," she answered promptly. "Am I not generous with mine? And I have given you a lovely daughter."

"Maeve *is* lovely," Niall agreed immediately, paternal pride rearing its head. "And sweet-tempered, and soft-

spoken, and eager to please . . . all the things Keely most
decidedly is not."

"And do you love her the less for it?"

Niall, smiling, shook his head. "She is a proud, strong
woman, Cheysuli to the bone. . . ." He grinned at Deirdre,
slipping into the Erinnish lilt. "And I'd be wanting her no
other way."

"And the boys?" Deirdre's green eyes, across the rim of
her silver goblet, were demurely downcast, but Niall knew
her far too well.

"Aye, and I know what you are trying to tell me,
meijha—that I should want *them* no different, either.
Mostly, I do not. But there are times. . . ."

"Times," she said. "Like now? The bathwater, I'm sure,
is cold, and yet you sit here and drink your wine. You are
no better than your sons, my lord Mujhar."

"But you see, I *am* Mujhar. The banquet must wait for
me." His fingers were in the lacings of her gown. "The
banquet must wait for us *both*."

Deirdre smothered a giggle. She was, she thought, too
old for giggles now. "And your sons?" she asked. "What
about your sons?"

"At this particular moment, I am less concerned with my
sons than with the knots you have tied in your laces. Have
you taken up celibacy?"

The giggle broke free of her throat. "No. Very definitely,
no." She reached down, took his belt-knife from its sheath,
presented it to him hilt-first. "My lord Mujhar, must I be
plainer still?"

Niall, smiling, accepted the knife and deftly cut the first
lace. "The banquet," he said calmly, "will be indefinitely
delayed."

Deirdre sat very still. "To make certain your sons will
be present, of course."

"Of course," he agreed equably, and cut the second knot.

Two

The tavern was one of Mujhara's finest. It lay in High Street, where business catered to the aristocracy of Homana; where boys with brooms swept the cobbles six times a day and poured water on the puddles of urine left by horses, sweeping again, so customers did not have to concern themselves with the condition of their boots. The Rampant Lion was clean, well-lighted, well-run, and enjoyed an excellent reputation, faring well even among stiff competition.

Rhiannon had not expected to get the job as wine-girl at The Lion. But she had paid six copper pennies for a bath two days before she applied, pinned up her hair in the way she had seen ladies do, and put on the cleanest dress she owned. Carefully, she had told the tavernkeeper in her best accent that she was of good family, but lacked means; was there a place for a young woman who needed to earn a living in a *respectable* establishment?

She was delighted when her looks and well-practiced refinement won her the position, and she worked very hard to keep it. She was born of poor people; she had thought to spend her years in poverty and whoredom. But the gods had blessed her with cream-fair skin, thick black hairs and wide black eyes, and a form that would win any man's regard.

It did not fail her now. She passed easily among the tables, serving the fine wines The Rampant Lion specialized in. The Falian white, considered by many to be the finest vintage available, sold best. But the sweet Caledonese red and the rich, dark vintage of Ellas did nearly as well. The ales and lagers found fewer throats; Homanan nobles had a taste for wine, rarely imbibing lesser brews, and almost never the common liquors, such as *usca*. It was considered too harsh among the nobles, who boasted more refined tastes.

Nonetheless, it was *usca* Rhiannon was instructed to bring to a rectangular table of polished hardwood near the wide-bolled trunk of the roof-tree in the middle of the common room. She set the stoneware jug in the precise center of the table, put down the pottery cups without the crude clacking sound heard in most taverns, where the wine-girls knew no better, and watched as the three young men poured the blue-glazed cups quite full. It was obvious, from the way they drank it down, *usca* was no stranger to their throats.

She curtsied as gracefully as she knew how, hoping for a generous tip. They could afford it, she knew; she had an eye for wealth. These three young lords dressed less ostentatiously than many others in the common room, clothed in subdued if rich velvet and soft-worked leather, but there was gold around their necks as well as in their ears. At least, in *one* ear. On them all, only the left bore ornamentation.

They were all fine looking men, she thought; the gods had blessed them with good bones and fine, clean lines in their handsome faces, accentuated by strong, straight noses and well-defined mouths. All men, she thought, if young still, lacking the hardening that years and experience would bring them. Rhiannon's taste ran to *men,* not pretty boys; these three were aesthetically satisfying as well as highborn, and more than comfortable in the belt-purse.

One, however, was clearly Cheysuli. Though he was the first shapechanger Rhiannon had ever seen, she knew. She had heard stories about them; how they slept with animals instead of women and so could shift their shapes, not being wholly human. A man could tell them by their color and their gold; Cheysuli were uniformly black-haired, dark-skinned, and their eyes, as his, were always a clear, uncanny yellow.

But where was his animal?

Rhiannon looked carefully, searching discreetly for the beast that was his other self. But the only thing visible beneath the table were their legs. Six of them, altogether, all knee-booted and thigh-muscled under taut, soft leather breeches of excellent cut and quality.

She glanced up, frowning, and saw his eyes on her. Rhiannon sucked in a startled breath. Yellow was not enough, she decided; not *nearly* enough to describe Cheysuli eyes. They were yellow, aye, and odd enough in that, but there was something about them that made her back away a step, clutching her linen apron.

He looked at her, and she froze, unable to take a step.

"Aye?" he asked, when she continued staring.

A human voice. No growl. No bark. No whine.

Transfixed, Rhiannon did not answer.

"Aye?" he asked again, and the slanted black brows drew down.

He was, she thought, a demon, all black and bronze and yellow.

"Are you a lackwit, Brennan?" one of the others asked. "She works for more than kind words and copper pennies." Almost absently, he rattled dice and rune-sticks in a wooden casket. A heavy sapphire signet ring glistened on one long finger. He had the hands of an artist, she thought; the hands of a musician.

"Of course." The shapechanger reached into his belt-purse and took out a silver piece. Without looking, he offered Rhiannon the coin.

When she did not take it, he looked at her again, turning away from the sticks and dice the other threw. The silver was quite bright against the dark flesh of his fingers.

"I think," drawled the man with the casket, "she has only just seen her first Cheysuli." He grinned and looked up at her. "Let alone three at once."

Three? Rhiannon looked at him quickly. He was black-haired, aye, and his skin was as sun-bronzed as the shapechanger's, but his eyes were decidedly blue. *Very* blue; the sort of blue that put her in mind of spring, and the richness of the sky. They made her think of love, his eyes; so did the smile he smiled.

Disconcerted, she looked away from him as well. To the third, where she knew herself safe at last. He was all Homanan, obviously, with tawny blond hair and dark blue eyes; his skin was Homanan fair. And when *he* looked at her it was not to frown as the shapechanger did, or to smile an invitation as the second one did; no, none of those things.

When he looked at her it was to look at *her,* to find out what she wanted.

Well, what *did* she want?

Rhiannon put up her chin. "Aye," she agreed plainly. "I've not seen a shapechanger before."

"Cheysuli," The shapechanger put the coin on the table, where it glinted against polished wood. "Not 'shape-changer,' *meijhana* . . . unless you *mean* to insult us."

There it was again: us. She frowned, flicked a glance at the blue-eyed man with the fortune-game, looked quickly away as his smiled slowly widened. And the fair-haired man merely laughed.

"So much for believing the Homanans trust us," he said. "Well, Brennan, how does it feel to have a woman *afraid* of you, instead of trying to keep your favor for more than a single night?"

"Cruel, *cruel,* Corin," the man with the casket drawled, and yet his smile belied the words. "You will have me thinking you are jealous of your oldest *rujholli.*"

Rhiannon thought the fair-haired man—Corin, the other had called him—was her age, which made him all of twenty. The other two, she was certain, were older yet, by at least a year. The shapechanger looked at her. "*Are* you afraid of me?"

Rhiannon swallowed. "Aye."

Somehow, she had hurt him. She saw it quite clearly, and instantly. There was little change in his expression, but the eyes were eloquent. Such an eloquent, eerie yellow.

"Well," he said, after a moment's thoughtful silence, "perhaps you would do well to serve the other tables, and send some other girl to us."

Oh, gods, if that were to happen, she would lose her place for certain! "No," she said quickly. "No. I—I'll serve you." She nodded in the direction of the jug. "You have your *usca* now. You won't be needing more."

"Will we not?" Tawny Corin smiled and lifted his pottery cup. "You judge us too quickly, *meijhana.*"

There it was again, the strange, foreign word. Shape-changer? Rhiannon thought it likely. No doubt when they were together, they spoke in growls and barks.

"Brennan frightens the girl, and now Corin *flirts* with

her." The third young noble laughed. "What is left over for me?"

Yellow-eyed Brennan looked up at Rhiannon. "Do you wager?" he asked calmly, without the trace of a smile. And yet she saw one clearly in his eyes; it was meant for the man with the fortune-game. "Say aye, and you will make Hart's evening complete."

"No, no," the other—Hart—demurred. "You leave out what comes *after,* when a lady is involved."

That, Rhiannon understood plainly enough. Shape-changers they might be, but obviously it was not true they only lay with beasts. She knew desire when she saw it, as well as the prelude to it.

"No, I don't wager," she told them curtly. "Not even with silver pennies." And she went away, leaving the coin upon the table.

As one, they looked at the spurned gratuity. In the light from hanging lanterns, the silver royal gleamed.

"Well," said the one called Hart, "I wonder if she would come back for it if she knew what it was worth. Silver penny indeed!"

As he made as if to pick it up, Brennan hid it beneath one palm. "Wager with your own coin," he said grimly. "Or have you none left?"

"None left," Hart said cheerfully. "A run of bad fortune." As if on cue, one of the rune-sticks rolled.

Corin's snort was eloquently condescending. "Only bad fortune because I was the better man when you tried to beat me this afternoon." He picked up the stick and dropped it back into the casket. "Which means Brennan and I must pay for the *usca.*"

"*You* can," Brennan told him. "I came here because I knew better than to let you two go out alone, not because I wanted to go drinking."

"And yet you are." Hart indicated Brennan's full cup. "Hardly water, *rujho*—I can smell it from here."

Corin smiled. Brennan merely shrugged. "All men make sacrifices."

"And you more than most?" Corin demanded. "Oh, aye—when you will have Homana!"

Brennan sighed; it was an old bone of contention. "You will have Atvia."

"And I, Solinde." Cheerfully, Hart scooped the dice and sticks back into the wooden casket. "Three princes, we, with glory yet to come in addition to fine titles. But I think, right now, I could do with less glory and more wealth." He eyed the silver royal. "Are you certain you want the girl to have it, after what she said?"

"I want the girl to have it," Brennan agreed. "And if you so much as *try* to take it when I am not looking, I will cut a finger off."

"If you are not looking, how will you know?"

"Because I would tell him." Corin shrugged as Hart scowled darkly at him. "What would you expect?"

"A little support, *rujho*."

"Brennan is your twin, not I. Look to him for support." Corin downed more *usca*.

Hart's scowl deepened. "Why do you resent it, Corin? You have a twin in Keely."

"Who says I resent it?" Corin retorted. And then, grimly, "Keely is a girl. We are close, aye, as close as you and Brennan—but she is still a girl. It makes a difference, *rujho*."

"Keely is a *woman*," Brennan corrected absently.

Hart laughed. "Aye, she is. Or would you name yourself a boy, Corin, even now at twenty?"

"*She* does not see herself as a woman," Corin stated flatly.

"No." Hart's brows climbed beneath raven hair. "No, she sees herself as a warrior." His smile was amused. "The only trouble with *that* is, the gods saw fit to give her a woman's body."

Corin frowned. "She has no desire to be a *man*. She just prefers to be something other than a fragile thing like Maeve."

"Keely *is* nothing like Maeve," Brennan agreed.

Hart snorted indelicately. "No. And I will lay a wager on it that Sean of Erinn, when he claims our warrior sister, will have a difficult time taming her."

"Keely will never be *tamed*," Corin said plainly, "and you will lay a wager on anything." He scowled blackly at Hart. "As to *that*, I would trust my life to Keely sooner than most men."

"Aye, aye, so would I." Hart set the casket down in front of Brennan. "Care for a game, *rujho?*"

Brennan's eyes narrowed. "I thought you had no coin."

"I have what Corin owes me." Hart looked at his astonished younger brother. "I won twenty-five crowns off you last week."

"*When?*"

"When we wagered on how soon Brennan would be thrown from his new stallion." Hart grinned at his older brother. "The third jump, remember? I won the bet."

Brennan glared back. "You bet *against* me?"

"No. I bet *on* the horse."

Brennan slapped his hand down as Corin reached toward his belt-purse. "Do not put a penny on this table. You know better than to encourage him."

"But he *won*," Corin protested.

Brennan leaned toward him across the table. "*Not a penny,* Corin."

Hart patted the casket. "A suggestion, *rujho*—let the game decide. I win: Corin gives me the money. *You* win: Corin gives *you* the money." He grinned, blue eyes bright. "Surely a fair way to decide."

Brennan sighed and leaned his face into one hand. "One day," he muttered, mostly against his palm, "*one* day, Hart, you will regret ever learning how to play these games."

Hart rattled the casket. "Care to wager on that?"

"Care to wager on *that*?" Corin looked past them both to a table just beyond their own.

Accordingly, Hart and Brennan turned to see what had caught Corin's attention. It was Rhiannon, Rhiannon and a young aristocrat who obviously wanted more from her than wine.

As he grabbed her, pulling her onto his lap, Rhiannon cried out and tried to lurch away. The wine jug she carried slammed against the edge of the table and shattered, spilling gouts of blood-red liquor across the table and onto the young nobleman's fine clothes.

He shoved her away, swearing as he leaped to his feet. Rhiannon stumbled against the table and thrust out both hands to keep herself from falling. As she clutched at the wine-soaked wood, a shard of broken crockery cut her hand.

Even as Rhiannon, trembling, backed away from the furious lord, he followed her. He seemed not to notice that the hand she clutched against her breasts left blood smears on her apron, nor that she was plainly mortified by what had happened and terrified of him. He spoke to her angrily in a foreign tongue, then slapped her across the face so hard he sent her staggering into another table.

But his move had been anticipated.

Brennan caught her, steadied her, held her.

Rhiannon sucked in a frightened breath as she saw who had rescued her. And then she saw how she had smeared blood on his black velvet doublet. "Oh, my lord—I'm *sorry*—"

"You should not be. Not *you*." Gently he set her aside and rose to tower over her. She had not thought he was so tall, but then she was quite petite. "It is *his* place to apologize."

Rhiannon shot a startled glance at the foreign lord. No, she thought, it was *her* place to say the words. "My lord—"

"No." The shapechanger shook his head and stirred black hair against his shoulders, against the nap of his matching doublet. His hands fell away from her waist and Rhiannon saw the black leather belt at his, weighted with plates of hammered gold. On his left hip a knife was sheathed. The gold hilt was smooth, shining and lovely; its shape was of a mountain cat. But even as she opened her mouth to protest yet again, he looked at the foreign lord. "Apologize to her."

The young man's hair was curly and dark, oiled with a scented pomade that turned it glossy black. His nose was slightly prominent, with a crooked set that made his brown eyes appear set too far apart. His fine silk-and-velvet clothes, once pale cream and jonquil, were now variegated a sickly purple-red.

Rhiannon nearly giggled.

The bent nose made it difficult for the foreigner to look down it in a straight line, but his attitude was made plain nonetheless. In accented Homanan, he said, "I apologize to no tavern-drab."

"Apologize," Brennan repeated. "You frightened her, struck her, hurt her. It is the least you should do."

"By Obram, I will not!" the other cried. "Do you think

I am required to do such a thing? *I* am the nephew of the King of Caledon!"

"Prince Einar's cousin?" Brennan nodded as the other stared. "It means you are Reynald, then; I thought you looked familiar." His smile was neither friendly nor amused. "My lord, I suggest that while you remain in Homana, you subject yourself to Homanan custom. Apologize to the girl."

Reynald plainly was unintimidated. "I will not," he stated flatly in his accented Homanan, and made a gesture that brought the others at his table filing out to flank him. Knives and swords glittered with gems, but the weapons were clearly lethal even in their ceremonial flamboyance.

As one, Hart and Corin rose.

Reynald smiled. "You are three. We are eleven."

"He *counts*," Hart observed.

"He smells," Corin added. "What is that oil on his hair?"

At that, the tavern-keeper came out from behind a cask of wine. "Please," he said, "this is not necessary. I will recompense you for your clothing, my lord."

Reynald stared down his crooked nose. "And for the insults from this man?"

The tavern-keeper looked at Brennan helplessly. "My lord, please—"

"Please *what?*" Brennan asked irritably. "It was his fault; you saw it. He deserves no recompense."

"He deserves to be booted out of here and back to where he came from," Corin announced flatly. "Are you forgetting, my foreign lordling, that you are in *our* land?"

"Precisely," Reynald agreed coldly. "Is this the way you treat your guests? Is this the way you treat a man who is to play host to the Mujhar himself this very night? Is this the way you treat a member of the Caledonese royal family?"

Hart smiled. "Does Einar know you are here?"

"My tavern," the tavern-keeper moaned.

Brennan placed a hand on Rhiannon and thrust her gently toward the man. "Bind her wound, if you please. This should not take long."

Reynald snapped something in Caledonese to his nearest guardsman. The man drew a knife and lunged.

Brennan avoided the Caledonese smoothly enough and

let the man's momentum carry him through his initial lunge. On the way by, Brennan planted clasped hands in the back of the guardsman's neck and smashed him to the floor. The man went down and did not move.

Brennan's brothers looked down on the body at their feet. Hart nodded sagely; Corin merely grinned.

A blood-red ruby set in gold glowed on Brennan's finger. He smiled at Reynald and hooked thumbs in the plated belt that clasped lean hips clad in raven velvet. He was considerably taller than Reynald. Behind him, Hart matched him in height and weight; Corin was shorter and slighter, but looked tenacious as a terrier.

"*Now* will you apologize?" Brennan calmly asked.

For answer, Reynald cried out angrily, snatched up a cup and hurled the contents in Brennan's face. As Brennan swore and wiped his eyes, the nine remaining Caledonese guardsmen spread out to encircle the three Homanan princes. Brennan abruptly found himself pressed back against his own table. As his eyes cleared, he found a knife blade at his throat and felt the prick of a sword tip in his spine.

"Still unconvinced?" he said in passing to Reynald, and lifted a wrist against the knife as he spun to dislodge the sword.

Corin, closest to the door, ducked yet another knife as it slashed toward his face, and quickly drew his own. Blades clashed, caught, were twisted; Corin's hilt remained in his hand while the other man's did not. The Caledonese stared in consternation at his empty hand.

Pleased, if a trifle surprised—it was his first encounter in anything other than practice—Corin grinned happily and turned to seek out another foe.

Hart, caught between Brennan and Corin, almost immediately found himself cut off from either of them, hemmed in on three sides by Caledonese. His indecision was quickly banished; Hart leaped up onto the table, cracking runesticks and scattering all the dice of his forgotten fortune-game. A swordblade darted toward his right leg, but he avoided it easily, skipping over yet another. Four of the enemy approached; Hart quickly acknowledged the folly in remaining on the table providing an easy target and sought a quick escape route. A glance upward showed him the only means.

Hart leaped for a low, thick limb of the massive roof-tree. He caught it, swung his body out and over his attackers easily, and dropped on them like a mountain cat on its prey.

Tables overturned as the fighting spread to encompass the entire common room. Jugs and cups shattered, spilling rivers of wine across tables, benches, the hard-packed earthen floor with its carefully stamped insignia of the rampant Homanan lion.

Brennan, having dispatched the Caledonese whose sword threatened his spine, abruptly somersaulted backward over a table to avoid another swipe and landed on his feet, knife in hand. He had not meant to draw it, preferring to avoid edged weapons in the midst of such a stupid, silly brawl, but it seemed he had no choice. And so, shrugging a little, he threw the knife in a glittering arc at an enemy, and saw the guardsman fall at Reynald's feet. He was not dead, Brennan knew, because the knife—though hilt-deep—was in a shoulder, not his heart. Accurate as always; he nodded in satisfaction.

The satisfaction did not last long. A second guardsman leaped for him, knife in hand. Brennan caught handfuls of the yellow Caledonese livery, ripping the tunic as he tried to thrust the guardsman against a table. But he lost his grip as the silk tore, slipped in spilled wine, and fell heavily to one knee.

The Caledonese knife blade sliced easily through velvet sleeve to flesh beneath, cut deeply, then caught on the heavy *lir*-band above Brennan's left elbow.

The guardsman tore the knife free to strike again, scraping steel against gold. The velvet, shredding, gave way; the rune-worked gold was suddenly clear for all to see, with its flowing mountain cat clawing its way free of metal.

Blood flowed freely to fill the incised runes. Brennan swore in the Old Tongue, forgoing his Homanan, and made himself ignore the pain. As the man thrust again, looking for flesh instead of gold, Brennan pushed himself up from the floor and slammed a shoulder into his chest.

"Brennan!" Hart called. "The knife—"

"—did little damage!" Brennan shouted back. "Look to yourself, *rujho!*"

Hart did, neatly avoiding a sword swung perilously close to his right hand. He immediately jammed the threatened hand against his ribs and kicked out with a booted foot. He stripped the sword from the enemy's grip.

Corin, outnumbered rather more quickly than he had imagined, dragged himself out from under a senseless Caledonese and slashed weakly at the closest yellow-clad leg he could find. The blade bit into the leather boot sluggishly, doing little damage, but it caught the attention of the wearer. Swearing in indecipherable Caledonese, the guardsman stomped down on Corin's bared wrist and knocked the knife from his hand.

Pain shot the length of Corin's arm. "*Ku'reshtin!*" he cried, outraged, "let me *up*—"

Just as outraged by Corin's attempt to stab through leather to his leg, the guardsman merely put more weight on the trapped limb.

Corin let out a string of Cheysuli obscenities, then—too proud to lose but not too proud to ask for help—he shouted for his brothers.

When neither answered, he realized abruptly they had their own battles to fight and *he* was solely responsible for his. It was not a pleasing thought; he had grown accustomed to shouting for one or the other of his brothers, if not both, whenever necessary. Now, unhappily, Corin came to the disturbing realization that occasionally there was no one to rely on save himself.

"By all the gods of Homana," he muttered to the floor so close to his face, "why did we leave the *lir* in Homana-Mujhar?"

The guardsman glared down at him. "What are you saying, Homanan? Begging my mercy already?"

Corin, sprawled belly-down with the trapped wrist stretched out in front of him, twisted his head to look up. "Mercy?" Astonished, he gaped at the Caledonese. "I will give you *mercy*—" Abruptly, putting the aching wrist out of his head entirely, Corin lurched up and locked his left arm around the heavy leather boot. Before the guardsman could retreat, Corin had ripped open his knee with a savage bite.

The Caledonese let out a howl of shock and pain and stumbled back, freeing the wrist, and nearly ripped Corin's teeth from his mouth. Corin, kneeling as he flexed his swelling wrist, was privately amazed at his success.

Then a hand came down, caught his russet velvet doublet and jerked him to his feet. "You cannot win battles on the *floor*," Hart said mildly.

"I won *that* one." Corin grinned at the cursing Caledonese. And then he stopped grinning, because the man with the bitten knee lunged past Corin and upended Hart entirely. "*Ku'reshtin!*" Corin cried, and flung himself on the enemy.

Hart, squashed beneath both of them, tried ineffectively to wriggle free. At last he resorted to swearing at the enemy *and* his brother. "Corin—get—*off*—"

"I am *trying* . . ." Corin scrambled backward awkwardly, planting a knee against Hart's left thigh, and dragged the Caledonese with him. Hart, wheezing, sat up slowly and clasped tender ribs.

The tavern door, so very close to Hart, slammed open. He winced instinctively, hunched his shoulders, and hugged his ribs even harder. Boots thudded against the hardpacked floor and swords rattled out of sheaths. Hart, catching a glimpse of crimson silk and leather-and-mail, felt the beating of his heart abruptly stop.

He squinted up at the men hesitantly, then closed his eyes. Aye. It *was* the Royal Mujharan Guard. Part of it, anyway.

"*Jehan* will have our heads for this," he commented in cheerful resignation, and smiled innocently at the nearest of his father's men-at-arms.

Brennan, consumed with gaining a victory over a Caledonese who simply *would not* go down, felt the lance shaft across his throat. Gently it pressed, so gently, warning him subtly, but firmly enough to threaten the fragility of his windpipe.

Slowly, Brennan let his hands drop back to his sides. In pleased surprise he watched his opponent stagger, straighten, collapse onto the floor. The Prince of Homana nodded, smiled, turned slowly within the cage of the lance to face his new opponent.

Abruptly he froze. Leaping out of the crimson tunic over

the leather-and-mail was a black Homanan lion, rampant: his father's royal crest. It matched perfectly the black-etched lion in Brennan's ruby signet ring.

The Homanan guardsman recognized his prisoner at the same time. The lance fell away. "My lord!"

Corin, as yet unaware of the new arrivals, scrambled out from beneath two now-prone Caledonese guardsmen. His face was smeared with blood, but his eyes were suspiciously bright. He grinned, delighted. And then, as he stood up, the grin slipped away.

Brennan faced a guardsman in the Mujhar's black-and-scarlet livery. Hart, looking none too pleased with affairs, leaned against a table and clasped his ribs. His handsome face was bruised, and one eye—the right—was plainly swelling and would soon turn black.

Corin looked at his brothers. He looked at the sudden stillness in the tavern. He looked at the four Mujharan guardsmen flanking him. And then he sighed and sat down on a wine-stained bench to cradle his injured wrist.

Three

Reynald of Caledon strode stiffly through the center of the common room, stepping over the downed bodies of his royal escort and kicking aside fragments of broken crockery. His foreign face was set in an expression of distaste, irritation and arrogance; his dismay at the results of the fight was evident even as he tried to hide it.

He drew himself up before the Mujharan guardsman who had set the lance shaft at Brennan's throat. Pointedly, he ignored Brennan altogether. "Your name?" he demanded.

"Dion," the guardsman answered. "Captain of this contingent of the Royal Mujharan Guard."

Reynald's dark brown eyes narrowed. "The Mujhar's men?"

"Part of his personal guard," Dion answered. "Attached to the palace itself."

The foreign prince nodded. "I am Reynald, cousin to Prince Einar of Caledon," he said flatly. "I wish to press charges against these three Homanans—I want you to see to it they are put in chains and locked away until justice can be levied. I intend to ask the Mujhar himself to hear my testimony."

"My lord, it is your privilege to do so," Dion said quietly. "But may I suggest you reconsider—"

"No, you may not, and I *will* not," Reynald answered. "I came here with my escort to enjoy an evening's entertainment in what I was told was a fine establishment." He cast a withering glance around The Rampant Lion. "These men intruded, provoking a fight, and I demand reparation for this affront to my honor, and that of my cousin, Prince Einar."

"Oh, is Einar here?" Brennan asked lightly. "I did not see him."

Reynald glared. "Because he is not present means nothing. You have injured my honor, and—as I am a member of the Caledonese party here to celebrate the Mujhar's reign—what insults me also insults my lord prince."

"Your pardon, my lord." It was Hart's turn. "But I fail to see how *you* were injured in any way. You let your escort do your fighting for you."

"Aye," Corin interposed before Reynald could answer. "You and Brennan *could* have settled it between you, but you provoked a fight. *You* gave the order to attack." He paused. "I think. It was in Caledonese, but it *did* serve to make your escort attack, whatever it was you said."

Color blazed in Reynald's saturnine face. "I was required to protect myself. This man meant to provoke *me*." His outflung hand indicated Brennan.

"My lord?" Dion looked at Brennan.

Brennan opened his mouth, but Reynald spoke before he could. "My lord?" he mimicked, glaring at Dion. "You give him more honor than you give me."

"Aye," Dion answered smoothly; it was easy to see his opinion of the Caledonese lordling, regardless of his neutral expression and tone. "I mean you no disrespect, my lord, but this man will one day be my king."

Reynald shut his mouth with a snap. He looked sharply from Dion to Brennan. "King," he echoed. There was, suddenly, the faintest trace of doubt in his tone.

"One day," Brennan agreed. "Not for a long time yet; my father the Mujhar is, thank the gods, a spectacularly healthy man." The faintest of twitches jerked the corner of his mouth; he was purposely underplaying his hand, which served to make it all the more devastatingly effective.

Reynald looked first at Hart, then at Corin. And all of a sudden the color drained out of his face. "Obram save me," he whispered, "you are all the Mujhar's sons. I remember, now—"

"You remember, *now*." Hart grinned. "A bit slow, are you, Reynald? We met only yesterday, did we not? In the Great Hall before the Lion Throne?"

"Where you wished our father *the Mujhar* best wishes for continued health." Corin pointedly emphasized their link to royalty. Reynald was the sort of man to understand such arrogance, having his own fair share of it.

"Chains, I think he said," Brennan told Dion. "Did you bring any with you?"

"No, my lord. Should I fetch some?" Clearly, the captain was enjoying Reynald's discomfiture.

Hart felt his ribs. "Enough," he said. "I think Reynald sees our point. And I think it is time we returned to Homana-Mujhar, before our *jehan* sends men out looking for us." He stopped short and looked at Dion. "Who *did* send you?"

"*I* did." Rhiannon stepped forward. The linen apron still bore bloodstains, now darkening, and her hand was wrapped in a clean cloth. "It was my fault this nonsense began. I thought I should be the one to stop it, so I ran to the palace and fetched them." She looked at Brennan. Her eyes lingered a moment on the earring in his left ear, now exposed by hair pushed away from his face. "I—I was ungrateful before," she said in a low voice. "You did this for me." She wiggled fingers showing at the edges of the cloth wrapping. "I didn't want you to get hurt—*any* of you." Her eyes touched briefly on Hart and Corin, but moved back to Brennan almost immediately.

Hart laughed. Corin's mouth twisted wryly.

Brennan smiled slowly. "Then you have *my* thanks," he said, and looked at Reynald. "I think we have arrived at an impasse, my Caledonese lordling. You may, of course, press charges—we *did* extinguish most of your royal escort, three to ten—" he grinned, "—but perhaps we may simply let bygones be bygones, and meet over the banquet you and your cousin Prince Einar are supposed to host in my father's honor tonight." Brennan paused. "And if we do not go now, we shall be quite late."

Reynald looked at the remains of his royal escort. Several of the men were clearly unconscious. Others were merely stunned, beginning only now to pull their wits back together. Two were on their feet, unwounded; they scowled sullenly at their fallen comrades.

Their lord, in his wine-stained silks and velvets, summoned what dignity he could muster. "Come," he ordered the two men still on their feet, and immediately departed the tavern.

Corin watched him go, then turned back to Hart. "What about the others?"

Hart grinned his lopsided, charming grin. "He is nephew to the King of Caledon, *rujho*, and cousin to Prince Einar. It is not for *him* to concern himself with men wounded in his defense."

"Ah." Corin, duly enlightened, nodded.

Brennan sighed and untied his belt-purse. He handed it over to the tavern-keeper. "For the damages." And then he worked a ring from one of his fingers. It was not the ruby signet of his rank, but a smaller sapphire set in silver. When it was free of his finger, he put it into Rhiannon's hands. "To replace the 'silver penny.'" He smiled warmly. "You see," he said, "Cheysuli are not so bad."

She stared after him as he preceded his brothers out of The Rampant Lion. And then she kissed the ring.

The Mujhar, stepping into one of the soft gray-dyed kneeboots, looked up sharply as Taggart finished speaking. "They did *what?*"

Taggart's face was very stiff. He repeated his final statement. "They destroyed most of Reynald's escort, my lord."

"'Destroyed.'" Niall straightened as a body-servant knelt to adjust the droop of soft leather. "Is anyone *dead?*"

"Not so far as we can tell, my lord. It appears several of the Caledonese are wounded, but none seriously." Taggart folded his hands behind his back and waited.

Niall stood stock still in the center of the antechamber that held most of the clothing suitable for a Mujhar. He preferred the soft leather jerkin and leggings of the Cheysuli, but all too often he was forced to wear Homanan apparel. Tonight was such a night.

"My lord . . ." The body-servant held up the other boot.

Niall glanced down, frowning in distraction. "Ah. Aye." He accepted the boot and pulled it on, then waited as it was properly adjusted. "All three of them?" he asked.

Taggart nodded.

"Even Brennan," Niall murmured. "Oh, curse them for fools, all of them. I do not *need* this tonight—*most of all* tonight." He waved the body-servant away and paced across the room to the doorway opening into his bedchamber. Serri was, yet again, asleep on the bed.

"My lord, Dion reported that it did not appear to be entirely the fault of the princes. And if my lord Reynald truly *did* provoke them, there must have been good reason."

"Reason, perhaps, but not good reason," Niall said grimly. He shook his head, still bare of its heavy circlet, and swung back. "I cannot believe *Brennan* took part in this idiocy. It is not like him. Hart and Corin, aye—they would hardly balk at a fight, regardless of provocation— but Brennan?"

Deirdre swept into the room from another entrance. "My lord Mujhar, your favoritism is showing."

"Is it?" Niall absently admired the rich blue gown that fit her slender body so snugly. Her brass-bright hair was twisted up on her head in a knot secured with thick pins of silver wire, and she wore yet another of his gifts, a silver chain crusted with diamonds and dark blue sapphires. It glittered against her throat. "Aye, well . . . even *you* must admit it is unlike Brennan."

"What have they done, your sons?" Deirdre smoothed the fit of his black doublet, quilted with jet and seed pearls.

"They have torn up a tavern—one of the *better* ones, I might add—and accounted for multiple casualties," Niall answered. "In short, they may have permanently destroyed any hope for a renewal of the trade alliance between Homana and Caledon."

"Have they, then?" She patted the silver chain of office that stretched from shoulder to shoulder, each wide link cleverly fashioned into a rampant lion. A remarkable distance from shoulder to shoulder; privately, Deirdre smiled.

"You do not seem to understand." Niall moved away from her to face Taggart again. "Where are they now?"

"In your private solar, my lord." Taggart paused. "I think they knew you would wish to say something to them. They went there on Prince Brennan's suggestion."

"Wise Brennan," Niall remarked darkly. "Aye, I wish to say something to them. Go and fetch them, Taggart. Fetch them *now*."

Taggart was clearly surprised. "*Here,* my lord?"

"Here."

"Aye, my lord." A bow, and he was gone.

"Niall," Deirdre said uneasily, "what it is you are meaning to say to them?"

"Whatever comes out of my mouth at the moment." He

took her arm and escorted her into yet a third chamber, a private withdrawing room.

"You will be giving them a *chance,* then." But she did not sound at all convinced.

Niall indicated she was to sit down in one of the X-legged chairs. "Promise me, *meijha,* you will leave the punishment to me."

"In other words, you are wanting me to be silent." She scowled at him as she sat down, but it lacked the determination to have much of the desired affect. " 'Tis for you to do, then," she agreed. "They are your sons, not mine." And she folded her hands primly in her lap.

"Oh, gods," Brennan said when Taggart had told them where they must go. "He *is* angry."

"And are you a woman or a warrior?" Corin demanded crossly. "We are too big to *spank,* Brennan; why do you dread facing him so much?"

"Probably because only rarely have I had to be reprimanded. It is *you* who have spent so much of your time in his bad graces." Brennan turned on his heel and marched out of the solar.

"So has Hart," Corin said defensively, following. Still he cradled the sore wrist, wondering if it were cracked or merely badly bruised. "I am not the only one who has been sent before our *jehan.*"

"Is that a point of pride?" Brennan asked acidly.

"Your arm hurts," Hart announced, bringing up the rear. "You are irritable, *rujho.*"

"If I am irritable, it is because I am plagued with a young *rujholli* who lacks the wit to know when to humble himself," Brennan declared. "He will only make it worse, if he gives our *jehan* defiance instead of contrition."

Corin swore in disgust. "It was *Reynald's* fault, not mine. And I was the last to join the fight. *You,* Brennan, were first."

"Aye," Hart agreed. "And that is precisely why I think he will *not* be so angry. He is accustomed to our scrapes, Corin. But with Brennan involved in this one, I think he will believe it had merit."

Brennan sighed. "That is something, I suppose." And he

swung into the open doorway to the Mujhar's royal apartments.

Niall watched them file in. Brennan first, of course; as always. The eldest was plainly out of sorts in clothing as well as temper; though he tried to hide both by forcing his face into a calm, neutral expression and attempting to straighten the fit of his velvet doublet. Niall saw wine stains, blood stains, gaping rents. Through the remains of the left sleeve, *lir*-gold gleamed faintly.

Hart, now second in line, looked much worse. His dark blue doublet was as stained and torn, but his face was badly bruised and already showed the beginnings of a black eye. There was no blood or wound visible, but he walked with the odd, stiffly upright posture of a man afraid to move anything above his waist. Ribs, then.

As for Corin, the youngest trailed the other two as if to defy his father, jaw jutting out to advertise his unwillingness to accept responsibility for his actions. It was a familiar posture to Niall, who murmured inwardly that one day, if it pleased the gods, Corin *might* grow up—and was relieved to see the son who looked so much like him showed no signs of serious physical discomfort. Even if he did favor his right wrist, which looked suspiciously swollen.

Brennan glanced briefly at Deirdre, so silent in her chair, and halted before his father. Niall stood before one of the casements, hands folded behind his back. He waited as Hart halted, and then Corin, who promptly sat down on the nearest stool.

Hart leaned a little in Corin's direction and hissed, "Stand up."

Corin stubbornly remained seated. He stared at his father with an unrepentent, unwavering gaze.

Inwardly, Niall sighed. "One at a time," he said aloud. "Who shall be first?"

Brennan opened his mouth to answer, as always, first, but Corin got there before him. "It was a girl," he said flatly, indelicately, and made both his brothers scowl their disapproval. He colored. "It *was*."

"A *girl*." Somehow, Niall had not quite expected that. Generally it was something more, or something else.

Hart wet his lips. "A wine-girl," he said. Then, as if hearing how ludicrous it sounded, he added, "But not a common sort of wine-girl, or a common sort of tavern."

"Far be it for my sons to frequent a *common* tavern with merely *common* wine-girls." The Mujhar's tone was deceptively mild.

Brennan was not deceived. His eyes narrowed as he tried to judge his father's mood; Niall was pleased to see none of them could do it. He smiled and outwaited them.

"There was also a Caledonese *ku'reshtin*," Corin added. "Anyone will tell you."

"Will *you?*" Niall asked.

"I just have."

"Corin—" Hart began, in warning.

Niall waved it away with a raised finger that silenced his middle son immediately. "Say on."

"He hit the girl," Corin told him seriously. "He nearly knocked her down, and she did not deserve it. She had already cut her hand on the broken winejug."

Hart nodded. "He refused to apologize."

Niall's left brow lifted; the right one, divided by the talon scar, was mostly hidden beneath the diagonal slash of leather strap that held the patch in place. "A wine-girl asked apology of a Caledonese prince?"

"No," Corin said lightly. "That took Brennan, of course."

"Ah." Niall's single eye flicked to his eldest son. "Then it was *you* who began it?"

Brennan did not flinch from the tone in his father's voice, which managed to express surprise, disappointment, disapproval, all at once. "Aye," he answered clearly.

"You."

"I," Brennan agreed. "*Jehan*—he was unnecessarily rude. He hurt her."

"So you stepped in and defended her honor, if such still exists."

Deirdre opened her mouth as if to protest, shut it, waited for the interview to be finished.

Brennan frowned at his father. "Are you saying that because she is a wine-girl, she is undeserving of aid when someone mistreats her?"

"No," Niall answered. "I am saying that I hope she was

worth the loss of a trade alliance between Homana and Caledon."

Brennan grasped the implications more quickly than the others. *"Oh."*

"Aye. *Oh.*"

"Do you mean it?" Hart asked. "Prince Einar will refuse to negotiate because of this?"

"Possibly."

"But you do not *know* that," Corin observed shrewdly. "Do you, *jehan?*"

"There is a possibility the negotiations will be postponed, even canceled. There are certainly precedents for such things, when princes meddle in politics even though they are more suited to drinking wine in uncommon taverns."

"Usca," Corin corrected quietly. Hart looked at him as if he had lost his wits.

Niall nodded a little. "Perhaps you were correct to defend the wine-girl's honor; I will not protest that. It is good manners, if nothing else. But I *will* protest the disregard you had for the delicacy of relationships between realms. I will also protest your inability to recall that diplomacy is necessary in nearly every situation, certainly this one. And I will most decidedly protest your inability to remember that Cheysuli warriors *do not brawl in taverns."* He paused, marking their shocked faces. *"Princes* do not brawl in taverns. *My sons* do not brawl in taverns." Again he paused, and heard the echo of his voice ringing in the chamber. "Do I make myself clear?"

Corin stared at him defiantly. "We have done it before."

Hart moved closer to Brennan, taking a definitive step away from his younger brother.

Slowly Niall moved from the casement. He walked to his youngest son and paused before the stool. And abruptly, before Corin could speak or make any sort of protest, Niall reached down and grasped the injured wrist, snapping Corin to his feet.

"Jehan—" But Corin, though clearly in pain, broke off his protest when he saw the expression on his father's face.

"You have spent twenty years in Homana-Mujhar, sharing in the bounty of your birth," Niall said in a tone that, for all its gentleness, implied more displeasure than shouting might have. "Your *jehana* was Princess of Atvia in her

own right, bred of Cheysuli warriors and Homanan kings.
I care little enough what you may think of me, or what I
do—but you *will* respect the blood that flows in your
veins." Niall drew in a breath that did nothing to dispel
the rising anger in his tone. "That blood you have spilled
all too often in petty tavern brawls. It must stop, Corin. It
must. Rid yourself of this resentment and hostility and conduct yourself as a prince and Cheysuli warrior should." He
paused, looking for something in Corin's blue eyes. "It is
not worthy of you," he said, more quietly.

Corin set his teeth. "And *I* am not worthy of *you.*"

Niall released the injured wrist instantly. His jaw slackened momentarily and something odd glinted in his good
eye; something that spoke of shock, of memories and unexpected pain, in addition to the sudden flaring of an intense,
abiding regret.

Deirdre wanted to go to him at once, but refrained. It
would undermine his authority completely if she showed
his sons how much Corin's words had hurt him; now, at
this moment, Niall needed all the strength and resolution
he could find, if he were to command their respect and
obedience.

The Mujhar turned away a moment, then swung back to
face them all. He looked at Hart and Brennan, ignoring
Corin as if he had nothing more to say to him. Or as if he
could not bear to look at him and see the son who so
closely resembled the young Niall in coloring as well as
insecurity.

"What I have said to Corin applies equally to you," he
told his twin-born sons. "I have raised none of you to behave as common soldiers on leave, fighting over petty
slights and imagined insults, nor as crofters spending their
few coins on liquor and wine-girls . . . *nor* on foolish wagers." His eye flicked to Hart, then returned to Brennan.
"I expected such behavior out of you least of all."

Brennan stood very straight, but his shoulders lost
their set.

Quickly Hart spoke up. "Blame him no more than me,
jehan."

"No," Niall agreed. "But *less* than you, aye. It was your
idea to go there, was it not?"

Hart opened his mouth, then shut it. After a moment,

he nodded. "We meant only to drink a little, *jehan*. Not to fight. You know I would rather throw the dice and runesticks than fight."

"Reynald deserved it, *jehan*," Corin said flatly. "And if the rest of the Caledonese royal house is like *him*, you do not wish to make an alliance with them anyway."

"Do I not?" Niall looked calmly at his youngest son. "I see—I am to base the future of Homanan economy solely on the personalities of Caledon's rulers. At least, so *you* say."

"*Jehan*—"

"Corin, I think you have very much to learn about dealing with other kingdoms," the Mujhar said gently. "And I suggest you begin now, because in two or three years you will be going to Atvia to take your rightful place as heir to Alaric's throne."

"Atvia," Corin said in disgust. "And if I would prefer to remain here?"

"Well, there is a choice," Niall said. "You may remain here as a dispossessed, disinherited son, or accept your *tahlmorra* and go to Atvia."

Corin's eyes narrowed. "I might also stay here with the clans, *jehan*. You cannot dispossess me of my heritage, nor disinherit me from my *lir*."

"I would not need to dispossess you of your Cheysuli heritage," Niall told him quietly. "A warrior turning his back on his *tahlmorra* is solely to blame for his disinheritance, which also includes loss of the afterworld." He paused a moment. "Corin, this serves nothing and is not necessary. What *is* necessary, however, is for all of you to acknowledge that you have been immature and irresponsible, and to accept your punishment."

"That depends on what it is," Corin muttered beneath his breath, as Hart glared at him openly.

"It is that I forbid you to attend the banquet this evening."

"That is *all*?" Hart blurted, and winced as Brennan kicked him covertly.

"In not attending the banquet, you will keep yourselves to your respective chambers," Niall explained, "and you will remain in them until I give you leave to go out of them. No banquets, no taverns, no Clankeep." He fixed his eye on each of his sons individually. "No horses," he said to Brennan. "No wagering," he ordered Hart. And lastly, to Corin, "No visits from any of Deirdre's ladies."

"For how *long?*" Brennan demanded indignantly, forgoing all the diplomacy he had so carefully cultivated. "If I leave Bane for even a day, all my progress will be undone and I will have to begin again."

Hart frowned. "And how am I expected to pass the time, *jehan,* while I wait for your leave to go?"

But Corin laughed. "Enforced celibacy, *jehan?* Well, it will only leave the ladies all the more eager for me when I *can* share their company again."

Deirdre smiled serenely. " 'Tis hard for my ladies to be eager when their positions are in jeopardy."

Corin stared at her in astonishment. "*You* would do that?"

"To support the Mujhar, I will do anything," she said calmly. "Just as all of his children should, sons and daughters alike."

That enforced silence among them as nothing else had.

Niall nodded. "You may go," he said quietly. "Meals will be sent up from the kitchens."

In silence, his three still proud but decidedly chastened sons filed slowly out of the chamber.

Four

Corin shut the door to his chambers with a resounding thud, knowing it childish, but satisfied with the action nonetheless. And then he regretted it almost instantly, because he had employed his right wrist in the motion and the wrist was less than pleased.

He cursed, examined it briefly, decided it was very sore and bruised, but not broken. Still, it would keep him from arms-practice for a week or more, and that he did not appreciate.

Have I only myself to blame?

Why? came the familiar liquid tone of his *lir* within the pattern of their link. *What have you done now?*

He looked for Kiri and found her lumped in the center of his draperied bed. She was little more than a knot of red fur, with sharp jet nose tucked firmly beneath a black-tipped tail.

Corin sighed and sat down on the edge of the bed, staring disconsolately at his wrist as she worked the fingers. *I have involved myself in a tavern brawl, which is beneath me—or so I am told by my jehan—and have drawn Caledonese blood, which may result in damaged trade ties between Homana and Caledon.* He paused. *I have also been incredibly rude and disrespectful to my* jehan.

Have you?

"Aye," he said aloud, with conviction. "Kiri, why is it I always say things I regret? *Especially* to my *jehan?*"

Because your mouth works independently of your brain. The vixen rose, shook her glossy red pelt into order, came over to sit beside her *lir*. Her expression was made quizzical by black mask and slanted amber eyes. Lir, *one day you will learn.*

"Will I?" He sighed and flopped backward, stretching

out on the huge bed. "He threatens to send me to Atvia in two or three years, *lir* . . . and the gods know I have no wish to go."

Atvia is your place, the fox said. *You will be its king. Is that not a fine thing, and worth much pride?*

"A fine thing, aye," Corin said on a deeper sigh, "and undoubtedly worth much pride. The trouble is, I have little enough of that. I look at Hart and Brennan and see real warriors and princes, while I am left to feel inferior."

All nonsense. Kiri settled her chin on his muscular thigh, slanted eyes closing. *You have a* lir . . . *you have* me—*how could you possibly feel inferior?*

"A habit that often happens when a warrior receives his *lir* late," Corin retorted. "I was sixteen, Kiri, as you should well recall—both my *rujholli* were thirteen. I had three years in which to fear I would never receive one, while Brennan flaunted Sleeta and Hart learned to fly with Rael."

And the Mujhar had nineteen years. Kiri's tone plainly said Corin's complaint had no foundation.

A fist banged on the door. Corin knew the sound extremely well. "Keely," he called, "now is not the time to gloat."

There came a muffled shout from the other side. "I am not here to gloat—" His sister's voice broke off a moment, then renewed itself. "What have you done *now*, Corin, that would cause me to gloat?" Without waiting for his leave to enter, she pushed open the heavy wooden door and slipped through, shutting it decisively. She stopped dead; elbows jutted out as she locked hands on hips. "Oh, *rujho* . . . not another fight."

"No." Corin struggled up. "I am in this state of disrepair because Deirdre's ladies could not keep themselves from me." He looked down at his torn, soiled russet doublet. He smelled of wine, smoke, and lantern oil.

"Did you win?" Keely asked.

"All three of us won."

"Three . . ." Her blue eyes, so like his own, narrowed. "Hart, of course . . . and Brennan? *Brennan?*"

"Brennan." Corin began to work at his right boot, desiring to strip it off. "He came with us to keep us from trouble, he *said*—and then promptly began the fight with Reynald."

"Reynald? Einar's brother?"

"Cousin." A twinge of pain shot through his injured wrist, and he swore. "The *ku'reshtin* tried to force himself on a wine-girl, and then when she refused his attentions he slapped her. She broke a jug and cut her hand."

"And Brennan came to her rescue." Keely's tone was dry; her expression indicated she, as much as Corin, was less than enamored of Brennan's status as eldest—and favorite—son. "How like him."

Corin swore again as he wrestled with the recalcitrant boot. "Keely—come and help me with this."

She swept across the room, shaking her head, and bent to catch the heel and toe of the brown boot in both hands. Only then did he realize she wore a rich copper-colored gown of silk and velvet instead of customary leathers; her tawny hair was braided Cheysuli fashion, pinned against her head and all achime with golden bells. A topaz and garnet torque clasped a slender, elegant neck.

Keely grunted, tugging on the boot, then caught his eye. Instantly color flared in her face. "Must *you* stare, too?" She was clearly annoyed as well as flustered. "Deirdre *insisted*—she said I could not attend the banquet in leggings and jerkin."

"Well, no," he agreed. "Keely—" He grinned, shrugged, laughed aloud. "So much for the independent *rujholla* I know so well."

"*Ku'reshtin*," she muttered, tugging on the boot again. "They will have *you* bathed and oiled and perfumed before you know it, and where will you be then?"

His mouth twisted in a grimace of disgust. "No," he said. "I am banished to my chamber."

The boot came off. Keely straightened stiffly, gaping at him as she clutched the leather in both hands. "What? You—banished? *Who* has banished you?"

"The only one who can," he answered wryly.

"He did *not.*" The bells chimed as she shook her head in disbelief. "Why?"

"I am in disgrace."

"Because of the tavern brawl?"

"Aye. He was—less than pleased." Corin sighed. "He has every right to be, I think. We *did* bruise Reynald's pride a little." He smiled. "We bruised it a *lot.*"

"Reynald deserves it," she said flatly, bending to remove his other boot. "Einar as well—do you know *I* have to be his partner at the banquet?" In disgust she jerked on the boot, which elicited a curse from Corin because it jarred his wrist. "Let him have *Maeve,* if he requires a princess to prop up his foreign pride."

"I think his pride will be propped up enough when he sees three empty chairs," Corin muttered. "He will know why, and doubtless he will gloat."

"Then I will see to it he cannot," Keely said firmly. A final twist freed his foot. She dropped the boot to the floor and sat down at his right side, leaving his other to Kiri. "Let me see your wrist."

He held out his arm. Keely carefully peeled the sleeve of the velvet doublet and the silken undersleeve back, baring the swollen wrist. Her fingers were gentle but matter-of-fact; like a warrior, she had little patience with injuries.

"Not broken," she said, after a moment, and pushed the arm away.

Corin scowled. "And will you be so solicitous with Sean, when you are wed?"

"Sean will take me as he finds me; he is not marrying a nursemaid," she said darkly. Then she made fists of her hands and banged the air with them. "Oh, *gods,* Corin, I have no wish to go to Erinn! I have no wish to be *cheysula* to some Erinnish island princeling!"

"Aye, well, our *jehan* pays little enough mind to what we do and do not want," her brother said grimly. "I said I had no desire to go to Atvia, and *he* said it was my choice if I went, or remained here and became a dispossessed, disinherited son."

Keely's mouth twisted in disgust. "But if *Brennan* were to ask. . . ."

"He has no need to ask; Homana will be his. He goes nowhere." Corin sighed and rose to undo the fastenings of his ruined doublet. After a moment of struggling with his left hand, he appealed to Keely once again. As she clucked her tongue over his helplessness and undid the fastenings, Corin craned his head out of her way. "But at least Brennan was banished to his chambers, too."

Keely's fingers paused. "Brennan was?"

"All three of us."

"He *was* displeased, then."

"As he will be if I keep you here longer." Corin pushed her hands away. "I will call a body-servant—Keely, you must go. Give Einar a taste of your wit."

"With sweet Maeve on his other side?" Keely shook her head. "He will think me a waspish shrew."

Corin merely raised eloquent tawny eyebrows.

"*Ku'reshtin*," she muttered, and took herself out of the room.

Hart soaked in a hot bath, drank half a decanter of wine, then suffered his ribs to be strapped by his body-servant. Once the man was done and dismissed, Hart went over to the polished silver plate hung on one of his bedchamber walls, and stared somberly at the bandages that made it so difficult to breathe. But the linen strapping did not draw his attention so much as the black eye. He fingered the bruising gingerly.

"You," he said somberly, "are a poor son. A poor son and a poorer prince. You know better."

Almost at once he felt restored. There. He had admitted his shortcomings; now he could get on with his life without excess guilt. He tried a smile at the battered face in the plate, found it did not hurt as much as he thought it might, and turned away.

You know better, but it does not stop you, chimed the voice that served as his conscience. All Cheysuli had them. They were known as *lir*.

"No," Hart agreed lightly. "Why should it?"

The hawk shifted on his perch in the corner nearest the big tester bed. Rael was white save for the jet black edging on each individual feather, and his eyes, which were the color of palest ale.

It should if it is wrong, the hawk pointed out.

"Was I wrong?" Hart, still nude from his bath, plucked the clean leather leggings from his bed and very carefully pulled them on. He grunted, swore, cast aspersions upon the parentage of the Caledonese who had so squashed him. And then he recalled that Corin had had as much to do with it as the foreign guardsman, and promptly included his brother in his deprecations. "How could I be wrong, Rael; I was only defending myself."

It would be redundant to say you should not have been in the position to have *to defend yourself*, Rael commented, having said it regardless of redundancy; it was often necessary with Hart.

"Enough," Hart said succinctly. He rubbed his hands through heavy black hair still damp from washing. In the candlelight the *lir*-gold on his arms, now bared, gleamed. The light lingered on incised lines of intricate feathering; on the exultation of a hawk in flight, wings spread to curve around the wide, rune-bordered armband. In honor of the *lir* Hart now attempted to silence.

"Do you reprove your own *lir?*" asked Ian from the doorway. "A distinct admission of guilt, *harani* . . . you are slipping. And if you tell me you deserve this exile from the banquet, I shall *know* you have gone mad."

Hart grimaced. Before his uncle, all his new-found contentment fled. "No, no—I will save you from insanity, *su'fali*. What I did was necessary, and certainly not deserving of punishment."

"Ah, I am set at ease." Ian grinned. He was five years older than his brother, the Mujhar, but like most Cheysuli he did not show his age. His hair was still black, save for a single silver forelock that fell to hide his left eyebrow, and his flesh still taut over pronounced musculature, with only the faintest of creases fanning out from yellow eyes. In blue-dyed leggings, boots, and jerkin, as well as *lir*-gold at left ear and on his bare arms, Ian was all Cheysuli physically, though he claimed a splash or two of Homanan blood.

"You have seen my *jehan*, then." Hart sighed. "He told you it was my idea to go to the tavern, I am sure."

"No." Ian shut the door and leaned against it, folding his arms. "He did not *need* to tell me—when I heard a tavern was involved, I knew it was your idea." He smiled in response to Hart's grimace. "Corin may be the impulsive one, rebelling against this or that, but he follows more than he leads. Brennan, of course, knows better than to leave Homana-Mujhar when his *jehan* has asked him expressly not to, unless given a very good reason for disobedience. And Keely was *here;* had it been her idea, she would have gone." He shrugged. "Whom does it leave, Hart? Maeve?"

Hart's response was a snort of derisive amusement. Then

he sighed and scratched absently at his bandages. "I am so obvious, then."

"To me, aye," Ian agreed. "To others, no. You have the odd ability to hide yourself even as you stand before numerous people. I think it is something you enjoy."

"No, no, not always." Hart shook his head. "I do not hide myself from you, *su'fali.*"

"Only because I have watched you do it, and know *how* you do it." Ian smiled. "Even Niall does not see it."

"Because he sees little of any of us."

"You discredit him, *harani.* He sees Brennan, because Brennan is his heir, and he must. He sees Corin because Corin is frequently contentious, often purposely. And Keely, of course, because Keely stubbornly refuses to acknowledge that others perceive her as a woman, when she would rather be perceived as a Cheysuli.

"And in Maeve he sees Deirdre." Hart sighed. "Favorite son, favorite daughter."

"I did not think it bothered you."

Hart looked at him in surprise. "It does not, *su'fali.* I am content enough with my lot—*more* than content with it. I only meant he makes no secret of his prejudice."

"When you are a *jehan*—and a king—you will see why it is difficult for him to reconcile affection with authority," Ian told him. "It was so with your grandsire, and now your *jehan.*"

"I do not see *you* reconciling such things with children, *su'fali,*" Hart shot back. "Where is your *cheysula?* Where is your *meijha?* Are you so inspired by your *rujholli* that you neglect your own responsibilities?"

Ian, unoffended, merely smiled. "I am not dead yet, *harani.* There may well come a time I bestow a *lir*-torque on one particular woman. But until then—"

"—*until then*, you leave half the women in Clankeep yearning for you." Hart grinned. "Not to mention a few of Deirdre's ladies."

"That, I think, is Corin's province rather than mine."

"Not all of them, *su'fali.* I am not blind."

"No. Only distracted by the lure of the fortune-game, and other such profitless time-wasters." Ian shook his head. "Do you wonder why the Mujhar grows impatient with you? You act as though you have no concern for the blood in your veins. You are as much a part of the prophecy as the Mujhar, my young *harani;* as much as Brennan, Corin, and Keely. If you think to shrug it off with games, you will soon learn that a *tahlmorra* can make itself known at a very inopportune time."

"As with you?" Hart faced Ian squarely, all the levity banished from his bruised face. "As it did with you, when the Ihlini witch took your *lir* and your will and forced you to lie with her?"

At once he regretted the words. The story was one few people knew of, and fewer spoke about. No Cheysuli warrior—least of all the Mujhar's brother and loyal liege man—wished to admit he had been ensorcelled by an Ihlini. Knowing that the ensorcellment had involved sharing Lillith's *bed*—against his will, made powerless through temporary *lir*lessness—was a wound that did not heal. Even a yearly *i'toshaa-ni* ritual had failed to cleanse him of the humiliation.

And now his favorite nephew had thrown it in his face.

"*Su'fali*—" Hart took a step toward Ian, then stopped. "*Su'fali*—forgive me. I should not have spoken." In disgust, he scraped a splay-fingered hand through drying hair. "There are so *many* things I should not say or do."

"Aye," Ian agreed grimly. "And one day, perhaps, you will learn to say and do none of them."

Hart watched his uncle go. And then he roundly cursed himself, with elaborate eloquence.

The Prince of Homana stood by his great bed and looked down on the sleek black mountain cat sprawled across it with an elegance only her kind knew. The heavy rope of tail curved around one haunch. It did not twitch, nor did her tufted ears, but Brennan knew she was awake. He had sensed it within the link the moment he entered the room.

"I should have taken you with me," he said in weary disgust. "I should have taken you to keep me from trouble, even as I went with my *rujholli* to keep *them* from trouble." He sighed again. "As you see, the results were less than spectacular." He reconsidered. "No. They *were* spectacular. I should say, less than satisfactory."

The cat opened one golden eye. *It was not you,* lir. *It was your* rujholli.

"That changes nothing. *I* started the brawl."

With reason?

"Of *course* I had a reason." Brennan scowled at her. "I am not Hart, who does it out of ignorance while in the heat of greed. I am not Corin, who does it out of perversity. I am *me*, rememer? The eldest, the maturest, the most trustworthy of all the Mujhar's sons." He paused. And then he swore. "I should have let them go alone."

And if you had?

"Oh, there would have been a fight regardless, I think. Which is precisely why I *did* go with them." Brennan sat down on the bed. "Gods, Sleeta, I sometimes think I will go mad."

It is not your responsibility to be jehan *to your* rujholli, she pointed out. *They have one already.*

"Aye, aye, I know." Brennan picked at the ruined sleeve of his black velvet doublet. Beneath the blood-crusted fabric, his arm stung. He could not tell how deep the knife wound was. One-handed, he tried to undo the fastenings and found he could not. He went to the door and shouted for his body-servant.

The man came quickly enough, but so did Maeve. She dismissed him at once, even when Brennan protested, and declared she would tend her wounded brother herself. The body-servant accordingly brought hot water, clean cloths, and salve, and Maeve set about stripping the doublet from Brennan.

He helped her as best he could, shouldering out of the velvet once she peeled it from the silken undertunic, and perched on the three-legged stool when she told him to. Deftly, she washed the wound with soft cloth and gentle fingers.

"You should remove this gold." Maeve tapped a fingernail against the *lir*-band.

"No."

"I think you will hardly give up your rank or warrior status if you do," she said absently, dabbing carefully at the crusted wound. " 'Tis only one, Brennan."

He smiled as he heard the faint Erinnish lilt in her voice. The oldest of them all at twenty-three, Maeve had spent all but two years in Homana, but the close relationship between mother and daughter had resulted in an occasional hint of Erinn in her speech.

"You will soil your gown," he told her, trying to pull the heavy yellow velvet away from leather breeches stained with blood and dirt and wine.

"I can change it. Wait—forgive me!—" as he hissed in pain, "—there. Only a little blood."

He craned his head to inspect the wound. The slice divided his flesh with neat precision, ending somewhere beneath the armband. He recalled the scrape of steel on gold.

Brennan flexed the muscle. It hurt, but seemed unimpaired. "Just tie it up, Maeve. I will be well enough."

"Patience, patience, my lord prince." She smiled and slanted him a glance out of green eyes. "How can you go to a banquet with an arm left to bleed all over the guests?"

"Easily, as I am not invited." He worked at the heavy armband a moment; tugged it from its customary place above his elbow and slid it onto his forearm, where it dangled like a bracelet. The candlelight caught gold, flashed, washed the bronzed flesh with an ocher tinge. The flesh that was usually hidden under the band was lighter, though hardly fair; Brennan frowned and touched it, disliking the nakedness.

Maeve stopped sponging the wound. "Not invited!"

"Let us say—*un*invited." He scratched at the pale flesh above his elbow. "*Jehan* has decreed we are to remain in our respective chambers until he decrees otherwise."

"Hart and Corin, again," she said darkly, and sighed. "Brennan, one day you will come to their aid and they will get you slain."

"Is that a reason to ignore them, then?" He winced. "Maeve, that is living human skin, not the tanned hide of an animal."

"They take advantage of you, Brennan. And they always have. Especially Hart." Her lips were pressed flat as she carefully rubbed salve around the wound, pressed the flesh together, wrapped it snuggly with linen. He thought the grim expression ruined the symmetry of her features. Like her mother, Maeve was green-eyed, blonde, attractive in a bold, handsome way. There was no mark of Niall upon her. Maeve personified the Erinnish side of her heritage, lacking even the faintest trace of Cheysuli gifts or coloring.

And that is one thing Keely can gloat over, he reflected. *My proud Cheysuli rujholla may lack the color, but none of the gifts. The Old Blood gives her a distinct advantage.*

"Well," he said aloud, "I can hardly let Hart go out by himself when I know he is likely to get into trouble."

"Aye, you can," she demurred. "He is not your *lir*, that you have to attend him always."

"No, not my *lir*. But twin-born, which is a link at least as binding as what I have with Sleeta." Brennan watched her face. "I mean no offense, *rujholla*, but you cannot begin to understand what is between children of the same birth."

Her fingers, tying off the linen, stopped moving. Stiffly, Maeve moved away to stand directly in front of him. "No," she agreed in an odd, flat voice. "No, I cannot. No more than I can understand why two of my brothers *and* my sister resent me so, simply because I had the great good fortune to be the only child born of the union between the Mujhar and his light woman."

"You cannot accuse *Hart* of resenting you," Brennan told her. "He resents no one. All he thinks about is how best to win his wagers."

Her mouth twisted. "Such consolation, Brennan—that you do not leap to deny the resentment on Corin's and Keely's part."

He sighed and reached out to catch one of her hands. It was stiff, and very cold. "Maeve, you know them. Corin resents the world, I think, for making him thirdborn instead of first; Keely resents that she has no voice in her disposition." He pulled her more closely to him, until a fold of her skirts brushed against one knee. "You are free of a cradle-betrothal. You are free of the responsibilities of helping to fulfill the prophecy. You are free of the need to prove yourself able to live up to self-expectations. But mostly, you are free to be yourself, which is what Keely wants more than anything."

"She *is* herself!"

"No. Corin understands this better than I—Keely and I do not agree on much, as you know—but I think Keely desires to be more than *cheysula*, princess, *jehana* . . . I think she wants to know the freedom most men have, to be whatever they choose to be, and do what they wish to do."

"*You* do not. *You* were cradle-betrothed. By the gods, Brennan, you will marry Liam of Erinn's daughter just as Keely will wed his son! How can she say you have more freedom than she does? How can she resent *me* simply because I am not discontented by my place in this life?" Maeve pulled her hand out of his and turned her back, skirts swirling. And then she swung around to face him once again, brass-bright hair whipping in its loose net of gold wire and glittering topaz gemstones. "Would she trade places with me, I wonder, in her desire for contentment, if she knew she would be called the *bastard* daughter of the Mujhar and his Erinnish whore?" .

"*Who* calls you that?" Brennan was abruptly on his feet. The tears that glittered briefly in Maeve's eyes were enough to make him long to take his sword from its rack upon the wall.

"No one. Everyone." Maeve gestured sharply with both hands, expressing helplessness. "No one to my face, of course. They value their lives too much, knowing better than to say it near members of the House of Homana. But—I have heard it. Muttered. Whispered. Sometimes said quite clearly, when I go to Market Square."

"Maeve, you know he would wed her if he could. You *know* he would make her Queen of Homana, and you legitimate. And he will—when Gisella no longer lives."

"You speak of your mother, Brennan."

"I speak of the half-breed Cheysuli witch he married," Brennan said plainly. "I speak of the madwoman who bore him children, then tried to give them over to Strahan the Ihlini—and *would* have, had *jehan* not caught her at it, preventing the travesty." He shivered in distaste. "Gods— when I think of what I might have become had she succeeded. . . ."

"Dead," she said hollowly.

"Or worse." Brennan wanted to spit.

"Worse?" Maeve stared at him. "What could be *worse?*"

"We would be made minions," he said flatly. "Minions of Strahan; of Asar-Suti, the Seker, who made and dwells in darkness." He could not help the instinctive movement of his hand toward his knife. "He would cause us to be *minions*, Maeve; and to sit as puppets upon our respective thrones, allowing Strahan to rule in our places. To rule— and to destroy."

Five

"Two days," Hart said emphatically. "How much longer do you think I can last, mewed up in my chamber like a disobedient child?"

Corin, seated cross-legged on the floor of his chamber with Kiri in his lap, upside down so her belly could be properly scratched, looked at his brother expressionlessly. "For one, you are not *in* your chamber, you are in mine— and I think the idea was that you *were* a disobedient child."

"Aye, well, enough is enough," Hart said crossly. "I think he has forgotten us. Surely he could not expect us to remain night and day in our chambers."

"Surely he could," Corin corrected. "I am no fonder of my chamber than you of yours, but there appears to be no solution—" He stopped short. "I know that expression, Hart—what are you thinking?"

Hart grinned. "That we are Cheysuli warriors, and there is indeed a solution. That it is time we employed it." He scratched idly at his sleeveless Cheysuli jerkin, dyed a soft amber brown; the bound flesh beneath it itched. "That it is time I found a game before I lose my wits."

"I thought you had no money."

"There are the twenty-five crowns you owe me."

Corin grimaced. "Aye, that again." He waved a hand. "There, in the brass-bound casket—I think there are twenty-five."

Hart crossed to a table. He tipped the lid of the casket and nodded, eyebrows raised; there were considerably more than twenty-five. Supple fingers dipped in, deftly counted out twenty-five pieces of gold, tucked them into a leather belt-purse already tied at his right hip. "Thank the gods for a thrifty *rujholli*."

"No more thrifty than the next man," Corin retorted,

scrubbing affectionately at Kiri's belly fur. "It is only that I avoid the games you thrive on."

"Aye, well . . . shall we go find one?"

Corin's hand stopped moving. "You are serious."

"Aye." Hart nodded. "Shall we go?"

"Now?" Corin glanced out the nearest casement and saw the sun was already down. "Our *jehan* has expressly forbidden this sort of thing, Hart."

"Aye." Corin studied him. "That does not bother you in the least."

"Aye, it does. But not enough to gainsay me." Hart grinned and patted the now-filled belt-purse. "How will he know, *rujho?* We will go out like thieves and come back like thieves. Only wealthier."

Corin scratched slowly at his jaw, considering. "What of Brennan?"

"I asked." Hart shrugged. "He swore, called me a fool and every other name he could think of, Homanan and Old Tongue alike—and said he would leave us to our folly."

"*Us.*" Corin scowled. "He was so certain I would go?"

"Quite certain."

"*Ku'reshtin,*" Corin commented without heat. "Well, I think he has the right of it." He let Kiri get out of his lap, then stood. "Where do we go, *rujho?* Not The Rampant Lion again."

Hart laughed. "No, no, even I am not so foolish. No, I think we should go to a different part of the city, just to be safe in case our absence is discovered, and *jehan* sends the Guard again." One finger caressed the heavy knife hilt at his left hip. "I thought we might try the Midden."

"The Midden!" Corin, aghast, stared at him. "That is hardly our part of Mujhara, Hart. The Midden is infested with thieves, cutpurses, assassins. . . ." He shook his head. "No wonder Brennan said you were a fool."

Hart grinned his lopsided grin. "I did not precisely tell him that is where we are going."

Corin grunted. "The Midden is dangerous."

"Aye, it is." Hart merely continued to grin, and caressed his knife again.

After a moment, Corin's answering grin banished the scowl. He nodded. "But let me shed these useless velvets, *rujho*. If I go to the Midden with you, I go as a Cheysuli."

He stopped short of the nearest clothing trunk. "You *do* intend to take Rael."

"Of course. He is even now perched on the curtain wall, awaiting our arrival."

Corin glanced at Kiri. For a moment his eyes were oddly detached, as he went into the link. Then he sighed. "Kiri says we are every bit the fools Brennan claims, but she will come. If only to protect me from myself."

"Rael said something very similar," Hart reflected. The *lir*-gold gleamed on his arms. "Hurry, *rujho*. I need a game."

Hart and Corin slipped down the spiraling stairs in a tower near the back of Homana-Mujhar. The staircase was only rarely used by any member of the family, being primarily intended for the household staff; Hart was certain if they met anyone, they could bluff their way past.

It might have worked, except Corin—in the lead—ran smack into a shadow-shrouded body at the bottom, near the door that would pass them out of the palace proper into the inner bailey.

Corin swore, fell back a step; Hart bumped him and jostled him forward.

"I knew you would come this way." Brennan's voice; he opened the door partway and let the diffused light of bailey torches spill into the tower. Corin blinked. Kiri's eyes reflected oddly in the distorted light. Sleeta was a plush velvet shadow in the darkness, golden eyes staring fixedly at Hart and Corin.

"Are you here to try and gainsay us?" Hart demanded. "*Rujho*—"

"No," Brennan said clearly. "Have I ever been able to stop you before?"

"Once," Hart said. "You tripped me; I hit my head and was knocked half senseless."

Corin snickered. Brennan nodded reminiscently. "But I caught you off-guard then, and I have not been able to do it since. We are too well-matched, now, in size *and* experience." He peered out the door. "I think the way is clear."

"You are *coming?*" Corin was patently astonished.

"*Lir* or no *lir*, I can trust neither of you to look out for your welfare. Aye, I am coming."

"And if *jehan* catches us?"

"He will no doubt have us executed," Brennan said lightly. "Now, where is it we are going?"

Corin glanced over his shoulder to Hart, who shrugged a little.

"*Where?*" Brennan asked suspiciously.

"The Midden," Corin said. Hastily, he added, "Hart's idea."

Brennan looked at his blue-eyed twin in silence a moment. And then he said, very quietly, "You are even a greater fool than I thought."

"I need a *game*," Hart said. When Brennan only stared at him, he slipped past both brothers and stalked outside, *lir*-gold agleam in the torchlight.

They went horseback to the edges of the Midden, the border between lesser and greater Mujhara in attitude as well as advantages. The mounts they left at a small livery, then went ahead on foot. They walked the narrow, night-blackened streets like shadow-wraiths, moving through the depths of the moonless night. Sleeta padded silently at Brennan's side, only her great golden eyes betraying her presence. Rael was a faint shimmering blur overhead; Kiri, quick, delicate Kiri, trotted at their backs.

Others moved in the darkness as well, soft-footed, silent, silk-smooth; men well-versed in the art of deception and subterfuge. No one spoke a word.

The cobbles under their boots were muffled beneath layers of dirt and the remains of old droppings, packed into the seams and hollows formed by rounded, timeworn bricks. The winding street smelled of old ale, urine, the close confinement of people unused to washing. In corners they heard scuttling and squeaking; occasionally the yowl of a tom cat protecting his territory.

The dwellings themselves were all of wood, set cheek-by-jowl in crooked corners and dogleg turnings. Candles glowed here and there, a lantern, occasionally a torch. But the night held dominance.

Corin twitched his wrist experimentally. A shiver of anticipation coursed down his spine; he felt the sting in his armpits. "Where do we go?" he asked quietly.

Hart shrugged. "A tavern—any tavern. No place in particular."

"Well-planned," Brennan muttered. "*Jehan* would be so proud."

"Perhaps we should have brought Keely instead of you," Hart retorted. "The gods know she has more willingness than you to explore the unknown."

"Perhaps you should have," Brennan agreed. "Then there would be four fools in place of three."

"Leave Keely out of it," Corin warned.

"She *would* have come," Hart said.

"Aye," Corin agreed. "And then we would have to concern ourselves with how many rude-speaking men she would be likely to cut, to teach them better manners."

"There," Hart said abruptly, stopping short. "A tavern." Corin and Brennan also stopped, keeping to the shadows.

"There?" Brennan asked in disbelief.

"Why not?" Hart returned. "See you the sign-plate?"

The sign-plate in question dangled crookedly from a length of leather thong. There was no wind; it did not creak or spin or swing. It seemed to swallow what little light there was in the street, and throw it back toward the three Cheysuli princes.

"I see it," Brennan agreed grimly. "I think I can *smell* it, also."

" 'The Pig in the Poke,' " Corin read aloud. "How appropriate."

Brennan shook his head. "I am not taking Sleeta in there."

"Then leave her outside to wait with Kiri and Rael," Corin said. "They will be close enough if we need them."

"Come," Hart said impatiently, and stepped out to lead the way across the street.

Brennan brought him up short by catching one bare arm. "Wait you, *rujho*—I think we would do well, before we go, to agree to one thing."

"Aye, aye, what?" Hart's impatience was manifest.

"That we leave our knives sheathed," Brennan said clearly, catching Corin's eyes as well. "In this sort of place, if we show steel we will likely have it fed to us."

"By the gods, Brennan, you will have me thinking you *are*

a woman instead of warrior!" Corin exclaimed in disgust. "Have it fed to us, indeed—we are *Cheysuli*, Brennan."

"We are also in a part of Mujhara where I doubt very much anyone will be much impressed by our rank or race," Brennan answered grimly.

Hart sighed and glanced over at the tavern. "I have no intention of showing steel, *rujho*—only enough gold to buy my way into a game."

"And I am willing to wager the game will be much different here than at The Rampant Lion."

"Wagering, are you?" Hart grinned. "Come, *rujho* . . . let us go in where your willingness to wager may be translated into *winning*." Without waiting for an answer, he headed across the street as the *lir* secreted themselves in the shadows.

The door caught on ridged dirt as Hart pushed it open; pushing harder, he knocked it off the uneven floor. His momentum carried it through to slam against the wooden wall, which served to stop all conversation in the common room and fasten everyone's attention on the new arrivals.

Brennan, just behind Hart, looked over the room, judging rapidly. And muttered beneath his breath, "We should have left the horses closer."

"And have them stolen?" Corin, last in, asked it very quietly as he shut the door, then turned back to face the room along with his brothers.

The Pig in the Poke was as unlike The Rampant Lion as could be. It was unlike any tavern the princes had ever been in before, and quite suddenly they came to the realization that their lives had been sheltered indeed. A few lanterns, stinking of cheap oil, depended from the roof-tree, which littered the floor liberally with debris and divots hacked out with knives and swords. The candles were tallow, not wax, and next to useless, giving off a smudged, greasy flame that burned only sluggishly. Thick smoke climbed up the limbs of the tree to hang in the air like a blanket. The common room stank of old ale, stale beer, and unwashed bodies, as well as desperation and hostility.

Hart indicated an empty table not far from the door. It was stained dark from age and spilled liquor, sticky with wine residue, scarred from weapons and spurs. Hart caught hold of a bench and dragged it over the earthen floor made uneven and treacherous by divots and hardpacked ridges. He sat down and placed his hands on the table; his fingers twitched, as if needing the rune-sticks and dice.

Brennan and Corin followed a moment later. And when at last the tavern-keeper came over, silence still ruled the room.

He was not tall but incredibly broad, brown-haired, and brown-eyed, with wide, spatulate fingers. His tunic and trews were spun of rough homemade yarn, nubbed with numerous flaws, and wine-stained. There was little fat on his body, save for a belly that overflowed trews and stretched the tunic tight.

He showed the resin-stained teeth in his mouth, but it was not precisely a smile. "You be far from your Keep."

"A man in search of a good game will go as far as necessary," Hart said calmly. "Have you one to offer?"

The tavern-keeper looked at each of them, one at a time. His dark eyes were shrewd and judgmental. "Have I a game to offer? Well, I might. Have you *gold* to offer?" The eyes were on the *lir*-bands weighting three pairs of arms.

Hart wet his lips. "Oh, aye, you may say so, and safely. Enough to play. Now—the game?"

Brown eyes couched in creases stopped evaluating Brennan and Corin entirely, making Hart their sole subject. The tavern-keeper said nothing at all for several long moments, and then his unfriendly face loosened a bit. Not a smile, in no way, but an expression of comprehension as he saw how Hart's brown fingers tapped incessantly against the dirty tabletop.

"Your beasts," he said, in his lowborn dialect. "I'll not have any in here, where decent men are drinking."

Corin straightened almost imperceptibly on his stool. One hand dipped below the tabletop and stayed there, until an unwavering stare from Brennan, across the table, made Corin take his hand away from his knife.

Brennan looked up at the tavern-keeper. "They are *lir*, not beasts."

The man shrugged wide shoulders. "Beasts, *lir*—what do I care what you call those sorcerous things from the netherworld? All I know is, I won't have 'em in here."

"Then perhaps you should not have *us* in here." Brennan stood deliberately.

Corin looked up at his waiting brother, then shoved his bench back to rise. He stopped. He lingered there, halfway, and looked at Hart. "*Rujho*—"

Hart made no move to join them, and the tavernkeeper laughed. "Still wanting your game, are you?" He nodded a little. "Aye, I can see it. So, it touches even the wondrous Cheysuli." He turned. "Baram—this Cheysuli be wanting a *game*."

"Hart," Brennan said quietly.

Hart shook his head. "Go, or stay. *I* stay."

Brennan watched the man cross the common room. "Hart no. This place stinks of trouble. It stinks of *murder!*"

"Not so easy to murder a Cheysuli, I think." Corin sat down again.

Briefly Brennan touched the linen binding on his left arm, absently checking the knots Maeve had tied. Then, with a muttered imprecation, he sat down once more.

"Three to one?" Baram asked.

Brennan shook his head. Corin, seeing Hart's intensity, indicated he would stay out of it as well. He and Brennan both had seen their middle brother in such a state before; it was better to let him play alone, against one or more opponents. He had little time for those who merely dabbled.

"One to one," Hart said intently, and the tavernkeeper set down the house casket.

Baram touched the casket with a forefinger, then drew it away. He was black-eyed and gap-toothed, with a hideous scar on his chin. "You," he said gruffly.

Hart picked up the casket and upended it, pouring the dice into his left hand. There were no rune-sticks, only ivory dice now yellowed with age and dirt. The marks on them denoting a numerical system were mostly worn away.

Hart examined them, nodded briefly to himself, poured them back into the casket. Ivory rattled as he set the casket down. "The game," he said, and waited.

"Counting game," Baram answered. He paused. "Count?"

"I count."

"Throw thrice. Each. High two of three wins." He shrugged. "Simple enow."

"Simple enough." Hart nodded. "Throw."

They played through quickly, with nothing said past what had to be said. Brennan watched uneasily as other men in the tavern came closer to watch, leaving their own games behind. Corin drank wine and watched the dice as they rattled and danced on the table.

After some time spent trading coin back and forth between them—Hart's twenty-five gold crowns, Baram's inconvenient assortment of coppers and silver royals—Hart leaned forward. "Not good enough," he said. "Shall we make it more interesting?"

Baram looked at the pile of coins glinting by Hart's elbow. Their winnings were evenly split, with neither man showing dominance over the dice. "Aye," he said at last.

Hart tapped his pile. "All."

Baram grunted. "Throw."

Hart threw tens, fives, twos; Baram twelves, eights, threes. Brennan watched the pile of coins in front of Hart go into Baram's pocket.

Hart frowned a little, tapped fingers on the table, nodded to himself. "Again," he said intently.

The Homanan slowly shook his head and pointed a crooked finger. "No gold, shapechanger. Nothing left to wager. Don't throw on promises."

Hart tapped his right forefinger on the table. The sapphire signet flashed in the smudgy light. "I have something left."

"No," Brennan said sharply.

Baram looked at the ring, at Brennan, at Hart. And he laughed. "Done," he said, and threw the dice.

Six throws, and the ring was forfeit. Baram put out his hand.

"No!" Brennan's own hand flashed down to catch Hart's, preventing him from stripping off the ring. "You are mad," he said flatly, "*mad* to think I will let you pay a debt with this. This ring signifies your title."

"I can get another." Hart tried to withdraw his hand from Brennan's grasp and did not succeed. "There must be hundreds of these stones in the treasury, Brennan; I can have another made."

"No." Brennan looked at Baram. "Will you take gold in place of this?"

"Gold?" Baram considered him silently a moment. "D'ye mean to make good his wager *for* him, then?"

"I do."

"Now?" Baram asked. "*Right* now?"

Grimly, Brennan nodded. "I have the coin."

"No." Baram's eyes went back to Hart, and he grinned his gap-toothed grin. "You said gold, shapechanger," he gestured toward the *lir*-bands on Hart's arms, "so I'll be taking those."

"*Ku'reshtin!*" Corin cried. "Do you think—"

"No." Brennan's sharp gesture cut him off. He sat very still on his stool. "I have gold crowns in my belt-purse, Homanan, and that is what I will pay you with. Nothing else."

Baram's determination was manifest. "I want those bracelets, shapechanger—and no man here can say I didn't win 'em *fairly*."

Hart's color was bad. "These—" he stopped, wet his lips, touched his left armband in something very like a caress. He started over. "These were never at stake," he said. "Never. I owe you, aye, and you will be paid—but not with *these*."

Brennan unlaced his belt-purse and threw it onto the table. It landed with a heavy thump and a satisfying clink of gold. "There. More than enough to cover what he owes you."

Baram's hand shot out, scooped up the purse, hid it somewhere on his person. "Now," he said, "I'm paid. But I'm still waiting for *those*, and there're enough of us here to see that you give 'em to me."

"Try," Hart suggested, and before anyone else could move, including his brothers, he caught the table and overturned it.

Casket, cups, and winejug flew in Baram's direction. Corin ducked, rolled off his stool, came up with knife in hand, knowing Brennan's ban on edged weapons no longer held true. Not at all; Corin saw the glint of a knife in *Brennan's* hand across the way. But he had no more time to watch for either brother; men were coming for him, and he saw steel in their hands.

Oh, gods, he thought, *I will have to slay a man.*

"Brennan—*behind you*—" Hart shouted, and then he

had no more time to shout at his brother. Baram himself was on him with a long-knife in his hand.

A stool, on its side, rolled at Brennan's heels. He tripped, as he was meant to; staggered back, trying to plant his feet and regain his balance—a man, no *two*—reaching for him from behind—

Sleeta—he cried within the link, *gods, Sleeta, I never thought*—

Corin felt the wooden wall at his back. Shoulder blades, leather-clad, scraped; he pressed back, back, wishing he could somehow slide through the cracks in the boards. There was no more choice left to him, none at all; he bled from a cut across the back of one hand, and the two Homanans came at him again.

Hart twisted aside, caught Baram's wrist. As the Homanan struggled, cursing, Hart wrenched his arm back until the cords in Baram's neck stood up. Cords gave; the knife fell out of his hand.

The stench of spilled oil and greasy flame filled the common room. Someone cursed; another called that there was *fire*.

From outside the tavern came the scream of an angry mountain cat.

"Kill them, kill all of them!" the tavern-keeper shouted. "Kill them before they shift their shapes!"

Brennan, outnumbered, was slammed down against the floor. Beneath him, a wooden cup jammed against his spine, so that he writhed away from the pain; the knife was knocked out of his hand.

Defenseless, he kicked out and tried to twist away, but the two men had stretched him so that there was no leverage. All he could do was thrash helplessly as a faceless man bent down to slide the knife through leather, flesh, past muscle into the belly wall.

He dared not lurch upward. *Dared* not—gasping with effort, Brennan summoned everything he could of concentration, thrusting his consciousness out of the room, away, *away*, to somewhere deep in the heart of the earth.

Gods, gods he cried in silent appeal, *let the magic come— let the power be tapped*—

Corin ducked a knife swipe; threw himself forward, beneath the arm . . . with all his strength he jammed his head into the belly of the Homanan. Breath expelled, the man fell backward, knees folding; Corin bore him down, braced quickly, shoved the knife deeply into the heaving belly. The Homanan cried out, thrashed futilely, cried out again.

Corin threw himself off, rolled, came up; blocked the second man's attack by catching the Homanan's wrist. Quickly, hardly knowing what he did, Corin sliced deeply into soft flesh of the underside of the outstretched arm. Blood flowed; flesh and tendons parted without a sound.

Hart bent, coughed, tried to breathe through the pain of sore ribs now doubly bruised. Smoke filled his throat as it filled the room, reaching cloying fingers into eyes, nostrils, mouths, even as it clogged the corners. Dimly he saw flames as they ran up the walls, danced along the roof-tree, dripped down to splatter on overturned tables and stools.

"Get out," he gasped. "Brennan—Corin—" He broke off as someone wrapped arms around his legs and pulled him down.

Hart struggled, felt hands insinuating themselves between his legs; groping, trying to grab, to wrench, to *rip*, using tactics of the sort Hart, honorably trained, had never, *ever* considered.

Outraged, he threw an elbow that caught the man in the face, smashed his nose; sent the Homanan tumbling backward, crying out.

Less beleaguered than Brennan and now twice as angry, Hart called up the earth magic and left behind his human form for the one with hooked beak and curving talons.

—the one that will lend me flight; that I can use to rake eyes from the enemy, to pluck them from their Homanan skulls—

Corin saw the flames, the smoke, the bodies. He saw the blurring of Hart's human form into the void that swallowed the space where he had stood a moment before; into the nothingness that was shed, replaced, made whole once again, only lacking the familiar shape of a man. Arms were wings, legs talons; the shout Hart began the shapechange with became the piercing cry of a hunting hawk—

—and was joined a moment later by the scream of a cat, as Brennan left behind *Brennan* to become an echo of his *lir*, tawny instead of black, but dangerous, so dangerous; so intent on his prey, as he raked claws across the nearest face, that Corin knew he had gone too far.

Too close, too close—oh, Brennan, no—not you—of all of us, not you—

Corin turned, stumbling, and reached for the door, for the latch, clawing it open; jerking open the door and thrusting it against the wall. Inwardly he called for Kiri. Aloud, he shouted for both his brothers' *lir*, and fell sideways, slamming a shoulder into the door; coughing, *coughing*, as smoke boiled out of the tavern into the darkness of the night.

Kiri, Corin said within the link, *Kiri, tell the* lir *to make them stop—tell them to stop—this place will become our pyre—*

The vixen understood at once, instantly passing the message to Sleeta and Rael. Corin knew better than to think he could talk sense into Brennan or Hart in the throes of the fight; especially as they were too angry, too blind to see the danger of remaining inside the tavern. Even with flame climbing the walls and running out along the roof to touch the dwelling next door, his brothers would not forgo the fight. Not now.

He heard screams from inside. He turned, saw someone afire. How the man danced; how the man screamed, as he tried to run and could not, trapped by the trunk of the burning roof-tree.

Limbs, burned through, broke off, and parts of the roof began to rain down. Flame shot through the openings and engulfed the upper floor.

"Corin—" Hart, coughing, staggered out. Ash smeared his face; light from the flames set his *lir*-gold to gleaming. "Corin, is Brennan out?"

"No," Corin answered tersely. "Gods, Hart, this is *your* doing."

"Mine—" But Hart stopped the protest at once, swinging back toward the interior of the tavern. "Brennan!"

Rael flew out, followed closely by Kiri. Then Sleeta, unaccompanied.

Hart swore, plainly afraid. Corin caught his arm to prevent him from going back in, "No, *rujho*—no!" and Brennan stumbled out in human form.

Coughing, he nearly fell. "Dead," he gasped. "Dead, or dying—gods, *all of them*—"

"And most of the street." Hart's voice was clogged with phlegm. He coughed, spat; hugged aching ribs.

"No reason for us to mimic them *or* it," Corin said firmly. "We have ourselves and our *lir* . . . I suggest we go."

Brennan, moving out into the street, craned his neck to look over his shoulder. "They would have slain us . . . they would have had the gold off all our arms, planting steel in our bellies."

Hart tried to laugh and could not. But the sound was not one of humor. "Justifying their end?" he asked Brennan. "Do not bother, *rujho* . . . no more than anyone will when *we* are dead."

"If we do not go *now*, we may well end up that way." Corin's hand on Hart's wrist was not gentle. "Is it left to me, then? Well enough, the youngest to the oldest: *run*—"

They ran. And with them ran—and flew—their *lir*.

Six

They were lined up before the Lion Throne of Homana, his sons, in the Great Hall. Like little soldiers, Niall thought, all prepared to accept their punishment. Except he was quite certain they had not even considered the punishment he intended to levy on them.

The cushion beneath his buttocks did nothing to soften the confines of the Lion. The great wooden throne swallowed him up almost entirely, which was not a simple task considering his size; he reflected it must have been the same for Carillon, his grandsire, whom he so closely resembled.

He looked at his sons, standing three abreast before the Lion, in front of the firepit that began some six feet from the marble dais to stretch the length of the hall. He looked for guilt, regret, comprehension; he looked for some indication they understood how serious was the situation. But they had practiced for him, showing him stiff Cheysuli masks in place of faces, all of them, even blue-eyed, fair-haired Corin, who lacked the dark skin as well.

They had practiced, and he could not read their expressions. Until he told them how many were dead.

"At last count," the Mujhar said quietly, "there were more than twenty-eight bodies. It could be more; they are still searching in the rubble." He paused a moment, looking at his sons. "No one is quite sure; the entire block was destroyed."

Now the masks slipped. Now the faces were bared. Shock, disbelief, denial; a profound, sudden and absolute comprehension of where the responsibility lay.

Niall shifted slightly, redistributing his weight within the embrace of the massive Lion. "I think the time for explanations is past. I think the assignment of guilt is unnecessary. Certainly apologies, however heartfelt, cannot begin to replace the lives and property lost. So I will request no explanations, no apologies, no admissions of guilt. I request only that you listen."

None of them said a word. Brennan, he saw, stood quite rigidly, staring blankly at an area somewhere in the vicinity of his father's left foot. Niall watched a moment as his eldest son tried to cope with the shock, the comprehension, the tremendous burden of responsibility he would, as always, try to assume. Even if it was only partially his.

Corin was plainly stunned. The color was gone from his face so that his tawny hair seemed a darker gold than normal. All the muscles stood up in his arms, flexing around the *lir*-bands; behind his back, Niall knew, Corin fisted his hands again and again, as hard as he could until all the muscles burned, protesting; inflicting discomfort to help the comprehension that what he now faced was real, and not some dream of his imagining. Niall had seen him do it before.

Lastly, he looked at Hart. Hart, whose insatiable taste— no, *need*—for gambling had, until two nights before, done little more than rob him of his allowance as Prince of Solinde; yet now it robbed people of their property. Of their *lives*.

Niall pushed himself out of the throne, bracing palms against the clawed armrests. He felt old, old and stiff, reluctant to rise and face them as a king, a Cheysuli, a father. And yet he knew he must.

He stood on the marble dais before the Lion Throne of Homana, personifying the strength and authority of his realm, and fixed his middle son with a single hard blue eye. "I think it is time I stopped looking the other way. I think it is time I stopped rebuilding half the taverns in Mujhara with money from the Homanan treasury, and—occasionally—my *personal* coffers. I think it is *past* time I forced you to become the man your *tahlmorra* intended you to be."

Hart did not flinch. "Aye, *jehan*," was all he said, and very quietly.

"I might wish you had been so acquiescent *before*, Hart." The mouth flattened a little. "Aye, *jehan*."

"Well, then, as you are so acquiescent *now*, I must assume you will start for Solinde in the morning with good heart and good cheer."

The color slowly spilled out of Hart's face. "Solinde—?"

"Tomorrow," Niall confirmed, "where you will remain for the space of a year."

"*Jehan*—"

"You will be sent to Lestra, where you will—I hope, I *pray*—begin to learn what it is to be a prince . . . a man with responsibilities . . . a man who cannot afford to drink and dice and brawl." He paused. "Do I make myself clear?"

"Aye . . ." And then, in shock, "*But*—"

Yet again, Niall cut him off. "Your allowance will be strickly administered by the regent who now governs in my name. He will be advised that he is not to underwrite your gambling habit *in any fashion* . . . that if you somehow lose the last copper penny of your monthly allowance, you will bear the responsibility for repaying the debt. *You*, Hart. Not Brennan, not Corin, not Ian, Maeve, Keely, or Deirdre. Certainly not me. And *certainly not* the Solindish treasury. Is that clear, also?"

"A *year* . . ." Hart's tone was hollow.

"Aye. You are hereby forbidden your homeland for the space of a twelve-month, unless I send for you myself."

"Exile." Bitterness, now, beginning to creep in. "First our *jehana*, now me."

"The circumstances are unrelated," Niall said coldly, "though I begin to wonder if there is more of Gisella in you than of myself." Abruptly, he stopped himself. "You will leave first thing in the morning."

Brennan took a single step forward. "*Jehan*," he said. "No. I beg you. Say you will reconsider!"

"You are to hold your silence until given leave to speak," Niall said evenly. Brennan flinched visibly and did not move or speak again.

It was Corin's turn; Corin, who so rarely knew when not to defy his father. "And I am to go to Atvia, am I not?" he asked bitterly. "I am to be exiled too, like Hart. For a year."

"For a year," Niall confirmed. "The circumstances are much the same, I think, even if the individual problems differ; you need to learn to accept the responsibility for your own actions, *and* your manners, which can injure others. And if you think to deny me—as I see you intend already, judging by your expression—I suggest you think back to the deaths you caused only two nights ago."

"It was not entirely my fault," Corin said angrily. "Lay no blame, you say. Well, I *will*. You may blame the cutthroats who tried to slay us, *jehan*—the men who were willing to stick us and watch us bleed for the price of our *lir*-gold!"

"You will leave in the morning," Niall said quietly. "But before you arrive in Atvia, there is a task I would have you perform."

"Task?" Corin stared at his father. "You send me away, then ask me to perform a task?"

"One I think you will be pleased to do, as it concerns the Prince of Homana."

Corin frowned. "Brennan?"

"Did you think I would forgo punishing him because he is the oldest? Because he is the heir to Homana?" Niall shook his head. "No. I said I would assign no guilt, and I do not. Neither do I weigh it by the things you have done in the past, all of you. Brennan is equally responsible, and he will share equally in the punishment."

"Equally?" Corin demanded. "I think not. There is nowhere to *send* him. Homana is his to rule, one day; you cannot exile the man who will take your throne."

"I *send* him nowhere, that is true," Niall said quietly. "But I can still make certain he begins to accept the responsibilities you and Hart must also accept. And it is up to you, Corin, to assist me." He paused. "I thought you might be willing to assume the task, once you realized it was within your province to alter the freedom of your oldest *rujholli*."

Corin glanced at Brennan, who stared stoically at the throne, avoiding his father's eye altogether. "How?" Corin asked finally, looking again at Niall.

The Mujhar turned to the Lion and resumed his seat, sitting back against the ancient wood. "You will stop at Erinn on the way to Atvia and deliver a message to Liam, Lord of the Idrian Isles. You will say to him the time has come for our realms to be formally united in marriage as well as in alliance." The single blue eye flicked to Brennan. "Liam's daughter is twenty-two, now. It is time the Prince of Homana secured the Lion with additional heirs."

Color rushed into Brennan's face. The yellow eyes were suddenly intent, and intensely feral. "You do not use a betrothal or marriage as *punishment!*" Brennan snapped angrily. "It does you little honor, *my lord Mujhar*, and gives none at all to Aileen."

"You have at least a six-month, if not more, in which to arrange your affairs and learn what it is to be a prince," Niall said. "Until Aileen arrives, you will attend me in all council sessions, at all trade negotiations, during the hearings when I entertain petitions put forth by Homanan citizens. I think you will be too busy to concern yourself with what does and does not constitute honor, in Mujhars or other people."

"After twenty years and more, you separate us so easily," Hart said blankly. "I cannot believe it."

"*Together*, you have done little more save drink and brawl and bring disgrace to your names as well as this House," Niall answered. "Apart, perhaps, you will learn what it is to be a man. To be a *Cheysuli warrior*." As one, in stunned silence, they stared at him, Niall abruptly stood up from the throne. "I do not doubt there are things you wish to say to one another without benefit of my presence, so I will take it from you."

Niall's sons watched in silence as he strode stiffly from the Great Hall. But as the silver doors thudded closed, the silence was ended most distinctly.

"Did you hear him?" Corin asked in angry astonishment. "Did you *hear* him? 'I think the time for explanations is past.'" He swore loudly, with great eloquence. "We were given *no* chance to defend ourselves, *no* chance to tell him precisely what happened—he merely stands before that travesty of a lion and tells us what we are to do with our lives, as if *he* has the ordering of them?"

"He does," Hart said remotely. He walked to the dais, turned, sat down upon the top step, propping booted feet wide on the second one. "He is the Mujhar of Homana, and our *jehan*."

"Aye, he *is* Mujhar," Corin snapped, "and, *as Mujhar*, one of his responsibilities is to hear both sides of the story." He swore again and kicked at the gold-veined marble dais. "You would think we *planned* the fire, they way he talks."

Brennan stood at one of the stained-glass casements,

staring blindly through colored glass to the bailey outside. He seemed oblivious to Corin's rantings.

"Gods," Hart murmured. "*Solinde*—"

"—and Atvia." Corin kicked marble again, as if he meant to dislodge a portion of his father's skull. "What do I want with a lump of rock in the middle of the Idrian Ocean?"

Brennan's hand traced the outline of one of the patterns in the glass. "Twenty-eight lives," he said. "*Twenty-eight.*"

"You would think he considers himself one of the *gods*, the way he stands before us and pronounces how we will spend the next twelve months of our lives," Corin said in disgust. "*I* think—"

"*Do you think I care what you think?*" Brennan abruptly spun from the casement and, before Corin could blurt a protest, crossed the hall to grab the front of his jerkin. "Do you think I care that you feel *inconvenienced* by having to accept your title in fact as well as name?" He pushed his brother back two steps, forced him up the dais, planted him solidly in the throne. "*Twenty-eight lives were lost, Corin* . . . it should not matter to you that those lives were spent in the Midden instead of Homana-Mujhar or Clankeep. It *should not matter!* They are *dead*, Corin . . . dead because of us!"

Corin inched back into the Lion, trying to escape Brennan's hands. "*Rujho*—"

"No," Brennan said tersely. "No explanations. No defense. In this I will be like our *jehan*." He took his hands from Corin's jerkin as if he could not bear to soil them. "We went there against our king's express orders, defying our *jehan* as well, and because of us an entire block was destroyed. Twenty-eight lives were lost, perhaps more. By the gods, Corin, how can you sit there and rail against our *jehan* with that guilt on your shoulders?"

"Let him be," Hart said wearily. "Oh, let him be, Brennan. I can think of better ways of spending our last day together than trying to levy even *more* guilt upon our youngest *rujholli*."

"Not more," Brennan shot back. "*Some* guilt . . . because I think otherwise he will dismiss this tragedy as not worthy of his time, his concern, simply because he has *more important* things to consider." Brennan's tone was filled with eloquent contempt. "Such as which of Deirdre's ladies should he seduce *next*."

"I care!" Corin cried. "I *care*, Brennan—more than you can know. And *aye*, I do have something else to consider . . . something that may not have occurred to you. And even if it had, likely *you* would not consider it worth the worry."

"What?" Brennan demanded. "What else is there to consider?"

Corin's lips drew back briefly, baring teeth. In his anger, his ferocity, he was suddenly more animal than man, though he remained in human form. "I am afraid," he said through gritted teeth. *"Afraid."*

"Afraid?" Brennan stared at him in astonishment. "Aye, it will be different in Atvia, and will take time to adjust, but—afraid?"

"Aye, afraid!" Corin cried. "Are you forgetting, then, that our *jehana* is there? Mad Gisella, Queen of Homana, who tried to give her children to Strahan the Ihlini?" He had their full attention now, as he looked from one to the other. "Aye," he repeated, "afraid because I will have to see her, to *face* her. . . ." He drew in an unsteady breath. "I will be required to breathe the same air as that half-breed, blood-tainted Atvian/Cheysuli witch, who *willingly* would have given us over to that Ihlini *ku'reshtin*, so he could twist us all—so he could turn us into minions for his amusement, to use as *puppets!*"

"Enough," Brennan said gently. "Enough, Corin—no more." His anger was banished, his contempt replaced with compassion. "Perhaps I judged you too hastily." He sighed and scrubbed at the lines of tension settling in the flesh of his brow. "Gods, save us from each other . . . save us from sword-sharp tongues."

"Save us from the Ihlini." Corin shut his eyes and leaned his head back against the throne. "Gods, *rujho*, I do not want to go. . . ."

"No," Brennan agreed. "Nor would I, in your place. Not even if you promised a casket of gold."

"For that much gold, I might." Hart's smile fell away almost at once. "No, no, forgive me for that . . . *I* am the one who put us in this position. Blame me, no matter what *jehan* says. Let me carry the guilt."

"Would you?" Brennan asked. "No, I think not. It is not in you to accept guilt, *rujho*, even if you comprehend that you are responsible for it."

Hart recoiled visibly from the comment.

"Well," Corin said in resignation, "for all I rail about it—and will—I think the distribution of sentences just. You go nowhere, Brennan; all you must do is wait for a *cheysula*. Not so bad, I think, but then it was not your idea to go to the Midden, and you did what you could to prevent us from becoming involved in an obviously dangerous situation. A wedding should not be so bad; the gods know Deirdre is bearable. Aileen is her *harana*, so if they are anything alike you should not find the marriage too onerous."

"No," Brennan agreed, "though I might wish the time to be of my own choosing."

"But he has taken that from you." Corin nodded. "He has taken it from us all." Abruptly he shoved himself out of the Lion. "I think I will defy him one last time, just so he does not forget me *too* easily—"

"Corin, *no!*" Brennan cried. "Why make it worse than it is?"

"Do you mean to refuse to go?" Hart asked in surprise.

"No." Corin straightened a jerkin still rumpled from Brennan's expression of anger and frustration. "I mean to go, because I must. But I mean to go *now*, rather than in the morning."

"Small defiance," Brennan said curtly. "You cut your nose to spite your face."

"Perhaps." Corin headed down the steps and toward the hammered silver doors at the end of the Great Hall. "But at least it is a decision I can make for myself. Besides," he swung around and walked backward, spreading his hands, "this way I will be home one day sooner." And he was gone, running from the hall.

Brennan said a sharp, brief obscenity in the Old Tongue that still, for all its brevity, managed to express his emotions very clearly.

"Three become two become one." Hart stood up from the dais. "Not a good wager, *rujho*, when the point of the game lies in *adding*, not subtracting." He sighed and walked aimlessly toward the silver doors. "No," he said wearily, "not a good wager at all."

"Hart." Brennan's voice stopped him at the doors, echoing in the vastness of the hall. "In a year, a *year*—we will be different people."

Hart leaned a shoulder against one of the heavy doors. "Aye," he agreed, "but still Cheysuli. Still *rujholli*. That is what counts, I think." He smiled sadly, pushed through, was gone.

After a moment Brennan turned to look at the empty Lion, all acrouch on the dais; the Lion of Homana, deprived of his Mujhar. Brennan looked at the old wood, the fading giltwork, the massive paws with their curving claws. He sighed. "You and I," he said, "will have to come to an agreement. You do not strip me of all my freedom, my good sense, my desire to be a man as well as Mujhar . . . and I will not bring dishonor to your name. To my House. Or to my people." He shook his head slowly. "And never again to my *jehan*."

But the Lion made no answer.

Deirdre was in her private solar, stitching on a tapestry with four of her ladies when Niall came in. She glanced up, saw his face, instantly dismissed the women. Before Niall could say a word, Deirdre was up and guiding him to a chair.

"I am well enough," he protested, as she pressed him down into the cushions.

"Are you, then?" she asked lightly. "I'm thinking not. I'm thinking you have, from the look of you, stared death in the eye, and lost." She made certain he was comfortable in the chair. "You'll be sitting here until *I* say you may rise."

Loose-limbed, he sat in the chair and stared blankly at the tapestry frame. "What is that?"

"Something I started a month ago. Something to go in the Great Hall, one day, when I am done." She knew very well his real interest did not lie in the tapestry; she knew also that Niall came around to things in his own way, in his own time. Prying would serve neither of them. "You see? Lions. Homanan lions, as you have told me; fierce, proud, loyal beasts, challenging all who *dare* to threaten their realm." Her voice wavered a moment as she looked at his ravaged face. "Niall—"

"Why so many?" he asked, staring at the tapestry. He bent forward to examine it more closely. "So many lions, Deirdre—and is this the Lion Throne?"

"Aye." She touched the design not yet fully stitched. "It seems to me some of the stories should be put down in yarn, and then hung up where all can see them. The recounting of the legends. Shaine, Carillon, Donal . . . you and your sons. . . ." her voice trailed off. "All the Lions of Homana."

"My sons." And Niall sat back again, pressing one hand against his face. "Ah, *gods*, Deirdre—what am I to do? How am I to bear it? How will I last the year?"

She stood very still before him. "You have sent them away, then, Hart and Corin."

"I had no choice." The words were little more than pain, mumbled against his hand. "They gave me no choice, *meijha*. So many lives lost. So many *innocent* lives; not everyone in the Midden is thief or murderer. Some were little children." Abruptly he stripped off the patch that warded the empty socket and bent forward rigidly. "Ah, gods—it hurts—"

"Your head?" She moved forward, knelt, threaded fingers in his hair. She pressed his face against her breast. "Oh, Niall, I would be giving anything to take it from you, this pain. After all these years . . ."

His breath was loud in the chamber. "No—no—not just my head . . . when the old pain comes on me, it is generally bearable. But *this*—" He sighed. "This is more. This is what it is to be a *jehan*, regardless of rank or race."

"Aye," she said, "aye. There is pain with all the pleasure."

"A year," he said hollowly. "Gods, I said a *year*. Hart and Corin banished . . . and Brennan made to wed."

She stiffened a little. "You'll be sending for Aileen."

"Aye. Corin is to stop at Erinn on his way to Atvia." Suddenly, he pulled away from her. "And perhaps I should have considered that *you* might want to go."

After a moment, she shook her head. "I'll not be denying that I want to see my homeland. But this is Corin's punishment; there is no place for me on board. Liam will understand."

He sat back again, asprawl, rubbing the ruined flesh near

his empty socket. "They gave me no choice," he said wearily. "What was I to do?"

"What you did, I think," she answered, settling down at his feet in a puddle of pale green silk. " 'Tis not for me to say yea or nay on this—they are not *my* sons—but I will agree with you nonetheless. Boys must stop being boys. Even when they are men."

"If you had seen Brennan's face . . ."

"Aye, well, if 'twas anything like the other times, he was there for the others, not himself."

"No, not that . . . no, I mean when I banished Hart. I think that was a worse punishment for Brennan than telling him he must wed and take on more responsibilities."

Deirdre sighed a little, stroking his rigid hand. "Aye, aye, perhaps it was. They are so close, Hart and Brennan . . . the time apart will be hard on them."

"Hard on me," he said unevenly. "For all they have done a monstrous thing, I know I will hate myself every day I took at Brennan and Keely, and see their accusing eyes."

"Brennan and Keely must tend to Brennan and Keely," Deirdre told him firmly. "*You* must look to yourself."

"And you?" he asked, reaching out to clasp her fingers. "Gods, Deirdre . . . what would I do without *you?*"

She smiled and kissed the back of his hand. "*I'll* not be telling you. For if I did, you might find reason to be rid of an aging Erinnish spinster."

He smiled. "Aging, indeed. Not what *I* would say; I who share your bed."

But she saw the anguish in his eye, and knew it would last forever.

PART II

Brennan

One

On a night with no moon, men gathered. Light was conjured from torches, from lanterns; distorting faces that, by day, by good light, were simply *faces;* Homanan faces, some young, some old, some neither, being not yet fully formed, leaving youth behind while lingering yet on the doorstep, not quite ducking beneath the lintel to enter the common room of manhood.

But now, by torchlight, by lanternlight, the faces were leeched of humanity, of sanity, of the expressions that, everchanging, reflected happiness, sorrow, pride, regret, and all those subtleties lying between. Faces that were no longer *faces,* but aspects of dedication, fanaticism, and the desire to right a wrong.

Within the ring of looming trees stood stave torches, thrust into the ground to form a second circle, a ward against the darkness. Within the ring of torches, men clustered. And within the ring of men, a boy was made to lie down on cold, hard stone. No. Not a boy; no longer. A warrior, now; he had received his *lir.*

Against the stone, he shivered. They had stripped him, the Homanans. They had taken jerkin, leggings, boots, as well as his knife. They had taken it all, leaving him with nothing, save the knowledge that they could get no gold, because he had only just received his *lir.* There had been no Ceremony of Honors in Clankeep, to honor his name, his *lir,* his newfound warrior status.

And would be none, ever, now.

It was full dark, long past the time he should have been back at Clankeep. But no one would come looking. He had left his father's pavilion four days earlier in search of his *lir,* knowing only he had to go, to assuage the craving that set his blood afire. No one would come looking, no matter how late it was, because it was a part of the ritual, to stay from home until the link was made.

Rings within rings: trees, torches, men. And in the center, himself. On an altar once serving as a part of sacred rituals, *Cheysuli* rituals, Firstborn rituals; now the altar, in its nook of towering trees, was forgotten by his people. Remembered only by Homanans, who meant to pervert its use.

Upon the stone he trembled, and shut his eyes against the darkness, the torchlight, the looming faces, with their aspects of fanaticism. He shut his eyes against the fear for himself, because another fear outweighed it. They would slay his *lir*, he knew. First. So they could see what it was for a Cheysuli warrior to lose his other self. And then, as he was consumed by grief for the loss of his *lir*, his newfound other self, they would slay the new warrior as well.

Beneath his naked back his flesh knew the touch of stone, and of blood. The altar reeked of it, stained black and red and brown, sticky with old and new.

Hands held wrists and ankles. Even his hair, so he could not thrash head against stone in a futile attempt at breaking free. Hands held him: Homanan hands. Deigning to touch his Cheysuli flesh, because soon enough his blood would wash them clean of taint.

"Bring the wolf," someone said. A man. Young, from the sound of it; the voice was cool, not deep, not high. Smooth as clover honey.

The boy on the stone jerked against human manacles. All held firm.

"Into the light," said the voice.

"No," the boy whispered; it was the first sound he had made.

The wolf was brought to the altar, into the ring of torchlight. A young male wolf, hardly more than a cub; like the boy on the stone, he had not quite crossed the threshold between youth and adulthood. And, like the boy, now never would.

The jaws had been wired shut. A chain was wound about the ruddy throat, snugged taut. He struggled, whimpered, dug the air with hind claws even as the front ones reached for flesh. But the man who held the wolf was large and strong, and used to big dogs; the cub was no match for him.

"No," said the boy again. Begging now, forgoing all the

pride of his people. Forgoing all save the need to see the cub made safe, unharmed, set free.

A hand touched the boy's brow, smoothing back damp hair. The palm was cool, almost soothing, like the voice. "We must," the voice said; the same one, the same voice, that had beckoned the wolf cub brought. That had beckoned the boy held down against the stone.

"There is a reason for what we do," the voice said. "A need. This is not idle whimsy, nor ignorant reprisal for the loss of the Homanan throne to a Cheysuli king. No. This is part and parcel of what must be done, in order to restore the balance of justice. To restore *rightness*." The voice paused. "Can you understand that? Can you understand that I do not hate you, boy, nor even hate your race? No. Hate is not what fuels me, other than using it when I must; in its place, hate has its uses. No. I do this because there is a need. Homana's need."

The hand was gentle against the boy's sweat-sheened brow. He tried not to listen, but he heard in spite of himself.

"There was a mistake made more than sixty-five years ago, when Carillon named Donal his heir," the voice continued. "Having no son of his queen, Solindish Electra, he turned to the closest male relative: a Cheysuli halfling got on his cousin, Alix, as much a halfling as her son. But there *was* a son, you see. There *was* a son . . . a wholly Homanan son, with no trace of Cheysuli blood."

The hand stopped moving; fell away. Fearfully, the boy waited, sensing a new tension in the air even though the voice remained calm, cool, quiet.

"Twenty years ago my father found Carillon's bastard. With the Homanan woman who bore the boy, my father went to face the Mujhar, Donal himself, to ask that the line of succession be restored to its proper path. And there within the walls of Homana-Mujhar, before Council, the woman was murdered by a man loyal to the Mujhar; my father was slain as well, by Niall, then Prince of Homana." The voice broke off. The boy heard only silence, but felt the thrumming of growing impatience that radiated from the others. And then the voice went on. "That man now rules, boy, the *royal murderer*, when it should be Carollan's place. And so there are those of us who will see to it Niall is deposed in favor of Carollan: the grandson replaced by the son." The voice paused again, then renewed itself. "That is how it should be, boy . . . *that* is how it should be. How my father, Elek, wanted it, before Niall murdered him."

The boy on the stone summoned all his courage. "Keep *me*," he said, "keep me. But let my *lir* go free."

"The *lir* is an aspect of your power," Elek's son said. "A manifestation of the wrongness that plagues this land. You are bound in life, boy—that much I know of Cheysuli . . . now you will be bound in death."

"He is so *young*—" and the boy abruptly shut his mouth, bit his lip to seal it; no more would he beg Homanans.

"He is young, and so are you," said the clover honey voice. "But if we let you grow to manhood, and him to adulthood, you will be more difficult to overcome. I do not devalue the strength of the Cheysuli, nor the dedication of your warriors. Indeed, I salute your people, boy, well and truly. How could I not? Look what they have done . . . look how cleverly they have stolen the throne in the guise of recovering what once was theirs."

"Then I will take *lir*-shape," the boy threatened, "and you will *see* what I can do—"

"Now," said Elek's son, and the man with the cub in his arms drew his knife and swiftly cut open the ruddy throat.

As warm red blood rained down, the young Cheysuli cried out. And *cried*.

"Now." And another knife flashed in the torchlight.

The man who called himself Elek's son watched as the altar drank its fill. Blood spilled over the edge of the stone and was poured against the ground. The splatter was loud in the darkness.

After a moment, he nodded. "It is time," he said calmly, "we turned to larger prey."

"Shansu, shansu," Brennan whispered tenderly, soothing her silk-soft shoulder with a gentle, beguiling hand. "Be easy, *meijhana* . . . be easy. . . ."

Her flesh quivered beneath his seductive hand, as if in answer to his tone.

"Shansu," he whispered softly, stroking slowly, so slowly, "no need to be afraid. I swear it. I swear it. Any oath you

choose . . ." Her flesh responded again. Brennan smiled
slowly, warmly, in a manner of immensely patient desire
and unconscious invitation. He was, in that moment, consumed utterly by the sole purpose of seduction. "Be
easy . . . be *easy*—"

But the mare was not seduced. Without warning, she
exploded in a flurry of activity that indicated *her* sole purpose was to rid her back of the man who sat astride it.

Brennan clamped legs against mare in an instinctive bid
to maintain his seat. He had buckled on a Cheysuli saddle,
lighter and less confining than Homanan gear, but also offering less latitude for error. With the mare in open revolt,
the Cheysuli saddle—little more than a shallow pad of
leather and sheepskin with wooden stirrups attached by
strips of leather—was next to useless as a means of staying aboard.

The mare, gray as smoke, ducked delicate head between
equally delicate forelegs and squealed in a decidedly
unladylike fashion. Dark eyes rolled. Tipped ears flattened.
Deceptively powerful rear legs elevated silken hindquarters
like a ballista hurling a stone.

Brennan, flopped forward against his will, tried to scram-
ble backward as she threw her head up, flinging it rearward.
Pale mane whipped yellow eyes, bringing royal tears; by an
inch only, Brennan missed having his nose smashed against
his face, forever altering aristocratic good looks. As it was,
a series of bone-jarring bucks served to twist his spine
alarmingly, threatening to cripple him.

Dimly, he heard the clatter of hooves on stone, the
grunts of equine rage, the shouts of running men as he
tried to weather the storm. The squat buildings of the
stableyard, built of the same rose-red stone that gave
Homana-Mujhar its pastel patina, performed a dance of
their own. He saw only bits and pieces of the curtain wall,
the sentry-walk, the beamwork of stable roofs. Straw cushioned the yard, and dirt, but cobbles lay beneath both.
Hard stone cobbles, promising a painful landing. He had
seen it happen to others.

The mare sucked in another great breath and leaped
sideways, lurched backward, lunged forward yet again. She
wanted to run, but the snaffle in her mouth—for all its
relative gentleness—prevented her; that, and Brennan's

skilled grip upon the reins. It was a deadly dance: infuriated horse against determined warrior.

We each of us have too much to lose, Brennan thought briefly, as he lasted another of the mare's spine-twisting bucks. *Pride, too much pride . . . hers will be tarnished if I win, mine if she does—*

And abruptly, Brennan won. The mare stopped fighting the bit, the reins, the hands. She sidled uneasily a moment, first to the right, then to the left, scraping hooves against cobbles, and then quieted, snorting, long-lashed eyes half-shut as if to acknowledge defeat.

But Brennan, not daring to move as the mare slowly settled, knew better. It was too soon to trust the gray.

She shook her head. Swished her flax-pale tail. Snorted. Eyed the men gathered in the stableyard. Brennan could feel the mare's debate: *Do I throw the man now, or later?*

Later. As Brennan urged her gently into a walk, she circled the yard quietly.

Round and round. The buildings blurred together as the circling continued. With each revolution the mare grew calmer, more relaxed, and so did Brennan. He was aware of the eyes watching him and the gray, waiting for something to happen. Curious, expectant eyes, brown and blue and black, all of them, save for the single pair of green ones.

Maeve. She stood in the stableyard amid the grooms and sweepers and lads, clad in blue woolen skirts, closefitting leather tabard belted snug, and soft house boots.

Carefully, he eased the mare in his sister's direction. With gentle persuasion, the gray tapped delicately across the cobbles and halted. Brennan looked down on Maeve, whose brass-bright hair, loosely braided, shone brilliantly in the sunlight. "Aye?"

She smiled, thumbs hooked into her belt in a distinctive imitation of Brennan's habitual stance. "I was sent to give you your freedom."

"Freedom?" He brightened. "*Jehan* sent you?"

"Aye." Maeve did not use the Old Tongue except on rare occasions. "He said I was to tell you he has rescinded his orders against you working your horses." She grinned. "Probably because he looked out a casement and saw you doing it anyway."

Brennan scowled. "This is not precisely *working*—at least, not when one trains a racing string. This was little more than making certain I would not be killed when *jehan* finally said I *could* start working them again." He sighed. "Thank the gods he has come to his senses . . . it has been four weeks since I *touched* any of them, let alone ridden them, and you just saw the result yourself. Now perhaps I can set my racing string back into order and begin winning again."

Blond brows rose. "I thought races were Hart's purview."

"Wagering on races is," Brennan agreed. "Racing for purses is different. I do not bet. I ride." His face was grim; Hart had been gone a month, and the separation made Brennan irritable. "Gods, if only I could go to Clankeep—" He broke off and looked down at Maeve sharply. "I *will* go. I should have gone before. Even *jehan* cannot deny me a part of my heritage."

"No," Maeve agreed calmly. "Keely wondered how long it would take you to realize that."

Heat rose in his face. *Leave it to Keely*— "Aye, well, now I have. And so I go. The mare needs work." As if in answer the mare stirred; Brennan leaned forward to stroke the glossy smoke-pale neck. *"Shansu, shansu . . ."* He straightened as she settled once more. "Come with me, Maeve. How long has it been? A month? Two? Too *long*, whatever the length of time; you used to go all the time."

His sister's expression was curiously arrested, as if his suggestion and accompanying question had caught her entirely off guard. Then she twisted her mouth briefly, hiding most of her emotions behind a carefully blanked face, but Brennan saw the glint of something in her eyes. Regret? Resentment? Fear? He could not be certain, even as she answered.

"No, no—I think not," she said easily. "There is much here for me to do."

Brennan heard an underlying note of tension in her tone. He reacted accordingly, as he did without fail where Maeve was concerned. "What has Keely been saying?"

"Keely?" Maeve frowned briefly, then shook her head. "Oh, *no*, no, not Keely. 'Twas—" And abruptly, she snapped her mouth shut. "No more of it, Brennan. I'll be staying here."

"What is so pressing that you willingly forgo a visit to Clankeep?" he asked in bafflement. "You used to nag me to go with you all the time."

"The tapestry," Maeve answered at once, too quickly. "The tapestry of lions my mother has begun. I promised I would help."

"Tapestry?" Brennan shrugged, bemused. "Maeve, I am sorry—"

"No, no, I do not expect you to know anything about it. It is a woman's thing, why would you? But, well . . . it will be beautiful, and glorious, and a thing our descendants will prize forever. . . ." She paused as her words trailed off and frowned a little, as if troubled by the faint forlorn note in her voice, then self-consciously tucked a loose strand of bright hair behind one ear. " 'Tis a thing of pride, Brennan, in race, heritage, tradition . . . a history woven of all the bright colors of our people: Cheysuli, Homanan, Solindish, Erinnish—"

Maeve stopped short, seemingly lacking the proper words. Brennan saw the turmoil in her face. And then, more quietly, controlled again, she went on. But he knew the lightness of her tone was little more than a well-practiced facade. "Well, 'tis a thing of magnificence, and I thought perhaps I should help. 'Tis nothing of the magic in me, but the pride is there regardless."

The mare tapped one hoof against a loose cobble. It rolled, clinking faintly; the mare bobbed her head and snorted down delicate, velvet nostrils. Brennan, tightening reins slightly in automatic response, looked down on his older sister and regretted more than ever that she had none of the gifts of their race. With them so evident in Keely, who took such great pride in her Old Blood that tact was nonexistent, it was harder than ever for Maeve to deal with her lack.

Perhaps if she did not live in a palace full of Cheysuli kin— But he let the thought die away. It would be no better at Clankeep, where only Cheysuli dwelled.

Brennan sighed. "Well enough, Maeve. Stay here and help Deirdre with her tapestry of lions. But I think you are a fool to turn your back on your heritage, no matter what the reason."

Brilliant color suddenly flamed in her face. "What would

you know of it?" she cried. "You with your *lir* and your gold and your yellow eyes—you with honorable welcome wherever you go—" Maeve clapped hands over her mouth as the hectic color drained out of her face and left it strained and pallid. "Gods," she blurted, "I did not mean to say that. Oh, Brennan, you know I do not mean it. Not for you. Never—" And she turned so abruptly, skirts swirling, that she startled the mare into a sideways leap that nearly unseated Brennan.

By the time he had recovered his balance and had the mare settled again, Maeve was gone. He saw startled eyes and perfectly blank faces, knowing each stable lad busily tried to name what ailed the Mujhar's daughter. He would give them more to talk about if he hastened after Maeve. And so he did not. He soothed the mare carefully, summoned Sleeta through the link, and rode out of Homana-Mujhar.

But not without worrying.

Two

Home. The word reverberated through the link from Sleeta to Brennan clearly. Equally clear was the big cat's satisfaction and pleasure as she lashed her tail to and fro and rubbed her jaw against his kneecap. *Home,* lir . . . *at last.*

He had tethered the gray mare at the indigo pavilion the Mujhar claimed, as Brennan had none of his own. For a moment, he lost himself in the sensations of being in Clankeep again, surrounded by folk who felt as he did, thought as he did, believed as he did. In Mujhara, things were different. There he was a prince, the heir to the Lion Throne, and that knowledge altered perceptions of him. Here he was nothing more than a fellow warrior, though that was more than enough.

Pavilions surrounded them, huddled in clusters of dyed and painted hides stretched over poles. Nearby a flank of the gray granite wall curved its way through the wood, bedecked in its ivy-and-lichen cloak. Smoke from cookfires drifted, tendrils rising to catch on tree limbs, tangling, like skeins of yarn; once freed, the tendrils were torn into the hint of a haze that drifted on the breeze. Brennan smelled roasting venison, boar; the tang of honey brew. His mouth watered in response.

Home. To Sleeta—to any *lir* perhaps—it was the closest thing to a home any of them claimed. And yet Brennan knew a brief inward stab of guilt. Clankeep was not *home* to him. It was a place of dreams, of his past and his future, the womb of his race, the security of his kin, and yet it was not quite a home, because he had not made it so.

You could, Sleeta said. *It is not too late. There is much time for you to reacquaint yourself with our heritage.*

She was warmth engulfing his leg, one sleek shoulder pressed against a legging-clad knee. He could sense her anticipation singing through the link, nearly drowning him. If it pleased Sleeta so much, he would not deny himself the chance to spend time in his people's place.

Home, Sleeta purred.

"Well," said a quiet voice behind them, "which of the royal get *is* it? Corin? No—the color is wrong. Hart, perhaps—no, no, as you turn I see your eyes are yellow, not blue. Well, then, it must be—Brennan?" The tone was eloquently ironic, and yet it lacked the note of friendly raillery someone else might have used to underscore the words, if only to make certain Brennan understood it was a jest. "I see any of you so rarely, it is difficult to know which princeling is which."

Brennan knew better than to laugh or smile or clap the speaker on the back, accepting the jest in good-natured competition. Because the speaker was Teirnan, his cousin, and Teir's irony—as well as the competition—was meant in deadly earnest, if cloaked in velvet instead of steel.

Brennan sighed, turning to face his cousin, and heard Sleeta's low-pitched, throaty growl. Teirnan was without his *lir*, so the hostility was clearly directed at him, not at the small-eyed boar Sleeta abhorred. And Teirnan knew it.

His mocking smile altered, but only briefly. He made a rude gesture of dismissal that Sleeta ignored, as he knew she would, but he followed the ritual all the same. Sleeta hunched down, tail thumping the beaten ground, and stared at him out of implacable golden eyes. Watching. Waiting. As if she counted the hours until she could kill him with impunity.

Brennan drew in a weary breath. The confrontation was only the latest in a long series. "Teir—"

"What is it this time, cousin?" Teirnan forbore the Old Tongue, as if to emphasize Brennan's frequent separation from the clan. "Do you require additional assurances that you are indeed the man intended for the Lion?"

"No. *You* require those," Brennan said bluntly. "Teir, are you still convinced that you would do better than I? I thought the last time I came, when the *shar tahl* spoke to us both, we settled all this nonsense of bloodlines and legacies."

"I am no more convinced you should inherit than you believe *I* should," Teir answered flatly. "Why should I be?

Shar tahl aside, facts are facts: I claim all of the rootstock bloodlines you do, but mine are untouched by Solindish or Atvian taint. There is Old Blood in me, and Cheysuli blood, and Homanan. Enough, I think, to fulfill that part of the prophecy pertaining to proper heritage."

"I think not," Brennan said gently. "Solindish and Atvian *taint* notwithstanding, it is required." Gritting his teeth, he managed to smile with infinite patience, though he was fast losing his share. "We have been through this time and time again, Teir—even when we were children! Look to the clan for your legacy. The Lion will be mine."

"My *jehan* says—"

"Your *jehan* is an empty, embittered man," Brennan declared shortly, forgoing his usual tact. "Ceinn worked against my *jehan* just as you work against me, and all out of a perverse desire to be someone he is not meant to be. Since he no longer has the option of thwarting my *jehan* through a disbanded group of Cheysuli zealots, he uses you. He twists you, Teir, like a green willow bough. And one day you will break."

"Disbanded, are we?" Teir retorted. "I think not, cousin. I think the *a'saii* live again!"

Brennan stared at him in astonishment. He thought first to charge Teirnan with a bluff, but Teir's tone was too thick with triumph, too assured. His pupils had shrunk so that his eyes were mostly yellow, intently cunning and feral as a wolf's; Brennan knew better than to discount him or his words. Not in something this important; something that could have an incredible impact upon the future of Homana.

Slowly, Brennan was able to pass words through the constriction of shock and growing anger in his throat. "You *ku'reshtin*," he said softly, "do you mean to say there are Cheysuli who work to bring down the prophecy?"

"Not bring it down. Serve it." Teir's face was shaped much like Brennan's, reflecting shared ancestry, but his bones were a trifle sharper, more predatory; his flesh was more accustomed to settling itself into expressions of calculation and ambition than anything more sanguine. "Only a fool foments rebellion out of simple greed," Teir said quietly. "My *jehan* and the *a'saii* desired Ian to hold the Lion. They still do—Ian lacks the Solindish and Atvian taint—but there is no more hope that he would assume the throne if the Mujhar were slain. So I tell you this, in preparation: we intend no harm to befall Niall *or* his sons, any of them, or his daughters, even his bastard girl." Something flickered faintly in his eyes, was gone. "Without bloodshed, we intend to take the Lion and give it over to the warrior whose blood best deserves to rule."

"Without bloodshed." Brennan wanted to spit. "Do you think any of us would politely step aside and let you have the Lion?"

"Aye," Teir said, "if Clan Council told you to."

"Clan Council—" Brennan stared. "Have you gone mad? Cheysuli Clan Council *supports* our right to rule!"

"Only so long as the members believe that right is yours," Teirnan said. "But if they no longer believed it, cousin, and bestowed that right upon another branch of the bloodline, what *would* you do? Fight? Become kin-slayer in the name of greed and power?" Teir's voice was steady and quiet, lacking the fanaticism Brennan might have expected. In its place was a calm matter-of-factness as he spelled out the consequences of such an action. "You would divide the world, *cousin,* and make it a place of two races yet again. Cheysuli. Homanan. Set again at each other's throats."

"The Homanans would have nothing to do with it," Brennan threw back. "This is a thing between Cheysuli factions—"

"Is it?" Teir smiled. "So easily you dismiss the very people you intend to rule. Have you forgotten how we are outnumbered? We always were, always have been—and Strahan's Ihlini plague twenty years ago stole half our numbers again. It leaves the Homanans with a vast superiority, cousin. If we took to fighting for the Lion in the name of the prophecy, what is there to stop the Homanans from declaring a new *qu'mahlin* and stealing it back for themselves? Would you risk that?"

"Would *you?*" Brennan was so angry he wanted to knock Teirnan's teeth down his throat and make him choke on them. "If you throw down my *jehan*—even if you *set him aside* through action of Cheysuli Clan

Council—you destroy the prophecy. You leave the Lion to the Ihlini.''

Teirnan's eyes narrowed. "At this moment, we are less concerned with the Ihlini than with the proper disposition of the throne. Strahan has been in hiding for a very long time. Who is to say he is not dead?"

"Who is to say he *is?*" Brennan tried to steady his voice. "If you begin to discount the Ihlini, *cousin*, you are no warrior at all, but a fool. A *dead* fool; at least I will not have to concern myself with what idiocy you may yet attempt."

"You had best concern yourself with your future without a title," Teirnan retorted. "No more Prince of Homana. Just a man, like any other."

"Walk softly," Brennan warned. "You soil your own leathers with such words; we are cousins, Teir, and I am as Cheysuli as you. I am not 'like any other,' and never will be." He smiled as Sleeta rose, stretched, sat down to rest a part of her bulk against his left leg. " 'Just a man'? I think not. Not while I claim a *lir*."

Teirnan looked at the cat. Briefly hostility and acknowledgment warred in his face. And then he masked himself again, all civility. "I mean you no harm," he said. "We are bloodkin and more, being children of the gods, but you must understand that it is only a matter of time. While Niall sits on the Lion parceling out his children to this realm and to that, dividing Homana's strength, there are those who will come to see there are better ways of serving the Lion. Of serving the prophecy."

"You serve your own ambition," Brennan answered curtly. "Oh, I have no doubt there are others like you, desiring a change no matter what the consequences— there are always those who thrive on discontent—but you are in the minority."

"This year, aye," Teirnan agreed. "And probably next. But what of the year after that? Or the next after that?" He smiled. "The *a'saii* are very patient. That is the nature of our race."

And always had been. Brennan knew his history well enough: the Cheysuli, warrior-born and bred, were nonetheless cognizant of how carefully considered, meticulous change was used for the betterment of a realm. Once his people had given up their claim on the Lion to the very Homanans who feared them, because they wanted no civil war. And when Shaine's royal purge had nearly destroyed the race, the Cheysuli quietly, patiently waited out the *qu'mahlin* until Carillon united his newly-won realm. Slowly, so slowly the Old Blood emerged again, and was mixed with Homanan, Solindish, Atvian. The prophecy was nearly complete.

And now it was threatened again. From within as well as without.

"You are a fool." He spoke without heat, knowing only that he could not allow Teir to comprehend how very real was the threat of the *a'saii*. "A fool, and if I could do it, I would spill from my veins the blood that makes us kin until I was free of you."

"Would you?" Teirnan smiled. "And what would Maeve say, to lose me yet again?"

A chill washed through Brennan, followed by the heat of anger. "Maeve has nothing to do with this!"

"Does she not?" Teirnan laughed. "I thought she did. I thought you *knew*—"

"Knew *what?*"

"That the last time she came to Clankeep, she agreed to become my *meijha*."

Impelled by rage, Brennan moved before Teirnan could. He was conscious only of clamping his hands around his cousin's throat and driving him to the ground, where he nearly crushed the fine bones beneath the flesh so like his own. "*Ku'reshtin*—"

"Ask her!" Teirnan rasped through Brennan's assault. "*Ask* her, cousin! Do you think she would lie to *you?*"

Brennan pressed him against the ground. "She would never—she would *never*—not with you—not with such as *you*—"

"Ask her," Teirnan challenged. "But also ask her why she will not come to Clankeep. Ask her why she will not honor her vow."

"If she made one—*if* she made one—I will release her from it—I will *release* her from it—"

"Freely made—" Teirnan struggled, but fading breath robbed him of his strength. "—freely made, Brennan, and only she can break it. Only Maeve, or me. And I would never do it."

"Why not?" Brennan demanded.

"Because you want me to." Teirnan's laugh was torn from a badly bruised throat. "She never will. She is too honorable to do it. I am not. For a good enough reason, I will. But—for now it serves me . . . it serves me to see how angry and helpless you are—"

"By the gods—" Brennan choked. "By the gods, I swear if you ever harm her, by word or by deed, I will soil my hands with your blood. Kinslayer you may make me, but that is a burden I would gladly bear for the sake of my *rujholla*—"

"Bastard," Teirnan mocked. "The Homanans call her bastard."

Lir. It was Sleeta, quietly intruding. *Lir, if you mean to do it, do it. If you do not, then let him go. Do not be irresolute.*

You would like me to slay him, he said. *I can tell.*

No. But the tone was distinctly reluctant. *If you slay him, you take on the responsibility of a fool. And you deserve better than that.*

Inwardly Brennan laughed, though it had little of humor in it. And then he released Teirnan and rose to stare down at the gasping warrior. "This will be settled," he said. "This thing between you and me and Maeve. It will be settled for all to know, regardless of the outcome."

Teirnan levered himself up on one elbow. "Ask her," he whispered. "Ask her if she was unwilling. Ask her if she was forced, when she came into my bed."

It cost Brennan dearly to shrug indifferently. "If she was," he said, "you are dead."

As Teirnan glared up at him from the ground, Brennan turned to fetch the mare, who fidgeted by the pavilion. *Sleeta,* he said, *we go home.*

The cat did not protest against leaving her own so soon. The cat said nothing at all.

Three

At sunset, the gray threw Brennan near the outskirts of Mujhara and left him to lie in the dirt, half-stunned, as she galloped toward the city. After a moment he sat up, spat out blood from a bitten lip, stared after her dazedly and cursed, if none too fluently; his tongue was also bitten.

Your fault. Sleeta sat not far away, tail curled fastidiously around one raven haunch. The tip flicked once, twice, was still. *You were paying more attention to your cousin's words and not enough to the mare.*

Brennan scowled and glared after the mare, massaging a sore shoulder. He did not look at the cat.

After a moment she flicked an ear. *Are you damaged?*

After a lengthier moment: "No." Grudgingly.

Embarrassed, then.

"Aye," he agreed morosely, staring toward the city that now hid the offending mare. From here he could not see the walls, for Mujhara had grown so much that the city proper—that portion that lay within the walls—had been swallowed by other dwellings huddling about the fringes, cluster upon cluster, until the new had nearly overtaken the old.

Well, what did you expect? She is horse, not lir. *She has no understanding of such things as dignity and protocol.*

Brennan slanted the mountain cat a glance of disgust mingled with amusement. Trust Sleeta to put things in perspective, though hers was often quite different from the views of others.

"Aye, well, she will have learned such understanding. When I am done with her."

If she goes back to Homana Mujhar.

That brought a frown. "Aye. She would be worth stealing."

But only if she can be caught first, Sleeta pointed out. *How many have your patience, your skill, your gentleness—*

Enough, he sent through the link, unable to suppress his laughter. *Enough, Sleeta—I know what you do. But I assure you, the only damage I have suffered is to my pride, and that will recover soon enough.*

Not if the Prince of Homana is discovered wallowing in the dust with a dirty, bloodied face.

That brought him to his feet faster than anything else, if a trifle painfully. He dusted leggings, straightened jerkin, attempted to clean his face, dabbed blood from his split lip, tried to ignore the sore shoulder, and sighed. "Prince or no, I deserved this. I know better than to trust the gray; still, Teir gave me cause to be distracted. That *ku'reshtin* . . ." Anger renewed itself. "If he *ever* harms Maeve—"

Sleeta sought to placate. *I think he would not be so foolish. Aside from you, there are other* rujholli *involved.*

"Aye. But one is gone to Solinde, the other to Atvia." A wave of loneliness suddenly swamped him. "Oh, gods, *lir*—without Hart I am half a man, and so alone—"

You have me.

He looked at her. She sat primly in the dirt, eyes half slitted against the setting sun. Outwardly she seemed unperturbed, but within the link he sensed her readiness. Sleeta waited for something.

Brennan smiled. "Aye. I have you. More than any man might ask for, even of the gods."

The tail flicked once; he had said what she wanted to hear. *Of course. I am Sleeta.*

Laughing, he thrust a hand into the firm plushness of her pelt and stroked her large, wedge-shaped head, losing himself in the silken velvet of her coat. He was a man for women above all things, but even a wondrously pleasing bedpartner could not fill him with such infinite satisfaction as his magnificent *lir.*

He sighed and tugged an upright ear. "Ah, Sleeta, what would I do without you . . . ?"

The mountain cat merely purred, as if the answer were implicit.

Brennan slapped one raven shoulder. "Onward, *lir.* Sitting out here will get us no closer to the palace. And I am hungry—it has been hours since I ate, and it is nearly time for dinner.''

Sleeta licked one paw clean of dust, rose, stretched, padded toward the outskirts. Brennan matched his pace to hers.

The boots he wore were eminently unsuitable for walking any great distance, Brennan discovered quickly, particularly when one was already stiff and sore from an awkward enforced dismount. Hungry, footsore, and decidedly out of temper, Brennan paused in one of the winding streets—now ablaze from new-lit torches—and bent to tug the offending folds out of his left boot. They were his favorite footgear for working horses, but only when he was *in* the saddle, not out of it. Already he had blisters.

You might have gone in lir-*shape*, Sleeta commented.

Brennan, braced against the wall of the nearest building, nodded briefly at the greeting of a passer-by. *Not within the city. You know Homanans never can tell the difference between* lir *and animals of the wild—likely they would slay us both before thinking to ask if we were human or animal.*

Sleeta was a blotch of darkness in the shadows, though the torchlight set the gloss of her coat agleam. She blinked, implacable as ever; though the link offered each of them an uncanny, unfettered means of communication, even to sensing emotions quite clearly, there were times Sleeta was shuttered against him. For all she was utterly devoted to him, she was also a very private animal.

Brennan pressed a hand against his belly. "If I do not eat soon . . ."

Then eat, Sleeta suggested practically. *I am not one to deny my* lir *a meal when he is clearly so close to wasting away.*

Brennan grunted. It would take more than missing two meals to strip flesh from his frame. He lacked some of his father's sheer bulk, perhaps, but none of the height the Cheysuli habitually claimed, or the musculature. He was clearly a warrior: fit, firm, physically well-suited to the lifestyle of his fellow Cheysuli. But Brennan thought some of it came from frequent arms-practice and daily sessions with his horses in addition to simple bone and blood inheritance; Hart, so very much like him, generally appeared a trifle softer, though not precisely *soft*. And Corin—shorter, slighter than either of them—was built much more compactly.

A warbow, Brennan thought. *Hart and I are Homanan swords, long and lethal, while Corin's power is hidden in subtlety.*

A vision of his brothers rose before him and hung in the air as if to taunt him, to strip bare the thin skin hiding his loneliness. Hart, his other self, was now in Solinde; only the gods knew how he would hold his own in the land of the enemy. He would probably wager his life on it. And Corin, quick-tempered, quick-tongued Corin, would undoubtedly embroil himself in difficulties of his own unique design, in Erinn and Atvia.

"Erinn." Brennan spoke aloud. "Gods, Sleeta—Aileen will soon be on her way!"

"What did you say?"

For a moment Brennan thought he had gone mad; he could swear the cat had spoken aloud. And then he realized the question was from the young woman pausing by his side. She was wrapped in a thin dark cloak, but the hood slid from her head to display plaited black hair, glossy as Sleeta's pelt, and he saw a face he could not place at once, though he knew he had seen it before.

"No," he said, "I spoke to my *lir*." He gestured to Sleeta, and saw the young woman's eyes widen as she looked at him more closely.

"You!" she said in surprise. "Oh—my lord—" And she dropped into an awkward curtsy that puddled skirts and cloak in the dust of the cobbled street.

Startled by the unexpected homage, all Brennan could do was stare. And then as her upturned face was made clear by the torchlight, he recognized her.

"The girl from The Rampant Lion!" He reached down, caught a hand, pulled her up. "There is no need for that. . . ." He paused, though he did not release her hand. "Forgive me, *meijhana*, I have forgotten your name."

Her hand was cold in his. "Rhiannon," she answered softly. "Oh, my lord, I have dreamed—" Abruptly she broke off, snatching her hand out of his and yanking the hood up to hide most of her face. "I am sorry—I must go."

"Rhiannon—wait!" He caught a fold of her cloak to

gainsay her, felt the thin cloth tear and cursed himself for being such a heavy-handed fool. He could well afford to buy her a hundred cloaks—and better ones than this—to replace the one he had torn, but he understood something of pride. The look in her eyes told him she had a fair share of what he himself claimed.

"I must go, my lord." She said nothing of the cloak that now gaped at her shoulder, where the hood had parted from the rest. "If I am late . . ."

"Then I will come with you, and if you are late because of me, I think the tavern-keeper will hold his tongue." He smiled at her and tried to pull the torn pieces of cloth together. "Have you food at The Rampant Lion?"

"Of course, my lord—though none so fine as you are accustomed to." She stood very still as he resettled the cloak. She did not look at him, keeping black eyes demurely averted; two gently insistent brown fingers beneath her chin drew her face up into the light where he could see it more clearly.

Something glittered against the fabric of her tunic. Brennan caught it, held it up: his ring. The sapphire set in silver he had given her in gratitude for bringing the Mujharan Guard during the altercation with Reynald of Caledon, who had gone home weeks before.

"You want it back." She reached up to strip the thong over her head; he stopped her.

"No. No, it was freely given to you. It is yours, Rhiannon. For as long as you wish to keep it."

"As long—?" She laughed a little. "Forever, my lord. Of course."

"Of course." He grinned. "Come then, *meijhana*—or the tavern-keeper will rail at us both." And he tucked her arm into his elbow and escorted her to The Rampant Lion as if she were the finest lady of all the Mujhar's court, while Sleeta padded beside them.

It was the first time since he could remember that Brennan had crossed under the lintel branch of The Rampant Lion without one or both of his brothers. Rhiannon was lovely and sweet and struck almost speechless by the Prince of Homana's royal presence—but she was not Hart. She was not Corin. And he missed them both acutely.

The tavern, as always, enjoyed good custom, though Brennan had seen it busier. A few men huddled together at a corner table over some sort of dice game—*where is my* rujho? he wondered sadly—while others of a more solitary bent drank quietly at separate tables. Sleeta's presence among them garnered sharp looks and startled expressions, but it was no longer unheard of for a warrior and his *lir* to walk freely in Mujhara, and soon enough the men turned back to their business.

As they entered, a young man—black-haired, brown-eyed, of pleasant expression—came out from behind a curtain divider and fixed Rhiannon with a playfully displeased scowl. "Lady, lady," he chided, though without heat. "What am I to do when there are men who call for your efficient table service, and you are not here to please them?"

Color suffused her face instantly. "I—I am sorry, Jarek. I will stay late, to make up the time."

He laughed. "Aye, you will, if only to keep me company while I count the ale barrels." Jarek's good humor remained, but his smile did not quite extend to his eyes as he looked at Brennan. "Should I lay blame for your tardiness on this man?"

"You may," Brennan agreed, knowing full well—and understanding even better—why the tavern-keeper's manner bordered on unacknowledged hostility. "And rather than have Rhiannon remain later than she should, I will compensate you for her time." Fingers dipped into the plump belt-purse on his hip. "Name your price."

Jarek glanced at Sleeta, then back at Brennan. Redfaced, he smiled ruefully, shrugged, spread his hands. "What would I ask of a Cheysuli warrior save gold? But only in coin, of course; I would not presume to covet that you wear upon your arms." Still, he could not keep his eyes from the bands. "Be welcome in my tavern, warrior, and leave what you wish as a gift for Rhiannon when it comes time for your departure. That will be compensation enough."

"*Your* tavern?" Brennan took his hand away from his belt-purse. "I do not recall having seen your face before. And I am a frequent patron."

Jarek frowned a little. "Forgive me, warrior, but I do not recall *your* face. And this tavern has been mine these past six weeks."

Rhiannon's voice was quiet. "He bought it, my lord, not long after—the fight."

"Ah." Brennan shrugged. It did not please him to recall the battle with the Caledonese, since one thing had led to another, and now he was brotherless, even if only temporarily. "Well, blame me for her tardiness. I delayed her. And now—lest I perish—may I request a meal? And wine. Red wine. Fine Ellasian wine." Smiling, he moved to the closest empty table and sat down. Sleeta settled herself behind his bench and stretched out, a gleaming, breathing rug.

"At once," Jarek smiled, bowed, gestured. "Rhiannon will do the honors."

"Aye, aye, of course." Again she curtsied to Brennan, with more grace this time, and hastened off to fetch the wine.

Jarek did not leave at once, though he watched Rhiannon depart even as Brennan did. Then he turned back, pale brown eyes assessive. He smiled; his tone was easy, carefully noncomittal, which was a story in itself. "She gives you great honor, warrior. I thought the Cheysuli did not put much weight in things such as curtsies and titles."

Brennan sensed Jarek's unspoken challenge clearly, though it lacked true hostility. Even if they were more than employer and employee, which seemed likely, Jarek no doubt knew Rhiannon would inspire much interest on the part of wealthier, high-ranking suitors. He believed his position within her regard precarious.

But Rhiannon did not strike Brennan as the sort of girl who would throw over one good man merely to stalk another with greater fortune.

"The Cheysuli do not," Brennan agreed easily. "The Homanans do. Rhiannon is Homanan, and therefore honors the title rather than the man." He smiled as Rhiannon came back with a jug of wine and a hastily-polished silver mug; he could see where she had spat upon it and rubbed it with a cloth.

"My lord," she said, filling the mug, "here is your wine— the best I could find." She glanced sidelong at Jarek. "Your private cask, Jarek, from the back of the cellar."

"*My* cask—"

"He is the Prince of Homana!" she hissed, and smiled

self-consciously at Brennan. "My lord, what victuals can I bring you?"

Sipping wine, Brennan shook his head. "No matter," he answered when he had swallowed. "Fresh meat, new bread, some cheese . . . have you any fruit?"

"Raisins from Caledon," she said brightly, and then abruptly they shared the same vision: Reynald, cousin to Prince Einar, with his ruined escort around him. As one they laughed, and Jarek quickly took his leave, too quickly; his spine was stiff as iron.

Jealous, Sleeta remarked lazily from behind.

With cause, Brennan told her. *The girl is worth the jealousy.* And abruptly, thinking of Maeve trapped in Tiernan's web, he reached out and caught Rhiannon's hand before she could leave again. *"Meijhana—"* he lowered his voice to spare her embarrassment. "—is he good to you? Does he pay a fair wage? Does he have—expectations?"

She knew what the last meant clearly enough. Vivid color washed into her face, then fell away, leaving her pale and lily-fragile.

"Jarek is a good man," she said evenly. "As for expectations—aye, and why not? It *is* a good wage, and I am grateful for his generosity."

"How grateful?" he persisted. "And for how long?"

She jerked her hand away. "Why, my lord? Will you pay more? Will you keep me longer? Will you fulfill *my* expectations?"

He was aghast at her interpretation of his interest in her welfare. "Rhiannon—no. *No*, I swear, I do not ask because I want you for myself." And abruptly cursed himself; he told her the truth, but too bluntly. What woman *wanted* to hear a man did not desire her in his bed? "Wait you," he said clearly, aware of color rising in his own dark face. "I meant only to ask if he *forced* you. No more."

"Why?" Her heart-shaped face was stiffly set, but delicately proud.

He thought at first to lie for Maeve's sake, but did not. He felt Rhiannon worth the truth. "Because there are men in the world who will stoop to force a woman's will, and I would not want to see Jarek do it to you."

It took her by surprise. No doubt she had heard all manner of invitations in her employment, as well as crude suggestions; she did not expect a man to concern himself with her welfare outside of what she could do for him in bed.

"No," she said. "No, he does not force me. "It—it was wanted. . . ." She looked away from him, though her fingers crept up to touch the sapphire ring. He thought it unconsciously done. "He is a good man, Jarek, better than any other I have known."

Brennan nodded, releasing her hand. "Then I am pleased for you, *meijhana.*"

"He is kind, and fair, and generous," she went on. "I am not made to work all night *and* day, like the girls in other taverns. I am given one day out of seven for myself. And all the meals I could wish for. He even gave me this—" She lifted a fold of the cloak, then blushed bright red as they both recalled how easily the cheap fabric had torn under Brennan's hand. "He is a *good man,*" she declared desperately, clenching her hands in the cloak.

Brennan smiled a little. "I am convinced, *meijhana.* You are eloquent in your assertions."

"I must go," Rhiannon said in a muffled tone. "There is work to be done." Abruptly she swung to take her leave, and in doing so she knocked the winejug over. It spilled wine across the table to splatter on the floor, red as blood.

Brennan stood at once, avoiding the pungent torrent. He righted the jug even as Rhiannon tore off her ripped cloak to sop up what she could of the spillage. "Oh—*my lord*—"

"Stop fretting," he ordered firmly, seeing tears gathering in her eyes. "I am not wet, and there is more wine in the cellars. *Shansu, meijhana*—the world will turn again."

"*Clumsy,*" she said, half angrily, gathering jug and soaked cloth into her slender arms. And she was gone before he could speak again, dripping wine to mark an unintended path.

Flighty sort, commented Sleeta.

No, no, only overwhelmed by my title, Brennan explained, a trifle sadly, as he sat down again after checking his bench for wine puddles. *It happens so often, lir—too often for my taste. It seems I am never able to see the true person underneath all the awe and awkwardness.*

"My lord." It was Jarek, with a new winejug in his hands. "My lord, Rhiannon has explained her clumsiness. I beg you, spare her your anger. She is a good girl, and meant no harm."

The obsequious manner was new, ill-fitting, and unwanted. Brennan's mouth twisted in displeasure. "And do you think I want her beaten? Do you think I expect her to lose her place? It was an accident, tavern-keeper. Even if I were soaked, do you think I would want her punished?"

"How can I say, my lord?" Jarek returned stiffly. "Men who are princes often want things others might not." He jerked his head to indicate other patrons. "For a six-week now I have served the aristocracy and wealthy men of Mujhara. Do you think I have not seen all manner of retribution? Have I reason to expect you might want none taken?"

"Perhaps not," Brennan agreed coolly. "As it happens, you have no reason to expect anything of me. Except, perhaps, my custom, which The Rampant Lion has always enjoyed. Unless, of course, you choose not to serve me now."

"Do you want her?" Jarek demanded bluntly, forgoing anything approaching diplomacy or respect for a title; now they were merely men. "Do you intend to take her?"

Brennan sighed. "She named you a good man, Jarek. She named you a fair man. I am not disposed to argue it—she sounded quite convinced—but I *am* disposed to say you are a fool." He took the jug from Jarek's rigid hands and poured his mug full. "I am not in the habit of taking women from other men. Particularly if they are content where they are."

Jarek did not look away as Brennan drank. "You could offer her much more. And she is deserving of it."

Brennan drained half the mug, then set it down. "Every man and woman has a *tahlmorra*, Cheysuli and Homanan alike. If the gods intend better for her, she will have it. Otherwise, it will be none of my doing."

"She is—special." Jarek's tone was desperate. "My lord, I have no wish to lose her, not to any man . . . but I want what is best for her."

"It does you credit," Brennan told him after a moment. "But have you never thought that what is best for her may be the man she has?"

"It is *your* ring she wears around her neck."

"And your bed she warms." Brennan sat forward on the

bench, resting forearms on the table. "If she wanted me in place of you, there are ways she could make it known. Ways she could make it happen." He shrugged. "She need only come to the palace and ask to see me on some pretext; I would receive her. Women have done it before. They do it every day." He held Jarek's eyes with his own. "When a man has wealth, power, rank, title—any or all—there are women who want to share it, even if for only a week, a night, an hour. They barter with their bodies in hopes of gaining favors. In hopes of gaining wealth. And some even dream of permanency." He poured more wine. "I am not celibate. I enjoy the courtship dance as much as any man. But neither am I a stud who likes the mares to force themselves upon him."

"Rhiannon—has not." Jarek's tone was harsh, strained.

"No. Do you think she ever would?"

Jarek looked away. "No. No. She is not a woman for that." He sighed heavily. "But—"

"Tend your custom, Jarek," Brennan said deliberately. "Rhiannon has need of you."

"And you?" Jarek asked.

He smiled. "I only have need of my *lir*."

Four

The food was excellent, the wine even better. Now, sated, content, drowsy, Brennan watched Rhiannon move smoothly around the common room tending Jarek's custom, and reflected that except for poor quality clothing and a certain naive innocence in her manner, the young woman could easily pass for one of Deirdre's ladies. She was well-spoken for an uneducated commoner and her courtesy was boundless, even with those men who chose to make sport of her or those who attempted to arrange a tryst. *Certainly she is lovely enough to grace Homana-Mujhar—* Abruptly he caught himself. He had pointedly told Jarek the Prince of Homana had no intentions of elevating Rhiannon out of her present circumstances, and here he was considering what it would be like. But he could not deny that he was attracted to her; for all Rhiannon's quiet, demure demeanor, he sensed she was also a passionate woman.

Who are you to contemplate bedding the girl when your Erinnish bride will soon be on her way? Sleeta asked, casually deliberate.

He sighed. *Who am I, indeed? Hypocrite, I think. Or merely befuddled by too much wine.* Brennan scrubbed his brow. *We should go home, Sleeta—there are questions I have for Maeve.*

He pushed himself up from the bench, recalled Jarek's solution to compensation for Rhiannon's tardiness, dug into his belt-purse and set a gold royal on the hardwood, knowing it worth considerably more than a week's lodging and full meals.

Generous, Sleeta commented, rising to stretch all her elegant lean length in the glow of candlelight.

Worth it— He smiled as Rhiannon came to halt before

him. "Jarek serves excellent wine and victuals, *meijhana.*
And you provide most attractive table service."

"Oh, my lord—are you going so soon?" Color sprang up
in her face, as if she felt her question too personal, or
too revealing.

"I must," he told her, "but I will come again." *If my*
jehan *allows me to,* he reflected wryly.

Slim fingers grasped the sapphire ring on the thong
around her throat as her eyes locked on his, and understood what she saw there. "I—I am Jarek's woman, my
lord—" She broke off, then went on, as if determined to
make things very clear. "You—do understand. . . ."

"I understand." He smoothed a strand of loosened hair
away from her cheek, slipping it gently behind an ear naked
of adornment. "Let us be friends, then, *meijhana* . . . if you
will allow it."

"*Allow it—!*" Rhiannon's laugh was half-swallowed. "Oh,
my lord—whoever would deny you friendship?"

Brennan's smile was mocking. "My cousin," he told her
wryly. "And I am assured there are others, as well." He
looked past her to Jarek, watching them from beside the
curtain divider. His face was a mask, but Brennan saw
something in the eyes that spoke of many things a desperate man might know. "Tell Jarek I am not without honor,"
Brennan said. "Tell him I respect what others hold dear."

"Aye." Rhiannon nodded. "The gods go with you, my
lord."

"*Cheysuli i'halla shansu,*" he returned, smiling at her
confusion. "A wish for Cheysuli peace."

Rhiannon nodded again, then abruptly turned away.
Brennan walked out of The Rampant Lion.

He was but a street away from the gates of the palace
when Sleeta growled a warning. Within the *lir*-link it was
incoherent, more cat- than *lir*-like, as if the threat were
something she might know in the world, and not a thing of
men and women.

Brennan spun in place, hand to knife, and saw the cat
crouch and hackle, ears flattened against her head. The
growl issuing from her throat was a sound he had never
heard from her, and it set the back of his neck to prickling.
Sleeta—

"Lir—" That much was coherent. *Lir—lir—*

All he could think of were Ihlini.

"Sleeta—?" He backed up, pressed his spine against the nearest wall, tried to slow his racing heart. He thought of shouting—the watch could be just around the corner, and the Mujharan Guard was one twisting street over—but did not. It would have been lost in Sleeta's unnerving scream.

Dogs! It overwhelmed the link and flooded his senses with Sleeta's rage and fear. *Dogs—dogs—men—*

"Sleeta!" Her consuming emotions—visceral, primitive, little more than instinctive responses and reactions—nearly destroyed his own precarious balance. And he was in human form; if he assumed *lir*-shape he was almost certain to be overcome by Sleeta herself as well as the threat she sensed. *Lir, lir*—within the link, in hopes of reaching her— *lir, what is it? Where?*

The hounds—the hounds—

—and suddenly the hounds were on her, jaws agape . . . he could not count them all . . . grayish shapes in the darkness, legs and teeth and claws . . . baying, baying . . . biting . . . trying to take her down, trying to tear her throat—

"Now," commanded a voice. "Now, while he is distracted."

—and Brennan knew then they wanted *him*, not Sleeta, not Sleeta at all, except as a means to distract him, to turn his attention from *them*, who meant to catch him, hold him, rob him—

Or do they mean to slay me?

And all the while the hounds barked and growled and Sleeta screamed her anger and fear and hatred.

He tried to turn. He tried to defend himself. But his reflexes were curiously slowed. Only limply did his fingers clasp the knife hilt, offering no defense. Vision blurred. He cursed and thought to summon *lir*-shape regardless of Sleeta's straits, but hands fell on his arms, his wrists, his throat—fingers threaded themselves in his hair and knotted there—so much weight, so much power, all thrust against him, pressing him back against the wall.

"Sleeta—!" But hands closed his mouth, mashing lips against teeth.

—*Sleeta*—But he knew he could not touch her, could not reach her, not with all the hounds—

—failing: *Sleeta*—

"Strike him down," someone ordered. "One cat is threat enough; do you wish to contend with two?"

And he thought: *I know that voice*—

But the voice said nothing more. And if it had, he could not have heard it. With a club, they struck him down.

He did not know where he was. For one horrible moment, he did not know *who* he was; and then he knew, and recalled the attack, and realized he had not been robbed at all, or beaten, or slain. Instead, he had been *taken*.

Sleeta—?

He tried to move. Iron rattled. Darkness pressed down against his eyelids, blinding him entirely. There was no sound save his ragged breathing, and the scrape of his bootheels against the floor as his leg muscles bunched in panic.

Sleeta—?

But there was nothing within the link; no answer, no stirring within the pattern he knew as Sleeta.

Oh, gods—lir—

Nothing.

He lay flat on his back. The stone beneath him was cold, hard, unyielding. The stone around him was equally so; he was inside, then, not out. He could tell by the closeness that weighed him down, the faint echo of the iron as it chimed. Cuffed at wrists and ankles, all he could do was stare blindly at what he might name a roof, had he the light to see it.

"Sleeeetaaa—" The word was a sibilant hiss in a tone akin to panic.

There was nothing in return. No sound. No stirring in the *lir*-link.

Panic took his wits. He surged upward against the iron, trying to break cuffs and chain; fell back again when he thought his head might burst. Pain threatened to blind him, except he was blind already. His belly cramped, tried to spew out all the food and wine he had consumed at The Rampant Lion; would have, had he not clamped throat and teeth against it.

"*Lion* . . ." The gasp whispered in the darkness, running along the stone.

Jarek. *His* voice had given the order. Had he been so insanely jealous as to order his rival imprisoned?

Brennan bit back a groan. The blow had split open the flesh of his forehead and nearly cracked his skull. Even thinking of movement made his belly squirm.

Sleeta?

Again, the appeal went unanswered.

Oh, gods—not my lir . . . oh, gods, I beg you, let her be alive. . . . And he realized, to his surprise, the petition was born not of fear for his own death, but because he could not comprehend what the world would be like without Sleeta. She deserved to survive, even if he could not.

No light. Only darkness, and stone, and the weight of an unknown future.

Blood rolled into one eye, the right; his spasmodic lunge against iron had opened the wound again.

Spare my lir, he begged—

—and slipped again into nothingness.

He awakened shouting. The words he did not know, being little more than gibberish; he shouted, he *shouted*, and the sounds bounced back from the stone and beat against his ears.

He stank of his own sweat. And he knew the smell. The stench filled up his nose and he knew it, he *knew* it, recalling how once before he had been trapped, trapped and completely terrified, so utterly *terrified* he had screamed and cried and soiled himself, beating boy's hands against naked walls—

—*the lir. All the lir, with beaks agape and claws unsheathed, all of them, beating wings against the air, against his head, his face, his eyes—all of them trying to throw him into the oubliette, the Womb of the Earth—to throw him down and down and down, until he died of fear alone, because everyone knew there was no bottom—*

Gods, he was afraid.

—*lir and lir and lir, shrouded in shadow, cloaked in secrecy—he heard them . . . he knew they were there, each and every one of them, speaking to one another, telling one another he was not fit to be the Mujhar's son because he was afraid, and Cheysuli feared nothing—*

But *this* Cheysuli did.

—so afraid, as the walls closed in. So AFRAID—

The memory washed up from the blackest depths of Brennan's inner self, battering at his awareness until it broke through to crash upon the cliffs of consciousness, and he remembered it all. Once, and once only, he had been enclosed as he was now, against his will, made helpless. There had been no iron, no purposeful imprisonment, but the result had been the same. The *fear* had been the same.

Then, there had been no *lir;* he was just a boy. Now, there was no *lir;* Sleeta could not be found.

He caught his breath on something very much like a sob. With no light, no world, no freedom, no *lir*, he would surely go mad.

—so much weight—

Sinews stood up in ridges, twisting beneath his flesh. Again and again he jerked limbs against the iron, until his wrists ran wet with blood.

—out—out—OUT—

"*Sleeta—!*" he shouted, and the sound came back to engulf him. To swallow him whole again.

Later, when he came back to himself: "*—afraid.*" The voice was smooth as clover honey, but honestly surprised. "*Look at him, Rhiannon!*"

Brennan did not move, did not speak, did not open his eyes to look. He lay in absolute stillness, tensed and rigid, in iron manacles and blood, and thought himself gone quite mad.

It could not possibly be Rhiannon—

"You struck him too hard," she said.

Let it not be Rhiannon— And yet he knew it was.

"It needed doing," Jarek answered. "But that has nothing to do with *this*. He is terrified."

"Too hard," Rhiannon repeated. "You have knocked him out of his head."

—oh, gods, no—

Jarek's tone was thoughtful. "I have heard of it before, once or twice . . . a fear of being enclosed. But—in a Cheysuli warrior?"

"They are as human as the next man," she said sharply. "Do you think him a sorcerer? He is just a man."

"*Shapechanger*, Rhiannon. And—as the zealots would have it—pretender to the throne."

Rhiannon did not answer.

Lir—? he asked; he begged.

"He will be fit enough for the sacrifice," Jarek said. "Whether he is in his head or no, the gods will not care. Give them blood: they are content."

Brennan struggled to understand. *Pretender to the throne?*

"And you?" she asked. "Will *you* be content to know you have slain the Prince of Homana?"

"If it serves," Jarek answered, "and it will. Oh, it will."

"There are two other sons. The Mujhar is rich in sons."

Thinking: *I have been a fool—the woman has made me a fool—*

Jarek: "And poor when all are slain." Movement. The clink of iron links as Jarek tested the bonds. "Not so soft a bed, is it? Cold, hard stone . . . iron for the bedclothes . . ." He laughed. "What was it he called you?— *meijhana?* Perhaps a bedding name . . . a sweet Cheysuli love-name."

"It means 'lovely one,'" Rhiannon said; then, laughing: "Do you know none of their Old Tongue? You, Jarek, who claim to know them so well? Even *I* know a little."

And I know less than nothing— Within the link, Brennan sent again to Sleeta. *Lir—lir—where are you?*

But nothing answered him.

"Go, Rhiannon. There are things to be said that do not require your presence."

"No?" Her tone was bitter. "Are you done with me, then, now that I have served your cause?"

"We may find use for you again," he said smoothly. "Now go."

"He is in pain, Jarek. You struck him too hard."

"By this time tomorrow, he will never know pain again. Now, *go*." Movement. The susurration of cloth; bodies moving. And then Jarek spoke again. "Well, my lord prince, do you intend to pretend senselessness forever? Have you no questions to ask?"

Brennan opened his eyes. A dish of oil with a twist of wick filled his prison with smoky light. He saw squat stone walls, very low, and a half-doorway barely large enough to admit a man hunched over, with runes carved around the opening. He had seen a similar place once before, much younger, when the *shar tahl* had carefully tutored the Mujhar's sons in clan history. He frowned, then banished it at once as the expression pulled at the wound in his hairline.

And then he knew. A cell. The sort of cell a priest inhabited, not prisoner. But the runes around the low door were Old Tongue, not Homanan; this place, then, was of the Firstborn, and very old. Now freely profaned by Homanan zealots.

Questions, Jarek had said. Oh, aye, he had one: *"Why?"*

Jarek nodded. "A good beginning, my lord." He shifted his position, moving from a squat into a kneeling posture, and Brennan saw past him to the doorway. Seated just outside was a Homanan, clearly on guard even with Jarek present. They took no chances. "There are many answers. One is that Cheysuli are demons and must be returned through death to the netherworld of Asar-Suti, from whence they issued." He smiled as his overdramatized voice echoed faintly. "Another is that the old gods of Homana have turned their eyes from us, requiring blood sacrifice to restore their favor." Jarek's grunt of laughter mocked the statement. "And yet a third requires the—*reduction*—of those now close to the throne, to make way for the rightful ruler." He glanced briefly toward the guard.

Brennan's head pounded. But for the moment astonishment kept the fear of enclosure at bay. "Have you gone mad? I can refute each of those ridiculous reasons!"

"Can you? The first two, perhaps—I no more believe you are a demon than I am myself, and the old gods perished long ago—but I do subscribe to the final reason for your assassination, my lord." The guttering flames from the oil lamp scribed shadows in Jarek's face. "I personally have nothing against your race. Cheysuli have as much right to live in this land as Homanans do, but—"

"Then *why*—"

"Why?" Jarek's tone was intent. "Because through a miscarriage of a twisted prophecy and the blind acquiescence of Homanans overcome by Carillon's legend, Cheysuli now hold the Lion Throne. And that, my lord Prince of Homana, is why you—and others of your kin—must die."

Brennan stared at him. "You *have* gone mad!"

"No," Jarek's demeanor remained unruffled. "There is a man in the world much better suited to rule Homana than your father."

"*I* have gone mad," Brennan muttered in disbelief. "This is nothing but a nightmare—"

Jarek merely smiled. His expression was oddly bland, as if he enjoyed giving nothing away except what he chose, and for specific reasons.

And suddenly, with ice-cold clarity, Brennan recalled his cousin. "You are Cheysuli—?" It was question, statement and accusation all at once.

Jarek's brows jerked upward; something flickered briefly in pale eyes, then disappeared. He laughed. "Do I *look* Cheysuli, my lord?"

In the distorted shadows, his face was alien, full of planes and hollows. He was black-haired but brown-eyed, a pale ale brown; in poor light, around the rims, almost a yellow-gold. And though his skintones lacked the sunbronzing characteristic of most Cheysuli, so did Corin and Keely.

"Cheysuli," Brennan said, shivering once in shock, "and in league with Teirnan, with the *a'saii*—" He looked at the man waiting just outside the low door. "You use the Homanan zealots to mislead any who might work against you, who might suspect what you are doing. . . ." Iron chimed. "Everyone knows the story of Elek's murder—how he supposedly died by the hand of the Prince of Homana . . . and you use it. You use it and other lies to twist the trust, to twist the prophecy—you use the Homanan zealots to throw down the rightful House and replace it with your own."

"Do we?" Jarek shrugged. "No, my lord. I am in league only with those who believe Carillon bequeathed us a better living legacy than the one who now holds the Lion."

"*Living* legacy—" Brennan went very still. "Then if you are *not* Cheysuli, and you are not *a'saii*—" He stopped. "You mean Carillon's bastard son!"

"Carollan," Jarek affirmed. "Son of the last *Homanan* Mujhar, and dispossessed king."

"Dispossessed! He was never *acknowledged*—and even if he had been, he could not rule. He is deaf and dumb, Jarek!"

"That does not alter the fact he bears the proper blood.

It does not alter the fact that he can sire sons who are *not* deaf and dumb."

Brennan rolled his head against the hard stone beneath his head. "This is madness, *madness* . . . this was settled twenty years ago, when my father and Caro met. There is no ambition in him. There is no desire for anything more than a peaceful life. And he has it, with Taliesin . . . do you mean to tear him away from it? To *force* the Lion on him, even if he does not desire it?"

Jarek's face and manner were not those of a madman, nor a zealot. He was quietly, wholeheartedly dedicated to his cause, lacking the fanaticism that might tip him into madness. He was utterly committed. Brennan saw in him the same quiet fire that burned in Teirnan, and wondered again if he was being purposely misled.

Jarek glanced over his shoulder at the Homanan guard, then turned back and wet his lips. "Twenty years ago my father was murdered by yours, my lord. Within the halls of Homana-Mujhar, before Cheysuli Council, Niall struck down my father to keep him from overturning the Cheysuli claim to kingship. For that cause, my father died. I swore an oath to carry out his commitment, and I mean to do it. No matter what the cost."

"Elek was sacrificed by his own people," Brennan said wearily. "My *jehan* held the knife, it is true, but only because in the crush of fighting someone put one into his hand and then forced him to stab Elek. It was carefully planned that way to implicate my *jehan*."

"I would expect Niall's son to say nothing else." Jarek smiled faintly. "It is old history, my lord, but history is a living thing, bequeathing life and knowledge to others, and the fuel to carry out ambitions and commitments. Time grows short—Carollan ages, and with each passing day Homanans forget the Lion belongs to them, not to the Cheysuli . . . not to Niall, nor to you, nor to the children you might sire upon your Erinnish queen." The light flickered, nearly died. "It is our *tahlmorra* to wash the Lion clean of Cheysuli claim, and give it to Homanans once again."

"*Tahlmorra*—" Brennan could not summon the means to spit. "If you do this—if you do this to me or to anyone else—the gods *will* turn their eyes from you!"

"Then all the better we appease them with blood sacrifice." Jarek picked up the dish of oil and told the other man to go.

Brennan tensed in his shackles. "You cannot simply slay me out of hand . . . in war, *aye*, but like this? In the name of *Carollan*?"

"But we can." The light was stark on Jarek's face. "You questioned if I could be Cheysuli, working with—*a'saii*?" He nodded, went on. "Perhaps this will convince you otherwise. For a six-month, now, we have been catching and slaying Cheysuli—not warriors, unless we are forced, because too many *lir* deaths would be remarked by other *lir*—but women and children. It is necessary." He bent closer, lowering his voice. "Now we reach higher, touching the royal family itself, to show no one is invulnerable. That even the highest can be overtaken." He paused. "Left to me, alone, I would devise another means. Death is death, but there should be dignity involved. Sacrifice is barbaric . . . but also useful. For those who thrive on such things, it serves to keep the fire burning. And we do need a fire, my lord—bright and hot and clean—if we are to burn the Cheysuli infection from the wound you have made in Homana."

"*Jarek—*"

But Jarek was gone, and he took the lamp with him.

Five

Eventually, Rhiannon came. She set the place alight with a single candle and knelt by him in shadows. Her palm was cool on his brow. Gently she parted sweat-stiff hair, pushed it back to bare the wound.

He jerked away from her.

She drew in a startled breath, twitching in shock. Abruptly she twisted to look over her shoulder toward the low entrance, as if she feared discovery.

Did she think he did not know?

He wanted to say: *leave me alone*, but he could not find the words. Thinking: *if I cannot be free of the place I am imprisoned, let someone share it with me.*

"Oh, my lord . . ." Her black eyes were blacker still in the shadows of his prison. "My lord—"

He cut her off. "Where is my *lir?* What have they done with my *lir?*"

"They have put her elsewhere. My lord—"

"Is she *alive?*"

"Aye. Of course." A smudge of dirt marred her face. "They want you whole. For the sacrifice. They will not slay her before the proper time."

He bared his teeth. "I cannot *touch* her. There is no Sleeta in the link!"

The flame danced, guttered, nearly went out; Rhiannon's hand was trembling. "I swear, she is alive. I *swear* it, my lord. Confined, as you are, but well enough."

"I cannot *touch* her!"

"Perhaps it is the drug." Plaited hair hung over her shoulders, braided ropes of glossy hair, threaded with crimson ribbon. "The wine—Jarek's wine, the second jug—it was drugged, my lord. To dull your Cheysuli magic."

The candlelight was kind to her face. Black hair, fair

skin, long-lashed eloquent eyes— Inwardly, the fear and fury rose. "By the gods, woman, you tricked me! You sucked me into this madness of Jarek's making."

"No! Oh, no, I swear . . ." Tears welled up into her eyes. "I knew noth—"

Brennan's mocking laughter cut her off. "Oh, aye, give me tears! No, no, woman, not again . . . I will not succumb to your posturing of innocence yet *again*."

"My lord—"

"I heard you," he accused. "You and Jarek, discussing my health and welfare, and the plans for my demise. Do you think I am a twice-born fool?" Iron chimed as he fisted grimy hands. "Go, woman. Hie yourself back to the man who is so kind, so generous, so—"

"Listen to me!" Her desperate hiss set the candleflame aguttering and cast distorted shapes upon the curving wall behind her. "Listen to me, my lord, when I deny knowledge of Jarek's plans . . . when I deny willing participation—"

"Oh, aye, you knew nothing." He writhed in his chains and knew again the helpless fear of a man entombed. "Oh, Rhiannon, I commend you; you played your part so well. I fell into the trap like a green boy sick for love of his first woman—"

"What do you want me to say?" she demanded. "Shall I swear by your gods? By the Mujhar? By *this*?" Light caught the sapphire ring dangling from its thong and set the gem-stone aglow. "Then I will swear by you, my lord prince— by Brennan of Homana, firstborn of the Mujhar's sons, and destined one day to sit upon the Lion Throne."

"So glib," he retorted. "You spew out titles and destinies like a *shar tahl*, woman, but I will not be suborned by you again."

Rhiannon briefly bared small white teeth in a feral dis-play of frustration. "You *fool*—I came here to give you what aid I can, and you spend your strength on insults!"

Brennan's laugh was a short bark of sound. "Fool, am I? No more 'my lord' this, 'my lord' that, now that the truth is out."

"At the moment, *my lord*, there is little in your state to recommend your heritage *or* your divinity!"

"Divinity . . ." This time the laugh was genuine. "Aye, not much of a man in this malodorous shell, is there?"

"I came to help," she said curtly. "Tell me what you would have me do."

He rattled his chains. "Set me free, Rhiannon. Prove you are innocent of my accusations." Thinking: *What lie will you tell me now?*

"Jarek has the key."

He wanted to strike the innocence from her face. "Are you not his whore, then? Have you no bed skill, that you cannot tease the key from him? Better yet, *steal* it!"

Color flamed in her face to rival the candlelight. "Jarek— is my first man," she said stiffly, with an odd integrity. "It has only been but a month . . . teasing is—not something I do very well." Her knuckles were white on the smoking candle.

He wanted to shout at her, to shake her, to force the truth from her. And yet, against all odds he believed her. "And if you do not try to tease, cajole, *steal*, Jarek will have me slain." He saw how her chin trembled convulsively. More quietly, he said: "Do you want that knowledge to compete with the memory of the ring I gave you?"

One hand closed over the ring and clenched it so hard the sinews stood up beneath the flesh. "If I am caught—" She stopped. "If I am caught, *three* will be sacrificed."

Brennan closed his eyes and felt the sweat sting the wound on his forehead. He would not deny the truth, even if he thought she might believe him when he told her Jarek would never consider such a thing. Jarek might.

Once again he tested his bonds and found them firm as ever, biting into weals and making them bleed again. He turned his head from her and ground his teeth, trying to keep himself from begging. If asking were not enough, begging would merely diminish what little pride he had left.

"My lord—" This time when she touched him, he did not pull away. "My lord, Jarek said you were afraid of places like this."

All the breath spilled out of his mouth. "I am." It was easier than he had believed; the fear did it for him. "This place—this *weight*—" He stopped short, shut his eyes, smelled the fear-stench again. "When—when I was but a boy, very small, I was trapped in a place not so different than this—all stone, cold stone, so much darkness and all the *weight*—" He swallowed, nearly gagged. "I had forgotten, thank the gods, *forgotten* . . . until now. . . ."

"Oh, my lord."

"Rhiannon—" He stopped, began again, not caring that this desperation was manifest; that the sound of his fear filled up his prison. "I beg you—*get me free!*"

Her fingers briefly squeezed the cold flesh of his arm. "I will do what I can do."

And she left him alone in darkness where he could cry in privacy.

Rhiannon did not come again. There was no freedom, no miracle that conjured a shackle key from the air to unlock his cuffs. There was no escape in sleep or unconsciousness. There was only the consuming knowledge that time passed too quickly, and that at the end of another day he would be dead, sacrificed in the name of Carollan, his great-grandsire's bastard son.

Curse you, Carillon . . . curse the loins that sired a son on some baseborn Homanan drudge instead of on Solindish Electra—

And yet he knew an insane amused irony in that curse, for without the loins that had sired Carollan—deaf, dumb Caro—there would have been no Niall. No Brennan. No need for Cheysuli rule at all, for there would have been a *Homanan* heir.

And no need for sacrifice. Uneven stone pitted his flesh through Cheysuli leathers. *Oh, Sleeta, give me the strength to die as a warrior dies, not hating myself for losing control in this fear of small, harmless places—*

Footsteps. Torchlight, reaching in through the low opening to set his prison aflame. And the shape of a man, ducking down, bending to enter, to kneel at his side with an iron key in his hand.

"My lord, your time is come upon you. The gods are thirsty tonight."

"Put no hands on *me.*"

"What? And leave you here to go mad from close confinement?" Jarek unlocked ankle shackles. "Lest you forget, my lord, we have your *lir* as well. Try to escape, and she shall surely die." His face was mostly hidden in distorted shadows. "The drug was strong." Calmly, Jarek set iron aside. It rang in the tiny cell. "An herbalist who has knowledge of such things recommended a mixture of ingredients deadly to most men, but merely temporarily—if powerfully—discomfiting to a Cheysuli. One ingredient you may recognize: the root called *tetsu*."

Muscles spasmed. "*Tetsu* is deadly!"

"Does it matter?" Jarek laughed. "No, no, not when used with certain other herbs—the root is dangerous, but not deadly in proper proportion. Still, it exerts a powerful presence, does it not? Cut off from your *lir*, you are no different from a Homanan." The wrist cuffs were unlocked. "Come out, my lord. The gods await."

"And if I stay?" Brennan flexed painful wrists and set his teeth against the cramping of his calves. "If I choose to remain here, what will you do?"

"Brick up the door and leave you to die a madman." Jarek shrugged. "It would discommode the gods briefly, perhaps, to lose so princely a sacrifice, but there are others. And who is to say the sacrifice be limited to the Mujhar's *sons*? There are daughters, too—"

"No!" he cried, and heard it briefly echo. "No, not my *rujholla*. Jarek—"

"Then come out, my lord. Come out into the air, where you can breathe again, and know yourself *alive*."

Alive. For how long? Still, he stood a better chance of escape out of the cell than in.

Jarek moved aside and gestured Brennan to exit first. He went, stooped and cramped, and felt fresh air upon his face. No chains—he was *free*—

Flames were in his face. He thrust up a hand to ward his eyes, felt heat and the lick of dripping oil. He staggered, thought to run, felt hands upon his arms; the strength of Jarek's drug still lingered in his system.

Behind the flames, he saw faces. Strangers all, ten, twenty, thirty or more of them, but he knew them. He knew them by their avid eyes and feral expressions; their commitment to Jarek's cause.

Nowhere did he see Rhiannon.

The men closed on him. "Come, my lord," Jarek said, as they forced him to the altar.

It was old, dark stone, stained black with the blood of murdered Cheysuli. Beyond the flames of the torches his captors carried he saw other torches, ten of them, thrust into the earth to form a ring around the stone. All the earth was beaten into dust beneath the trees around the altar; now his blood would muddy it.

He stiffened, tried to twist free, was shoved toward the altar.

"Your *lir*, my lord," Jarek said quietly. "Do not forget your *lir*."

They lifted him, even as he struggled; thrust him up onto the stone; pinned him on his back.

"Justice," Jarek said.

"You are mad—*all* of you, mad!"

"The rightful line restored . . ."

"Carillon himself declared Donal heir in lieu of sons," Brennan appealed. "He wed Aislinn, Carillon's daughter, who bore him a son . . . whose *son* sired a son."

"The Lion shall have a *Homanan* Mujhar again . . ."

Brennan writhed; they held him down. "*I* am Homanan!" he shouted. "I am the Lion's get!" And he thought in sudden, ice-cold clarity. *But if they succeed—if I am slain— there is still my* rujho . . . Hart *can be Mujhar* . . .

And the prophecy perpetuated.

Jarek still spoke, softly, calmly, as if he had practiced it many times. "Elek's death shall be avenged . . . his memory replenished in the blood of his royal murderer's son."

Brennan cursed them all, but they understood none of it. They did not know the Old Tongue.

"Carillon's son shall have the Lion—"

"*I am Carillon's great-grandson!*"

"—and the Lion shall know the proper line again, the gods-blessed Homanan line. . . ." Jarek's smile was odd. And then he began to laugh, but the laughter was odder yet.

Brennan rolled his head against the stone. "Fools and madmen, *all*—"

Grinning, Jarek gave the order. "Strip him of his armbands."

He was stripped.

"Fetch the cat."

Sleeta—Sleeta—Sleeta—

Jarek stepped close. Torchlight glinted off the knife. "Your earring, my lord." And touched blade to ear as he took the lobe into his hand and stretched it down, as if he meant to cut the earring free.

Brennan spat at him. "In the name of the sun and the wind and the rivers, the earth and the sky and the seas—"

Jarek laughed.

"—name of the Hunter, the Weaver, the Cripple—"

And Jarek *laughed*.

"—I curse you, Jarek son of Elek—*I curse you to die the death of a lirless man, beneath the jaws and claws of a beast*—"

Jarek bent close, still laughing, and bared his teeth in a mocking challenge. "Levy all the curses you desire on *Jarek, son of Elek*, my lord. They will not touch *me*." His eyes were black in the whipping torches, but the rims were a clear, eerie gold. "What I do, I do in the name of Asar-Suti, and *he* holds precedence over all your petty Cheysuli gods!"

"Ihlini!" Brennan cried.

"Now!" Jarek roared, overriding Brennan's shout.

Now, Sleeta echoed, as the *lir*-link blazed to life.

Brennan, tearing free of them all as out of the darkness the cry of a hunting cat rose, hardly noticed that Jarek's knife sliced through weighted flesh and severed his lobe. Pain was something he no longer acknowledged. Only anger. A terrible, burning anger that swallowed his knowledge of self and tipped him over the edge.

—down—

Rage fed the flames.

—down—

He did not know his name. He did not know *her* name, only that she was there, *here*, lending him needed strength, giving him what he needed; what he had to have, to use, to wield in the name of his anger.

Anger and something more. Something he knew as fear.

He reached out for the strength, the fear, the rage; touched it, snared it, hugged it to his breast.

—now—

Before an Ihlini, he knew, his Cheysuli gifts were muted nearly to nothingness, but now—oddly—he felt stronger than ever before.

—now—

Jarek no longer laughed. "Slay him!" he screamed.

—*now*— Brennan whispered. And within the webwork of the link, he tapped Sleeta and all the terrible heritage of his race.

In the guise of a tawny mountain cat, he shredded Jarek's throat.

Six

—run—run—run—

A litany in his head.

—run—run—

On four feet, curving claws raking divots of debris, the tawny cat ran. Running with him, Sleeta; black on black in the darkness of the night.

—run—

Deep in his chest, he coughed. Wreaths of vine and underbrush fouled his course, lacing his eyes with the whip-snag of tiny branches. Thorns caught at his pelt, breaking, clinging, burrowing into his flesh.

Still he ran. Flowing, like honey through a flame.

And then, unwanted, came the memory of what he had been, of what he had *done*, and he tumbled out of *lir*-shape into the man-shape known as Brennan.

He landed on one elbow; it gave, folding beneath his weight, and threw him over onto a shoulder, his left one, and then all the pain he had forgotten came rushing back again to set his bones afire.

Tangled in deadfall, he lay breathing heavily. His belly convulsed with it, until the grunting and gasping subsided, and he knew what he was again.

Man.

Brennan pressed himself up. Damp leaves formed a clammy cloak on naked arms against the night. He shuddered once, twice; gagged, and nearly spewed the contents of his belly onto the forest floor.

"Too fast," he croaked, touching his pounding head. "Too soon . . . agh, gods, my *head*—"

Sleeta's eyes were oil lamps in the darkness. *Lir—lir—* She pressed her chin against his shoulder, rubbing as if to offer strength and sympathy.

The pain of his abused head nearly took precedence over the *lir*-link, which frightened him. He tried to set it aside and think only of Sleeta, but the pain was so bad even his teeth hurt with it.

Lir. Sleeta leaned against him.

Forcing himself to ignore his own discomfort, Brennan tried to assuage hers, soothing her with gentle hands and tender words. Through the link they were reunited, reconfirming their need of one another; the cat's fear, shock, and weariness were echoes of his own.

"Gods . . ." In human speech, it was the only word he could manage. He was disoriented, tangled up in the sensations of cat mixed with man, until for a moment he could not distinguish himself, being neither human nor feline, but *thing.*

An owl hooted from near by. Another answered; in the distance Brennan heard the rising howl of a wolf, the yapping of his pack. He drew up both knees and rested his forehead against them, willing the pain to fade.

Lir. Sleeta again, still pressed against him. His hand touched matted fur, sticky blood, fluid seeping from an open wound. And he was outraged at the sacrilege.

"Sleeta—" This time the words began to make sense. He knelt, gently examining her head, throat, shoulders, carefully fingering ribs and belly and haunches. In the darkness much of her disrepair was hidden, but he knew she was not unscathed. The dogs had taken their toll. *"Ku'reshtin,"* he muttered. "Setting hounds upon a *lir.*"

Effective. Sleeta licked at his neck. *They distracted me from you.* She paused. *Blood,* lir. *Did he set the hounds on you?*

Brennan carefully touched his left ear. No more lobe, no more earring. Only blood marked the place where he had borne the cat-shaped ornament.

No hounds, lir. *This was done by man. This was done by Ihlini.*

No! Sleeta's shocked response was immediate. *I would have known an Ihlini.*

So I thought, he agreed grimly. *But in the past other Ihlini have walked unknown into Homana-Mujhar itself . . . who is to say what spell was cast to blind us to the truth?*

She was fretful from pain and incomprehension. *The gods*

*set us to guard the Cheysuli, to know enemy from friend, to
recognize ill intent.*

And to know Ihlini?

That more than anything else.

Brennan sat very still, not even daring to move his hand
against her pelt. In but a few words Sleeta had said more
of the purpose of the *lir* than he had ever heard from her
before. As a child he had been taught that a *lir* was a gift
of the gods, something incredibly special; the bond between
warrior and animal was a blessing no one else could possibly comprehend, a thing to be cherished above all else.
Such handing down of absolutes left little room for questions, even less for answers. The *lir* themselves had always
been oddly secretive about so many things.

"Why?" He asked it aloud because somehow it made it
more substantial; he asked it gently, casually, because he
was afraid she would give him no answer if he sounded too
intense. "Why are you to know Ihlini above all else?"

Having more power, they offer more threat. Sleeta licked
his shoulder.

It was not the answer he wanted; it told him nothing he
did not know already. "Surely anyone with power offers
equal danger."

Her breath was warm. *Who is his own worst enemy?*

"*I* am my own, of course—that tells me nothing." And
then he stopped speaking. His fingers dug deep into the
thickness of her pelt. "Unless, of course, you are confirming
my *jehan*'s contention that Cheysuli and Ihlini are
bloodkin."

Sleeta butted her head against his shoulder. Lir, lir,
enough . . . can we not go home?

Home. Did she mean Clankeep or Homana-Mujhar?
"Sleeta—" But he did not finish his question because he
heard movement in the forest.

He thought at first it was the Homanans come to find
him, to throw him down again on the altar to complete the
sacrifice. He thrust himself to a crouch, legs drawn up to
push himself into headlong flight, but he did not run. The
world spun slowly out from under him, and he fell awkwardly over onto one hip, keeping himself upright only by
dint of one rigid, outstretched arm.

No, Sleeta said. *Think before you run.*

He did as told, and understood what she meant him to understand. No, what he heard was not the noise of Homanans hunting him; not those fundamentalist fools. The unveiling of Jarek as Ihlini would be enough to send them fleeing. If there was one thing more horrifying to a Cheysuli-fearing Homanan than a warrior assuming *lir* shape, it was an Ihlini sorcerer.

No wonder Jarek spouted all that nonsense about Carollan—he used it to cover his real intent, to hide himself in the others.

He crouched in the darkness with Sleeta crouched beside him. And then the cat gently butted an arm. *The girl, lir . . . the one who got me free.*

Rhiannon. So she *had* done as she had promised.

The noise came closer. No doubt she thought she moved quietly, using all the stealth she could, but to Brennan, warrior-bred and trained, her progress was easily followed. She had not learned to move randomly, to stutter-step, to wait, to move again, as if an animal. She rustled, snapped boughs, snagged vines and underbrush. He waited until she was close enough, and then he said her name.

Her startled reaction sent her crashing back two steps and then she was caught fast, clothing and hair snagged on twisted boughs. He heard her rapid breathing and the tearing of thin fabric as she sought to free herself.

"*Meijhana*—no. There is no need to flee *me*." And he rose out of his crouch to stand, one hand splayed against the trunk of a conifer to keep him from falling down.

"My lord?" All movement stopped. "Brennan?"

"Aye. And my *lir*, whom you were good enough to release."

He heard more cloth shredded, the clink of something metallic, the ragged eagerness in her breathing. And then she was free and stood before him. Debris littered her braids, clung to her clothing, marred her face. But she smiled, and laughed, and held out glowing gold.

"Yours, my lord. When all the others ran, I took them to give to you."

He had not thought to see the *lir*-bands again. Nor had he allowed himself the time to think on what the loss represented. Although the *lir*-gold did not make him a man or a warrior in place of a boy, it was still an integral part of who he was. The loss would have shamed him as much for his manner of death as wearing them honored his manner of living.

"*Leijhana tu'sai,*" he whispered. "Oh *meijhana*, I owe you so much. For Sleeta . . . my life . . . for these. . . ."

Her eyes avoided his. "I could not find the earring, my lord. Perhaps—if we were to go back—"

"No. It does not matter. I lack the lobe in which to wear it." He smiled ruefully at her hiss of realization. "These are enough, *meijhana*. That I promise you." Slowly he slipped hands through the heavy gold circlets, one by one, and slid the bands up past his elbows until the gold was locked against living flesh. The bands were cool for only a moment, and then they warmed, remembering their customary place, and he was whole again. "*Leijhana tu'sai,*" he said again, tracing the cat-shapes in the metal.

Rhiannon shrugged a little. "The return of your gold is still not enough to repay the pain I have caused you and your cat. If I had known what Jarek intended—" She stopped short, and tears welled into her eyes. "Oh, *gods*— how could I have been so blind, so *stupid* . . . how could I not have seen what he meant to do?"

He reached out and caught the back of her head against the palm of one hand and cradled it gently. Slowly he pulled her in until she pressed her face against his soiled jerkin, clinging to his arms. At first she held herself stiffly, plainly made uncomfortable by his rank if not by his compassion. Slowly he gentled her, as he had gentled so many fillies.

"*Shansu,*" he said softly. "Peace, *meijhana*—I think no less of you for your grief." Yet even as he said it, he wondered if he meant it. In the clans, grief was an exceptionally private thing. A Cheysuli showed none where others might see it.

Traditionally. *But traditions change* . . .

The tears did not last. Rhiannon moved back, out of his arms, and wiped her face, succeeding only in smearing grime across both cheeks. Twigs and leaves clung to her braids. But he thought he had never seen a woman who looked lovelier, even in disrepair.

"Oh, my lord—" She reached up and touched fingertips to his neck where the blood from his stolen lobe had crusted. "My lord, they have used you so cruelly. First your poor head, then the drug, the chains . . . now *this*." She caught one of his arms as he wavered and tugged gently, urging him down. "Sit, my lord, I beg you. It is clear you are close to collapse."

"Is it?" Awkwardly, grateful for her assistance, Brennan sat down. Sleeta lent him warmth by pressing against one side; he wrapped an arm around her and gloried in her presence. "Gods, what I did—" He broke off as the world turned yet again, and bit back a curse as he tried to stay upright.

"Lie you down," Rhiannon said. "Here—I will help—" And she moved quickly as he toppled, taking his head into her lap. Tentatively she stroked sweat-stiffened hair back from his forehead. Her fingers were cool and light, and the pain was not so bad beneath her touch.

"Sleep, my lord," she said. "No more harm will come to you."

He smiled, though he did not open his eyes. "You sound so certain, *meijhana*."

"I am. No harm, my lord Brennan—I promise. Your *lir* is here, and so am I."

For the moment, there was nothing more he wanted.

He dreamed of darkness and close confinement, and the knowledge of his fear. Weighed down, he could not move. Only his voice knew freedom, and even that was denied him. Muzzled by a deep, disturbing sleep, the only sound he emitted was a throttled wail, a muffled plea for release.

"My lord."

The woman's voice intruded. From a distance he heard it. He reached out for it, trying to catch it and cling to it like a babe to a mother's breast.

"My lord—" *She paused.* "Brennan . . . *Brennan*—wake up. I am here. I am here. I promise."

He struggled toward the voice. Something touched his face: a hand, warm and kind, offering him compassion. He reached out, caught it, clung, and the darkness began to recede.

"Brennan—"

And he came up out of the dream into reality again, and caught her against his chest, pulling her body beneath his,

*knowing only one way to banish such gods-cursed fear; how
to prove he was alive, alive, after coming so close to death.*

"Please—" he whispered, and then abruptly he was
awake.

—oh, gods—

Even as he moved to relieve her of his weight, of his
uncharacteristic *demand*, her hands pulled him back
down. "No."

"But—you know what I meant to do—what I *would* have
done, whether you wanted it or no. . . .

"I know." She reached up to catch a lock of his hair.
"Do you think I am unwilling?"

A dozen questions spilled into his mind. He wanted to
speak of Jarek; of the line between lust and love; of the
differences in gratification and gratitude. He could give her
so many reasons for what he had so nearly done, and what
his body still wanted him to do. But looking into her face,
into her eloquent eyes, he saw no desire for explanation.
She knew as well as he. She wanted as much as he.

She locked her hands into his hair and pulled his head
down, down, until her breath caressed his face. "I did not
love him, Brennan. That much I promise you."

For now, it was enough.

He gave Rhiannon into the care of serving women when
they reached Homana-Mujhar. Sleeta he tended personally,
as always. And, at last, he turned his attention to himself,
tarrying in a hot bath even when his kinfolk came knocking
at his chamber door with questions regarding his health,
word of his battered appearance having been passed among
the servants and so to his kinfolk. He sent them away with
promises of a full explanation, and fell asleep in the cask.

At last he faced his kinfolk in Deirdre's airy tower solar,
though now it was dark outside. He was more than willing
to give an explanation now that he was clean again, clad
in fresh leathers and smelling of cloves instead of fear and
close confinement. But he did not begin at once, because
Ian stepped close and stopped him short with a hand upon
his arm.

He inspected Brennan's left ear attentively a moment.
"A clean cut," he said after a moment. "You are lucky.
You might have lost the entire ear."

Maeve, standing near one of the tripod braziers, grimaced and touched her own, as if sharing a measure of his pain. Keely, sitting crosswise in one of Deirdre's chairs, combed unbound hair away from her face with stiffened fingers. Her blue eyes were very thoughtful.

Deirdre, playing hostess, poured wine into a cluster of cups and began to hand them out. As she came to Brennan, he saw how tightly set was her mouth. She said nothing at first, giving Ian his portion, but he seemed to sense she intended to and moved away smoothly. It left Deirdre and Brennan confronting one another over a cup of blood-red wine.

He took it from her, but her fingers pressed his own. "Next time," she said quietly, "let the bath wait."

"I was *filthy*—"

"I know. And I am saying, let it wait." Her green eyes were steady, unyielding. "Think of your father instead of yourself."

He opened his mouth to protest, to repeat how badly he had needed the bath, but he shut it in silence instead. A glance at his father, waiting quietly in a chair near the fireplace, underscored the intent of Deirdre's words. Niall would say nothing, but there was suddenly acknowledgment in Brennan's mind that he had worried him deeply and unnecessarily, even if for only the brief length of time required by the bath.

He sighed. "Aye. Aye, I will." He touched Deirdre's shoulder briefly in thanks, then went to his father. The others would hear clearly enough, but it was to Niall he would speak. "I am well, *jehan*. I swear. There is discomfort—" he shrugged "—but it will fade."

Niall looked up at him from the chair. "Who put you in irons?" he asked quietly.

"Irons!" Maeve stared. "What does he mean, Brennan?"

The others, clearly, had seen only the lobeless ear. The Mujhar had seen his wrists with their bracelets of flesh rubbed raw. And now everyone else did as well.

Keely abruptly swung her legs around, rose and crossed to him. Forthright as ever, she grabbed one of his hands and pulled it out where she could see it and his wrist clearly. He felt her fingers spasm briefly in shock, and then she let him go.

"Who *dared* to chain you up?" Her tone was level, on the surface unemotional, but he heard the truth beneath the sound. Anger. Outrage. An abiding disbelief.

"His name was Jarek," Rhiannon said, and shut the door behind her.

As one, all turned and stared at her. Even Brennan did not move to her at once, though he meant to, because he was too startled. He had known she was attractive, but the women had made her beautiful.

Awkwardly, she curtsied deeply. Heavy skirts—a deep, rich blue—draped on slate-gray stone. Her hair, bound back smoothly in a single braid, coiled like glossy black rope against soft wool. "My lord Mujhar—" And abruptly, she lost her balance.

It was Ian, closest, who caught her arm and raised her. Her face blazed with brilliant color. She allowed Ian to hold her stiff arm and did not attempt to move again, as if afraid she might embarrass herself further.

"Be easy, *meijhana*," Ian told her kindly, offering her his warmest smile. "There are times formality is required, but this is hardly one of them." His fingers squeezed her arm gently. "Be welcome among us, lady."

Brennan looked at his uncle instead of Rhiannon. It was no secret among Deirdre's ladies—and therefore the rest of the palace—that the Mujhar's brother was a man worth having, as friend or bedmate—or both—but Ian had never shown any indication of desiring permanency in feminine companionship. Certainly he did not now, but there was no mistaking his attentiveness to Rhiannon.

He would do the same for any woman . . . and then: *She must be twenty-five years younger than my* su'fali!

Smoothly Brennan moved forward and offered his hand to Rhiannon. She took it at once, and he could not hide the smile of subtle triumph as he turned her away from Ian.

He presented her to his father. "This is Rhiannon, *jehan*. Because of her courage, I am here to stand before you."

"You have my thanks," Niall said quietly. "*Leijhana tu'sai*, in the Old Tongue. But will you be more forthright in an explanation than my son? We still are woefully ignorant of circumstances."

"Why was he in irons?" Maeve demanded. "Do *you* know, Rhiannon?"

"Gently," Brennan suggested. "Rhiannon is ally, not enemy."

Rhiannon's hand was cold in his. "I know," she said, and proceeded to tell them in a quiet, steady voice.

When she was done, the silence was palpable. And then the Mujhar began to swear. Quietly. Calmly. Inventively. In perfect eloquence he levied every curse against the Ihlini he could think of.

"Well," Ian said dryly when Niall was done, "there is no need for *our* retribution. Surely this is enough."

"Track them down," Keely said tightly. "Track them *all* down, and slay them all as you slew Jarek."

"Jarek was Ihlini," Brennan reminded her. "For all we know, so were the others."

"How?" Maeve asked. "Could they *all* hide themselves behind Homanan faces? Even before the *lir?*"

Brennan shrugged. "Sleeta did not know him for Ihlini. It is clear Strahan has learned well the spell that shields Ihlini from the *lir.*"

"And it makes them all the more dangerous," Ian said.

Niall shook his head. "I am not certain that is so. That Jarek was shielded, aye—but the others? I think not. It requires something tangible from a *lir*—a tooth, a claw, a talon, a feather . . . how many *lir* have died in Ihlini hands?" He sat forward in his chair. "Tynstar had Cai, my grandsire's hawk. Strahan had four teeth from Storr, Finn's wolf. But not enough, I think, for all of them."

"He might have had more than enough," Brennan said. "He told me that although they preferred to sacrifice women and children to avoid alarming the *lir*, they did kill a few warriors."

"An endless supply of *lir*." Ian, stark-faced, shook his head. "It is not impossible. It may be all *were* Ihlini, not Homanan at all. Jarek simply used the story of Elek as a ruse."

"But why?" Rhiannon asked. "If all were Ihlini, why act as Homanans at all?"

"Think," Ian said. "How better to infiltrate a realm than by portraying yourself as a *part* of that realm?"

"Even before people you intend to murder?" Keely asked. "That makes no sense at all, even for what I have heard of Strahan."

Ian shrugged. "I cannot say *why* Strahan does any of the things he does. But if he is true to himself—true to the Strahan *we* know—he will use every device in his ken to harm us." He nodded at Rhiannon. "Had she not freed Sleeta, thereby returning the power of *lir*-shape to Brennan, Jarek and the others would not have been unmasked. We would still be ignorant of the truth, because Strahan's allies take infinite care to keep us in ignorance." He spread eloquent hands. "How best to do that? By playing out the role."

Keely shook her head. "I still say it is senseless. I cannot see why any of them bother to portray themselves as Homanans when they mean to slay us regardless."

"Because you have no guile in you," Deirdre said.

Keely looked at her in surprise. "What?"

"No guile," Deirdre repeated. "You're a woman for saying what you mean."

"Even when silence is preferable." Brennan smiled at his scowling sister. "Admit it, *rujholla*—you would sooner charge in shouting your name and intention for all to hear, than to work in silence and subterfuge."

"So should everyone," she retorted. "What good is there in crawling on your belly when there are legs to carry you?"

"And what is wrong with waiting to move until all the facts are known?" Maeve asked. "Keely, you are too bold, too quick to say that you think when you would do better to wait."

Niall silenced the brewing battle with a raised hand. "Enough." The single word was sufficient.

Brennan made good use of the opportunity to put in his own thoughts. "It is possible Jarek acted alone. Now that I think on it, he seemed very aware of how the others might preceive him, as if he had to think about how he phrased things so as not to give himself away. To me, he was always Homanan, in speech and attitude." He paused. "At least—until he *chose* to divulge himself, and then the others scattered."

Niall looked at Rhiannon. "It is for you to tell us what you know of Jarek. Everything. Hold nothing back, or you may deal us a blow Strahan would be proud of."

Rhiannon's face was pale as she stared at the Mujhar.

Her hand, in Brennan's, was still very cold. He squeezed it to lend her reassurance; quickly she looked at him, smiled faintly, then withdrew her hand entirely and nodded to the Mujhar.

Niall opened his mouth to speak again, but held his question as Deirdre touched his arm lightly. "A moment, my lord. Let the girl—and the rest of us—find a seat." She poured wine into the remaining cup and passed it to Rhiannon. "You're not to be holding us all in so much awe," Deirdre told her kindly, green eyes alight with humor. "Underneath all the gold and prickly pride, these Cheysuli are no different from you and me."

Rhiannon clutched the cup. "But—are *you* not?"

"Cheysuli?" Deirdre's brows rose. "No, no, not I. Erinnish, I am, no more. There is no magic in my bones."

"Nor in mine." Maeve did not smile, though her tone was even enough. "We are remiss in our gratitude. For what you did in Brennan's cause, all of us are grateful."

Rhiannon fixed her eyes on Brennan's face. What she felt was clear for all to see. "There was nothing else I *could* do."

Ian fetched a chair and brought it forward, thumping it down behind her. "Sit you down, *meijhana*." His smile was exceedingly charming; the glint in his eyes was clearly intended for Brennan's benefit. "Be at ease, as I insist—and tell us whatever you can of Jarek."

Slowly she sat down, clutching her cup of wine. She did not drink. She waited, watching as her hosts found places to sit, and then she drew in a breath so deep it made the sapphire glint in the candlelight. "He was a kind man—to *me*." Blood rushed into her face as clearly she heard the incongruity in her statement. "He said nothing to me of Elek, my lord Mujhar. He kept his affairs very private, aye . . . but how many men share such things with women? Even the women who share their beds?" Color deepened in her face; she glanced briefly at Brennan, then looked away. "He served Cheysuli willingly in the tavern. I heard no words of hatred or hostility."

"Nor did I," Brennan confirmed. "Even when he and the others threw me down on the altar, there was little of true *hatred* about it, and nothing of madness at all." He shrugged. "Again . . . up to the point he gave away his race by admitting he served Asar-Suti, Jarek was loyal, dedicated, openly commited to the bastard's cause . . . and I believed him. There was no reason not to."

Niall nodded. "I think you may have the right of it. He misled them purposely so he could, if he had to, blame *them* for your death. He would admit the truth of his identity to none who was not Ihlini." His eyes softened as he looked at Rhiannon. "Not even to you."

"What else?" Ian asked white-faced Rhiannon quietly. "Think of him in a new light, *meijhana*, and surely you will discover something in his conversation, his behavior . . . in the company he kept."

Rhiannon frowned thoughtfully. "Once, he said something of his birth. He said he was bastard-born." She shrugged. "I thought nothing of it—I too am bastard-born—but he said it mattered very much in the scheme of things. That in the end, the bastard blood would give him power no one else could hold." She glanced at Brennan. "It was not a claim I paid much attention to—until I heard him tell my lord he would bring down the House of Homana. And then I knew what I had to do."

"Thank the gods," Maeve murmured.

Niall shook his head slowly. "Power from his blood . . . for all we know, he may have been *Strahan's* son."

"Does it matter?" Keely asked. "He is dead."

Ian shrugged. "Dead, aye . . . but I will curse the nameless bitch who bore him anyway."

Rhiannon looked at him sharply. "But I *do* know her name," she said. "I thought it pretty, so I remember it easily." Rhiannon smiled a little. "His mother's name was Lillith."

As one, they looked at Ian.

Seven

"You cannot be certain," Niall declared. "*Rujho*—you cannot."

Ian's face was a peculiar chalky gray. "How not?" he asked hoarsely. "Am I to ignore the obvious?"

"What is obvious?" Niall demanded. "Do you think Lillith kept herself celibate before *or* after you?"

Ian looked blankly at Rhiannon, who stared back in growing alarm. "Have I said the wrong thing?" she asked. "Have I said something I should not?"

Brennan intended to speak, to calm her fears, but Ian moved to stand before her, neatly shouldering him out of the way.

"Rhiannon." For a moment Ian said nothing more, locked up within some private battle, and then he blew out a breath between constricted lips and knelt down in front of her. *"Meijhana—"* He took one of her hands into both of his. "Can you tell me how old he was?"

"How old?" She stared in bafflement at Ian, then glanced up at Brennan as if to ask instruction. But he could offer her nothing.

Ian was singularly intent. "How old was Jarek, Rhiannon?"

"My age," she answered. "Twenty."

"Twenty," Ian repeated blankly. He turned his head to look at Niall. "The age is right . . . and he was bastard-born of an Ihlini *jehana* whose name we know is Lillith. What other proof do you require?"

The Mujhar looked infinitely older. "Perhaps none," he said wearily, rubbing at the ruined flesh around the patch. "Perhaps we have all we need."

"Aye." Ian's face was oddly blank. "It was what she

wanted. A child of us both, to mix the blood, the heritage, the *power*—"

"And now he is dead." Niall's voice was steady. "Why hate yourself the more when the need for it is passed?"

Ian's posture was incredibly rigid as he released Rhiannon's hand and rose. Brennan, watching him in growing alarm, thought he had never seen his uncle so shaken, or so vulnerable.

"Thank the gods," Ian said. He looked at Brennan. "*Leijhana tu'sai, harani*, for ridding us of another Ihlini—an Ihlini abomination!"

For all the words were brutal, Brennan heard the anguish in Ian's tone. He knew better than to believe it derived from grief, but there was more than dispassion as well.

How does a man deal with the death of a son he never knew? Brennan slowly shook his head. "*Su'fali—*"

"Surely you recall the story," Ian said harshly. The mask slipped from his face; Brennan saw the hostility that was so uncharacteristic of his uncle. "I was stud to Lillith's mare. She ensorcelled my *lir*, ensorcelled me . . . she *stole* the seed from me. Do you think I will grieve for that misbegotten spawn?"

Looking at him, Brennan saw an angry man who tasted the bitter fruit of shame. It was a new aspect of Ian, whose place in the household was one of abiding warmth and affection. He was *kinspirit* as well as kin.

It is as if he wishes to flagellate himself since we will not do it for him. "*Su'fali—*" Brennan began again, thinking to ease Ian's anguish, and realized there was himself to think of as well. Ian could not, for the moment, see past his own feelings to those of his nephew. "*Su'fali*, you are saying I killed a *kinsman*."

For a brief arrested moment there was acknowledgment in Ian's eyes, and then it was quickly banished. "Ihlini. No more than that."

Slowly Brennan shook his head. "But he *was*. He was an enemy, aye, but we shared blood. He was my cousin, just as Teirnan is. It does matter, *su'fali*."

Ian's look was intense. "Then I will put it another way," he said with elaborate distinctness. "If you had known he was my son as he began to carve you to pieces on that perverted altar, would you have hesitated to kill him?"

A neat trap— But Brennan shook his head. "No, *su'fali*. No."

"Then do me the courtesy of attempting to understand my feelings," Ian said curtly. "I will not weep for a man who was born of my seed, but decidedly not of my beliefs and loyalties."

"Ihlini and Cheysuli," Keely said rigidly. "Gods, who is to say what arts he might have had? What magnitude his powers?"

"Firstborn," Maeve said tightly.

"No." Niall's answer was quick and definitive. "No, not a Firstborn. He lacked the other blood; therefore the prophecy was unfulfilled . . . and even if it *had* been, do you think the gods would countenance an accursed kinslayer on the Lion?"

Brennan's belly twisted. "Kinslayer," he said hoarsely. "Am *I* not accursed, then?"

He saw their eyes upon him. He could not read them, even as well as he knew them, because what they all considered was something entirely new. Killing enemy Ihlini, Homanans, Solindish, and Atvians in service to the prophecy was one thing, and well accepted, but slaying kin? It carried a heavy weight.

Niall slowly shook his head. "Weigh yourself against Jarek, Brennan, and tell me which man deserved to die."

"Easy enough," Keely said sharply. "*Rujho*, you cannot doubt it. You are heir to the Lion Throne. Would you give it instead to Jarek?"

"No." He looked at his uncle, whose face was masked to them all, and yet the world was in his eyes. "No, I would not give the Lion to any man such as Jarek. But—" He paused, still looking at Ian. "*Su'fali*, surely you must wonder what he might have been if you instead of Lillith had had the raising of him."

"Must I?" Ian shook his head. "No, I must not. Else I will begin to question my conviction that Ihlini and Cheysuli cannot possibly coexist, within a realm or within a conscience." His eyes were on the Mujhar. "You say that once we were brother races, *rujho;* that the gods sired us both. And I say they did not, being gods of uncommon sense. But if you have the right of it . . . if we *are* brother races, intended for cohabitation once again when the prophecy is

fulfilled . . . then how do I live with it? How do I live with
the knowledge that my son tried to murder yours?"

Brennan saw clearly that a measure of Ian's pain was his
father's. Half-brothers only, sharing so little and yet so
much; he wondered if their bond was anything like the one
between himself and Hart.

"Then I will answer for you," Ian continued, as Niall did
not respond. "I could not live with it. And even if you have
the right of it after all, and one day we are expected to lie
down with Ihlini again . . . I would sooner give myself over
to the death-ritual than acknowledge one as my kin." Ian
looked at each of them, one by one: Niall, Deirdre, Maeve,
Keely, and Rhiannon. Lastly he looked at Brennan. *"Leijhana tu'sai,"* he said firmly, and then he put down his cup
of wine and walked silently out of the solar.

The Mujhar sat down again and scrubbed at his rigid
face. "Ah, gods, spare my *rujho* this pain. . . ."

"My lord." It was Rhiannon, speaking softly, and Niall
turned his head to look at her. "My lord, is this true? Jarek
was his *son?*"

The Mujhar sighed. "It is an old story," he said gently,
"and a very private one. But aye, it seems likely Jarek was
Ian's son."

"Then he also was Cheysuli? Like you. Like the Prince
of Homana?"

"And one step closer to the Firstborn," Keely said flatly,
answering in place of her father. She tossed back a gulp of
wine, then shook her head in disgust. "So, the Ihlini think
to destroy the prophecy from *within* instead of without. A
Cheysuli sire, an Ihlini dam, and children who do the bidding of the Seker."

"A formidable mixture," Niall agreed grimly.

Rhiannon frowned. "I do not understand."

Keely cast her an impatient glance, then looked at Brennan. "You would do well to tell her, *rujho*. Her ignorance
is appalling."

"Keely, enough," Deirdre said quietly. "Are you thinking everyone knows what the Ihlini are to us?"

"Us?" Keely asked. "You are not Cheysuli."

"Keely, that *is* enough," Niall said sharply. "I will tolerate no insults to Deirdre *or* Rhiannon."

Keely recoiled, looking startled. "No! Oh, *no*, I meant

no insult. Deirdre, I did *not.* I only meant you had less to fear, not being a part of the prophecy."

Deirdre's smile was crooked. "Aye, 'less to fear.' I'm only needing to worry myself over all of your father's children, as well as the father himself."

"Something *you* should think about," Maeve told her younger sister darkly.

"Aye, so I should." But Keely did not sound particularly repentant.

"Well," Deirdre said. "I'm thinking 'tis time I showed Rhiannon what there is to learn if she is to enter my service."

Rhiannon stared. "Your service?"

"My service," Deirdre repeated. " 'Tis hardly payment enough for saving the lives of the Prince of Homana and his *lir*, but I think 'twill be a beginning. If you are willing."

"Willing?" Rhiannon echoed. "Do you mean I am to stay here, with him—with *you?* I need not go back to the tavern?"

Deirdre smiled and slanted Brennan a bright, knowing glance. "There is a place for you here, if you want it," she told Rhiannon kindly. "You deserve better than serving wine to amorous young lordlings in tawdry taverns."

Brennan raised his brows. "*I* was always polite, and The Rampant Lion is not tawdry."

" 'Tis for Rhiannon to decide."

Keely grunted. "Even *Hart* would not lay a wager on that."

Brennan felt the familiar stab of loneliness.

Rhiannon looked at him directly a long moment. And then she rose and curtsied to Deirdre. She was slim and lissome in the rich blue gown. The rope of heavy hair swung against her hip. "Aye, lady, I will stay."

"Good." Deirdre's beckoning gestures encompassed Maeve and Keely as well. "Come then, there are things you must be learning. We'll be leaving the men to themselves."

Maeve and Rhiannon moved to the door at once. Keely, scowling darkly, finished her wine in a single gulp and then thumped the cup down on the nearest table. "Foolishness," she muttered, and was the last one out of the room.

Brennan smiled a little as the door thudded closed to

punctuate Keely's temper. "Do you regret it, *jehan?* Siring such unruly children?"

Niall grinned. "There *are* times. . . ." He let it trail off and stretched out his legs, slumping back in the chair. Candlelight glinted off the cup still held in his hand. "If the gods are willing, you will know the same trials I do. But in the end it is worth it . . . too long was the House of Homana poor in children, poor in healthy sons." He shook his head. "Because of my unruly children, I am able to make just distribution of our holdings; and improve for our House the trusts held by other kings. Within one generation I am able to secure threefold the path of the prophecy. Believe me, that is something."

Brennan nodded. Idly he looked into his cup; his wine was untouched. He drank down half of it in two gulping swallows, then dropped into the nearest chair. His ear hurt, and his head, and the rest of him as well. "There is more," he said at last. "I saw Teir at Clankeep. He was his usual self."

Niall shook his head in disgust. "I thought Ceinn knew better than to raise his son on resentment and bitterness. It does no good—the *a'saii* are disbanded."

"Teirnan says they are not."

The Mujhar went very still. "Not," he echoed. "And do you say they again espouse a change in the succession?"

"With an *additional* change. Ceinn and the others may have wanted Ian to take your place, *once*, but this time Teir wants the Lion for himself."

"The fool. The young, arrogant fool!" Niall thrust himself out of the chair and paced to one of the casements. It was full night outside, but the glow from bailey torches banished total darkness. What he saw Brennan would not venture to guess, but then he was not certain his father looked at anything other than memories.

"He says they will appeal to Clan Council, charging that Teir's blood has precedence over ours, *jehan*." Brennan shook his head. "He seems not to care that a division within the clans could well divide Homana."

"Teirnan never could see farther than his own immediate desires," Niall said in disgust. "Ceinn was shrewder . . . he said they wanted *Ian* on the Lion, or—when it was obvious Ian would never claim it—the first son 'Solde bore." He sighed and rubbed at ruined flesh, obviously troubled by old memories and grief. "Never did he claim it for himself. So—now he gives that son leave to win it—or steal it—however he can."

"Jehan—"

The Mujhar's tone was weary more than angry. "If he knew what it was to sit in the Lion Throne . . ." But he did not finish, turning instead to face his oldest son. "Well then, I think it is time to have him come to Homana-Mujhar."

"Here?" Brennan frowned. "Why?"

"I discounted the *a'saii* before, because I was foolish enough to believe my place secured," Niall said. "I was, after all, Cheysuli and Homanan, a part of the prophecy." He smiled in wry self-deprecation. "It nearly got me slain. I will not do it again . . . not when my son is at risk."

Brennan stared at his father thoughtfully for a long moment. Then he slowly shook his head as he understood the ramifications. "You are taking Teirnan hostage against the *a'saii.*"

"Am I?" Niall's bland tone divulged nothing of his thoughts.

Brennan could not look away from the man. He had seen the Mujhar on many occasions dealing with all manner of circumstances, political and personal, but never had seen him so intently purposeful while seeming so unconcerned.

"He might not come, *jehan.*"

"I think he will. If I know anything of Teirnan at all, he will come to prove himself. To prove what he is to *us.*"

"I can *tell* you what he is," Brennan murmured darkly.

Niall smiled and walked slowly over to Deirdre's tapestry frame. He studied the pattern intently for a moment, then turned back to Brennan. "I cannot expect you to be boon companions any more than Ceinn and I were. But perhaps you can—*influence* him."

Brennan scowled. "I can think of better company."

"Doubtless so can he."

The scowl evaporated, replaced by a wry smile. "And if Ceinn objects? He *is* Teir's *jehan.*"

Niall raised his tawny brows. "And I am Mujhar of Homana. On occasions such as this, there *is* some value in rank."

Brennan laughed aloud. "I think you *want* Ceinn to object."

"There is no pleasure in discord." Smiling, Niall lifted his cup and drank.

Son looked at father in detached appreciation. He did not much resemble Niall, being wholly Cheysuli in bones and color while the Mujhar was wholly Homanan, but they often thought alike, spoke alike, experienced similar feelings. There were times Brennan thought his father knew what he was thinking.

He scrubbed at his brow; weariness threatened to make him incoherent. He rose and set the cup down on the nearest table. "*Jehan*, if you will give me leave, I am for bed."

"Brennan."

At the door, Brennan glanced back. "Aye?"

"You have bedded the girl."

Brennan took his hand off the latch and turned to face his father more fully. "Aye." He felt a brief spasm of guilt as he recalled the initial circumstances, but it faded instantly. In the end, what he and Rhiannon had shared had not been a thing of force or mere gratification at all, but of entirely different dimensions.

The Mujhar's single eye was oddly opaque, but unwavering. "Perhaps I would do well to remind you that although *meijhas* are accepted in the clans, Aileen is not Cheysuli."

He thought he was too tired to be truly angry, but a trace of resentment flared. And was gone almost at once. He knew very well that if it were not in deference to Aileen's Erinnish sensibilities, his father would never interfere in his son's personal life.

"I have no intention of offering insult to Aileen," Brennan said quietly, "any more than I intend to make Rhiannon my *meijha*."

The Mujhar relaxed almost imperceptibly. He smiled. "Go and eat. And sleep. I intend to send men tomorrow to learn what they can of this Homanan idiocy concerning Caro—it may be nothing more than something created by Strahan for effect—but I will excuse you from it *and* from Council in the morning."

"*Leijhana tu'sai*," Brennan said fervently, and pulled open the heavy door.

*   *   *

He slept heavily for part of the night and then awoke, sweating, as he felt himself slide toward the abyss. Sleep was banished. He sat up in bed and stared blankly at the draperies dripping from the framework of his bed and knew if he did not resolve his fear once and for all, he would never sleep well again.

Sleeta was a lump of warmth and blackness at the foot of his bed. Even in deepest winter he required no heating pans; Sleeta was more than enough. Through the link he felt her drowsy inquiry, and told her to go back to sleep. What he intended to do required solitude, or the accomplishment—should there be any—would be tainted.

Brennan pulled on leggings, jerkin, soft houseboots. Moonlight slanted through casement slits, providing more than enough illumination for a man with Cheysuli vision. He went out of his room into the torchlit corridor and took the first down-winding staircase he came to.

In the Great Hall, the Lion crouched on the dais. Brennan hardly glanced at it; nocturnal visits in childhood had inured him to the eerie, lifelike stare of wooden eyes. And it was not the Lion that drew him now, but something else entirely.

Brennan kicked charred wood and ash from one end of the firepit, sweeping clean of debris the circular iron lid set flush against stained brick. He thought briefly of using a torch for a lever; dismissed it and bent to grasp the twisted handle. He muttered a plea for help, then braced himself and jerked upward.

The hinged lid yawned open and folded against the rim of the pit with a muffled clang. Ash rose; Brennan coughed. The exertion emphasized his need for rest and recovery. Raw wrists stung as other muscles clamored to protest abuse.

Brennan stood on the edge of the stairway leading deep into the earth. It had been sixteen years since he had descended the one hundred and two steps to the underground vault called the Womb of the Earth.

Aloud, he quoted a tenet of the clans: *"If one is afraid, one can only become unafraid by facing that which causes the fear."*

The words fell away into silence.

He sucked in a deep breath through a throat that threatened to close. "Prince of Homana? No. More like prince of cowards."

There was no disagreement.

Brennan swore. He caught up a torch from the rack and thrust it rigidly before him. It roared in the mouth of the stairway.

"Down," he said aloud, and made himself follow the order.

He counted. Each step took him nearer the Womb, farther from the Lion. Deeper. Until there was no light at all from the Great Hall, only the flames from the torch, and he knew it was not enough.

Brennan stopped. Sweat stung his armpits and dampened the hair against his face. The torch shook from the rigidity of his grip, distorting illumination. All he could see was blackness ahead and the promise of close confinement.

Down.

More steps. One by one, he descended them, until there were no more. He stood in a closet made of rune-worked stone. Slowly he put out one hand and pressed the keystone.

The wall fell inward, as he knew it would, and the vault revealed itself to him. The torch roared, spat flame, threatened briefly to snuff out. But it did not. And when he could, Brennan stepped into the vault.

The walls ran wet with torchlight. Gold veined the creamy marble and lent life to the *lir* imprisoned there. Brennan saw wings and claws and beaks and eyes, all frozen in the stone. Each wall, from floor to ceiling, was alive with marble *lir*.

"Ja'hai," he muttered aloud. But the gods made no indication they heard his instinctive plea for acceptance.

Sixteen years . . . and I am no less afraid at twenty-one than I was at five.

Brennan took three steps forward, then two more. He stood at the edge of the oubliette. The torchlight did not begin to touch the darkness of the pit. He could see nothing past the rim.

There were stories about the Womb. Legends that said a man, meant to become Mujhar, was required to be born of the earth herself, of the *Jehana*, and this was the birthing place. No one knew if the stories were true, or merely imagery handed down by the *shar tahls* to make certain everyone would remember. Brennan himself could not say, although he had heard one story more than once; that Homanan Carillon, needing the blessing of the gods, had of his own accord gone into the oubliette. And come out again, whole, but with a greater understanding of what it meant to be Cheysuli, even though he was not.

"Homanan," Brennan said aloud. "But I am Cheysuli; is there really a need for such sacrifice?"

"Is there, my lord?"

He stood very still on the edge of the oubliette, taking great care to maintain his balance. When he could move again without fear of falling, he turned.

Rhiannon stood in the open doorway. She had exchanged gown for linen nightrail and woolen robe. Wrapped in deepest blue, cloaked in a mantle of raven hair, she blended into the shadows.

In her eyes was the knowledge of what they had shared the night before, and the desire to share it again. She was not a bold jade such as many of the court women, but neither was she a coy woman whose mouth was filled with innuendo. That she believed herself in love with him, he knew; perhaps she was. But he was not in love with her.

She did not move from the doorway, as if she understood quite well that to enter was to intrude upon something sacred, something of ancient and binding power. "I went to your chamber and saw you leave it, so intent you did not see me in the shadows. You looked so troubled—" she shrugged, excusing her boldness easily, "—I followed. I found the stairway in the firepit, and knew what you meant to do."

"Did you?"

"Aye." She raised her chin slightly. "Whatever you may think of yourself in the aftermath of what Jarek did, you remain a brave man. A man of pride and strength and determination, not one to let a thing like fear cripple his *tahlmorra*." She smiled. "Deirdre is a remarkable woman, my lord. She answered my questions before I asked them, and told me what it was to love a man so bound by a prophecy. She told me how to share a Cheysuli with his *tahlmorra*."

He would not spare her the truth. "And did she also tell

you that within a matter of months there will be a Princess of Homana who will share those things with me?"

"Aye," Rhiannon said.

He had expected tears, disappointment, resentment. She gave him none of those things. What she gave him was pride to match his own, and integrity, and an honesty he so rarely saw in Homana-Mujhar, except when he spoke with Cheysuli.

He smiled a trifle sadly. "Where is the innocence?"

A tinge of color entered her face. "Do not mistake me, Brennan. I want nothing more than what I had last night. You wanted it—*needed* it then . . . and I think you want it now."

He did. For different reasons, perhaps, but he would not lie to himself any more than to her.

"Her name is Aileen." His words were brutal by design; he offered a final chance for withdrawal.

But it was not accepted. "I know," she said evenly. "*My* name is Rhiannon."

He took her hand. He led her out of the Womb of the Earth. He brought her to his chambers. To his bed.

To something he did not, could not regret.

Eight

Teirnan threw himself down in the Lion Throne. He grinned, caressing the ancient wood, then laughed aloud in joyous exultation. "Do you *know* how long I have wanted to do this? Can you guess?"

Brennan, who did not particularly care, merely shook his head.

"For as long as I can remember." Still Teirnan stroked the clawed armrests, glorying in the texture of age-polished oak. "Since my *jehan* first told me I was kin to the House of Homana."

Brennan's mouth twisted in irony. "And how carefully did he tend you, Teir? How subtle was he in impressing upon you his belief that you should rule in my place?"

Teirnan luxuriated in the throne, sitting back so that his head was shadowed by the gaping lion's mouth. "There was no subtlety at all, cousin. I am the son of dead Isolde, *rujholla* to the Mujhar . . . my blood cries out for the Lion."

Brennan, arms folded, paced slowly to the dais and climbed it, posting himself directly before the throne. "There are no *a'saii*, are there? Only you. And Ceinn, of course—but I think Ceinn's teeth were pulled many years ago, when my *jehan* named him *shu'maii* in his Ceremony of Honors."

Teirnan's hands clenched the claws of the Lion. "I have as much right to it as you."

"Do you?"

"My blood hearkens back to the days of the Old Mujhars, the *Cheysuli* Mujhars, who had no need to marry unblessed foreigners in order to secure Homana. It was ours already, given us by the gods themselves."

"And the Ihlini?" Brennan shrugged as Teirnan broke off to stare at him in shock. "I do not deny that through

Ceinn your blood is purer than mine . . . that because of Ceinn, you count some of the oldest and *cleanest* blood in your heritage." He tipped his head to one side in a brief gesture of idle acknowledgment. "After all, even your *jehana*—kin to the Mujhar himself—had decidedly mixed blood, while yours is admittedly less so." Brennan was motionless, holding him with the understated gentleness of his tone. "But if you wish to sit here and prate about it how you are improved by such purity, recall that it was precisely *because* certain clans refused to marry out that this dynastic manipulation became necessary. This realm to that realm, this warrior to that woman . . ." He shook his head. "Perhaps you should also consider that it becomes more and more likely we *are* bloodkin to the Ihlini."

"No." Teirnan was deadly serious as he pulled himself out of the throne. "You speak heresy, Brennan."

Brennan shook his head. "I speak of probabilities."

"How can you *say* that?"

"Look at the *lir!*" Brennan said. "Will they attack the Ihlini? *No*—even though they will do their best to destroy anyone else who means us harm. Will they tell us why? *No*—all they ever say is that they follow the law of the gods." He drew in a breath, understanding things more clearly himself even as he spoke. "It does seem entirely possible, *cousin*, that the reason that law exists is to keep children from slaying children—"

"Children—?"

"The children of the gods." Brennan exhaled slowly. "I find it hard to believe the gods would give their children the weapons with which they might kill one another when what their parents desire is for them to live in accord."

"But Ihlini kill Cheysuli!"

"And Cheysuli kill Ihlini." Brennan drew in a breath of dull acknowledgment, understanding it at last. "But without benefit of the *lir*. Without benefit of a full complement of powers . . . so that the battles are battles of *men*, and not the get of the gods, who have more power than perhaps they should to live in a world of men."

Teirnan's breath rasped loudly in the hall. "It cannot be," he said.

"How can it *not* be?" Brennan asked. "You know the prophecy, Teir. Its aim is to merge bloodlines and unite deadly enemies. We know the four realms: Homana, Solinde, Erinn, and Atvia. Even now we are closer to fulfilling that portion of the prophecy. I will hold Homana. Hart will have Solinde, Corin Atvia, and Keely will wed into Erinn. As for the two magical races, who else can they be but Cheysuli and Ihlini?"

Teirnan's face was gray. "May the gods strike you down!"

"Why?" Brennan asked. "It was the gods who gave us the prophecy."

Teirnan backed up a step and ran into the throne. He stopped abruptly, rigidly, and stared blindly at his cousin. His face was a death-mask.

"Teir," Brennan said with abiding patience, "I do not advocate we go to Strahan with words of peace in our mouths. But I think perhaps my *jehan* has the right of it: the time is come for the Cheysuli to begin acknowledging *all* Ihlini are not dedicated to Asar-Suti. There are those who serve themselves because they believe in peaceful unification as much as our prophecy demands it."

"Unification," Teirnan echoed.

"Blood merged with blood," Brennan told him. "And a chance for lasting peace."

Teirnan looked at the Lion. He touched it again, exploring it with his fingers. His face was immobile in its intensity, the angles hard as stone. "What will happen when the prophecy is fulfilled?"

Brennan frowned; Teirnan was leading up to something. "Peace. Cohabitation. The Firstborn will live again."

"*Aye.*" Teirnan overrode his words. "Aye, they will— and do you know what will happen?"

Brennan raised his brows. "Who can say? Their power will be complete . . . there will be no weaknesses."

"And what of us?" His cousin asked intently. "What of the Cheysuli, who *do* have weaknesses?"

"Teir—"

"Blood merged with blood, until the new overtakes the old. Do you see what will happen? There will be no more need for us!"

Brennan started to put out a restraining hand, thought better of it. He could not predict what Teirnan might do. "The gods would hardly guide us to fulfillment only to discard us when we have reached it," he said dryly. "We have been such faithful children."

"Faithful, aye . . . perhaps *too* faithful." Teirnan frowned and fingered the hilt of his Cheysuli long-knife. "Aye, I have heard some of this heresy you spout. Niall has made it no secret for the last twenty years. Peace, he says, as *you* have said, with the coming of the Firstborn. But what else? What *else*, Brennan? Have you not heard that we are also to lose our *lir?*"

"I think that is exaggeration."

"Oh? It was the Mujhar who said it, and his loyal liege man, our *su'fali*." Teirnan shook his head. "I think perhaps the heresy may hold a kernel of truth. For all I and others have continually denied it, including the *shar tahls*, I think perhaps we *are* to lose our *lir*. And for that—for that *alone*—I think we should reconsider what the prophecy really means."

Brennan sighed. "Is this nonsense compensation for your pride because you know you will never hold the Lion? Teir—"

But Teirnan shook his head and stepped abruptly away from the throne. "I renounce it."

After momentary astonishment, Brennan opened his mouth to compliment his cousin on recovering his senses, but said nothing as Teirnan spoke again.

"I renounce it. I renounce *you*. I renounce anything to do with the House of Homana, even Maeve."

The latter had already been settled; Maeve had admitted to making a vow to become Teirnan's *meijha*, but in ignorance of his ambition. Discovery of it had driven a wedge between them, and she had not returned to Clankeep. Neither did she have, she said, any intention of honoring her vow; Teirnan's declaration was therefore an empty one.

Brennan sighed. "Teir—"

"Do you see?" Teirnan demanded. "We will be diminished. We will be *used up*. There will be no more need for flawed children when the Firstborn live again."

"You *fool*." Brennan's disgust was manifest.

"Am I? No. I think I am the only one who understands fully what will happen." Teirnan moved away from the throne again. "You have the right of it, Brennan; there were no *a'saii*. Only an overly ambitious cousin. But now—

now I think the need is come again. . . ." Teirnan rubbed his face with both hands, as if to make certain he fully understood the consequences of what he intended to say. "I renounce the prophecy."

Shock turned Brennan icy. He shivered violently. "You *cannot!*"

"Why? I am bound by nothing more than my willingness to serve it. Now I choose not to do so."

"If you renounce the prophecy you turn your back on the clans, your race, your *tahlmorra*—"

"Then I will do so."

"Teirnan!" Emphatically, Brennan shook his head. "You deny the afterworld."

"I begin to think *this* world is more than enough." Teirnan moved past him and descended the dais steps to the stone floor. Before the firepit, he turned to face his cousin. "I thank you for your frankness, Brennan. For explaining how necessary it is for us to breed Firstborn on Ihlini, and how the results will change the world. Because if you had not, I would still be blindly serving a prophecy that will undoubtedly insure the destruction of our race."

"I could gainsay you," Brennan told him angrily. "Here, in this hall, we could settle this idiocy."

Teirnan swung to face him squarely, beckoning him on with empty, eloquent hands. "Then come, cousin. But if you do, be certain the fight will be to the death." Teirnan's eyes blazed with a feral light. "If you truly mean to gainsay me, then you will have to kill me."

They stared hard at one another. Teirnan's face was alight with some inner exultation, a kindling of new and abiding commitment. Brennan looked at him in disgust coupled with frustration, and considered calling his bluff.

But there is every chance Teirnan does not bluff. And if he does not, and I should kill him in some stupid, pointless battle, I become kinslayer yet again. He shook his head. *Teirnan is not worth it.*

"Go," Brennan said harshly. "But remember that you are now a clanless man. Your rune will be painted out of the birthlines. Your name will be struck from the histories. Your *jehan* will have no son."

It was a powerful inducement to make a warrior recant

his renunciation. But Teirnan was not induced. "Unless he should come *with* me."

"Ceinn would not—" But Brennan broke off. It was possible Ceinn *would*; he had raised this rebel. It was also possible others would; Brennan was realistic enough to know there were warriors who might prefer the old order to the new.

Teirnan smiled a little. "Aye. I see you understand."

Brennan's mouth was dry. "You would willingly divide the clans?"

Teirnan shrugged. "I offer an alternative. It will be their choice."

"It will be *no* choice!" Brennan cried. "What kind of warrior are you?"

"*A'saii*," Teirnan said evenly. "Clanless, runeless, and free—*free to serve myself*."

It was all Brennan could do not to shout at him. "You profane this place," he said in a deadly tone. "You dishonor your *jehana*."

"Isolde is dead," Teirnan said curtly. "As for profaning this place, I will take myself out of it."

Mute, Brennan watched his cousin go. He could find no protests in the face of such deadly determination. And when he was alone again, save for the massive throne, he went to it and sat down. It was not the first time. He and the Lion were on good terms.

"He will change his mind," Brennan told it, as much to reassure himself as to placate the Lion. "He will never leave his clan." But there was no answering reassurance from his conscience. Uneasily, he touched the lobeless ear. "Perhaps I should tell *jehan*."

Brennan did, over the Mujhar's evening meal, which Niall took alone in his private solar; Deirdre was otherwise occupied. His father pushed aside his platter of unfinished food so sharply his knife rattled against the silver. "I cannot *believe* you were so foolish as to incite Teir to such idiocy! You know what he is like."

Brennan sat slumped over the table, chin propped up on one hand. He was disgruntled enough; his father's displeasure made him feel worse. "Aye, well, I think we need not worry. Teir often says much but does very little."

Niall's tone was decidedly cool. "That is your opinion after carefully considering what would happen if he did precisely as he threatens?"

"How could he turn his back on so much?" Brennan asked in guilt-born exasperation. "His clan, his race, his *tahlmorra*—"

"Obviously he is willing to do so. For all he gives us impotent threats much of the time, *this* one may be real. How many warriors do you know even *jest* about such action?"

Brennan scowled. "None, but—"

"*But.*" Niall's tone was distinctly harsh. "I suggest you leave for Clankeep now and see if you can repair the damage."

"*Jehan—*"

"I myself will go in the morning. This sort of threat will be of concern to the clan-leader as well as the *shar tahl.*" Niall scraped his stool back and rose, his meal unfinished. "Well?"

Belatedly, Brennan also rose. He was grateful they were alone so no one else could see his frustration. "Teir will do nothing tonight. Why not let me go with you in the morning?"

"Because I have told you to go *now.*"

Brennan sighed and shoved the stool out of his way. "Aye, *jehan*—aye, *aye*," he muttered, and strode angrily toward the door.

"Even kings must take responsibility for the consequences of their own actions," Niall said as Brennan opened the door. "Begin now, and it will be that much easier when you are Mujhar."

His heir shot him a look of deep disgust and closed the door with a resounding thud as he stepped into the corridor. *Lir, we have been sent on a foolish errand.*

Sleeta was one floor up in his chambers, but the link dissolved the separation. *We?* she asked pointedly.

Do you berate me, too?

She sighed. *Where are we going, lir?*

Clankeep.

Her tone brightened. *Then I will bestir myself.*

Upon Brennan's orders his newest horse was brought,

saddled and ready. It was late afternoon and the weather was cool; winter was not so far away. The stallion, all black save for a splash of white upon his nose, sidled and snorted, stomping noisily on the cobbles. His eyes rolled as he espied Sleeta, who waited on the steps.

"My lord, I can saddle another," the groom said as the stallion's lips peeled back to display large teeth.

Brennan avoided the bite. "No. I am in the mood for Bane." He caught the reins and swung up into the Cheysuli saddle, clamping legs against sleek sides as Bane laid his ears flat back and essayed a tentative sideways leap. "The Mujhar rides out in the morning."

"Aye, my lord." The groom stepped away quickly, dodging flying hooves as Bane commenced dancing across the bailey. Brennan rode out the worst of the stallion's customary protest, then signaled the gates open. "I cannot say when I will return," he called, and let the stallion go as Sleeta bounded through.

He was at the border dividing meadowlands from forest when Rhiannon caught up to him. After the first short gallop across the plains to work out frustrations and Bane's bad temper, Brennan had slowed the stallion to a walk. Rhiannon clearly had kept her mount at a run; the bay mare was lathered with sweat.

He waited until Rhiannon had caught up before reaching across to grab one rein. "You know better," he said sternly. High color stood in her face. She was breathless, black eyes alight with exhilaration; the wind had blown tendrils of hair free of confining braid.

"I know better," she agreed, "but there was no help for it. You did not heed my call to wait."

He frowned. "When did you call?"

She laughed. "When the horse tried to smash your knee against the gatepost. You were swearing, my lord; I am not surprised you did not hear me."

He smiled ruefully. "Aye, well, I am somewhat fond of my knee, and the gods know I have more need of it than Bane." He released her rein and jumped down from his horse. "Dismount, *meijhana*—the mare should be walked."

"Aye, of course." She slithered out of the saddle in a

tangle of tassled boots, blue skirts, and midnight mantle. The heavy rope of hair was lost in the folds of the mantle, but he saw a glint of silver ribbon threaded through the plait.

He reached out and caught one slim hand, pulling her close. Rhiannon, laughing, stretched up for his kiss, then locked hands around his neck to pull him closer yet.

"Do you mind?" she asked as he released her. "I wanted to be with you. So often I must spend all my time with Deirdre or the ladies, when I would rather be with you."

He felt a twinge of guilt. It was no secret that Rhiannon shared his bed, yet the Mujhar held his silence. Brennan had no doubt Niall knew, but perhaps he knew also that repeated reminders of Aileen's imminent arrival would merely promote discord.

"I do not mind, *meijhana*, but you may find it tedious. I am sent to Clankeep to settle things with my rebellious cousin."

"Teir is a fool," Rhiannon declared. "Maeve loves him— had he any sense, he would try to gain the Mujhar's favor so he can take her for a wife."

"Then perhaps *Maeve* is the fool." He turned Rhiannon toward the wood. "Come, *meijhana*—the mare needs cooling."

She fell in beside him, leading the tired mare. "Where is Sleeta?"

"Gone ahead. Hungry, she says, but she will not be far."

Fingers twined. They walked in companionable silence, leaving behind the open plains for the shadows of the wood. The track was wide and beaten smooth; Clankeep was no longer closed to those who were not Cheysuli. Homanan goldsmiths came to trade for ornaments, and other craftsmen as well.

"There was another reason," Rhiannon said quietly. "The Mujhar meant to send a man to tell you, but I said *I* would go." She looked up at him gravely. "Word has come. Aileen's ship has sailed from Erinn."

Brennan nearly missed a step. Behind him, Bane nibbled irritably at his shoulder.

"I wanted to be the one to tell you."

He looked down at her. Her face was mostly averted,

but he heard the merest trace of a waver in her voice. *"Meijhana—"*

"I know," she said. "I have always known. You will marry her."

"It was a cradle-betrothal." He sighed. "It was more than that, *meijhana*—it was agreed before I was born."

"I know." She shrugged, speaking brightly. "I am no one. I could bring you nothing. Nothing but—" She hesitated, then halted and turned to face him squarely. One hand was splayed across her belly. "Nothing but this child."

He caught her shoulders and held her firmly in place, ignoring the mare's snort of fright and Bane's rolling eye. "Are you certain?"

"Quite certain, my lord." Rhiannon's smile was odd. "Does it please you?"

"How *not?*" He was astonished that she could ask it. "A *child*, Rhiannon . . . how could I not be pleased?"

"A *bastard*, my lord."

"Do you think I care about that? A child is a child."

Rhiannon laughed. "And an *Ihlini-Cheysuli* child? What do you say to that?"

His fingers locked in the folds of her woolen mantle. *"Ihlini—"*

One cool hand was a shackle on his wrist, clinging, pressing, *squeezing*, until the flesh began to protest. "Ihlini," she said distinctly, "Ihlini *and* Cheysuli. Why else do you think I wanted you?—why I made you want *me?*"

She was a woman, and weaker than he: angrily Brennan tried to break her grip, twisting sharply; to shock and dismay he found he could not. Because even as he moved, thinking to thrust her violently away, he felt the explosion of pain through the link.

Sleeta was nearly incoherent. *Lir—lir—lir—*

Even as Brennan tried to twist free again, meaning to run toward the source of Sleeta's anguish, Rhiannon prevented him. With one hand only, fingers spread rigidly against his breastbone, she coolly forced him off the track and against the nearest tree. "Back," she said only, supremely indifferent to his aborted bid for escape.

Lir— The cat's helplessness was his own, transmitting itself through the link with frightening ease and accuracy.

Though Rhiannon exerted little pressure, Brennan was slammed against the tree.

"Sleeta—"

"She is ours." Deftly Rhiannon pulled the reins free of his clutching hand and freed both horses, sending them away with a burst of purple flame from negligent fingers. "I suggest you do not try to struggle, for Sleeta's sake if not your own. My servants hold her now."

He wanted to overpower her. He wanted to snap her elegant neck. But Sleeta's welfare was paramount in his mind, and there was no doubting Rhiannon's confidence. He dared not try to move, or risk his *lir*'s life as well as his own.

Sleeta?

Lir—lir—Ihlini— And abruptly her pattern was broken, like a candle snuffed rudely out.

Rhiannon's hand still rested on his breastbone, promising violence. That she used some form of arcane force, he knew; she was strong, *too* strong. The rough bark of the tree ground against his spine, even through the leathers. Within he raged at her; without he made no effort to escape or attack.

"Good man," she said, "good warrior. Do not move and she will live."

"Slay her and you slay *me*."

"Empty threat," she answered. "I *have* what I want of you."

He tried to reach Sleeta through the privacy of the link, but nothing answered his frenzied search. There was emptiness in the pattern. "You have already killed her!"

"No, my lord. Not yet. She has been overcome by brutal force, but she lives. For now. Until we are through with you."

"How do you intend to kill me?" Bitterly. He could not believe he had been so gullible.

"Strahan wants you alive."

"*Strahan—*" He nearly gaped. "This is Strahan's doing?"

"Strahan's *suggestion*. My doing." Rhiannon smiled and reached up to caress his face even as he tried to jerk away. "It could have been worse, Brennan. Much worse. Seduction is better than force."

His lips peeled back from his teeth in an instinctive expression of feral disgust. He thought he might be ill.

"Lillith believed I could not do it," Rhiannon said quietly. "She feared I was too young, even by human standards. But then my mother forgets that Ihlini women are born to seduction as Cheysuli are born to the *lir*."

His muscles spasmed beneath her hand. *"Lillith—"*

"—is my mother. My *jehana*, you would say. As Ian is my *jehan*." Rhiannon laughed softly. "We are cousins, you and I—in addition to being bedmates."

"But—*Jarek*—" Brennan stopped. He required no explanation. In the face of her triumph and confidence, he knew she spoke the truth. "Not Jarek at all . . . nothing but misdirection, to make us believe ourselves safe . . . it was *you* all the while. . . ."

"It was me all the while." Rhiannon smiled. "Jarek was a fine diversion. Thinking *him* Ihlini, you did not look at me." She laughed. "A clever plot to take you . . . send Solindish Jarek into Homana as a *Homanan*, where he would pose as Elek's son to win Homanan aid. And then we would take you in the name of Carillon's deaf-mute bastard."

"Was it your idea to let Ian believe Jarek was his son?" he asked bitterly. "Your idea to let *me* believe I was kinslayer?"

She pursed her lips. "The first? No. It was my mother's idea; a gift, she said, for Ian." Rhiannon smiled. "As for allowing you to believe you were kinslayer, well . . . it made you more vulnerable to me. That was my idea."

He drew in a deep breath, longing to spit in her face, but knowing better. Ihlini held his *lir*. "A complex and clever plan."

"It took a great deal of time to lay this plan—more to execute." She shrugged. "But then *time* is nothing to us." Black eyes narrowed. "And now we go, my lord. Strahan grows impatient."

His struggles were futile, and he knew it; Rhiannon's power over Sleeta was too pronounced. But he ignored the pressure against his breastbone and caught her wrist, thinking to snap it in two, to shatter all the bones. Or to crack her fragile skull with a blow from his other hand.

And yet he could do none of those things. Even as he

tried to move, he found his body would not answer. His hand fell away from her wrist; he slumped against the tree, pinned by slender fingers. In her eyes was triumph and the knowledge of burgeoning power.

Angrily he bared his teeth in a feral, mocking smile. "Valgaard is a long ride from here. If you think it will be *easy*—"

"Who said anything of riding?" Rhiannon pulled something from beneath her gown; he saw a glint of familiar silver. It was the ring he had given her, but the sapphire glowed an eerie purple instead of clear blue. "We Ihlini have better ways."

He managed to laugh, albeit was little more than an impotent bark of sound. "You forget; I am Cheysuli. Your sorcery will not work."

"*You* forget, my lord—I am Cheysuli also." She smiled. "Ask why Sleeta did not know me. Ask why I hold you so easily. Look into your mind and find the link I have forged through careful and subtle means, all done in the throes of passion, when you would not notice my intrusion."

He rolled his head against the tree in desperate denial. "You cannot. . . ."

"Can I not?" She was magnificent in her pride. "But I *can*, cousin . . . the merging of our blood gives me a new dimension of power altogether, when that blood is also joined with Asar-Suti."

Her serenity alarmed him. "But you are not a Firstborn—"

"No. Not yet. But closer. Closer even than you. Because in the end, it will be the blood of our child—of Ihlini-Cheysuli children—who will hold dominance in Homana. Dominance in the world."

Rhiannon unhooked the silver chain that had replaced the ring's original leather thong. And though he tried to twist his head away, she clasped it around his neck. The chain was ice against his throat.

One last time—

"Brennan." Calmly she interrupted his futile attempt at *lir*-shape. "I do not love you, but neither do I hate you. What I do, I do to serve my race, as much as you serve yours. We are kin, close kin, and I have no wish to spill your blood; I share more than a measure of it. Ian is in us both." She caught his hands and linked her fingers with his, even against his will. "But we cannot control the Firstborn unless we make our own."

"Ihlini—" He writhed against the tree.

Rhiannon kissed him. And then the world was gone.

Interlude

Where she walked, smoke followed. Disturbed by the motion of heavy skirts, it tore apart like a webwork of lilac lace, then repaired itself in her wake to renew its delicate dance.

Godfire hissed in the whorls of glasswork columns. Down and down, around and around; light glistened in the twisted strings of the Seker's magnificent harp. She thought once to touch the closest column to see if it would sing, but she did not. It was not for her to do.

She walked, and the smoke followed. All the way to the rent in the flesh of the earth, where flame instead of blood issued forth in a blinding glare. Beyond it, poised on the rim of the Gate, stood her mother and her uncle.

On the near side, Rhiannon halted. She folded her hands in her skirts.

Lillith smiled. In her daughter she saw herself, and took pride in the girl's loyalty as well as her loveliness. "How soon will the child be born?"

"Seven months. Brennan was—most accommodating."

"And you?"

"I?"

"You are young," Lillith said kindly. "Cheysuli and Ihlini are bloodkin, born of the same gods, and meant to lie together. It is understandable if this was—difficult. There is no shame in wishing it could be another way."

Rhiannon lifted her delicate chin. "Was it difficult for *you*, when you seduced my father? Was it hard to break that immense Cheysuli pride?"

"Ian's pride was never broken," Lillith answered. "*He* may have thought so, but it was *lir*lessness he felt, nothing more." She paused. "When you speak of breaking pride, remember that what is theirs is also ours."

"They will never accept it," Rhiannon said. "Never will they accept us as anything more than enemies."

"Good," Strahan said coolly. "If the day ever comes that an Ihlini and a completed Cheysuli lie down together *willingly*, the Seker is defeated. The gate will be sealed forever, and the Firstborn shall rule the world. We will no longer exist."

Rhiannon frowned. "What is a 'completed' Cheysuli?"

"One with all the necessary blood, save our own." The glare increased, leeching shadows from Strahan's face, then faded away to a dull glow, as if the god listened. "The prophecy is a true one, Rhiannon. The Cheysuli weave it like a tapestry, and the pattern is nearly completed. But we can still alter it. We can tear away the brightest yarns, as we have torn away Brennan, and use them to fashion another."

Lillith nodded. "Link by link, we must shatter the chain."

Godfire hissed; the flame rose, swelled, died away again.

"What will you do to him?" Rhiannon asked.

"Break him," Strahan answered. "Then mend him most carefully."

"How?" she asked intently.

Strahan's eyes narrowed. "Have you a suggestion?"

Rhiannon's laughter echoed amidst the columns and set the glassy strings to thrumming. "Lock him away," she said. "Lock him away in a small stone place . . . with no light, no *lir*, and no hope at all for escape."

PART III

Hart

One

Solinde was an inhospitable, barren land, Hart thought, until he left behind the borderlands and entered wooded hills. The wide track leading out of Homana into Solinde traded plains for huddled hills, winding like a tunnel through heavy vegetation. Thick and deep, the shadows held dominance over sunlight.

He was thankful he had exchanged sleeveless jerkin for something a bit more substantial. The doublet, dyed a rich emerald green and belted with bronze-plated leather, was of stiffer leather than a Cheysuli jerkin and, though still immensely comfortable, its long sleeves provided warmth against the breath of a fall day. In the wood, in the shadows, the chill seemed to seep through flesh into his bones.

Hart shivered as the trees closed in, branches reaching for his face. The tunnel shrank and the shadows deepened, until he felt singularly oppressed. All around him were trunks and limbs and vines. The wood smelled of decay.

Lir, he said uneasily; Rael was out of sight.

Here. The hawk answered instantly. *Above you, lir, above the trees, where it is bright and warm in the sunlight.*

Hart tilted his head back and searched, but all he could see was the screen of limbs, a latticework thrown up by trees and vine and shadow. *Perhaps I should leave the horse behind and go on as a hawk.*

And then you would arrive without all your finery.

Hart laughed aloud, casually patting the saddlepacks that clothed most of his stallion's rump. "Little enough of that, I fear. Aye, I *could* have brought every trunk, but what is the sense in that? I have leathers, food and a fortune-game . . . what else do I require?"

Good sense, Rael retorted. *Or am I expected to supply the wisdom while you supply the gold?*

"I intend to *win* the gold, not supply it," Hart explained. "Sweet Solindish gold . . . I hear it is red as copper, but with twice the weight and thrice the value of Homanan."

Then you will need thrice the amount of your allowance to make the games worthwhile, Rael countered. *Sooner wagered, sooner lost.*

"I win, *lir*. I win."

Tell it to the Mujhar.

Hart scowled blackly at the branches overhead, trying to see the hawk, but gave up after a fruitless search. Feeling oppressed yet again by the wood, he pulled up and held the stallion in place.

All was silence initially, as if the wood paused as he did, waiting to see what he would do. And then the impression passed and the wood was a wood again, full of familiar song. And even one Hart welcomed: the splash and gurgle of a stream.

"Water," he said aloud, then leaned forward to pat the stallion's chestnut shoulder. "Not as good as wine or ale, I'll wager, for *me*, but it will do for us both until we reach Lestra."

He guided the horse off the track into the thicker wood, tearing vines and bracken as they went, beating their way through brush. It gave way at last to spongy ground and the rocky bank of a wide, shallow stream. Hart swung off his sorrel and turned him free to pick his way through rocks into the water; he himself balanced precariously on a flattened boulder and bent to scoop up handfuls as he braced himself with one splay-fingered hand.

The water was cold and sweet. Hart lingered even as the stallion did, ignoring the chill of his fingers. He was weighted with bow and quiver in addition to his long-knife, but at least he wore no sword. Even though he had learned it in deference to his Homanan rank, he much preferred fighting with Cheysuli weapons.

Hart felt the vibration first even as the stallion did, transmitting itself through the water. And then the sound, close upon its heels; the splash of hooves in water, running, and the clop and clack of rocks torn free of their customary bed. He pressed himself up as the stallion stumbled through the rock-choked stream to the bank on the far side, to shy away into the shadows. Hart stood his ground silently, knowing a Cheysuli's very stillness was protection in itself.

Lir. He appealed to Rael for information.

A rider, the hawk answered. *In flight from yet another.* And then. *A woman, lir. In crimson, mounted on white.*

He saw her, then, come running out of the shadows. She was a palette of white and scarlet: hair white-blond, gown bright red, the mare unsullied white. She hunched in the saddle, bent low over the mare's neck, and the vivid mantle billowed behind as she urged the mare onward.

The mare would fail soon, Hart knew, or trip and fall, snapping slender forelegs, perhaps even her neck. The streambed was treacherous with rocks and deeps and shallows; it was only a matter of time.

She was by him. And then he stepped out into the center of the stream, water lapping just above booted ankles, and unstrapped his Cheysuli warbow.

Lir.

A single man, Rael answered. *Not far, not far, coming on.*

Coming on. Hart nocked an arrow, drew the black string back to his ear, and waited.

The rider came on, splashing through deeps and shallows. It was clear he did not see Hart, so intent was he on his prey. Hart waited, waited; watched the horse come closer, coming on, *coming on*, churning water into spray.

And when the man was close enough, Hart ordered him to hold.

The rider drew up in shock, brown-haired, brown-eyed, staring with mouth agape as he tried to control his mount. And then he shut his mouth, reaching for his sword, but did not unsheathe it, did not spur on as he saw the arrow was intended for his throat.

"Hold," Hart repeated.

The man spat out a spate of Solindish Hart could not decipher. But the emotions were clear: anger, astonishment, outrage.

"You tempt me," Hart said quietly.

It was plain the Solindishman understood Homanan. Color rose in his face. Impotently he raised a clenched fist, but it was conspicuously empty of knife or sword. In accented Homanan, he said, "It is my duty, my *task*—"

"And now your duty is failure," Hart answered. "I have

no knowledge of the place you are from—Lestra, perhaps?—but I suggest you go back to it."

"Homanan!" the man cried. "It is my *responsibility*—"

"Go back," Hart said calmly. "Gods, but you do tempt me."

The Solindishman glared angrily past Hart toward the prey he had lost. Then he muttered an imprecation in throaty Solindish and jerked his horse into a rearing pivot and an awkward departure that splashed Hart liberally with water.

He returned the unused arrow to his quiver, hooked the bow over a shoulder and turned to face the woman.

She had not gone far past him, or else she had come back. The white mare stood in the center of the stream, sucking water gratefully; the woman sat erect in the saddle with crimson skirts and mantle all tangled on equipage, while her hair came free of its braid. Her expression was serious, yet it did not hide the flawlessness of the delicate bones of her face.

Fragility personified. But Hart thought he might be wrong. He had seen her ride.

"My thanks," she said gravely, gathering up her reins. For all her fingers were slender, they handled the mare competently. And tightened, wary, as he splashed through the water toward her.

The mare eyed him in alarm and shied two steps, until the young woman checked her with a rein. Hart halted at once. From closer range, the incandescence of her beauty was incredible. It unfolded like a lily in the sun, then dominated its surroundings. Ice-white hair, ice-blue eyes, with glorious, flawless skin.

"You have done me a service." Her accented Homanan only attracted him the more.

Hart grinned. "Saving your life, or your virtue? Aye, you might say so."

"No." Her long-lidded eyes were gray-blue. "No, he meant me no harm. What he said of his duty, his task, his *responsibility*—all was true. But not as you believed. He was bodyguard, not ravager. Certainly not assassin."

He stared up at her. *Gods, but this woman is enough to charm the teeth out of the Lion, and he would give them willingly*— He smiled. "Lady—he was not? Then what service did I do you?"

Her laughter set the world ablaze. "Freedom—you give me *freedom* . . . at least until the others come searching for me." Some of her gaiety was banished. "And they will. They will."

He could well imagine they would. *He* would. "So, you allowed me to chase away the man who guarded you." He laughed out loud in genuine amusement, appreciating her wit. "The man must now be cursing me for a fool, or himself."

Her eyes were full of laughter. "Aye, cursing us all—or cursing those who set him to his task." Almost abruptly, the humor spilled out of her face. An odd grimness replaced it. "But do they expect me to do nothing, meekly accepting their will?"

He heard a trace of bitterness in her tone and wondered if perhaps she *had* intended to use him to rid herself of her hound. "You said nothing, lady," he told her quietly. "And if I had slain him, what would you have told those who gave him his duty to ward you against enemies?"

She shook her head decisively. "No. No. I would not have let it go so far." She tightened reins and prepared to go. "My thanks, Homanan. But my business is better left to me."

He caught one of the reins, stepping closer. "And what do you give me for your freedom?"

She frowned. "Give?"

He shrugged. "I have done you a service. Now I ask payment, lady."

"If *you* think—"

"I do." He pulled the mare closer. "A kiss, lady. Small token of your gratitude, payment for my service." He grinned, arching suggestive brows. "Not so much, I think."

"More than you *know*, from me." One booted foot kicked out and caught him flush on the jaw.

He staggered back, swearing, and lost his grip on her reins. By the time he could see clearly again, the woman had spurred the mare on and was gone.

Rael, he said. "Rael!"

Not so far, lir. *Mount your horse and catch up*.

He whistled the stallion out of the trees and splashed

through the stream to the bank, swearing all the while. She had caught him squarely, snapping his head sideways toward his right shoulder; neck muscles protested in unison with the jaw. Had she been man instead of woman, she might have broken his neck.

Were she man instead of woman, you would never have asked a kiss.

Hart, swinging up into his saddle, laughed aloud as he heard the hawk's tone. *No, I would wager not.* He urged the chestnut through the water onto the bank on the other side. *Where,* lir? *Which way?*

Westward, along the track. Riding toward Lestra.

The mare, he knew, was tired, and had drunk too much water to sustain a comfortable gallop for long. His own mount was rested; he would be on them soon enough.

He was. Rounding a curve in the tunneled track, he saw a flash of white tail ahead. Closer, closer yet; divots of dirt and turf were thrown up into his face. He ducked down and let the stallion shield him even as he ran.

The girl looked back once, then again. Her face was lost in the tangle of unbound hair; like the mare's tail it streamed out behind, a whipping pennon in the wind. Hart, grinning as the stallion closed, saw the girl reach up swiftly and catch her hair at the nape of her neck, winding it swiftly into a single plume. And then she stuffed it beneath the neck of her gown with both hands, the mare running free, and caught reins again to pull the mare off the track into the shadows of the wood.

Hart nearly rode by the broken opening in the vines. A decisive hand on the reins checked the stallion into an abrupt slide on his haunches, and then Hart spun him and sent him crashing after the mare.

Lir? he asked.

Hard to see, Rael answered. *She twists and turns, but still heads westward.*

"Lestra," Hart muttered, and swore as vine leaves slapped mouth and eyes.

No more track, save for what he could break open in her wake. No more headlong run, but leaps and stumbles instead, as the stallion tried to negotiate bracken and fallen trees. The world was a maze of green and brown and black, all shadows in the daylight, with little or no sun to illuminate their passing. The sound of his own mount obliterated hers. It was only when he saw a flash of white and crimson that he knew he drew closer again.

A quick glance over her shoulder; the curve of one fair cheek. And grim determination in the line of her lovely mouth. He saw her jerk the mare offstride and then turned her northward instead of west.

She will kill the mare yet— But the thought was never finished. The mare's passing startled a hare from cover and he broke. The stallion, startled, leaped sideways, stumbled, ran directly into a huge felled tree and, in trying to leap it off-balance, merely succeeded in snapping front legs. His rider was thrown headlong out of the saddle into the nearest tree.

Lir— But the light of the world was snuffed out.

A sound. A voice: a woman's, with desperation in her tone. Telling him in accented Homanan to wake up, and then when he did not, pleading something else in indecipherable Solindish.

Solindish.

His eyes snapped open. He was conscious almost at once of extreme discomfort, all tangled in vine and bracken and clawed by boughs and limbs. His head throbbed unmercifully; he recalled, dimly, that it had collided with a tree trunk.

He shut his eyes again. *Gods, but my head hurts. . . .*

He heard a rustle in deadfall and underbrush. Through his lashes he saw the bright colors of her clothing, now dulled by debris and mudstains. That she meant to come to his side was plain; equally plain was that Rael, a flurry of wings and talons, would not allow her to.

"Oh, wake up," she begged. "Wake up and call off this hawk!"

Rael swept down again from the tree and slapped a wingtip across her raised arm, driving her away once more.

Enough, Hart said dryly. *Have you no eyes*, lir? *The girl is magnificent—let her come as close as she wants.*

Rael's relief was tangible as it thrummed throughout the link. But his tone belied the truth. *Was this a ruse, then, to trick her into giving you your payment?*

Have you ever known me to willingly suffer so much pain in the name of a woman?

Rael lighted on a tree limb. *No*, he said dryly, and folded his wings away.

Hart opened his eyes again. "If I try to move, lady, will my head fall off? Or is it still attached?"

She twitched in surprise, then shifted a trifle closer. "Alive, then," she said in relief. "Oh, I thought I had killed you."

"No." He levered himself carefully up on one arm and wished he had not; his head throbbed alarmingly and a bough stabbed him in the ribs. "Well, perhaps you did." Tentatively he fingered his forehead. "Gods, lady, I would say you need no bodyguard, nor even *my* protection."

She said something in Solindish, then shook her head. "I meant no harm to you. I wanted to *escape* you, aye, but not at the cost of your life."

"And my horse?" Hart looked over to where the chestnut lay. The stallion's breathing was labored. That he had exhausted himself trying to rise with his shattered legs was plain; Hart cursed aloud in the Old Tongue with as much eloquence as he could muster. "You acquit youself well," he said shortly, and pushed himself out of the underbrush with another bitten off curse. He wavered and clutched the tree for support. But the stallion's plight was more imperative than pain; grimly he unhooked his bow and jerked an arrow from his quiver, walking unsteadily to the chestnut.

"The hawk—" she began.

Hart did not so much as glance at her. "Rael will not harm you." He nocked the arrow.

She rose, skirts tangled on her boots, and came to stand beside him. "Had I the strength, I would do it myself."

Mocking: "Aye, lady. Of course." He raised the bow and drew back the string.

Released. It sang briefly, so briefly, and then the stallion was dead.

He hooked an arm through the bow, settling it across his back, and bent to unfasten the saddlepacks. The horse was slack in death, and very heavy; Hart had to expend more energy than he had left to free the saddlepacks. His head ached, and he sat abruptly to avoid falling down.

"Give them to me. I will put them on my mare." Slender

hands beckoned him to comply. "Where do you go, Homanan?"

"Lestra. Lady—there is no need for that."

She took the packs anyway and slung them across her mare's white rump, buckling them onto the saddle. Then she brought a skin of wine and knelt beside him. "She is not accustomed to carrying two. You will ride, and I will lead."

"Nor is there need for *that*." He drank, returned the skin, rose unsteadily.

She swept the glorious hair away from her face and showed him lifted brows. "And do you intend to *fly?*"

Hart laughed. "Aye, lady, I do."

She nodded calmly, plainly doubting him. "Even *Ihlini* cannot do that."

He looked at her sharply and recalled this was Solinde, the realm the Ihlini called home. Here they lived with impunity. "Thank the gods," he said curtly. "No, such things are for the Cheysuli."

"Aye, but—" She broke off. The color ran out of her face, leaving her wan as death. She looked quickly at Rael, then back at Hart. In silence she asked the question.

"Aye," he told her, "I am. Rael is my *lir*."

She pulled her mantle more closely around her slender body, as if to ward off a chill. "I thought—I thought him merely well-trained, when he would not let me near."

"*Lir* are not trainable; they do what they will do." He resettled his bow and quiver. "And now, lady, I suggest—"

But she did not allow him to finish. "I have heard they have yellow eyes. Yours are decidedly blue."

He raised his brows. "Doubtless you have heard many things . . . *some* of them may be true." He smiled as he saw her frown of indecision. "Aye, most Cheysuli have yellow eyes. I do not because I am also Homanan. But the rest of me is Cheysuli."

She looked at Rael again. "You become *him*."

"No. I become another. Rael remains Rael."

She looked at his hands, at his fingers, at the shape of the bones of his face. As if she searched for some clue that would make him bird instead of human. Raptor in place of man. "The Ihlini have said—"

He overrode her. "Do you traffic with Ihlini?"

She stiffened. "This is Solinde, not Homana! The Ihlini have freedom here."

"Freedom to raise a rebellion? To rule this realm in place of those who should?"

"What is it to *you?*" she asked angrily. "You are a Homanan, a *Cheysuli* . . . what is Solinde to you? You have no stake in what happens in my land!"

"Do I not?" He smiled. "Oh, but lady, I think I do . . . because one day I will rule it."

"*Will* you?" She faced him squarely, tangled hair hanging to knees, skirts caught high on her boots. "You say so, to *me?*"

"I will say so to anyone, because it is the truth." That she was genuinely angry, he knew, because it was shouted from her posture and the expression in her eyes. He had seen such anger before, such cold, controlled anger, born of a true hostility shaped by war and heritage. He had seen it in the clans, in the older warriors who had come through Shaine's *qu'mahlin* and decades of Solindish-Ihlini wars. But he had not thought to see it in her. "Lady, I do not lie in hopes of impressing you—"

"Oh, no?" she asked. "Men have done it before. *Homanans* have done it before. Why should I believe you are any different?" Icy eyes swept him from head to toe; contempt was implicit in her posture. "I think your sincerity requires practice, Homanan. You are not particularly convincing."

Hart stared at her. She was either completely unaware of her disarray, or else so angry she did not care. *Or else she realizes that nothing could dull her beauty.*

He wet his lips. "Lady—" he began patiently.

"No one rules Solinde," she said coldly. "No one. A regent sits in Lestra claiming right of authority from Homana's Cheysuli Mujhar." One arm gestured toward the city and a rigid finger divided the air. "But is that a ruler?— *no*. A travesty, no more. We are a proud land, shapechanger, and unused to kowtowing to a foreign Mujhar who rules out of ignorance, holding Solinde in trust for a man we do not—*cannot*—know. So, shapechanger, when you tell me lies for your own amusement, to impress me or otherwise, it bears no fruit at all. I am impervious to such things."

"Impervious to the truth?" Without waiting for an answer he moved past her to the mare and dug into his saddlepacks. When he had found the thing he sought, he turned back again and put it into her hands. "There, lady—the truth."

She stared at the thing in her hands. It was small for a thing of so much significance, and yet the shocked tears that sprang to her eyes belied the seeming worthlessness of it. "This is the seal," she said, "the Third Seal of Solinde!"

"Aye."

She stared at him; all the color had left her face. "The Trey was broken when the war with Carillon was lost. When Bellam was slain." Her heavy swallow was visible against the fragile flesh of her throat. "The regent has one seal, the Mujhar the other two. But—*this* is the Third Seal!"

He had not expected her to know it so precisely, only to know the cipher. Nor had he expected the seal to have such an effect on her, that she would stare at him in shocked discovery. He had every intention of telling her who he was, if only to prove he was not a liar, but it seemed she already knew.

She clasped the seal against her chest, shielded by pride and hair. "So." Her voice was cool, dulled by shock and hostility. "*So*, the Mujhar at last sends his wastrel son to sit in judgment on Solinde."

Wastrel son. It hurt. Worse than he had expected. "Lady—"

She backed away a step, edging toward the mare. "If I took this . . . if I took this with me and sent men back to murder you—"

"—you would be executed." He moved too swiftly for her, catching her hands in his own. "Aye, lady, wastrel son that I am, I am also the Prince of Solinde."

She laughed. She laughed so hard she cried, and then thrust the seal at him. "Take it! *Take* it! Without the other two it is nothing. Even in *my* hands!"

"Lady—"

But she was free of him, shedding his hands easily as she

leaped for the mare and scrambled into the saddle. Curtained by hair, there was little of her face he could see. But he heard her words all too clearly.

"Hart, *Prince of Solinde*, know you that battle has been joined!"

And before he could speak, she was gone.

Two

Oil braziers burned in every corner of the room, casting a pall of clean bright light that obliterated the shadows of early evening. It glittered off the silver and crystal wine decanter, off the fine-mesh ceremonial mail shirt showing at hem and sleeves of his rich blue Solindish overtunic, off the polished silver plate that conjured his reflection: black hair, still damp from the bath, starting to curl against his shoulders; bright blue eyes in an angular face of burnished bronze, not even remotely Solindish; and a somewhat rueful set to the mouth as he pushed hair aside and studied the swelling on his forehead. The pattern of the tree bark was impressed in his flesh.

Hart sighed, turned from the plate and faced the man who waited so quietly, so patiently, by the table near the fireplace. "I *will* survive," he said mildly as he saw the man's expression. "I promise."

The pale brown eyes watching him narrowed minutely, fanning outward a webwork of tiny creases. Tarron, regent of Solinde by authority of Niall the Mujhar, was not a man who gave up his thoughts without careful deliberation. But neither was the newly arrived Prince of Solinde ignorant in the ways of reading men, even lifelong politicians; Hart had learned to discern the inner man in dozens of dicing games.

Tarron inclined his head slightly. "As you say, my lord—surely you would know better than I."

Surely I should . . . Hart agreed inwardly. *As surely as I know my head is likely to fall off.*

Rael, settled on his oaken perch in a corner of the royal chambers, remained eloquently silent. Hart ignored him altogether and smiled blandly at the regent, hoping to turn Tarron's irritation into good humor. His abrupt arrival in *lir*-shape had ruffled feathers other than his own, figuratively speaking; Tarron, he felt, was displeased more by the lack of pageantry associated with the arrival than by the sudden usurpation of his own authority. Hart knew a messenger from Homana must have arrived before him, if only to prepare Tarron, because his father would have seen to it.

Jehan *would know better than to spring me on Solinde— on on Tarron—unannounced.* Hart's smile widened to a crooked grin of wry humor as he recalled what the girl had named him. *But I wonder what the regent thinks now that the* wastrel son *has arrived?* He gestured toward the polished table and two padded chairs. "Sit you down, regent," Hart suggested, and did so himself.

What Tarron thought of his lord's wastrel son remained unspoken as he seated himself at the table and accepted the wine Hart poured. The regent's ascetic face was smooth and serene again, a polite, politic mask. He was older than the Mujhar himself, Hart knew, having served as councillor to Donal before Niall's ascension and Tarron's subsequent appointment to Solinde. He was well experienced in dealing with men of all ranks and races. Even Cheysuli.

"Is all to your liking, my lord?" Tarron inquired.

Hart laughed, amused by his attitude. They faced one another like two men in a fortune-game, seated across the table with nothing at all to bind them together save a royal command. They did not play with dice, they did not wager, but the game was surely on. "Aye, and how not? Since my somewhat unusual arrival less than two hours ago, I have been bathed, clothed, fed, examined by a chirurgeon, and ensconced within royal apartments as luxurious as my own in Homana-Mujhar." A gesture encompassed the chambers. "The servants have been so thick around me I can scarce move my elbows for fear of blacking an eye or knocking loose a tooth. Only *now* am I given room to breathe, and I find myself attended by no less than the Mujhar's regent himself, when I would do well enough on my own." His mouth twisted wryly. "If I said no, you would have it all done over again, and *that* I could not bear."

Tarron did not smile. "You *are* the Prince of Solinde."

Hart laughed aloud. "Aye. But even *you* must know my reputation; it is what puts me here instead of Homana-Mujhar." He leaned forward, looming across the table. "I am Hart, the second son, the *wastrel* son, who spends his gold and wits in taverns, dicing his life away. I am the man responsible for setting the Midden aflame, though unintentionally, and for killing thirty-two people—men, women, children. And I am punished for it: I am sent to rule Solinde." He sat back again, all humor banished, flopping against the chair. "But where does that leave Solinde, regent? Where does it leave *you?*"

Tarron did not hesitate. "It leaves me in fear for the future of this realm," he said quietly. "It leaves me wondering if the Mujhar's prejudice interferes with his intellect. And most certainly, in these past two hours, I have seen nothing in you that assuages my fear, and *everything* that leaves me wondering how I can possibly do what my lord has commanded, and teach a hopeless reprobate how to govern." He paused. "Even a *royal* one."

Hart stared at him a long, rigid moment. He had expected anything but censure from the man; Tarron was too well-versed in the delicacy of politics and the exigencies of rank to ever be so blunt and risk his entire career. But Hart knew better than to believe he had misheard, asking to have them repeated; the words had been explicitly distinct, displaying neither malice nor bitterness, only heartfelt sincerity.

That kind of honesty was a thing Cheysuli honored. But Hart was more than Cheysuli. He was also Prince of Solinde.

"Ku'reshtin," he said without heat, more surprised than offended. "Is this how you spoke to Donal?"

"Your grandsire never required it," Tarron answered quietly.

Hart gazed at him thoughtfully. The regent wore understated clothing of plain, unrelieved black, as if to downplay the importance of his rank. His dark brown hair was graying at the temples and brushed back from a face almost stark in its severity of expression, but it was derived of sharp bones rather than of nature. And yet Hart sensed little or no humor in the regent; he wondered if Tarron recalled the follies of his own youth.

Unless there were no follies. He sighed a little and tapped fingertips against the wood of the table. "No doubt you feel I deserve it; perhaps I do. Perhaps this is why my *jehan* sent me to you. Perhaps I am to develop some sense of guilt for past indiscretions, merely by seeing the condemnation in your eyes." Hart sat up and pushed the chair back to rise, scraping wooden legs against marble floor. "And perhaps I *will*, one day—but not just yet."

Belatedly Tarron rose as Hart moved to open the door. "My lord—where are you going?"

"Out," Hart said succinctly. "The urge for a game is upon me, and the sweet perfume of a smoky tavern."

"My lord—"

Rael, Hart summoned, ignoring the regent's protest; the hawk flew out of the open casement even as Hart walked out of the room.

He went out of the palace and into the bailey, following blurted directions he had asked of a Solindish servant. Lestra's royal palace was enough like Homana-Mujhar that he had no difficulty finding the bailey and hence the guardroom; when he paused by several off-duty soldiers lounging by the entrance, he saw they assessed him indifferently, not knowing who he was. Anonymity suited him well enough, at least for the moment.

"I am looking for a game," he told them, tapping his heavy belt-purse significantly. "Not here—undoubtedly your captains prohibit wagering within the castle walls— but elsewhere. In the city. Can you suggest a tavern?"

They were Solindish, not Homanan, for their woolen tunics were indigo banded with silver braid, not the crimson and black livery of the Homanan Guard. Four pairs of eyes reassessed him, noting the richness of silken overtunic, the glitter of costly mail, the quality of leather trews, silver-buckled belt, polished kneeboots. To them, Hart knew, he was an enigma: a Homanan garbed Solindish. It altered their responses.

And if they knew I was Cheysuli? He smiled; Rael had perched himself on the roof of the guardroom.

"Homanan tavern, or Solindish?" one of the soldiers asked in accented Homanan.

Hart shrugged. "Does it matter?"

The Solindishman, red-headed and green-eyed, showed his teeth briefly in a humorless smile. "It matters. Lestra is a Solindish city, for all the Mujhar might have it otherwise; the Homanans cluster together like chicks about a hen."

"Avoiding the fox, no doubt." Hart smiled benignly and spread upturned hands. "By all means, let it be a Solindish tavern. Wagering has a tongue all its own."

The four men exchanged glances, murmuring among themselves in low-pitched voices. Finally the spokesman shrugged and looked back at Hart. "The White Swan," he said. "Not so far from here. Do you require escort?"

"Is it customary?" Hart asked evenly. "Without one, is a Homanan likely to be accosted?"

Again they exchanged glances. The red-haired man smiled. "In the shadows, one man is very much like another."

Hart grinned back. "A chance I might have to take . . . but I know a little Solindish. Perhaps this phrase might be enough?" And, though the accent was horrendous, he told them, in their own tongue: *"A Cheysuli never walks alone."*

On their benches, they straightened. "Cheysuli—" blurted one, staring. Two of his comrades muttered in Solindish; amidst the mostly alien words Hart heard his own name twice.

The fourth man, the redhead, slowly rose and faced him. They were of a like height and similar build, though the shapes of their faces and coloring was entirely different.

"My lord," the redhead said formally, "word of your arrival has been given out. But I think we expected another sort of man. The animals . . . all the gold—" He broke off, shrugging awkwardly. "There are stories, my lord."

Hart laughed. "My things were misplaced earlier today. Fine as it is, Solindish clothing is somewhat more elaborate than Cheysuli leathers." He tapped his left arm. "Beneath all this silk and mail and linen lies the gold you refer to. As for my *lir*—" he gestured "—Rael is always with me."

All four craned their heads and saw the hawk, little more than a silvered shape upon the edge of the roof.

The redhead looked back. "Shall we escort you, my lord?"

"No, Rael is escort enough. Simply give me directions to The White Swan."

"You might do better at another tavern, my lord."

"A tavern catering to the chicks clustered around the hen?" Hart grinned as the other man reddened. "The White Swan, soldier."

He was given explicit directions, and a warning.

"The White Swan is a supremely *Solindish* place, my lord," the redhead told him. His discomfort was quite plain. "You may not find the welcome to your taste."

Hart grinned. "I am Cheysuli, soldier; even in Homana, even *sixty years* after the ending of the royal purge that nearly destroyed us, we know the taste of hatred and prejudice. But I have learned that where a man may not be welcomed, his wealth always is."

After a moment, the Solindishman smiled. "Aye. The custom is no different in Solinde."

Hart thanked him, saluted him, left the palace entirely and entered Lestra proper with a winged shadow overhead.

The White Swan was, he thought, one of the finest taverns he had ever entered, certainly as nicely appointed as Mujhara's own Rampant Lion. Good wax candles in clay saucers stood on every table, lighting food or play. The beamwork of the ceiling was higher than most, which pleased Hart immensely. Cheysuli height often resulted in the need for constant ducking, for Homanans were almost uniformly shorter, and built taverns accordingly. But here he could stand and move with impunity. He admired the clean, sweeping lines of the blond beams; whitewashed walls made the tavern look large and airy instead of cramped and dark.

Rael he left outside perched atop the roof, knowing better than to invite immediate trouble by taking the hawk inside. The windows were of thin, costly glass; had he need of Rael, he could summon the bird easily through either one.

If I am to judge the stakes of the games by the richness of my surroundings, the winnings will be well worth any rudeness I may encounter.

But he encountered none at all, save the curiosity extended any stranger entering a tavern patronized by friends and comrades. The cut and quality of his clothing, particularly the ceremonial mail, marked him a wealthy Solindishman, obviously a noble, and worthy of attention because of that alone. The hawk-shaped earring was mostly hidden in his hair, but Hart believed that even had his eyes been as yellow as Brennan's, no one would have named him

Cheysuli. This was Solinde, even though ruled by Homana; no one expected to see a Cheysuli in the heartland of Ihlini.

The tables were mostly full. None was entirely open, though not all boasted a full complement of gamblers or other patrons. But Hart knew he could not very well invite himself into a game; his lack of Solindish—and command of flawless Homanan—would instantly mark him an enemy to those men who chose to regard the Homanans as such.

One of the wine-girls came up to him and curtsied briefly in deference to his obvious wealth. What she said he could barely discern, for he spoke very little Solindish even after childhood tutoring—he had been a supremely indifferent student—and only very slowly; she chattered at him like a magpie. He knew better than to attempt an answer in her tongue. Instead, he drew from his belt-purse a heavy coin: the gold royal of Homana. He placed it in her hand and shut her fingers over it. "There is more," he said distinctly, "much more, for the man who gives me a game."

The Homanan words silenced the tavern instantly. As one, shocked faces looked up from games and drink to stare at him, and then the shock turned slowly to hostility.

The girl tore her hand from his. The falling coin rang dully against the hardwood floor. She backed away from him, wiping her hands on her skirts, and stopped only when she fetched up against a table. She was black-haired, black-eyed, pretty; she reminded him vaguely of the girl from The Rampant Lion, who had been so impressed with Brennan. But that girl had been Homanan, and this one was clearly Solindish, with all attendant resentment of her foreign overlord.

Hart was imperturbed. It was no more, no less than he had expected, after what the soldier had said of the Swan. Calmly he untied his belt-purse and dangled it before them all. He shook it once, twice; the clash of gold and silver was plain for all to hear.

"A game," he said, "not a war."

They stared, did Solindish eyes. Out of hard, eloquent faces, full of hatred, full of anger; of a burning, brilliant resentment that seemed to intensify as he waited.

Supremely Solindish, the soldier had said. Aye. That was one way of putting it.

Perhaps I have misjudged them . . . perhaps something is

stronger than the lure of gold or gems. Disappointed, he began to tie his belt-purse back on his belt.

"*I* will give you a game," said a voice in accented Homanan.

Hart brightened even as there was murmuring from the others. He heard one word mentioned more than once, and thought it might be a name.

It was. The man rose, scraping his stool against the hardwood floor, and gestured Hart to join him. "I am Dar," he said. "I give you no welcome to the Swan, for it it is *ours*, and only ours, but I will give you the opportunity to buy your life back."

Hart paused. "Buy my life back?" he echoed.

Dar did not smile. "It was forfeit the moment you asked for a game."

Hart looked at the others. All remained clustered at their tables, but no games were played, no wagers laid, no food and drink consumed. The atmosphere of the place was decidedly unfriendly, but he smelled the tang of anticipation as well. They waited for something, the Solindish. They *wanted* something specific, just as he desired a game.

He looked back at Dar. "I said a game, not a war. I am not here to rehash old battles, nor discuss political things. I have no interest in either. I am here to wager, nothing more."

The other studied him briefly, marking height, weight, strength, and the indefinable self-confidence of a Cheysuli that others called arrogance.

The Solindishman nodded slightly, as if his decision were made. "You asked for a game without knowing the stakes," he said coolly. "Know them now, and clearly: for a Homanan, what he wagers is nothing less than his life."

Hart looked at him closely. Dar was perhaps a year or two older than himself, sandy-haired, brown-eyed, with strong, bold features that marked him a singularly dedicated man, no matter what the cause. Like the others in the tavern, he wore clothing and appointments of good quality—tawny leather trews, russet quilted velvet doublet, a belt-knife hilted with gold. Obviously, The White Swan catered to the wealthy and high-ranking. Just as obviously, Homanans were unwelcome regardless of wealth or rank.

His own assessment finished, Hart nodded a little. "A

good way of winnowing out the undesirables," he said lightly. "How many men did it cost before the Homanans learned to go elsewhere?"

Dar did not smile. Neither did he hesitate. "Two," he said, with deliberate clarity and succinctness.

He was not a man much intimidated by others, particularly when a game was in the offing. Hart knew the type well, relishing their eagerness for play as much as his own. The Solindishman's baiting bothered him not in the least; if anything, it added a fillip to the game.

Hart shrugged negligently, aware of the familiar flutter in his belly. It spoke of risk and danger, of success and failure. It sang a song of possibilities; of hope and need and desire. But he showed none of it to Dar, knowing better. "And so it shall remain," he said lightly, striding to the table to hook out a stool and plop his belt-purse down upon the table. Pouring out a stream of gold and silver, he sat down and looked at Dar. "Match it," he said gently, "with red Solindish gold." He paused as the other slowly sat down. "Unless, of course, you stake your own life as well as mine."

For a moment the other hesitated, arrested in midmotion. There was a brief flash of recognition in his eyes, and then it was gone. "Oh, no," Dar said quietly. "I am Solindish, not Homanan; I am of the *occupied* race, not of the oppressor. My life is not required." The irony was subtle and yet exceedingly clear to Hart, who chose to ignore it altogether.

"Let us play man to man, not soldier to soldier; wagerer to wagerer, not oppressor to occupied," he suggested. "The game is all that matters."

Dar's sandy brows rose to disappear beneath thick hair. "The game? Well, since it is *your* life we wager, you may choose the game."

"Considerate." Hart looked at the wine-girl, standing so close to his shoulder. The others had drawn near as well, clustered in ranks around the table. He had seen it happen before in games of high stakes; men who could not or would not risk so much preferred instead to watch, gaining a measure of the pleasure without the threat of loss. He smiled at the girl. "Have you a fortune-game?"

She was patently unimpressed by his charming smile, which might have perturbed him had he not been more caught up in the need for the risk, the chance to play the odds and win. Her lips drew back. *"Homanan!"* was all she said.

Dar laughed. "Translation: the Swan has no Homanan games."

"Then I will play a Solindish one," Hart said evenly. He studied the other without bothering to hide it, knowing Dar assessed him as openly. It was all a part of the eternal dance. After a moment he nodded. "I judge you an honest man, Dar—I think you would prefer an honest win."

Dar rubbed an idle thumb along his lower lip. "You judge quickly, Homanan. Too quickly, perhaps?"

"I think not. I have seen your kind before . . ." Hart grinned at narrowing brown eyes and tautening jaw. "Aye, I have, just as you have seen me before, in many men. Why bother to deny it? When it comes to it, Solindish, the *game* is more important than the man who plays it—*or* his loyalties."

The Solindishman laughed, eyes suddenly alight. For the moment, the quiet hostility was banished. "Aye, so it is. Perhaps we are more alike than we know, for all it paints me an unflattering color." He drew out his own belt-purse and opened it, pouring out the rich red gold of Solinde. The shape and weight as well as the color was different than Hart's Homanan wealth, and the value, coin for coin, was uncalculated, but it no longer mattered. They both knew the other for a man who wagered for the love of it, the *need* of it, not for the actual value of the winnings. "There you are, Homanan—red gold against your life."

It was red gold indeed, deeper, brighter, richer than Hart's yellow Homanan hoard. He ached to touch it, to feel its texture, its warmth, knowing what it represented. Not money. Not wealth. But victory over the game.

Dar grinned. With a single finger he flipped over first one coin and then another, so that they rang against one another. In the heavy silence of the common room, the siren song was eloquent.

Hart smiled. For the moment, they were *kinspirits*.

Dar turned and said something to the girl, who disappeared a moment and came back with a small wooden bowl. She set it down on the table; it was filled with flat, bone-colored oblong stones the size of a man's thumbnail.

Dar pulled several stones from the bowl and set them down on the table. Each bore a shape incised and colored, save for one blank one. "Bezat," he said. "A Solindish rune-game. Very simple; even a Homanan may learn."

"Did the others?" Hart asked. "The two who died?"

Dar's smile was faint. "They learned not to wager what they could not afford to lose."

"Show me," Hart said intently, thinking only of the game.

After a moment, Dar did. "You see the marks. Each rune represents a thing from Solindish folklore; I will not bore you with the stories, or we will be here all night and most of the next." He grinned. "Let it suffice you to know the runes have value within the context of the game: the moon, the sun, the plow, the scythe, famine, plague, war . . . and, of course, death." He touched the blank stone. "This supersedes the others. No matter what value the others give you, even the highest, this takes precedence." His expression was carefully noncommittal. "You do understand?"

"I understand death very well," Hart answered readily. "And I understand that in *this* game, for a Homanan, the death is literal."

After a moment Dar nodded. "We draw eight. The moon, sun, plow, and scythe rank higher than famine, plague, or war, but there are fewer of them. We match my stones against yours: the highest grouping wins."

"And the death-stone?"

"Stones," Dar said clearly, emphasizing the plural. "*Bezats*. Fewer yet, but hardly timid."

"How many times do we play?"

Dar shrugged. "As many as you like . . . ordinarily. In *this* case, with these stakes, should you turn up a bezat—" he smiled, "no more games are possible."

Hart smiled back, unmoved by the possibilities. His luck would see through. "Once," he said, and a flutter of anticipation pinched his belly. "*Once*. To make it worth our while."

"Once," Dar agreed. "You will draw eight stones, I will draw eight stones—both of us drawing blind . . . and then we give them to one another."

Anticipation was smothered by shock. Hart went cold. "Are you saying you will draw *my* stones? The ones on which I wager?"

Dar laughed. "But of course! Therein lies the game. You wager that I will give you good stones, while I do the same with the ones you draw for me."

Hart no longer smiled. "Then my life—*literally*—is in your hands."

Dar shrugged casually. "It is the luck of the draw."

Hart grabbed the bowl and upended it, spilling stones across the table. One by one he turned them over, baring rune after rune. There were suns, moons, and other things—four stones were blank as death.

"Did you fear all of them were blank?" Dar smiled and nodded as Hart began to drop them back into the bowl. "Did you fear you *had* misjudged me?"

Hart was deliberate as he replaced the stones. One by one, they rattled into the bowl as he watched Dar's face. He knew very well he could refuse to play, but he would not. It was poor manners; worse, it marked him a coward and cheat, when he was neither. If anything, the stakes made him reckless.

A true test of a man's mettle, and certainly of his skill. If I beat this Solindish ku'reshtin, *I can win back a measure of pride for the Homanans, who have been so readily insulted in this tavern. Moreover, I can win back respect for those who died.*

But even more than that, much more, it was the challenge.

Hart flipped the last stone into the bowl. "It is a foolish man who wagers without knowing the stakes, *or* the contents of the game. And I am not a fool." No longer did he smile. "I have accepted your stakes; now I accept the game."

Dar looked at the wine-girl. "Stir them," he said, in clear Homanan. "Stir them well, Oma."

She put a slim hand in the bowl and stirred the contents, steadfastly keeping her eyes on Hart's face as if to emphasize her honesty. When she was done, she lifted the bowl in both hands and held it out over the table, so that neither of them could see in as they drew the stones.

"You may draw first," Dar said politely. "If it is a bezat—a death-stone—I lose at once, and the game is done."

And if he draws a bezat for me . . . Hart smiled. He

reached in, drew a stone, placed it face up on the table in front of Dar. It bore the rune for famine.

"Not good," Dar said conversationally, tapping a finger against the tabletop. "Beaten, should I draw you a sun or moon, a plow or scythe."

"Draw," Hart said.

Dar did so, turning up the rune for scythe, representing a generous harvest. Through seven stones they went, one by one: suns, moons, famine, and war . . . and then Dar drew the final stone for Hart.

He put it down in the center of the table, turning it from one side to the other, so that both were clearly visible to Hart and all the rest.

"Bezat!" the wine-girl cried.

"Bezat!" the others echoed.

Dar drew his knife and placed it in the center of the table, next to the blank death-stone. "Bezat," he said quietly, and took his hand away.

Hart looked at the stone, at the knife, at the man. And then he began to laugh.

Three

Dar's eyes narrowed. "It is a fool who laughs in the face of death, or a very brave man. Which are you, Homanan?"

Still Hart laughed, though the initial burst of amusement faded, and then the laughter died away. He shook his head, grinning, and idly stirred his pile of Homanan gold and silver. "Neither, I think . . . or perhaps a little of both."

No one else spoke, though Hart was aware of the tension in the common room. The others stared hard at him, scowling, or looked to Dar in expectation. The knife blade gleamed a promise in the candlelight.

"Did you think I jested?" Dar inquired in an elegantly dangerous tone of voice. "Did you think, when I spoke of your death as the stakes of the game, I meant nothing of what I said?"

"Oh, I *know* you meant it," Hart answered, smiling. "I can smell the stink on all of you, this desire for my death." Again he stirred the coins, admiring their patina in the candlelight. Still he smiled a little, but mostly to himself; he preferred not to provoke the Solindishman further, and yet a part of him did not care. He met Dar's eyes and shrugged. "But I have learned that even a life may be purchased—or bought back—when the loser is wealthy enough." He paused. "Or has other means to force it."

Dar himself smiled. "There are three men behind you with knives in their hands. And more behind them."

Hart shrugged, shaking his head. "It makes no difference. The force I speak of has nothing to do with weapons."

"*Mine* does." Dar touched the hilt of his knife with a single eloquent finger.

Hart laughed. "Effective against a man, perhaps, but what about a hawk?"

"I think—" But Dar stopped short, interrupting himself.

He looked at Hart in silence a long moment. And then, though his expression did not change, the tone of his voice altered perceptibly. "Cheysuli," he said flatly.

"Aye," Hart agreed.

Silence filled the room. And then was swallowed by murmurs of shock and muttered Solindish epithets.

Dar's nostrils were pinched, his mouth drawn flat and tight. For only a moment his fingers remained near the knife, and then he took his hand away. "Cheysuli," he repeated. "An accursed shapechanger in our midst."

"Now," Hart said, "shall we negotiate this loss?"

Dar smiled tightly. "It *was* a loss," he said, "and you knew the stakes. Your life against the stones. Cheysuli, Homanan, it does not matter. The wager stands."

Hart matched his tone. "I have only to summon my *lir*."

"Do it." Dar laughed as Hart frowned his incomprehension. "Do it, shapechanger—or should I say, *try*." His glance went past Hart to another man. "Even *I* know that a Cheysuli has no power before an Ihlini."

Hart swung on his stool and felt the knife blade against his throat. He sat very still, but he saw the man Dar's glance had indicated. "Ihlini?" he demanded.

The man inclined his head politely, though his smile was coolly derisive. "This *is* Solinde, is it not? Here, we go where we will go, just as you do in Homana."

For the first time since entering the tavern, Hart went into the *lir*-link to contact Rael. And instantly felt the blankness that signaled Ihlini presence and canceled out the link.

Oh, gods—oh, lir, what have I done now?

"Now," Dar said gently, "shall we speak again of the wager?"

Oh, gods, where is Brennan when I need him?

On his stool, Hart swung back around to face Dar, wary of the knife so near his throat. He forced a smile and tapped the pile of silver and gold. "Surely there is enough here to buy my life from you."

"No." Dar's tone did not waver.

"This is worth—"

"Worth*less*," Dar said distinctly. "This is Solinde, Homanan; do you think your coin has value here? I have seen how you look at our red Solindish gold; how you covet it with your eyes." His own narrowed. "Eyes *which*, I might add, are blue instead of yellow. Cheysuli? I think not. I think you are a liar who lives on the legends of other men."

That touched prickly Cheysuli pride. Hart went rigid on the stool, but dared not move with so many knives prepared to take his life. He scowled blackly at Dar. "And is every *Solindishman* the same color?"

Dar's mouth twitched. "But I have heard so much about the beast-eyes of the Cheysuli. . . ." He grinned, unable to suppress his amusement. "Glare at me all you wish, Homanan—blue eyes are less effective, I think, than yellow."

"Ku'reshtin!" Hart snapped. "Were there no Ihlini here—"

"But there is," Dar said coolly, "and your claim has no validity."

Hart stripped black hair behind his left ear. "Oh no?"

The Solindishman shrugged negligently. "Many men wear similar adornment."

Hart gritted his teeth. "Then give me leave to show you *other* adornment."

Dar laughed. "If you wish. But if you mean to show us your *weapon*, Homanan, recall there are women present."

Even Oma laughed, eyeing Hart with derisive amusement. Heat coursed through his body and stung his armpits, but he rose slowly and unbuckled his belt with careful deliberation. He dropped it and the heavy knife on the table, then stripped out of the rich blue tunic. It left him aglitter in silver mail, and he saw a flash of irritation in Dar's eyes as well as envy in the eyes of others.

"I am laced," Hart said tightly.

Dar gestured. "Oma, unlace him. Tend him as benefits a *Solindish* lordling."

The girl's fingers were deft as she undid the laces of the mail shirt. When she was done Hart shrugged out of it, letting it slide to his stool where it lay in a shining pool of exquisite mesh. Ceremonial only, it was lighter than traditional Homanan ringmail, but was more than he cared to carry.

It left only the quilted linen shirt used to keep the links from his flesh. Quickly Hart divested himself of it and draped it casually over Oma's shoulder, though she immediately threw it to the floor. He smiled, knowing no man—or woman—in The White Swan would dare call him liar now.

Dar kept his face expressionless, but there was no hiding the grudging acknowledgment in his eyes as he looked at the massive *lir*-bands. There were mutters in the room, but he nodded. "Well enough, blue-eyed or not, you have the right to call yourself Cheysuli. But it does not change the wager."

Hart pointed. "There is my coin. If it is not enough, be assured I have the means to get more."

"I have already said Homanan gold and silver has no value here," Dar said patiently. His eyes were still on Hart's armbands. "*Cheysuli* gold, however—"

"No." The refusal was distinct.

"Then what?" Dar asked idly. "You say you have the means to buy your life from us, and yet you offer nothing."

No, I do have something, though undoubtedly Tarron will not like it. Hart drew in a deep breath. "Then I will buy it with something emminently *Solindish.*" He pointed to the leather belt-purse. "There is something in there which should more than cover the worth of my life, Solindishman."

Lazily Dar reached out and took up the leather pouch, upending it. He shook it; a ring fell out onto the table. It rattled, rolled, stopped. It was solid gold, red Solindish gold, and large enough to hide half of Hart's forefinger when he wore it. But he had never worn it.

And now I never will.

Oma bent close to look; Dar's rigid hand thrust her rudely away from the table. In the light from the fat wax candle, the heavy ring glowed.

"The Third Seal," he said in disbelief.

"Part of the Trey," Hart agreed. "Enough, do you think, to purchase the life of the Prince of Solinde?"

"There is no Prince of Solinde—has been none for eighty years or more, ever since Bellam's son Ellic was killed by Shaine the Mujhar." But Dar's tone was dulled by shock and comprehension. Slowly he reached out and took up the ring, turning it so the light fell fully on the incised pattern that formed the Third Seal of Solinde, and the key to almost limitless power. "No prince," he said distinctly, "until the Lady Ilsa weds and bears a son." He looked at Hart in dawning recognition. "There was a man, she said—a Cheysuli warrior, who carried the Third Seal . . . a man she nearly killed."

So, her name is Ilsa. Hart smiled crookedly and pulled hair aside, baring swollen brow and ugly scrape. "Nearly. But not, quite."

Dar tipped the ring into his palm and rolled it back and forth. "With this, a man could rule Solinde."

"No. Even *she* told me that much: without the other two, this one is not so important. And the other two are safely held by the regent and my father."

Dar looked at him thoughtfully. "Niall is your father."

"Aye. My *jehan.* Mujhar of Homana." He glanced at Oma and the others, marking how attentively they watched him. The hostility had altered significantly to shock and wonder. He found he preferred the latter. "I did not come of my own accord," he said, for their benefit as much as for Dar's, who held his life. "I was sent. I am to learn to rule Solinde . . . and I want it no more than you do.

Dar looked at him sharply. "You do *not?*"

Hart shrugged. "Not now. Later, aye—I have been bred and raised for it, and have no intention of turning my back on my *tahlmorra*—but as for now, my interest lies in other directions." He looked at the ring in Dar's hand. "Is it enough?"

"To buy back your life?" Dar's tone was incredulous. "This is worth much more than you can imagine, my Homanan-Cheysuli princeling. This is worth a woman."

Hart frowned as Dar began to laugh. "A woman?"

Still laughing, the Solindishman shook his head. "Ah, shapechanger, how you amuse me with your ignorance. Obviously you have no aptitude for ruling, else you would have steeped yourself in the politics of Solinde. And I refuse to be your tutor." He grinned. "Your life is duly bought. Take your borrowed clothing and your hawk and all your worthless Homanan coin and get yourself back to the palace."

He had never been dismissed so arrantly by anyone, even his father, who had more right. And yet he dared not vent his anger on Dar or any of the Solindish; in a way, he acknowledged their right to treat him as they did. He knew nothing of them at all, or their realm, and yet he came expecting to rule them, whether he wanted to or not.

In taut silence, Hart put on the linen shirt and gathered up mail, silken tunic, belt, and belt-purse. Then he turned and walked out of the tavern.

In the morning Hart went to see the regent and briefly explained the circumstances of the evening before, glossing over the very real threat to his welfare and stressing instead the need to learn more about the woman called Ilsa, who could give Solinde a prince merely by wedding and bearing a son. He expected Tarron to express relief at his escape and compliment him on his resolution; instead, Hart was mildly startled to see the regent of Solinde gape unattractively, banishing his habitual dignity.

Tarron grasped the arms of his chair and thrust himself out of it stiffly. "You lost the *Third Seal?*"

"In return for *my* life, I allowed Dar to keep it," Hart explained again. He shrugged. "One ring is as good as another. Have a duplicate made; it will serve as well."

"*Will* it?" Tarron's face was red, though the color slowly faded to white. He sat down again, but the motion lacked anything akin to grace. The regent stared blindly at Hart. "You have no conception of what you have done."

Hart sighed. He was restless, wanting little more than to go out of the palace and into the city again, leaving behind the responsibilities Tarron intended him to assume. Hands on hips, he faced the regent in Tarron's private council chamber. "What I have done? Aye, I think I do. I think—"

Tarron did not wait for him to finish. "*I* think you have placed all my work in jeopardy . . . possibly even the entire succession." He shook his head in disbelief. "The Mujhar warned me—he *said* you required watching until you learned the importance of your role. But I thought surely he exaggerated—" He shut his eyes. "By the *gods*, you have given over the Third Seal into the hands of those who would wrest this throne from your father . . . from those who would gladly see you dead so they can crown their *own* candidate Prince of Solinde. . . ."

"Tarron—"

"Be silent!" The regent sat upright in the chair and glared at Hart, who gazed back in astonishment. "Hold your tongue, *my lord*, while I try to think of a way to make certain you may keep the head that wags it!"

Hart scowled. "May I remind *you*—"

"May I remind *you*?" Tarron snapped. Then, more quietly, "Listen to me, my lord, and perhaps you will see that I am less concerned for your rank and personal pleasure than for your life."

After a moment, Hart nodded and sat down in the nearest chair. "I will listen."

Tarron sighed a little. "To put it as succinctly as possible: you understand, of course, that Solinde is an occupied land in vassalage to your father. All judgments concerning the welfare of this realm are made by him, and him alone, although he encourages and acts on advice from me as well as other Homanans he has placed to administer the governing of Solinde."

"Of course."

The regent nodded. "It is a necessary practice that documents requiring triple seals—the Trey of Solinde—must be sent to Mujhara for the Mujhar's acknowledgment. For all the days of his rule, Niall the Mujhar has held the First and Third Seals of Solinde, while I held the Second. Nothing in Solindish law can be done without the Trey, the *complete* Trey. No orders can be carried out, no armies paid, no judgments rendered to the petitioners who gather at court for such things. Without the Trey, the wheel stops turning." Tarron drew in a calming breath. "He gave you the Third Seal so that you could have an active role in governing the realm that one day you will rule absolutely, with no fealty paid to Homana."

Hart sat upright. "Do you mean he intends to give me *sole* responsibility? But—I thought I would rule in his name . . ." He frowned. "I thought things would continue mostly as they are."

The regent's smile was bleak. "How many times has he told you Solinde would one day be yours?"

Hart shrugged. "As long as I can remember, but—"

"But nothing," Tarron said flatly. "On the day of his death, you will become king in your own right. Solinde will be *yours*, my lord. Yours. To do with as you will."

Hart snorted inelegantly. "And if I choose to give it back to the Solindish?"

"So be it." To his credit, Tarron did not flinch. "Although you may have done that already."

Hart grunted skepticism. "How?"

"You gave over the ring, my lord. The seal. And into the hands of one of the men most likely to order your death."

Hart shook his head. "Dar had the chance last night. He let me live."

"Because while the lady delays her decision, he has no power. Only *promised* power—whatever man she weds becomes Consort, and a son by him on Ilsa will be named Prince of Solinde. Power, my lord, is often gained through marriage. Or through children."

Hart grunted. "That I know well enough. Of five children, my *jehan* betrothed two of us before we were ever born."

"And you, my lord?"

Hart grinned. "A free man, Tarron, with no marital obligations."

Tarron did not match his humor. "If the lady weds before you are fully accepted, she provides a threat to your security."

"If she weds *Dar*."

If she weds any man, although she will *not* wed 'any man.' She is too highly born. Too close to the old Solindish line of succession; her grandmother's mother was youngest sister to Bellam, the last king of Solinde." Tarron tapped his hand on the chair arm. "Dar is only one of several Solindish lords who desire to wed the lady, although it is said he has a better chance than most. He is young, handsome, wealthy—and dedicated to Solindish rule."

Hart scowled at the regent. "I know the solution as well as you, Tarron. You intend to tell me that *I* should wed her, if only to keep her out of Solindish hands."

"I intend to tell you no such thing," Tarron retorted. "For all I know, you may prefer a Cheysuli woman. So long as the lady weds no man, your path is safe. We watch her very closely, my lord—more closely than she likes. And she shows no signs of choosing any man."

"But she *is* aware of what it could mean to Solinde?"

"Very aware," Tarron said grimly. "My lord, tread gently. I have seen the lady . . . I understand very well how a man could lose his head over her. But if you press her for anything, anything at all, she will bolt. And, most likely, she will bolt to the closest den."

"Dar's." Hart nodded thoughtfully. "An interesting position, regent. If I pursue her, she bolts. If I *ignore* her, she may simply go to the same den more slowly." He smiled. "What would you propose?"

Tarron's voice was steady. "I would propose that you get the ring back from Dar, my lord, before he puts it to use. With it, he stands a better chance of winning the lady. With it *and* Ilsa, your time in Solinde is done."

Hart swore beneath his breath. He was of no mind to wed, not even for the sake of a realm. Let Brennan make the sacrifice with Aileen of Erinn, and Keely with the girl's brother, Sean. His choice would be his own, and the timing of it.

The Third Seal— Abruptly he brightened. "There *is* a way I might be able to get it back, and without bloodshed. But it will require something from you."

Tarron did not hesitate. "Anything, my lord."

Hart smiled warmly. "Change my Homanan gold for Solindish."

Four

"My lord," the servant said, "the messenger will speak only to you, though he sends this with me."

Hart, more concerned with the dice he tossed across the table than the messenger's intentions, glanced only absently at the speaker. But his interest sharpened as he saw the palace servant carried the saddlepacks lost to Ilsa. He rose at once and took them from the man, relieved he could finally trade borrowed Solindish clothing for familiar Cheysuli leathers. "Have him come up at once."

The man bowed yet again. "My lord, he waits outside, in the bailey. He says he may not leave the gift intended for Hart of Homana, nor bring it into the palace."

Hart, digging leathers out of the packs, looked at the servant in distracted surprise. "A gift?"

"Aye, my lord."

He shrugged and resumed his search. "Well, then, I shall go down and tend to this gift. Tell the messenger I am coming."

"Aye, my lord." The servant departed at once.

Hart found the leathers he wanted and dumped the packs across the table, scattering dice. Quickly he stripped out of his borrowed finery and into leggings and jerkin, buckling on a wide leather belt tooled with runic glyphs. The buckle was heavy gold set with lapis; the knife he retrieved from the Solindish belt and slid it home in the Cheysuli sheath. Bare-armed at last, his race was plain to see.

No more doubts from Dar or his ilk, he thought in satisfaction. *Now, lir, shall we go?*

We go, Rael agreed, and lifted from the perch.

The gift was nothing at all a messenger might bring inside the palace, being a tall chestnut stallion with four white stockings and flaxen mane and tail, who eyed Hart with intense interest as he came into the bailey. At the stallion's head stood a man in blue-and-white livery, the royal colors of Solinde.

Though he was not the expert in horseflesh Brennan was, Hart nonetheless knew well enough the stallion was magnificent. The chestnut's height was impressive, as was his conditioning; a deep chest, long shoulders, and strong legs bespoke his stamina. Fox-red ears tipped inward toward one another, and his brown eyes were large and intelligent. He stood quietly enough, but there was a quivering expectancy about him that told Hart he required a rider who was alert to equine tricks.

Another way to attempt my death? Hart smiled as Rael drifted down to perch upon the bailey wall. Quietly he approached the stallion and gently caught his head with both hands, cupping nose and jaw. The firm flesh quivered at once; the stallion lifted his upper lip to display awesome teeth as he tried to catch an unwary finger.

"Shansu," Hart said quietly. "You and I will settle our differences another time; for now, you will leave my fingers intact." He nodded to the messenger. "I am Hart of Homana, now the Prince of Solinde."

The man's face was a polite mask, though his tone was civil enough. "My lord, I am given no title other than your name. It is my lady's contention that there is no other than your name. It is my lady's contention that there is no Prince of Solinde."

"The Lady Ilsa is stubborn." Hart laughed.

The man ignored that. "The Lady Ilsa sends to say this stallion cannot replace the one you lost, but will nonetheless provide a means of transportation. She acknowledges her part in the loss of your mount, and repays the debt freely." He held out the reins perfunctorily.

Hart accepted them, automatically stroking the firm layers of muscle lying beneath the flesh of the stallion's underjaw. "Tell the lady I am honored by her gift, if not by her refusal to acknowledge my Solindish title." He did not really care if she chose to ignore his status, but it was all a part of the game. "And tell the lady I will one day claim her forfeit."

"My lord, I will." Ilsa's messenger fell back as Hart swung up into the saddle. The gear was Solindish and unfamiliar, but he found it not uncomfortable. The stallion bunched massive hindquarters and essayed a single side-step, then relaxed beneath Hart's quieting touch.

He grinned down at the messenger. "You may tell the lady I am pleased indeed."

"Aye, my lord."

Hart signaled and one of the stable lads came running. "Have word sent to the regent that I am about the business we discussed. I may return very late." And then he summoned Rael and rode out of the double gates.

Rael's dubiousness became patently clear as Hart reined in before The White Swan. *Are you certain?* the hawk inquired.

Quite, Hart answered. *If Dar is not here, I will look for him elsewhere. But he must be found, and the seal won back.*

There are other ways, lir.

And do you suggest I turn thief? Hart asked wryly. *Worse, yet, murderer?*

No. I suggest you think about what you intend to do.

Hart laughed and jumped off the stallion. *I intend to take you inside with me, and enter into a game. What other thinking need I do?*

Rael's tone was resigned. *More than that, I think.*

Hart tied off the stallion and waited for Rael to settle upon his forearm. The hawk was large, too large; it was not a comfortable position, but an impressive one—for the moment, precisely what he wanted. Once inside, Rael would find another perch.

The stallion snorted and shook his head, clattering brass appointments. The setting sun glinted off the metal, flashing in Hart's eyes. He turned away and thrust open the door.

He had not expected a welcome and did not receive one. Casual glances turned into frozen stares, and once again he heard the cacophony of the common room die into expectant silence. A single word through the link loosed Rael into the room, and the great hawk lifted to stir the air against staring faces. He flew to the rooftree and perched himself upon it, shedding a single black-edged feather.

"Dar," Hart said only.

As one, the faces turned from him to stare at the man who walked out of the shadows into the candlelight. Stand-

ing, he was at least as tall as Hart, though his quilted Solindish doublet and padded trews hid much of such things as
true weight, frame, strength. Hart's snug Cheysuli leathers
did not.

Dar carried a silver goblet in one negligent hand. On his
forefinger Hart saw the heavy ring he himself had lost but
three nights before. Dar smiled faintly, and it was not without its share of honest amusement taken at no one's expense, least of all at Hart's.

"I thought you might be back." He waved a hand at the
nearest table. The patrons deserted it at once.

Hart jerked his belt-purse loose and held it up in the
light. "*Solindish* gold," he said pointedly. "Red Solindish
gold."

Dar grinned. "Bezat, my lord? Or did you find the stakes
too high?"

Hart crossed the room and hooked a stool free. "Bezat,"
he agreed calmly. "You had your chance at my life, and
accepted payment in its place. This time we play for gold."

"Until I have won all of yours, and then you will wager
something else." Dar sat down. "I know your kind, Cheysuli. You live for the wager, the *risk*—everything else is too
tame." He slapped the flat of his hand down upon the table.
"Oma! The bowl!"

She brought it at once and thumped it down on the table.
Hart grinned at her and was rewarded, as he expected, with
a muttered Solindish curse between small Solindish teeth.

Dar laughed, ordering a jug of wine and a cup for Hart.
"She is all sting and no venom. Be assured, if you want
her, you have only to win my gold. Oma goes with the man
who has the most."

Hart busied himself with stirring the contents of the
bowl. "My taste runs to fair-haired women."

Dar looked at him sharply, but Hart's face gave nothing
away. He placed his own belt-purse on the table. "My taste
runs to women, period. I have no preferences."

"None?" Hart smiled blandly. "But then, a man who
aspires to wed the Lady Ilsa might not even see the others."

Dar did not smile. "You have learned well in three days,
my lord."

"To survive in Solinde, I have to." Hart pushed the bowl
in Dar's direction. "Stir them?—or shall I?"

Tight-mouthed, Dar stirred, and Hart drew the first stone for him.

They played the hours away, burning the candle down to a stub. Red Solindish gold changed hands many times, making one man a pauper, another wealthy, and then went the other way with the draw of a single rune-stone. Blank bezats held no threat for Hart, who had weathered the first high-stakes game and felt the others far too tame. But he would not risk himself again.

When at last he and Dar stared at one another across a pile of stones—red-eyed, dry-mouthed, stiff from hunched postures—no man could be called a victor. Each shared equally in the wealth.

Dar scraped his stool back. "Enough, shapechanger. The cock will crow within an hour, and my bed beckons me."

"One more time," Hart said intently. "Once more, Dar."

The Solindishman shook his head. "I have wasted enough time for now—"

"Then I will see to it there is no waste." Hart shoved his pile of gold forward. "All of it, on but a single game."

Dar looked at the gold thoughtfully. Then he shrugged, dismissing it. "Not worth the effort."

"Wait—" Hart rose. "If we *made* it worth the effort?"

Brown eyes narrowed. "With what? You will not risk your Cheysuli gold; you have said so." He looked across the room at Rael, still perched on a limb of the roof-tree. "Unless you mean to put up your hawk."

Hart was incredulous that Dar could even think it. And then he laughed, realizing the man could not possibly know what the hawk was to him. "No," he said clearly, and thrust his left hand into the air. "Sooner this than my *lir*."

Dar shrugged. "Then again I must say, what have you to offer?"

Hart looked down at his right hand. On his finger glittered the heavy sapphire signet ring of his Homanan rank. Quickly he stripped it off and tossed it into the pile of coins. "This."

A light came up in Dar's brown eyes. It was not the ring so much, Hart knew, but the sudden desire for higher stakes, *high* stakes; they both of them lived to walk the edge of the blade.

"More," Dar said quietly.

Hart laughed. "You do not have nearly enough to match it. The wager would be no wager."

Dar's eyes narrowed. "Try me," he said. "I will match in worth whatever you have to wager."

Hart assessed him a moment. Then, smiling, he said, "A horse."

Dar shrugged. "I breed the finest horseflesh in Solinde. It would be difficult to offer me better than I have."

"Judge him for yourself. He is tied just outside."

The Solindishman's mouth twitched in amusement. "So prepared to lose . . . well enough, let us judge the worth of this horse."

Hart led the way outside. Once there, he was pleased to see the look of shock on Dar's face. "My horse, Solindishman. Worth enough, do you think?"

"That is *Ilsa's horse!* I myself bred him, raised him, trained him . . . I *sold* him to her only because she refused to accept him as a gift." His face was white with anger. "How does he come to be with you?"

"A gift," Hart said lightly, "from the lady to me."

Dar's breath hissed. "You *lie!*"

"Send a messenger to ask her." Purposely, Hart kept his tone light. He had known all along divulging the source of the stallion would force Dar's hand, although he had not known the man himself had bred the stallion. It made the challenge all the sweeter. "If you will recall from the lady's story of our meeting in the wood, my own mount broke both forelegs and had to be destroyed. This horse was sent to replace him."

"*This* horse—" Dar was nearly incoherent as he swung to face Hart directly. "Name your wager, shapechanger. This horse is worth more than the gold I offer."

Blandly, Hart smiled. "The Third Seal of Solinde."

After a moment of taut silence, Dar said something succint in explicit—and idiomatic—Solindish. Hart's grasp of the language extended only to a few halting phrases; slang was beyond him. But the tone told him more than enough.

"Undoubtedly I am whatever you claimed I am," he said cheerfully. "Now, shall we go back inside and settle this?"

Dar looked at the stallion, who tugged at his reins and tried to reach out to the Solindishman. It set white dents of anger at the corners of Dar's mouth. His eyes were black as he stared at Hart. "You risked the Seal without knowing its worth," he said flatly. "I am not so foolish—I *know* its worth. Do you think I will risk it on a thing so inconsequential as a *game?*"

"Perhaps not," Hart said calmly. "But will you risk it for a woman?"

Dar spat at the ground, just missing Hart's boots. "*That* for your game!" he said tightly. "Inside, shapechanger, and we shall *see* who gains that woman."

In silence, they played a final game of Bezat. Hart did not look at the Solindish ring that sat atop the pile of red gold in front of Dar; he did not dare to. Nor did he look at his own pile, upon which waited the sapphire ring he risked as well as the horse. The stakes were not anything like the game in which he had risked his life, but he found it no less fascinating. If he won, it would prove there was a place in the world for his gaming.

If he won. If he *had* won.

But he did not.

Dar laughed aloud as he turned over the final runestone. No bezats, but the worth of his stones outweighed the worth of Hart's. And so the man who had risked more won more; Hart was left to stare at the gold that was now Dar's, knowing the sapphire and the horse were lost also.

The Solindishman raked red gold across the table amidst hearty congratulations. The Solindish ring he slipped onto his forefinger again; the sapphire he tossed to the winegirl, Oma. "There!" he cried, in Homanan for Hart's benefit. "A token of my thanks, Oma, for good service throughout the years."

Hart found himself on his feet. "That ring is worthy of more respect, Solindish!"

"Is it?" Dar shrugged. "It is Homanan, is it not? And I say again, *this is Solinde.*" He poured his winnings into his belt-purse. "I will tell the lady how little you thought of her gift, shapechanger; so little you wagered it in a silly gambling game." His smile was eloquently derisive. "Ilsa does not entirely approve of such feckless pursuits, being so personally involved in something as important as the future of her realm."

"What of *you?*" Hart demanded. "Will you tell her how often *you* wager your wealth in silly gambling games?"

Dar laughed. "I thought I would leave it to the lady to reform me." He tied the now-bulging purse onto his belt. "I bid you good night and good morning, shapechanger . . . and my thanks for a worthwhile game."

Inwardly, Hart swore. Outwardly, he took his *lir* and left, hating the laughter that followed him.

In private chambers, the Homanan regent of Solinde perused parchments attentively. He read through one carefully, nodded thoughtfully, set it aside for further review. The next he scanned, then put it atop another pile. Briefly he glanced at the young man who waited impatiently near the table.

"You—lost?" Tarron nodded before Hart could answer. "Aye, I thought that was what you said. Well then, we must live with the fact the Third Seal is in the hands of the enemy, and we can no longer govern Solinde." His faint smile was wintry. "I have written to the Mujhar."

Hart swore, then scowled at Tarron. "There is still a chance I can get it back from him."

"In yet another game?" Tarron sat back in his chair. "My instructions from your father are quite clear, my lord. I am to give you no money other than the allowance he will provide."

"Payable how often?"

Tarron smiled. "Once a year."

"Once a year!" Hart nearly gaped. "How am I to make it last the entire twelve-month? Has he gone mad? Have *you* gone mad? How am I to live?"

"By learning not to wager it in foolish fortune-games." Tarron picked up another parchment. "My lord, if you will excuse me, there are things I must attend to."

"Then give it to me now."

After a moment, the regent glanced up from the parchment. "My lord?"

"My allowance. Give it to me now."

"I think not, my lord. It has not yet arrived from Homana."

Hart bit back another curse. "Then loan me the coin until it comes, and pay yourself back from that."

"I think not, my lord."

"Tarron!"

The regent set down the parchment. "Aye, my lord?"

Hart stepped very close to the table. "I can order you," he said quietly. "I am your liege lord."

Unexpectedly, Tarron laughed. "No," he said, "you cannot. Because you *are* not. My liege lord is Niall of Homana."

Hart glared at him angrily. "Do you think I have no resources, regent? Do you think I *need* your coin? No. *No*. I have gold, good Cheysuli gold, and plenty of gemstones, in wristlets, buckles, rings—countless other baubles. Do you think denying me coin can keep me from the game?"

Tarron's face was austere, yet oddly compassionate. "My lord, you are welcome to strip your caskets of every piece of jewelry you possess; it changes nothing. You may *beggar* yourself, my lord, but it will not change my mind. I have my orders from the Mujhar."

Pushed too far, Hart bared his teeth at the regent. "And when I am king in his place?"

The answering tone was very calm. "The day that happens, my lord, I will excuse myself from your service."

Hart's anger evaporated instantly, replaced with cold shock. He stared at the man in dawning acknowledgment. "You hate me that much."

"What is there to hate, my lord?" Tarron asked. "No. I dislike you, aye, because you waste yourself. I know your father well; I know his good sense, his mettle, his generosity. I know the Prince of Homana; he is a responsible, mature adult who will do as well as his father when he assumes the throne. But what do I know of you?" He spread his hands. "I know you prefer taverns to council chambers, games to governing, personal gratification to responsibilities. Certainly there are many men who feel as you do. But none of them are Prince of Solinde."

Guilty, Hart chafed beneath the gentle reprimand. "Aye, aye, I know—and one day I *will* become the man you think I can be—"

"But not yet?" Tarron did not smile. "If you are not very careful, you will not live long enough to become that man."

Hart pressed both hands against the regent's table and leaned forward. "I can win the ring back, if you let me," he promised, working hard to charm the man. "I *know* I can. And I will. All I require—"

"No."

"Tarron—"

The regent was not charmed. "No."

"You *ku'reshtin*—"

But Tarron cut him off. "My lord, if you will forgive me, there is much I must attend to. Without the Seal, many things must be handled with delicacy and deliberation." He gestured toward the stacks of parchments. "Unless you care to aid me—?"

Hart merely laughed at him.

Tarron nodded. "Well enough, I shall deal with it. But if I may suggest it, my lord, you might wish to consider what you will wear to the feast."

Hart, heading toward the door, turned to look at him blankly. "The feast?"

"The feast to celebrate your arrival, my lord. In one week's time." Tarron waved a negligent hand. "All the Solindish nobility will be here, as well as all the Homanans in the city."

"*All* the nobility?"

"Aye." Tarron's face was oddly expressionless. "Including the Lady Ilsa, and all the lords who wish to wed her."

"Ku'reshtin," Hart muttered. "I know what you mean to do."

"Do you?" Tarron's raised his brows. "I think perhaps not, my lord. What purpose would your marriage to Ilsa serve if you refuse to rule Solinde in the realm's best interests? What purpose if you died unexpectedly? She would still be Princess—or even Queen—and it would make it that much easier for the Solindish to throw us out of Solinde." He smiled thinly. "Such a wedding might well prove a disaster."

Hart jerked open the door. "I may be the wastrel second son, *regent*, but I am not stupid. And if you think I am blind to your backward attempt to push me *into* this marriage, you are the stupid one."

Tarron merely laughed. Swearing, Hart banged the door closed behind him.

Five

Hart walked quietly into the Great Hall of Lestra's palace with Rael perched upon his left forearm and saw the faces, one by one, turn to stare. Conversations eddied, trailed off, died out as the gathered Solindish nobility and the Homanans who governed them recognized the Cheysuli Prince of Solinde. And then the noise began again: whispers, murmurs, comments, in Homanan and Solindish, until Hart could no longer quite control the amusement that threatened to overtake his painstakingly practiced solemnity.

Those who know you, know better. Rael said pointedly.

Aye, but how many here know me? Tarron? No. He only believes he does. Dar? He knows me only as a mark. As for the lady . . . inwardly, Hart sighed, *by now surely the lady knows me only as a fool who risks her realm in silly games.*

The chamberlain mounted the white marble dais and formally announced the Prince of Solinde. Hart, unaccustomed to such pageantry arranged solely for his benefit, winced visibly, then recovered himself almost instantly. His years in Homana-Mujhar had taught him that kings conducted themselves with decorum at such formal festivities even when they did not feel it. He was not a king yet, but he needed the practice. Besides, the Solindish would expect it.

Now? Rael asked.

Now, Hart agreed. *The better to impress them.*

Accordingly, Rael lifted from Hart's arm and circled the huge hall, banking toward the high-backed chair set upon the dais. Women cried out at his passage and men set hands to knives; Rael swept relentlessly to the throne and settled himself upon the carved back. He spread his wings and shrieked aloud his dominance, then settled, folding his wings away, and surveyed all down the sharp hook of his deadly beak.

Hart moved toward the dais, mounting the steps even as the throng fell back. He was aware of the whispers and hissed questions, as well as the subtle hostility on the part of the Solindish. From the Homanans he sensed only a quiet, abiding pride; if they did not relish the thought of having Homana held by shapechangers in place of Homanans, they at least were willing enough to put the Solindish in their place by using the reputation of the Cheysuli.

He turned, trying to still the flutter of nervousness in his belly. Never before had he faced so many people as a ruler. Even in Homana he was only the second son, the prince who would trade his home for foreign lands. He was not Brennan, whose duties included nearly as many rituals and formalities as his father, the Mujhar. In Homana, he was simply Hart; *Prince* Hart, perhaps, by dint of his birth, but he had been easily overlooked. Now, he found he *could not* be overlooked, even if he preferred it.

How they stare, all the eyes.

He drew himself up, though his posture did not require it. And then he smiled. "I am Hart," he said quietly, pitching his voice low; he had learned from his father the art of making men listen by underplaying the moment. "Hart of Homana, second-born son of Niall the Mujhar, and styled Prince of Solinde." He saw narrowing eyes and tightening faces among the Solindish; how glibly he stole their title. "I am sent to learn kingship in the land I will rule; to learn how to govern a people in vassalage to Homana." Solindish mouths drew taut and flat, though some of the faces were conspicuously blank so as not to give anything away. "It is my wish that Solinde know peace, not war; that the hostilities of the past be buried along with those who have died." He drew in a steadying breath. "It is my personal desire that the overweening ambitions of the Ihlini be laid bare for all to see, so that there need be no discord in a land that deserves far better."

That, as he expected, sparked shocked murmurs and curses of disbelief among the Solindish; the Homanans merely watched him curiously.

"It is known to Cheysuli and Homanan alike that the Ihlini call Solinde their homeland," Hart continued quietly.

"It is not my intention to banish them from it, because not all serve Asar-Suti. But it *is* my intention to halt the hostility that they foment, and let Solinde remain *Solindish*—instead of a servant of the Ihlini."

All the eyes stared back, divulging nothing and everything; Hart realized, somewhat belatedly, that he had learned more from his father than he had thought.

He smiled, spreading his hands. "Enough of such talk; I am more in mind of a celebration than a declaration of war. Let the dancing begin." And abruptly he stepped down from the dais into the gathered throng.

It did not take long for Tarron to make his way through the couples who danced, or those who stood in groups and discussed politics. The regent, clad in habitual black, stepped to Hart's right side and said, quietly, "My lord, perhaps it would have been better if you had worn Solindish garb. Perhaps you should have left your hawk in your chambers—"

"—and perhaps it would have been better had I not attended at all." Hart smiled coolly at Tarron. "Would you say so to the Mujhar, regent? Would you bid him dress Homanan when he is a Cheysuli warrior?"

The brown eyes reflected shock. "My lord—"

"I am not my *jehan*," Hart said quietly. "I do not mean to be. But I am, first and foremost, *Cheysuli*. If I choose to wear leathers instead of velvets, I shall. If I choose to take Rael even into my bridal chamber, I shall. *I shall*, regent, do precisely as I please when it comes to my personal conduct." He caught up a cup of wine from a passing servant. "The Solindish will have to accept me as I am, Tarron. So will you."

"So much *gold*, my lord." Tarron's distaste was plain. "They will say you are a barbarian."

Hart grinned. "At least a wealthy one." He sipped wine, watching the regent over the rim of his cup. He was not surprised Tarron found his garb displeasing, for he was a man who abhorred ornamentation. The regent's black clothing, though of good cut and quality, was very plain. Hart's soft leathers, equally black, were also equally plain—except he had put on rune-scribed wristlets, torque, plated belt, sheath, and knife, all of heavy gold.

Tarron's mouth was flat. "And how long will you keep

it?" he asked grimly. "You will lose it all in a fortune-game."

Hart grinned. "Here it is called Bezat."

The regent's jaw bunched as he gritted teeth. "My lord, if you will excuse me—"

"No." Hart smiled blandly. "It is time you made the introductions, regent, as you are the one who knows all the Solindish nobility. May I suggest you begin with those lords who desire to wed the Lady Ilsa?"

Tarron stared back. "*Now*, my lord? *All* of them?"

"Those who desire to wed the lady," Hart said evenly. "Those whom you think may well have a chance."

Tarron's expression gave away nothing. "Aye, my lord. Of course."

Over the next two hours Hart met more men than he cared to acknowledge, and yet he had to. In execrable Homanan they greeted their newly-arrived prince and bid him courteous, insincere welcome, politely offering whatever assistance or companionship he might require. And as he opened his mouth to answer the first of them, he realized he dared give him only Homanan, or he would never be understood.

Jehan—and Brennan—always said I should pay more attention to my language lessons . . . that one day my ignorance would catch me up. . . .

Hart looked at the gathered Solindish aristocracy. Uncomfortably, he realized that the vanquished always were required to give up more than land or status. They gave up language and culture as well, replacing both with the preferences of the victor.

How was it during Shaine's qu'mahlin? *he wondered idly. How was it for the clans that had to flee Homana to live in foreign lands?*

"My lord." Tarron again. "My lord, may I present Dar of High Crags, born of one of the oldest lines in Solinde."

Hart came out of his brief reverie to find Dar standing before him in silence. The Solindishman's smile was blandly polite, offering nothing more than the courtesy demanded of his rank, but Hart saw the glint in his brown eyes and the twitch of amusement at the corner of his mouth.

"Dar of High Crags," Hart repeated. "How old a line is it?"

"Very old, my lord," Dar answered politely. "At least as old as the Lady Ilsa's; my kin has served hers for more than seven centuries."

"And in all of that time has none of you ever wed into the royal house?"

The barb went home. Dar's eyelids flickered, but he managed a benign smile. "History changes from one night to the next, my lord . . . surely you know that better than most. Is it not true that the Cheysuli ruled Homana for a thousand years, then gave it over to the Homanans?" He paused for the benefit of Homanan ears. "And *now* you take it back?"

"In accordance with the wishes of the gods," Hart said smoothly. "Have you not heard of our prophecy? Surely you have, Dar . . . surely the Ihlini in service to the Seker have made certain you know *of* it, if not the truth." He sipped wine. "The Wheel of Life is a thing no man may fully know, except that the gods have a purpose when they set it into motion."

"Tahlmorra." Dar nodded. "Aye, I have heard of the fatalism that rules your race. And I have heard how blindly you serve it."

Tarron cleared his throat. "My lord of High Crags—my lord prince—"

"I think you may leave the lord of High Crags with me," Hart interrupted, without taking his eyes from Dar's. "Are there not things you must attend to?"

"Aye, my lord." In obvious relief, Tarron bowed quickly and departed.

"Neatly done." Dar scooped a cup of wine from a passing servant.

Hart was not ready to change the subject. "There is a purpose in all things," he said quietly. "All things, Dar . . . even the handing over of a Solindish throne to a Cheysuli warrior."

The woman's voice was cool. "And was there a purpose in risking my horse in a *game?*" she asked. "And the Third Seal, *my lord*—what purpose in losing that?"

Hart inclined his head to acknowledge Ilsa's arrival. "He was my horse, lady—freely given. As for the Seal, well—" He shrugged, grinning ruefully "—had I known it was the price that bought your willingness to marry, surely I would never have risked something so valuable."

She gazed at him wide-eyed in unfeigned astonishment. "My willingness to *marry?*"

Dar interrupted smoothly. "Lady, he seeks only to turn the subject. That he should be so thoughtless as to risk your horse on the very day the gift was received, or to risk him *at all*—"

Hart looked only at Ilsa. "You might ask him," he suggested. "You might ask him how he considers the ring as a way of securing you for a *cheysula.*"

She frowned. "A what?"

"Wife," he amended. "Do you intend to marry him?"

Dar's hand was on Ilsa's arm. "That is none of your concern, shapechanger."

She slipped free easily, obviously well accustomed to avoiding the possessiveness of men, and turned to face Dar squarely. "But it is *my* concern." Delicate color deepened in her face to compete with the frost in her eyes. "Is it true, Dar? Do you think I will wed you because you hold the Seal, when it should be mine regardless?"

Brown eyes narrowed minutely, weighing the need for frankness against the requirements of diplomacy; Dar discarded his elegant courtier's manner instantly. "I think you will wed the man best able to help Solinde," he said flatly. "You *must* wed such a man—a strong, loyal, dedicated Solindishman, who wants only the best for his land . . . a man who can forge the warring factions into one united front—"

"And take Solinde back from Homana?" Hart interposed. As they stared, he shook his head. "You reckon without the Cheysuli, who *require* this land—or at least the bloodlines from it."

"And do you require *me?*" Ilsa demanded icily. "The last of Bellam's line, born of the oldest House of Solinde . . . how could you overlook *me?*"

"How could I?" Hart grinned. "Not easily, Lady Ilsa— no more easily than Dar."

She looked from him, to Dar, back again. And then she laughed, surprising both of them. "And do you think I would wed either of *you?*"

"Ilsa—" Dar began.

Still she smiled, though her eyes remained cool. "No," she said, "I would not. I want no man who values games over the welfare of Solinde."

"Then I will stop," Dar said flatly. "I will stop altogether, here and now, no more to waste my time and wealth in foolish games of chance."

Ilsa turned to Hart. "What of you?" she asked. "Will you make me the same promise?"

Without hesitating, Hart shook his head. "No, lady, I will not."

Her mouth twisted, briefly ironic. "Honesty from *you*, at least, displeasing though it may be." She looked at Dar. "You are all you have described—strong, loyal, dedicated, and capable of uniting Solinde. I will indeed require a man with the same abilities, *but I will choose him myself.*" Coolly, she smiled. "I find it shameful that Solinde demands a *man* to rule when a woman could do as well—and I am deserving of it." She put out a slender hand. "Give me the ring, Dar. You know it is rightfully mine."

He spread eloquent, empty hands. "Alas, I have left it home."

Her tone was very grim. "Dar—"

"Ilsa." He cut her off. "We are old, old friends, and older adversaries in this game of men and women. You ask for honesty? I give you honesty . . . *I give you a truth you may not like.*" He glanced at Hart as if regretting his presence, but continued regardless of it. "The Third Seal is mine, won fairly from a man who did not know what he risked. He lost. He lost it *all*, including his only chance to marry the woman he needs to marry, in order to hold this realm. But I won. *I won.* And I keep what I win, regardless of who else might want it . . . *unless they are willing to pay the price.*"

She was awash in candleglow. In crimson and gold she set the hall ablaze; rubies glittered in braided hair. But they could not compete with the determination in her eyes, or her pride. That and her dignity were palpable. "I am Ilsa of Solinde," she said evenly. "I can rule without the ring."

"But not without a Consort." Dar sipped wine; his eyes were alight with inner amusement. "The lords of Solinde will require a male heir as soon as is humanly possible, lady, to insure the succession. It seems to me you have need of me as much as I of you."

"But I can take another man," she reminded him gently, patently unaffected by his challenge. "Where will that leave you?"

"Without," Hart said succinctly.

Dar shook his head. "She will do what is required. Ilsa has pride, integrity, honor . . . and an incredible sense of duty." He bowed his head in a courteous salute. "In the end, rather than leaving it to others, she will make the decision herself."

"Then leave me to it!" Ilsa said sharply. "Leave me altogether!"

Dar bowed. "Aye, my lady. At once."

As the Solindishman left, Hart looked at Ilsa in mild surprise. "A sharp tongue, lady."

"With him, I need one." Ilsa took the cup of wine out of Hart's hand and drank down what remained, eyes aglitter over the rim. Abruptly she pressed the cup back into his hands. "Dar always makes me angry, which makes me all the angrier."

Hart skillfully eased her through the throng, guiding her slowly toward a quiet corner. "Are you enemies, or bedmates?"

Ilsa looked at him sharply. "Not bedmates," she said dryly. "Nor enemies, to tell the truth." She sighed and sat down on the padded bench against the wall, deftly spreading crimson skirts to decorously cover gem-crusted leather slippers. "Since we were young, there was talk of uniting our houses. It was believed that Dar could provide Solinde with the strong leadership she requires." She slanted him a glance from eloquent eyes. "You know, of course, that we prefer self-rule. We want no foreign overlord."

"I know. And were there no prophecy, I might be disposed to grant it, once in the position to do so." Hart shrugged as he sat down beside her. "But I am not, and I am a dutiful Cheysuli. I serve the prophecy."

"Why?" she asked bluntly. "If it does not please you, turn your back on it."

"Because I aspire to the afterworld." Hart grinned and leaned back against the wall, stretching out long legs. "Out of character, she is thinking. A man who wagers the Third

Seal of Solinde could not possibly concern himself with what happens after death." Then, more solemnly, "But I do. Every Cheysuli does. The gods have given us a place here in the world, and promise a better one when we are dead." He smiled wryly. "We need only be faithful children."

"Faithful to a daydream dreamed too many years ago." But Ilsa's smile removed the sting of the words. "So, you serve your prophecy in hopes of reward after death. It seems such a futile thing . . . and perhaps a little childish."

"I am not a child."

Ilsa looked at him a long moment. "No. I think you are not."

He gazed out at the people: at those who danced; who clustered to mutter of politics; who advocated rebellion and the taking of his life. "We are an old race," he said finally. "Thousands and thousands of years. We are children of the gods: it is what *Cheysuli* means." Still he stared, though his vision blurred and he saw only colors and candlelight. "The Homanans tried to slay us all, to annihilate us entirely, in a purge that lasted decades . . . the Ihlini have done it again and again, through sorcery, plague, intrigue. So many centuries of hatred, prejudice, fear . . . so many years of being the hunted, not knowing if we would survive." He blinked and turned his head to look at Ilsa. "We survived because of the gods. Because of the afterworld. *Because of the prophecy.*" Silently he turned a spread-fingered hand palm-up. "All of it shapes our lives. Without it, we would perish."

She said nothing for a long moment, seemingly unable. And then she shook her head. Rubies glistened in her hair. "How is it a man—a Cheysuli—who is so dedicated to this prophecy can risk himself in a *game?*"

Hart laughed; it was a single burst of sound. "Because I cannot help it."

Ilsa frowned. "Cannot?" She shrugged. "I say, simply *stop.*"

" 'Simply stop,' " he echoed, and grinned to himself.

"If you pride yourself on the discipline of the Cheysuli—"

"I pride myself on nothing." Abruptly he rose to tower

over her. "Lady, we speak of private things. Let us dance instead."

Ilsa rose also, but disdained to take his outstretched hand. "No," she said coolly. "I think I would rather not." She turned to go, took four steps, turned back so abruptly rich skirts swung against the floor. Golden girdle chimed. "Dar has the right of it," she warned with infinite distinctness. "In the end, regardless of how I feel, I will do what is best for the realm."

Hart watched her rigid back as she slipped into the crowd and was lost. He was more than a little stunned by her sudden retreat—no, it was not a retreat. She had simply *left* him; he was not a man much accustomed to women leaving him.

Not-accustomed to it at all. Morosely, he searched for her in the throng. Had she gone to Dar? Possibly. He thought it entirely possible—until Dar himself approached.

He carried two silver cups in his hands and offered one to Hart. "I swear, there is no poison. It would cheat me of my wager."

Hart, still stinging from Ilsa's rebuke, slanted her foremost suitor a black scowl. "No doubt the bet is against me."

Dar grinned. "Not entirely, though it does involve you." He tipped his head in the direction of the departed Ilsa. "Shall we drink to the lady, my lord, and to her unerring tongue?"

Reluctantly, Hart smiled. And then he laughed ruefully. "Aye, she has that. And uses it on us both."

They clanged cups and drank; the wine was dry, hearty, powerful. Hart liked it very much.

"The lady has used it on *me* for many years," Dar remarked. "It is time she had a new target, though not a permanent one." His smile offered a challenge. "Are you interested in my wager?"

"And if I said I was not?"

"You would be a liar, and I think you are not that." Dar smoothed a lock of sandy hair away from his eyes. "For all we are Cheysuli and Solindish—and rivals to one another— I think we are much alike," he said lightly. "Once, had a man suggested that, I would have slain him outright; Cheysuli and Solindish? But I am a man for realities if nothing else; you are here, you intend to *stay* here, and—short of having you slain—there is little to do about it."

Hart grunted. "You might still try."

"To slay you?" Dar shook his head. "I think not. I think it would result in too much trouble, for me and for Solinde. No. No killing. Perhaps a wager will do as well."

Hart sighed. "What wager?"

"One worth our time, my lord. One worthy of *both* of us." Dar paused. "I propose we place a wager on the lady . . . and on ourselves."

"Dar—"

The Solindishman gestured expansively. "Deny it all you wish, but I have seen that expression before when a man looks at Ilsa. It has been on my *own* face often enough." He shrugged and smiled ruefully. "You want her, *I* want her, every man in *Solinde* wants her. But only half a dozen stand a chance, and only one will get her."

"You," Hart said dryly.

Dar grinned. "I am willing to wager on that."

Hart smothered a laugh as he lifted the cup to his mouth. He drank, thinking it over, and watched the anticipation light Dar's eyes. *He is as bad as I. . . .* After a moment, he sighed. "What is the wager, then?"

Dar's face was very intent. "For all she says she will marry who and when she pleases, Ilsa knows full well it cannot wait much longer. Perhaps a month at the most; the lords already request a decision from her." His eyes shrewdly assessed Hart's carefully arranged noncommittal expression. "She need only wed a Solindishman—myself, or another of equal wealth and station—in order to unite the warring factions of this realm. We cannot hope to win Solinde from Homana until we are as one, and there is only one way of uniting us: under a single man."

"You," Hart said, tasting ashes in his mouth.

"Or my son." Dar's tone was steady. "Under our laws, the man who weds Ilsa does not become King of Solinde, he becomes Ilsa's Consort—a position lacking the magnificence of a proper royal title, perhaps, but none of the power accorded his place beside Ilsa. Nor will she be Queen; Solindish law requires a male sovereign. But a son born of the lady and her Consort *does* become king upon his majority." He smiled. "Until he reaches that majority, his father acts as regent."

"And if she weds me?"

To his credit, Dar's expression did not alter. "If Ilsa weds you, it would alter the traditional lines of succession. No doubt you would claim yourself King . . . since Solinde is a vassal to Homana, it seems likely that title would not be contested." He shrugged. "We have been soundly beaten repeatedly by your ancestors. I doubt there would be any rebellion."

Hart shook his head. "There is no wager, Dar. Ilsa would never allow Solinde to be ruled by a Homanan."

"Would she not?" Dar stared grimly into his wine. "Do not discount yourself, shapechanger. There are those in Solinde who do not want another war, preferring peace even to self-rule. They are very persuasive. And Ilsa—" He broke off, scowling blackly, then continued. "Ilsa is guarded by those who desire peace."

Hart recalled the man who had accompanied her the day they had met. A Solindishman whose task it was to guard her, and who allowed her so little freedom in order to protect her welfare.

He looked hard at Dar, assessing the man's intentions. He knew Dar wanted Ilsa, wanted Solinde, wanted self-rule. He knew also that Dar enjoyed the challenge of a wager as much as he did, which was substantially indeed; he could not live without it. But he did not know how far Dar was prepared to go.

Idly, Hart drank wine. "What are the stakes?" he asked.

"The highest," Dar answered. "I wager with my life."

Hart looked at him sharply. "Your life," he echoed, disbelieving the man.

"Aye," Dar agreed curtly. "Let it stand so: if Ilsa chooses you, I will give up my life and give back the Third Seal of Solinde."

"I do not want your life."

Dar's eyes did not waver. "If you do not take it, my lord, be assured I will do what I can to throw you down from the throne of Solinde."

Hart knew the Solindishman meant it. "I do not want you for an enemy."

"If you win, you will have one."

Hart sighed. "Aye, aye, well enough—if I win the lady, you forfeit the Seal and your life. But what of me? What if *you* win the wager?"

Dar smiled. "You go home to Homana."

Hart stared. "Go *home*—"

"Alive. Unharmed. Quite well . . . very much as you came." Dar, still smiling, shrugged. "But you will forfeit your claim on Solinde."

"And if she chooses neither?"

"Then we will find another game."

Hart chewed at his bottom lip, hearing the siren song of the challenge. *If I lose Solinde, my* jehan *will forfeit* me—

But he found himself clasping Dar's forearm; the wager was made and accepted.

Six

Hart awoke with the haunted feeling of something gone wrong. He snapped out of sleep and into daylight so abruptly it left him disoriented, and then he realized the disorientation had less to do with the sudden awakening than from late hours and excess drink; he and Dar and three other Solindish lordlings had wasted most of the night closeted in a private chamber, gambling and drinking, while the rest of the guests disported themselves in the Great Hall.

A pang of guilt pinched his belly; such behavior in Homana-Mujhar would be considered unconscionably rude, particularly as the celebration had been in his honor, and he sincerely doubted he would have been allowed to slip away. But here no one dared attempt to dissuade him or otherwise remark on his behavior.

Hart sighed grimly. *Save for Tarron.*

But Tarron had said nothing, because Hart had taken care to slip away unnoticed, too hungry for a game to consider the consequences.

Consequences. The haunted feeling came back. Hart, tangled in tumbled bedclothes, frowned up at the draperied canopy of the tester bed and tried to name what caused his discontent.

Abruptly, he remembered.

His eyes popped open. *The wager . . . the wager with Dar, on Ilsa.* Swearing, he rolled over onto his belly and buried his face in feather-stuffed bolsters, half hoping he could smother himself and forget all about Dar and his infamous wager. *Oh, gods,* lir . . . *I have wagered away my freedom!*

Rael stirred on his perch. *Have you?*

Hart groaned aloud and clenched fingers in the silk of

his bedclothes. *The wager with Dar, on Ilsa—on who will win her hand—* He groaned again, feelingly. *How could I have been so foolish?*

The last is easy to answer. Rael's tone lacked sympathy. *When the craving is on you, you are no man, no warrior, no prince—you are nothing more than a hound smelling a bitch in season . . . save the bitch is no dog at all, but the wager itself.*

After a moment Hart lifted his face out of the bolsters and turned his head to stare at the hawk through the gauzy draperies. "How eloquent," he said grimly; there was no humor in his tone.

How do you know you have lost your freedom? Rael asked. *In order to lose it you must win the woman, and there is nothing that leads me to believe you will.*

Unexpectedly, the dry summation hurt. Hart frowned. "Nothing?"

Nothing. Rael's pattern within the *lir*-link was infinitely assured; for once he did not offer the crutch of meaningless reassurance to his irresponsible *lir*, though the habit was hard to break.

Hart sat up and tried to drag the hangings aside, swearing as fabric tangled and obscured his vision of Rael entirely. Finally he ripped them apart and climbed out of the huge bed, naked save for *lir*-gold.

"Nothing?" he repeated, elaborately distinct.

Rael heard the subtle challenge in Hart's tone. He stirred on his perch and fixed his *lir* with a bright eye. *Tell me what you offer the woman, then.*

"A title. Improved status. Greater respect in the realm." Hart shrugged, spreading his hands. "Power as well, though not as much as I hold."

What power do you hold?

He smiled, victorious. "I am the Prince of Solinde."

Who spends his time wagering on improbable outcomes such as who the last of Bellam's line will wed. Rael couched his words in brutal candor. *Say again what you offer the woman, lir—and then realize that she can have precisely the same if you are sent home to Homana . . . or if you are dead.*

It banished the smile entirely. Hart felt as if one of Brennan's horses had kicked him in the belly—no, not a horse, and not the belly. It was one of Rael's talons, and he stabbed lower than the belly, aiming for something very different, something personal, something eminently more vital.

"Rael—"

Think, lir. *For once. See yourself as others see you.* Rael paused. *No. See yourself as the lady herself must. And tell me again you have wagered away your freedom.*

It curdled the wine in his belly. Hart turned from the hawk and went back to the bed, clutching one of the testers for support. It was never pleasant listening to others decry his habits, but he had always had the enviable capacity to cheerfully dismiss the comments, the fraternal and paternal lectures, knowing no one stayed angry at him for very long. He was not a man for moods and high temper, as Corin was; neither was he willing to shoulder all the burdens of his rank and future, as Brennan had always been. What he offered was friendly camaraderie, cheerful companionship, generosity of spirit. He was not a bad man. He was not a bad brother, bad son, bad friend, or bad warrior.

"But I *am* a bad prince."

Rael did not answer. Hart shut his eyes and set his forehead against the wooden tester, regretting the wine he had drunk. More than that, he regretted his willingness to overlook so many things in pursuit of personal pleasure.

After a retrospective moment Hart turned back to the hawk. "She will not have me."

No.

"And if she takes Dar in my stead, as is likely, the wager is lost . . . and I will be sent out of Solinde in disgrace."

Much as you were sent out of Homana.

Again the talons stabbed into him.

"If I go home, having lost Solinde—" Abruptly Hart sat down on the bed, realizing the enormity of his situation. "Gods, Rael, if I lose Solinde because of something so infinitely trivial as a *wager*—"

If you lose Solinde for any reason, lir, *you alter the prophecy.*

It snapped Hart's head up. "No," he said firmly. "*No.* I will not allow you to give that guilt to me."

And if it is the truth?

"How?" Hart challenged. "I am a second son, the *middle* son, obligated to no betrothal. It does not matter who I wed, how many children I sire—or who *they* wed. Let Brennan know that burden, *lir* . . . I need not."

The wine has replaced your wits. Rael's tone lacked the bite of earlier comments, sliding instead toward customary patience and wry acknowledgment of Hart's shortcomings. But it did not make his words less telling. *Whether you wed a Solindish woman does not matter—it does not matter if you wed at all—but it* does *matter if you hold Solinde. The prophecy involves four realms, not three. If you lose Solinde now, it will be lost forever . . . and the Ihlini victorious.*

Hart swore feelingly, knowing guilt as well as consternation. "If only there were no wager . . . then there would be no risk."

Is that not the point of the wager?

He raked tousled hair with rigid fingers, trying to make sense of the circumstances; knowing it unlikely. "Aye, aye, always before it was the risk, the *chance* I might lose, and the pleasure in knowing I had won—or *would* win, next time. But now—" Hart shook his head. "This is different. The game is different. The stakes are too high—" Trapped, desperate, despairing, he swore again. "Gods, Rael, it is the *ultimate* wager . . . and now I cannot enjoy it."

Which do you mourn? Rael asked gently. *The loss of that enjoyment, the loss of your freedom . . . or the loss of a realm?*

Hart did not answer at once. He stared blankly into the room, lost inside his head, knowing only that his need of the game had accounted for more than his current predicament. For the first time he fully acknowledged that he alone was responsible for the fire, for the loss of life in the Midden. Regardless of the *kind* of people they were, they had not deserved to die because of his selfish irresponsibility.

"Thirty-two people," he said hollowly, and his mind fashioned a vision: Brennan, standing before the stained-glass casements in the Great Hall of Homana-Mujhar, visibly stunned by the loss of life; Brennan, shouting at Corin that it did not matter if he felt inconvenienced about having to go to Atvia when people were dead; Brennan, feeling more keenly the deaths of the people in the Midden because he was a *responsible* man.

Oh, rujho, *I wish you were here to tell me what to do.*

But Brennan was not. And so Hart did his own *responsi-*

ble decision-making for the first time in his life. He put on his clothing and went to see the subject of the wager.

Hart was admitted at once into the city home in which Ilsa dwelled and was shown to a small walled garden. At first he did not see her, wondering if he was meant to wait for hours while his impatience grew; then he *did* see her, and his fine intentions went out of his head. He could think of no way to speak plainly with her, to tell her of the wager that reduced her to chattel instead of independent woman, knowing how she would feel. And knowing what she would say.

And so, lamely, he smiled, and drew for strength upon the abundant charm he had used unthinkingly so often in the past.

Only the night before he had seen her clad in brilliant crimson, ablaze with gold and rubies. She had been elegant, incandescent, incredibly beautiful. He found her no less so now, though the fine gown, gold, and gems were gone, replaced by nubby wool skirts of a cream and russet weave and an amber-colored tunic belted with supple leather. She wore scuffed boots in place of soft slippers, and there was mud on one cheek. The glorious white-blond hair was bound back in a single tight-plaited braid, tied off with brown leather. Around her face the shorter hairs came loose, straggling, curling, tangling, serving only to make him want to smooth them back.

Looped over one arm was a basket full of flowers. A profusion of delicate, black-eyed moss roses, ruffled like crumpled parchment, all of bright golds, rich yellows, pastel apricots. In her right hand she carried small silver scissors connected to her belt by a fine-linked silver chain. She rose, intently tucking flowers into the basket, and then turned toward him only to stop short.

"Come out with me," he said. "Come ride with me, Ilsa."

Winged brows rose. "Ride with you? On what, my lord? You wagered your horse away."

He crossed the garden walk and put out his hand to take the basket from her, bending to set it down beside the path. Her wrist was slender in his larger hand, almost to the point of fragility. She seemed delicate as a lily, and yet her spirit and pride burned brightly as his own.

"Aye," he agreed, "I did. Foolishly, selfishly, I sought to goad Dar into a wager that would win back the Third Seal, knowing he could not turn his back on the knowledge you had given the horse to me. And the gambit was successful."

"Except you lost the horse."

"Losing is always a risk, Ilsa. Even now." He did not release her wrist. "The palace is rich in horses, though none so fine as the one you gifted me. I have another." He smiled. "Come with me, lady. Come out of the city and know a little freedom once again."

"We have nothing to say to one another."

"Oh, lady, we do." His thumb rubbed the top of her forearm, glorying in the delicate texture of her skin. "Come with me, Ilsa. Please."

Coolly she pulled free of his hand and its intimacy, bending to scoop up the basket. She hooked both arms through calmly, as if to put up a barrier between them. "I will order a horse saddled for me. You may wait, my lord."

And he did, somewhat impatiently, wondering why women took so long to ready themselves for a ride when the wind would only muss them almost instantly. But Ilsa did not, and when she appeared he discovered she had not changed at all, save to clean the mud from her face and to put on a fitted leather doublet with silver-rimmed horn buttons. Engaged in working hands into snug gloves, she hardly looked at him as she walked past him toward the front entrance.

Hart exited with her. "You need take no guard. My *lir* and I are enough, I think, to ward you against most dangers."

She slanted him a cool glance over one shoulder as she turned toward the white mare she had ridden at their first meeting. "Are you? I think a man need only offer you a wager, and you would name *me* as the stakes."

He stopped short, staring at her in shock. *She knows . . . oh, gods, she already knows, and this is nothing more than a travesty.*

But Ilsa gave no sign, no hint she knew anything of the wager between Hart and Dar. She merely waited for him to hand her up into the saddle, and when he did not move to do it at once she led the mare to a mounting block and

did it on her own. Belatedly, Hart hastened to lend her a
hand, though now she did not require it.

The white mare nosed him, pressing muzzle against neck
and blowing even as he tried to turn her head away. He
looked up at Ilsa, backlighted by the sun, and opened his
mouth to speak. Then abruptly turned away.

Hart swung up into his saddle and waited for Ilsa to fall
in beside him. It was midmorning and cool; the air chilled
his bare arms and lent an icy sheen to his *lir*-bands. He
had brought nothing out of Homana save Cheysuli leathers.
Solindish clothing would be warmer, but he preferred familiar garb.

How can I tell her? How can I explain?

Rael offered no answer. In silence, Hart escorted Ilsa out
of Lestra and into the countryside beyond.

He found it no easier when they were free of the city.
He *did* find it easier to forget about the wager altogether,
losing himself in the pleasure of the moment. And so
he did.

Ilsa was an accomplished rider, as her flight through the
wood had proved. He did not hold back now; together they
galloped across the turf and lost themselves, for the moment, in the sheer joy of good horseflesh. Running on, *running on*, he could forget all about wagers and risks and
titles, thinking only of how the stallion should move beneath him; how fast, how smooth, how willing. For an unblessed human, it was the closest thing to *lir*-shape.

The moment was spent too quickly. Hart eased his mount
from a gallop to a canter, then to a walk, even as Ilsa did.
In companionable silence they listened to the horses blow,
jangling bits and shanks and ornamentation. He could smell
the acrid tang of his stallion's sweat, the scent of flowers
in the turf, the promise of summer coming. It was a good
time to be alive. Better yet, it was a good time to share it
with a woman.

"Is that your hawk?" she asked, pointing.

He glanced up and saw the shape against the sky; the
outspread wings and lazy spiral. "Aye. Rael. He keeps his
distance today, knowing this is a thing between man and
woman, requiring no *lir*."

She looked at him sharply. "He *knows* such things?"

Hart laughed. "Did you think him mute? A pet, or a

tame bird like those kept mewed up at the palace?" Grinning, he shook his head. "No, lady. A *lir* is far more than anything you might imagine. Rael is an extension of myself, though his conscience is his own. We are bonded. He speaks to me, I to him, though it is all done silently."

"And does he value games as much as you?"

He heard the dry tone in her voice. So close to the edge of contempt; it hurt. "No," Hart said quietly. "Rael does not. Rael *does*, however, suggest I turn to things more important, such as learning how to rule."

"Then indeed, he is wiser than you."

"The *lir* always are." He felt safer discussing Rael than his irresponsibility. "Do you know nothing of them?"

She shrugged. "I know only the things I have heard: that they are magical animals with awesome arts, allowing the Cheysuli to assume shapes other than their own." Her glance betrayed no distaste, but quiet curiosity. "You can really become a hawk? With wings and feathers and talons?"

The laughter was gone. "Aye."

"Does it hurt?"

Hart frowned. It had been so long since he had thought of *lir*-shape in terms other than an automatic exchange of human form for raptor that the words were harder to find than ever. In Homana, the Cheysuli were no longer the enemy, but part and parcel of the present. No one required explanations.

"There is no *pain*," he said thoughtfully. "Not as you know pain. But there is an oddness, an alienness, when I put off my human shape for another." He shrugged a little. "Knowing what I will become, it does not frighten me. I will come through it; I always do, and back again. But the first time, not knowing, is frightening and exhilarating all at once." He looked at her intent face, wishing he could share *lir*-shape so he need not struggle for words that were inadequate no matter how glib his explanation. "From birth we are told that to be whole we require a *lir*. And although we have no reason to anticipate being left without one, the hidden fear is always there . . . the fear that somehow the gods have forgotten to prepare the animal that is to become your *lir*." He shrugged. "The first time you assume *lir*-

shape, you are so eager the fear recedes and you think only of the need, not the fear of what you do."

Ilsa looked into the sky to watch Rael's soaring flight. "And when you are a hawk, what do you feel then?"

The answer was instant. "Freedom." As she looked at him, he smiled. "*Freedom.* No more am I earthbound; no more do I require legs, feet, horse, or other means of transportation. I have only myself, *requiring* only myself . . . and I become the freest thing alive."

"But you are still a man."

"Mostly. I keep my human thoughts and feelings, although I experience things as a hawk. Human instincts are augmented, not overcome. I know I am a man in the form of a hawk. I am still Hart."

She turned from Rael to him. "Is there danger in it?"

He shrugged. "There is a question of balance. A Cheysuli in *lir*-shape is both and neither; it *is* possible for him to lose himself to the animal form, but it only rarely happens. It is something we are carefully taught, this balance." He saw the comprehension in her eyes, and the realization of the dangers. "I will not lie to you, Ilsa. If a warrior in *lir*-shape should grow too angry, relying too much on animal instinct instead of both, he can tip over the edge and lose humanness altogether."

"And remain an animal."

"Or something made of both." He plaited the mane of his bay stallion, thinking through the best way to explain to her what he had learned quite young. "It is one reason the shapechange is more difficult in extremity. In pain, a man might lose himself. In anger also, and sheer exhilaration. The shapechange requires concentration, and responsibility. There is always the risk that a warrior in *lir*-shape may become something other than himself."

"And risk is something you understand very well." Ilsa smoothed hair back. "I have known Dar nearly since birth; his family has served mine for centuries. I have seen how it is with him, this need to risk his wealth in wagers. The coin means little to him, other than representing victory over the odds." Briefly, her mouth twisted ironically. "I see much the same in you, although you are worse. Dar enjoys a good wager, but I think you *need* it."

"For as long as I can remember." He did not smile, not

try to avoid the topic. "I do not lose myself in *lir*-shape, perhaps, understanding the need for self-control . . . but a wager is different. I *do* lose myself."

"And so the balance is broken, and you tip over the edge." Ilsa looked at him squarely. "Last night you told me you take pride in nothing. I think you lied, albeit unknowing. If nothing else, you take pride in being Cheysuli; in the ability to become a hawk and know the freedom of the skies."

He did not look away. "Aye."

"Then I offer you a challenge, my lord. I offer you risk." Ilsa smiled a little. "Put it aside, Hart. Set aside this need of the game, and look instead to becoming a prince in fact. Solinde is in the palm of your hand. Grasp it, my lord, or surely you will lose it."

"It is *out* of my hand," he said. "Blame me, blame Dar, blame us both, but we have undertaken a wager that will end this controversy over Solinde. One of us will be the victor, the other the vanquished . . . with you and Solinde in the middle."

Ilsa went rigid in her saddle. "What have you done?" Her face was taut and pale. *"What have you done?"*

Hart drew in a deep breath. "I came to see you intending to tell you the truth at once. I delayed it because it was easier, as always, to avoid speaking of it at all, and because I wanted to spend time with you. And so now the time for truth is on me once again, I find I have no more desire to spoil what is between us than I did before."

"Hart—"

"You must wed," he said clearly, overriding the beginnings of her protest. "And wed soon, for the sake of Solinde. For all I avoid responsibility whenever possible, I am no stranger to political intrigues and marriages. Three choices face you, Ilsa: wed me, wed Dar, or wed another powerful Solindishman with the ability to help you hold Solinde."

She said nothing.

Hart did not look away. "If you delay, my own hold on Solinde increases; are they not advocating you wed within a month?" Grimly he nodded, though she remained locked in rigid silence. "If you wed Dar, Solinde will one day revolt; he has as much as promised it. If you wed another

Solindishman, there will always be those who advocate rebellion. If you wed *me*—"

Ilsa cut him off. "Why?" she asked flatly. "Why would I wed you? You offer me nothing, my lord wagerer . . . you offer nothing to Solinde save irreverence and irresponsibility."

"The wager is this," he said quietly. "If you wed me, Dar gives over the Third Seal—and his life. If you wed Dar, I am sent home to Homana . . . and Solinde remains Solindish."

"Under a Homanan regent!" Color spilled into her face, then out again. "Dar put up his *life?*"

"Aye, lady—at his own behest. I do not want it."

"But you accepted the wager!"

"I am on the edge of the blade," he said clearly. "If I go home to my *jehan*, having lost Solinde, I will have lost him as well. Worse, I will have destroyed the prophecy." Hart nodded slowly. "Aye, Ilsa, I accepted the wager. Dar gave me no other choice."

"What choice did you give *him?*" He saw tears in her eyes. "If he loses this wager, he loses his *life!* I think that is more important than a Cheysuli prophecy—"

"One life is little when balanced against a race," Hart told her quietly. "Hear me, Ilsa, when I tell you that above all, I serve the prophecy. Wastrel that I have been, I am fully committed to this. Aye, you spoke of pride—and I *do* take pride in something. I take pride in the prophecy."

"So you leave the choice to me," she said bitterly. "Yet again you turn your back on responsibility and reduce the future of Solinde to a wager and a woman's choice of husband." She said something more, equally bitterly, but the words were Solindish, and he did not know them. He knew only that he had angered her far more than even he had anticipated.

"Ilsa—"

"Did Dar put you up to this?" she asked abruptly.

He considered lying, knowing the truth made him appear vindictive. But he nodded. "It was his suggestion."

Ilsa shook her head, pushing hair out of her face in irritation. "You are a fool, my lord prince of wagerers. Dar knows me too well, and he has learned you also. As he expected, all my pride screams at me to wed Dar if for no other reason than to *force* your loss, and your subsequent loss of Solinde. And I would . . . if my better judgment would allow it." She looked at him squarely. "If only to pay him back, I should refuse him. But it would cost him his life, and that I cannot bear."

"There is an alternative," Hart said quietly. "Wed another man entirely."

"*What* other man?" Ilsa asked bitterly. "There is no other man in Solinde who can do what Dar can to rally the Solindish to war again. We are too weary of such things. Niall and those before him have defeated us soundly too many times. Without the right leader, what good would it do us now?" She shrugged. "But Dar could do what is necessary, and would. If I wanted this war, I would be a fool to wed a Solindishman other than Dar." He saw the turmoil reflected in her eyes, in her features. "But if I wed you to save my land from war, it costs me Dar. And that price I will not pay."

"Then wed no one."

Ilsa's sharp laugh was little more than a sound of despair. "If I do not choose *someone*, I will be forced to it. The situation warrants it; they have not done it only because they respect me personally, and my heritage. But for Solinde, to thwart Homana, they will. They will have no other choice."

"Ilsa—"

She gathered her reins and turned the mare toward Lestra. "Forgive me, my lord, but I desire solitude. I have no taste for your company."

He knew better than to allow her to depart under such circumstances. But he knew also that to stop her was to destroy all hope of winning her. And so he let her go.

Seven

Tarron's move to assemble more parchments was arrested in mid-motion. "I must have misheard you. You want *what*, my lord?"

Helpfully, Hart gathered the parchments from the table and placed them on the stack in Tarron's arms. "I want you to teach me how to rule. It *is* what I came for."

"No," Tarron said plainly, "you came because you were *sent.*"

Hart scowled at him. "Aye, aye, all right—I came because I was sent. But I am done with shirking my responsibilities. Teach me how to rule."

"Have you seen the Mujhar do none of it?"

Oh, aye, he had, in bits and pieces. But he had steadfastly refused to attend council sessions, petition hearings, and other assorted requirements of kingship, perfectly willing to let Brennan do it all instead. He had a rudimentary knowledge of what constituted governing—the ruler had to sit in judgment on citizens who had disputes, settle treaties between other realms, levy taxes, tribute, and so on, plus innumerable other duties—but when it came down to it, he had not the faintest idea what was expected of him. Particularly in a foreign realm.

"Teach me," he said only, hoping it was enough.

Apparently it was, although Tarron eyed him doubtfully. "Well enough, my lord; follow me. I am bound for a hearing regarding a petty dispute between two northern Solindish lordlings. They are feuding over a boundary formed by a river; the river has changed its course, and now they dispute ownership of the land it has laid bare."

Dutifully Hart followed Tarron out of the chamber into a corridor, though his heart was not in it. He opened his mouth to beg off, then shut it sharply. It was time he learned to accept tedium as gracefully as his father and brother.

"Without the Third Seal, what can you do?" he asked.

Parchment crackled. "Delay," the regent said succinctly. "No real business can be conducted without it, but until I hear from the Mujhar I cannot let slip the news the Seal is lost. We must hope the Solindish do not grow restless over countless delays and obfuscation . . . I think they will not understand why it is you lost it in a *game.*"

Hart ignored the latter. "And if Dar has already let it be known?"

"It would certainly serve his own interests." Tarron nodded as guardsmen in Homanan livery swung open the heavy wooden doors of the audience chamber. "But perhaps this will serve yours, my lord; if you are the one to make the decision, it will let the Solindish know you are indeed planning to rule." He nodded greetings toward the men waiting in the chamber and made his way to a table on a dais.

"Me?" Following, Hart kept his voice low. "I have no experience in such things."

"I suggest you get it, my lord, as any man does: by listening, and by determining which party deserves the judgment rendered in his favor." Tarron put the stack of parchments on the table and stepped away, motioning Hart to accept the only chair. "And now, my lord, I leave you to it."

Astonished, Hart watched the regent turn and walk away. He wanted to shout after him, to *order* him back, but he would not, not before the Solindish lordlings who waited to present their case.

Oh, gods. Lamely, he smiled at the lords. They stared back grimly, hard old men, prepared to humor no one. *Oh, gods.* But he summoned what he could of his courage and sat down, intending to do whatever it was a ruler did to the best of his ability.

Even if he had none.

After dark, Hart ordered a horse and rode to The White Swan. He felt after a day spent listening to two old Solindish lordlings arguing who had more right to the new parcel of land—mostly in incomprehensible Solindish no matter how many times he requested Homanan—he deserved an evening's entertainment. But he made up his mind not to wager, only to while away the hours in a hospitable tavern.

Or even an *in*hospitable tavern.

By now most of the regular patrons were accustomed to his presence. He still was not precisely welcomed, but neither was he greeted with hostile stares and crude comments. Now most of them shrugged and turned back to their games, leaving him to his own devices.

Unless Dar was present. But this time, for the first part of the evening, he was not, so Hart sat by himself at a table and drank ale, forgoing wine entirely.

The wine-girl, Oma, made a particular point of flashing the Homanan signet ring in his face whenever she could. Eventually he called her over and offered to buy it back, but she merely grinned and shook him off. She was too shrewd to give in so easily, and too pleased by the grim frustration she caused him. And so in the end he gave it up entirely, turning back to his ale, and lost himself in contemplation.

Until Dar came.

The Solindishman glittered with silver and sapphires at collar, cuffs, wrists, fingers, and belt, ice against indigo velvet. The royal colors, Hart knew, and wondered if Dar had dressed for him in the spirit of the wager. But then he spoke, and Hart knew he had dressed for no man at all.

"I have been with Ilsa," he said calmly, sitting down at the table without bothering to wait for an invitation. "A most sumptuous meal, and served by the lady herself." A raised finger brought Oma with a cup and his favorite wine. "She told me an interesting tale."

"Did she?" Hart drank ale.

Dar waited for Oma to pour his cup full, then waved her away. Over the rim of the cup he assessed Hart. He sipped thoughtfully, then thumped the cup down onto the table. "So, you thought to win her through frankness."

"I thought to be frank with her for the sake of honesty and honor, not because of the wager," Hart said quietly. "Let us end it, Dar. It is a travesty. It is unfair to Ilsa *and* Solinde."

Dar did not smile. "Then declare it a forfeit. Go home to Homana in the morning, and do not come back again."

Hart matched him stare for stare. "You know I cannot."

"I know you *should* . . . and, one day soon, you will. When I have won."

"You are so certain of her, then?"

Dar smiled. "What choice is there, shapechanger? She wants me to live—she told me so herself—so she will not choose you. She would prefer Solinde remain Solindish; again, so she will not choose you. She would prefer a man she knows as Consort, so she will not choose one of the other lords." He drank again, then leaned forward intently. "She will name *my* name, shapechanger. Be certain of it."

Hart smiled. "Then why are you so *un*certain?" His smile widened as Dar's lids flickered. "No matter what she may have said to you tonight, you still are not sure. You still have doubts. You know there is a good chance she may choose me after all."

"Ilsa will do what is right for Solinde."

"She will do what is best for all concerned." Hart poured more ale into his cup. "It is how such decisions are made; one weighs all issues, and then one decides which best serves all involved." It was what he had done with the old lords and their river dispute, though he could offer nothing until the Seal was recovered.

Dar said nothing for a long moment, then shouted for Oma to bring the Bezat bowl. But Hart shook his head as the stones were offered.

"No?" Dar's sandy brows lifted. "*You* say no?"

"I say no." Hart drank ale. "The game begins to pall, Dar . . . I will pass."

Dar slapped his belt-purse down on the table. Red gold chimed.

Hart smiled. "No."

Dar stripped his fingers and wrists of gem-studded silver. Still Hart smiled. "No."

"What do you want?" the Solindishman asked. "The Seal is already wagered." He smiled suddenly. "The stallion. You want to win back the stallion Ilsa gave you."

Slowly Hart shook his head.

Dar's brown eyes narrowed. "Then *what?*"

"To watch you squirm," Hart said softly, "and now I have seen it without wagering even a silver penny." He pushed his stool back, scraping it against hardwood, and rang down a red coin on the table to pay for his ale. "You *will* lose, Dar. Ilsa. Solinde. Your life. Because I have learned when to stop, and you have not even begun."

Dar rose abruptly. "Shapechanger—"

"Cheysuli," Hart said gently, and walked quietly out of the tavern.

He was in a private room adjoining his bedchamber, slumped in a chair and lost in thought, when a servant knocked at his door. He considered ignoring the knock, then gave it up and went to the door.

"My lord." Not a servant at all, but Tarron. "My lord, a message has come from the Lady Ilsa. She requests your presence at once." He paused. "I know the messenger; the summons is genuine."

"Now?" It struck him as odd she would send a message at night, though it was not late.

"Aye, my lord." Although perfectly polite, the tone in Tarron's voice told Hart the regent thought it just as unusual. "The message is that a decision has been made, and she would have you and Dar of High Crags know it at once so the travesty may be ended." Tarron frowned. "My lord—"

Hart raised a silencing hand. "Do not ask, regent. When I return, you will have your answer. It may please you—or it may not." He chewed his bottom lip a moment, thinking deeply. "Tell her messenger I will come at once."

"Aye, my lord." But still Tarron lingered. "If there is anything you wish to confide in me, be certain I will hold it in strictest confidence."

Hart smiled. "I trust you, Tarron. But this is between a man and a woman—no, between *men* and a woman—and until I know the lady's answer, there is no sense in confiding anything. When I can, I shall."

The regent inclined his head. "Aye, my lord. Of course." And he was gone.

Hart shut the door and turned to look at Rael, perched on his now-empty chair. "Well? Do I dress to celebrate, or to exile myself from yet another realm?"

If you delay to change your clothing, she may change her mind.

Hart grinned. "Aye. And if she has chosen in my favor, I would do well not to give her that chance." He nodded thoughtfully and opened the door again. "We go, *lir* . . . to gain a *cheysula*, or lose a realm."

He thought of Brennan as he ordered a horse saddled and brought. No doubt his *rujho* would compliment him on his decision to take a *cheysula*, even if it was not his decision at all. Brennan would tell him he was finally growing up, maturing, becoming the man he was meant to be.

He sent a wry glance heavenward. *Brennan would no doubt tell me I am only answering my* tahlmorra.

And perhaps you are. Rael, sounding insufferably smug, circled over the bailey as the horse was brought.

Hart sighed and swung up, gathering reins hastily as the bay stallion stomped and snorted his displeasure at having his evening meal interrupted. Hart took a deeper seat and reined him in, calling his thanks to the groom, and went out of the bailey at a long-trot.

Iron rang on stone as Hart guided the bay through the winding streets of Lestra. Ilsa's dwelling was not far from the palace, but the journey took too long nonetheless; his belly was so twisted up he was afraid he might never be able to eat again. He could not begin to predict Ilsa's decision, though he had been foolish enough to wager on it. And, the gods knew, wagered more than he could afford to lose.

Much more, he thought hollowly as the shadows and torchlight played tag along the walls. *Fool that I am, I should have known better. It is no wonder* jehan *banished me for a year; I have been gone but three months, and already I have risked a realm, myself . . . the prophecy.* He gritted his teeth. *Rael, what do I tell him if the wager is lost?*

The truth. Rael responded. *No matter what the punishment, the loss of Solinde is worth it.*

It was not the comfort Hart sought. Disgruntled, he withdrew from the link altogether.

One of Ilsa's servants waited outside as Hart drew the stallion to a halt. He dismounted slowly, delaying the moment of truth, and handed over the reins. Rael perched himself upon the roof. No light showed from the house, for all the windows were shuttered against the night air. Hart drew in a breath so deep it made him light-headed, and then he knocked on the door.

He was shown to a private receiving chamber warmed

by a blazing fire and was offered wine, ale, or *usca*. He declined all, too nervous to drink, and asked when the lady would present herself.

"As soon as my lord of High Crags arrives, my lord," the servant answered, and bowed himself out.

"Except the lord of High Crags is already present." Dar stepped out of a curtained antechamber. With him were six men, all in Solindish livery.

Oddly, Hart felt relieved. At last the man had shown his true colors. "Where is Ilsa?"

"Ilsa has gone to bed," Dar said quietly as one of his men moved to lock the door from the inside. "Ilsa has done her part of this night's work by summoning you here; the rest is left to me."

Hart nodded. "And what are your plans, Dar? To pack me off to Homana before the wager is settled?"

Dar grinned and waved a casual forefinger. His men moved closer to Hart. "Which wager, shapechanger? The one between you and me—or the one I struck with Strahan?"

That, Hart had not expected. He was unsurprised by the six men who clearly meant him no good, but he had not considered that Ihlini would enter into it. "What has Strahan to do with this?" he asked curtly, trying to ignore the tightening of his belly. "*You* are not Ihlini; Rael would have known it."

"No, I am not Ihlini," Dar agreed. "But I *am* an ambitious man, as well as one desirous of winning favor with those in power, and Strahan offered me something I could not pass by. Of course, he couched it as a wager; he said he did not believe I could do it. So now I have done it, and he will pay me my price." Dar grinned. "One way or another, the lady will be mine."

Hart felt strangely relaxed. There were no Ihlini in the room, and Rael was on the roof. Although the windows were shuttered against his entry, his closeness still lent Hart all the power he needed to assume *lir*-shape. Dar had badly underestimated his enemy.

"Dar—"

But he was given no chance to finish his sentence. Six men laid hands on him, and none were gentle.

"Bring him here." Dar indicated the ironwood table.

Hart resisted, but six to one were not good odds. "Dar, it is easy enough to trap a man, but not so easy to trap a hawk—"

"Draw your sword." Dar ignored Hart altogether, speaking to one of the men. The Solindishman did so, waiting attentively.

Rael— Triggering the link, Hart drew on the magic in his blood.

"Hold him," Dar said. "Stretch out his left arm so the flat of his hand is on the wood. *Quickly!*"

Hart tapped the power.

Smoothly, Dar drew his knife and stabbed it through the splayed hand, pinning it to the table. "There," he said. "Shapechange *now,* shapechanger."

Pain burst in his hand and set the world afire. Too shocked to do anything more than gape, Hart knew the shapechange was banished. As he had so clearly told Ilsa, a man in extremity lacked the required concentration.

Dar's eyes were dilated black. "Once you told me you would sooner wager your left hand than your *lir*, shapechanger. Well, you have lost the wager. And now you have lost the hand." He signaled the man with the sword. "Hack it off. *Now.*"

The blow was swift and very clean, slicing through flesh and bone to stop short in the ironwood. And painless, so stunned was Hart. Standing only by dint of the men who held him up, he stared at the arm that now ended at his wrist.

Rael—Rael—RAEL—

Dar made a moue of distaste. "So much blood," he said. And then he himself fetched the iron from the fire and slapped white-hot tip against stump.

Hart meant to scream. But it died aborning as he collapsed into the arms of Dar's men.

Interlude

Lillith looked down on her brother. Strahan knelt on one knee at the rim of the vent, at the edge of the Gate itself. One hand was outthrust, palm down, as if he intended to summon Asar-Suti himself. As perhaps he did; white flame licked up, touched, curled around the fingers, gloved his hand entirely, then deepened to lilac, to lavender, to deepest lurid purple. In its reflection, Strahan smiled his beautiful, deadly smile.

She saw a tendril of flame slip beneath the cuff of his doublet, beneath the white edge of his linen shirt. Where it went she could not follow, for it cloaked itself in his clothing; then, abruptly, it blossomed at his collar, caressed the flesh of his neck, touched a gentle fingertip to the sharp-edged line of his jaw.

Still Strahan smiled. Even *she* no longer smiled, but he was lost to her utterly, caught up in eerie intercourse with the god of the netherworld, who made and dwells in darkness. Still he knelt, smiling, as the flame flowed out of the Gate to his hand, then upward to his neck, and began to lap at his face.

Strahan's lips parted. A thin, tensile wire of flame touched, withdrew, touched again, then flowed up to shape his mouth into something more than flesh. Emboldened, more tendrils appeared, and within, a matter of moments Strahan's face was alive with a webwork of fragile purple lace. It overlay his features, shaping them into those of another man—or into the god himself.

"*Strahan*—" But Lillith stopped herself. It was not her place to remonstrate with her brother, who was the god's own chosen. It was her place only to serve, accepting all that was asked, offering whatever she could.

Strahan laughed. He was ablaze with delicate fire, and

yet fabric and flesh was untouched. Kneeling, he was an incongruous torch; laughing, he was far more than merely human, even by sorcerous standards.

And then, abruptly, the webwork came undone. Tendrils withdrew, untying knots; untied, the knots fell into disarray. Within moments Strahan was merely Strahan, and the god was gone from him.

He shut his eyes and released a shuddering breath of deep satisfaction, as if he had lain with a woman. Head bowed, he made his obeisance to the god, and then he rose to face his sister across the glowing Gate.

"Done," he said. "Dar has won his wager."

"One you are pleased to lose." Lillith sighed herself; he seemed perfectly normal again. "And the woman? Will you pay his price?"

Strahan smiled. "Dar is an overly ambitious man with overweening pride. One day he and his pride will stumble over those ambitions, and he will fall."

It was not precisely the answer she wanted; perhaps he was still caught in the thrall of the god, speaking of things she could not know. "How will you break this one?"

Strahan shrugged. "I think it is already done, or very nearly so. The Cheysuli can be a hard, seemingly heartless race, even with their own; the clans require *whole* men as warriors, unmaimed—whole in flesh as well as spirit in order to maintain the viability of the race. Much like animals, they cull the pack of the weakest in order to protect the rest." Again he shrugged. "Perhaps they have the right of it; *I* have no use for the weak."

Lillith, smiling secretly, thought it an understatement. "And how will you 'mend' this one?"

Strahan laughed. "By offering him a reason to live again. Service to me can make him whole, though not in the way he might wish. But by *then* it will not matter—he will be too firmly bound."

Deftly she smoothed the velvet of her skirts. "Only one—the youngest—remains. It is time I went to Atvia."

Strahan looked at her, but she knew he did not see her. "Safe journey," he said only, then knelt again at the edge of the Gate.

PART IV

Corin

One

Faster. Faster. *Faster—*

He bent low in the saddle, low, so that the pommel ground into his belly and his cheek was pressed against the stallion's dampening neck. Whipping gray mane stung Corin's eyes until they teared; he found release in it, knowing he need not be ashamed of tears shed because of irritation to the eyes themselves, and not anguish of the heart.

Faster—

The world was a collage of green and blue, brown and gray, all blurred together by tears. He clutched leather reins and pushed them forward against the stallion's neck, giving him his head. On and on the blue roan ran, doing his rider's bidding.

Beneath clamped legs fluid muscles bunched, rolled, stretched, tautened, fed by the pumping of the stallion's great heart. Corin tasted dirt and horsehair; smelled the acrid tang of sweat and wet blankets. In his ears was the song of a winded horse; the rhythmic pounding beat of iron-shod hooves against hard-packed road. In his heart was anguish.

Oh, gods—forbidden my home for a year— And he squeezed the stallion yet again with legging-clad legs, urging him faster yet.

You will kill the horse.

For a moment Corin did not recognize Kiri's tone. He was so caught up in the sound and rhythm of the horse and the weight of his own pain that he had neglected to think of the vixen.

He turned his head against damp horsehair and peered over his shoulder. Far behind, in the sienna-colored dust of his passing, he saw the rich red flash of his *lir.*

If not the horse, you will kill me.

That stopped him as nothing else could. Corin sat upright in the saddle, gathering reins, and eased the stallion down. Slowly, carefully; for all he was angry and hurt and frightened, he had no wish to ruin the roan.

If he had not already.

Slowly. Slowly. From gallop to canter, canter to trot, trot to winded walk, head dropped, nostrils sucking and blowing great gulps of air as the stallion tried to answer the demand of his heaving lungs. Guiltily Corin freed his right foot from the stirrup and swung it over the roan's damp, blue-washed rump, letting his weight linger briefly in the left stirrup and against his thigh. He did not halt the stallion but let him walk on, knowing the roan needed careful tending if he was to recover completely.

Corin dropped off and kept moving, dragging reins free of the dangling head to lead the horse onward. Sweat ran down the roan's face. Lather flecked chest and flanks. He stumbled over hooves but newly-shod.

Still walking, Corin half-turned and looked over a shoulder for Kiri. No longer did she run, trotting instead; he could see the brush of her black-tipped tail swinging behind her hocks. Closer now, he could see the glint of eyes in her mask, and the lolling of her tongue.

Remorse surged up at once. *Oh, lir, I am sorry. I should know better than to punish you.*

Save your apologies for the horse. I have a choice; he does not.

Corin looked again at the roan stallion. He had served well and faithfully for three years, and was rewarded with thoughtless, cruel behavior. Walking on, not daring to stop until the stallion was cooler, Corin ran a soothing palm down the proud nose and promised him better treatment.

Guilt clenched the wall of his belly yet again. *It is no wonder* jehan *feels it necessary to punish me . . . I give him reason enough.*

Then stop, the vixen suggested.

"How?" Corin asked aloud, clearly frustrated. "There are times I grow so angry I cannot control myself, knowing only that I have been wronged. And when I try to explain, *jehan* will not listen."

What is there to explain when your behavior has ac-

*counted for the lives of twenty-eight people—perhaps even
more?*

The guilt rose higher in his belly, reaching out cruel fingers to grasp, twist, pinch. "That was Hart." He had meant
it to defend and accuse all at once, but his tone was subdued instead, full of acknowledgment. Aye, twenty-eight
people dead, probably more, all because he and Hart had
insisted on going to the Midden, which was a place none
of them frequented for a very good reason.

Well, it *had* been Hart's idea.

And yet he had contributed.

"To save my life," he said aloud. "They would have slain
us all."

Kiri caught up and trotted next to his left leg. Briefly she
pressed a shoulder against him, then dropped aside again.
Courage, lir—*the Mujhar disputes your self-defense less than
the reasons for your presence in the tavern. All of you dis-
obeyed orders—that is the bone of contention. Had you not,
no one would be dead.* She paused thoughtfully. *Or at least
they would be dead by their own murdering hands, and not
by careless fire.*

"No one *meant* it to happen," he murmured unhappily.
"And yet *jehan* refuses to listen to that, hearing only that
his sons were involved in yet another tavern brawl." Corin
shrugged a little, rolling shoulder blades uncomfortably in
an attempt to assuage his guilt, or to push it away. "Had
he given us the chance, we might have been able to help.
He might only have stripped us of our allowances, giving
them to the survivors, rather than of our freedom."

Lives cannot be bought. Kiri's tone lacked even a trace
of sympathy. *As for freedom, you would not know it if it
bit your nose from your face. A man can only know true
freedom when he understands or experiences its loss, so the
value becomes greater.*

Corin slanted her a resentful glance beneath half-shut
lids. "Are you finished?" he asked grimly.

Are you?

Corin sighed heavily, expelling acknowledgment along
with breath. "Aye," he said unevenly, "I am. One way or
another, I will have to learn to depend only on myself. And
right now, that does not please me. Another man would
not depend on me—how can I? I know what I am as much

as anyone else." He kicked a stone out of his path and watched it skitter across the road into the turf of the meadowlands. The stallion was so winded he did not even notice. "I am, betimes, sullen and resentful, selfish and moody, unresponsive and angry. Or so my *jehan* has said, and Deirdre, and Ian, over the scope of years. No doubt others have said more, and worse." He sighed. "I like it no more than they, but I cannot help myself."

You are already helping yourself.

Corin drew in a breath that filled his belly with doubt. "And you? What of you, Kiri? Do you stay with me only out of duty to the gods, and not through loyalty to me? Do you dislike me for my temper?"

I dislike your temper, not you, the fox said quietly. *As for staying with you, what choice have I? I was chosen for you and you for me . . . there is a purpose in all things the gods do. As for personal loyalty, why question it? I would not leave you even if you beat me.*

"I would never beat you!"

Yet you beat the horse in the name of your fear and anger.

Corin looked at the horse in the stallion. The roan breathed more easily and was no longer wringing wet, although he was hardly fully restored. Corin stroked the blue-white nose again, scratching the heavy jaw, and promised he would never ride him so hard again.

Lir.

Corin glanced around. Kiri had stopped, standing in the center of the road, and stared upward into the sky. Corin did likewise, holding the stallion back, and lifted a hand to shield his eyes against the sun.

"Hawk—" he said. His pulse quickened; was it Hart sent to fetch him back? Corin had left a day early. Had his *jehan* repented of his sentence?

But he knew better. Niall had made it a royal decree as well as a parental one; the banishment would hold for the precise number of days it took to fulfill twelve months.

The hawk spiraled, drifted, floated down, and Corin nodded as the blur of the shapechange swallowed the raptor. His senses, as always, reeled momentarily, then settled; the disorientation faded quickly as the hawk exchanged bird-form for human.

Keely grinned. "Did you think I would let you go out of Homana alone?"

He stared at her. "You cannot mean to come *with* me!"

"Why not?" She spread her hands. "There are no duties incumbent upon me except to give my *rujho* whatever aid and support he requires.'

Corin looked at her. She was slim and wiry in snug Cheysuli leathers, dressed like a warrior though there was no doubting she was a woman; the brass-buckled belt hid nothing of slender waist or the smooth swelling of breasts and hips. Gone were the days she could stuff her hair beneath a huntsman's cap and swagger like a man with impunity. Now she did neither, for her tawny hair hung free in a plaited braid, and she made no attempt to swagger. She had no need of it; as much as any of them, Keely claimed inbred pride and confidence of carriage.

He smiled, and the smile spread slowly into a grin. Trust Keely. . . . "You should not come," he told her, though it lacked true conviction. "The banishment is my punishment, not yours. In this we need not share."

"We share in everything, *rujho*." Her blue eyes were very steady. "*Everything*—except, perhaps, your taste for bedding women." Her mouth hooked ironically. "That I leave to you."

"*Your* taste runs to bedding men?"

The humor slipped perceptibly. "My taste runs to belonging only to myself," Keely said grimly. "If that means I keep myself apart from men, so be it. I am willing."

He grunted. "Sean of Erinn may have something to say about that."

"Sean of Erinn will have nothing at all to say." Keely was very calm, *too* calm. "Sean of Erinn will take what he gets—or look to wedding another woman entirely."

Corin laughed. "If he *does* get you, Keely, be certain he will take you." He used the word in the crudest sense, knowing it might be the only way she would hear what he had to say. "Aside from needing an heir for Erinn, he might wish to enjoy his *cheysula*."

" 'Enjoy,' " Keely said grimly. "Indeed, 'enjoy.' I hope he will *enjoy* a foot of steel in his belly if he presses me when I have no desire for it."

He shouted aloud with laughter. "Since I think you will

be naked in your marriage bed, Keely, it might be difficult to hide a knife." Corin raised a hand as she started to protest. "Have you come to discuss your personal dislike for the betrothal, or my own banishment? You will forgive me, I trust, if at the moment I am less inclined to sympathize with *your* plight when I have my own."

Abruptly she was contrite. "Oh, Corin, I know. It is so unfair! *Jehan* had no right to do it, no right at all . . . how *can* he do it? How can he send two of his sons out of Homana into things they cannot know?"

There were times he wished he shared more of Keely's temperament in addition to coloring. She was outspoken and high-spirited, and equally subject—as he was—to outbursts of hot temper, but she was more charitable, more generous in her feelings. She thought less of herself than of others, and always supported him without thought for what such support might mean to her father's opinion of her.

"He can do it," he said, "because he is our *jehan*, and because he is the Mujhar."

"Rank excuses nothing," she flung back instantly.

"Aye," Corin agreed wryly, "and *jehan* would say it certainly does not excuse the behavior of his sons."

Trapped, she glared at him. "Do you *want* to go?"

"No," he said succinctly. "Do you?"

Keely opened her mouth, then snapped it shut. After a moment she shook her head a little. "Defy him. What could he do to you? You are his son. Moreover, you are a part of the prophecy."

"A dutiful son does as his father commands. A part of the prophecy knows better than to defy him."

"But *you* have never been dutiful," Keely retorted, "and who is to know what your *tahlmorra* is but you—" She shrugged. "Come back to Homana-Mujhar and face him down, Corin. Defy him. Refuse to go. He cannot have you tied up and hauled bodily to Atvia. It would soil his own honor as much as yours." Keely grinned. "If we *both* faced him—"

"If we both faced him, it would only underscore the need for discipline," Conn said grimly, "and all the while Brennan would be standing there like the dutiful son—nodding, agreeing, supporting our *jehan*—because that is what he does best. *Jehan* need only look at his heir to see the sort of son he desires, and then he *would* order me tied up and hauled bodily to Atvia.''

Exasperated, she glared at him with rigid hands clamped on hips. "Then what *do* you intend to do?"

"Go to Atvia." He sighed and rubbed the roan's muzzle. "With a stop in Erinn, as *jehan* has ordered."

Keely's eyes narrowed. "You would do well to listen to yourself sometime, *rujho*. On one hand you blow and bluster and threaten to do this or that . . . on the other you meekly give in and do what you have been asked—or told—to do. If you *intend* to do as told, why make so much noise in the first place?"

For an answer, Corin turned sharply and walked on, taking the stallion with him. And then he stopped short, swinging to face her again. "Listen to *yourself*," he suggested curtly. "It is no wonder Deirdre despairs of ever making a woman out of you."

"Oh?" Her tone was infinitely deadly.

Corin indicated her clothing. "Do you ask why? You are in leggings every time I see you, disdaining skirts or gowns . . . you talk our *su'fali* into teaching you the knife and sword and bow when the Homanan arms-master will not . . . you absent yourself from Homana-Mujhar to run wild in the wood . . . you spend no time with Deirdre's women, learning how to behave as the Lady of Erinn must. . . ." He shook his head. "You drink *usca*, Keely, and dice nearly as much as Hart—"

"—and nearly as well." She smiled grimly. "Go on, Corin. Do not stop now."

He signed. "And you persist in denying a willingness to wed a man who will one day be king of Erinn and, through you, a part of the prophecy. You deny your own *tahlmorra*, and then tell me to do the same with mine."

"It is hardly a denial of willingness when I do not *wish* to wed him," she said coolly. "As to the others, I will not deny that I would be as soon forswear womanly things altogether. Given a choice, I would be warrior in place of wife."

"And man in place of woman?"

Keely laughed in genuine amusement. "No, you fool— even *you* seek the easy answer! I have no desire to be a *man* . . . what I want is to be myself. I want the freedom to choose what I will do instead of fulfilling expectations of my behavior." She shrugged. "I would do better in the clan than at Homana-Mujhar, but even there I would not know the freedom I crave. There are no women warriors . . . and I am the daughter of the Lion. They see that before all else." She sighed and tugged pensively at her braid. "Shall we go, *rujho?* I ache to see Hondarth. I have never been *anywhere* but Clankeep or Mujhara."

Corin considered ordering her home; discarded it at once. He considered *suggesting* she go home; he knew better. For all she prated of having no freedom, she claimed more than most. It took a stronger man than he to enforce his preferences when Keely's determination was so firmly entrenched.

I will leave it to Sean. Corin surrendered, nodding. "I am walking, for the moment. The roan needs rest."

"So I see." Keely shook her head. "Better you shout at me, next time, than burden your horse with your anger. At least I know when to defy you."

"Defiance," he muttered. "Is that all you know?"

"Better to ask the same of yourself." Sweetly, she smiled at him. "Shall we go? Hondarth beckons."

He raised his brows and pursed lips thoughtfully. "Hondarth will never recover."

But he said nothing more as he started walking and Keely fell in beside him. His *lir* trotted ahead, head dipping as she sniffed grass and dirt. The day was warm, the sun bright, the sky infinitely blue. Moreover, he was *Cheysuli;* it made him a man truly blessed.

Abruptly, unexpectedly, Corin was content. If he had to go to Atvia, at least he had the best company he could think of.

They sold the stallion in Hondarth, much as Corin hated to part with him. There would be no room on the ship for a mount, and he could get another in Atvia. He would have sent the roan home with Keely, except she refused to go back. And so with their purses considerably plumper, they stopped before a tavern.

Keely gestured. "As good as another, *rujho.*"

He looked askance at her. "A waterfront tavern? I think not. We would do better to go farther from the docks."

She stood with booted feet planted. "I want wine, and I am hungry. If you fear trouble because I am a woman, remember I have a knife."

"See how I shiver from fear?" Corin asked dryly. "I think the men who frequent taverns of this sort will hardly be deterred by a knife in a woman's hand."

She shrugged. "Then I will resort to *lir*-shape, if they force me. Corin—let us go *in*—" She caught his jerkin and dragged him toward the door, even as he craned his head to look for Kiri.

Inside, Keely had the good sense to release his jerkin, which he absently pulled back into shape. He thought briefly, in case of trouble, he would claim her his woman: a glance at Keely's face made him think better of it. In sleeveless jerkin, leggings, and boots much like his own, with identical coloring and similar features, no one would believe it. Their kinship was too evident.

Keely sniffed. "Fish."

"Hondarth *is* a seaport." Corin glanced around the tavern. He had seen better; he had certainly seen worse. The light was dim, but not nonexistent. Nothing led him to believe they courted trouble. There were no covert glances hiding ill will, no rude comments on Keely's apparel, no private jests about the vixen who flanked one side. The patrons looked at the newcomers curiously, as anyone would, then turned back to private business without excess incivility.

"A table." Already Keely was striding toward it, boot heels thumping against hardwood floor. Men watched her, elbowed partners, made comments, but they watched with an appreciation significantly lacking in rudeness or raillery.

Corin let out a breath, surprised to discover he had been holding it. All his life he had done what he could to keep his headstrong sister free from trouble, and sometimes he succeeded. But the task was more difficult when she seemed purposely to flout convention. He did not entirely blame her—he himself would go mad as a woman, confined to women's work—but neither did he fully understand her dedication to defiance. She *was* a woman—should she not behave as one?

She is also a Cheysuli, and gifted more than most, Kiri reminded him. *She has the Old Blood in abundance. Do you expect her to behave as a dutiful Homanan woman?*

The thought of Keely portraying herself as a meek, docile woman thinking only of her man's pleasure made Corin grin. But he was doing an injustice to the female portion of Homana's population; they were not *all* meek and docile. Certainly enough of Deirdre's Homanan ladies were spirited, in bed or out of it.

Women. Following his sister, he cast an assessive glance around the tavern. If there was a likely wine-girl present, he might pass the night pleasurably indeed.

And then he recalled Keely. Glumly, he reflected he could hardly tell his sister to hunt up a private room for herself while he disported himself with the wine-girl. It would only invite trouble. He sighed. With Hart or Brennan things were much less complicated; although Brennan tended to keep himself to court ladies, neither he nor Hart were averse to spending time with wine-girls, and they certainly made no protest when Corin did. But Keely might.

He reached the table. She was already seated, hunched forward on a stool, and looking about with interest. Corin could not remember a time he had taken her into a tavern, even in Mujhara; away from the palace, away from Clankeep, they generally frequented inns or roadhouses, where the clientele was different.

Corin hooked out a stool and sat down slowly, one hand touching Kiri's heavy ruff. Her presence, he saw, had been noted, remarked on, accepted. If there were mutters of beasts and shapechangers, he heard none of them. And yet he recalled the stories of how his grandsire, Donal, had met only hatred and prejudice when he had come to Hondarth.

A step sounded behind him. He thought nothing of it until he saw Keely's hand slip to her knife, and then he half-turned. He was stopped by a big hand on his shoulder.

"Be ye Cheysuli?" asked the man with the paw of a bear, or so it seemed to Corin. "Or a Homanan masquerading as such?"

Corin tried to shake off the paw. Keely, he saw, was leaning forward as if to rise; beside him, Kiri's lips peeled back to show sharp white teeth. "Why?" he asked coldly. "And why should it matter which?"

"Because if ye be Cheysuli, I'll be buying you a drink, you and the lass. If ye only *play* at it, lad, I've no business with either of ye."

The accent was familiar, though far thicker than Deirdre's fading lilt. Corin grinned, and even Keely began to relax. "Erinnish?" he asked.

"Aye, lad, name o' Boyne. But ye have yet to answer *my* question."

Boyne was a huge, bearlike man, black of hair and beard, though gray generously salted both. His nose was bent from some accident—or fight in the far past, and he lacked two teeth to boot. But the smile was genuine, lighting dark eyes as Corin nodded.

"Aye, Cheysuli, both of us." He gestured. "Will you join us?"

Keely's jaw was tightly set; he saw the reprimand in her eyes. But it was too late. Boyne had plopped his bulk down on a bench and was shouting for fresh wine.

He grinned at them both, eyes alight as he looked at Keely. "*Captain* Boyne," he said, "sailing home to Erinn on the morning tide. But when I saw the fox and all your gold, I knew ye must be Cheysuli, and I said to myself I must buy ye a dram before I sail."

"Why?" Keely's tone was cool.

He raised black brows. "Because o' the ties between our countries, lass, why else? Erinn's own fair Aileen will wed into the House o' Homana, and Prince Sean will take the Mujhar's Cheysuli lass for his bride. 'Tis good manners to drink to such happiness, lass!" He reared back as a wine-girl thumped down a jug and three cups. He poured generous measures, then handed them out. "To Aileen and her Cheysuli prince; to Sean and his sweet lass!"

Following his lead, Corin raised his cup. Keely's motion was considerably slower, but Boyne seemed not to notice as he clacked his cup against theirs.

" 'Sweet lass,' " Keely said sourly, and tossed back a gulp of wine as if to wash away the taste of unpleasant words.

Boyne leaned forward. "Aye," he said, "sweet lass. Would Sean be having any other?" He grinned, guffawed, slapped the flat of one huge hand down upon the table. "Hot for her he is, too, our lusty lord . . .' twill only be a matter of weeks before he sends for her. He's a man now, our Sean, and of no mind to wait longer for his bride. 'Tis time he started a son!''

She lifted one tawny brow in an eloquent arch. "Is that how he values a woman, then—by the children she can bear?"

" 'Tis her only value, lass . . . what *else* can she do?" Boyne gulped wine, then set his cup down so hard the remaining contents slopped over the rim. "Mind ye, I can hardly be speaking for my lord, but I *can* say he's no wilted flower. He'll be wedding her, bedding her, getting a son upon her . . . within a year, I'm saying." He slopped more wine into his cup, then thrust it upward again. "To all the fine wee bairns!"

Keely set down her cup and refused to drink. Corin, knowing Boyne meant well and that to refuse was rude as well as unnecessary, sipped his own and tried to ignore the look on his sister's face.

"We too are sailing for Erinn in the morning," Corin began, intending to ask passage of the flamboyant captain. But Keely interrupted.

"No," she said coolly, "*we* are not. Only my brother sails."

Astonished, he nearly gaped.

Keely's smile was excessively insincere. "I am needed at home."

"Have you gone mad?" It did not bother him that Boyne was an interested onlooker. "You said you were coming *with* me!"

Keely sipped her wine thoughtfully. "I have changed my mind," she said after a moment. "Is it not what a woman does? Certainly the sort of woman Boyne's beloved prince might prefer."

He scowled at her. "You might have changed it *before* I sold the roan."

Keely shrugged. "I will buy him back."

"And if he is sold already?"

"Then I will *steal* him back." Keely grinned at Boyne to remove the sting from her words; the big man's answering smile was fatuous.

For all she protests womanly behavior, she knows how to use it when it suits her, Corin reflected irritably. "Keely—"

"We will speak of it later," she said calmly. "As for now, I want some food."

Boyne nearly overset the table as he rose to shout for service.

Later, when they were alone in the small room Corin had rented, Keely faced him squarely. Never did she avoid a confrontation or deserved punishment; nor did she now.

"Why?" he asked.

She watched in silence as he sat down on the edge of his cot and drew off his boots, one by one. The belt with its long-knife was next; the remaining leathers he would sleep in.

"You heard him," she said finally, working at the lacing that bound her braid. "You heard that big-mouthed fool of a man, bellowing about how his lusty prince was hot for his Cheysuli bride." She stopped fussing with the knots and crossed her arms instead, all her unexpected vulnerability suddenly evident. "*You* heard how he will wed her, bed her, and get a son upon her—all in the space of a year!"

"Aye, well, I think Boyne exaggerates out of habit." Corin scooted back on the cot and leaned against the wall as Kiri jumped up and settled herself next to him. "He enjoys the sound of his own voice, Keely, little more. There is no malice in him. Only goodwill."

She sat down on the edge of the other cot, no more than four feet from his own. "I cannot go, Corin. I *cannot*."

"You are afraid."

She did not demur. "Aye."

"Of what? From what Boyne said, Sean is a good man . . . kind to dogs, horses, children—" He grinned. "In all likelihood he will be as kind to his woman."

But he had erred in thinking humor might soothe her. All it did was drive her farther from him, knees drawn up to shield most of her face as she hunched against the wall. "I want none of it," she said. "No wedding, no bedding, no children . . . I want *none* of it, Corin! All I want is to be myself, and if I go with you to Erinn, I will lose myself that much sooner. At least this way I may wait until Liam of Erinn and *jehan* decide it is time."

"Sean himself may have a say in it. And if he does—"

"If he does, let him do it the way it is always done," she

said bitterly. "He will have to tell his *jehan,* who will in turn send to ours . . . it will buy me a little time. If I go with you, that time is halved." She sat up straight and stared at him. "I cannot afford to lose it, *rujho* . . . not even a single day."

"But there *will* come a day—"

"I know." She cut him off. "I know. But that day is not tomorrow." Keely bent forward and jerked her boots off, dropping them to the floor. "I am sorry, Corin—but in the morning I go back."

He nodded as she blew out the single candle. In the darkness he heard the crack of the leather webbing that bound her mattress to the frame. In the darkness he heard the sound of her uneven breathing, and knew she was more frightened than he.

And he swore to himself that when he arrived in Erinn with his words of Aileen's betrothal, he would also speak of his sister's.

Two

Boyne stood next to him at the taffrail as sea-spray broke over the prow of the ship and splattered them both liberally. "There, lad—d'ye see it? 'Tis called the Dragon's Tail. 'Tis what divides Erinn from Atvia—a league or two of ocean, and centuries of war."

Corin clutched the rail. The Dragon's Tail was a narrow channel winding its way between two islands. Winds lashed the water into heavy chop, turning much of the shoreline of both islands into jagged teeth instead of smooth beaches. But lest the fisherfolk lament such harshness, there were also two natural harbors, sheltered and less treacherous.

"I did not know Kilore and Rondule were so close," Corin remarked in surprise. Next to him, Kiri pressed against his leg.

"Aye." Boyne, beside him, leaned on the rail, wind whipping graying hair into dark eyes. "Legends are saying once the islands were joined into a single kingdom ruled by a fair man. But that fair man's younger brother was desiring a kingdom of his own, and so they fought." Boyne grinned and spat over the taffrail into the slate-gray ocean. "They battled day in and day out, day in day and day out, till each realized if they kept it up, there would be no men left to lead. And so they agreed to fight no more."

When Boyne did not continue, Corin glanced at him. "But that does not explain how two islands were made out of one."

The big man tapped his badly bent nose. "I'm but warming to the tale, lad . . . ye never rush a good story, now, or ye'll be ruining the ending."

"Forgive me." Corin smiled in amusement. "I will leave the telling to you."

Boyne nodded. Thoughtfully, he stared toward the Dragon's Tail. " 'Twas the younger brother's doing. Not satisfied with the truce, because it gave him nothing he didn't have already, he sought the power to overcome his brother, the king. He begged the aid of a powerful sorcerer, bargaining with his soul. And when he had slain his brother and won the war, he was king by conquest." Boyne grinned. "The only thing was, now the sorcerer wanted his soul. Since no man, newly crowned, is wanting to give up his soul, he said no."

Corin nodded. "And so the sorcerer took his due."

"Oh, aye. He split the kingdom in twain and took the soul of the king."

"Leaving two kingdoms in place of one, and no men to rule either of them."

Boyne grinned. "Each brother had a son. Each cousin took a throne. And to this day their descendants are fighting over a single title."

"Lord of the Idrian Isles." Corin nodded. "That much I *do* know." He wiped spray out of his eyes and tasted salt. "What happened to the sorcerer?"

Boyne frowned dramatically, black brows knitted. "Well, 'tis said he got the soul he was promised. But 'tis also said he soon grew tired of such pettiness and turned his back on it all. Some say he died; others are saying he went belowdecks and became king of the world down there." An eloquent gesture accompanied the final sentence.

Corin looked at him sharply. "Do you mean Asar-Suti?"

Boyne shrugged and turned to call out an order to one of his sailors. When he turned back, he was frowning. "I'm not knowing the name, lad. All I know is the story. Whether there's truth in it, I'll not be saying one way or another."

"Asar-Suti, the Seker, who made and dwells in darkness," Corin mused thoughtfully. He glanced at Boyne, knowing what he said would sound like a tale to rival the captain's. "The Solindish Ihlini worship him as the god of the netherworld. In his name, they try to take Homana to make it part of his earthly kingdom."

Boyne shrugged. "I'm not knowing so much of Ihlini, either, being Erinnish-born. But they could be one and the same: sorcerer and god."

It was a new concept to Corin, who was accustomed to

viewing sorcerers as men—or women—with magical power, but no godhood. If indeed the sorcerer had become Asar-Suti, then what was to prevent other sorcerers from doing much the same?"

Strahan made a god? Corin felt a chill at the base of his spine. He looked at Kiri. *What becomes of our gods if the Ihlini make their own?*

The vixen's thick, bright pelt ruffled in the wind. *It is a question I cannot answer.*

He looked at her more sharply. *Cannot, or will not?*

Bright eyes glinted as she turned away. *One and the same,* lir. *I have no answer for you.*

Again Corin thought of Strahan. He had been raised on stories of the man who led the Solindish sorcerers, those who served Asar-Suti. The Mujhar had said more than once that not all Ihlini did, and that only those sworn to the Seker were men to be wary of. But Strahan was different. Strahan was more than merely sorcerer, being blessed with an uncanny charm that beguiled good and bad alike. He was already extremely powerful because of his dedication to the Seker. If his reward for such service and dedication was godhood, then he offered more than idle threat to the Cheysuli and the prophecy.

"Kilore," Boyne said. "And now, lad, I must tend my ship."

Distracted by his thoughts, Corin watched the Erinnish giant go. It had been a long time since he had thought much about Strahan or the Ihlini, or even the prophecy. That he was a link in it was old news. Except for Maeve, all of Niall's children were; it was why Strahan had tried to kidnap them as infants with Gisella's participation. But Boyne's fanciful tale had reawakened old memories and questions.

Twenty years ago my jehana *tried to give her children to the Ihlini. No doubt he had a use for us then. But what of now? What would he do with us now?*

And then, as abruptly, he forgot about Strahan and his half Atvian mother because the ship was docking.

Corin clutched the rail and stared. Kilore the city spilled along the waterfront like a tangle of seaweed, streets, and wynds interlocking to form a webwork he did not think he could ever decipher. And above the city, thrusting up in a jagged line of palisades, were the white chalk cliffs his father had mentioned so often. Kilore was a place of mist and magic, Niall had said, and Corin saw at least half of it was true. Shrouded in dampness, the cliffs formed a bright white curtain wall against the darker world.

And atop it, almost ominous in its bulk, stood the fortress from which the city took its name: Kilore itself, Aerie of the Eagles.

"Kilore!" Boyne called, and then added considerably more in Erinnish, which Corin understood well enough, thanks to years spent with Deirdre.

I wish I were arriving home, like Boyne, instead of here. Corin looked up at the castle and tried to suppress his nerves. *I wish I were doing anything but playing messenger for my* jehan, *and proxy suitor for my* rujholli.

The ship was secured handily, the ramps lowered, the unloading commenced. Corin, having nothing more than a set of shoulderpacks, proceeded down one ramp with Kiri trotting behind.

Fish, she said fastidiously.

Corin smiled crookedly. Aye, fish indeed. Deirdre had told him much of Erinn's economy depended on fish, and the stench made it more than evident. He smelled fish, old and new; sea salt and seaweed; the effluvia of ships toiling for months on the Idrian and beyond. There was nothing romantic about voyaging, Corin thought, when one looked at realities.

He and Kiri picked their way around nets and coils of rope, conscious of the shrieking of the gulls and the chatter of fisherfolk going about their work. It was late afternoon; the tide was in and so were the fishing boats. He and Kiri, wandering along the quayside, were distinctly in the way.

"Hai, Cheysuli!" Boyne called, and Corin turned back as the captain strode across the docks in his rolling sailor's gait. "Will ye be looking for someone in particular, or biding your time for a spell?"

Corin, who had told the Erinnishman no more than his name and destination, shrugged beneath the shoulderpacks. "My business is with the castle."

Boyne's black brows rose. He was a garrulous man but not a stupid one; he knew better than to ask questions that were none of his concern, and had not during the voyage.

But it did not stop his thoughts, and he chewed idly on a tattered thumbnail. "Aye, well, I'll not be keeping ye from it, then. I thought to buy ye a wee dram o' ale or wine in the grogshop before I saw to my own business."

Corin looked up at the Aerie. No, not yet. He smiled at Boyne. "No, captain, it is my turn to buy for *you*. Shall we go?"

Boyne looked down at Kiri. "What of the vixen, then? Will ye leave her on my ship?"

"Kiri goes with me."

The Erinnishman shrugged. "Aye, aye, and welcome to her. Come along, then, lad. Let us be wasting no more time flapping our mouths when we could be swilling ale." He clapped Corin a buffet on the shoulder that nearly knocked him down and strode off toward a row of buildings not far from the quay.

Boyne was engaged in another of his lengthy, colorful tales when a woman's angry voice distracted both of them. For a fleeting instant Corin thought she was protesting Boyne's loquaciousness, then realized there was more to it than that. It stopped Boyne dead in his tracks.

"Here!" he called, looking toward a narrow wynd that twisted down toward the sea. "Hai, lass, *here*—"

The woman's protest was silenced at once, and forcibly. Boyne slapped Corin on the shoulder and took off at a run, filling the wynd with his bulk and voice. After only a moment's hesitation, Corin followed.

Three men, Corin saw as he turned a corner—and a woman bundled in blankets. Near the end of the wynd, close to the quay. One of the men turned to face Boyne; the other two lifted the women off her feet and effectively controlled her struggles.

After a brief exchange between Boyne and the spokesman for the others, Corin realized civilities had been abandoned.

Boyne shouted with mocking laughter. "Oh, aye, and my mother was a queen!" He turned to Corin. "Yon man is saying the woman is drunk, and they're taking her home to her husband. But *I* know better than that—she shouted for help, and there was no drunkenness about it. And if these men are Erinnish, I'll be giving them my ship! Atvian, more like, trying to spirit away an Erinnish lass for evil purposes." He advanced a step. "Come, lad, 'tis a lass in need of us."

Kiri, Corin said within the link, and the vixen darted past Boyne's opponent to the others. Even as Boyne engaged, slapping away the knife that appeared in the Atvian's hand, Kiri was nipping at ankles amidst kicks and curses.

Corin grinned and waded into the fray himself. As Boyne settled his score, reducing their number to two, Kiri forced the men to neglect their prisoner. It was easy enough for the girl to tear herself away even as Corin and Boyne converged on the remaining opposition.

Boyne's fight did not last long. Corin's took longer, since he lacked the other's sheer bulk and strength. But as Kiri continued to nip at ankles, Corin smashed the Atvian's nose and sent him reeling off balance. A second blow snapped his head back and took his senses from him. He collapsed on the cobbles.

"Aye, *aye,* lad, 'tis the way of it!" Boyne clapped him on the shoulder. "We've saved the lass from the scum!"

Boyne's "lass" still sat on the ground where she had landed, half wrapped in dark blankets. Slowly she levered herself up on elbows, feet flat, knees drawn up, skirts tangled around her boots. She stared up at them both, then put out a hand to yank heavy skirts decorously into place.

Corin reached down an open hand. "Lady, will you come up?" He caught her, pulled her, steadied her as she rose, clasping one arm around her slender waist.

She was pale and a trifle shaky, but apparently unharmed; slight, but decidedly not fragile. Another woman might have cried or fainted or both; this one did neither. She eyed him closely a moment with incredibly bright green eyes, shrewdly assessing intentions, then pushed tangled hair—very *red* hair—away from an oval face. She blew out an explosive sigh of relief that also melted the tension out of face and limbs.

Guardedly, she smiled; the mouth was eloquent in its mobility, wide and willful beneath a straight, bold nose. She was not a beauty, not as Corin reckoned women—her coloring was far too flamboyant—but she was a striking girl, the kind of girl whose vibrant liveliness of spirit made beauty unimportant. Almost without thinking, he found himself responding.

"*You're* not Erinnish." She glanced at Boyne. "You are, captain, but the lad's not."

"No, lass, he's Homanan. Cheysuli, more properly." The big Erinnishman grinned at her expression of surprise, then replaced it with concern. "D'ye fare all right, lass? Did they have time to harm ye?"

She withdrew her hand from Corin's and deftly smoothed clothing into place, tightening snug belt, twitching the folds of her skirts, resetting the fit of tunic and underblouse. She wore the plain garb of a fisherwoman, and yet Corin had felt the softness of her hand, which did not at all coincide. No more than her carriage or her manner; he had seen the like in Keely.

And, by Keely, he knew her. Inwardly, he smiled. *Highborn, if not the highest.*

"They were meaning no harm," she said grimly. "They wanted me for Alaric, I'd lay a wager, and not for their own."

"Atvian scum!" Boyne turned his head and spat. "Come, lass, we'll be taking ye to your husband or your father; one or the other'll be wanting to know of this."

She tried to untangle the mass of hair and could not; the task required a brush. Distractedly she combed it back with her fingers, grimacing as she found additional tangles. The curling ends shifted against her belt. "I have no husband. My father's not in Kilore, nor is my brother or mother—which made it all the easier for the *skilfins.*" She cast a scowl at the unconscious men. "But 'tis my fault as much as anything else; I should not have come down alone. I know better, as my father is one for telling me. And now he can tell me again." She shrugged and smiled a rueful smile. "For all I hate to say it, he may have the right of it. All Alaric *needs* is leverage, and I nearly gave it to him." And then she stopped short, as if she had said too much to men who could not understand, and cast a bright glance at Corin. "Why does a Cheysuli come to Erinn?"

"Business with her lord."

Straight red brows jerked upward. She was not subtle in her thoughts, but he found it rather engaging. "With Liam, then? Well, 'twill have to wait. He's on the other side of the island tending to disputes." She jerked her head upward to indicate the fortress. "Will you come up, then? 'Tis where I'm bound." She looked at Boyne and grinned. "You as well, captain. 'Tis grateful I am for your service, and you're both due reward. What would you say to a meal in the Aerie, and a purse of gold apiece?"

"In the *castle?*" Boyne stared. "Lass, lass, ye shouldn't be promising things ye can't deliver."

"But I can," she said calmly. She glanced at Corin briefly, saw his expression, and her bright eyes twinkled. "But then I'm thinking *you* might understand."

He grinned. "Aye, lady, I do. And I think Boyne will, also, although you will steal his tongue. I have heard him speak of you; I think he worships someone other than the gods."

She grimaced wryly and indicated her mussed appearance. "Not for much longer, I fear." One of the Atvians groaned and shifted on the cobbles. She scowled. "Let us tarry no longer. We'll be leaving the rats in the gutter . . . they'll crawl home to their master and suffer for their failure."

"Lass—" Boyne stopped her as she swung away, ready to march out of the narrow wynd. "Lass—the *castle?*"

"The castle," she agreed. "D'ye think you're not fit for it?" And as he nodded, she laughed and took his arm, turning him toward the cliffs. "Not fit to face the eagle when you've saved one of his fledglings?" She paused. "Except the eagle is not in the Aerie, nor any of the others. *I* shall have to do."

"Boyne." Corin fell into step as Kiri trotted beside him. "Have you not told me what the Princess Aileen looks like?"

The captain grinned as he slackened his pace to the girl's. "Aye, lad, many times. 'Tis only from a distance I've seen her, mind you, but 'twas enough." He grinned and tucked her slender arm into his elbow. "Red-haired she is, like this lass here, and I've heard her eyes are green as Erinn's turf."

"Turf," the girl echoed morosely, twisting her mobile mouth into something akin to an offended wince, although the laughter in her eyes belied the truth of it. "Ye might at least compare them to *emeralds,* man, not *turf.*"

"*Your* eyes are the emeralds, lass," Boyne said gallantly. At that she burst out laughing and stopped him in his tracks. "Ye great-hearted, blathering fool, can ye not hear what this Cheysuli is trying to say? *I* am Aileen, man . . . *I* am the Princess of Erinn . . . turf-green eyes and all."

Boyne gaped. "You're *not*."

"I am," she said solemnly, but her bright eyes were alight with humor. "And when I invite you to take supper with me and accept a purse of gold, you *will* do as I say."

"Oh, *lass*—I mean, *lady*—"

"Fie on that blather," she said cheerfully. "Come up with me, captain, and let me thank you for your courage."

Grinning at Boyne's discomfort, Corin possessed himself of silence. But he wondered what Brennan would say when he met his Erinnish bride.

Three

Although Aileen struck Corin as an unaffected, uninhibited girl, she was also a princess and well understood the responsibilities of rank. Once within the towering walls of Liam's fortress, Corin and Boyne were shown to guest chambers to refresh themselves before the meal. It took neither of them long—Corin bathed and put on fresh leathers, Boyne bathed and put on his well-worn flamboyant silks because he had nothing else—and then they were escorted into a private hall made ready for the evening meal.

Corin was impressed. Both his father and Deirdre had said Liam was not a man much concerned with show, preferring simplicity over elaboration, and Kilore itself reflected the tastes of simple men. But in a short amount of time Aileen had ordered her guests treated with the utmost respect and hospitality, the meal and hall prepared, and her servants had quickly complied.

A figured white cloth covered the wide table. Iron gimbles filled with candles hung from massive roof timbers, providing a wash of illumination that glittered off glass and silver. Covered platters looked like silver turtles steaming. Servants neatly attired in Liam's green livery waited quietly, indicating that Corin and Boyne were to be seated. And then Aileen came in.

Gone was the fishergirl in homespun wool and knee boots, with unruly red hair an unbound mass of tangles. In her place was the Princess of Erinn, gowned and garbed appropriately. And yet she maintained a simplicity in dress and manner, for there were no jewels or haughty ways, merely a simple green gown, a slender fillet of gold threaded through shining hair now free of snarls, and a wide, impish smile.

Corin rose with alacrity, although Boyne's matching response was so abrupt it overset his chair. One of the servants hastened to right it as Boyne, unheeding, gaped at Aileen.

"Lass," he rumbled, "oh, *lass*—"

Aileen's brows rose expectantly as he stumbled to a stop; when he appeared incapable of continuing, she laughed and bade them both be seated.

Good manners, Kiri approved.

Corin put a hand down as he sat and passed it through the vixen's ruff. As always, the touch soothed him. *Do you judge her in Brennan's place?*

I merely comment. Kiri settled her rump on the floor next to Corin's chair and curled tail fastidiously around black paws.

"We'll be dining first," Aileen told them, "and then I'll be asking all the things I want to know."

The meal was superb, particularly after weeks of ship's stores, which were intended for longevity and ease of storing rather than for flavor. Corin's table manners reasserted themselves after the long voyage, but Boyne suffered from inexperience. He quaffed wine freely, consumed incredible amounts of rare beef, partridge, eel, oysters, and a variety of fish. Corin and Aileen, with more refined appetites, finished long before the captain, and exchanged amused grins as Boyne continued his culinary attack.

At last he shoved his platter away and belched contentedly. "Aye, lass—*lady*—'twas a meal fit for a lord. My belly is in the way of being grateful."

" 'Twas only the beginning of showing you my own gratitude." Aileen motioned the servants to begin clearing as she rose. "If you'll come with me now, I'll be showing you the rest."

She led them to an antechamber well-warmed by a huge brick fireplace. Plush pelts covered the stone floor and tapestries cut the chill from thick walls. There were chairs, small tables, two wooden cabinets carved in Erinnish knotwork patterns. Altogether the chamber formed a homey, comfortable place, reminding Corin of Deirdre's solar.

Aileen motioned them to sit, then withdrew something from one of the cabinets. As she turned, Corin saw two leather pouches in her hands. Her expression was solemn as she faced them, but her green eyes were alight. "I know

neither of you did me the service out of greed or ambition,"
she said, "and you weren't hoping for reward, either—not
from a fishergirl all wrapped in dirty blankets—but I'll be
giving you a token of my gratitude regardless. And I'll not
be hearing modest refusals from you, either—would ye say
them to my father?" She looked each of them in the eye,
forbidding them to answer, and handed out the pouches.
"You'll be staying the night as my guests."

Boyne stared down at the pouch, dwarfed in the palm of
his huge hand. He chewed at his lip, scowling blackly, then
sighed and tucked the pouch away with the air of resignation. Aileen, watching his struggle, smiled and went to him.

"And as a measure of more personal thanks, a kiss." On
tiptoe she still had to urge him to bend, and kissed him
squarely on the cheek when he acquiesced. Boyne turned
scarlet.

Aileen laughed and stepped away. "Off with ye, captain,
I'm no blind fool; you've been at sea a long time, and no
doubt you'd rather be spending the night with a lady. Well,
'tis a host's responsibility to provide hospitality, woman or
no; I think you'll be pleased with the girl."

Boyne's color deepened. "*Lass*—"

"In my father's place, I am host," Aileen said cheerfully.
"I know my duties, captain."

In the face of her matter-of-fact announcement, Boyne
was clearly unable to answer. And so he backed toward the
door, bowed awkwardly, and went out at once, bagged
coin clinking against one massive thigh.

Aileen laughed, eyes blazing amusement, and turned to
Corin.

"Did you really send him a woman?" he asked, wondering what she intended for him.

Her laughter was arrested. "Aye," she said in surprise.
"D'ye think I am a liar?"

"No, no, but—" Suddenly uncomfortable, he shrugged.
"It—seems odd to think of a woman sending a man a girl
to share his bed."

"'Tis not a habit of mine," she answered cheerfully.
"But I spoke the truth: there are customs of hospitality,
regardless of sex, and that is one. I *could* send him back
to the waterfront, but I thought a night in the Aerie might
be worth a drink or two in the taverns." She shrugged

disarmingly. "My father is a lusty, plain-speaking man, and so is my brother. I know a man's needs, and so I tend to Boyne's." Her mobile mouth moved into a crooked smile. "Besides, 'twas Moira's *desire* to bed him. She told me so as I bathed."

Corin laughed aloud. "Then what of *me,* lady? Do you tend my needs also?"

She eyed him thoughfully, then flung a gesture toward a chair. "Sit, sit; Boyne was easy to predict, but you are harder to know. And I have never met a Cheysuli."

She poured wine as he sat down, handed him a heavy goblet and settled herself in a chair opposite his own. The fire- and candlelight was kind to her coloring and features, enriching the former and enhancing the latter; Deirdre also wore Erinnish green frequently, but now that he saw the color on Aileen, Corin felt Deirdre's choice less suitable.

He set the pouch of gold on the table and made a gesture indicating polite refusal. "Your words were well-spoken and I admire their intent, but I cannot accept your reward."

She arched a single eyebrow. "Too proud, then? Or is it that Erinnish gold means less to you than those bracelets on your arms?"

Absently Corin touched one of the heavy *lir*-bands. "No, nor am I too proud, though you may think otherwise." He shrugged slightly. "Let us say it is—unnecessary."

"Why?" she asked bluntly.

Corin smiled. "Your father and brother are not the only plainspoken eagles in the Aerie."

Aileen laughed and swung a foot. "No, no, I have my share of a forthright tongue as well. 'Twas the price of living with my father." Her eyes did not waver from his. "Why is it unnecessary?"

"Because for a kinsman to do less is unconscionable. For him to do it for reward is unspeakable."

The foot stopped swinging. *"Kinsman."*

"Corin," he said, "as I have told you. But it is Corin *of Homana* . . . I am the Mujhar's son."

"Niall's son!"

"Aye."

She pursed her lips thoughtfully. And then shook her head. "But we're *not* kin. Through my aunt we would be, but Niall and Deirdre are not wed." Her expression was cool. "He holds to Gisella, does he not?"

"He holds to the laws of Homana," Corin told her calmly. "You honor the customs of hospitality, Aileen . . . *he* honors the laws of the land he rules."

She sipped wine, then shrugged and thumped the goblet down on the table. "So, you've come to see my father. Official business? Or personal?"

Her eyes were watchful, no matter how casual her tone. He opened his mouth to tell her the business concerned her betrothal to Brennan—and found he could not. "It is for me to speak with your father."

Aileen's smile was slow, but no less eloquent. "I *am* his daughter."

"I have been charged with this message—for the Lord of Erinn—by the Mujhar himself." He thought the evasion was answer enough, and not so far from the truth.

She considered it, tilting her head slightly. Candlelight blazed off the gold fillet and the glory of her hair. And then she shrugged slightly, dismissing the topic entirely. "Well, 'twill have to wait regardless. My father is, as I have said, on the other side of the island. He could be home tomorrow; he might come home in a month."

Corin thought of Keely. "Sean is not here?"

Aileen shook her had. "Sean has a new ship, the *Princess of Homana*." She sighed and swung her foot again. "Men and ships—who can say how long he will be gone? 'Tis her maiden voyage . . . but he should be back by spring." Her eyes were steady. "In time to have Liam write the Mujhar about the betrothal between son and daughter."

Corin drank hastily to cover the rigid expression on his face. He could not very well tell Aileen *his* sister wanted no part of *her* brother; it would be rude as well as an insult. Plainspeaking she might be, and Liam, but in negotiations between the royal houses such bluntness was deemed unwise.

"She is lovely, your fox," Aileen said, looking at Kiri curled on the bear pelt beneath Corin's feet. "And so quiet; I'd be thinking she'd prefer the out of doors to castles."

He smiled. "She does. So do most Cheysuli; it is the *lir*-shape in us. But a warrior adapts, and so does a *lir*."

Aileen bent forward to take a closer look. "We know of

Cheysuli, of course, but little of your animals. My father says Niall had none when he was a guest here so long ago."

"Guest?" Corin grinned. "You bend the truth, Aileen. My father was held hostage against Alaric of Atvia."

She laughed ruefully. "Aye, aye, *hostage* then, but will you be telling me he lost by it? In the end he got his Atvian wife, but he got my aunt as well. *And* a bastard daughter."

He inclined his head to indicate concession. "Maeve and Deirdre thrive. Bastard or no, she is his favorite child."

Aileen's brows rose. "*You* are not?"

"Hardly." Corin felt the familiar bitterness rising. "Maeve is Deirdre come again; my father adores his Erinnish *meijha,* and the daughter as well. As for *me,* I come last in his regard."

"Why?" Aileen frowned. "Why do you rank your brothers and sisters? Does he not love you all equally?"

"There is little to love in me." Corin blocked out her face with the goblet, drinking deeply. "Equally? No." He shrugged. "There is Brennan, who is the heir to Homana and therefore the most important of us all." Though he tried, for her sake, to mask the resentment in his tone when he spoke of Brennan, he heard its echo regardless. Quickly, he went on. "There is Maeve, dutiful daughter of his beloved *meijha.* And Hart, who is as good-natured as he is irresponsible, and impossible to dislike." He smiled. "And Keely, impetuous, passionate Keely, who tests his patience with her wild ways, and yet pleases him with her spirit. As for me," Corin shrugged, "I am, perhaps, my own worst enemy . . . but I cannot help it." He looked at her over the rim of his goblet, seeing himself through her eyes, and found he did not like it. But he did not look away. "There are times I hate myself, and therefore I make it easy for *others* to hate me."

Aileen looked straight back at him. "Then 'tis up to you to change it."

He waited for the upsurge of anger or resentment. It was a solution others had suggested many times, and each time it had made him blacker of temper than ever. But before Aileen, he found himself regretting his contrary moodiness for the first time. And sincerely desiring to change it.

He smiled ruefully. "I have said more to you than anyone

save Keely, and half the time she *supports* me instead of suggesting I change my behavior."

"It does a person no good to abet his insecurities," Aileen said flatly. "My brother is the proudest, most honorable man you could ever meet, and yet he's hot-tempered and hasty as well, and equally plainspoken. If I stood by him when he is wrong, nodding and 'ayeing' and buttressing his flank, I'd be doing him a greater injustice than Sean his victim." Her tone was one of understanding courtesy, and yet there was also an inflexible note of determination. "I'd make of him a tyrant, believing in only himself without granting others the right to disagreement or other forms of self-expression . . . and 'tis a poor man *that* makes."

Corin laughed sourly. "My father has said as much, and Brennan as well . . . but it makes more sense coming from you."

" 'Tis usually the way of it." Aileen shrugged. " 'Tis why 'tis important to listen to your kin. Let *them* show you what you are and what you do, so you give others no opportunity." She paused a moment, watching him. "And then you won't be having to sit there across from me, wishing there was a hole you might crawl into."

He grinned and rubbed at an eye. "Gods, but you are good for me. Brennan is fortunate—" And he broke off, realizing that yet again his brother would take precedence over him. And this time, this time *particularly*, he resented it badly. More than ever before.

But you have known all along she was intended for your rujholli, Kiri told him. *For all the days of your life.*

Rigidly, he stared at Aileen. And then he set the goblet down unsteadily and rose. "If you will excuse me . . . it was a long voyage, and I would like to retire."

Aileen stood quickly and awkwardly, bewildered by his sudden withdrawal. "Oh, aye—of course." She frowned. "Corin—"

"I am weary, Aileen," he said curtly, and saw the color blaze in her face.

Her eyes glittered with an acknowledgment of his rudeness. "Then go," she said coolly. "The servants will show you to your chambers."

With Kiri, Corin left.

* * *

He was a child again, in his dream, overlooked because of his age. Around him the women gossiped, clucking over the latest of Hart's habitual pranks or Keely's willfulness; praising Maeve's sweet temper and Brennan's maturity. But they said nothing of him, nothing of Corin at all.

In his dream he heard their praises, and Brennan— Brennan—Brennan.

Corin awoke. He touched Kiri sleeping at his side. And then fell into darkness again.

Older now, but no less overlooked unless he made them look. And he did, whenever he could, using wits and will-fulness, forcing the women to look, to see, to hear, even if the result was punishment, because then its name was Corin . . . then they spoke his name. Even if cursing it.

Asleep, he reached for Kiri, who heard him whenever he spoke. And even when he did not.

In the dream, he was himself, no longer a child but the Corin he saw every day when he looked in the polished plate. And suddenly he was the polished plate; he saw himself, as if he were someone else entirely, outside looking in, and the Corin he saw was a stranger.

But not a stranger at all. Corin stood in the Great Hall, before the Lion Throne, facing the Mujhar of Homana, the man who had sired him. Alone, he faced him . . . and then he was not alone, for with him was a woman, a slim, red-haired woman with eyes clear and green as emeralds—green as Erinnish turf—and the woman's hand was in his hand, and she faced the Mujhar, as he did, and together they re-cited the private Cheysuli vows that bound a warrior and his woman.

Bound . . . bound . . . bound—

—Until Brennan stepped out of the shadows and tore Ai-leen's hand out of his.

"No!" Corin cried. "No—not *again!*"

And he was awake, and knew it, and knew what he had dreamed.

Four

The dream haunted Corin for days. He did his best to ignore it, to push it away into the recesses of his subconscious, but its aftertaste remained, like the sour flavor of sweet wine turned to vinegar. When he looked at Aileen, he saw the woman who had recited the Cheysuli vows with him before the Lion of Homana, defying Niall himself. And defying her betrothed as much as Corin did himself.

Theirs was an uneasy companionship at best. Aileen hosted him with as much hospitality as she could muster in the name of her absent father, but the uninhibited generosity was gone. She eyed him warily at times, like a dog with an unkind master; other times she relegated him to obscurity, too busy to pay him mind. But occasionally he saw an odd sort of compassion in her eyes, as if she began to understand him and what made him the man he was.

At last the dream lost its immediacy, freeing him to relax, and Aileen responded at once, as if she had been waiting.

The relationship changed. The companionship deepened. They shared the things good friends shared, things kin shared, things he shared only with Keely. But he sensed a bond between them that superseded mere kinship, much as the one with Keely. With Aileen he was another man, freed of resentments and irritability; freed of the insecurity of being the third-born son. Here there was only Corin. No Brennan. No Hart. No ranking according to birth. Here there was merely *Corin*—

Corin and *Aileen*, who saw what he was and cherished it. As much as he cherished her.

Four weeks after his arrival—to celebrate, she said—Aileen took him out to ride along the headlands overlooking the Dragon's Tail. Kilore fell away from them, dropping below the horizon as they moved ever westward. The massive stone fortress gained invisibility; with it fled the last vestige of moodiness. He laughed again, unencumbered by doubts or recriminations, when Aileen told him a tale about her brother, and gloried in the banishment of the dream that had so plagued him. Free of it, he was also free of Brennan.

Until Aileen said his name and conjured him between them.

Such a simple question: "Is Brennan much like you?"

They had run their horses, tearing across the headlands, laughing into the wind and calling out challenges. Now they walked them, afoot, reins looped through their hands. Ahead of them, Kiri trotted; between them hovered Brennan.

"No," Corin said curtly.

She waited for more. When he gave her nothing, she looked at him directly. "D'ye hate him so much, then?"

He opened his mouth to refute the question at once. But nothing came out. Nothing at all; the denial died aborning. He had never thought of it as hatred; even now he felt the word incorrect. But he would lie to her no more than to himself.

"He is my brother." Purposely, he used Homanan in place of Cheysuli.

Aileen's mouth twisted. "Kinship has little to do with like and dislike, when it comes to a man's heart."

Corin sighed. The wind came up from the ocean below and curled over the rim of the cliff to buffet them both. He smelled sea and salt and fish.

"I asked for *me*." Aileen said quietly, "thinking of myself. But now I ask for Corin."

He looked at her sharply. And then at once away; he could not bear to see the compassion in her eyes.

"No," he said finally. "No, I do not hate him. I dislike him, but I dislike myself more for giving in to it."

Wind threatened to tear her hair free of its braid. Shorter strands teased her eyes. She stripped them back automatically, one hand still leading the horse. "Why?" she asked quietly.

Corin fought his own losing battle with wind and hair. "Because . . . because he is *Brennan*."

Aileen laughed. "Such a black scowl, Corin! Is he truly so bad?"

"No. He is truly so *good*." He shook his head, feeling a vague sense of guilt. Only Keely really knew how he felt, because of their birth-link, and because she shared a measure of his resentment. She and Brennan were no closer than *he* and Brennan, although she was less bothered by troublesome resentments. Corin thought it was because Keely, being a woman, knew there was no chance she might inherit the Lion; in Corin's case, he was prevented only by the order of his birth. "I should say nothing more, Aileen . . . he is your betrothed, and it does no good to color your opinions of him when you should form them fairly."

She laughed. "D'ye see? You don't dislike him as much as you think . . . if you did, you'd not be defending him to me."

He sighed again, deeply, giving up the final vestiges of decorum. This was a subject he had avoided from the beginning, unable to raise it with the woman Brennan would wed. But if Aileen wanted frankness, he would give it to her.

"Since I can remember, it was always Brennan *this*, Brennan *that* . . . Brennan, the Mujhar's son; Brennan, the Prince of Homana; *Brennan*, heir to the Lion. Part of the past and of the future: Cheysuli and Homanan." He slanted her a glance, fearful he might offend her, but saw only that she listened without judging. "All my life he has been held up as an example of what a man can and should be—what *I* could be if I tried!—and I am so weary of it. If he had earned it, I would not care so much, but it is because of his birth . . . because he was born *first*—" He broke off, stripping tawny hair out of stinging eyes. "It might have been Hart. *Hart* might have come first, and then *he* would be heir to Homana"

"Or you." She said it calmly. "Is that what you're resenting so much? That you were not born in place of Brennan?"

Corin stopped dead. The horse nearly walked over him, but he did not care. "Aye." He did not avoid her eyes. "*Aye*, Aileen, it is. I have always wanted the Lion."

She turned to face him. The wind ripped hair from her

face and bared it for him to see. "But you'll be having *that*."

He followed the line of her lifted arm. Beyond her hand he saw the island across the Dragon's Tail. "Atvia," he said sourly, "is poor proxy for Homana."

Slowly she lowered her arm. "D'ye want it because you *want* it? Or because your brother will have it?"

He stared at her. He had never considered that view of his desire. He knew only that for as long as he could remember, he had wanted Brennan's place.

He looked at Kiri. *Oh, lir, is that it? Do I want what Brennan has only because he has it?*

The fox did not answer. Corin shivered, discovering something within himself he did not like at all; acknowledging it for the very first time, and liking it no better.

If I had what Brennan has, would I be content? Or would I search for new unhappiness and ways of expressing it?

Corin looked at Atvia across the choppy gray water. Slowly he sat down, giving the horse his head, and stared out into the skies. "I want power," he said. "I want freedom. I want contentment. But—mostly I want the chance to be myself without being weighed against my *rujholli*."

Aileen released her horse and sat down beside him, deftly settling her skirts. "Not so much," she said. "You're not in the way of being a greedy man."

The island across the channel was awash in spray and sunlight, tinted with myriad colors. "Atvia is a land of strangers," he told her. "A land of old hatreds and resentments, of wars and vassalage . . . I will not be welcome there."

"No," she agreed. "But for a man who wants power, you might look on it as a challenge. You can go *in* a foreign prince, and come out a beloved king."

"Beloved." He smiled. "What king is beloved?"

"My father," she answered quietly.

Corin sighed. "And, I think, mine."

Aileen stared into the distances, seemingly lost in thought. Her voice, when she spoke, was quiet, but he heard the subtleties in her tone as loudly as if she shouted. "If Brennan is anything like you, perhaps I can be content."

"Anything like *me*?" He stared at her in shock. "Aileen—

no . . . Brennan is *nothing* like me, and you should be grateful for it!''

"Why?" Now she looked at him. "Should I be grateful because he lacks your complexities? Because he lacks your depth of emotions? Lacks your *passion?*" Her eyes did not waver. "Should I be grateful because there is no need for him to say what is in his heart?"

"And if the heart is *black*—"

"Not black," she said quietly. "Only bruised by childhood resentments, and I'm thinking those can be easily banished."

Corin shook his head. "Brennan is more suited to the Lion. He thinks before he speaks, speaks before he acts, then acts responsibly. He understands what makes a man feel the way he does, and respects that man for his feelings. He *listens*—" Abruptly, Corin broke off. And then he began to laugh. "Oh, gods, *woman*—do you see what you have done? From telling you why I dislike my *rujholli* I am become his champion!"

"I'm thinking he needs none," Aileen told him. "And— I'm thinking too that Atvia's gain is surely Homana's loss."

Corin thought not. Corin thought something else entirely, and found he must express it. Slowly he drew in a breath. "And *I* am thinking that my loss is Brennan's gain—" He broke off a moment, then went on bitterly. "Except you cannot lose what you never had."

They stared at one another for a long moment, unable to look away, knowing only that he had said what was better left *un*said, between *them;* between the woman meant for his brother and the man who wanted her for himself, even as he had wanted so many things Brennan had. But this time, *this* time, he wanted less to win her *away* than simply to win her, period.

Slowly, she put out her hand and touched his, gently; he felt the trembling in her fingers. "For that, I am sorry."

Corin pulled his hand from hers and made a gesture: an upturned hand, palm bared, fingers spread. *"Tahlmorra lujhalla mei wiccan, cheysu,"* he said grimly, "and I can change the fate the gods have given us no more than I can change the order of my birth."

*   *   *

He stood before the Lion Throne and faced the man within it. Not his father; Niall was gone. In his place was Brennan.

Corin inclined his head. "My lord, " he said politely, "I wish to steal your queen."

He sat up with a muffled shout. All around him was darkness and the swathing of the bed. And once again, as always, he reached out for Kiri.

Lir, oh, lir, I think I am going mad.

No, the vixen said, *you are only losing sleep.*

He was. Each night. He slept, dreamed, wakened, then repeated the cycle. He was ashamed of some of the dreams. He had thought, fleetingly, of bedding one of the serving girls, if only to banish the dreams, but the thought died nearly the instant it was born.

What he wanted was Aileen herself, not one of Aileen's women.

Corin rolled over onto his belly. *If I went to Atvia now—* But he knew he would never go. While Liam was from the palace, he had every right to wait. No one could suspect him of remaining for anything else.

Not even Aileen could.

He slept. He dreamed. He awakened.

"My lord," he said politely, "I wish to steal your queen." In his hand there was a sword—

Aileen touched his shoulder and the vision fled at once. "Where are you, Corin? I see the look in your eyes."

He blinked, knowing himself back in Kilore. No more Lion, no more Brennan. Only Brennan's betrothed.

"Nowhere," he said curtly, rising from the stool.

They had shared a meal, exchanged favorite stories of mishaps suffered by their kin, told tales on one another, recalled childhood games. Now they sat before one of the giant fireplaces within a private chamber, and he knew they tempted fate.

"Corin—"

"Will Liam never come home?"

Aileen, still seated, stared up at him as he turned to pace away. Back and forth he moved, restless and angry, swallowed by desperation. She saw it in him, and grieved.

"I can send for him," she said at last. "I didn't do it before only because you said there was no need for urgency."

"No. No need for urgency." He stopped pacing and swung back. "What I *need* I cannot have."

Clearly she understood him. She did not look away. "Who is saying you cannot have it?"

"Brennan—"

"Brennan is not here."

Corin watched her rise. No more than three paces separated them; he knew he dared not take them. Yet hoped *she* would, so he could live with the guilt. And knew it was unfair.

"Aileen—"

"You came unknowing," she said, "intending nothing. I received you in place of my father, offering nothing more than courtesy. And, eventually, compassion and understanding. From that grows the vine that tangles us in its thorns."

"Then I will cut us free."

Aileen's smile was bittersweet. "Will you, now? But how?"

"By telling you the message I have for Liam is that the betrothal is to end." He saw the whitening of her face. "A wedding is desired; Brennan requires an heir."

Aileen said nothing for a long moment. And then she clenched her hands in the folds of her heavy skirts. " 'Tis a sharp knife, Corin . . . sharper than the thorns."

"Brennan will bind the wound."

"And who will be binding *yours?*"

"Oh, gods—*Aileen*—"

But she took the paces and closed the space between them, closing his mouth as well with cold, slim fingers. "No," she said, "no. I'm wanting no cruelty from one another, nor *for* one another. Ah, Corin—will ye *hold* me? I've been wanting it so long—"

He held her, as she asked, thinking he might fool himself into believing he did it *only* because she asked, but he knew better. He knew. He was lost, and so was she.

And so was their innocence.

Lir, Kiri said, and someone threw open the door.

They broke, but not quickly enough. And then the dogs were begging for Aileen's attention, so many dogs, all wolfhounds, pushing them apart, and he knew Liam was home at last.

"Lass," her father said mildly, and then he looked at Corin.

Oh—gods—

Liam grinned and strode into the chamber, parting the sea of dogs. He was a big man, a strong man, with Deirdre's brass-bright hair and Aileen's green eyes; wind-chafed, weather-burned, hardened from years of warfare. He was fifty, Corin knew, but the years did not weigh him down.

"Niall's lad," the lord of Erinn said in a vast and abiding satisfaction. " 'Tis in your face and your color, though you lack the height and weight." He caught Corin in a brief, bearish hug, then set him back for perusal. Green eyes glinted; beyond him, white-faced, Aileen stared. "I see none of Gisella in you."

Corin drew in a deep breath. "My lord—"

"So, have you come to woo my lass?" Liam strode to a table and poured wine. "Or is she already won?" He grinned and raised his cup. "To Brennan and Aileen, future king and queen of Homana."

For one insane moment Corin wondered if it were possible to keep Liam in ignorance. Hart, he knew, might try it, merely to win a wager.

But this was not a wager; Aileen was worth far more.

"No," he said hollowly.

One thick blond brow rose. "No?" Liam echoed. "Will you not let me drink to your happiness?"

"You may drink to the happiness of *Brennan and Aileen*," Corin said with as much control as he could muster. "But I am not part of it."

Liam lowered the cup. "Are ye daft, lad? D'ye insult my daughter so soon after you kiss her?"

"My lord." Corin moved to face Liam squarely, no longer able to see Aileen. "My lord, you saw what you saw. But I am not Brennan."

"Not—" Liam broke off. He set down the cup with a thump; wine slopped over the rim. "Then who *are* you, ye *skilfin*, and why were you kissing my daughter?"

"I *am* Niall's son, my lord . . . he has three, if you will recall. I am the youngest of them."

Liam's levity and high spirits were banished, replaced

with a frowning intensity. The sheer power in the man's gaze made Corin want to squirm. But he held his ground, unmoving.

"Corin," Liam said finally. "That much I know from Niall's letters." He flicked a glance past Corin to Aileen and his mouth tautened. "Well, lad, have you come to tell me Brennan and Hart are dead, and *you* are heir to the Lion?" His tone was harsh. "I'll accept no other explanation for why you would take the liberty of kissing Brennan's betrothed."

"Will you take this one?" Aileen spoke for the first time since Liam had entered the room. She moved forward to stand by Corin, facing her father even as he did, but with less courtesy. "Will you accept it when I say I'll be taking Corin in place of Brennan?"

Corin snapped his head around to stare at her in shock.

Liam's brows rose. "*Will* you?" he asked mildly. "D'ye think it so easy, then?"

Corin had expected more than that from him. But when he looked back at Liam, he saw the light tone did not entirely dispell the intentness of his manner. He put Corin in mind of a mountain cat feigning indolence until it was time to leap.

But who is prey? he wondered uneasily. *Aileen, or myself?*

"Not easy," Aileen said, "but right. I know it was a political thing, the betrothal . . . I have no quarrel with that. But I'm saying we need only wed me to Corin in place of Brennan."

Liam turned idly and walked around the table to the immense fireplace. He stared into the flames, putting his back to them. He wore black hunting leathers and golden spurs; blond hair was tumbled against his shoulders, combed by the wind of his ride. Around him, wolfhounds gathered.

"Corin is pledged to Atvia."

It was all Liam said, and to the flames. Corin and Aileen exchanged puzzled glances; she shrugged a little, indicating ignorance of the reason for Liam's odd manner.

"Aye, to Atvia," she said finally, when it became apparent her father intended to say no more. "But 'twould be a good alliance, my lord . . . 'twould help to forge peace between the realms."

" 'Twill be for others to do, when Alaric and I are dead." Liam turned, warming his back, and Corin saw the Lord of Erinn was not as indifferent as he sounded.

Not indifferent at all . . . he merely waits for the proper time.

"What would it alter?" Aileen asked. "Brennan and I have never met, nor even exchanged letters. He won't be missing what he never had, nor made any *effort* to have." She gestured. "There is Ellas, Falia, Caledon . . . let him have one of *their* princesses instead of Erinn's only one."

Liam's eyes flicked to Corin. "D'ye want her, lad?"

He raised his head. "Aye, my lord, *I do.*"

Liam looked down at his dogs. "I could write Niall," he said absently. "I could write him . . . could be telling him the very things you've told me . . . perhaps it *could* be arranged—" he looked up from his dogs, "—but then 'twould be the end of the prophecy . . . the end of the Cheysuli."

In shock, Corin stared back at him. In despair, he saw the truth in Liam's compassionate eyes. *He* knew, did Liam; he understood very well. Better than Aileen, who heard only the denial; better even than Corin, who knew a great shame in overlooking the obvious. In nearly betraying his blood.

"Are ye daft?" Aileen asked. "How could it be the end of anything? And what does a prophecy have to do with *us?*"

"Aileen." Corin wanted to touch her, but did not dare it. "Aileen, I have told you of the prophecy . . . how it governs Cheysuli lives."

"Aye, *aye,* " she said impatiently, "you've told me all about it. 'Tis a fine, shining thing, Corin, and worthy of dedication, but what has it to do with *us?*"

"With *you,*" he said clearly. "The first son you bear Brennan will be another link in the chain, taking us one step closer to fulfillment."

Aileen shrugged. "And if I bore your son, would it not please the gods as well?"

Corin slowly shook his head.

"Why *not?*" she cried. " 'Tis a son they want, is it not? Then I'll *give* them that son!"

"Aileen." Corin drew in a breath. "It comes down to Brennan. It comes down to you. I do not figure in it."

"And why not?"

"Because—" he gestured emptily. "Because it has to do with how the blood is mixed. Brennan is Cheysuli, Homanan, Solindish, and Atvian. You are Erinnish." He sighed. "The prophecy requires—"

"But *you* have all those bloodlines, Corin!"

"But I am not the Prince of Homana!"

They stared at one another, transfixed by pride, by anger, by anguish. And then Aileen made a gesture of defiance and determination. "Does it matter *so much* that I wed the Prince of Homana?"

"Aye," he said wearily. "It all begins with Homana . . . one day it will end with Homana."

"Aileen." It was Liam, very quiet. "Aileen, has he taught you nothing of the Cheysuli? D'ye see nothing of his pride, his honor, the strength of will that rules his life?" He looked older now, and saddened by what he said. "Niall spent a twelve-month here, and in that time I learned a little of the Cheysuli—enough to respect them *and* their determination."

"D'ye not respect *me?*" she asked. "D'ye not think me capable of judging a man? Why *else* d'ye think I want him?"

"Then ask him," Liam said gently. "Look at him and ask him."

After a moment, Aileen turned to Corin. "D'ye say you're not wanting me?"

She would never be beautiful, but he was blinded by her pride; by the brilliance of her spirit. "You showed me what it was to look out of myself to others," he told her gently. "You showed me how to be myself, not judging myself against others, or what others wanted *of* me. You taught me to be free in spirit if not in body, bowing to necessity, and to accept the latter with grace." He smiled a little. "Lastly, you taught me to love my brother, and for that I am very grateful. *Leijhana tu'sai, meijhana* . . . but I cannot steal his queen."

Aileen's face was a white blotch against red hair. Her

eyes swam with tears. But she said nothing, nothing at all; she merely turned and walked from the room.

After a moment, Liam put a large hand on Corin's shoulder and gripped it briefly, then released him. "Until this moment I never regretted what Niall and I did, promising sons and daughters to one another. 'Tis the way of royal houses; the requirements of rank." He picked up Corin's forgotten cup of wine and put it into his hands. "But it seems we dealt too lightly with unborn souls."

Corin stared into the lukewarm wine. "I came here to tell you my *jehan* desires the wedding to go forth." He looked at Liam. "Aileen is to make ready for the voyage."

There was pain in Liam's green eyes, and more than a share of regret. Slowly he reached out and took the cup away. "Go to her, lad. She's a spirited lass, saying what she thinks, and likely she'll have harsh words for you . . . but *go*. I'll not be making the mistake my father did when Niall was sent from Deirdre. Go to Aileen and say your goodbyes. It won't be enough, but at least 'tis *something*."

All Corin could do was nod. And then he left the chamber.

At last he found her on the battlements of the fortress. If she cried he could not tell; the wind scrubbed her face clean of everything save the starkness she turned on him.

Her fingers clutched the brick. The line of her spine was rigid. "Go, Corin. I'm wanting to be alone."

"That is a lie," he told her plainly. "What you want is for me to say I was wrong . . . to say I'll take you regardless of consequences . . . to say I want you badly enough to steal my *rujholli's* betrothed."

The mobile mouth was tightly drawn. "But you won't. *You don't*."

He stood next to her, turning to stare out at the sea that pounded Erinn's shores. "I want you," he said simply, knowing no other way, no *better* way, to put it. "If it is not enough that I say it without qualifications, then I am sorry for you. But I know you better, Aileen . . . I know you better than anyone save Keely, if in an entirely different sense."

"Do you?" They were close enough to touch, but neither moved to do it.

"Aye." The wind carried most of it away. "I know that if I turned my back on my kin, my race, my *tahlmorra*, eventually you would hate me. Perhaps even tomorrow." He turned to her, scraping leather knife sheath against the wind-scoured stone. "There are women in the world who would be pleased to have such sacrifice made in their names, but you are not one of them."

Her hair was a banner in the wind, whipping back from her face. "No," she said, "I am not . . . but I almost wish I could be."

A laugh rose from deep inside of Corin; a single gust of sound. "If you were," he told her, "if you were, I could never love you the way I do."

Aileen swore bitterly and banged the wall with her fist. "Why is it," she cried, "why *is* it I meddle where I should not? Why is it I took it into my head to ease a man's pain, to show him what it is to know contentment within oneself?" Slowly she shook her head. "If I'd left you alone, never trying to understand you, never trying to ease that pain, we'd not be in this coil!"

"Why is it you took it into your head to show me that underneath all my childish resentment, I really care for Brennan?" Corin sighed and rubbed aching eyes with rigid fingers. "Well, we have fashioned me into someone I can live with, and now I must live without you."

"Brennan," she said bitterly. "Each time I look on him, I will think of you. Even in *bed*—"

It was a vision he had purposely pushed aside, and now she brought it back in all its intensity. He could not bear it. "Aileen, *stop*." He caught her wrists. "Stop. You punish *me* as well as yourself."

All the anguish was in her face, but so was her pride. "And when I call him by your name?"

Corin shook his head. "Aileen, I swear, when you meet Brennan you will understand. You will never mistake him for me. We are so different, so very different . . . temperament, coloring, preferences . . . so many other things." He swallowed tightly. "I promise you, Aileen, it will not be an empty marriage."

She jerked her wrists away. "I might prefer it that way."

All the pain rose up. "Do you think I want that?" he cried. "Do you think I want to spend my life knowing you hate every moment with my *rujholli*, when there is nothing for me to do? *No*, Aileen. I would sooner believe you content enough than living your life in sorrow, lost in some futile hope that someday I might come. It would twist *you*, twist *me* . . . it would destroy any hope of happiness for either one of us."

"So," she said, "you tell me to go to Homana and wed your brother . . . to be his wife and bear his children . . . to be everything to him that I want to be to you."

"Aye," he said harshly. "That is what I tell you."

She drew in a deep, unsteady breath. "You are a hard man," she said, "and I wish I could soften you. But in doing it, I would destroy the thing I love."

"Aileen—"

She thrust up a silencing hand. "No more," she said. "No more from you, I say. And now I must go . . . 'tis time I began to pack."

He watched her go. And when she was gone, when he stood alone on the battlements, he slid slowly down the stone to sit with legs drawn up, staring blindly at his knees.

Later, Liam came to him in his chambers. "Come out with me, lad. Now."

"*Out* with you—?"

But Liam did not answer. He motioned Corin to follow him out of the chamber and immediately left it, dogs trailing in his wake, and after a moment Corin went as well.

They left Kilore entirely, riding across the headlands with an escort of giant dogs, and also Kiri, a blotch of rust and black against emerald turf. Liam said nothing at all of his intentions, nor what he expected of Corin; he merely rode, wrapping himself in silence, and Corin rode with him.

At last Liam halted. Before them was a grassy tor, swelling out of the turf, and Corin saw a crude stone altar on its crest. He thought they might dismount and go up to it, but Liam remained in the saddle. In his eyes was the opacity of memories recalled.

" 'Tis of the *cileann*, this place," he said finally. "The oldfolk of Erinn, born of ages past. The tor is sacred, blessed with ancient magic . . . can ye not feel it, lad?"

"Aye, my lord. I do."

Liam looked at the tor. " 'Twas where I took Niall when

he went out of Erinn to Atvia . . . leaving my sister behind."

Pain rose; he would leave Liam's *daughter* behind. Thinking: *You forget, my lord. Niall left her, but Deirdre came to him later. I cannot hope for the same.*

"I was angry, lad . . . angry with Niall, with Deirdre— angry with myself." Liam grimaced. "I thought it a waste, that a man such as your father had to bow to the dictates of his *fate* and trade Deirdre for Gisella. I saw what was between them as clearly as I see the thing between you and Aileen. And I cursed it, and them, and myself, because I knew I would have to end it." He fell silent a moment, and the wind teased his hair. "Lad, 'twas no easier for me then than it is now. And I understand it no better. But I know it must be done. Niall taught me that much, and you have reminded me."

The horse stomped under Corin, who soothed it absently. "I am nothing like my *jehan*. I wish I might be, that I could offer her better; or that I was firstborn, so I would be more like Brennan—" He broke off. "But even then, I could offer her nothing."

"And you're a blind man, lad." Liam turned his horse. "Come, then. One day you will be king in Alaric's place; we must speak now of trade and treaties, while we have the time."

Silently Corin followed, while the wind blew down the tor.

Five

She was, he thought, the most beautiful woman he had ever seen. The power of her allure touched him as it had touched all men, nearly engulfing his wits. But he knew better. He knew *her:* Lillith of the Ihlini, sister to Strahan himself.

Corin drew in a steadying breath as he dismounted in front of the palace steps. A boy took his horse. Alone, afoot, afraid, he faced the sorceress.

She stood at the very top of the steps. She watched him. And she smiled. "You are well come to Rondule."

"Am I?" He made himself mount the first step.

"But of course. Are you not the Crown Prince of Atvia?" A second step. "That is for Alaric to say."

"But of course." Still Lillith smiled. "If Alaric *can*."

Corin paused, then forced himself to climb. "An odd thing to say."

"Not when you have seen him." She wore blue, deep, rich blue, girdled with silver and pearls. Large, irregular pearls, some creamy, some gray, some black, with a tinge of silver-blue. More threaded the weave of her braid.

Closer, ever closer, until he could see the silver tips of her nails; the kohl-smudged lids. The eerie youthfulness of features and form.

This woman seduced my su'fali.

Corin looked at her as he climbed. He began to understand how. *Lir*less, Ian had stood no chance. Her power was manifest.

Lillith smiled. "I see you have brought your *lir*."

Someone, some*thing*, touched an icy fingertip to his spine. He did not like the way Lillith looked at Kiri. To change the subject, he said, "My *jehan* sent word I was coming."

"No," Lillith said. "I already knew."

He stopped short. He was but three steps below her. She was young, he saw, genuinely *young*. Not older. Not age, masquerading as youth. He had only to compare her to Aileen to know that the sorcery was powerful indeed. It did more than lend her the *illusion* of youth and beauty, it gave her both in full measure. The Seker was an unstinting god.

Oddly, he recalled Boyne's story. The tale of a sorcerer become god. The memory made him shiver.

Lillith smiled. Calmly she stood at the top of the steps, giving nothing away of her power, but showing it all the same. "There is no doubt who sired you."

He had heard it before. He and Keely had both inherited Niall's coloring—blue eyes, tawny hair, fair skin—and a resemblance in facial structure, but neither claimed his frame. Keely was tall for a woman, but nothing more; he himself was considered short for his Cheysuli heritage, being less than six feet. Brennan and Hart both topped him by a handspan.

"And no doubt who sired *you*."

Lillith laughed. "And did you know Tynstar well?"

"Only by reputation."

"With *him*, that is all that is needed."

Her tone was a trifle cooler, her black eyes more assessive; Corin disliked intensely the sensation of being judged. It was bad enough when his father did it; worse when done by an Ihlini. "Lillith—"

"Come in," she said abruptly. "There are matters to discuss, and better places to discuss them."

He wanted to refuse her, to leave her and go somewhere she could not touch him, even with her eyes. But an innate sense of self-preservation and a desire to play the game very carefully kept him from blurting it out. This was Atvia, not Homana. Lillith had been Alaric's light woman for a very long time, and was Ihlini to boot; her influence would be well established by now. Until he knew better how things stood, it was not his place to quibble.

At least until reason is plainly given. He followed Lillith in silence.

She took him to a private chamber within the heart of the palace. The servants they passed bowed quickly to Lil-

lith, but watched him with curious eyes. He wondered how
Lillith had known he was coming; he wondered if she had
not, and simply said she had. Mostly, he wondered how he
would manage to last the year.

"Here." Lillith indicated a carved, high-backed chair.
The room was shadowed, lacking windows, illuminated
only by candleracks. Most were unlit, like the fireplace.
It dulled the colors of the tapestries and robbed the room
of welcome.

He sat down. Kiri took her place by his feet, sitting rigidly in front of his legs. She watched the woman intently
as Lillith poured wine.

Corin shook his head as the cup was offered. Lillith did
not withdraw it. "A fool will often go thirsty."

"But at least the fool will live."

Briefly she looked at Kiri. She smiled. "You *are* a fool,
Corin. Why should I stoop to poison when I have other
means? And why, for that matter, should I desire to take
your life? You are more useful to me alive."

"Useful?" Lillith still held out the cup; he stared at her
over the rim.

She did not answer at once. Instead, she gazed thoughtfully at the cup she held, as if troubled by his refusal. She
lifted it to her own lips, sipped distinctly so he could see
she did indeed drink the wine. And then, idly—as if it were
no more than an afterthought—she tipped the cup over and
poured out the wine.

Corin jerked back into the depths of the chair, trying to
avoid the torrent. Even Kiri dodged aside. But there was
no need. In midair, as the wine spilled out of the cup, it
turned into coils of lavender smoke.

"One need not concern oneself with unwanted residue,"
Lillith said obscurely, and threw the cup to Corin.

He caught it, as she meant him to, and then cursed himself for following her lead. He leaned over the side of the
chair to put the cup down on the floor; as he did, stretching
out his arm, the cup began to change.

Aghast, he jerked his hand away. But the cup followed.
In his hand the silver melted, reformed, braceleted his flesh.
Cursing, he tried to fling the silver away, but it had formed
a rigid cuff around his wrist. A seamless, shining shackle.

"I will be very plain," Lillith said quietly. "If I wanted you, I would take you. There is nothing you could do."

His hand trembled, then spasmed. "Take it *off*—"

Lillith shook her head. "For now, I will leave it. It will be a reminder, so you do not forget who holds the power here." She turned from him and moved to the nearest chair, spreading blue skirts as she settled into black cushions. She did not seem to notice that he was transfixed by the silver cuff, unable to look at her. "I want you to understand very clearly how things are in Atvia."

"Lady, I *do*." He fisted his hand and thrust it into the air, displaying the shining shackle.

"Good." Lillith smiled. "I have no intention of robbing you of your birthright."

He frowned before he could hide it.

"No," she said, "why should I? You are Alaric's grandson, kin to Osric and Thorne and Keough, and all the lords before them. I would be a fool if I stripped Atvia of her rightful blood."

"Then why are you *here?*"

"Because it pleases me to be here." Lillith's tone was bland.

"As it pleased you to seduce a *lir*less Cheysuli?"

Black eyes glinted. "Does Ian dream of me?"

"No more than I will, Ihlini." He tried to ignore the silver on his wrist. But it was cold, so *cold*. "What is your purpose? Why do you stay with Alaric? If you speak the truth about my inheritance, you must know I will not want you here."

"By the time you inherit this realm, there will be no *need* for me here."

"Lillith—"

"We must speak of the future, Corin," she said quietly, overriding him easily. "Alaric is an old man. His wits fail. Atvia suffers from the lack of a strong hand at the helm. If something is not done, Atvia will fall to those who wish to conquer her and take her for their own."

He frowned. "Who would benefit from conquering Atvia? The realm owes fealty to Homana."

"Liam would take the island in a moment if he knew of Alaric's weakness. It has nothing to do with Homana; Atvia and Erinn have battled for years."

That he knew well enough. But he shook his head. "No, I think Liam—"

"*No.*" she said plainly, "you do *not* think. You know nothing of Liam at all, having met him only yesterday."

"My *jehan*—"

"Your father has not seen Liam in twenty-two years," Lillith said flatly. "And even then, he knew him as Prince of Erinn, not the lord himself. Power changes men. Power will change you." She spoke coolly, without excess emotion, expressing things the way his father might. He found he did not like it; Lillith was enemy. "I will not waste my time trying to convince you Liam means Atvia harm," she continued. "You would never believe me. But I will say this: unless a strong man assumes the throne, Atvia will fall. If not to Liam, to someone else." She paused, and her tone was subdued. "There are other realms in the world besides those we know."

It was an odd statement. To Corin, the world was made up of a handful of realms: Homana, Solinde, Erinn, Atvia, Ellas, Falia, Caledon, and the Steppes. In childhood, he had learned a little of them all. There had been no others named.

"And you want *me* to assume the throne. Now. Ahead of time."

Lillith's shrug was eloquent. "Alaric's time grows short."

"Then why precipitate it?"

"For the reasons I have given."

"No," he said flatly, "there must be something more." He grasped the ensorcelled silver with his left hand, sensing a disorienting ambience in addition to the icy touch, and tried to twist it off. But the silver was solid, inflexible, hugging his wrist as firmly as the *lir*-bands hugged his arms.

"It would serve you," she said. "Take the throne now, establish your claim . . . make certain Atvia understands *you* are the lord. Give the people no chance to be swayed by foreigners."

Foreigners. Again she spoke of external threats. And yet, to his knowledge, there *were* no foreigners; the world was made of eight realms, those he had already named. Four of them were part of the prophecy.

But this was Lillith. "You are lying," he said curtly. "You

are Ihlini, and you are lying, and I want no part of your plots."

"But Atvia is your responsibility, Corin."

She was so cool, so calm, so *certain* of her influence. "Not yet," he answered firmly. "Alaric is lord until the day he dies, and I go home in seven months."

"Alaric will be dead within seven *weeks*," Lillith said gently. "Unless, of course, I should prefer it be seven days—or perhaps seven *hours*."

Corin swore, pushing himself from the chair. The silver was heavy on his wrist, heavy and cold, unneeded ballast for his spirit. "So help me, Ihlini, I will have you sent from Atvia *now*—"

Lillith also rose. They faced each other across a space no wider than five paces, knowing centuries of contention.

Corin frowned as he stared at her. He badly wanted to ask Kiri's advice, but their link was blocked by Lillith's nearness. "What do you want?" he asked. "What is it you want, Ihlini? My cooperation?—you know I will never give it. My departure?—on Alaric's death the realm is mine, regardless of where I am. But you stand here and tell me to reach out my hand and take the throne; you hint you will put Alaric out of my way. Collusion? No. I will never condone his death. And yet I wonder . . . I wonder *if* I refuse it, *if* I go, does it serve some unknown Ihlini purpose? Do you tell me to stay, to take the throne, only because you know the asking will make me go?"

Lillith laughed. "Have I confused you, Corin? Do I show you the two-sided mirror?"

"You show me the perversity of your race," he retorted. "Do you think I will listen to you?"

"If I choose to speak, you will." Lillith gestured and the door flew open to slam against the wall. "Simple tricks," she told him derisively. "The old gods saw to it the Ihlini could not level most sorceries against their brother race, but some small powers remain."

"And Asar-Suti?" he asked. "Does he promise godhood in exchange for servitude?"

For a moment, a moment only, Lillith's color changed. And then she smiled, smoothing her skirts, and gestured for him to go. "A servant will show you to your chambers."

* * *

There was little for the servant to do with Corin's shoulderpacks other than remove the contents and put them away in trunks and casks. Corin, watching in silence, realized there was little about him that denoted his rank. He had come away from Mujhara with few belongings; under the circumstances, he had not wanted to ride with a baggage train. Now he was dependent upon Alaric for such things as extra clothing, and he did not like it.

Had I thought about it, I might have planned more carefully, he told Kiri, and then flinched away from the interference in the link. Lillith's presence was everywhere in the castle, imbuing even the walls with the stink of sorcery. Outside, at greater distance, he had no doubt the link would be re-established, but within the walls of the castle he was cut off from his *lir* in everything save physical contact.

The servant bowed himself out. Corin, hardly noticing, went instantly to Kiri. He sat down on the bear pelt by the bed and gathered the vixen into his arms. She was warm, alive, affectionate, but he badly missed their interior dialogue, the link that gave him the ability to change his shape. He felt stripped of half his identity. "Gods, Kiri . . . I am so *alone.*"

As he bent down, she pressed her muzzle against his neck. He felt cold nose, warm breath; smelled her familiar musky scent. Bright amber eyes seemed to tell him all was well, but it served only to make him even more restless and ill at ease. Suddenly Kiri seemed no more than a tame fox, little more than a pet. It made him angry, resentful, uneasy; it robbed him of his sense of *self*, so important to the Cheysuli.

Is this what it was like for my jehan? *Lirless all those years, despairing of ever knowing the magic of our race . . .* Corin shivered once. *Gods, I could not bear it . . . this is bad enough, and I know it is temporary.*

Against her fur the silver wristlet gleamed. He felt his fingers curl, tighten, *fist*, until he wanted to smash it into the nearest wall. It did not matter that he would shatter delicate bones; he wanted only to rid himself of the shackle Lillith had put on him.

"No chain," he said aloud. "No *chain*, but this is more than enough."

He turned his hand over, baring the underside of his arm. The silver was seamless, displaying no joints; a solid ring of metal. Corin pulled his knife, slid the tip of the blade beneath the cuff and tentatively pried. The shackle was very snug, leaving no room for the blade. Steel scraped on silver; a subtle stinging told him he sliced hair instead of metal.

The door swung open.

Corin, seated on the floor with Kiri in his lap and the knife in his hand, prepared to send the servant away. But when he looked up, scowling, he saw plainly the woman was not a servant at all.

Cheysuli was the first word that came to his mind. And then another: *jehana*.

Corin said it aloud. And then, awkwardly, he sheathed the knife and rose, turning Kiri out of his lap.

He had, he thought, prepared himself for the meeting. On the voyage from Hondarth he had, every night in his bunk, carefully considered what he would say and do when he saw Gisella. But now, seeing her, he could do nothing at all.

"Which one are you?" she asked. "Which son does he send?"

For a moment his tongue was locked in silence. Having heard of Gisella's madness from his father, his uncle, and others, he had reconciled himself to incoherence, wandering wits, perhaps even tantrums. But not such clarity. Never such conciseness.

"Corin," he said hoarsely. "Third-born of his children."

"Mine, too," Gisella said. *"Mine, too, Corin."*

He drew in an unsteady breath. He was accustomed to his father's disfigured face, even beneath the patch; to the wear derived from worry and the experiences of his past. And somehow Corin had unknowingly transferred much of it to Gisella, expecting to see identical signs in her flesh. But there were none.

At thirty-nine she did not share the same uncanny youthfulness as Lillith, but she was not what Corin expected. She was, plainly, Cheysuli; the Atvian was unseen. Black hair was pulled back from her face, displaying the widow's peak that lent her features an odd elegance. There was no hint of silver, no trace of age in her coiled braids. Her flesh was taut and dark, unlined except for a delicate tracery at the edges of yellow eyes. Most striking of all, having borne two sets of twins, she retained the slenderness inherent in Cheysuli women. And she certainly claimed the posture.

Corin and Keely were Niall; now he saw Brennan and Hart.

"Jehana," he said again, and wished that he had not.

"Jehana," she mimicked, shutting the door behind her. "Aye, I am your *jehana.* Gisella of Atvia; Gisella, *Queen of Homana."*

"Aye," he said carefully, wary of her mood.

"I have ordered the packing begun."

He blinked. "Packing?" He felt a fool, cursing himself for his inability to say more than a single word.

Gisella smiled. "It is time I was a wife to my husband again."

"Wife—" He stopped himself, drew in a deep breath, tried to keep his tone uninflected. "There is no place for you in Homana."

"Then I will make one." Yellow eyes glittered a moment; he was reminded of Brennan and Ian. Of a predator stalking its prey. Gisella, watching him, laughed. "They told you I was mad."

Corin was foundering quickly. "Aye," he said plainly at last, giving up on diplomacy.

"Do *you* think I am mad?"

She waited expectantly, clearly unoffended by the possibility he might say he believed she was. He wondered what *he* would say if it were given out that *he* was mad. "All I know," he said slowly, "is that you tried to give all of us to Strahan."

"Is that proof of *madness?"* Gisella asked. "It was not what Niall wanted, nor any of the Cheysuli, but it hardly makes me mad. It makes me an *enemy."*

"Are you?" He stared at her. *"Are* you an enemy?"

"Would I give you to Strahan now?" She laughed. "Oh, no, *no.* That time is passed. I would rather keep you."

That pleased Corin no better; he pictured himself a lapdog on her leash. *Or a dogfox in a cage.* He looked at Kiri uneasily, wishing they could converse.

Gisella moved into the room almost idly, playing with the girdle that clasped slender hips and spilled down the front of her skirts. She wore red, deep, rich red, and rubies set in silver. "That time is passed," she repeated. "The time now is for me to stand at Niall's side . . . to share my husband's bed." She turned abruptly, catching him off-guard. "To send that whore from my place."

Anger rose instantly. "Deirdre is my *jehana*. You will not call her a whore."

He had never, to anyone, claimed Deirdre was his mother. From childhood it had been made plain that Deirdre was mother in blood only to Maeve; that she was not *cheysula*, but *meijha*; not queen, but beloved of the Mujhar. The lines of descent were too important for dissembling or convenience, even among the Cheysuli; all of Niall's children knew Gisella was their mother. But he would not claim her now.

"*Meijha*," Gisella said sweetly. "*Meijha*, then, if you like. It changes nothing. *I* am Queen of Homana. *I* am Niall's wife. I am mother to his children, and I intend to assume my place."

"He will never have you." He was adamant in his certainty.

"Homanan law will *make* him." Gisella's eyes were on Kiri. "I will go before the Homanan Council and I will plead my case." Her voice was quiet and even. "I am the forgotten wife, the forgotten *Queen*, conveniently pushed aside in the name of Niall's lust. I bore him four healthy children—three of which are *sons*—and I have borne exile meekly, with no thought to disagree." Her eyes were eerily feral. "But now I weary of such treatment. I desire better. I desire the place to which I am entitled, the privileges of my rank, the respect and honor of my husband." Her lids half-shuttered her eyes, but he saw the yellow glint. "I desire to know the love of all my children."

"Get out." He was shaking. "Get out of my room. Go. I want nothing to do with you—"

"But you do." Gisella stood before him. "You do, Corin. You want to love me. You want to have me love you in return. You want a mother, a *jehana*. You want a *cheysula* for your *jehan*. You want things to be right in your world, so you can feel good again. You want to know that all those years were not wasted; that indeed, your mother loves you. And *would* have loved you better, had your father allowed it. Had he not sent me away for the sake of an Erinnish princess."

"You would have given me to Strahan—"

"What other choice did I have?" Her shout stopped him cold. "What choice, Corin? Lillith raised me. Lillith shaped me. Lillith *told* me to."

"Lillith is Ihlini," he said tightly. "What did you expect?"

"I expected—and received—*love*," Gisella told him. "It was what she gave me. It was what my father gave me. In the name of that love, I did what I was told."

"To *Strahan*—"

Gisella looked away. "I was confused," she said softly. "Confused, afraid—so *afraid*." She crumpled the silver girdle so that the links bit into her flesh. "I did what I was told."

Corin stared at her for a long, stricken moment. And then he backed away. Hugging himself, he backed away. Knowing himself as confused.

And perhaps equally afraid.

"Go." He stared at the floor. "Just—go."

She went. He heard the chime of silver links, the rattle of clashing rubies, the swish of heavy skirts. He heard the door thud closed. And then he was alone.

Alone with the wondering.

Six

Alaric of Atvia was indeed an old man, though Corin could not venture how old. A few years more than sixty, he knew, and yet he seemed much older. His hair was white. His frame was wracked with palsy. When Corin compared him to Liam, but fourteen years Alaric's junior, the contrast was astonishing.

And somehow *frightening*.

He had been called to attend his grandsire in one of the massive halls. He had gone immediately, in deference to the courtesy Deirdre and Niall had taught him, but he did not like it. And now, facing the man, he liked it even less.

The old man, the old *king*, was a pile of bones in an oversized chair. Rich cloth adorned the bones, but it did not hide the fragility of his flesh or the brittleness of his spirit. The loss of many teeth altered the line of mouth and jaw. The flesh over the nose had thinned so that it was little more than a blade-thin beak jutting out of a hollowed face. His brown eyes were rheumy, nearly swallowed by drooping lids, and he stank of insidious decay.

One hand stabbed out peremptorily, indicating a place before the throne. *"Here!"*

Uneasily, Corin approached. Even with Kiri warding one leg, he wanted to take his leave.

"Here!"

Corin stopped before the throne. The hand with its rigid finger was little more than thinning hide stretched over bone. He could see dark, mottled blemishes and knotted sinews beneath the flesh.

"Here." The hand was lowered at last.

Corin waited. He could think of nothing to say, of nothing to *do*, other than to force himself not to stare. And so he looked at Alaric's feet, wishing himself anywhere but where he was.

"Gisella says you are my grandson."

"Aye."

"*Look* at me, boy! Tell me what you see!"

Startled by the thready shout, Corin looked at the man. "My lord?"

" 'My lord,' " Alaric mimicked. " '*My lord*' indeed! *Tell me what you see!*"

Corin's short-lived courtesy vanished; he did not like this man. "I see death," he snapped. "Death, decay, disillusionment, and the destruction of a man."

"Tell me what you *see!*"

"An *old man!*" Corin cried. "The man who killed his *cheysula* . . . the man who destroyed his daughter . . . the man who lay with an Ihlini witch in exchange for petty power!"

"*What* power?" Alaric demanded. "What power do I hold? Atvia? No. Sorcery? No. The control of my wits and body?—*no!* Lillith has stolen them all."

Corin frowned. This was not what he had expected. Alaric had always worked *with* Lillith, trying to shape the downfall of Homana. "You reap what you sow," he said shortly.

Alaric laughed, although the sound was unlike any Corin had ever heard. And the tears ran out of his eyes. "The seed of my destruction was sown so many years ago," he said. "More than forty, when Lillith first came to Atvia."

"You should have sent her away."

"At the time, she served a purpose." Alaric's fallen mouth moved into a travesty of a smile. "I gave her freedom. I gave her power. I gave her everything she wanted, and willingly. There was no coercion. She used no sorcery on me. We worked toward similar goals." He bent forward, coughed; spittle flew out of his mouth. "I even gave her my daughter."

"And now she wants your throne." Corin tried to keep the distaste from his expression.

"Lillith *has* the throne in everything but name." The old man thrust himself more deeply into the huge chair, thin hands gripping armrests. "She is done ruling through me. Now she wants *you*."

Cold radiated outward from the silver on his wrist and encompassed his entire body. "No," Corin said. "Do you think I would give in to her? I am not as you."

"But I am *in* you." Alaric smiled again. "Will you tell me there is no ambition in you? No desire for power? No need to rule other men?"

"Grandsire—"

"Will you tell me you do not want it?" Alaric's acid tone, though diluted by age, retained enough of its arrogance and spite to stop Corin's protest dead. "Will you stand there, blood of my blood, and tell *me* you do not dream of holding the Lion Throne?"

Appalled, Corin stared.

"Aye," Alaric said. "*Aye* . . . I know what you feel. Because *I* felt it . . . *I* desired it . . . I even dreamed of it. We know better, you and I. There is more to this world, much more, than petty island kingdoms. There are places such as Homana."

"You are disgusting," Corin said. "A disgusting old man awash in the stink of his death. Atvia will be mine on your death because I am your grandson, not because I *need* it—"

"But you do. You *do*." With great effort Alaric grasped the armrests and pulled himself out of the chair. He was stooped, twisted, wracked. But the flame of his hatred blazed. "She drains me . . . *drains* me to feed Gisella . . . to replace her addled wits. Once it is done, I am dead. And then she will turn to you."

"Grandsire—"

"She means to send Gisella to Homana," Alaric said steadily, "where they will see that she is *not* mad, not mad at all, merely the victim of Niall's lust for Deirdre of Erinn. And because there are Homanan laws governing the rights of husbands and wives, the lives of kings and queens, they will make him take her back . . . they will make her Queen again, not knowing what she is." Tears ran down his face. "My beautiful, addled daughter. . . ."

"*Grandsire.*" This time, Corin overrode Alaric. "Do I understand you? Lillith is using *you* to restore Gisella's wits?"

Alaric tapped his head. "It grows emptier by the day—"

Lillith laughed. "So it does, old man. I think your time grows short."

Corin spun even as Alaric sagged and fell back into the chair. Lillith stood in the open doorway, one hand on the door, and then she swung it shut.

Kiri's upper lip lifted. Hackles rose. Corin could not touch her through the link, but there was no need; what both of them felt was obvious, requiring no conversation.

"Old man," she said, "are you unhappy with your lot?"

Alaric mumbled something.

"Old man," she said, "you knew it would come to this."

The old man stirred uneasily in his chair. Between them the tension was palpable; Corin wanted to back away, to leave the hall entirely, wanting no part of this.

"Old man," she said, "it was what you wanted. To see your daughter made whole."

"Gisella," Alaric whispered, and the tears ran down his face.

Lillith looked at Corin. "He asked it," she said. "He begged it of me: to make his daughter whole. To restore her wits so he could see the woman she might have been, had he not destroyed her mother."

"I know the story," Corin said hoarsely. "Alaric shot her out of the sky. Bronwyn was in *lir*-shape, a raven, and he shot her out of the sky."

"Not knowing it was her," Lillith said quietly. Her hands were folded in dark green skirts, hiding the silver-tipped nails. "Not knowing the fall would steal the wits from his unborn daughter, whose birth was so rudely precipitated." Her eyes were on Alaric, huddled formlessness in the throne. "He begged it of me, Corin: to make his daughter whole."

Corin swallowed back the bile that tickled his throat. "For how long?" he asked. "How long will it last?"

Lillith shrugged. "Once Alaric dies, the wits die. The power is not unlimited. Gisella will become what she has been from the moment of her birth."

"Mad," Corin said.

"We are all a little mad." Lillith approached the throne. She put her hands on Alaric's head. "Oh, my lord, I promise the pain will end. In a day, two, three, you will not know its name anymore. You will only know sense-lessness."

"*Knowing* she will go mad, you send her to Homana."

Lillith barely glanced at Corin. "It will be sweet to trouble Niall."

Beneath her hand, Alaric stirred. And Corin, looking into the face of approaching madness, found he could no longer. He turned and walked rapidly from the hall with Kiri close beside him.

Lillith's laughter followed him. "Welcome to Rondule."

With Kiri, he left the castle. He ignored the servants who asked how they could serve him; ignored the soldiers stationed at the gates who offered to fetch him a horse. He ignored them all, too intent on escaping the castle, and said nothing at all to them. He went out of gates, out of the walls, out of Rondule entirely, climbing to the headlands. To the top of the dragon's skull.

He shut his eyes and reached for the earth magic with all of his strength. And as it came tumbling forth, surging up to fill his bones with power, he summoned his other self.

Now— His eyes snapped open.

It hurt. It *hurt.* Perhaps it was Lillith's proximity that twisted the power, perhaps it was something else. But the shapechange was slow and sluggish, wracking his bones with pain.

He gasped. He fell, kneeling on the turf, and tried to thwart the pain. But it came at him in waves, as if intending to keep the earth magic from reaching him.

Kiri—Kiri—Kiri—

He gagged, then retched, as his belly twisted. He felt the shapechange start, then stop, then waver, then withdraw, only to try again. What he was he could not say, knowing only that if it continued he would no longer be Corin at all, but someone else. Some*thing* else; beast instead of man. Or something even worse.

He cried out, hearing the echoes of an eerie yapping howl. Sweat blinded him, distorting his vision. Kneeling on the turf with arms outstretched, fingers clawing at the dirt, he saw the silver on his wrist. Lillith's seamless shackle.

Muscles knotted. Cramped. Spasmed. Altered shape, then altered again.

This time, Corin screamed.

Kiri.
Here.

Kiri.

Here. Her nose pressed against his neck.

Lir—

I am here.

He was stiff. He ached. Flesh, muscle, bone, all ached with unremitting pain. Not blinding, screaming pain, but the deep-seated ache of a body abused within and without. Corin felt as though someone had stretched all his muscles out of shape, binding them tightly around the bones of an ancient man, to form a new one entirely.

Or was he a new *thing?*

He stirred. *"Lir—"*

Here, she said. *Here.*

He opened his eyes. The world was the world again, though he could not speak for himself. He lay curled on his side, arms and legs tucked up, and stared in shock at the woman.

Girl, more like. She sat not so very far away, clad in gray wool skirt and blouse, leather tabard, boots. And she bared a knife in her hand.

Corin blinked. She did not vanish into the air. She remained seated and silent, watching him warily.

He tried to move and found it incredibly painful. Gritting his teeth, he forced arms and legs to straighten. It drew a hiss of discomfort from him. The girl, he saw, frowned. The knife glinted in her hand.

He swallowed. His throat was dry. Even his teeth hurt. He tongued them, relieved to find human instead of vulpine. He *felt* fully human. But he knew he could not be sure.

"Am I a man?" he asked, and heard the croak that issued forth. It stirred him into a movement his body was yet unready for; he fell back, gasping, and wished he had not tried. "Am I a man?" he repeated; this time the words made sense.

"With two arms, two legs, a head," the girl agreed. "Did you think you might not be?"

He sighed. "Aye . . . aye, there was a chance." Slowly he sat up, locking his jaw against the stiffness, and felt a little of it fading. Perhaps once he was up and moving, things would return to normal. He looked at nails, fingers, hands. Then he touched his face.

"Man," she told him firmly. "What else might you be?"

Corin touched Kiri, who sat so close beside him. "Fox," he told her. "Like this one, though dog instead of vixen."

Her eyes narrowed. She was brown-haired, brown-eyed. Not pretty, not plain, though her features had a familiar cast as well as an uncanny, arresting power. Oddly, she reminded him of Aileen. "Are you Cheysuli, then?"

He nodded. "Aye. Kiri is my *lir*."

After a moment of consideration, she slid the knife home in the sheath attached to her belt. "I heard you shouting," she said. "I heard you *screaming*. So I came to see what caused it, and found you there, on the ground, all balled up like a newborn babe." One hand splayed briefly across her abdomen; the gesture was eloquent, divulging much to Corin. "But when I found you, I saw nothing that caused such pain. Nothing except the fox, and *she* wanted only to protect you."

Corin rolled shoulders, head; flexed hands. Everything responded, though a residual ache remained. "I tried to assume *lir*-shape," he said. "Something prevented me. Something twisted the magic." He looked more closely at her, seeing a look in her eye that hinted at wariness, and something close to fear. "I promise, I mean no harm."

"Something might mean *you* harm," she said flatly, pointing to his wrist. "That is the witch's handiwork."

Corin smiled. "You do not appreciate Lillith?"

The girl shivered. "I would sooner live without her." She pressed herself up from the ground, shaking out gray skirts. "There is a tower not far from here . . . an old watchtower, built to warn us of Erinnish invaders. But it is mine, now; will you come? I think you could use the rest."

Corin got up slowly, hearing joints and tendons snap. He could not recall ever feeling so stiff and sore, not even after lengthy arms practice with Hart or Brennan, or even against his uncle.

She took him to the tower on a cliff overlooking the Dragon's Tail. The edge of the world, it was; jagged, craggy, promising death to the man who fell over it. He could see Erinn from here, and the palisades, showing their chalk-white faces. It made him think of Aileen.

The interior was clean, washed white with lime. The tower was round, supporting only a second story. A wooden stair was tucked behind the studded door, winding to the upper floor and beyond, up to the watchtower roof. There was a table, benches, chests, and baskets of wild-flowers. Also the dome of a tiny fireplace where she un-doubtedly cooked her food. It was a cozy, airy home unlike any he had ever known.

She served him bread, cheese, ale. Her name was Sidra, she told him; she owned a goat, some chickens, grew vege-tables, made cloth out of wool on her loom. In town she traded for the other things she might need.

He looked at her in surprise. "You are *alone?*"

"Aye," she said; her chin rose a little.

"Why? Have you no husband"

"No husband."

"And no man to protect you?"

"I protect myself."

"With what, that knife?"

"I have also a sword," she said clearly, looking toward one of the trunks.

Corin thought of Keely, so proud of her weapons-skill; of her independence. But Keely, he thought, had sound reason for both. She was skilled with sword and bow and knife, because her brothers and uncle had taught her. As well as her father's arms-master before Niall had stopped it.

"Sidra," he said quietly, "what are you hiding from me?"

She sighed, staring down at the table as she turned her cup in restless circles. "No man will harm me," she said quietly. "No man who knows who I am, and my father takes care to make it known."

"Why?"

She lifted her head to look at him. "I am Alaric's bas-tard daughter."

Seven

"*Alaric's* bastard?" Corin stared at her in surprise. And then he began to laugh.

Sidra was unamused. Color stained her cheeks and set her ale-brown eyes to glittering; she moved to rise, but he reached across and caught her hand.

"No," he said, "no. Forgive me. I do not laugh at *you*, but at the situation." He suppressed another laugh, though the sound threatened his throat. "How old are you, Sidra? Eighteen? Nineteen?"

"Nineteen." She removed her hand from his. "Why do you ask?"

"Because you are my *su'fala*." He smiled at her frown of incomprehension. "Aunt," he told her plainly. "Gisella, who is your half-sister, is also my mother."

This time there was no quick color in Sidra's cheeks, but a draining of it entirely. "Gisella's—" She broke off, staring at him blankly, and then she thrust her stool away to rise and move from the table. "Cheysuli . . . aye, now I see it. Gisella's son—*one* of them . . . would your name be Corin?"

He affirmed it with a nod.

Sidra sighed, combing brown hair absently. She did not braid it like so many other woman, but wore it tied back with a strip of leather. Mostly free, it curled to her hips. "Corin," she murmured, "Crown Prince of Atvia . . . if the witch lets you have it." She turned back sharply. "You do understand what she does, do you not? The witch? My father's Ihlini whore?"

Corin recalled very well what Alaric looked and sounded like. He wondered how much Sidra knew. "I have seen him only today."

"Then you *do* know." Abruptly she sat down again, leaning forward against the table. "He was not like this, Corin—not always. Oh, aye, I have heard all the stories—you have little reason to love Atvia *or* my father—but I swear, he was not always as you see him. That took *her*."

"Sidra—"

"I saw it," she interrupted. "I saw what she did to him, and what it meant, and I told him. I *told* him to send her away, to make her *stop* it, so she would not destroy him. But I should have known. I should have reckoned with her power over him." She shrugged a little, pulling slender shoulders forward; the gesture was eloquent as a sign of her helplessness. "Lillith had me sent from the castle."

"Against Alaric's wishes?"

Sidra sighed heavily, staring blindly at her cup of ale. "By then he had no more wishes—no more power to demand them of her. But she is not a fool; she used no sorcery against me, nor tried to have me slain. No. She simply sent me *here* . . . where I am away from my father."

Corin could not reconcile the Alaric of his father's stories and the Alaric of the girl's. "Forgive me, Sidra—but I do not see him as you do."

"No." She scraped a nail against the wood and drew an idle pattern. "No, you would not." She fell silent again, then flicked him a glance from under heavy-lashed lids. "It was after Gisella went to Homana to marry the Mujhar. The Lord of Atvia, being lonely without his daughter, turned to other women. My mother was one of them. And on her he sired a daughter, whom he named Sidra." Her mouth hooked down briefly. "My mother died. He took me in. There was no secret of my birth, but he did not care. He loved me, and made it known."

"What happens when he is dead?"

The question was cruel, but she did not avoid it. "What more than *this?*" she asked. "I have no place in the succession. My mother was a simple Atvian girl whose beauty, briefly, caught the eye of Atvia's lord. She was nothing to him. Once, *I* might have been, but Lillith ended that." Sidra shook her head. "I have nothing to offer Atvia."

"Except the child you carry."

Again he saw the telltale hand splaying itself across her belly. "How do *you*—"

"You give it away yourself." He mimicked her gesture distinctly. "I have seen it before."

Sidra looked away from him. "It was one of my father's guardsmen. He is gone, now—sent away by the witch . . . but at least she leaves me the child."

"For now." Corin shook his head. "I have grown up in the midst of political intrigue, Sidra. Bastard you may be, *and* the child, but it bears royal blood. If it is a son, what is to keep the people of Atvia from deciding to follow him instead of a stranger who shifts his shape?"

She stared. "Do you think it will threaten *you?*"

"You yourself said Lillith allowed you to keep the child—at least for now. But once it is born, and if it is a son, what is to say she will not take it for herself? Surely a child would be easier for her to control than a Cheysuli immune to her power."

"Immune," Sidra echoed. "Is that why you wear her wristlet?"

He had forgotten. Now, reminded of it, he felt the weight on his wrist. Cold. It was so *cold*. Bleakly, he shook his head.

Unexpectedly, Sidra smiled. "Aunt," she said in amusement, "to a man who is older than I."

He might have smiled back, but he was thinking of Aileen.

"What is it?" Sidra asked. "What troubles you, my lord?"

It was the first time she had used his rank. It was customary, and something to which he had grown accustomed since childhood, but it was odd coming from her. "Corin," he said. "I was thinking of a woman."

"Ah." She nodded, sighing. "Even as I think of a man."

His hand was lost in Kiri's pelt as she sat by his stool. "Did he know there was a child?"

"No." Sidra poured more ale and drank. "No, he left before I could tell him. Before I knew for certain."

"And if you sent word to him now?"

Her eyes filled with tears. "I could not begin to say where he is. The witch would never tell me."

"And Alaric?"

Sidra brushed the tears away quickly, as if disdaining them. "I doubt he knows. I doubt it was his doing."

"I might ask him for you."

Hope colored cheeks and glistened in widened eyes. "*Would* you?"

"I promise nothing," he told her gently. "I will ask. But I doubt Lillith would tell me anything more than she has told you."

Sidra nodded, staring down at the hands she twined in her lap. "Anything is welcome."

Corin rose. "I should go back. I left somewhat abruptly." He was still stiff, still sore, but the rest had done him good. "I will see what I can find out, and bring you word as soon as I can."

"Oh, my lord, thank you!"

Corin shrugged as he turned toward the tower door. "It is the least I can do after what you did for me." Kiri trotted past him out into the afternoon. It grew late, and dark; the sun slipped low in the sky and was hidden behind a wall of heavy clouds. The wind had an icy bite.

Sidra, framed in the doorway, watched Corin go. "Be wary of the witch."

"Here, I am wary of everything." He lifted his hand in a farewell wave and turned away from her. And then, abruptly, he stopped. "Why not come *with* me, Sidra? Ask Alaric yourself."

"*With* you!" She gaped inelegantly. "I told you how I was turned out of the castle!"

"This time you come at my invitation. If Lillith desires to turn you out again, she will have to contend with me." He put out a beckoning hand. "Come with me, Sidra. We will approach Alaric together."

She did not hesitate. She slammed the door shut behind her and ran down the path to join him.

Lillith's black eyes glittered. "You are a fool," she said coldly.

They faced her in one of the private receiving chambers. Corin had meant to take Sidra immediately to Alaric and had very nearly succeeded, but Lillith ruled the castle. Guardsmen had halted them at the Lord of Atvia's door. In short order, at Lillith's command, they had been forcibly escorted to the chamber.

Corin did not flinch beneath her stare. He was too angry.

"What I *am*, Lillith, is Alaric's grandson and heir to Atvia's throne. If you think to keep *me* from him, you had better reacquaint yourself with the succession."

"He is dying," she said plainly. "He has the night to live, or perhaps tomorrow. I can think of better ways for you to spend your time than bringing bastards here."

"I will bring whomever I choose," he retorted. "She has more right here than you."

"She was sent from this castle at her father's behest—"

"*Your* behest," Sidra said sharply. "Why not let me see my father? Let *him* say if he wants me here or not."

Lillith looked at Corin, ignoring Sidra altogether. "She has no place here. There is no provision for bastards in this castle."

"I will make provision."

"How?" Lillith asked. "Who are you to do so? A stranger. A foreigner. A *shapechanger* sent from the Mujhar, who sucks Atvia dry of wealth. Do you expect a welcome? Do you expect to be loved? Do you expect to *rule?*"

"By the gods, Ihlini—"

"By *my* god!" Her voice rang out to fill the chamber. "You are a long way from Homana, Corin. You are a long way from your gods." Before he could speak, Lillith crossed the room to him. She put her hand on his wrist and the silver blazed to life. "You have no power here. But do you feel mine?"

The pain was intolerable. He felt it run through body like fire, eating at every joint. Yet somehow, dredging up what remained of his waning strength, he managed to pull away. And in doing so, he retaliated. Before Lillith could avoid it he struck her full across the face.

She staggered and nearly fell. He saw the mark of his hand upon her; saw the fury in her eyes. Never had he witnessed such hatred. Never had he seen such control.

"What can you do?" he taunted. "I am a *Cheysuli*, witch."

Lillith threw fallen hair back from her face. Corin's handprint was vivid red against the pallor of her skin. "What can I do?" she asked. And then, oddly, she laughed. "I can *watch*, Cheysuli. That will be more than enough."

It chilled his bones. "Watch *what?*"

But she was gone, leaving them alone in the chamber.

"Gods," Sidra said weakly, "I thought she meant to kill you."

"Come," he told her grimly, "it is time we saw your father."

He took her to see Alaric. But her father was already dead.

"No," Sidra said, as they stood outside the chamber door.

"Aye," the guardsman told them. "Only a moment ago."

"Was Lillith here?" Corin asked curtly.

"My lord, she was. She was with him when he died."

"Convenient," he said flatly, and moved to go inside.

The guardsman dropped his halberd across the door. "No, my lord, I beg you—let them prepare him first."

"Or let them hide the signs of Lillith's touch." Corin put a hand on the halberd. "Guardsman, move aside."

"My lord—" But the door was opened, and Gisella came out of Alaric's chamber.

Corin fell back a step. *"Jehana—"* And cursed himself instantly.

She stared at him blankly. There was nothing in her eyes save grief, and an odd opacity. Corin recalled what Lillith had said about Gisella's borrowed wits. Now Alaric was dead, his mother would revert to madness, to the woman who had so willingly agreed to give up her children.

"Dead," Gisella said. "Dead—dead—dead—" But she broke off the refrain. She looked at Corin expectantly. And then she began to smile. "Have you come to take me home? Has he sent you to take me home?"

Corin suppressed a shudder. *"Jehana—*no. Not to Homana. Your place is here—"

She stopped him. She put out a hand and touched the tawny hair that reached his shoulders. "My beautiful boy," she said. "My strong, beautiful boy . . ."

He wanted to move away, to avoid her entirely, disliking the look of her eyes, but she had backed him against the wall. And even as he tried to pull away her hand, she locked fingers in his hair.

"Jehana—"

"Stay here," she said, "stay with me. No Homana. *Atvia.* Atvia is my home. Stay. *Stay.* Niall has all the others . . . *you* will stay with me—"

He nearly gagged as he jerked her fingers from his hair. "*Jehana*—let me *be*—"

"*Corin will stay with me*—"

He caught her wrists and thrust her away, sacrificing some hair. But he was free of her at last. And before she could reach out again, before she could trap him again, he turned and lurched away. He could not bear to face her.

"My lord." Sidra caught him halfway down the corridor. "Corin, wait—"

He pulled free of her hand as well, wanting no one at all to touch him. "Gods," he said. "*Gods*—" And he fell against the wall, turning his face from her.

"I know," she said, and he saw the tearstains on her face. "*I know.* Come with me, Corin."

She took him away. She took him out of the castle. She took him to the tower, and gave him bitter ale. She herself took two sips, then pushed her cup away. There was grief in her eyes, and weariness; a stark, bleak look. But after a time it faded, and it was his turn to deal with it.

He sat on the floor and gathered Kiri into his arms. "He was nothing to me," he said blankly. "Less to me than to you."

"I know," she said gently. "To me he was always kind, but I know what he has done."

He cradled the vixen against his chest, needing Kiri's strength. "I never wanted Atvia. I have known for as long as I can remember that one day it would be mine, but I never wanted it. I wanted Homana instead."

"It is your home," Sidra said.

"More." He stroked Kiri gently, lost in reverie. "More. It was not just that I longed to stay in a familiar place . . . it was that I wanted it for *mine*. To hold. To rule. To love. I wanted to be Prince of Homana instead of Prince of Atvia." He tilted his head and rubbed his cheek against Kiri's fur. "I wanted Brennan's title. I wanted Brennan's birthright. And now I want his woman."

Sidra sat very still.

"I went to Erinn to tell her it was time she wed my *rujholli*, and fell in love with her myself. Knowing she was Brennan's. Wishing she might be mine." He stared blindly into the gloom of Sidra's tower. "But she must wed the Prince of Homana."

"Oh, my lord . . . I am so sorry for you."

Corin sighed and shut his eyes. "*He* will have Aileen. *He* will have the Lion. *He* will have Homana."

Night had come down fully. It had begun to rain. Sidra rose and lit a second candle, shielding it with her hand. She turned and looked at him over the flame. "We needed to know," she said. "We needed to have the key." And then she opened the door to Lillith.

The storm was in the room. "Strahan wants you," she told him. Behind her were Atvian soldiers.

Corin looked at Sidra.

"*Strahan's* child," she said.

He did not waste time thinking. Almost at once he was up and running with Kiri darting ahead. Together they stumbled up the stairs to the second story, then higher still, heading for the roof. He unlocked and threw back the trapdoor at the top of the ladder, boosted Kiri through, lurched through himself. Slammed the door down, knowing they would break through.

Slashing wind and rain stripped his eyes of vision. He was soaked through in an instant. Cursing, Corin made his way to the low wall and peered out into the storm.

Everything was blackness. No stars, no moon, no torches. He could not see the edge of the cliffs. He could see nothing at all.

Behind him, the door was thrown open.

"Kiri—" he said aloud. "Let me go first, *lir*—let me break your fall."

He caught the edge of the wall. Climbed over, clinging to the rocks. Boot toes grabbed for footholds. The stone was wet, slick, unforgiving. In a moment he would fall.

He heard the shouting of the soldiers. And let go.

He fell, scraping bare arms. And then he landed, toppled, fell—pushed himself up again, wet, muddy, aching. He stared up at the wall, fighting the rain, trying to see the vixen. Now she could jump. Now he could catch her. Without him, the fall would kill her.

"The fox is taken." Cutting the darkness he saw a lurid glare of purple light and Lillith's silhouette.

"*Kiri*—"

"Give yourself up," she called. "He has no plans to kill

you any more than to kill your brothers. Strahan has need of you."

He knew better than to surrender. If Strahan wanted him whole, the Ihlini would never harm Kiri. Corin knew it would be difficult, but there was a chance he might free his *lir*.

Provided I free myself.

Accordingly, Corin turned and ran.

Through the rain and the wind and the darkness—

—and fell off the edge of the world.

There was no time for even a scream.

Interlude

The glare from the Gate backlighted Strahan, making him little more than a shape before her eyes. She could not see his face. She could not see his expression. But she heard the satisfaction in his tone.

"One, two, three." He paused. "Though I might have wished the youngest was less damaged."

"He will heal," Lillith told him. "It was—unexpected. There was no one who could stop him. I think he was as surprised as any of us when he fell from the top of the cliff."

Strahan considered it. "I think it will have its uses . . . if, for nothing else, to help me sway the others." Light was a nimbus around him. "I think it is time to begin."

Lillith smiled. "Who will be the first?"

Flame licked out of the Gate, fell back in a shower of sparks. It illuminated Strahan's face. "First I must test them, one by one, to learn who is the weakest link. None of them will be easy. It will be a task of discovery . . . I must be very gentle. Nothing will be done in haste." He knelt. His back was to her. She saw him bend over the rim of the Gate, extend a hand, then he rose to face her again. In his hands was a silver cup. It was filled with viscid liquid and a pungent purple smoke. "I think the first-born shall be the first."

Lillith drew in a breath. "He will be the hardest of all."

The cup glowed silver-purple. "What I have to offer Brennan may not be enough . . . it is possible he has overcome his fear. But I can use his brothers . . . I can use his twin. The bond between them is nearly as strong as that between warrior and *lir*."

"And do you think Hart will break?"

"He may be the easiest. What I offer *him* is continuity

as a Cheysuli. They are an immensely proud race, as we have reason to know, and more intractable than they should be." Strahan smiled and rubbed thoughtfully at his bottom lip. "But now he lacks a hand. Now he is *maimed.* Lacking a hand, he lacks a race . . . I think it should be enough."

"And if *Hart* does not break?"

Over the cup he looked at her. Smoke wreathed his face, but the eyes were still paramount. "Then all will be left to Corin. With one, I can break them all." Strahan slowly nodded. "He is an ambitious man, and jealous of the eldest. It is a formidable weapon. It should not be difficult."

Lillith frowned. "Do not misjudge them, Strahan. None of them is weak."

"But all of them have *weaknesses.* And I intend to exploit them."

It did not erase her frown. She was older than her brother by nearly two hundred years. She knew the Cheysuli better. She knew them very well.

Lillith looked at her brother. Strahan drank from the cup.

PART V

One

The door was opened. Light spilled into the cell. Brennan, hunched against the wall, shut his eyes at once.

"Come out," the voice said.

The syllables were strange. Brennan did not at first know them, hearing only sound. And then he pieced them together, understood them, stared through the crack he made in the shield of his fingers.

"Come out," the voice repeated.

He pressed himself against the wall and tried to climb inside it.

"Bring him out," the voice said, and hands were laid upon him.

They got him as far as the door. Light fell full upon him. To a man who had lived too long in darkness, the flame was intolerable.

But no more so than the fear.

He was poised on the threshold, blinded by the light. He turned his head aside, shutting his eyes, trying to avoid it; a torch was held nearer yet.

"*Behold* the Prince of Homana."

The voice was Rhiannon's voice. Brennan opened his eyes.

Alone in the darkness, he had lost track of time. He knew it had been weeks; he had not expected months. But she was big with the weight of his child.

"Behold the *Prince of Homana*." Her tone mocked him. Then she gestured to those who held him. "Take him at once to Strahan."

Slowly it penetrated. He was out of the cell—*free* of the cell—they had taken him out of the cell. The stink of it clung to him, but the scent of hope replaced it.

They took him up endless spirals of winding stairs. He

was weak from inactivity, cramped from the tiny cell, bound up by the burden of fear. He knew he was not mad; he knew also he was not quite sane.

More stairs. And then at last a door. They opened it, thrust him through, shut the door behind him.

Brennan spun, staggering, and tried to claw open the door. They had shut him up *again*.

His nails broke on the wood. The latch did not give beneath his desperate fingers. The door was securely locked. It was no less than he should have expected. He closed his eyes and pressed his face against the wood, trying to calm himself, but the fear was ever-present.

It was all he had known for months.

Finally he turned. Expecting anything, he set his back against the door. But the room was empty of men or women. No one inhabited it. Brennan drew in an unsteady breath.

The chamber was small, but large to him, after captivity in his cell. The walls were black—Valgaard's dominant color—but soft rugs carpeted the floors even as tapestries brightened the walls. Fire blazed in the fireplace. There were chairs and tables and candleracks, all ablaze with light. It made him squint; he was yet unaccustomed to light.

And then he smelled the food.

His belly cramped instantly. They had not starved him, preferring instead to keep him alive, but the food had been much less than he was accustomed to, and the diet very plain. His body cried out for better, and now it was offered to him.

Brennan stared at the silver platters. Hot meat: beef, venison, pork, and poultry. Fresh bread: brown, white, hard, and soft, redolent of fresh baking. Wheels of cheese: creamy ivory, pale yellow, ocher-gold. Baskets of fruit: apples, grapes, pears, peaches, plums, and countless others. Beakers of wine and ale and *usca*.

Quickly he crossed to the table, reaching out to scoop up the food. He grabbed a goblet of wine. Tore off a chunk of beef. And then, even as his belly cried out, he ate and drank none of it.

His hands trembled. Wine slopped over the rim of his goblet, dripping on his boots. The aromas were overwhelming.

He dropped the beef onto the platter. Set the goblet down. It overturned in the unsteadiness of his hand, ringing against the wood of the tabletop. All the wine spilled out in a river of blood-colored liquid.

Brennan backed away. And then, still shaking, he sought a chair and fell into it, leaning forward to press his face against his hands.

The flesh was slack and lifeless. His nails were rimmed in black. He smelled the stink of himself. He was awash in the filth of his cell. The Brennan he knew was gone.

And his belly cried out for food.

"You insult me," Strahan said.

Brennan started. He had heard nothing, nothing at all, and yet the door was open. And then Strahan closed it and came to greet his guest.

"I offer you food." He indicated the table. "I offer you wine, ale, bread. Yet you touch none of it."

Brennan had spoken to no man for weeks, for no one had spoken to him. All he could do was stare.

Strahan's eyes narrowed slightly. And then he smiled, and sat down across from his kinsman.

Brennan had not, until now, ever seen the Ihlini. He had been raised on stories of the man, on tales of his sorcery, but never had he seen him. And now that he did, now that he sat but four paces from him, he realized the stories paled beside the man. Strahan was power incarnate.

The eyes, Brennan thought. *Gods, what evil eyes.*

One blue, one brown, set slightly oblique in a face built of flawless bones. His beauty did not in any way make him effeminate, but the features were as arresting as those of a beautiful woman. Straight, narrow nose, winged black brows; the fall of raven hair, held back by a silver circlet.

He was a man who ruled through beguilement, and Brennan felt its touch.

Strahan looked at him. Looked at him and smiled. "You should see yourself."

Brennan did not need to. He knew what Strahan saw; what he had ordered shaped to precise specifications.

The Ihlini's skin was fairer than Brennan's. Slender white hands were ablaze with brilliant gemstones: ruby, sapphire, emerald. A diamond and a bloodstone. His nails were clean and buffed. Idly, he leaned his chin into one hand and tapped at his upper lip.

Brennan did not know at which eye to look, and so he looked at neither.

Strahan sighed a little. His leathers, soft and gray, were far cleaner than Brennan's soiled brown ones. He smelled of scented unguents more fragrant than Brennan's stink.

"It is unfortunate," Strahan said quietly, "that you have come to this state. A prince should never be brought so low, nor a Cheysuli warrior."

Brennan locked himself up in silence.

Strahan gazed at curiously. "Was it the Womb of the Earth that did it? I have been there, you know. I have seen the marble *lir*, the bottomless oubliette, the rune-carved walls of the narrow passageway." He nodded. "I myself have never been afraid of small places, but it must be a difficult thing to bear. Particularly for a Cheysuli." He paused. "Particularly for *you*."

Brennan was no longer in the room. He was back in the Womb, seeing the marble *lir*. Seeing the oubliette. Learning the meaning of fear.

"It must be terrifying to know yourself locked in, unable to leave . . . to know yourself trapped and helpless, alone in a tiny place. Knowing no one can hear your screams. No one can soothe your fear. No one can bear it for you."

Brennan's breathing quickened. Rigid fingers made knots of his hands.

"And so filthy, too," Strahan said sympathetically. "Such humiliation, on top of all the fear. Having to relieve yourself in a corner like an animal instead of like a man . . . contending with dungeon vermin . . . smelling the stink of one's own body." He shifted in his chair; gemstones glittered on his fingers. Glittered to mirror his eyes. "Hearing things . . . seeing things . . . and too afraid to sleep."

Brennan shut his eyes.

"And knowing all the time such a simple thing will free you."

Brennan opened his eyes.

Strahan leaned forward and took up a cup of wine. "Will you serve me, Brennan?"

Brennan's scalp itched. Lice infested him. All he could do was stare.

Strahan drank wine.

Brennan drew an unsteady breath. The room was warm, dry, brightly lighted, filled with the beguiling aromas of food and drink. His body cried out for kindness again. His battered spirit demanded it.

Strahan put down the wine. "I have a smaller cell."

Brennan flinched, and hated himself.

"More suitable to your condition."

Brennan wet cracked lips. "No," he croaked, prepared to argue it.

Strahan rose. "You will excuse me, I am sure; there are things I must attend to. My servants will escort you back."

He turned away. A casual flick of one finger caused the door to swing open. Men waited there.

"The prince prefers his cell." Strahan's tone was one of complete indifference.

Men surrounded him. They lifted him out of the chair and put him on his feet. Before he could speak a word, before he could begin to struggle, they had taken him from the chamber. Back down the winding stairways into the depths of Valgaard's bowels.

At the cell door, he rebelled. But they were too strong for him. The door was opened. They flung him through. They locked it on his outcry.

Brennan stared blindly into the darkness and knew Strahan was not finished. And then he began to shake.

A second door was unlocked. A second man brought out. Him also, they took to Strahan.

The sorcerer turned from the casement as Brennan's brother was ushered in. He looked at Hart's gaunt face, looked at the leather-wrapped stump, looked back at the haunted eyes. "I apologize," he said kindly. "Dar was overly enthusiastic."

Hart was plunged back instantly into the room at Ilsa's dwelling. To when they had pinned his hand to the table. To when the blade had fallen. To the moment he realized he no longer had a left hand. And the memory of the pain.

Rage boiled up inside. But he said nothing at all; he would not give Strahan the satisfaction.

"It makes you angry," Strahan said. "Do you think I cannot see it?"

As was becoming habitual, Hart cradled the stump in his remaining hand, pressing it gently against his chest in an unconsciously vulnerable gesture of retreat and self-protection.

Strahan indicated food and wine. "Will you eat? Will you drink? I should hate to see it go to waste." And then he paused, as if arrested in mid-motion. "But of course, I had forgotten . . . someone will have to cut it for you."

Humiliation tied Hart's belly into knots and briefly, too briefly, colored his face a deeper bronze. It took all his strength to keep the anguish from his tone. "What do you want me for?"

"Sit down, my lord of Solinde . . . I see an alarming pallor in your face."

Hart fully intended to ignore the suggestion. But the pallor was unfeigned; shock coupled with fever had served to sap his strength. Slowly he seated himself, preferring the chair to falling down. He found the motion uncomfortable; he was accustomed to using two hands.

"Does it hurt?" Strahan asked. "Is the loss of a hand anything like the loss of an ear?"

Hart looked at him in shock. He had forgotten that Strahan had only one ear. The other had been cut off in a fight with one of Hart's own kinsmen long ago on the Crystal Isle.

Strahan hooked long hair back and bared the side of his head. "We all suffer losses, some of us more dramatically than others." He moved the hair back into place. "It was my misfortune the ear was lost entirely. Had I found it, the Seker might have made me whole . . . but I was somewhat pressed for time."

Hart stirred. "If he is as powerful as you claim, why did he not simply make you a new one?"

"Flesh born of flesh," Strahan said. "The original was required."

Hart looked down at the stump of his wrist. He *felt* the hand there, and yet when he looked he saw nothing at all. When he moved it, nothing grasped. But the reflexive pain was undiminished.

"I know, of course, the loss of a hand precludes you from returning to your clan." Strahan's mouth shaped the words with a deep and abiding compassion. "We Ihlini are not so harsh. A man's mind may be useful even if the body is not."

Hart gazed blindly at the hand that no longer existed.

"But it would be so difficult for a maimed warrior to contribute to his clan," Strahan remarked. "How can you use a bow? How can you mount a defense? How can you ward your woman and children against the enemy?"

Hart did his best to ignore him, but the gentle probing found its mark.

"And, of course, as part of the prophecy . . . well . . . what is left to you?" Strahan poured wine. "What is there for you to do? How can a warrior serve when he is no longer recognized as a warrior?"

Hart stirred at last. "My *jehan* lost an eye."

Strahan made a dismissive gesture. "Oh, aye, he did . . . but then he had another."

"I have another hand."

"A hand is not an eye." Strahan paused. "What will they do?" he asked. "Will they strip you of your gold? Blot out your rune in the birthlines? From the path of the prophecy?"

Breath caught in Hart's tight throat. He felt the slow churning of his belly.

"Will they tear down your pavilion? Take *cheysula* or *meijha* from you?" Strahan paused. "Or will no Cheysuli woman be allowed to speak your name?"

"Stop," Hart whispered.

"Will they strip you of your *lir?* Or will the *lir* go regardless?"

"Stop." Hart said.

"There is no place for you, Hart. You are now a clanless warrior, unable to serve your race."

Hart stood up so fast he overset the chair. *"Ku'reshtin!"* But before he could move to strike him, Strahan caught hold of his wrist.

"No," the sorcerer said, and closed his fingers on the leather that warded the healing stump.

The pain was excruciating. Hart wavered on his feet.

"No," Strahan said, "I can offer you better."

Sweat ran down Hart's face to mix with tears of pain. "You offer me loss of honor . . . the loss of who I *am*—"

"Service to me will replace it."

Hart tore his wrist free, then hugged it against his chest. Pain robbed him of the words. All he could do was shake his head.

Strahan sighed. "You Cheysuli are so stubborn. Nearly as stubborn as I." And before Hart could answer, he summoned men to take him away.

The hand was cool on Corin's brow. It took the heat away. For so long there had been heat. Heat and unbearable pain. And now Strahan took it away.

"You are a fortunate man," the sorcerer told him gently. "You very nearly died."

The eyes transfixed him utterly.

"But you are better now. The bones begin to heal. I think you will walk again, though possibly with a limp." Strahan paused. "Do you recall what happened to you?"

Vividly, Corin did. "I fell." The voice echoed the weakness in his body. "I fell off the dragon's skull." He gazed clear-eyed up at Strahan. "She said it was *your* child."

Strahan's winged brows lifted to touch his circlet. And then he smiled. "May the Seker grant it perfect health."

Corin itched. He ached. He wanted badly to get up, but knew he could not. "Kiri?" he said plainly.

"Mine. She is well, I promise you." Strahan made a sign and a stool was instantly brought. He sat down close to Corin's bedside. "You understand, I am sure, why I wanted you."

"You want Atvia."

"But only for my lord. I am not a greedy man." Strahan smoothed the covers. "Is there much pain, Corin? I can drain it from you."

Corin recalled how Lillith had drained Alaric of wits and life. He said no distinctly.

Strahan smiled, and then he laughed. "Why do you think the worst of me? If I wanted you dead, I would have left you at the bottom of the cliff, to wash out into the sea. Perhaps to wash up on Erinn's shores, where Aileen could grieve over you."

Corin shut his eyes. "I will not give you Atvia."

"Atvia, for the moment, is quite within my grasp." Strahan's palm touched his brow again. "I was thinking of Homana."

Corin's eyes snapped open.

"Aye, I thought that might get your attention." The fingers dripped with ice; the fever began to fade. "Sidra tells me you want your brother's bride. That you want your brother's title. That you want your brother's throne."

Corin bit his lip. "Take your hand from me."

After a moment, Strahan did. The pain renewed itself. "The Seker is a generous god. What a man wants, he often bestows."

"Then why does he not simply *give* you the realms you want?" The level of pain was rising. He was transfixed by Strahan's stare. "Why does he not simply *take* them?"

"Through men like me, he will." Strahan tore back the covers to bare splints and linen wrappings. "Both legs, Corin. And ribs I cannot count. You are fortunate the bones of your head were left intact, else I could offer you nothing."

"You offer me nothing I will accept." Corin threaded bruised fingers through his hair and stripped it back from his face, pulling hard purposely to deflect the pain from his mending bones. "I will heal. The pain will die. You offer me nothing at all."

"You will heal. The pain will die. But I can offer you much more. I can offer you what you want."

Corin grunted his irony. "Homana is not mine to give."

"And if it were?" Strahan asked softly. "If I offered to share it with you?"

"Share *what?*" Corin demanded. "You will make me a minion regardless, and then I will need no throne."

Strahan carefully covered him up again. "A minion has its uses, but so does a living man. I would prefer to use the latter."

Corin turned his head away.

"I can turn your legs to jelly," Strahan said softly. "*You* have the power to heal, but I can undo it all. With only the touch of my hand." Jewels glittered on his fingers.

"You have my *lir*," Corin said hoarsely. "How can I hope to refuse you? What pleasure is there in it for a man like you?"

"You should hope instead to aid me." Strahan touched Corin's head. "I will be here if you need me. Dream a while, my lord. Dream of your red-headed princess . . . dream of your brother's throne."

Corin slipped into darkness. He dreamed of his brother's bride.

Two

Light spilled into the cell. Strahan stood in the doorway. "A gift for my stubborn kinsman."

Brennan turned his back.

"Surcease from your fear."

The voice was endlessly tender. Brennan shut his eyes.

"Behold," Strahan said. "I show you the life of a warrior."

Brennan stood facing the wall. Spread fingers touched fetid slime; nails dug into slick stone in an effort to beat off beguilement. He hated the cell. Hated what it did to him. Hated himself because of it. He had grown used to the stench, but not inured to the distaste. It made him want to vomit.

And then the wall moved. Stone melted away. Brennan opened his eyes.

The world unfolded before him.

Homana. The grassy plains outside of Mujhara, stretching east toward Clankeep. He was free of Valgaard at last—free of the tiny cell—free of consuming fear. All around him lay the world, a bright and shining world, made of earth and sky and sun and moon and the warmth of a summer day.

Brennan's breath hissed out of his mouth. Filth sloughed off of him. Fresh leathers adorned his body. He was young and strong and full of life, bursting to run free.

Then come, Sleeta said. *What keeps you from it,* lir?

And he ran, he *ran,* trading human flesh for feline, knowing the endless freedom of *lir*-shape. Running on, through meadowlands, woodlands, forests, shedding the weight of fear. All he knew was freedom and the promise of the day.

Gods, he exulted, *this is the best of all—*

And then all was snatched away. All was torn apart. All was swallowed whole by the darkness of the cell.

Beneath his hands was slime. Banished was his freedom, traded for degradation.

"Sleeta," he said only.

"Come out with me," Strahan said. "There is something you should see."

Brennan was too dazed to mark his way. He knew only that Strahan's servants took him up stairs, then down them, then through narrow passageways. Eerie *godfire* glowed, negating the need for candles. Beneath his booted feet fell away stair after stair, shallow, hollowed, smooth, worn down after decades of use. Or was it centuries?

Down, down, down. Briefly, he thought of the Womb of the Earth. But this was far deeper. Blacker. It stank of the netherworld.

One man before him, one behind. Fleetingly, he considered an attempt at escape. But it fled the moment he thought it; he was in no condition to try such folly. Captivity had worn him to the bone just as time had worn the steps. Even a child could knock him down; Strahan's men were not children.

Down, down, *down.*

Something gibbered in the wall.

Brennan's breath was an audible rasp. He tried to silence himself, but the months had stripped him of control. He was frightened, and it showed. Strahan knew his man; knew how to diminish his pride.

Down.

And then the servants stepped aside.

On the threshold, Brennan halted. He thought to turn and run, but a door closed quietly behind him. Through the columns, an echo ran.

"Behold," Strahan said, "the Presence Chamber of the god."

Brennan looked down the columned corridor, stunned by the vastness of the cavern. It unfolded before him into a multitude of vaulted glasswork ceilings, arch upon arch, each reaching higher then the last. Much like the rune-carved hammer-beamed timbers in the roof of Homana-Mujhar, the cavern displayed a filigree of fretwork. A lattice of delicate glass, set aglow from the glare of the Gate.

Something hummed through whorled columns. *Godfire* rose, then died.

"Come forth," Strahan said, *"and behold the Gate of the god."*

Steadily, Brennan walked. Behind him, humming followed.

Beyond the Gate, Strahan waited. He wore black leathers and a velvet doublet of deepest, blood-red purple. *Godfire* glowed in the creases. On his brow, the circlet blazed. Raven hair cloaked shoulders.

Brennan walked steadily on, transfixed by the maw in the earth. Around its lips flames danced, licked, beckoned; the spittle of the god was foul.

"There," Strahan said. In his hands was a rectangular black-lacquered box alive with writhing crimson runes.

Brennan halted. He was but two steps from the rim of the Gate, but he did not look. Strahan faced him across it. Between them lay the glowing sphincter of the Seker's netherworld. The realm of Asar-Suti.

He was *afraid*. But in that moment, anger swallowed fear. "One might think," Brennan said, "the Seker would *smell* better."

Strahan's smile vanished.

"One might *realize*," Brennan said, "that a Cheysuli cannot be broken." He paused. "Not by his brother race."

The runes ran in frenzied circles around the edge of the box until there were no runes at all, only a blur of lurid light red as blood. Strahan's expression was unreadable.

"Lock me up," Brennan said. "Lock me up forever. But I will never serve you. Not in madness *or* sanity."

Strahan's winged brows rose slightly, touched the curve of the gleaming circlet. It was of gnarled, twisted shapes, wracked in blood-born silver. "I am suitably impressed by your confidence." One eloquent finger tapped the lid of the wooden box; the runes fell back into place. "I admire your strength of will. But I make no idle boast: I can break a Cheysuli. And I intend to do it."

"How?" Brennan asked. "You hold my *lir;* so be it. I can do nothing to free her. You may slay her if you choose; doing so frees me forever, and you will lose me entirely."

"There will be no death-ritual," Strahan told him. "No escape from the madness *lir*lessness will bring. Do you sentence yourself to that?"

Madness was anathema to the Cheysuli. The loss of control in *lir*-shape or out of it was considered inexcusable, in addition to being potentially deadly. A Cheysuli warrior made *lir*less was, in time, little better than a beast; death was preferable. And so the ritual had been born. But in order to make the ritual have meaning, suicide was taboo. A paradox. And clearly, Strahan knew it.

Brennan had been raised to respect the customs of his race. At his Ceremony of Honors, following the bonding with Sleeta, he had accepted the responsibilities of a warrior knowing full well that even the Mujhar of Homana owed his life to the will of the gods. The ritual bound Niall's heir as well as others, and he had accepted it.

And now, his commitment was tested.

"You have spent the better part of several months attempting to drive me mad," Brennan said. "*Lir*lessness will succeed where imprisonment could not, but of what use am I then? What good is a mad Mujhar?"

Strahan's smile was sweet. "More malleable than one who is sane. Look at Shaine." A tendril of living flame licked up from the Gate, touched his boot, tapped, as if to remind him; fell back as Strahan nodded. "Look at Shaine, your distant kinsman, who once gave *us* Homana-Mujhar because he preferred Ihlini to Cheysuli."

"But Carillon took it back . . . it *and* Solinde. Your homeland, Strahan . . . and now a vassal to the Cheysuli." Brennan shrugged. "Do your worst, Ihlini. I can hardly gainsay you, but idiocy may thwart you."

"And if I chose to kill the cat with an excess of—civility? What would you say then?"

"That I will suffer," Brennan answered. "No doubt I will beg you to stop. But when you *have* stopped, and I have my wits about me, the cycle will start again."

Strahan shook his head. "You do not understand. I do not *need* you sane . . . I can control a hollow man easier than one stuffed full with Cheysuli pride."

"Then why this mummery?"

Strahan sighed. "An amusing divertissement. But now, shall we to the bargain? You may find it interests you."

Brennan merely shrugged.

"I want Homana," Strahan said. "Through you I can have it."

Brennan shook his head.

"In good time, *you* shall have it; I will not take Niall's life. Let him live out his years . . . I have as many as I need." Strahan's eyes narrowed. "The bargain, Brennan: serve me, and I will spare your father's life. I will spare the life of your *lir*. I will give you the years of your life and beyond, through the benificence of the Seker."

"I have no desire to live forever." Brennan folded his dirt-crusted arms. The *lir*-gold was dulled by grime, but it did not dull his determination. "I will not accept your bargain."

"Not even to save your kin?"

He dared give Strahan no advantage. Brennan set his teeth. "You can only kill them once. *Then* where is your power?"

"I can destroy the prophecy."

"You have tried so many times."

Strahan sighed. "This, I see, leads nowhere."

"No." Brennan smiled. "What have you left, Ihlini?"

"*This*," Strahan said, and opened the wooden box.

Through the smoke, Brennan looked. And then he stared in disgust at Strahan, his distaste as plain as his bafflement.

"Do you not recognize it?" Strahan asked.

"A human hand," Brennan said flatly. "Ensorcelled, no doubt; else it would have decayed by now."

"More than a human hand. It is a *Cheysuli* hand."

As he was meant to, Brennan looked again. His belly knotted itself.

Strahan closed the box. "I should be very careful. Hart may want it back."

When he could, Brennan breathed again and swallowed back the bile. "There was no ring," he said tightly.

"He wagered it away." Strahan looked past Brennan. "Why not ask him yourself?"

Brennan swung around. Through the columns came his brother. At his left wrist there was no hand.

"I have the power." Strahan spoke with infinite kindness. "Serve me, Brennan, and I will make him whole."

"*Rujho!*" It was Hart, whose voice echoed shock throughout the cavern. "Gods, Brennan—not *you!* I thought he had only me!"

Strahan smiled warmly. "Welcome to the Gate."

Hart barely spared a glance for the Ihlini. He ran forward toward Brennan. *"Rujho—"* But he slowed as he reached the Gate. The light was odd on his face, limning gauntness and despair. "Brennan, are you whole?"

Brennan swallowed tightly. "More so than you," he said. "Oh, gods, *rujho*—" Abruptly he turned away.

"Brennan!" Hart halted raggedly. Shock made him awkward. "Do you already cast me out?"

"Ask him!" Brennan spun and thrust out an arm toward Strahan. "Ask *him*, Hart!"

Hart turned toward the Ihlini. Shock at seeing Brennan had overtaken the immediacy of his disability, but now it was obvious that Brennan had been told. He had *expected* it. And it obviously made a difference.

Emptiness overwhelmed him. Despair was overpowering.

"I offer your brother a choice," Strahan said, "now I will give it to you."

Hart sighed wearily, too weary to protest as he stripped fallen hair out of his gaunt face. Cheysuli were characteristically angular, formed of remarkably striking bones, but captivity, illness, and strain had fined Hart down too far. If the dark skin were any tauter, the cheekbones would cut through flesh. "You asked him for Homana. Now you ask me for Solinde."

"But your bargain is different." Strahan's fingers splayed across the lid of the box, tapping idly. "He says there is no inducement to make him accept my service. But you are a different man. What would *you* have of me?"·

Hart's laughter had the edge of madness in it. "My freedom," he said promptly. "The freedom of my *rujholli.* No further dealings with you."

"Unacceptable." Strahan smiled. "Serve me, Hart. Accept the Seker as your lord."

"And destroy the prophecy." Hart shook his head. For all he meant to sound fierce and adamant, unimpressed by Strahan's words, he knew he sounded precisely what he *was*: badly frightened, nearly worn through, on the brink of breaking down from the loss of hand and clan. It took all he had to speak steadily, betraying nothing of what he felt inside the dwindling shell. "You have taken my hand, Ihlini . . . you have stolen my heritage from me. I am, as you have said, clanless and unwhole. There is no place for me among the Cheysuli." He spread his arms and displayed hand and stump. "What have I left to lose?"

"Your *lir*."

Hart laughed at him, though it had a ragged sound. "Rael is *free* . . . Dar never caught him. Try again, Ihlini."

"He may be free," Strahan conceded after a moment, "but you are separated. Eventually, the *lir*-bond shall grow thin, *too* thin . . . grow brittle, *so* brittle . . . until it cannot survive, and *breaks*."

Hart drew in a deep breath. "So be it, Ihlini. Madness— and eventual death—is preferable to serving you and your noxious god."

Strahan tilted his head toward Brennan. "The life of your twin-born brother."

Hart looked at Brennan. He saw the rigidity of the body, the bleakness in yellow eyes. He looked for some suggestion, some hint of what Brennan desired him to say. But there was none. Brennan looked soundly defeated, co-cooned in futility.

That shook Hart more than anything else. He drew in another deep breath. "An idle promise, Ihlini. Brennan would sooner be dead than have me become your minion merely to save his life."

Brennan's smile was bittersweet.

Strahan considered it. He stroked the wooden box. "I will give you the girl."

Anger flared anew. "Is she not what you promised *Dar?*"

"Dar is expendable." Strahan brightened. "Would his life be enough for you?"

Hart drew in his left arm and hugged it against his chest. "You will kill whomever you choose, regardless of what I want. I would be a fool to accept such terms."

"Give in." Strahan suggested. "The service will not harm you. You will still be Prince of Solinde. Still have the white-haired woman. Still have your games of chance. What more could you want?"

Hart's hard-won demeanor began to slip. In his eyes was emptiness. "What I want you cannot give."

Brennan, clearly afraid, took a step toward him.

"No." Strahan's tone was a whiplash of sound that hissed in the glassy cavern. "This is *his* choice, now."

"No!" Brennan shouted. A tendril of flame flowed out of the Gate and slapped him to the ground.

A second gout deftly blocked Hart's move to reach his brother. It beat him back until he cursed aloud.

"Now," Strahan said, "tell me what you want."

Hart hugged his arm, swaying on his feet. "I want my clan!" he shouted. "I want the regard and honor of my race, not the ouster I am due." He thrust his left arm into the air and displayed the emptiness at the end of his leather-cuffed wrist. His arm shook with the tension of his rigid body. "With one blow of a sword, Dar had me stripped of my heritage. Maimed warrior, *worthless* warrior . . . not fit to be part of the clan. And so I am *kin-wrecked*—" He shut his eyes a moment, then drew in an unsteady breath and went on. "Where does it leave me, Ihlini? Why should I serve *you?*" Hart stood on the edge of the Gate, oblivious to its flame as the tears ran down his face. "You cannot give back my hand—no more than grow back your ear!"

Strahan opened the box.

In noisy silence, Hart stared at the hand in its bed of silk. There was no blood. The cut had been clean, leaving no gore at all. Oddly dispassionate, coldly assessive, he studied the severed hand. He marked scars won in childhood and arms-practice. The enlargement of one knuckle. The sinews beneath brown flesh. There was no mistaking the hand. He knew it was his own.

Instinctively he made an impossible fist. As the tremor spread through his stump, the hand in the box closed its fingers.

Hart cried out. He wavered on the brink. Flame licked up and drove him back, staggering, until he fell to his knees. He cradled his arm and rocked.

To and fro.

To and fro.

Oblivious to his brother.

Strahan's tone was gentle. "You have only to say you will serve me."

Hart hugged his arm and rocked.

Strahan looked at Brennan. "*You* have a choice as well."

Brennan knelt on the glassy floor. All he could do was stare at Hart, sharing a measure of his anguish.

"I will let you consider it." A flick of his hand built an encircling fence of flame to keep them near the Gate. Then Strahan walked away. As he moved, smoke followed. The columns sang their atonal song.

Corin leaned back on his elbows, gritting his teeth in response to the discomfort of ribs and legs. He was indeed fortunate, as Strahan had pointed out, to have survived the fall from the cliff. To survive the fever that followed. But he had, and now he healed; with healing came renewed and abiding anger: he was prisoner to the Ihlini.

And yet he was not in a cell. His room was small, but hardly bereft of luxuries. The bed was comfortable. The hangings were richly patterned, if in runic glyphs he did not know and feared to learn. The door was clearly unlocked. If he could walk, he might go free. But his legs were not quite healed.

He had tried, time and again, to contact Kiri through the link. But Valgaard was the font of Strahan's power; even Old Blood was neutralized. It would take wits instead of magic to win free of his captor's grip.

The door swung open. Corin tensed as Strahan entered. He saw rich dark clothing, rune-wrought circlet, the compelling mismatched eyes. And he knew the time had come at last to meet absolute power in human form.

The room lay in darkness in deference to his rest. But now Strahan bent over a gilded candle, blew, set the wick ablaze. The flame was purest purple.

Another. Another. Until the room ran with lurid *godfire*, the excrescence of the god.

Strahan stood over him. "The time is come," he said gently. "You must make your choice."

Corin slowly leaned back against piled bolsters and uncrooked his elbows, hearing the pop of weakened joints; feeling the fatigue of battered flesh. He tried consciously to ease the tension from his rigid body, knowing he would fail.

"I have something for you." Strahan put it into his hand.

Corin stared at it. A ring. A circlet of heavy gold, incised with careful runes, and a brilliant blood-red ruby held firm by taloned prongs. The ring of the Prince of Homana.

Chilled, Corin looked at Strahan. "You have my *rujholli*."

"Brennan. Hart. *You*." In the eerie light, Strahan's face was etched in fretwork shadows. "In addition to your *lir*."

Corin's eyes went back the ring. It was too large for him, he knew, because he had tried it on once. Brennan was taller, heavier, more strongly made than Corin; Hart was very like him. Their fingers were longer, stronger, browner. More Cheysuli than his.

Corin looked at his own signet. The emerald still glittered against his flesh. The gold shone brightly as ever, if perverted by the *godfire*. Strahan had not touched it.

"Trade," Strahan suggested.

His hand spasmed closed, trapping the ring in his palm. "This is *Brennan's* ring."

"Put it on, and it is yours," Strahan smiled. "And all it represents."

Corin swallowed tightly. "Is he dead? Have you killed him? Is that why you taunt me with it?"

"He is quite unharmed, and I do not taunt. I *offer*." Strahan paused. "If you want it, it is yours. You need only put it on."

"I am Crown Prince of *Atvia*."

"You are prisoner to me," Strahan moved a trifle closer. "There is no need for dissembling, Corin. I understand very well what it is to desire something very badly. I understand passion and ambition and the *need* for a thing fulfilled. Do you think I do this for pleasure?" His eerie eyes were black in the purple glare. "Brennan is unfit for his inheritance. Homana lacks a proper prince. There is a *need* for you."

"Unfit—" Corin clenched the ring in his hand. "What have you done to him?"

Strahan's gemstones glittered. "Shown him what he is: a man unfit to rule."

"Brennan is more fit to rule than any man I have seen!"

"More fit than you?" Strahan smiled coolly. "I think you discount yourself needlessly . . . and I think you misjudge *him*." He turned away briefly, paced three steps, turned back. And halted. "If a man is unfit to rule, should he not be replaced?"

"My *rujholli*—"

But the angry protest was overridden. "If a man is incapable of holding the Lion, should he be its master?"

"And if Brennan *were* unfit, Hart is next in line!"

"Hart will have Solinde."

Corin spoke distinctly. "My *jehan* was most particular in parceling out the realms. Mine is Atvia."

"*Your* realm, Corin, has been mine for several months, because of Lillith's power over its lord. But now Alaric is dead. His heir has disappeared. Into the confusion, I have moved to quell the fear." Strahan smiled. "There is no need for you there."

Corin sighed. "They would still turn to Hart. He is second-born. *I* would end up with Solinde."

"Hart will never be accepted in Homana . . . at least by the Cheysuli."

A chill touched Corin's neck. "What have you done to Hart?" Foreboding knotted his belly. "*Why* would they not accept him?"

"Becaused a maimed warrior has no place in the clans." Strahan shrugged. "Through great misfortune—he lost an important wager—Hart now lacks a hand. The Cheysuli will no longer honor him as a warrior. He is, as he himself says, *kin-wrecked*."

"Maimed—" Corin mouthed it. The ring bit into the flesh of his palm. "Oh—*rujho* . . . no—"

"Aye," Strahan said, "and none of *my* doing. So—you see?—Homana is in dire need of a prince. A healthy, whole prince, willing to hold the Lion—"

Bitterly, Corin finished it, "—in the name of Asar-Suti."

The Ihlini lifted a single eloquent shoulder. "A minor price to pay. Look what you will get Homana, the Lion . . . *Aileen*."

Corin's head snapped up; he stared at the sorcerer.

Strahan smiled warmly. "Need I remind you? She is to wed the *Prince of Homana*."

Gilded candles guttered. Flame danced and smoked.

Corin clutched the ring. "Show me," he said hollowly. "Show me my *rujholli*."

Strahan bowed his assent.

Three

The Gate emitted a deep gurgling belch, like a man suppressing laughter, as Strahan left the cavern. *Godfire* continued to play around the rim. Tendrils of it licked out of the hole, probed the air, withdrew in a splash of smoke. Caught in tiers of glassy arches, the echoed hiss was amplified.

Brennan rose, pressing himself to his feet with one thrust of a splayed hand. He went immediately to his brother.

Hart still knelt on the uneven floor, left arm hugged against his chest. The rocking had ceased, but not the rigidity of his body or the emptiness of his eyes. His face showed the strain of his captivity: pronounced hollows beneath high cheekbones, dark circles beneath blue eyes; a stark bleakness of expression that had nothing to do with captivity and everything to do with the choice Strahan had given him.

Gently, Brennan touched the crown of Hart's bowed head. "*Rujho*, I am sorry."

The sound of Hart's swallow was loud in the circle of flame. "The worst," he said, "the *worst* is knowing I can never fly again."

Brennan drew in a very deep breath, knowing there was nothing he could say to assuage his brother's anguish.

Hart turned his face up to stare at Brennan. "All of those other things I think I could learn to live with, given time—even being *kin-wrecked* . . . but to know I am earthbound *forever*—"

"I know." Brennan's fingers touched Hart's head. "I know."

"You do *not* know." Awkwardly, Hart got to his feet. "No warrior whose *lir* lacks wings can understand the freedom there is in the air, the manifest miracle of *flight*—" He broke off a moment, realizing he walked too close to the edge of control. "I do not discount Sleeta or your own *lir*-shape, Brennan, but it is not the same as mine."

"No," Brennan said. His eyes were on the leather-wrapped stump. "Hart, what happened?"

"Foolishness," Hart said bitterly. "Idiocy, and worse. I put myself in the hands of the enemy for the price of a stupid game."

"You wagered your *hand?*"

"No. Worse. I wagered Solinde." Hart drew in a deep breath, than blew it out. "It is complicated, *rujho*, and I am not proud of it. You can see the result plainly." Frowning, he looked more closely at his brother. "What has he done to you?"

"To me? To *me?* Nothing." Brennan turned away, paced a few steps, swung back. "Nothing that shows, *rujho* . . . he is too clever for that."

"Sleeta?"

"He has her. Somewhere here. Somewhere hidden." He shook his head. "Close enough to keep me from the edge of *lir*lessness and madness."

"But only just," Hart said flatly. "Do you think I cannot see it? I can see it in your *eyes*—"

Brennan waved it off. "Aye, aye," he said shortly, "but what of Strahan? I know why he wants us—to use as puppet-kings—but why this protracted mummery? Why not simply force us to do his will? He can. Easily. This is Valgaard, the Gate of the netherworld—his power is manifest. It should be a simple task—"

"Should be," Hart echoed, "but is it? Could there be a limit to his power? Does he require *willing* victims?"

Brennan's expression was a scowl of consideration. "He has other minions, but none of them are Cheysuli . . . none of them have the Old Blood—"

"But this is *Valgaard*. Why should it matter here?"

"Supposedly, it should not." Brennan shrugged. "Wishful thinking, *rujho*—but could it be that he needs more power to make a Cheysuli his? That one who fights his influence could drain him of his strength?"

"Strahan's strength seems boundless."

Brennan rubbed a hand through dirty hair. "Aye. But what other explanation? Why does he try to induce us when force should be enough?"

Hart stared toward the Gate. "Perhaps it is nothing more than a facet of his perversity. Which would please him more, *rujho*—a Cheysuli who was forced, or one who accepted service willingly?"

"Even Gisella was not forced."

Hart shivered once. "No. What need? Lillith twisted her so badly—"

"—at least, what was left from the unfortunate circumstance of her birth." Brennan's expression was unsettled; only rarely did he give over any time to thinking of his mother. "But this is different, *rujho*—"

"Aye," Hart said harshly. "He *knows* what inducements to use."

Brennan looked at him sharply, suddenly afraid. The note in Hart's voice, the expression in his eyes . . . foreboding was iron in Brennan's belly. "Hart, I can hardly *begin* to comprehend what you have lost—"

"Aye," Hart said curtly. "Look to yourself, *rujho*. My choice is my own to make."

And abruptly, the fence of fire died away.

Smoke boiled up from the Gate and carpeted the floor. It touched their knees, no higher; spread out to engulf cavern and corridor, wreathing glassy columns. Through the smoke came Strahan, holding the rune-worked box.

Hart's breath was harsh in his throat. Brennan looked away.

"Tahlmorra lujhala mei wiccan, cheysu," Strahan said as he walked. Echoes thrummed in the Seker's harp. "Such an all-encompassing statement, this thing of gods and fate. Have you never thought to question it? To free yourselves of such blind and binding service?"

Slowly, Brennan shook his head. "No more than you have questioned your own service to the Seker."

"Ah, but I have my reasons." Strahan paused between them, near the lip of the Gate. And then circled it calmly to stand on the other side. He smiled and made a gesture. "A full complement of Niall's sons."

As he meant them to, Hart and Brennan turned to look. And stared, rigidly, as Corin was brought into the cavern. That he could not walk was plain; both legs were tightly bound in wooden splints and linen wrappings. Ihlini carried him on a litter. He reclined against piled bolsters, but gripped the litter with both hands.

"You may blame me as you like," Strahan said, as Hart and Brennan turned back to him with anger in their faces, "but it is not my doing." He shrugged. "Broken legs mend. He will be whole soon."

"Provided he accepts the bargain you offer him," Brennan turned his head and spat. "You are *abomination*—"

"Am I?" Strahan smiled. He watched as his servitors brought the litter to a halt near the Gate and set it down. "I was thinking I might prefer to be known as *deliverance*."

Hart went to Corin. *"Rujho—"*

"I am well enough," Corin said. "For all I hate to admit it, Strahan does not lie. I am nearly healed." His eyes were on Hart's left wrist. "He told me—he *told* me—"

Hart's mouth twisted. "Strahan does not lie." He sighed. "You know what he wants from us."

Corin averted his gaze. "Aye. He has made it very plain."

Brennan came to the litter and knelt. "Corin—"

"Enough," Strahan said. "The reunion may come later. I want you to listen to *me*."

After a moment, Brennan rose. Hart turned to face the Ihlini squarely. On his litter, Corin watched.

"I am no more abomination than *you*," Strahan told Brennan. "What I do, I do for my god, my race, myself. I *believe* in what I do, because what I do is just."

"The destruction of the Cheysuli? The fall of Homana?" Brennan shook his head. "I think—"

"You do *not* think!" Strahan shocked them all with the abruptness and intensity of his passion. The sound reverberated in the cavern, threading its way among the columns of the Seker's monstrous harp. *"If* you thought, you would realize that what I do is no different from what you do, if for a different reason." Now his tone was cold as he looked at each of them individually. "When I was a boy, and very young, I learned what hatred was, and I learned that it had no place in what I was meant to do. *And so I do not hate you."* He drew in a breath, strung so tightly the others thought—prayed—he might snap. "I learned what it was to prepare myself to serve my father's god with absolute loyalty, knowing the way of the Seker was the only way for me. And when Carillon slew Tynstar and Electra, stripping me of my parents, I learned what it was to know of the desire for revenge—and how to *detach* myself from it so it did not affect my judgment, my needs, my loyalty to my god and to *his* needs."

"No doubt." Brennan said coolly. "We see the design quite clearly."

"Do you? I think not. I think you see only *yourself* caught within a trap, when the trap involves much more than a single man." Strahan shook his head. "You give yourself too much value, too much weight in the fabric of life . . . you are but a slub within the cloth, subject to rejection."

Brennan's brows rose. "If that were true—"

"—I would not want you?" Again, Strahan shook his head. "You are an ingredient, but hardly the dish itself."

"What is this nonsense?" Hart asked harshly. "What is this senseless talk of hatred, revenge, *cloth*—?"

Strahan's odd eyes were incredibly compelling. "I am no different from any of you. I serve my god as you serve the pantheon of your own, as dedicated to destroying the prophecy as you are to fulfilling it. Why? Because fulfillment destroys the Ihlini." He spread one hand; the other held the rune-scribed box. "You see? A *simple* answer for you: I believe in what I do every bit as strongly as you do in your prophecy. Does it make me a monster? Does it make me abomination? Does it make me different from you?"

"We do not kill people arbitrarily," Corin said curtly. "We—"

But Strahan's laughter overrode his retort. "Oh, *no?*" the Ihlini asked. "Then what of the thirty-two innocent souls who burned to death in the Midden? Was *that* done with purpose?"

For a long moment all any of them could do was stare, stricken. And then Hart stirred, knowing himself most guilty.

"But we do not set about destroying an entire race," he answered flatly. "What of the plague, Strahan? Twenty years ago it nearly killed us all. What of the *wars*, Strahan? How many hundreds of years has Homana fought Solinde merely to stave off the Ihlini? What of all the trap-links and other sorcerous things designed to bring us down?"

"War requires harsh measures," Strahan said, "and this *is* war. A battle for survival that you would fight as hard, if you were not so blind."

"What are we blind *to?*" Corin demanded in frustration.

"Yourselves," Strahan told him, looking from Corin to Hart to Brennan. "Once the Firstborn have come, we will be redundant. Ihlini *and* Cheysuli; the need for us is gone."

Brennan's disgust was plain. "I have heard that before." He thought of Tiernan and other similar sentiments. "It is idiocy, Strahan—why would the gods sentence us to death on the birth of other children?"

"It is the way of things." Strahan said. "When you breed a stallion and mare to improve existing bloodlines, you desire offspring combining the best of both. And then you breed get to get to *fix* the characteristics. It is the same with dogs, with sheep, with cattle . . . and one day, when you have the characteristics you want, you realize there is no need for the progenitors; they are obsolete. The new breed is much better." The light was odd on his face. *"It is the same with people."*

Corin laughed once. "You reduce the House of Homana to a collection of studs and mares."

"Look at your prophecy," Strahan snapped impatiently. "Are you blind to its commands?" Glibly contemptuous, he quoted. *" 'One day a man of all blood shall unite, in peace, four warring realms and two magical races.' "* He stared at them angrily. "Marry here, wed there, get the blood for the prophecy . . . look to no other kingdom because we need *this* one, to fulfill the prophecy." He shook his head in disgust. "A collection of studs and mares . . . what *else* do you think you are?"

None of them could answer.

Strahan nodded slightly. "You are all of you one of the final links in the prophecy. You combine the blood of three realms: Homana, Solinde, Atvia. You lack only Erinn, but children born of Brennan and Aileen will fulfill that portion, as well as children of Keely and Sean. And that leaves only the blood of the Ihlini." Black brows touched the circlet in an expression of delicate amusement. "The hardest feat of all, getting Cheysuli to lie with Ihlini."

Brennan's flesh went suddenly hot on his bones.

"Of course," Strahan continued, "the precedent *has* been set. By Ian. The unspeakable was accomplished once—and then again." He looked at Brennan. "And yet an impediment exists. The child will not quite be a Firstborn, lacking some of the blood . . . it will not *quite* be the human equivalent to fulfillment of the merging of power and bloodlines— but it *will* have a complement of powers greater than most of ours. And I will put it to good use in breeding it for my own."

"Then Sidra's child *is* yours," Corin blurted.

"Of course." Strahan smiled. "The Cheysuli have done well breeding so close to the prophecy, so I will adopt a successful strategy and use it for my own. Rhiannon's child shall marry mine, once the genders are in balance." His glance at Brennan was amused. "I doubt Brennan will freely participate again, but Sidra is young and I am potent. In time, I shall have the pair I require."

"Then let us go," Hart suggested. "Of what use are we to you?"

"To *me*, not so much. But to the Seker, aye. He wants the realms, and I will do what I can to win them from those who would keep them from him."

"*Why* does he want them?" Hart demanded. "Why all this greed, this overweening ambition? He *has* the netherworld—why must he want the rest?"

Strahan, for the first time, looked truly perplexed. "Why? Because he does." He shrugged. "It is not *my* place to question the ambitions of a god."

Corin nodded. "And when *you* are become a god?"

Strahan's motion was arrested. He looked at Corin blankly.

"Aye," Corin said, "I begin to put it together." He struggled to sit more upright on the litter. "A faithful servant, Strahan, working for the god—but when the task is done? When you have succeeded? Does he give you what *you* want?"

"What *I* want is immaterial—"

"A godhood of your own?"

"Godhood!" Brennan stared. "Is *that* what—"

"*I serve Asar-Suti!*" Strahan's shout reverberated in the

cavern. "He is my god, my lord, *the Seker*, the font of all my strength—"

"And you want parity." Corin smiled. "I understand an ambitious man. But I wonder . . . does Asar-Suti?"

Strahan's eyes narrowed slightly, but his smile remained unblemished. "And does Brennan know how much you want Aileen?"

Corin's arms collapsed beneath him. He slumped back into the pillows.

"Aileen?" Brennan said blankly. Then he looked at Corin. "*You* want—"

"He said you were unfit." Corin's tone was curt and characteristically defensive.

"Unfit! I? And you believed him?"

"Are you not?" Strahan asked.

Brennan nearly gaped. "I have spent nearly twenty-two years of my life learning *how* to rule—I doubt I am unfit!"

"Are you not?" Strahan repeated. "Think back, my lord of Homana . . . think back to your fear."

Brennan's color faded.

"Aye," Strahan said. "Your fear of small, dark places— the terror of close confinement . . . the diminishment of the *man* who becomes nothing more than a beast." He smiled. "Do you think I have not seen it? Rhiannon told me of it, and I have watched you in your cell."

"Enough!" Hart shouted, seeing Brennan's eyes.

Strahan looked only at Brennan. "I ask you to serve me willingly, as I have done before. Accept, and I will free you forever of this fear."

Brennan swallowed tightly. "No."

"Then live in it again . . . show Corin how *fit* you are to rule." Strahan raised his hand and Brennan's world was changed.

He was small, so small, so *tiny* in the abyss of the world. He knelt on the ground and hugged himself, wrapping himself in his arms, trying to withstand the pain and fear of knowing himself alone.

The vastness amazed him. It made him insignificant, reduced him to obsolescence. Alone in the world he knelt on a vast stone plain, watching the world around him, and saw it begin to move.

—how it *moved*—

Like a sphincter squeezing closed, it began to move upon him. Fold upon fold, swallowed by itself. The world grew smaller and smaller and smaller, until he could put out his hands and touch it, and then it grew smaller still.

All around him the world trembled. And then it touched him, even as he withdrew. It drew closer, *closer*, until he could not breathe without feeling its caress; without smelling the stink of its fetid breath and the slime of its glass-black skin. Awash in the power of helplessness, he felt the world draw closer.

—so small—

—he could not straighten legs—could not sit up—could not stretch out his arms—

All around him the world squeezed.

—so dark—

He was entombed within the world, and it was deaf to his cries.

Brennan fell backward, rolling from one hip onto his spine. Cramped thighs spasmed and trembled, jerking twisted tendons. His skull banged against the floor, released from the rigidity of his neck. He lay on the stone and shook, wet from the sweat of his fear.

Dimly he heard movement. But no one came to aid him.

"What kind of king," Strahan said, "fears confinement more than death? Fears it *so* much that it robs him of control?" He pointed slowly to Brennan's trembling body on the floor. "Do you, Corin, truly believe him fit to rule? Fit to hold the Lion? *To sire children on Aileen?*"

"Stop!" Corin shouted.

Strahan ripped open the box. "Accept service with me, and I will make your brother whole!"

Sickened, Corin stared. "Oh—gods—*stop*—

"You see what Brennan is—*I can free him of that!*"

"No more!" Corin cried.

"Take the Lion for me. Hold Homana for me. *Take the woman for yourself!*"

Corin clapped both his hands to his head. "Make him *stop*—"

Hart tried. Even as Strahan shouted something more, he lurched forward and threw himself across the expanse of the Gate.

Flame licked up. It bathed Hart briefly as he leaped. He

cried out, came down, landed hard on the other side, too near, *too near* the Gate—

Brennan, still weakened from his ordeal, struggled to hands and knees. "Hart—*no!*"

Strahan stood his ground. *"Corin—"*

"No—" Hart scraped his knees and boots against the rim of the Gate, grimacing in pain.

"I will give your brothers their lir—"

"Corin—no—" Hart gasped.

Brennan rose unsteadily. "Hart—get back—*Hart—*"

Abruptly, Strahan knelt on one knee before Hart. His hands held out the box. "Do you want it? *Do you want it?* You have only to say the word—"

"No—" Brennan shouted.

Strahan's smile was unearthly. "To be a whole Cheysuli, honored by all the clan—"

"Leave him alone!" Corin cried.

"—to be able to fly again—"

Brennan stumbled forward. "Hart—*get back—*"

Flame exploded from the Gate and blinded all save Strahan.

"—to know the freedom of the skies—"

Hart wavered on his knees. *"Ku'reshtin—"*

"Take *me!*" Corin shouted. *"I* will accept the service—"

"Corin—Corin, *no—*" Brennan tried to round the Gate. Flame licked out, slapped him down, smashed him against the floor.

"Take *me!*" Corin cried.

Hart threw himself at the Ihlini. Strahan fell heavily, landing on hip and elbow. A shower of sparks exploded from the Gate.

"He is forsworn!" Strahan shouted. "You heard what he said—"

Hart dragged himself forward, bodily preventing the sorcerer from rising. Steadfastly he ignored the rope of Ihlini *godfire* that caught an ankle and tugged, trying to jerk him into the Gate.

"He is *forsworn!*" Strahan shouted.

Hart's hand was on the box. Runes blazed up and writhed, then circled the rectangular box in a blur of uncanny script. Faster, *faster*, until the blur ran off the wood and leaped onto Hart's remaining hand. He cried out in pain, but did not release the box.

Brennan, badly disoriented, tried to stand up and failed. Nearly senseless, he crawled slowly toward his brother.

Hart jerked the box from Strahan's grasp. Twisting, he turned back toward the Gate. "—*my* choice—" he gasped, and hurled it into the flames.

The loss was new again. He felt the sword blade come down, divide flesh, muscles, vessels, shear easily through bone. He saw the blood. Saw the severed hand. Saw Dar laughing at him.

Pain.

Hart screamed.

One Ihlini servitor caught Brennan. A second dragged Hart off Strahan and pushed him back around the Gate. Strahan sat at the rim and laughed, one foot wreathed in icy Ihlini *godfire*. And then it crept up slowly, so *slowly*, to touch his knee, his thigh, his hip; caressed his genitals. And exploded in ecstasy as it swallowed the rest of him.

The fire died quickly before their astonished eyes. In its place was a delicate webwork of lavender lace, a lattice of living light that cloaked exposed flesh. Hands. Throat. Face. It even pooled in his mouth; licked out of nostrils as he breathed. Through it all, Strahan laughed.

He rose. He went directly to Corin; inclined his glowing head. And then knelt to catch the wrist that still bore the silver shackle.

"No more need for *this*." It caught fire, flowed off Corin's hand, pooled in Strahan's webworked palm. And then shaped itself into a silver goblet. "There." Strahan rose, turned, knelt again at the rim of the Gate. Dipped the cup. Came up with dripping *godfire*. His smile was for Corin alone. "I give you the baptismal cup . . . and good welcome to the world."

Corin's face was awash in the glow of the cup. His eyes were blue, all blue, with only a speck of pupil.

"Corin!" Brennan shouted.

Corin's gaze was transfixed by Strahan's altered appearance. The Ihlini offered the cup. Fingernails glowed. "Drink of Asar-Suti."

Hart struggled impotently against the man who held him.

"Corin, *no*—I threw it away—*I threw it away*—no need for this sacrifice—"

"Drink," Strahan said, and helped Corin hold the cup.

"Ku'reshtin!" Brennan shouted. "Did you do this for Aileen?"

"No." Corin said, "I do this for myself."

And drank of Asar-Suti.

Four

In Strahan's luxurious tower chamber, they faced the sorcerer. They did not sit, though he did, preferring instead to stand. Hart cradled his arm; Brennan waited rigidly.

The Ihlini stretched out elegantly booted legs. The unearthly living lace had died from his flesh, but there remained an aura of power. Subtle, but intoxicating; both Cheysuli felt it. Neither succumbed to it.

In his chair, Strahan smiled. "The game is somewhat altered."

"Is that what this is?" Brennan asked harshly. "An afternoon's entertainment?"

"It *is* entertaining." Strahan, chin in hand, slouched casually against the chair arm and braced his elbow on it. "Entertaining as well as enlightening . . . but no, not a game. For none of us, now; certainly not for Corin."

Hart took a single step forward. "What have you done to him?"

"I?" One winged black brow rose. "*I* have done nothing at all."

"That *bile* you made him drink—"

"The blood of Asar-Suti," Strahan corrected calmly. "And I made him drink nothing; did you see him turn away? Did you see him choke? Did you see him spit it out?" The Ihlini shook his head with its fall of raven hair. "No. He did none of those things. He drank it willingly, and was filled with the spirit of the Seker. *You* saw his eyes."

Brennan's temper flared. "He had no choice—"

"He had *every* choice." Strahan leaned forward in the chair. "He accepted my offer of his own free will. He *drank* of his own free will. I used nothing at all on him save persuasion, and *that*, my Cheysuli kinsman, is power no different from your own." He sat back again. The elaborate courtesy and negligent humor were gone, replaced by a sharp intensity. "Now. I have Corin; that is finished. What do I do with you?"

"Finished," Hart echoed. "*Finished?* If you think we will let it rest—"

Strahan's eyes blazed. *"I think you will do exactly as I tell you."*

It stopped both of them cold.

The Ihlini uncoiled and pressed himself out of the chair. He stepped very close to Hart, though he did not touch him, and held him in place with an unwavering stare. "It is your misfortune," he said clearly, "that you chose to destroy your own flesh. Now you are truly cut off from your people, and through your own doing. Blame *yourself* for that; I will have none of it!"

Hart wanted to fall back, but forced himself to stand still. This close to the Ihlini he could feel Strahan's power as if it leaked out of the pores of his skin.

"Your determination is commendable." Strahan continued, "and its seeming boundlessness is a trait I do admire. I *want* steadfast, loyal men, willing to sacrifice that which they prize most. But I think you misjudge my willingness to mold such men into the shapes that serve me best."

"Willingness." Brennan was elaborately distinct. "A familiar refrain, Ihlini . . . but why is it so important? If you have so much power, why not *force* Hart and me to do your bidding? Why *not* mold us into the shapes that serve you best?" He spread his hands. "Here we stand, sorcerer—why not shape the clay?"

Something flickered in Strahan's mismatched eyes. Briefly, so briefly, but Hart had seen it, and so had Brennan.

Hart's eyes narrowed. "You have us," he said intently. "What can we do to gainsay you? *Make* us the minions you want."

Strahan flicked a finger and the door slammed open. "You are dismissed."

Hart held his ground. Brennan moved to stand beside him.

Strahan's fair skin burned darker in slanted cheekbones. "You are *dismissed.*"

"All those threats," Hart said quietly. "All those promises . . . empty, all of them?"

"Is it that we *must* be willing?" Brennan asked. "Why else do you waste so much time an trying to break us physically, hoping to *persuade* us? Is it that an unwilling minion lacks something you need in us? Something peculiar to *us?*"

"So peculiar that without it, your efforts would be in vain?" Hart smiled. "I think we have beaten you, Strahan. I think we have won at last."

Strahan said nothing at all.

Brennan began to smile. "And what are we? Princes. More than Cheysuli, but *princes*, meant to inherit realms. Homana. Solinde." He nodded. "You cannot rule on your own, so you hope to rule through us. But there is no puppet-king if the king is *too much* a puppet—"

"You need us sane," Hart said intently. "You need us complete in wits. And if you *force* us to your service, we will lack the thing you require—"

"—and the people will throw us down." Slowly, Brennan spread his hands. "Kill our bodies, kill our wits . . . and you are left with nothing."

"So," Hart said, "where is the leverage now? If you kill Sleeta, Brennan will go mad. No minion in Homana; the people will not have it. Rael you do not have, so what is there for me?" He lifted his left arm. "I threw it away, Strahan—you cannot use my hand."

"Leverage?" Strahan nodded, turned away, swung back. "Aye, there is a need. And I do have it."

"What is there left?" Brennan asked.

"Corin," Strahan said, and their triumph poured away.

The youngest of Niall's sons stared at the man who faced him. For a long moment he did not know him, barely knowing himself, and then a name came into his head. *Strahan.* Strahan, called the Ihlini.

Strahan's outline was blurred. His face was a blaze of white, marred only by the holes for eyes, nose, mouth. And then the blaze became more distinct, and the holes dissolved themselves into things identifiable, and Corin knew whom he faced.

He shuddered once, like a man awakening from a deep, dreamless sleep. He was, he realized, ensconced within a massive chair, supported by tall back, tall sides, cushioned seat. It cradled his lax body like a woman a sleeping child.

Sleeping. Aye, he had been. Or something close to it.

Strahan stood before him, holding a cup in his hands. A black glass goblet, unlike the silver one that had held the blood of the god. This one smelled of wine.

"Drink." Strahan held it out. "It will help restore you."

Slowly Corin took it. The world was dulled to him, wrapped in swaddling clothes. He felt heavy, ponderous, movements slowed accordingly. His fingers closed on the cup, felt the warmth of the glass, carried it to his mouth. He drank deeply, sighed, felt his head thump against the chair.

Strahan took the cup away. "It takes time," he said, "to accustom yourself to it. You will know discomfort, but it will pass. I promise."

Corin looked at the sorcerer. He saw the fine planes of jaw, cheekbones, brow; the oblique angles of mismatched eyes. Such fine, delicate features, yet there was no mistaking his sex.

Strahan smiled and sat down in a chair opposite. "I thought it might be Hart," he said calmly. "I underestimated him, believing his need for his race would outweigh his dedication. But you will do well enough."

Corin swallowed heavily. His voice seemed very distant, as if another man spoke. "Hart is often misjudged. People see only his fecklessness, his desire for amusement. They look no farther than that."

Strahan considered it. "What will sway him, then? I cannot replace his hand."

"The loss of his place in the clan." Corin frowned a little. "You have cut away his anchor . . . he will founder on the rocks one day, no matter what he says. Offer him succor. In time he will repay it."

The Ihlini stroked one eyebrow. "And Brennan?"

"Him you may never win." Corin shifted in the chair. His bones tingled. He *itched.* "I know of no way to convince him. Brennan's particular strength lies in his unequaled loyalty to kin, clan, and prophecy." He shrugged. "It will make him a predictable Mujhar, but also a very good one."

"Then perhaps he should not *be* Mujhar." Strahan nodded thoughtfully. "I made you promises, and I intend to keep them. Brennan will undoubtedly become expendable . . . Homana will need a new king. You I can put in his place."

Corin rubbed at his tingling scalp. "Aileen . . ." He shivered. "What of *Aileen?*"

Strahan waved a hand. "With Homana and Solinde under my control, it no longer matters whom she marries. The prophecy will not be completed no matter what child is born." He shrugged. "I no longer need her. Alaric failed to spirit her to Atvia, and there was no time for a second try. Now there is no need. You may have her, Corin. It was a part of our bargain."

Corin blinked repeatedly. The chamber was bright, too bright; he squinted against the light.

"It will be difficult," Strahan said softly. "I will not discount the steadfast determination of your race . . . the arrogance of your convictions. But I need your brothers, Corin. May I count on you?"

Corin frowned. "There may be a way," he said. "Will you trust me to do it?"

Strahan showed even teeth in a silent laugh. "Trust? There is no need for *trust*. If I tell you to do a thing, you will do it without question. That is the way of the service."

Something flickered deep inside Corin. Mute denial. But it was snuffed out so quickly by apathy he hardly recognized it.

"There may be a way," he said again. "What they want most is freedom. Their need of it may overshadow their caution and distrust."

"Aye." Strahan nodded. "We shall devise a scenario, and then give them what they want."

Corin shut his eyes. The world was too bright to bear, his flesh too heavy to carry. "I can deliver them."

"Good," Strahan said. He poured himself more wine.

The cell was new to Brennan, though not so to Hart; larger, brighter, more comfortable than the tiny one Brennan had known for months. Two fat candles burned in corners opposite one another. A narrow cot lined one wall, which was, like the others, cool but dry, lacking fetid slime. The occupant, unlike his brother, had also been provided with a bucket in which to relieve himself.

Hart sat down on the cot and hunched against the wall, cradling his left arm. He stared into invisible distances.

Brennan saw the withdrawal at once. "Hart—"

"Gone," he said. *"Gone."* He looked at the emptiness where once his hand had been. "And I did it to myself."

Slowly Brennan sat down on the edge of the cot. He felt a vague sense of relief that *he* still had both hands, and guilt because he did. "If you had accepted Strahan's bargain—"

"I know!" Hart cried. *"I know, Brennan*—I do not require reminding!"

Inwardly Brennan recoiled, though his body did not move.

"I know," Hart repeated. "I know what I did was right. I *know* it was for the best—to remove the possibility I might succumb to the temptation—but knowing it makes it no better. Corin *did* succumb . . . what I did was for naught."

Brennan drew in a steadying breath. "Not for naught," he said quietly. "That bargain was offered me as well, before you were brought into the cavern. And once I saw your face, how the knowledge ravaged your spirit, I knew there was a very good chance Strahan had judged me too well."

"He promised you *my hand?*"

"To make you whole again, just as he promised you." Brennan scratched viciously as a louse ran against his scalp.

"What else?"

Brennan sighed. "The lives of all my kin." He looked at Hart. *"And* release from the fear."

Hart massaged his forearm above the cuff. He frowned a little, clearly reluctant to speak. "You never told me," he said finally, obviously hurt. "You never told me about your fear. You told me *everything*—"

"Everything but that." Brennan stared at the floor. "I was ashamed."

"To tell *me?*"

"To tell anyone." He flickered a glance at Hart. "You most of all; you are afraid of nothing."

Hart's face tightened; his mouth hooked down briefly in mute argument. "So you locked it away inside of you, until Strahan discovered the secret." He sighed heavily. "Oh, *rujho*, I am sorry . . . I might have helped you with it."

"For me to do." Brennan shrugged. "But now—" He stopped. "Oh, gods, Hart—what are we to do? How do we deal with Corin?"

"As we have dealt with Strahan."

"He is our *rujholli!*"

"And he has turned his back on his race to serve Asar-Suti."

"Has he?" Brennan asked. "*Has* he?"

"You saw his eyes. You saw how his legs were healed." Hart leaned his head against the wall. "You saw how he rose and walked; how he knelt down at the rim of the Gate."

"To make his obeisance to the Seker." Twitching in distaste, Brennan shut his eyes. "What will Strahan *do* with him?"

"Use him," Hart said flatly. "What else is leverage for?"

Brennan turned his head and looked at his brother. Before, overwhelmed by what the loss of Hart's hand represented, he had looked at nothing else, *seeing* nothing else. But now he looked, now he *saw*, and was shocked by the tension in the body so like his own; equally stunned by the pronounced lack of conditioning; Hart had lost weight, muscle tone, the hard fitness characteristic of a Cheysuli.

Worse, and indicative of something far graver than physical discomforts, Brennan saw Hart had also lost the high-spirited good humor that marked him different from any of Niall's other children.

It frightened him for some obscure reason. He did not expect Hart to be *amused* by the circumstances, nor particularly cheerful, but Brennan was accustomed to his brother's uncanny ability to find the good in the bad. He realized, in that moment, that for all he had longed for Hart to shed some immaturity, he treasured his brother's relentless search for diverting entertainment. And now that propensity was lacking.

Brennan forced a smile. "If we had us a fortune-game—"

Something flared in Hart's eyes. First shock, then recollection, then a deep and abiding anger that stunned Brennan with its virulence.

"*No* game!" Hart said viciously.

"Hart—"

"No game—" And he was up, thrusting himself one-armed from the cot, to pace the cell like an animal.

Brennan stared in shock. "Hart—what *happened* in Solinde?"

"This!" Hart thrust out his left arm. *"This*—and my stupidity . . . my incredible gullibility."

"Hart—*everyone* is gullible at one time or another."

"Not like this." Hart stopped pacing and fell back against the wall, pressing shoulders into stone. "Oh, Brennan, I was such a fool. They laid a trap most carefully, baiting it so well, and I gobbled it whole, not even bothering to *sniff.*" He sighed. "But I thought she was a pawn as much as I."

"Ah." Brennan sighed. "She."

"Never have I been such a blind, witless fool."

"You are not the first."

"But I should have *known* . . . I should have *seen* it." Hart closed his eyes. "All a wager, the *ultimate* wager, and I primed to be the loser, regardless if I won."

It was too obscure for Brennan, who was more concerned with Hart's well-being than his reference. "Aye, well, take consolation in the fact you did not give Strahan the *child* he wanted." He pushed himself back until he leaned against the wall. "The girl from The Rampant Lion—do you recall?"

Hart frowned. "The Lion? No. What girl? And what *child?*"

"The girl I rescued from Reynald of Caledon, Einar's illustrious cousin."

"Oh, aye, I recall." Hart frowned. "What has *she* to do with this?"

"She set a trap for *me.* A most intricate trap indeed." He hooked one arm across his face. "I made her my *meijha,* Hart. I sired a child on her."

"It does happen. But why—"

"She is Ihlini. Daughter to Lillith and Ian." He removed the arm. "The child who will lie with *Strahan's* child to give him the power he needs."

Stunned, Hart stared. "Oh, *Brennan*—"

"But I did not lose a hand." Brennan rose and went to Hart, hooking an arm around his neck to pull him close. "Gods, *rujho*—I am so very sorry—"

The door swung open. Corin came into the cell.

He was whole, lacking splints or bandages. He had shaved, bathed, was clean again, smelling of scented oil instead of the stink of Valgaard's bowels. His hair was washed, cut, shining, indisputably free of lice. His clothing was immaculate, and of a decided Ihlini cut.

At his side was Kiri. Behind him two Ihlini.

"I wanted my *lir*," he said, "and Strahan gave her to me."

Brennan unwound his arm from Hart.

Corin lifted his right hand and displayed the ruby signet ring that once had hugged Brennan's forefinger. "I wanted Homana," he said, "and Strahan promised me it." His eyes were odd, more iris than pupil, with an eerie, unfocused cast. "I wanted your title, I wanted your throne, I said I wanted your woman. And Strahan will give her to me."

"This is for *Aileen?*"

"Aileen and all the rest."

Brennan's belly rolled. "By all the gods of Homana—"

But Corin shook his head. "By the god of the nether-world."

"No—" Hart cried, but missed as Brennan leaped.

Corin was slammed back against the wall. Brennan's fingers dug deeply into the flesh of his throat. "I swear, I will save the Seker the trouble of freeing your soul of its shell."

"Brennan, *no*." Hart grasped at Brennan's arm and caught only cloth. "Brennan—"

The two Ihlini plucked Brennan from Corin and threw him across the cell. He tripped, fell, stayed down, legs asprawl as he hitched himself up on both elbows and stared unblinkingly at Corin, who gestured the two away. They went as far as the corridor.

"Your treatment is up to you." Corin told his brothers. "Certainly this sort of accommodation is not *required*."

"Provided we do what Strahan wants," Hart said sourly.

"There is that." Corin looked at the cot, the slops pail, the two dim candles. Then he looked at Brennan. "You have never been a fool. Not in all the years I have known you. Why be one now?"

Brennan turned his head and spat deliberately.

"Corin—" Hart moved forward, saw the Ihlini tense,

stopped and held his ground. "Corin, you *know* what he has done to you—what he made you do—"

"I did it of my own choosing." His eyes should have been dilated black in the shadows, but his pupils were non-existent. "There are things in this world I have always wanted, and this is how I get them."

"By stealing them." Brennan's tone was deadly as he slowly sat up. "My title, my throne, my *bride*—"

"Aye!" Corin hissed. "Why should *you* want her? You never even bothered to *write*."

Brennan stood and tried to pull his crusted jerkin into something resembling a proper fit. "Obviously you did more than that while in Erinn."

A thin white line banded Corin's mouth. "I did not come to speak of Aileen. I came to speak to *you*, to suggest the course you should take."

"To tell us, no doubt, that we should do as Strahan suggests," Hart said in dry disgust.

"It *is* best," Corin told him quietly. "You have the right of it, both of you." He flicked a glance at the silent Ihlini. "He does require men *willing* to become minions. Without that willingness, the Seker exerts force . . . the results are—unattractive." His strange eyes focused a moment, than resumed their eerie cast. "Strahan prefers to rule through men with minds, as you have said. But he *is* willing to do it another way." He brushed back a lock of hair, frowned, then continued. "If it becomes necessary, he will force you to accede, and use what is left of you."

"He can hardly rule through idiots," Brennan said. "The people will never accept us."

"For a while they would. You would not go mad right away." Corin shrugged. "It would take time, during which Strahan could firm his grasp on the thrones of Solinde and Homana. Eventually, of course, no wits would be left in your heads, and you would be locked away. But by then, the damage would be done." He looked from one to the other. "Why persist in refusal? It does no good, none at all . . . he will break you, and eventually you will die. *Lir*less, friendless, alone." He stopped short, frowned again, then sighed. "Consider this: accept him and rule with dignity, with integrity, or deny him and lose anything even slightly resembling freedom of mind and soul."

Brennan drew in a deep, deep breath. "There was a time, Corin, and not so many years ago, that you swore an oath before kin and clan. Your Ceremony of Honors, where you named as *shu'maii* by our *jehan*. Where you put on the *lir*-gold and accepted the responsibilities of a warrior, and all the loyalties it entails." His voice was very steady. "Do you stand here before me now and say you willingly *break that oath?*"

Corin did not blink. "I have sworn another."

Hart sat down awkwardly on the cot, as if his hamstrings had been cut. "No—no—*no*—"

"Oh, aye, he has," Brennan said coldly, "and I renounce him as my *rujholli.*"

Nothing moved in Corin's eyes. "You may renounce *yourself* for all I care, Brennan . . . it has been a long, long time that I have watched you play your part as Prince of Homana, coveting it myself. And now, in the end, it *is* mine—"

"How?" Brennan shouted. "If I *do* accept this service, Homana will still be mine!"

Corin smiled. "No," he said, "no. In the end, it will be mine. Your fitness to rule will be questioned. After all, is your *jehana* not known as mad Gisella?"

"She also bore *you.*"

"But I am not afraid of small, dark places. There is no doubting *my* sanity." He turned toward the Ihlini waiting in the corridor. "Do not wait. They will agree to nothing in front of you. Go to Strahan. I will bring them immediately when I have an answer."

The Ihlini turned and melted away into the shadows.

Brennan slowly shook his head. "If you think I will agree to anything you suggest, or step one foot outside this cell with *you*—"

"I think you will." Corin briefly massaged his throat. "You give yourself away. You are so willing to believe the worst of me. If I were Hart, you would not be so quick." He sighed, bent to touch Kiri, then straightened again. He smiled a little, though it had an ironic hook. "Aye, you *did* believe it . . . well, so did Strahan. At least I know last night was worth it."

Hart sat slowly upright on the cot. All Brennan could do was stare.

Corin sighed. "I spent all of last night with fingers down my throat, trying to rid myself of that foul, malodorous bile Strahan calls the blood of the god. But if you tarry any longer, I will have to drink it again . . . two cups remain before I am truly his." He gestured toward the door. "I *would* suggest we go."

Speechlessly, they went.

Five

Corin led them down a twisting corridor illuminated by torches set in infrequent iron brackets. The flame was pure and yellow, not lurid Ihlini purple, but Hart, accustomed to little light, and Brennan, accustomed to none, found discomfort in the illumination. They squinted, avoiding the pools of light; Corin's nearly pupilless eyes remained wide and strangely unfocused.

Brennan's walk slowed. At last Corin turned. "If we tarry—"

"What if we do?" Curtly, Brennan overrode him. "I go nowhere without Sleeta."

Corin smiled a little, glancing down at Kiri. "I know. I do not expect you to. Sleeta is in the cavern."

"The cavern?" Hart stopped short. "You are taking us *there?*"

"Would you suggest we depart through the front entrance?" Corin's tone was dryly disgusted. "Valgaard is a maze of tunnels and corridors, as well as secret exits. But I only know of one; I am newly come to the god, and Strahan does not tell me everything as yet." He looked at them more closely and saw doubt in grimy faces. "Oh, aye, I know—now you are uncertain. Well, the choice is yours. Come with me, or stay." Corin turned and went on as Kiri trotted beside him.

Hart swore. Brennan sighed and shook his head. And then he shrugged and pushed off the wall, muttering resigned imprecations.

"Kiri is with him," Hart pointed out. "If he meant to trick us, would she accompany him?"

"The *lir*-link is obliterated here," Brennan said over his shoulder. "She knows as much of his intentions as we do."

"But would he lead *her* astray?"

"He is not the Corin we knew. Who can say what he will do?"

They turned a corner and came up on him as he waited in the shadows. *Lir*-gold gleamed in tawny hair; armbands were hidden beneath sleeves of a dark gray doublet.

"What I will do," Corin said distinctly, "is take you out of here."

"Then do it," Brennan told him.

He led them into yet another corridor. It was short, too short, showing a dead end. But Corin halted, touched a stone, and a piece of the wall slid aside. Cool air rushed out of the tunnel. The nearest torch was snuffed out.

Brennan's breath rasped in his throat as darkness settled around them. Behind him, Hart stepped closer and touched his shoulder briefly in a gesture of support.

"Almost there," Corin told them, and went into the shadowed tunnel.

"The gods forgive me if I do our *rujholli* an injustice—" But Brennan did not finish. He merely followed Corin.

The tunnel soon gave way into an alcove cut into polished basalt. And the alcove gave into the stairway leading down to the massive cavern. *Godfire* dripped from seams of rock, splattering on the stairs. Corin went on without pausing, steadily descending.

In the distance, harp strings thrummed. Something gibbered in the wall.

He took them out of the passageway into the archivolted cavern and led them to the Gate. He paused at the glowing rim and pointed into the glare.

"Down *there?*" Hart demanded.

"I am with you," Corin said. He gazed at them both with an eerie, unfocused stare. "*I* can show you the way."

As one, his brothers backed away from the lip of the Gate.

Corin stepped closer. "It is your only chance."

"Ours—*all* of us?" Brennan's eyes narrowed. "Or only Hart and me?"

Corin frowned. "I am coming with you. Do you think I would dare remain?"

Hart chewed on a lip as he stared at the opening. "Through the Gate itself?" His tone was dubious.

Brennan's was distrustful. "Into the lap of the god."

Corin bent down. One hand reached into the gate and scooped up livid *godfire*. "Cold," he said, "*cold*. You will shiver, but never burn."

"No," Brennan said. "I will forgo that exit."

"Then why not try *this* one?"

As one, they spun in place. Strahan stepped out of basalt. *Godfire* edged his robe of deepest black. The silver on his brow glowed lilac-white in the glare of the Gate. Behind him was only shadow; no exit could be seen.

He gestured, indicating stone. "In there, Sleeta awaits. Why not go and see her?"

"Trap," said Brennan succinctly, unimpressed by Strahan's avowal.

"Is it?" Strahan moved closer to them, between the Gate and the glass of the cavern wall. Corin, at the rim, dropped down to his knees instantly in perfect homage. He bowed his head.

"Ku'reshtin," Brennan said bitterly, as Hart closed his eyes.

The Ihlini nodded slowly and put an approving hand on the tawny hair. "Well done, Corin. You have done as you said you would."

Corin turned his face up to Strahan. "And you have done as I *hoped*—" He lunged upward, off his knees, locking both arms around Strahan and pinning the sorcerer's arms. Even as Strahan twisted, Corin thrust out a foot to trip Strahan and tumble him into the Gate.

Flame gushed up. Strahan screamed something, and then the voice was silenced.

"Now!" Corin ran for the glassy wall.

"But nothing is *there!*" Brennan cried.

Corin and Kiri disappeared.

"I am not waiting." Hart ran for the darkness as well.

Brennan took a step after him, then stopped. He recalled too clearly the power that had reduced him to obsolescence. He recalled too clearly the fear that had engulfed him.

He shivered. Sweat broke out on his flesh.

And then the Gate disgorged the Ihlini, blazing like a pyre, and Brennan did not look back.

There was a seam, he saw at once. A fault in the stone, or else something cut by god or man. The naked eye could not see it, but the hand felt its gap. He slipped through and departed the cavern even as Strahan shouted.

He ran. The passageway engulfed him, scraping against bare arms. He heard the chime of *lir*-gold on basalt. It was a narrow, low conduit, alive with the stink of the netherworld. *Godfire* glimmered in crevices. For once, he was thankful; he would be blind without it.

He ran on, ignoring the knot in his belly. Small, dark place . . . and the only available exit.

"Hurry!" Hart called. The echo carried back, reverberating, and then Brennan saw them all. Hart. Kiri. Corin. And Sleeta just beyond, eyes aglow in purple *godfire*.

"*Lir*—" He tripped and nearly fell.

"No time," Corin said breathlessly. "The bailey is just beyond."

Brennan caught his balance. "Strahan is *alive*."

Corin's face was stark. Fear turned blue eyes black. "Then he can still *gainsay* me." He turned abruptly and thrust the hidden door open.

Cheysuli and *lir* spilled out of basalt into the bailey, footsteps echoing on cobbles. All around them was darkness and the breath of Asar-Suti. Stars were but a dim glow through the veil of malodorous smoke.

"I have forgotten what daylight is like." Hart remarked, half laughing. "Will we ever see the sun?"

"Not if we tarry here." At a run, Corin headed toward the gates with Kiri streaking behind. Hart caught Brennan's arm. With Sleeta, they followed their brother.

Stone shifted beneath their feet. It burst from under boots and threw them to the ground. Once, twice, thrice; each time they lost more distance. Some stone melted, clinging to their boots. Other cobbles exploded around them and rained down as smoking missiles.

Hart fell. Pain set his stump ablaze. The missing hand spasmed and tried to clutch at stone.

"Up—up—" Brennan dragged him from the ground.

Corin was at the gates. Frenziedly he threw the bar out of its brackets.

"No guards," Hart gasped. "Why does he post no guards?"

"Does an Ihlini require any?" Brennan dodged as a cobble exploded beneath his right boot, sending fragments of smoking stone slicing through the air. Splinters cut one cheek.

"Now—*now*—" Corin's shout was mostly swallowed by the shrieks and whistles of flying cobbles.

Massive gates tore loose of hinges and slowly began to topple. Corin scooped Kiri up and ran through as they crashed down. The sound of thunder filled the bailey; if Strahan did not already know precisely where they were, the noise would surely tell him.

Brennan gaped in astonishment as he and Hart ran on, pounding over the fallen wood. "By the gods—Strahan is using Valgaard *itself* to stop us!"

"Trying—" Hart rasped. "Oh—gods—I had forgotten *this!*"

They were through. The walls of Valgaard fell behind them; the field of fire lay before, stretching into the night. Fold upon fold of stone, all piled on one another; ripple here, curl there; a treacherous carpet of ensorcelled stone. The god had a sense of humor.

They ran. Staggered. Tripped. Got up and ran again, cursing the pockets of shadow that reached out to catch their boots. Cauldrons gurgled, fumaroles splattered, smoke issued forth from vents. It coated flesh, clogged throats, filled eyes with irritation. Coughing, wheezing, gagging, they stumbled through crumbling crusts and tripped over the spine of the earth itself, wrenched free of flesh and muscle. The viscera was foul.

Shadows loomed. Darkness incarnate, stretching across the ground. And then the rules were changed.

Unexpectedly, there was movement in addition to their own. They snatched hurried glances out of the corners of reddening eyes, and then the eyes abruptly widened. The field was a grotesque boardgame made by the god himself, and the pieces were alive.

"The stone—*moving*—" Brennan croaked.

Shadows altered. Darkness shifted. The pattern of fear mutated. Strahan's stone menagerie came to life in the sulfurous murk.

Hart recalled his father telling stories of how he had voluntarily come into Valgaard, alone, leaving behind even his *lir*, to make a bargain with Strahan. He recalled very clearly Niall's descriptions of the canyon of the god, cut so sharply from black basalt. As a child he had smelled the sulfur and squinted against the fumes, imagining Strahan's lair. Now he was in it himself, experiencing the same doubts and fears that Niall himself had known.

"Watch out for the stones," Corin rasped. "Remember how *jehan* told us they can move—?"

Brennan fell over a coiled protruberance. He landed hard, jarring his senses; a vent cracked open beneath him. Cursing, he tried to rise before the Seker's spittle burst forth.

Hart snatched one arm, Corin the other as steam gushed out of the vent. Together they dragged him free, scraping boot toes against rock, and forced him back into a stumbling run. Dodging paws and teeth and slashing tails, all formed of sinuous stone, they fled toward the defile that would give them exit from Strahan's domain.

"Not so far—" Hart panted. "Almost there—" Stone parted beneath his boots even as he spoke. He leaped, stumbled, staggered on, ignoring the angry gurgle.

Through the shadows Sleeta flowed like watered silk on velvet. Brennan longed to go into the link, to reestablish the communication he wanted so desperately, but such an attempt was futile so close to the Gate. Here the Ihlini was paramount, so long as he worshiped the god.

Corin swore as a wave of steam coated face and hands. He slowed, halted, rubbed hastily at stinging eyes. Tears rendered him incapable of seeing, and he dared not run blind.

Kiri yapped, then nipped at his ankles. And then he sensed the *presence*—"

"Corin—*run!*" Brennan cried.

He cleared his vision in time to see a monstrous gryphon bearing down on him, stone beak agape. Beneath the hiss of steam was the grate of stone on stone, and the yapping of his *lir*.

Corin twisted away, feeling the touch of ensorcelled stone as a wing cruelly caressed his scalp. He saw his brothers waiting, both poised to flee again. But their unwillingness to leave him renewed his fading strength.

"—coming—" he gasped, and ran.

And then, abruptly, could not.

He fell hard. Tried to rise. And then knew what Strahan had done.

"My legs!" he cried. "*My legs*—"

Jelly, Strahan had threatened. As Corin lay sprawled on hot stone, trying in vain to rise, he knew the healing had been recalled. There was no tremendous uprush of pain, no snapping of brittle bones, merely a return to what they had been before he had committed himself to the god. Nearly healed, but not completely; it left his bones fragile and his muscles weakened by confinement in splints and linens.

Kiri licked at his face. A cool nose nudged his neck and urged him desperately to rise. And then Hart and Brennan were lifting him, *dragging* him, as the world caught fire around them.

"—not so far—" Hart gasped, wrenching one-handed Corin's left arm across his shoulders.

"We will steal you from him yet." Brennan told Corin firmly.

And even though they dragged his feet, Corin shut his mouth on complaints.

Slowed by their burden, Hart and Brennan had more difficulty avoiding the Seker's grotesque mimicry of *lir*. None was especially mobile, being rock instead of flesh, but the advantage lay in being impervious to fumes and heat and flame. As Hart and Brennan slowed to negotiate the safest way with Corin, the monstrous creatures advanced.

Corin shivered. "Cold," he said. "—*cold*—"

Brennan's laugh was hoarse. "If only winter were this 'cold'—"

"Almost, *rujho*—" Brennan gasped, "—nearly through the defile—"

"Look!" Hart exclaimed. "Look above the opening!"

Brennan looked, saw the pristine line of white wings against the darkness, and laughed hoarsely. "Did you think Rael would *leave?*"

"—so long—" Hart croaked.

"*Put me down*—" Corin said. "Down—down—*down*—"

"Almost there—" Brennan's throat burned. "Nearly through—"

"*Down!*" Corin cried.

They carried him through the narrow defile choked with

steam and into a different world. This one too had suffered the presence of Ihlini, but here the damage was less extensive. Instead of stone there was soil, if thin and discolored in places. The trees were wracked by wind and whim, roots bared to the elements, but they were wood instead of stone, foliage in place of steam.

In Strahan's lair, it had been summer. Here it was winter, and frost lay upon the ground.

"That tree," Brennan rasped, and as they reached it carefully put Corin on the ground.

Almost immediately he tried to crawl away from them, heading unerringly for the defile.

"Corin—*wait*—" Hart caught an arm and was shocked at the rigidity of sinew beneath the flesh. "Corin—"

"—go back—" Corin gasped. "—go back—the Seker—"

More roughly than they intended, his brothers dragged him back and forced him into place.

"Look at his eyes," Brennan said.

Hart shook his head as he saw the shrunken pupils. "The poison is not wholly banished."

Corin tried to draw up his legs, but weakness and stiffness forbade it. "Gods—" he said, "—oh—*gods*—"

"At least he calls on *ours*," Brennan said dryly. "Hold him down, Hart."

"The farther from the Gate, the safer he will be."

"No doubt. But we need to wrap his legs—"

"We need to *heal* him," Hart said sharply. "But this close to Valgaard, I doubt we can summon the magic."

Corin shuddered beneath their hands. "—burning—" he muttered. *"—burning—"*

Above them, Rael shrieked in agitation.

"Whole legs or broken, we go," Brennan said firmly; together they hoisted Corin up again.

Distance closed the defile. With each step they left behind the field of smoke and stone, the brooding, glassy fortress and the Gate of the netherworld. Stars shone more brightly. The moon was freed from smoke and steam and painted a pathway for them.

"—down—" Corin begged.

"Not yet," Brennan told him through gritted teeth. "Not until we put more distance between you and Valgaard."

"The Seker—*the Seker*—" Corin shuddered in their grasp.

"Beat him off," Hart ordered succinctly. "Somewhere in that Homanan-fleshed body is the Old Blood, Corin . . .as much as in Brennan or me. Call on it. *Use it*—" He tripped, cursed, bit his lip against the pain in the stump of his arm.

And then, abruptly, the *lir*-links came blazing back into life, and all of them cried out.

"Down—" Brennan gasped, and they put Corin down as gently as they could. At once, Kiri pressed her muzzle into his throat. As Brennan opened his arms to Sleeta, he saw comprehension creep back into Corin's eyes.

Even as his twin knelt to grasp Sleeta against his chest, Hart rose. He moved away from his brothers, clearing the tangle of arms and legs and *lir*, and thrust both arms into the air. From out of the darkness came the white hawk he called Rael.

Lir—lir—*oh, gods. Rael*—Hart discovered an uncommon incoherence, even within the link. *Rael—Rael—Rael*—

Shansu, the hawk soothed. Shansu, *my* lir . . . *my proud, brave warrior*—

Do you see? Do you see? Hart appealed. *The Ihlini has ruined me*—

Rael soared closer yet. *I see strength and pride and an unrelenting determination to withstand the arts of Asar-Suti.*

Ruined, lir—

Shansu, the hawk soothed. *Oh,* lir, *it has been so long*—And he settled briefly, with infinite gentleness, on the handless, outthrust arm. He touched his hooked beak to Hart's shoulder, eyes alight, then lifted from flesh to seek the air again, saying nothing about Hart's tears.

On the ground, Brennan's arms were filled with cat. Bare flesh felt the dry texture of her pelt, fingers touched protruding ribs beneath taut flesh, eyes sought the truth in her own.

Sleeta, he began, intending to question her, and then put away words to lose himself in the renewal of the link. There was no need to ask her anything, all was present for him to discern through the thing that bound them. He knew fear and pain, anguish and anger, the pride that made her so strong.

All is well, she said. *All is well*, lir.

She was heavy, so heavy, though lacking her normal weight. Gently, she set her teeth against cheek and jaw and nibbled, more catlike than was common. One huge paw patted a thigh, the other kneaded a hip.

"Leijhana tu'sai," Brennan whispered. And could not say if he intended the thanks for Sleeta or the gods.

On the ground, Corin writhed. His bones were alive with fire.

Lir, Kiri said, *try harder to overcome it.*

He thrashed, and his legs spasmed. *The Seker*—he said. *The Gate—*

Think of me instead.

—burning— In the link, he felt her strength. *Gods, Kiri— it burns—*He hitched himself up on one arm, meaning to reach for her. Without warning, he vomited.

Abruptly, Brennan and Hart discontinued greetings to *lir* and turned to their brother again.

"We are too close," Hart said anxiously.

"Then send Rael to seek out safety, some place we can settle him until this crisis passes." Brennan's tone was sharp. "There is no opportunity for us to heal him until we have found proper refuge."

Instantly Hart went into the link. *We need a place of safety*, he said. *Some place Strahan has no power to find us.*

Done. Rael said, and soared eastward toward the Molon Pass.

"Shansu," Brennan told Corin. "I promise, *rujho*, Strahan will not win."

Hart felt Corin's brow. "Nor his malodorous god."

Corin's breathing was labored. "I thought if I made myself vomit the blood . . . I could win . . . could overcome the power—" He grimaced from unseen pain, baring teeth shut tightly. "Strahan wanted you so badly . . . I thought if I *acted* like he had won, if I tricked him, I could find a means to escape—" His head thrashed against the earth until Brennan trapped it and held it still. "I knew if I drank again, I would be truly lost—" Teeth bit into bottom lip. "I needed to know a way out . . . I let him think he had won, so he would show me—show me a hidden exit—" He spasmed. *"Oh, gods, it hurts!"*

"Hold your silence," Brennan told him gently. "There will be time for this later."

Corin's eyes were transfixed on Brennan's face. "But—you have to know . . . I *do* love Aileen!" His mouth warped into a rigid rictus of pain. "I *do* want her, Brennan . . . Strahan found my weakness."

"And uncovered your strength." Brennan's face was stark, though his tone reflected none of it. "There are things all of us want, Corin, even against our wills. Much of Strahan's power is that which we give him . . . he lets us make our own guilt, instead of forcing it on us."

"And I *did* want the Lion . . . long as I can remember—"

"Corin." Brennan bent close. "I swear, it does not matter. Do you think I could hate you for it after what you have done for us?"

"I could." Corin tried to smile. "In your place, I could. But now—*now*, I think . . . I think there will be no place for me—"

Hart caught his rigid hand. "Do not give in *now*."

"So *tired*," Corin murmured.

Lir, Sleeta said sharply. *The man.*

Brennan looked up quickly. And then gaped in astonishment. *"Jehan—?"*

Hart twisted to look. Like Brennan's, his face reflected shock. And then he expelled a breath, laughing a little. "Not *jehan*, Brennan . . . Carillon's bastard son. The deaf-mute."

"Carollan," Brennan breathed. "By the gods, I had forgotten he lived in Solinde."

Carollan approached at a jog. He was, like their father, a big man, tall and strongly built, though now age stole flexibility and fluidity of movement. His hair was gray, bound back into a clubbed braid. Unlike Niall, he still had two eyes of unwavering blue. Both were fixed on Corin.

He knelt as Hart and Brennan moved aside. His hands were infinitely gentle as he examined eyes, mouth, ears, wiping away the trickles of discolored blood.

"Jehan—?" Corin's head rolled weakly from side to side, until Carollan stilled it. *"Jehan . . .* has Strahan given you back your eye?"

The large hands were soothing. Carefully Carollan scooped Corin up, settled him against a broad chest, and started back the way he had come.

Hart and Brennan did not hesitate, but fell in to flank him on either side. With them went the *lir*.

Six

He was white-haired, but oddly youthful. There was no age in his face, none at all, though the expression in sky-blue eyes told of things seen in ages past as well as anticipating all the days of the future. He tended Corin with endless patience and gentleness, though he required Carollan's aid because of his ruined hands. Quietly courteous, he turned aside anxious queries from Brennan and Hart and gave all his attention to the youngest of Niall's sons. And at last, Hart and Brennan subsided into a forced, rigid patience.

Taliesin. They knew him well enough, though neither had met the man. More than man, at that: Ihlini, once servant of the Seker, harper to Tynstar himself, Strahan's father, and later to the son. Taliesin of the Ihlini, who lived apart from everyone save Carillon's bastard son.

Hart looked at the harper's hands. Such wracked, twisted things, incapable of functioning normally. There were some small things Taliesin could do, but more intricate chores called for straight, flexible fingers and hands with unknotted bones. Once he had made music for Solindish kings and queens and sorcerers; now he saved a Homanan king's Cheysuli son from death.

He looked at the stump of his wrist. How he hated the absence of his hand, the lack of fingers, thumb, palm; knowing the lack sentenced him to a life apart from his people. Slowly he sat back in the chair and scratched absently at his scalp, taking solace in Rael's presence upon the chair back, and yet knowing the *lir*-link was forever tarnished by his inability to fly. The lack of a hand, translated out of human mass into raptor's, meant the lack of too much wing; short hops, perhaps, would be possible, but to resemble chicken instead of hawk—

Hart shut his eyes. He was so weary, so *diminished* by

reaction . . . he needed rest badly, and solid food, and an escape from worry and fear.

A hand touched his arm. His eyes snapped open and he looked up at Brennan, who tried to smile encouragement and failed. By Brennan's face he knew his own; too pale, too gaunt, too dirty. And the eyes, though yellow instead of blue, were full of memories and more than a trace of confusion.

Strahan has touched us all— Hart sat more upright, then leaned forward as Brennan moved back to the pallet on which Corin lay. Taliesin had made it clear he required none of their help—Caro was enough, he said—but still they could not keep themselves from returning time and again to the pallet. To stare down helplessly at the one who had done most to thwart the Seker and the Ihlini, and all the while they had believed him traitor to their race.

Taliesin sighed, brushed back a strand of fine white hair, and turned to look at them both. Caro still knelt at Corin's side, unable to hear what was said; unable to speak of it if he could. "He will recover," the harper told them. "He started it himself, by forcing himself to vomit . . . the draught I have administered will ease the burning in his blood until it passes normally. It is a side-effect of drinking the Seker's blood; I experienced it myself. He is lucky he drank only one goblet, or we would be hard-pressed to win him away from Strahan." He sighed. "As for the legs, well, time will heal them of its own accord, but time is not a luxury any of you may lay claim to." He rose and slipped ruined hands inside the wide sleeves of his blue robe. "If I thought you would go without him, I would send you on to Homana-Mujhar."

"Why?" Brennan asked sharply. "Is something wrong in Mujhara?"

The harper sought and found a seat on a stool, settling himself with a calmness that belied the intent of his words. "Nothing that your return cannot help put to rights, although it will not settle things entirely. Your cousin has done too much harm in your absence. There is unrest in the clans."

"Cousin?" Hart frowned. "Teirnan? Why? What has Teir done?"

With feeling, Brennan swore. "He meant it, then, the fool."

"Meant *what?*" Hart scowled at his brother. "Enlighten me, *rujho.*"

Brennan made an impatient gesture. "He swore to renounce the prophecy because he refuses to acknowledge that someday Cheysuli and Ihlini must coexist, cohabit, in order to merge the bloodlines."

"Aye, well, I am not so fond of that idea, either. But— to *renounce* the prophecy?" Hart shook his head. "Teir is too quick to act sometimes, but to turn his back on what gives our lives meaning? I think not."

"I think *aye,*" Taliesin said gently. "He has done it, Hart. I hear little enough here in Solinde, and rumor is often blown out of proportion, but some truth leaks through. And you must recall that in *Solinde*, the people are willing enough to hear words of Homanan trouble."

"Which are?" Brennan prodded.

"That Teirnan has withdrawn from his clan," Taliesin answered. "He has struck his pavilion and formally petitioned the *shar tahl* to remove his rune-sign from the birthlines." So calmly he spoke of things Cheysuli. "He has gathered other malcontents and together they have gone from clan to clan, all across Homana, to win warriors to the cause of the *a'saii.*"

"Idiocy!" Hart's startled disbelief was manifest. "What does he think to do?"

"What he *hopes* to do is fracture the Cheysuli into separate factions, those dedicated to the prophecy and those who are newly turned against it." Taliesin shrugged. "Niall has done as I expected, once I had told him the truth of things. No longer could he—and Ian—believe implicitly in Ihlini *evil*, when only a portion of us worship Asar-Suti. They have acknowledged that we are not so bad after all, most of us, and that perhaps it would not be impossible to believe a Cheysuli could lie down with an Ihlini and bear children with all the required blood." In his eyes was serenity, though his words were heresy. "Some of you already have begotten children on Ihlini."

"But not Firstborn." Brennan's tone was taut. "And not willingly."

"You lay with Rhiannon willingly enough," Taliesin retorted gently, "though, admittedly, you were unaware of her heritage."

"And so are we to believe the Firstborn will result from *trickery?*" Brennan shook his head. "I am not Teir, harper, but I find it impossible to believe the day will come when Cheysuli and Ihlini can live in peace."

"Or lie down with one another?" Smiling, Taliesin shrugged. "The gods are not fools, Brennan . . . they arrange things deftly and with surpassing subterfuge, when it is required. I give you a prophecy of my own." His eyes were very distant. "There will come a day when a prince of the House of Homana takes to wife an Ihlini woman, born of Asar-Suti—"

"No." In unison.

"—and from that willing union will come the child known as the Firstborn, the boy who will one day rule."

"And this is what Teirnan fights," Hart said grimly. "I begin to understand."

"And will you join with him?" the harper asked. "Or take up your part in the prophecy?"

Hart shook his head. "I have no part. I am the middle son, unpromised to House or princess." Briefly, he glanced at Brennan. "Once I was Prince of Solinde. Once I was a warrior." He displayed the stump of his wrist. "Now I am a man without a clan."

"And Solinde a realm without a king." Taliesin's smile was inexpressibly gentle. "Whatever you may think of me because I am Ihlini, I hope you will also realize that I am a man who loves his country. The House of Solinde is in descent. It is time for a *new* House, built on strong, proud rootstock. Yours would do, I think."

"I am Cheysuli—" But Hart stopped short.

"You are many things," Taliesin told him gently, "and all of them of incalculable value."

Brennan saw mute, bitter protest rising in Hart's eyes and moved to make the explanation himself, knowing it was too painful for his brother. "Taliesin—I think you misunderstand. We were taught, in childhood, all Cheysuli traditions. All the customs, rituals, beliefs." He scrubbed wearily at his forehead. "One custom, cruel as it may sound, is that a warrior stripped by physical dismember-

ment or permanent handicap of his ability to perform a
warrior's duties voluntarily leaves his clan. He is—"

"—*kin-wrecked.*" Hart's clipped interruption stopped
Brennan dead. "It is not so heavy a sentence as the death-
ritual, perhaps, requiring no forfeiture of life—" his tone
was bitterly ironic, "—but what he *does* forfeit is his clan.
His kin, unless they choose to accompany him." Hart
shrugged one shoulder in eloquent acknowledgment of his
plight. "I can hardly expect the Mujhar and everyone else
of the House of Homana to follow me into self-exile."

Taliesin's blue eyes were oddly complacent. "A harsh
custom, indeed."

"Born of necessity." Again, Hart shrugged, as if trying
to dismiss the ramifications of the custom that made him
clanless. "The law of survival."

Thoughtfully, the Ihlini harper nodded. "I understand:
the weak can pull down the strong."

Brennan's tone was subdued. "In the days of our ancestors, when the world was very young, the weak were left
to die so the strong could continue." He did not look at
his twin, whom he judged strong enough despite the loss
of a hand; knowing the old custom, in its day, made sense
even in its cruel practicality. "A man dying of disease in
a time of famine eats food better given to another, and
perhaps causes two deaths in place of one."

Taliesin did not smile, but his tone was strangely sanguine. "I will not argue that, perhaps once, the times warranted such harsh customs. Certainly we Ihlini have made
difficult adjustments in order to survive. But the time you
speak of has passed. Hart is more than merely a warrior,
but also a Prince of Solinde." He shrugged, forestalling
incipient protests. "Besides, I think you should recall—
loyal fatalists that you are—there may be a *reason* for this."

Hart's face was stark.

"*Tahlmorra,*" Brennan said hollowly. "A word more eloquent than 'reason.'"

"Then, my lord, you might argue that the need for such
rigid adherence to an outdated custom has declined," the
harper suggested. "You might go before Clan Council, as
the *Cheysuli* Prince of Homana, and tell them the need is
no longer valid. Now is the time for a new custom, where

a man maimed can be valued for things other than physical abilities."

Hart looked at Brennan sharply, abruptly cognizant of what such change could mean to him as well as to others. Brennan was clearly stunned by the magnitude of the idea, but Hart knew it would not gainsay him. Yet he also knew better than to hope too hard for something that might not occur. Clan Council and the *shar tahls*, whose job it was to insure the continuance of tradition, were incredibly protective of Cheysuli customs; it was what made the race so difficult to destroy, from inside as well as without.

"The need *is* no longer valid," Brennan said thoughtfully. "Hart is as good a warrior as any Cheysuli I know, and there is no reason to believe the lack of a hand will gainsay him from his responsibilities." He nodded. "If I *were* to go before Clan Council—"

Hart shrugged. "Peacetime, *rujho*. If war were to return—"

"There will be no war again, ever. With Corin in Atvia and Keely wed to Sean of Erinn, who is left to fight us? Solinde?" Brennan spread his hands. "Would you levy war against your *rujholli?*"

Hart sighed and sat back in his chair, gazing up at Rael perched on the back. "No more than against my *lir*."

"And so the prophecy nears completion." Taliesin smiled and rose. "You are so close, you cannot see it. But you have, just now, completed a major requirement for fulfillment: four warring realms united in peace."

"Which leaves the two magical races." Brennan said grimly. "I think even the gods underestimated the strength of hatred between Cheysuli and Ihlini."

"I think the gods knew very well how strong that hatred would be," the harper countered. "A parent is not blind to resentments among his children." He looked from one to the other, starting with Brennan and ending with Corin. "There comes a time, however, when the children must outgrow them. And so it will be with Cheysuli and Ihlini." The harper moved toward the door. "It is for you to call on the earth magic to complete the healing of Corin's legs. You cannot wait for them to heal normally. And so I will go from here for awhile, so my presence does not hinder the magic."

The door was shut. "Gods," Hart said, "I am so weary, I doubt I can summon *anything*."

"For Corin, we will have to," Brennan knelt briefly and locked his hands into the pelt behind Sleeta's ears, drawing strength from the contact. Lir, *oh, lir, we are all so weary, so cursed weak, and yet we must all be strong.*

She shifted forward and pressed her head against his jaw. *You will be as strong as is required.*

Hart moved to the pallet and touched Carollan's shoulder briefly. *"Leijhana tu'sai,"* he said, knowing Caro could not hear; knowing also it did not matter, nor tarnish the gratitude. *"Leijhana tu'sai,* kinsman, but this is for us to do."

Carollan moved aside with alacrity, though there was nothing of subservience in it. He merely gave them the room they required, retiring to Taliesin's stool, and watched out of their father's eyes.

Brennan joined Hart at Corin's side. Kiri lay curled at his hip, pointed nose tucked beneath his slack hand. Her bright eyes watched the movements they made in preparing to summon the magic. Sleeta sat beside Brennan, pressing one haunch against his doubled leg. Rael did not depart the chairback, but his link with Hart was not weakened by such a brief distance.

"I have never done this," Hart said nervously.

"Nor have I." Brennan pushed a lock of fallen hair out of his face. "Come with me, *rujho*. Now—"

He slipped into the void quickly, too quickly; he knew fear and an overwhelming sense of helplessness. What if his ignorance cost Corin his life?

Lir. Lir. Sleeta was in the link with him, lending him a measure of strength and courage, though her own was stretched dangerously thin.

Hart! he cried in the void. *I need you,* rujho—

And Hart, abruptly, was there, tumbling through the emptiness like a cork caught in a millrace. Brennan sensed his fear was equal to his own. And inwardly he laughed; two frightened warriors meant to heal their unconscious brother, summoning a power neither had fully tapped.

We need a shar tahl, he told Sleeta.

You need to heal your rujholli. Delicate dictatorship.

Brennan sighed. Linked, he and Hart dissolved the contact with their bodies and sank beneath the level they knew as the world.

Down.

Down, until they touched layers of sentience they had not known existed. Such boundless power as they had never imagined.

Come with us, Brennan said.

We need you, Hart explained.

Sluggishly, Power stirred.

There is a man who requires your aid. Brennan told It. *A warrior, Cheysuli, born of the Old Blood, descendant of the Firstborn, ancestor of those to come again.*

In need, Hart echoed. *Touched by Asar-Suti, who would destroy the gods as we know them so he may hold dominion.*

Power raised Its head.

Come with us, Brennan invited. *Show the Seker that his power is nothing compared to yours.*

He needs you, Hart explained.

Power rose up and set them ablaze with a single touch. And then, too quickly, It hurled them upward, through all the layers and strata and broke them free of the world, where they saw a man on his bed of pain, and took it from him easily. Bones knit themselves into wholeness. Stiffened sinews grew flexible. Vessels pulsed with blood set free of the Seker's fire.

And then, as quickly, the Power was gone, and they were men again; exhausted, dirty, sick of the stink of themselves. And knowing they must go on.

Conscious, Corin gazed up at them both. *"Leijhana tu'sai,"* he said drowsily. Even as Brennan protested, he worked the ruby signet from his finger and pressed it into his oldest brother's palm. "Yours," he said as firmly as he could, and fell asleep with a hand locked in Kiri's ruff.

Hart lay back on the wooden floor, not caring that his sprawl was more than a trifle undecorous, nor that the floor was hard. He shut his eyes, sighed deeply, gave himself over to the luxury of complete relief for the first time in months.

"In the morning, we go," Brennan said hoarsely. "We cannot waste a moment."

"In the morning," Hart agreed wearily, and fell asleep himself.

Brennan laughed raggedly, stroking Sleeta's pelt. *If our jehan could see us now—*

He would cry, Sleeta answered. *But they would be tears of joy.*

Taliesin did not have the means to offer Brennan and Hart the sort of baths they needed, having no half-cask or carefully crafted oak tub, so they did the best they could. Water was heated in a cauldron over the fire and they scrubbed themselves down with harsh soap and harsher cloth, scraping away layers of filth. Taliesin gave them an herbal soap for their hair, to rid themselves of lice, but they forbore cutting it. It could wait; there were things more important than the length of their hair.

Teirnan. Brennan told his brothers what he could of their cousin's treachery, and his treasonous intent. Then, turn by turn, each confessed how he had been taken by Strahan, betrayed by love, lust, greed, ambition. They raised old resentments, hidden emotions, true feelings, and dealt with them as best they could. By the time morning dawned and it was time to leave, each had come to terms with himself in relation to his brothers; each believed he was a better man for it.

And each knew more than ever how binding was a *tahlmorra*.

Taliesin examined the stump of Hart's wrist, pronounced it healed, did not avoid the acknowledgment of persistent pain.

"And it *will* persist," he said gently. "The loss of a limb is something the mind does not fully understand. It will take some time before you stop reaching for things with your nonexistent hand, expecting to close your fingers upon it. It will take time for the sensations of a hand to abate. One moment you will swear it is still attached . . . the next you will know better." His own twisted left hand was gentle on the wrist. "I am sorry, Hart, but there is nothing to be done. Even the gods cannot give back that which was so decidedly destroyed."

"Asar-Suti would have," Hart said grimly. "Or so Strahan promised. It was his price."

"But not *yours*." Taliesin's blue eyes were kind in his

ageless, unseamed face. "Do not curse yourself for being an honorable man. You did what was required."

"Required." Hart sighed and replaced the snug leather cuff that warded the stump against injury. "Aye, required—*and* my own decision."

"And I tell you again to recall that—should Brennan fail to sway the Cheysuli in altering tradition—customs are different in Solinde. We do not throw men away." Taliesin turned away to look at Brennan and Corin. "You cannot afford to waste more daylight. Caro has food and water for you outside. Best go now."

Brennan's face was cleaner than it had been in weeks, but tension had etched permanent lines into the flesh. He frowned. "You are certain Strahan will not punish you for this?"

The harper nodded. "He has no idea where I am, and I use simple magic to keep it so. Strahan is too arrogant to recall the ward-spells I have used; he thinks in terms of conquest, not simple protection." He smiled. "He will not search far. He will be more concerned with placating the Seker, who grows impatient with men who fail him. He will spend his time in Valgaard, not seeking me." The eyes sharpened. "But I warn you, be wary of him still—he *will* seek another way. One day, he will try again to thwart you."

"Best go," Corin said.

Thanks were not enough, but it was all they had. And they offered it in abundance as Taliesin stood in the door and watched them go out into the frosted world. Three battered but gods-touched men, and their *lir;* cat, fox, hawk: the children of the gods.

Seven

In Deirdre's solar, Niall bent over her shoulder and placed a finger on the lion patterned in the tapestry. "Who is this?"

"Shaine," she told him, batting his finger away. "This one is Shaine, that one Carillon, *that* one—"

"Where am *I?*"

"Here." She pointed out the proper lion. "But 'twill be some time before I get to you. All those other lions, and the histories of each—" Deirdre grinned. " 'Twill be *years.*"

Niall sighed and straightened. "Aye," he agreed grimly. "And years before I know what has befallen my sons."

She looked up quickly, saw his face, set aside her massive tapestry. "Niall—"

"Months!" he exclaimed. "And how many of those were wasted? How many of those months did I believe Hart and Corin merely in their respective realms, learning how to rule, while I believed Teirnan and the *a'saii* responsible for Brennan's disappearance?" He cursed and strode angrily to the nearest casement, glaring out on the inner bailey. There was a commotion within the walls, but he was too distracted to wonder at its cause. "By the gods, I should have known. *Strahan* yet again, and eternal Ihlini meddling."

She stood behind him, wanting to touch him and not giving in to it; he was too angry and full of self-recrimination to accept any kindnesses. "And how *were* you to know?" she asked tartly. "You told me yourself the Ihlini have been quiet for years . . . why would you be having a reason to think of Strahan now?"

"Precisely because it *has* been years." Niall leaned his brow against the stone. "Gods, Deirdre . . . *my sons*—"

"I know." Now she touched him. "I know, Niall. But

you said yourself 'tis unlikely he'd want to *kill* them. Strahan's way is to use men instead."

"He wanted them twenty-two years ago . . . he nearly got them then. And now that he *has*—" Niall turned. "Oh, gods, I am so frightened. What sort of men will he make them?"

She sighed, knowing she could give him no answer. "When do you send the army to Valgaard?"

"In the morning." His hands rested on her shoulders. "Ian and I go with them."

Tight-faced, she nodded. "The gods grant—"

But whatever she desired the gods to grant was never stated. A servant, circumventing courtesy entirely, threw open the solar door. "My lord! *My lord!*"

"What is it?" Niall asked irritably.

Brennan stepped around the wide-eyed servant. "What he means to say, *jehan*, is that all of your sons are back." Kindly, Brennan moved the servant aside and held the door open himself as Hart and Corm and assorted *lir* made their way into the tower solar. The chamber was suddenly filled.

"All—" Niall said hoarsely.

"One, two, three." Hart grinned. "Unless Deirdre has contrived to add another in our absence."

"No," she said blankly. And then laughed aloud in joy.

Mute, Niall stared at his sons. One, two, three, as Hart had said. But they were not the sons he had sired and known for years. Something had changed each one, and profoundly. There was a tangible difference.

Brennan: much too gaunt and oddly haunted in yellow eyes, though his smile was genuine. His jerkin was soiled and crusted with countless unnamed things, and Niall had no desire to ask how it had become so; he had a good idea. His only desire was to see that Brennan was whole, and that was blatantly obvious. His hair was mostly clean, if too long, and he held himself with customary pride, but there was something about the way he moved that spoke of things unsaid even among his brothers.

Corin: bearded as an Erinnish brigand, looking less Cheysuli than ever, though there was, Niall noted, a subtle self-confidence Corin had always lacked, or was banished by bad temper. And though there was a tension in the way he moved, as if he waited for something, Niall saw no anger, no hostility, no reluctance to accept his place in the House of Homana. Clearly he had suffered; equally clearly, he had come to terms with himself.

And Hart, showing teeth in a familiar grin; showing something else in posture. All of them were clad in worn and dirty clothing, though clearly they had bathed a day or two before arrival, if only arms and faces; but there was more than a weary relief and elation in Hart's posture and attitude. He stood rigidly next to the door, left hand thrust behind his back as if he meant to hide something in it. Even as he stepped free of the door, letting it swing closed, he kept the forearm behind him.

But Niall would worry about them later. Now was the time for celebration and explanation. He expelled an eloquent breath of relief. "Oh, gods—all of my sons—*leijhana tu'sai*—"

"We have expressed similar sentiments repeatedly the last two weeks." Corin went to the nearest chair and collapsed into it, putting his feet up on a footstool. "I am footsore, hungry, and weary, but I feel happy for it."

Brennan went straight to Niall and put out an arm to clasp his father's. But Niall ignored the arm altogether, instead jerking Brennan into a rough embrace. "You do not know how many times I petitioned the gods for the safe return of my sons."

Corin laughed. "Well, they must have grown weary of hearing it. All of us begged them, too."

Niall's good eye was wet as he released his oldest son. The patch hid the other from sight. There was more silver in his tawny hair and deeper lines in the contours of his face, but the smile banished the age worry had added. "You are well? All of you?" He wanted to hug Corin and Hart as he had hugged Brennan, but Corin was settled and obviously oblivious to the gesture; Hart's posture warded him against familiarity, even from his father.

"Well enough," Brennan said. "But first, let us swear to you that we are not Strahan's minions sent to do you harm. Because of Corin, we are nothing but ourselves, if a trifle worn." He glanced briefly at Hart, turned back and sought a chair.

Belatedly, Niall pushed one over. Deirdre beckoned Hart to take her own, but he shook his head and remained at his post beside the door. Or intended to. The door was abruptly shoved open; Hart, thrusting out arms to keep himself from being crushed between wall and wood, saw his father's face go white.

But Ian was in the room. "By the gods, it *is* true! All of you are back!"

Silence met his outburst. He stopped short, staring at his brother, then slowly turned to look at the Mujhar's middle son, his own personal favorite.

Hart's face was stark. "I meant to tell you later."

Niall summoned his voice. "*Strahan* did that to you?"

"No, *jehan*. My stupidity did this to me." Bitterness crept in. "A heavy price, but I pay it."

From the corridor came an urgent voice. "Corin? *Corin!*"

Corin sighed. And then Keely prodded her uncle aside to force her way into the solar past the bodies near the door.

"Corin—" But she broke it off, turning to look at Hart.

"Why not announce it?" he said unsteadily. "Why not say it and be done with it: *The Mujhar's son is* kin-wrecked."

Abruptly, Brennan wrenched his eyes away to stare at the floor; he could not bear to see the pain in Hart's eyes.

"Come here," Niall said.

After a moment, Hart answered his father's bidding. He was conscious of all the eyes, but looked only at the single blue one of his father. *"Jehan—"*

"If you think I will love you the less because you lack a hand, you have no wits at all," Niall said clearly. "If you think I cannot comprehend the pain—physical as well as emotional—that such a loss engenders, look again at my face."

Hart felt dizzy. He drew in a deep breath, wet his lips, did not avoid the topic. "No, *jehan*. But you are Mujhar; they dared not send you out of the clan."

"That had nothing to do with it," Niall said gently. "An eye lost, as Taliesin pointed out to me, is not a mark of physical weakness nor deformity of the spirit. I am no less a man because I have only one. And while it is true that the loss of an eye does not affect a warrior as much as the loss of a hand, I do understand what you feel."

Hart looked at the floor, thinking mutinous thoughts.

"I *do*," his father repeated.

After a moment, Hart nodded.

"Sit down," Niall told him. "Keely, will you send for wine? I think all of us could use it."

"*Usca*," Corin said, and grinned at her exaggerated curtsy just before she went out the door.

"So." Niall sat down in the last of Deirdre's chairs even as she settled herself on the stool nearest his feet. "I am ashamed," he said flatly. "Ashamed I did not realize sooner the scope of Strahan's intentions. But when Brennan and Rhiannon disappeared so soon on the heels of Teirnan's defection, I feared *a'saii* interference, not Ihlini. Not after so much time." Bleakly, he shook his head. "I spent weeks trying to trap Teirnan, and all I did was waste time and effort. Yet until a crofter's half-wit son at last had courage enough to come forward and tell me he had *seen* Rhiannon spirit Brennan away, I did not comprehend what was afoot."

"Nor did I," Ian said grimly. "Blind fools, all of us—and it gave Strahan the time he needed."

Niall glanced briefly at Ian, who had sired Rhiannon, than looked away from the bleak guilt in his brother's eyes. He sighed, rubbing at old scars. "I knew then he would want you all, *each* of my sons, and that further delay might result in your deaths, or worse. And so I readied an army to march on Valgaard itself." Niall's smile was twisted. "We were to leave in the morning . . . but I think I may cancel the duty."

"Unless you wish to engage Strahan once and for all." Brennan shook his head. "A formidable foe, *jehan.* He needs killing, but I think it will take more than an army. Even of Cheysuli."

"Or less," Ian remarked. "Perhaps a single man, in place of that army."

"No," Niall said promptly. "For now I want none of my family anywhere near Valgaard or the Ihlini. We are together again for the first time in nearly a year, and I would prefer to enjoy it."

"Nearly a year?" Corin grinned. "Our banishment is incomplete, then . . . do you intend to send Hart and me away again?" He slanted a glance at his middle brother, who merely shrugged one shoulder and smiled vaguely.

Keely returned. "The wine is coming," she said, moving

to stand behind Corin's chair. "*And*, my lord Mujhar, if you intend to send Corin—or Hart—*anywhere*, you will have to contend with *me*."

Niall's smile was crooked. "Aye, aye, so I see. And no, I do not intend to send them anywhere, unless they want to go." He lifted a tawny brow in Keely's direction. "Did you tell Aileen Brennan is home at last?"

In his chair, Corin froze. He felt Keely's hands on his shoulders, pressing gently, as if to offer support. "She knows," Keely said briefly. "Everyone in the palace knows."

Ian nodded. "I sent Tasha to Clankeep with the news, so you may expect Maeve home by evening."

"Maeve is at Clankeep?" Brennan asked in surprise.

Niall frowned a little. "She wished to see the *shar tahl*. She swore the vows of a *meijha*, Brennan, in good faith, even if in poor judgment. Now that Teir has renounced his clan, she wishes to formally renounce the vows."

"Teir is a fool," Hart declared.

"Teir is more than that," Keely said grimly. "He is *kin-wrecked*—proscribed by the *shar tahl*, by the clan-leader . . . he is forbidden Clankeep, Mujhara—not that he would wish to come here anyway—and all the other clans." She grimaced. "Though he goes where he will, in truth, gathering other warriors."

"How many?" Brennan asked bleakly.

"Unknown." Ian moved aside as a servant came in with wine and goblets. He took them from him, dismissed the man, set everything on a table, and began to pour, handing out the cups. "There are rumors one day he has seven men, the next day seventy."

"He is shrewd," Niall said. "Much smarter than I believed. But Ceinn has suckled him on tales of the old days, when the race was exquisitely pure . . . Teirnan is now dedicated to the restoration of the old ways without benefit of the prophecy."

Brennan shook his head as he leaned forward to take the cup from Ian. "How can a warrior who has been raised to respect the prophecy turn his back on it? I admit that I am less than enamored of the need to cohabit with Ihlini, but to deny myself the afterworld? No." Brennan shook his head. "Teirnan must be mad."

"Not mad." Ian carried the requested *usca* to Corin. "Determined. We have been blessed, as a race, with a consuming dedication—to the exclusion of all else—to fulfillment of the prophecy. We have been accused, on more than one occasion, of being blind and deaf to the truth, locking ourselves away in insular arrogance, believing we know the only way." He looked at his brother. "*Some* might name us cursed."

Niall nodded thoughtfully. "Once, we believed no Ihlini could intend anything but harm to us. We learned differently from an old woman, an old *Ihlini* woman, who lived in Homana out of choice. And from an ageless harper, who showed me that an Ihlini formerly sworn to the Seker could renounce that allegiance in the name of peace and coexistence, and actually work *for* the prophecy."

"And still does so." Hart reached for wine with his left hand, stopped rigidly, put out his right. "It was Taliesin who gave us refuge from Strahan."

"And Taliesain, with Carollan, who gave us back our youngest *rujholli.*" Brennan smiled at Corin. "If you do not tell him all that you accomplished, even in front of Strahan, I *will.*"

Corin shrugged. "Another time."

Niall smiled. "That, too, has changed." His eyes glinted. "No more resentment of your oldest *rujholli.*"

Corin stared. "You knew?"

Silvering brows rose. "How could I not? Do you think I am blind? I knew very well how much you wanted what Brennan had. As for now?" Niall smiled. "I think you have learned there are more important things to concern yourself with than what your *rujholli* has."

"Such as survival," Hart said dryly. "The gods know we could have died a dozen times."

"I did." Brennan's tone was hollow as, for the moment, he was back in the tiny cell. He shivered, rose abruptly, put his unfinished wine down. "*Jehan*, there is more to tell you. But I think it will wait for another time." He straightened his jerkin. "There is something I must do . . . someone I must come to terms with."

Corin, thinking of Aileen, thrust himself to his feet. And checked as Brennan turned to look at him. Uncomfortable, he shrugged. "I—I intend to have a bath. I am filthy."

"'So are we all.'' Hart rose as well, sucking down the last of the wine in his cup. "I think I will catch up on lost sleep.''

In silence, Niall's sons filed slowly out of the solar, automatically sending *lir* ahead to bedchambers. Intent upon their thoughts, they paid no attention to one another. Not even Corin to Brennan, as much as he wanted to. Like Hart, he turned away, and Brennan went on alone.

It was midmorning. Sunlight spilled through stained-glass casements and painted the Great Hall a mass of liquid colors. But Brennan ignored the light, ignored the Lion, moving instead to the end of the firepit. He cleared wood and ashes, gripped the iron handle, peeled back the lid.

He stared down into the hole, watching the stairs fall away into darkness. One hundred and two of them. Far fewer than in Valgaard on the way to the Gate of the god.

Time enough for such foolish fear as I have known . . . never again will I give over such a weapon to the enemy.

But sunlight, however bright, did not touch the darkness. And so Brennan turned away, intending to light a torch, and saw her standing inside the hammered doors.

Red-haired. Green-eyed. Supple as a willow. She carried her head high on a slender neck; brilliant hair fell to curl around her hips.

"They were saying you were back.'' He heard Erinn in her voice, far more lilting than Deirdre's accent.

This woman, this girl, whom I am to wed, nearly cost all of us our sanity, because of Corin.

But he could not tell her that. Not yet. Perhaps not ever; too much, at this moment, lay between them. Because of Corin. "Back,'' he said. "Aye.'' Not knowing what else to say.

"And safe.''

"Aye,'' he agreed, "and safe.'' Then, giving in to it, "So is my youngest *rujholli*.''

She did not flinch, though clearly she had heard him. Nor did she answer, though she calmly walked the length of the hall from doors to firepit. And then she stood before him, considerably shorter than he, and he found, oddly, he wanted to apologize to her. Corin had said little enough of Aileen on the journey home from Solinde, shying away from the topic as if fearing Brennan might be further insulted by his words.

But Brennan was not insulted. At this moment, facing the stranger he would marry, he did not know what he was.

He drew in a breath. "You are in love with Corin."

"Aye," was all she said.

"And he in love with you."

Her lips tightened minutely. "Once," she said quietly. "I'm not knowing how long it lasted."

Resentment rose, then faded. Brennan smiled wryly. "It lasted," he told her sardonically. "I can assure you of that."

She said nothing. She was no beauty, he saw, and certainly not the kind of woman Corin generally sought for companionship. What she *was*, he realized, looking at her without benefit of prejudice, was proud as a Cheysuli, with a spirit that blazed as brightly. And he knew, seeing that pride, that spirit, Aileen of Erinn was as trapped by circumstances as the Prince of Homana himself.

How do I deal with this?

But there was no answer, not in her face. Nor, he knew, in his own.

Brennan sighed. "Corin is different," he said. "I saw it at once, when I could see again, but I did not recognize it. The circumstances did not, quite, lend themselves to contemplation." She gazed at him steadily, hands folded primly in the folds of her gown. And yet, somehow, he knew better. This was not Aileen he faced, but another woman entirely. A woman who knew how she felt no more than he himself did. "Different," he repeated. "Not all of it, I think, is from imprisonment. I think most of it is from you. And so, in the end, instead of blame, I must offer gratitude; it was what saved our lives."

She did not avoid his eyes. "It was not intended, none of it. I was meaning it no more than Corin. It—" she checked, sighed, went on quietly, "—just *happened.*"

Brennan thought of Rhiannon. None of that had "just happened," being carefully designed, but he understood what Aileen meant. And knew he could lay no blame. "I admire your honesty," he said abruptly. "I have had little of that, of late, from women." He paused. "You do know the story."

"Aye. Keely told me."

Trust Keely— But now was not the time. Now was the time for honesty. "Aileen—I cannot promise it will be easy. Arranged marriages are difficult enough, particularly cradle-betrothals, but now, with *this*—"

Her cool voice interrupted. "I'm knowing it as well as you, Brennan. D'ye think I've not spent my nights thinking about it, wondering what I would do when you and Corin came home?" A trace of inner fire lighted Erinnish eyes— green as emeralds, he thought—and he saw a hint of Aileen's passion. " 'Twill be as hard as we make it, I think."

Brennan did not couch his words in diplomacy. "And if Corin stays here? What then? Am I expected to *share*?"

The fire caught and burned, blazing in her eyes. " 'Tis between Corin and me, I'm thinking."

He laughed once, incredulously, on a gust of air. "Is it? Am I discounted so easily?"

Her skin was very fair, and he saw the bloom of color in her cheeks. Bright scarlet, competing with the brilliance of her hair. "He left me," she said. "He *left* me, my lord husband-to-be, because he would not steal his brother's betrothed. An honorable man, your brother; d'ye think he'd discard that honor *here*?"

It was a new light she cast on Corin. A few weeks before Brennan might have protested she did him too much credit; now, he did not think so. He had seen Corin's unexpected sense of honor on dramatic display in Valgaard.

"No," he said quietly. "No, I was wrong to imply it."

Some of her vitality drained away. "Were you? No. I'm thinking not. You believed what any man might, faced with such a coil." Aileen shook her head, wide mouth twisted. " 'Tis sorry I am, Brennan. We none of us asked for it, but it has all been spilled into our laps by your gods . . . by your capricious Cheysuli *destiny*." She sighed. "Keely told me you are a good man, if a trifle unimaginative."

He considered it thoughtfully a moment. Discarded the idea; he was whatever he was. "And did she tell you of my fear? The flaw in the Prince of Homana?"

Aileen stared back at him. And then she smiled a little. "If you're meaning he could put a cask of hot water and scent to good use, then aye, I see—*smell*—a flaw. But otherwise—no. Keely said nothing of a flaw. Nothing of a *fear*."

"Then I should tell you of it." He went to the wall, took a torch from the bracket, lighted it from a candle and returned to the firepit. "Come down with me," he said. "Come down with me, *meijhana*, and tell me how it was a bad-tempered, impetuous Cheysuli princeling won the heart of Aileen of Erinn." He smiled. "And I will tell you how it is Corin's oldest *rujholli* means to face his fear and destroy it."

Green eyes widened in surprise. "Are you really wanting to know?"

"No," he said truthfully, "but it will give me something to listen to instead of chattering teeth."

She frowned. "My teeth are not much for chattering."

"Mine are." He took the first step into the stairway. Turned to look back at the woman his brother loved, knowing, one day, he might learn to feel the same. "Will you come, Aileen?"

After a moment, she did.

Corin sprawled on his back in the center of his bed. It felt odd to be in it after so many months, smelling familiar smells, feeling familiar warmth and the softness of the mattress. He had known so little warmth and softness in Strahan's glassy fortress.

He sought Kiri with one hand, found her, lost himself in silent communion. It remained unbroken until his sister came into the chamber.

"Corin?"

He turned his head.

"You mean to go back to Atvia."

It was a statement, not inquiry. He thought about it a moment, then nodded. "I think so."

Keely moved closer to the bed. "And if I asked you to stay?"

The wall of his belly clenched. "Do you know *what* you ask?"

"I know." She stood rigidly beside the bed. "Aileen has confided in me." She shrugged a little, clearly tense. "We became close, Corin, being somewhat alike . . . she told me what had happened, and how." Abruptly she sat down. "Gods, *rujho*, I know how you must feel! But if you go to Atvia you will leave me all alone."

"I went to Atvia before."

"That was for a year. You would come home, I knew it—but now, *now*—" She sighed, shaking her head; the tawny braid shook itself. "You will go, and never come home again."

He stroked Kiri with resolution, locked away in silence.

Keely's tone altered. "You are *afraid*. I see it."

"Aye." He did not shirk the admission.

"You, Corin?"

"I have cause." He threaded fingers in Kiri's pelt. "Alaric is dead. Atvia lies open to whatever influence Lillith wields, and Strahan. And *jehana* also is there—witless, twisted *jehana*." He rolled his head against the bedclothes. "Someone must go, Keely . . . and Atvia is mine."

"Leave it to someone else."

"No."

"Corin—"

"I will not run from responsibility, nor bewail it. I have something of my own at last, something no one else may hold; Atvia is *mine*. It is for me to put the realm into order again, *my* task, to put light in place of darkness. It is for *me* to do; not Brennan, not Hart, not you." He shook his head again. "One day, Keely, you will learn that saying no is not always the answer. Nor is turning your back."

"Then you *will* go."

Corin sighed. "Aye."

Keely's tone was bitter. "Because the prophecy requires it."

"As much as it requires service of you. And you *will* serve it, Keely; no matter how difficult, how demanding, how much sacrifice is asked. You are not like Teirnan." Corin sat up and turned, swinging his legs over the edge of the bed. He still wore his boots; he did not care that he had soiled his bedclothes. "Be what *you* must, Keely, but let me do what *I* must."

She leaned against him slightly. "Then do it. I will not gainsay you; I am not such a fool as to say no to you now, after such a pretty speech. But *you* are a fool if you think I will not curse you for such newfound resolution."

"I am not a fool; I know you will." He flipped her braid behind her back.

Keely drew in a breath. "Will you see her before you go?"

"I thought to do so now."

She opened her mouth, then shut it, and would not meet his eyes.

After a moment, he nodded. "She has gone to Brennan."

"They—she said there are things to be settled between them, things Brennan must know of her, and things she must learn of him. She said if she left it until after she had seen you—" She broke off, plainly uncomfortable. "Oh, Corin—"

"Later, then; we will both of us be better prepared to say good-bye." Corin nodded; his "newfound resolve" was firm at last, and something he could live with. "And now, if you do not mind, I would like to take a bath." He bent over and tugged off his boots, one by one, welcoming the activity. And then, distracted, he looked at his sister in startled comprehension. "Oh, gods, Keely—one-handed, Hart cannot even do *this!*"

Keely turned her face against his shoulder in unspoken grief for lost hands and lost brothers, not knowing, for her, which was worse, or would be.

Hart pushed open his chamber door, leaned against it in weary numbness, at last moved aside and shut it. As always, he looked for Rael. As always, the hawk was on his perch, wings folded, perfectly groomed, content to wait in silence.

He sighed. He wandered aimlessly to the bed, sat down on the edge, stared blankly at the floor. He wondered vaguely if he was ill; depression was foreign to him.

"Gods," he said aloud; it seemed a most eloquent comment. Wearily he bent forward, reached to grab his boots, realized abruptly he no longer had the freedom to undress himself at his leisure.

It stunned him. But then for longer than he could remember, he had not been *required* to change clothing or boots. In Valgaard, there had been no need, and there had been no time on the journey from Taliesin's cottage to Mujhara except to dip head in a bucket and scrub face and hands—*hand*—clean.

Hart stared at his boot. At his hand. And at the hand that no longer existed. *"Gods—"* he said; he choked, and covered his head with his arms.

"Let me," the woman said, and he jerked arms away in shock.

Ilsa. He gaped at her like a fool.

Ilsa. In his room.

"Let me," she repeated, and knelt to remove his boot.

Awkwardly, Hart scrambled away. He found himself standing some ten feet from her, still staring, still made mute by her presence; filled with abject humiliation, that she had seen his helplessness.

And then anger began to replace it. "Go," he said curtly.

Ilsa rose. The incandescence of her beauty had not faded, and he felt renewed astonishment at the magnitude of it. "Hart," she said, "it does not matter to me."

He was shaking. "You knew."

"Dar told me what he had done." She was pale as death. "He thought I would approve."

"And you did *not?*"

"I was appalled." Her tone was even. At first he thought she spoke by rote, not caring what she said; beneath the tone he sensed a wire stretched to breaking. "I swear, I did not know what he intended. I did not know he would go so far."

"But you did not tell the Mujhar." He recalled too clearly his father's shock.

Even her lips were pale. "I could not find the words. Not after I learned how he lost his eye. To tell him his son had also been maimed by Ihlini treachery—?" White-faced, Ilsa shook her head. "I could not do it. I thought it better left to you."

He thought again of Dar. "You were in the house." As he intended, his tone accused.

Ilsa drew in a breath. Slender fingers shredded the gray-blue silk of her gown. "Dar came," she said. "We drank wine. We spoke of you. I told him I wanted no harm to come to you, nor to him, nor to Solinde. And he laughed, and said it would not; that the wager was merely a game." Her tone wavered minutely; she steadied it and went on. "I looked into his eyes, and knew he lied to me. But by then it was too late. The wine was drugged. I—slept." Color touched her cheeks; the glacial eyes were angry. "In the morning, he came in triumph, saying the enemy was removed. And he told me what he had done."

Hart longed to believe her. "Did he tell you all of it?"

"Aye." She did not look away as he displayed the handless arm before her. "He told me quite clearly, in his perversity, knowing I would be sickened, and seeking pleasure from it." Ilsa drew in a trembling breath. "I swear, *I swear*, I had nothing to do with it."

His eyes narrowed. "Why are you here? What did you tell my *jehan* so he would let you stay?"

Her eyes were startled. "The truth. That I desire you to come home."

"Home?"

Fingers twitched in a gesture of arrested acknowledgement. "To Solinde," she amended.

He nodded grimly. "Dar should like that."

"Dar should not," she said quietly, "knowing he will be executed."

That startled him out of his bitterness. He stared at her and saw the grief in her eyes, that she tried to hide and could not. "I am not dead. It was a *hand*, not my head." And he knew, as he said it, the first seeds Taliesin had so carefully planted were beginning to take root.

"It was treason," she said steadily. "He attacked the Prince of Solinde and otherwise threatened his person. I had no other choice but to petition the regent for Dar's arrest, and I did so immediately." She paused awkwardly. "It is for you to give the order, when the trial is completed."

"Me?"

"You are the Prince of Solinde."

He did not deny it. "Why a trial, Ilsa? So that others might argue in Dar's behalf? I should think the Solindish might prefer to be rid of me, regardless of circumstances."

"Some, aye," she agreed, "but not all."

"What of you?" he asked. "What of the last of Bellam's line?"

Ilsa drew in a breath. "I came here to bring you home—" quickly, she caught herself, "—to *Solinde*. I came to tell you that we are in need of a prince of the blood." Her smile was slight, but wry. "A prince not *entirely* of our blood, perhaps, but there is some. Electra was your kinswoman as well as mine, though we tend to overlook it; I am *not* the sole bearer of the blood of Bellam's House. It should, in the end, please those who argue against you." Briefly, Ilsa looked down at closed hands, "I came here to tell you I had chosen even *before* Dar arrived—it was why I sent the messenger—and that you were the one I chose."

"Did you?" It was rhetorical; he was not certain he believed her.

"Aye," she told him evenly, and held out her closed right hand.

After a moment, he accepted what she gave him. Heavy rings chimed. He looked down at the Third Seal. At the Second, which Tarron had held. And the First, that had been in Niall's keeping.

"The Trey," Ilsa said.

"I know what it is." He felt empty. "I do not think I can."

"There is also this." Ilsa held out her other hand. When he did not move to accept what she offered, she turned over her hand and opened it. Against her palm the sapphire glowed.

"My signet," he blurted, startled.

"I got it from the wine-girl after Dar told me she had it."

He smiled wryly. "She would not sell to me."

"She did not sell to *me*." Ilsa answered his smile. "I won it from her, Hart."

He stared at her in shock. And then began to laugh.

Ilsa smiled also, but the amusement faded quickly. "Will you come, Hart? Solinde has need of you."

"To give the order for a patriot's execution."

Her gaze did not waver. "If you would prefer—if it is a *test*—I will do it myself."

"As you would have put down my broken-legged horse."

Her chin rose minutely. "I do what must be done. There are requirements of state."

His eyes were oddly intent. "I have been told," he said slowly, "that in Solinde the customs are different."

"Aye." Her tone was guarded.

"I am told that *in Solinde*, it does not matter so much that a man lacks a hand. That a *king* lacks a hand."

Comprehension lighted her eyes. "My lord, in Solinde all that matters—*in kings*—is that they do not lack the wherewithal to sire children on their wives."

Hart smiled crookedly. "No," he said, "I do not."

She lifted a delicate chin. "Then will you come home with me?"

He studied her a long moment. And then he turned and set the Trey of Solinde down onto a table, and stepped closer to the woman. He took the sapphire signet from her palm and slipped it onto her thumb, knowing it too large for any of her fingers.

He did not smile. "Only if you wear this."

"The requirements of state." But there was laughter in her eyes.

Niall sat slumped in his chair. Nearly all of them were gone; his sons, his daughter, his brother. Only his *meijha* remained.

Deirdre stood behind his chair. She leaned down, caught his neck in both arms, hugged briefly. "*All* of them," she said; nothing more was needed.

"All of them," he echoed. "But *gods*, how changed they are."

"Were you expecting something else?" She asked it gently, knowing it would hurt him. "You, who lost an eye to the Ihlini?"

He sighed, reached up to catch her arms beneath his chin, held them. "Each," he said, "so changed. Corin, I think for the better, though there is pain in him; I saw it. And Brennan—something in his eyes, *something*—" He shivered. "And *Hart*—" Abruptly, Niall checked, took his left hand from Deirdre's arm and stared at it, studying palm, fingers, thumb. "Gone," he said hollowly, then dropped it to his thigh. "He will not stop, *meijhana*. I know him and his kind too well . . . the Ihlini will not stop."

She moved around the chair to stand close beside him, one hand stroking back silvering hair. "No."

"He will seek them out again, or me, or Ian, or someone else of the *proper* blood . . . he will seek them out, and take them, and do his best to twist them to his needs . . . to fulfill his god's desires."

"I know."

"Strahan *does not* give up."

"No." Deirdre knelt beside the chair and locked her hands around his forearm, feeling the tension in the sinew beneath the bare flesh. On his arms, *lir*-gold glowed. "But neither do the Cheysuli. Neither did your sons."

"No." Niall closed one of her hands in his. "*Leijhana tu'suai* for that." He sighed. Looked at the folds of yarn and tapestry. Studied it absently. And slowly, some of the tension drained away; amusement crept in to replace it. "*Which* lion did you say was me?"

Deirdre laughed, and showed him.

Epilogue

She walked steadily through the corridor of spiraling columns, passing beneath tier upon tier of glass forming interlocked arches above her head. So lovely, all of it, in its glassy magnificence; in its sharp-edged, threatening beauty. Much like her brother, she thought.

She saw him, then, where he had spent the entirety of the night, and all of the following day. It was night now again, although within the heart of Valgaard it was difficult to tell. When one wanted light, one needed only to summon the *godfire*.

Lillith did not. In darkness she walked to the Gate. There she paused, and waited.

He did not look up. He did not, in any way, acknowledge her presence. He sat cross-legged by the lip of the Gate, head bowed, staring fixedly into the hole. Black hair spilled over his shoulders. The glow of *godfire* touched the circlet and set it ablaze in the heavy darkness.

"So," she said, "they are gone. You have lost them yet again."

Strahan did not answer.

"Brooding will not help."

"I am thinking, hardly brooding . . . there *is* a decided difference."

She was relieved. He sounded normal. "Aye," she agreed, "there is, and I am glad you know it."

Strahan sighed. "What do you want, Lillith?"

"To offer condolences, if you want them; encouragement, if you need it."

"No and no." One pale, slender hand brushed nonexistent dust from a knee.

Lillith waited. He said nothing more. Perhaps he was brooding. "Strahan." She knelt down, spreading blood-red skirts, and looked at his face across the Gate. It was a mask in the glare, lacking definition. "You did try."

After a moment, he nodded. "And I will try again. Perhaps *this* time I will succeed . . . already I have a plan."

A plan. Lillith smiled. She felt anticipation.

At last he looked at her. "It does not matter: *time*."

She lifted winged brows. His face was so like hers, except for the mismatched eyes.

Casually, he said: "I have all the days of forever."

Daughter of the Lion

PART I

One

I was aware of eyes, watching me. Marking every step, every feint, my every riposte with the sword. Thinking, no doubt, I was mad; or did she wish she were in my place?

She had come before to watch me practice against the arms-master. Saying nothing, sitting quietly on a bench with heavy skirts spilling over her legs.

Before, it had not touched me, because I can be deaf and blind when I choose, so focused on the weapons. But this time it did. It reached out and touched me, and held me, with a new intensity.

In the eyes I saw desperation.

It was enough to pierce my concentration. Enough to get me killed, had it been anything but practice. As it was, Griffon's blade tip slid easily by my guard and lodged itself, but gently, in the buckle of my belt.

"Dead," he said calmly. "On your feet, but dead. And all your royal blood spilling out of those proud Cheysuli veins."

Ordinarily I might have cursed him cheerfully, or retorted in kind, or made him try me again. But I did not, this time, because of the eyes that watched in such mute, distinct despair.

"Dead," I agreed, and left him to gape in surprise as I walked past him to the woman.

She watched me come in silence, saying nothing with her mouth but screaming with her eyes. Green Erinnish eyes, born of an island kingdom very far from my own. But born into similar circumstances; bound by similar rules.

Though foreigners, we were kin. She had married my brother. I would marry hers.

Aileen of Erinn, now Princess of Homana, looked up at me as I stopped. Standing, we are similar in height; Chey-

suli are taller than other races, but she comes of the House
of Eagles, where men are often giants. But she is red-haired
to my tawny, green-eyed to my blue. Equally outspoken,
but without knowing the frustration I so often faced, because we wanted different things.

But now, she did not stand. She sat solidly on the bench,
as if weighted by stone, with both hands clasped over her
belly. Looking at her, I knew.

"By all the gods," I said, "he has you breeding *again!*"

I had not meant it to come out so baldly, not to Aileen,
whom I liked, and whom I preferred not to harm with hasty
words. But I am not a person who thinks much before
speaking, being ruled by temper and tongue; inwardly I
cursed myself as I saw the flinch in her eyes.

And then her chin came up. I saw the line of her jaw
harden, that strong Erinnish jaw, and knew for all she was
wife to the Prince of Homana, he did not precisely rule her.

But then, being Brennan, I knew he would not try.

Aileen smiled a little, though one corner curved down
crookedly. "In Erin, bairns *often* follow the bedding. 'Tis
the same in Homana, I think."

I glanced over my shoulder at Griffon, due more honor
than I gave him, but I was thinking of Aileen, and of things
better kept private. "You may go," I told him. "But come
again tomorrow, at the same hour."

Briefly, so briefly, there was a glint of something in
brown eyes, but hidden instantly. I regretted my tone, but
did not know what I might say to lessen the insult, since it
was already given. He was far more than servant, being my
father's personal arms-master, and therefore in service to a
king. And he owed no service to me, since only men are
trained in the arts of war. He had agreed to train the Mujhar's daughter only because he had lost a wager. In winning
it, I had won him, and all that he could teach.

He cleaned his sword, sheathed it, bowed to Aileen and
left. Giving her the courtesy he might have given me, had
I been deserving of it. But for now, Aileen's welfare was
more important than Griffon's feelings.

"He might have waited," I said curtly. "He has a son
already, and you nearly dead of *that.*" Grimly I caught up
a soft cloth, cleaned the blade, drove it home into its
sheath. "You have been wed but eighteen months, and a

child of it already. Now there will be another?" I shook
my head, speaking through my teeth. It was their business,
not mine, but I could not help myself; Brennan and I are
not, always, friends. "Aileen, he gives you no *time*—"

" 'Twas not entirely up to him," she told me sharply,
giving me back my tone but in her Erinnish lilt. "D'ye
think I had no say in the matter? D'ye think I'd let him
take me against my will, or that he would try?" Aileen
rose, absently shaking the rucked up folds out of her
skirts. "Are ye forgetting, then, that women can want the
bedding, too?"

It silenced me, as she meant it to. Aileen and I are close,
nearly *kinspirits*, and she knows how strongly I feel about
women being made to do certain things merely because
they are women. She knows also I have little interest in
bedding, being more concerned with freedom. In body as
well as in mind.

"He might have waited," I said again. "And you might
have let him."

She smiled. Aileen's smile lights up a hall; it lighted the
chamber now. "He might have," she agreed, "and *I* might
have, as well. But we were neither of us thinking of anything more than the moment's pleasure . . . 'twill come to
you, one day, no matter what you think."

I turned away from her and strode across to a sword
rack, put away the sheathed blade. I felt the rigidity in my
back; tried to loosen it even as I tried to force my tone
into neutrality. "When will it be born?"

"Six months' time," she said. "And 'it' will be a 'they.' "

I jerked around and stared at her. "Two?"

"Aye, so the physicians say." Aileen smiled again, speaking easily. "A family trait, I'm told. First Brennan and Hart,
then you and Corin. And now—?" She shrugged. "We'll
be seeing what we see."

She did it well, I thought. Only her eyes betrayed her.
"Two," I repeated. "You nearly died of Aidan, and he was
only one."

Aileen shrugged again. "I'm larger, now, from Aidan. It
should be easier this time, and the physicians are telling
me twins are always smaller."

I could barely stifle a shout. "By the gods, Aileen, you
nearly bled to death! What do the physicians say to that?"

It wiped the forced gaiety from her face. "D'ye think I don't know?" she cried. "D'ye think I *rejoiced* when they told me?" Such white, white flesh set in the frame of brilliant red hair; such green, frightened eyes, now dilated black. " 'Twas all I could do not to vomit from the fear . . . not to disgrace myself before them, even as I saw the looks in their eyes. They are afraid, too . . . but heirs are worth the risk, and Aidan is oversmall and sickly. There's a need for other sons." Fingers clutched the folds of her skirts. "Gods, Keely, what am I to do?"

"Lose it," I said succinctly. Then, more clearly, "Lose *them*."

Aileen nearly gaped. Then closed her mouth and wet her lips with a tongue that shook a little. "Lose them," she echoed.

"There are herbs," I said impatiently. "Herbs to make you miscarry."

Aileen's voice sounded drugged. "You want me to kill my bairns?"

"Better them than you." Sweat was drying on my face, against my scalp, beneath the leathers I wore: leggings baggy at the knees; sleeveless Cheysuli jerkin, belted snug; quilted, longsleeved undertunic, cuffs knotted at my wrists. I needed a bath badly, but this was more important. "Brennan has an heir. He needs a queen as well."

"Oh, *Keely*." With effort, she shook her head. "Oh—Keely—no. *No*. Kill my bairns? How could I? How could you even suggest it?"

"Easily," I told her. "If it is a choice between losing you or keeping you, I would sooner lose the babies."

"If you were a mother—"

I turned my hands palm-up. "But I am not. And, given the choice, I never will be."

Aileen sat down again, hastily. "Why *not?*" she asked in shock. "How can ye not want bairns?"

I peeled sticky hair away from my face and smoothed it back, tucking it into my loosened braid. Not wanting to offend her with my odor—and unable to sit close while discussing something so personal—I eased myself down on the stone floor and leaned against the wall. The room was plain, unadorned, nothing more than what it was intended to be: a practice chamber for war.

"Babies *require* things," I said. "Things such as constant

responsibility . . . they steal time and freedom, robbing you of choice. They are parasites of the soul."

"Keely!"

I sighed, knowing how callous it sounded; knowing also I meant it. "All my life I have fought for my freedom. I fight for it every day. And I will lose what I have won the moment I conceive."

" 'Tisn't true!" she cried. "Have I lost *my* freedom?"

"Have you?" I countered. "Before you left Erinn and came here to Homana—before you fell in love with Corin—before you married Brennan . . . what was your life like?"

Aileen said nothing at all, because to speak was to lose the battle.

"On the day you lay down with Brennan, Aidan was conceived," I said. "And from that day you became more than a woman, more than *you*: you became the vessel that housed Homana, because one day that child would be Mujhar. Your value was based solely on that, not on you, not on *Aileen* . . . but on that child—that bairn, as you would say—because babies born into royal houses are more than merely babies." I shrugged. "They are coin to barter with, just as you and I were before we were even born." I pulled my braid over one shoulder and played absently with the ends below the thong. It needed washing, like the rest of me. "I have no affection for babies; I would sooner do without."

"You'll not be saying that once you're wed to Sean."

She sounded so certain. *So* certain, in fact, it fanned unacknowledged resentment into too-hasty speech. "And how does it feel, Aileen, to lie in one man's bed—to bear that man his children—while loving yet another?"

Aileen jumped to her feet. "Ye *skilfin!*" she cried. "Will ye throw that in my face? Will ye speak to me of things ye cannot understand, being but half a woman—" And abruptly, on a strangled cry of shock, she clamped her hands over her mouth. "Oh, Keely . . . oh, Keely, I swear . . . I *swear*—"

"—you did not mean it?" Emptily, I shrugged. "I have heard it said before. To me and about me." I pressed myself up from the floor, brushing off the seat of my training leathers. "If I am considered half a woman simply because

I prefer to be myself, not an appendage of a man—nor a mother to his children—then so be it. I am Keely . . . and that is all that counts."

Some of the color had died out of her face. She was pale again, too pale. "Will you be saying all this to Sean?"

"As I have said it to you, I will say it to your brother." I crossed the chamber to the door, which Griffon had pointedly closed. "I am not a liar, Aileen, nor one who admires deception. I was never asked if I wanted to marry, but was betrothed before my birth . . . I was never asked if, being a woman, I wanted to bear children. It was simply *assumed* . . . and that, my lady princess, is what I hate most of all." I paused, my hand on the latch, and turned to face her fully. "But you would know." I spoke more quietly now; it was not Aileen with whom I was angry. "You *should* know, being made to wed the oldest of Niall's sons when you would sooner have the youngest. You would know how it feels to have things arranged *for* you, simply because of your gender."

Straight red brows were lowered over an equally straight nose. She is not a beauty, Aileen, but anyone with half a mind sees past that to her fire. "I am not a slave," she said darkly, "and neither am I a fool. There are things in life we're made to do through no fault of our own, but because of necessity, regardless of gender . . . and that *you* should know, being a Cheysuli." She paused, assessing me; I wondered, as I so often did, if the brother was anything like the sister. "Or are you Homanan today? Ah, no—perhaps Atvian, instead." Aileen stood straight and tall before me, her pride a tangible thing. "It strikes me, my lady princess, that *you* are whatever you want to be whenever it takes your fancy. Whenever 'tis *convenient.*"

She meant it, I think, to sting. Instead, it made me laugh. "Aye," I agreed, "whatever I want to be. Woman, warrior, *animal* . . . and I thank the gods for that magic."

"Magic," Aileen repeated. "Aye, I was forgetting that—but so, I'm thinking, are you. Because with the magic that makes you a shapechanger comes the price you'll be having to pay. And someday, you'll be paying it. Your *tahlmorra* will see to that."

I frowned. "What price?"

"Marriage," she said succinctly. "Marriage and mother-hood; how else to forge the link the prophecy requires?"

I grinned at her. "Ah, but *you* have done that; you and my oldest *rujholli.* Aidan is the one. Aidan is the link. Aidan will be Mujhar."

Evenly, she said, "Aidan may die by nightfall."

It stopped me cold, as she meant it to. "Ai*leen—*"

Her tone lacked expression. Like me, she masks herself rather than show her concern for things of great impor-tance. "He is not well, Keely. Aidan has never been well, ever since the birth. He may die tonight. He may die next year." She clasped her hands over her belly, swelling gently beneath her skirts. "And so you see, it becomes imperative that I bear Brennan another son." She paused, holding me quite still with the power of her eyes and the knowledge of her duty, of her *value,* by which men too often judge women, especially those they marry. "Two would be even better, I'm thinking, in case they are sickly also."

I thought of Aileen in potentially deadly labor, bringing forth two babies at once, for the sake of her husband's throne. I recalled it from before, with Aidan's birth; how she had bled and bled and nearly died, recovering so very slowly. And now she faced it again, but this time the threat was compounded.

Fear lurched out of my belly and found its way to my mouth. "Aileen, you could *die.*"

Her fingers tightened rigidly, clasping the unborn souls. "Men go to war. Women bear the bairns."

I unlatched the door and shoved it open. But I did not leave at once. "Do you know," I told her, "if I could, I would trade."

"Would you?" Aileen asked. "*Could* you, do you think?"

I paused on the threshold, one shoulder against the wood. "If you are asking me if I could kill a man, then I say aye."

Her face spasmed briefly. "So glib," she said. "I'm think-ing *too* glib; that you're not knowing what you can—or cannot—do, and it irritates you. It *frightens* you—"

I overrode her crisply. "I will do what I must do."

Slowly, Aileen smiled. And then she began to laugh as tears welled into her eyes. "So fierce," she said, "so *proud* . . . and so very, very helpless. No less so than I."

Denial, I thought, was futile; I closed the door on her noise.

Two

I itched. I wanted nothing more, at that moment, than to climb into a polished half-cask of steaming water, to soak away dried sweat, stretched muscles, irritation. But even as I gave the order for the bath and went into my chambers, untying the knots of my sweat-soiled undertunic, I was prevented. Because my father came in behind me, silently and without warning, and shut the heavy door.

"So," he said, "you have been learning the sword from Griffon."

For a moment, only a moment, I seriously considered stripping out of my boots and clothing anyway, just to see his reaction. I decided against it because, by the look in his eye, he would not be put off by anything, not even his daughter's nudity, until he had his say.

My hands went to my hips. "Aye," I agreed, saying nothing of Griffon's defection; he was, after all, my father's man, not mine. "I have made no secret of it."

"But neither did you *tell* me."

I thought it obvious, but said it anyway. "I knew you would tell me to stop."

"And so you should." He folded arms across his chest. "And so I do: *stop*."

I pressed fingers against my breastbone, tapping for emphasis. "I am not a fragile, useless female . . . I *know* how to fight. All my *rujholli* have taught me knife and bow . . . why should I not learn the sword?"

He leaned against the door, assuming an attitude of relaxed, quiet authority; he could order me, I knew, and probably would, but if I could give him a logical argument beyond refute, I might yet win. Sometimes I could. Not often. Not nearly often enough.

I looked at my father's face, seeing what others saw: lines

of care and concern bracketing eyes and mouth; the silvering of his hair, mingled still with tawny brown; the leather patch stretched over the emptiness that once had been his right eye.

But I saw more than that. I saw kindness and compassion. Strength of spirit and will. Loyalty and love, honesty and pride, and a tremendous dedication to his personal convictions.

Still, I could not give in so easily. He had taught me that.

He countered my question with one of his own. "Why do you *want* to learn the sword?"

I shrugged. "I do. I want to know them all, all the weapons men use in war . . . not because I desire to *go* to war, but because I have an interest in weapons." Balancing storklike on one leg, I twisted my knee up and tugged on the toe and heel of my left boot to work if off. "Why do you ask me such things, *jehan?* You never ask Deirdre why she weaves that tapestry of lions . . . nor Brennan why he enjoys training and racing his horses. You only ask me, because I care for things you and other men think unseemly to a woman." The boot came off; I dropped it and traded feet, feeling the chill of stone on my now-bare sole. "You are such a stalwart champion of fairness and justice, *jehan*—and yet you are blind to unfairness and injustice under your own roof."

"I hardly think it is unfair to ask my daughter to cease learning the sword," he said flatly. "By the gods, Keely, you have known more freedom than any woman born in the last fifty or sixty years . . . you have the gift of *lir*-shape, and you speak freely to all the *lir*. All that, and yet you also insist on tricking my arms-master into teaching you the sword."

I dropped the other boot to the floor, hearing the heel smack sharply against rose-red stone. "It was no trick," I retorted, stung. "Hart taught me how to wager . . . I won Griffon's service from him *fairly*."

He sighed and rubbed wearily at his brow, automatically resettling the leather strap that held the eyepatch in place. "Hart taught you how to wager, Corin how to rebel . . . it would be too much to assume Brennan taught you civility and respect—"

I cut him off even as I moved to stand on a rug. "Do

you want to know what Brennan has taught me, *jehan?* He
has taught me that a man has no regard for his *cheysula,*
thinking only of himself . . . by the gods, *jehan,* Aidan's
birth nearly killed Aileen! And now she must go through
it again, with *two?*" I shook my head. "Teach Brennan
restraint, *jehan,* and then perhaps I will allow him to teach
me civility and respect."

Weary good humor dissolved. "That is between Brennan
and Aileen, Keely. Your feelings are well known on the
subject; I think we will get no objectivity from you."

I yanked the knotted thong out of my braid and began
unthreading plaited hair violently. "Oh, and I suppose you
think making me put down the sword will transform me
into an obedient, compliant woman. One like your beloved
Maeve, perhaps, giving in to Teirnan when she knows
better . . . or perhaps even Deirdre, born to be a queen
and yet forced to be light woman to a king who will not
set aside the *cheysula* who tried to abduct his children." In
my anger I felt sweat-crisped hair tearing. "Do you know
what they call her, *jehan?* Not light woman. Not even
meijha, which holds more honor . . . no, *jehan.* They call
her whore. Deirdre of Erinn, *whore.*"

His face was very white. I had succeeded too well in
turning his mind from me to another matter. Part of me
regretted it—I had not meant to go so far—but part of me
was too angry to think clearly. Always, *always,* someone
comes to tell me what I should and should not be . . . gods,
but it makes me angry!

I faced him squarely, waiting. Knowing he was hurt and
shocked and angry, at least as angry as I, if for different
reasons. But he said nothing of that, having better control.
Having learned to shut his mouth. It was something I had
not, and probably never would. Though sometimes I wished
I could.

Just now, I wished I had. I hated to see him hurt. Gisella
was far beyond the ken or control of either of us; that
some Homanans spoke of her as the Queen of Homana and
claimed she should be by the Mujhar's side instead of
banished to Atvia meant nothing to us other than ignorance. They did not understand. They *could* not. For even
though she was labeled Mad Gisella, she was also the Mujhar's wife in Homanan law, *cheysula* in Cheysuli, and she

had borne three sons for the succession, as well as the prophecy. One and the same, these days; to many, it was all that counted.

And so Deirdre, whom my father loved more than life itself, was made to suffer the insults better ladled onto my mother, who had tried to give her children into Strahan's perverted power.

Her *sons,* that is. Her daughter, a mere girl, had counted for next to nothing. It was boys the Ihlini wanted.

He drew in a very deep breath. And smiled, though there was nothing of humor in it. "Meanwhile, my daughter has learned the sword, when I would prefer her not to."

"Too late," I told him crisply. "Would you have me but half-taught? Dangerous, *jehan* . . . Griffon would do better, now, to finish what was begun."

"And if I order him otherwise?"

I met him, stare for stare. "Does it matter? You will do it anyway." I unhooked the belt snugged around my waist, complete with sheathed knife, and slung it to land on my bed. "And I will find someone else to teach me." I was moving away as I said the last, intending to go into the antechamber where my bath was waiting, but he reached out and caught my arm, with nothing of gentleness in his grasp, and snapped me back around.

I nearly gasped, so startled was I by his demeanor. He was coldly, deadly serious, no more the father half-amused, half-tired of his rebellious daughter's antics. He was now more than father entirely, being Mujhar as well.

Being also Cheysuli warrior, with *lir*-gold on his arms and glittering in his hair. Tawny-silver instead of black, blue-eyed in place of yellow, but still he was Cheysuli. Like others, I often forgot it; he seems more Homanan in habits, until he takes care to remind us that in his veins flows gods-blessed blood as hot as it flows in mine.

"Though it suits you to ignore it—" He spoke very quietly; too quietly, for my peace of mind, "—when I tell you a thing I generally have a good reason for it."

My wrist was still in his grasp. "*What* good—"

"Be silent," he said, "and listen . . . if that is possible for you."

I did not answer the rebuke, having decided finally it was better, for now, to do as he asked, if only to get the confrontation done with. My bath was growing cold, my temper hotter by the moment.

His voice was very quiet. "I will not argue for the Homanans, who expect little more of their women than the obedience and compliance you mentioned, but I *will* argue for the Cheysuli, who give women more honor and respect." His grasp tightened on my wrist. "Has it never crossed your mind that women do not learn the sword because they lack the strength to use it?"

I waited only a moment, to lull him, and then I snapped my wrist free of his big hand with ease. Standing tall, balanced, braced, I cocked both arms up before me for inspection. The untied cuffs fell back, baring sinewy forearms. I could not help it; my hands were fists. "Do I look weak to you?"

He knew better. I am tall, even for a Cheysuli woman, and have not spent my years in idle pursuits. Tough and hard and strong, like a warrior, though without a warrior's bulk. "Lean and lethal," Corin had often called me. He had not, lately, because now he lived in Atvia, hundreds of leagues away. Closer now to Erinn than to Homana; farther from Aileen, whom he loved, or had; I no longer knew how he felt. He said nothing of her in his letters. I said little in mine to him.

"Weak, no," he conceded, "but strong enough? Perhaps. Perhaps not; you have never been in battle." He reached out again, this time with both hands, and took my wrists in a much gentler grasp. "I know, Keely. I have seen men shorter and slighter than you in battle, and they do well enough . . . usually. But matched with a larger, stronger opponent, they die. And even you must admit that most women are considerably smaller and weaker than men, particularly hardened soldiers."

"If they were allowed to do things other than mend clothing, make soap, bear babies . . ." I let it trail off, shrugging. "Who could say, *jehan*? And our history tells us Cheysuli women once fought beside their warriors."

"Aye, in *lir*-shape," he agreed dryly. "There is some difference, I think, between that sort of battle and the ones the unblessed Homanans fight."

I sighed, drawing my arms free again. "I have no wish to go to war, *jehan*, that I promise you . . . but I do wish to learn how to use a sword. All my *rujholli* did. Should I be denied simply because of my sex?"

"Are you *so* unhappy being a woman?" He had never asked it before, though my brothers had. Even Maeve once, my very feminine older sister, who allows body to rule head. "Do you wish that much to be a man?"

I smiled with infinite patience. "No," I told him gently. "I want only to be *me.*"

Clearly, he did not understand. No one had, yet, not even twin-born Corin, who knew me better than any.

He sighed. "I will strike a bargain with you, then. Meet Griffon as he should be met: as an opponent in battle, but with wrapped blades. And when you are done with the match, decide *then* if learning the sword is worth the trouble and pain."

He meant well. But all I could do was shake my head. "Anything worth doing is worth the trouble and pain. I am new to neither." I grinned at him lopsidedly. "And now, I think, it is time I took my bath. You have been too polite to mention it, but I am rank as a week-old carcass."

The Mujhar of Homana shut his eye. "I cannot begin to predict what Sean will say when he meets you."

I laughed. "If the gods are on my side, he will say he does not want me."

"And he would be a fool." He turned to open the door. "We have given you time, Keely, much time, and so has Sean . . . but it will come to an end. One day, perhaps tomorrow, the letter from Erinn will come asking the marriage be made."

Lightly, I answered, "Then let us pray for a storm at sea." And I went into the antechamber, calling for more hot water, as my father muttered something about gods and rebellious children.

I did not get my bath. Because even as servants came to pour in more hot water while I waited impatiently to strip, there came a commotion outside the door, in the corridor. My father had only just left; likely it was something that concerned the Mujhar.

And then I heard Deirdre's voice raised, and realized it concerned more than merely my father.

Still barefoot, I crossed to the antechamber door and

pulled it open, letting the voices spill in more clearly. Aye, it was Deirdre, and speaking urgently. There was fear in her tone.

"—with her history, it may be serious," she was saying. "Bleeding she is, and in pain. The physicians are doing what they can, but it may not be enough. Can you and Ian link to heal her?"

Gods, it was Aileen. And *bleeding* . . . gods, she would lose the bairns she wanted, and probably her life as well.

They knew I was there, if barely, too caught up in their conversation to pay me mind. Deirdre looked badly distracted, as was to be expected. Aileen was kin, close kin, being daughter to Deirdre's brother.

My father shook his head but twice. "Not Ian; Tasha has the cubs. Until she is free of them, he is bound by human standards. No *lir*-shape, no healing . . . I will have to do it alone." He frowned. "Brennan should be told. He will want to know—to be with her—"

"Not here," I said succinctly. "He went to Clankeep early this morning, blowing out one of his colts."

Now I had their full attention. Deirdre's face went whiter yet. My father cursed, briefly and powerfully. "Too far for Serri to reach Sleeta through the *lir*-link, to pass the message to Brennan . . . it will have to be done without him."

"I will go." It seemed obvious to me, and not worth the conversation. I left the doorway, scooped up my boots and tugged them on again, also buckling on my belt, knife sheathed. It took but a moment longer to grab a leather hunting cap from a chest, and I was with them once again. "I will send him home at once. Tell Aileen he is on his way already; it may calm her." Briefly I shook my head, putting on my cap and stuffing loose, braid-rippled hair beneath the crimson-tasseled peak rising above the crown of my head. Then tugged pointed earflaps into place, joggling red tassels. "Although why it should calm her to know the man who caused such pain is on his way—"

"Just go." I have never seen my father's eye so fierce. "Just *go*, Keely, without another word. You waste time and try our patience, and Aileen is worth far better than your scorn."

Aye, so she was. But it was not Aileen for whom I had

meant it. "Tell her," I said only, and started down the corridor at a run.

I did not stop running until I was outside, on the massive marble steps of Homana-Mujhar, and there I reached deep into the marrow of my bones, where the magic lies, and changed them. Trading human flesh for raptor's, woman's arms for falcon's wings.

I reached out, stretched, caught air—

—lifted—

Screeching aloud in exultation; in sheer, unbridled ecstasy, born of body and of brain.

—gods, oh gods, what glory—

—what glory it is to *fly*—

Three

He is nothing like our father, being black of hair, dark of skin, yellow of eyes. All Cheysuli, is Brennan, unable to hide behind the fair hair and skin of our Homanan ancestors. But he would never try; nor would any Cheysuli, for the gods have made us what we are, blessing us with the *lir* and all the magic that comes with the bond.

I myself do not share that bond precisely. I have no *lir,* but I do not require it. I am blessed instead with the Old Blood in abundance, the strain of the first clans who, settling in Homana from the Crystal Isle, did not mix with others, and so fixed the gifts. It was only after other clans outmarried that the blood weakened, making the true gifts random, that women lost the magic and only warriors bonded *lir.* And yet now we are *told* to marry out of the clans, to merge our blood with others, so that the gifts may be regained. I have little understanding of such things, and little interest; I know only that all of this specified marriage, as required by the prophecy, is supposed to give birth to the Firstborn again, the race that sired the Cheysuli. And, some say, the Ihlini.

Brennan, I knew, had his doubts. Honor-bound and dutiful, as are most Cheysuli, he served the prophecy unselfishly and kept his thoughts to himself, unless he shared them with Hart in frequent letters to Solinde. But there were times, looking into his supremely Cheysuli face, I wondered if indeed there might be Ihlini in it as well. Or ever would be, in a different, but similar, face.

He sat inside his pavilion, awash in the meager sunlight I let in through the opened doorflap, and stared at me in shock as I told him of Aileen. Unsympathetic, I watched as the color drained out of his face. On a Homanan, it is bad; on a Cheysuli, worse.

His hands shook. I watched as they shook, holding the cup; watched as they spilled liquor over the rim to splash against his leggings. Brennan did not notice, being too engaged in staring at me. Beyond him lay Sleeta, his mountain cat *lir,* sleek black Sleeta, velvet in coat, sharp as glass in opinion. Though we could converse as easily as she and Brennan, we did not; this was between *rujholla* and *rujholli.*

And then Brennan was up, tossing aside the cup, brushing by me without a single word, nearly knocking me aside, ripping the flap from my hands and calling for his horse. Irritably, I followed him; Sleeta followed me.

It was only after the horse was brought that he turned to me, and I saw something other than shock in his eyes. I saw desperation. "Too far," he said. "I will kill him if I run him all the way to Homana-Mujhar, and reach Aileen too late."

It was a supremely ridiculous statement, in view of his heritage. Dryly, I asked, "Why ride at all?"

Fixedly, he looked at Sleeta, as if rediscovering his *lir* and what she represented. "Aye," he said in surprise, then nodded vaguely. "Oh, aye . . . of course . . ."

"Brennan." I frowned, reaching for the reins he held in slack fingers, before he dropped the leather and lost the horse entirely; he is a mettlesome colt. "The way you are behaving—the way you look . . . are you saying you did not know? Aileen had not told you?"

"Aileen is often—private."

It was, I thought, an interesting way of summing it up. Married eighteen months, yet only because it was required, not freely desired; an arranged marriage, just as mine was. Aileen loved my twin-born *rujholli,* Corin, not the man she had wed. And Brennan? He is proud, my eldest *rujholli,* and stringently honorable. Though Aileen's virtue had been intact, her heart was clearly not. And he had not presumed to mend it. He had merely wedded her, bedded her, got a son upon her; a child for the Lion, and also the prophecy.

And now two more who might not live to be born.

"So," I said, "she is private. Well-matched, I would say; you have offered her nothing since the day you married her. But *she* offers you her life." I jerked my head in the direction of Mujhara. "Go, *rujho.* See to your *cheysula.* I will bring your cherished colt."

There were things he wanted to say, but he said none of them. Another time, perhaps; Brennan and I do not often agree, and our discord is sometimes of the spectacular kind. For now, all he did was turn on his heel and walk purposefully away, ignoring me quite easily, with Sleeta at his side.

But I had seen his face. I had seen his eyes. And realized, in astonishment, my brother loved his wife.

I did not leave at once for Mujhara. Perhaps I should have, but Aileen's travail frightened me. If the gods wanted her, they would take her whether or not I was present; I did not think I could face watching her die, nor have the patience to wait quietly in another chamber for someone to come and tell me she was dead. I would go mad with the waiting, saying things I did not mean, hurting people, probably Brennan; having seen his face, I thought he was deserving, at this moment, of more compassion than I was prepared to give him.

So I did not go. Knowing no matter what happened, no matter what I did, I would hate myself.

And then Maeve gave me the opportunity to focus my mood on someone other than myself; to contradict, as always, a woman who considers her world empty if a man is not present in it.

We are sisters, *rujholla,* separated by three brothers—for Maeve was born first of us all—and equally by convictions. Also by blood; though Niall's daughter, there is nothing of the Old Blood in Maeve, nor even of the newer, thinner blood that limits warriors to a single *lir* and women to no *lir* at all, and nothing at all of the gifts. Deirdre's only child reflects mostly the Erinnish portion of her heritage, blanketing the Cheysuli under brass-blonde hair, green eyes, fair skin . . . and none of the Cheysuli woman's tendency toward independence.

Yet of late she *had* shown a tendency toward living in Clankeep, which baffled all of us. Maeve, much more than myself, fit well into palace life, complementing Deirdre's unofficial reign as chatelaine in Homana-Mujhar with ease. She was the Mujhar's dutiful eldest daughter and, of all his children—it was well-known—his favorite, yet of late she had forsaken his companionship for the company of the clans.

We sat outside a slate-blue pavilion on a thick black bear pelt and tossed the prophecy bones. Not to wager—Maeve is not much for it; it is Hart's vice—but to pass the time, and to ease ourselves into conversation, since ordinarily we have so little in common that there is as little to discuss.

Maeve sighed, scooped bones, let them dribble out of her hand after a half-hearted throw. "Perhaps I *should* go. Mother will be so distracted . . . I could lend her aid—"

"Doing what?" I asked bluntly. "Deirdre will indeed be distracted, with no time for you; you would do better to stay out of the way, as I am."

Her mouth tightened. "You are not staying out of the way, Keely—at least, not in order to help. You are staying here because you are afraid." She smacked her hand flat down on the bones as I moved to scoop them up. "No, listen to me—you *are* afraid, Keely . . . afraid to see what it is a woman goes through to bear a child, knowing you will have to do the same." Maeve laughed, a little, shaking her head. "You are so contradictory, Keely . . . on one hand you are willing to take on any man in a fight, with knife or bow or sword; on the other, you are deathly afraid to lie with a man . . . to give over yourself to the bedding, to the loss of self-control, to the chance to love someone other than yourself—"

I raised my voice over hers. "You know nothing about it, Maeve—all *you* know is that Teirnan had only to clap his hands and you spread your legs for him—"

Maeve's face was corpse-white. "Do you think I have not spent the last year of my life regretting the vow I made to be his *meijha?*" Tears sprang into her eyes; born half of anger, I thought, and half of humiliation. "Do you know what it is like to lie down alone each night knowing the man I love is a traitor to his race? A threat to the Lion itself?"

Guilt cut me deeply; gods, why do we always argue? Why does she force me to walk the edge of the blade and then push me off with such talk? "Maeve—"

She scooped up the translucent, rune-scribed bones and hurled them violently away from us both. "Do you have any idea what it is like knowing you have been *used,* without regard for your own needs and desires, or your loyalties?" She stared at me angrily, tears spilling over. "No. Not

you. Never. Never *Keely.* Well, I *do* know what it is like . . .
and I have to live with it. Each day, each night . . . and
for the rest of my life."

I was humbled into silence by her passion, by her humiliation, which she did not trouble to hide, being as proud as
any of us. It is easy for me to dismiss Maeve because we
are so at odds with loyalties and convictions, so mutually
certain of ourselves. But for all there is little to bind us,
what does exist takes precedence over threats from outside.

"It will pass," I told her finally. "One day you will look
at yourself and realize that Teir won nothing at all. He lost,
Maeve. He lost you, the clans, the afterworld. *Kin-wrecked,*
he has nothing, save his *lir* and the knowledge that he is a
traitor to his heritage."

"What of his child?" she asked bitterly. "What of the
halfling got on the Mujhar's daughter?"

"But there is no—" I stopped. "Oh, Maeve—*no*—"

"Aye," she answered curtly. "Why do you think I am
here instead of Homana-Mujhar?" Maeve shredded bear
pelt. Her head was bowed; loose blonde hair hid most of
her face. "Why do you think I cannot bear to see my
father—" And abruptly she pressed both hands against her
face, shutting it away from me as she fought to hold back
the tears. "Oh, gods, Keely . . . what will he say? What
will he say?" Her words were muffled by her hands. "I
broke the vow, I *did*—and yet Teirnan came later, after he
had freely renounced kin, clan, prophecy . . . he came, and
I went with him . . . I lay down with him again, and now
there will be a child!"

In the silence after her outburst, I heard the echo of
Aileen's words: *"In Erinn, bairns often follow the bedding.
'Tis the same in Homana, I think."*

I wanted to be patient. I wanted to be compassionate.
But other emotions took precedence: frustration, disbelief;
an odd, abrupt hostility, that she could be *so* malleable as
to give herself to Teirnan after renouncing him before Clan
Council; that she could so readily dishonor our customs.
"You *knew* what he was—*a'saii,* proscribed by the clan,
kin-wrecked—and yet you went with him? Bedded with
him? *Knowing*—"

"—that I loved him." Her tone was dead. She had taken
her hands from her face. "Call me whore, if you like—

others will, I am certain—but I was not lying with him for coin. It was for love, for pleasure . . . and for the pain, knowing it would be the last time for us ever; knowing also that the risk was worth it, if only for the moment, for the *doing* . . ." She shook her head. "Maybe I am not so different from Hart after all, chancing risk for the lure of the risk itself . . . all I know is that nothing is left of what we had, nothing at all, now—he said so himself, and *laughed*— except the seed he planted."

I bit my lip on recriminations, finally gaining control. Instead, implying nothing, I asked if Teirnan knew.

Maeve shook her head. "That much, at least, is mine. He does not know, and *will* not. It was to humble me, I think; to prove he could put a leading rein on the Mujhar's daughter and make her do his bidding." Self-loathing pinched her tone. "There was no love in it for him—he is too Cheysuli for it, too much *a'saii*—only power. Only acknowledgment of my weakness, proof that the House of Homana is not immune to manipulation." Bitterness shaped her expression. "And so there will be a child."

I kept my voice neutral. "So there will," I agreed, "unless you take measures to rid yourself of it."

Maeve stared at me, much as Aileen had. "Rid myself—?"

Carefully, I said, "Surely you know the means."

It was a new thought to her. "I have told no one," she said blankly. "No one at all, save you . . . the *last* one I would tell, since you have no compassion, no empathy for anyone save Corin . . ." Maeve shook her head. "But now I *have* told you, and your answer is to say I should rid myself of the child."

Scowling, I got up and went a few paces away, retrieving, one by one, the scattered prophecy bones. "It is *one* solution," I told her. "Did I say you had to do it?"

"A child is a child," she said. "The seed is planted, but the harvest not yet begun . . . who can say what manner of son or daughter it will be?" Maeve's tone, now, was steady. Plainly, I had shocked her, as much as I had Aileen. "Should I measure it by the father? Should I make it proxy for Teirnan's sins, accepting his punishment?"

I wanted to throw the bones back at her. "Putting words in my mouth, Maeve? Trying to make me feel guilty? Well,

you will not . . . I am not foolish enough to say it is the
only answer, nor even the best. I know our history well,
Maeve . . . it was not *that* many years ago that Cheysuli
warriors stole Homanan women in order to get children on
them, because the clans were being destroyed by Shaine's
qu'mahlin." I sighed, finished picking up the bones, spoke
quietly; fool or not, she was my sister, and under the circumstances deserving of more than my derision. "Children
are valued within the clans, *rujholla* . . . no matter who the
jehan, your baby will be welcomed."

"He will hate me," she said hollowly.

"Teir?" I stared. "Do you really care—?" But I broke
it off, realizing she did not refer to our cousin. "Oh,
Maeve—no, no . . . of course he will not hate you. How
could he? You are his favorite. You are Deirdre's
daughter."

"The bastard gotten on his whore," she said tonelessly.
"Who will herself now bear a bastard, begotten by a Cheysuli who has renounced everything of his race but the magic
in his veins."

"Oh, no," I said dryly, "not everything. It is *for* his race
he does it, Maeve. That is what they all say, the *a'saii,* as
they renounce kin and clan and king." I sighed, kneeling
again on the pelt, pouring rattling bones from one hand to
the other. "Teir has been jealous of us all since birth, because of his *jehan,* who raised him on bitterness and greed,
and lust . . . lust for power, lust for domination; even, I
think, for the Lion. In the name of the Cheysuli, Teir and
the *a'saii* fight to turn back the decades, the centuries, to
the time Cheysuli held dominance, without outside
interference."

Maeve's eyes were anxious. "Do you think it is true,
Keely? He says fulfillment of the prophecy will give Homana to the Ihlini, destroying everything the Cheysuli have
lived for since the gods put them here. He says the only
way the Cheysuli can survive is to destroy the prophecy,
and then turn to destroying the Ihlini."

"They" and "them." Only rarely does Maeve refer to
Cheysuli as we or us. I wondered if she felt *so* apart from
the rest of Niall's children that she perceived herself entirely Erinnish and Homanan, not Cheysuli at all, regardless

of paternity. If so, it was no surprise Teirnan had held such a powerful sway over her.

"The only way we can survive," I said clearly, "is to make certain the prophecy survives, and to serve it. It is what the gods intended when they made it."

"Ah," Maeve said sweetly, "then we can expect an announcement of your marriage to Sean of Erinn any day."

The thrust went home cleanly, as she intended it to. In answer I dumped the bones into her skirt-swathed lap— Maeve would never wear *leggings!*—and stood. "As to that, it remains my decision, my say-so. Nothing so trivial resides in the prophecy of the Firstborn; I will do as I please in the matter of my marriage."

Maeve's brows arched up. "Nothing so trivial? An odd thing to say . . . 'tis common knowledge the best way of merging bloodlines is through children, and the prophecy is quite specific about merging those bloodlines. All that's left now is Erinn, Keely . . . and the only way Homana will get Erinn is through marriage—yours to Sean. I hardly think Liam or Sean would *give* Erinn to Homana merely to serve a Cheysuli prophecy; that will be for your son to do, when he is born." She paused. "The son who bears every necessary bloodline save that of the Ihlini."

From my belt I took my hunter's cap and tugged it on, stuffing hair into it. "If I bear that son—*if* I bear that son, ever—it will be of my own choice, not a directive from the prophecy."

Maeve shook her head. "You can't be having it two ways, Keely . . . either you serve the prophecy, or you don't. Either you are of the faithful, as is our father, our uncle, and our brothers, or you are of the *a'saii.*" She did not so much as blink. "Just like Teirnan."

I glanced at Brennan's restless colt, tied to a nearby tree. I wanted to fly, not ride, but I had promised to return the horse to Homana-Mujhar. "So," I said finally, "am I to believe it was the prophecy that led you on a leading rein into Teirnan's bed? Into the arms of an *a'saii?*" I shook my head before she could answer, tugging my cap on more securely. "No, *rujholla,* of course not. It was your decision, your *desire* . . . and so now the decision falls to me, as does my desire to be free to make my own choices."

Maeve's expression was bleak. "We are none of us free," she told me. "No matter who we are."

"But I am *Keely*," I said lightly. "A free Cheysuli woman, with magic in her bones."

Maeve sighed and shook her head. "You are as bad as Teir."

"Well, we *are* cousins." I untied Brennan's colt, briefly judged his temper, mounted carefully. "Maeve, if you want to come home, come home." The horse danced a little, ducking head and swishing tail; I cursed him beneath my breath, tightened reins, twisted my head to look back at Maeve. She stared after me blindly, tears swimming in her eyes. "Come home," I told her gently. "*Jehan* could never hate you. That I promise you."

Slowly, my sister nodded. "Tomorrow," she said. "Tomorrow."

Four

Brennan's colt was a fine animal indeed, a leggy chestnut with deep chest, long shoulders, powerful hindquarters. I could feel the speed living in him, and a bright, burning spirit, but it was raw, so raw, as yet uncut and unpolished. He was young, just shy of three—Brennan refused to race at two, saying it broke down leg bones not fully formed—and very green, wary of my touch. He did not know me at all, which left him confused and also clumsy, watching too much of me on his back and not enough of the track that stretched westward in front of his nose.

My task was to get him back to Homana-Mujhar without blemish, but he was making it difficult. He wanted to lunge, he wanted to spin, he wanted to bolt and run: all and yet none of those things. He was too distracted for any, merely teasing me with his nerves. It made my own stretch thin, along with my meager patience.

"Gods," I muttered aloud. "It will be *nightfall* before we are back."

It was, at best, late afternoon, judging by the low-hanging sun. If I let him run we would undoubtedly be home before it set, but I dared not let him go, even though he was begging to be set loose. I knew better. I also knew what Brennan would say—and precisely how he would say it if I ruined his colt's conditioning.

I considered briefly turning back to Clankeep, to stay the night and go home in the morning, but I was nearly halfway to Mujhara already. All it wanted was a little time, a greater store of patience—

"*Hold,*" someone said.

Startled, the colt shied violently sideways, then attempted to run away. He did not, but only because I jerked his head around to the left, dragging nose up to my knee. Twisted so, he could not free his head to bolt; it gave me time to regain control.

I said all manner of soothing, silly things to the frightened colt, most of them nonsense but effective because of my tone. When at last his trembling stilled I loosed his head again, but carefully, slowly, letting him know I was alert to any tricks.

I glanced at either side of the track, hugged by a tunnel of trees and close-grown foliage, but saw no one, only shadows. Still, it did not prevent me from speaking. With forced lightness—keeping in mind the colt's touchy temper—I spoke to no one in particular, knowing he would, nevertheless, hear. "Whoever you are, you *ku'reshtin,* have a care for my horse . . . *if* you have a care for your life."

I heard soft laughter, the hiss and rustle of leaves, the subtle sibilance of boot against deadfall. A man stepped out of the trees, out of the shadows, into waning sunlight gilding birch and beech and elm.

The colt saw him, snorted noisily, pinned ears, and rolled eyes. I soothed him with soft words and gentle hands, thinking it odd contrast to the quickening of hostility in my heart. For the stranger was more than merely a man, he also was Cheysuli. More, even, than that: my *kin-wrecked* cousin, Teirnan.

I looked at his face but saw Maeve's instead, twisted by anguish and self-derision, washed by tears of humiliation.

I looked at his face and saw a consummate Cheysuli: proud, unyielding, determined; as fierce in defense of loyalties asked, given and secured as any king could require, for he was bound by sacred oaths. So like all of us, my cousin, and yet like so very few. His oaths were to himself and to the *a'saii,* demanding a service in direct opposition to the sort freely offered, as Maeve had said, by my father, uncle, brothers.

And, as for my own?

I stared down at Teir from atop Brennan's mettlesome colt, thinking of my sister and the child yet unborn. Then leaned pointedly to one side and spat onto the ground.

"So tactful, as always . . ." He grinned mockingly, twisting his mobile mouth. "Niall should make you an envoy."

"Ku'reshtin," I said again. "What are you doing here? What do you want with me?" I looked past him for other

warriors. "Where are the rest of your malcontents, Teir?— or have they grown weary of your preaching and pettiness and gone home at last to their clans?"

My cousin shrugged. "*This* is home," he said, "every inch of Homana—every pebble, leaf, raindrop—as was always intended. We have made a new clan out of the old, with warriors and women more cognizant of how things were, how they should be, how they will be again." He lifted one shoulder, dropped it; eloquent negligence. "A clan lacking in prophecy, perhaps, but with an abundance of free will."

"What do you want?" I asked again, more curtly than before. "Have you come to trouble Maeve?"

Teirnan shook his head, folding bare bronzed arms across his chest. *Lir*-gold gleamed; the repeated pattern encircling heavy bands was the profile of a boar with curving tusks, interlocked within the symmetry. All Cheysuli, Teir, though his *jehana* had been part Homanan, and sister to the Mujhar. "If I wanted to trouble Maeve, I would at least know where to find her." Now he did not smile. "No. I wanted you."

"I have nothing to say to you."

"Nor do I care," he answered equably. "I came to *talk*, not listen . . . and you have never been known for a sweet tongue, Keely. A man could spend his time on better things than listening to you."

I shut my teeth on the answer I longed to give, *and* its emphasis. The colt was too nervous already, shouting would send him flying. Quietly, I suggested, "I could say the same of you."

"And will, given the chance." Teir's face, similar to Brennan's, was formed of sharper bones lying but shallowly beneath characteristically dark flesh. It lent him the look of a predator more so than anyone else of our House; I found it ironically appropriate. "Come down from that horse and hear what we have to say."

"We?" I glanced around pointedly. "I see only you, Teir—and no, I am not blind to other warriors, I am Cheysuli myself." A quick link-search gave me the means to smile in scorn. "Nor are there any *lir* nearby save your own, hiding in the shadows; say '*we*' again, Teir, and see if I am foolish enough to bite."

It wiped the amusement from his face and the irony from

his tone. We have never been close, Teir and I, and undoubtedly he had forgotten I could converse with his *lir* and that of any other warrior. It made a difference; I could see it plainly. He was reassessing me.

The mask was stripped away and cast aside. Teirnan showed me the face beneath it, naked and feral, with the conviction of a zealot. He was *a'saii,* deserving of nothing from me but renunciation. And, perhaps, my pity; he had cut himself off from his race.

But from none of his heritage. For now he was little more than a troublesome gnat nipping at the Lion, but I sensed he could in time make a dangerous enemy.

"Keely." His tone was flat, uninflected, yet compelling in its own way, underscoring his change in mood. "I came alone because I thought you might prefer it, being honorable in your own way—*and* me in mine." He did not so much as blink, speaking so easily about banished honor. "What I have to say could affect your own *tahlmorra,* and that is a thing best left between bloodkin, even among the clans."

I laughed at him outright. "You, Teir, speaking of my *tahlmorra?* I thought you renounced such things last year."

He took a single step forward, halted as he saw it made the colt sidle and snort. He was angry, *angry,* though he kept it carefully in check, which made it all the more evident.

"You," he said coldly, "know nothing of what made me do what I did, *nothing at all*—" Teir stopped short, clenched his teeth briefly, fought some inner battle. It only took a moment; he was not the sort of zealot controlled by ignorant passions, but by cold efficiency, a personal conviction. "And until you understand—until I have taken the time to explain it *clearly* to you—I suggest you do me the courtesy of holding your tongue." He paused, then smiled coolly, under perfect control again. Showing nothing of the anger that had flared so very brightly, if so very briefly. "And do yourself the service of not betraying your ignorance with such naive forcefulness."

"Ignorant, am I?" I flung back. "Naive?" I shook my head. "I think not, Teir . . . I know very well what you did, and why. You are a small, petty man, fed on the bitterness of your *jehan*—" The colt sidled again, restively slashing his tail as he responded to my tone. "Because of Ceinn's jealousy and your selfish ambition, you turn your back on our honor and try to create your own." I shook my head. "You are no different from Strahan, serving his noxious Seker—*he* wants power . . . *he* wants control . . . *he* wants the Lion Throne—" I fought the colt automatically, twisting my head this way and that as I tried to stare down my cousin. "Renounce everything you like, Teir, but know it will buy you nothing of what you desire, nothing of what you expect—" I leaned forward in the saddle, holding the colt with reins; holding Teir with will. "If you truly want to destroy the prophecy, why not go to the Ihlini? Go to the Gate of Asar-Suti and trade your manhood for Strahan's pleasure!"

He called me a foul name in explicit and eloquent Old Tongue. In response, I laughed. But then he jumped to catch the colt's bridle, my arm; to pull me down from the saddle. It was no more a laughing matter.

"*Teir*—"

But the colt had had enough. He tore himself free and ran.

How he could run, Brennan's colt . . . how he could bunch and stretch and *fly* in the fluent, fluid language of a horse bred only to race. I knew better than to attempt to curb his flight so soon. The track was clear, level, firm, though layered by crushed leaves. It was best simply to let him run a bit, wearing down the fear. He was doing what he was born for, though transcending human desires. Even Cheysuli ones.

I hunched in the saddle, leaning forward, and began to gather the reins. And then felt my cap loosen, threatening to fly off. One-handed, I caught it, crushed it against my head, one by one tugged the tasseled earflaps to snug it down again.

Too late I saw the rope stretched across the track. Black and taut, dividing the sunset, each end tied to trees; an invisible, treacherous trap. And I fell into it.

On a man, it would hit shoulders, scraping him out of the saddle. On me it hit my neck.

I landed hard on head and shoulders, bent in half like a toymaker's puppet, then completed the somersault and sprawled belly-down on the track.

At first I could not breathe. When I could, whooping and gulping spasmodically, I inhaled dirt, leaves, blood.

Oh, gods. Brennan's colt.

Oh, *gods,* my head.

—agh, gods—my *throat*—

Five

Hands tore me from the ground. I was stood on my feet, held firmly on either side—and gaped at. Like a motley-fool at a Summerfair.

Three men, dirty of teeth, hair, habits. And patently astonished by what their trap had caught. But not so surprised as to loosen their grasp of my arms.

Inwardly, I swore; outwardly, I coughed. Gods, but my throat hurt!

The men were thieves, plainly, and plainly intending to ply their trade by cutting my coin-pouch free of my belt. Except there was none. I had left it in my chambers prior to weapons practice, and had exited Homana-Mujhar too quickly to retrieve it.

Two of them held me easily, one on either side. The third faced me squarely, scowling horrifically and chewing the inside of one cheek. He was my height, pock-marked, gray of hair and eyes.

"A *woman*," said the man at my right: young, younger than I, smelling of too many days and nights spent drinking and whoring without bath or change of clothing.

The one on my left shook his head. He smelled little better. "We've no call to rob a *woman*."

Promising, I thought, until the third one spoke. "Woman or not, she's worth coin." He paused. "*Or* better yet."

*Un*promising; he was unlikely to drop his guard simply because of my gender.

Instead, he would drop his trews.

Still, the two who held me were clearly uncertain of their behavior, and it might just be enough.

I was half blinded by pain, in head and neck and throat. But I have never been one to let physical discomfort have its way until there is time for it; at the moment there was not. And so I swayed against the two men who held me, feigning weakness, and felt their instinctive attempt to right me. Smoothly I altered stance and balance—rolling hips, bunching thigh and buttock muscle—and cow-kicked out with my right foot toward the man who stood so invitingly flat-footed before me.

Full extension—I caught him square on the right knee and snapped it backward. He screamed and went down even as I wrenched free of his companions.

Like me, they had knives. But no swords, thank the gods; it gave me a decent chance. Perhaps better, if they were only indifferent with their weapons. But I thought not. Thieves are rarely unversed in fighting and weaponry.

I ran. Off the track and into the trees, into the twilight of early sundown, where the shadows lay thick and deep with nothing of light about them. *Lir*-shape, I knew, would provide a swifter escape, but I hurt so badly from my fall that the shapechange would require more concentration than usual, consequently more time. I knew better than to hope for the latter, and probably could not manage the former. I had caught them off-guard and put one of them down, but my store of tricks was gone. If they ran me to ground, I would have to fight them.

Behind me, I heard shouting interlaced with shrieks of pain. Also the telltale crashing of bodies through the brush. The quarry had been flushed, now pursuit was begun.

I swore aloud breathlessly, then wished I had not. My throat was afire with pain, inside as well as without. The rough rope had scraped me raw, shredding the flesh of my neck while also half-throttling me. I was lucky to breathe at all; it might have broken my neck.

My hunter's cap caught, came off, was left; I dared not stop for it. Now hair came tumbling down, snagging boughs and brambles, cluttering itself with leaves and twigs, growing sticky with juices and sap. Fear-sweat stung my armpits; breasts ached from nerves.

The shadows grew deeper as day shapechanged into evening. I fell, rose, staggered, tore vine-ropes out of my way. Wished myself, vainly, elsewhere, or at least a sword in my hand.

But mostly I wished for *lir*-shape; for wings in place of arms.

If I stopped running, perhaps I could summon the magic. But *if* I stopped running to try it, I chanced losing the lead I had. And all of my kin had taught me to treasure advantages, no matter how large or small; never to spend them foolishly, nor ever surrender them.

I crashed through brush into clearing, staggered to a halt. Facing me were men. Kneeling, squatting, hunching, all gathered around a new fire. All listening to another who held a sword in his hands.

The firelight blurred before me, glinting off knives and in eyes; from the accoutrements of rank. I blinked, fighting off weakness, clung to the nearest tree. They were, I thought, king's men; they had that look about them.

"Leijhana tu'sai!" I gasped. "Let me have that sword!"

As one they turned and stared, showing knives, swords, and startled eyes, and hard, strange faces. Some were bearded, some were not; all wore foreign clothes.

I put out my hand. "The sword." But it was more a question than command.

The man with the weapon smiled. There was little of it I could see in the rich red bush of his beard, so at odds with the blond of his hair. "Sword, is it?" he asked. "And you but a bit of a lass!"

Erinnish, I knew instantly, by the lilt of Aileen and Deirdre.

Cursing was loud behind me, accompanied by crashing. I spun, dragged free my knife, braced to meet the thieves. They broke free into the clearing, saw me, saw *them*, stopped short. And uneasily counted the numbers of the men who stood at my back. Even *Hart* would lay no wager;. I unlocked my jaw from itself.

The red-bearded man strode forward, nearly knocking me aside as he brushed a shoulder purposely. "Have ye business?" he asked of the thieves. "Or have ye come for the fun?" He made a sweeping gesture of his left arm as if to invite them in. At the end of it his hand touched me on the chest and pushed me back a step. "A bonny lass, aye, but she'll be serving us first. You'll have to wait your turn." He eyed them assessively. "Unless, of course, you'd sooner play the part of the maid yourself . . . we've just arrived from Erinn and we're not particular whom we rape. 'Tis been a long journey."

As he intended them to, the thieves backed away and ran. Now it was my turn to flee, though I chose another direction.

Two steps only; he caught me by the hair. "Lass, lass, don't go . . . don't you know the sound of a lie?"

I sliced his wrist with my knife. "I know the sound of a threat—let me go, *ku'reshtin!*"

He did so, with alacrity. I saw shock in long-lashed eyes. *"Lass—"*

In clipped, fluent Erinnish, I told him to shut his mouth.

He stared, but he did. And then brought up the sword and knocked the knife from my hand. *"Now,* lass," he said, "d'ye think ye might listen to us?"

"No," I answered promptly, and summoned the magic to me.

Tried to summon the magic . . . the Erinnishman clamped a hand on my right arm and the pain of it nearly sent me out of my senses. I bit into my lip to beat off the swoon and inwardly cursed my weakness.

"Lass," he said, "you're hurt. There's blood all over your neck—" Abruptly, he took his hand from me, "—as well as on your arm. Lass—"

Gods, but I *hurt.* "Let me go," I rasped.

He put up his swordless hand in surrender and took a backward step. "Then go," he said clearly, "though you'll get no farther than a step or two, I'm thinking."

My laugh was mostly a croak. "Who says I will *walk*?"

But the magic would not come. In dismay, I stared at him, then looked down at my arm. From shoulder to elbow the quilted undertunic was shredded, showing rope-burned flesh beneath. Watery blood spread across the fabric. The pain was increasing, not fading; no matter how hard I tried, I could not distance myself from it.

What kind of Cheysuli are you, to let pain take precedence over magic? Old Blood, have you? More like ancient *blood, and therefore all used up—*

Dizzily, I looked up at him. He was a huge man, larger even than my father. Blond of hair, red of beard, warmly brown of eyes. He put out a hand and touched me, clasping my left shoulder, and turned me toward the fire. "Lass," he said gently, "you're safe with us, I promise. Any woman who speaks gutter Erinnish as fluently as you deserves nothing but our respect; that, and our liquor. Will ye share a cup with us?"

He said nothing else of neck or arm or blood, merely guiding me toward the fire. I thought of protesting—he could very well be lying, no matter what he claimed—but I hurt too much to speak. Reaction was sweeping in; it was all I could do to stand.

He sat me down on a stump of wood, said something briefly to four of his men about warding the wood against thieves, then motioned to a fifth. A full cup was put into my hands. The smell was powerfully pungent.

He gestured again. Quickly cups were brought out from under leather doublets or untied from belts. I heard the gurgle of liquor poured, saw the cups passed around. Tried again to protest, found all I could do was shake.

"To the *cileann,*" he said, "and to our bonny lass, though she be foul of tongue and appearance."

"You *ku'reshtin*—" I was up, slopping liquor, then firmly pressed down again.

"Drink," he advised. " 'Tis a compliment, my lass. Are we so very much better?"

No, they were not. Not so filthy as I, perhaps, but not so very much better. Hard-faced, hard-eyed men, watching me intently, with pewter in their hands and steel at their belts.

"Who are you?" I asked.

He lifted one shoulder in a shrug. "What I told the others."

Still I did not drink, though the cup was at my mouth. "Erinnishmen," I muttered.

Blond brows rose. "You're knowing that already."

Suspicion briefly smothered pain. "Who *are* you?" I repeated. "Why have you come to Homana? What are you doing *here?*"

I saw glances exchanged, the masking of faces, the tautening of lips.

"King's men," I said flatly. "Or are you sent from Sean?"

It shocked them, each and every one, even the red-bearded man, who stared hard at me with a burning in his eyes, a fierce bright light that competed with the fire, with the glint of the sword in his hands. He did not hold a cup. He did not drink to me.

"From Sean," he echoed.

With meticulous effort, I rose. This time I remained standing. "Aye," I said clearly. "From Sean, Prince of Erinn. Liam's only son. Aileen's only brother. Do you know the man I mean?"

Plainly my irony stung him. But he said nothing in response, merely sheathed the sword at last. Slid it home with a hiss and click as he rose to face me standing.

I opened my mouth to speak again, but he forestalled me with a curtly silencing hand. "Do I know the man you mean? Aye, lass, I do—is there an Erinnishman who doesn't?"

"Well, then—" I began.

"*Well*, then," he echoed.

"Answer me," I said. "Have you come from Sean? I have a reason to ask."

"Reason," he muttered, "*reason!* So grand as ours, I wonder? So demanding a thing as our own?" He stared down his bold nose at me, arrogant as my brothers. Proud as a Cheysuli, and with at least a little of our honor. "And who are *you* to ask?"

Fair question, I thought. But I dared not give him the truth. "My father is Griffon, arms-master to the Mujhar."

"I didn't ask *his* name, lass."

Carefully, I swallowed. "Keely," I said blandly. "I was named for the Mujhar's daughter."

There was a stirring among the men. No one said a word, but I saw them speak nonetheless.

"Drink," I was told. And then, as I did not, he reached out and took the cup from me, drank half the contents down, gave it back into my hands. "There, lass . . . 'tis not drugged, I promise. But your color is going quickly, and I think 'twill help a bit."

I shivered. Blinked. Drank. It put tears into my eyes and set a fire in my belly. With a second generous swallow, followed by a third, some of the pain diminished.

"Better," he said softly.

Over the cup, I looked up at him. "Your answer," I croaked. "*Are* you sent from Sean?"

He looked at the others. Then down at me once more. "Aye," he said at last. "but not in the way you're thinking."

"No? How do you know what I think?"

"I can see it in your eyes, lass . . . and if you're of the castle, you'd know the girl you're named for. Likely you'd know how she'd feel."

It took me a moment to untangle his references. "If you mean the princess royal, aye—we have met. But as to how she would feel—?"

"If she knew why we were here."

I shrugged a single shoulder; the other was too painful. "She would think you sent from Sean to fetch her to her wedding."

"And would it be pleasing to her?"

I nearly laughed. "Probably not." Then modulated my tone. "She is a stubborn girl, the lady . . . she wants no part of Sean."

He nodded. "I have heard the same."

"*You* have heard—" I stopped. "He *did* send you, then!"

"Not in the way you're thinking." His voice was very steady. "I am not here as the prince's proxy . . . I am here as his murderer."

Six

I dropped my cup. "Sean is *dead?*"

Masked again and mute, he stared at me with eyes throwing back the firelight. I saw shame, guilt, and an odd vulnerability, as if he wished he could have said otherwise; especially to me.

All I could do was stare, was *gape*, like that motley-fool at the Summerfair, faced with an unknown thing. I heard again the words he had said, naming himself murderer, and wondered at my emptiness; at the lack of grief or distress. Shock aplenty, aye, but little more than that.

He watched me closely, assessively, waiting for my response. Undoubtedly expecting censure, or some other form of hostility, something to mark what I thought.

What I thought was unfair: *If Sean is dead, I am free.*

Shame flooded me with heat and set my nerves atingle, dancing inside my flesh. I turned unsteadily and walked away from the fire, from the men, unable to show them what I felt, to the edges of the clearing where the wood encroached again.

Thinking yet again: *If Sean is dead, I am free.*

And then I thought of Aileen, his sister; of Liam, his father, and of the others who loved him more than I was able, knowing nothing at all of the man.

I shut off my thoughts and swung back to face the fire. Saw the murderer and his men exchanging glances, telling secrets in silence, and it occurred to me to wonder if they knew precisely who I was, regardless of what I claimed.

Sean is dead, he says. He has killed the Prince of Erinn, and likely himself as well.

"How?" I asked curtly. "And why are you still alive?"

He sighed, stripping thick, unruly hair back from his bearded face. " 'Tis a long story, lass . . . have you the wits to listen?" Unspoken was the question: *"And do you really care?"*

Oh, aye, I cared. And indeed, my wits were failing. But I recaptured them with effort, fixed blurring eyes on the man. "You are, you have said, a murderer—"

"We're not knowing for *sure*."

I blinked. "But you just said—"

" 'Tis *possible*," he said flatly. "He was sore hurt, aye, with a broken head, and bleeding . . . but I left before the truth was known."

In other words, he fled. My face showed what I thought.

He did not look pleased by his admission. A brief sideways glance at the others showed him men clutching pewter cups but not so much as sipping, none of them, as if too ashamed of their part in this tale. Color stood high in his face, in what I could see of his cheeks between eyes and the edge of his beard.

There was a look, a *presence* to him—"King's men," I said plainly. "And you, I think, their captain."

The flesh by his eyes twitched. "Aye," he said, "we *were*."

I looked again at his men. I have seen their like in Homana-Mujhar, gathered in the baileys, lounging in the guardrooms, on furlough in Mujhara. Only four of them now; four had gone into the wood, making certain the thieves were gone. Every face was masked to me, showing me only what they intended, and that being little enough. Young men all, twenty-five to thirty, but each with that selfsame presence, that quiet *confidence;* all of them ageless in experience, in the knowledge of what they faced.

If he had killed the Prince of Erinn, what he faced was death. What *they* faced, I thought, was exile.

I was tired, so very tired, and the liquor had fuddled my tongue. At best I am often tactless; now I was nothing short of rude, though I hardly meant it to come out so plainly. "So," I said thickly, "you and those men who were with you sailed for Homana, just in case he *did* die, to avoid sentencing." I paused, sucking in a hiss of reawakened pain; I had absently scratched at my shredded neck. "Liam would have had you executed for killing his only son, his *heir*—" I broke it off; it needed no more embellishment. Clearly, he knew what it meant.

" 'Twasn't an easy choice." He stroked into place the heavy mustaches interlacing themselves with beard. So much hair on the man, head and face: bright blond and brilliant red. "Ye see, lass, 'twas only a bit of a thing, this fight between me and Sean . . . hardly enough for *dying*—" He sighed, looking unexpectedly weary. " 'Twas only over a lass."

Dull anger flared and died. "Only" over a lass; I scowled at him blearily. "It seems to me you have an uncommon familiarity with your lord's *name*, Erinnish, rather than his title."

He grinned, but with little humor. "Och, aye, Sean— *Prince* Sean, if you like, but there's little reason for it . . . we're pups of the same sire, though born of different bitches."

My wandering wits snapped back. "Liam is your father?"

He arched an arrogant eyebrow beneath a forelock beginning to curl in damp night air. "I could say something of *you*, lass, using names in place of titles . . . but aye, 'tis all of it true: Liam is my father." He paused. "The Lord of Erinn, if you prefer, *and* of the Idrian Isles."

The latter was due, in part, to Corin, who did not contest the title. His own was Lord of Atvia; he had told me it was enough.

Gods, I am so tired . . . I roused myself with effort. "Did Sean know you were his brother?"

Something flickered in brown eyes. "Liam freely acknowledged me at birth, making no secret of it. Sean and I were childhood playmates—there's but thirteen months between us—and later, when Liam made me a captain in his Guard, boon companions." He looked away from me. "We often went drinking together."

I said nothing at all, merely staring at the man who may—or may *not*—have killed his brother in a tavern brawl over a pretty wine-girl. It was not, I knew, unheard of; my own brothers had battled the odds in such places, and over women of like employment. They had even begun a fight that became far more, accounting, in the end, for the deaths of thirty-two people.

But that was another, older tale. This one still cut deep; the man, I saw, was bleeding, though perhaps he did not know it.

Then again, perhaps he did. Abruptly he was striding away from the fire, as I had, as if he could not bear to face it, or himself. He paused but a few paces from me, head bowed, fists on sword-belted hips; stared bleakly groundward, then frowned and bent to pick something up. My knife, I saw, and flinched at my forgetfulness.

Then froze. It was more than merely a knife. Cheysuli long-knives are particularly valued because only rarely does one go out of Cheysuli hands. A student of weaponry knows the design, the style, the *difference;* even, I thought, in Erinn.

And if the style of weapon did not give away its origins— *and* those of its owner—the hilt design might. Rampant lion with rubies for the eyes: the device of the House of Homana.

If he knew it, he knew me.

"You fought," I said lightly, hoping to distract him.

"We fought," he agreed, "to see who would win the lass. We have done it before, but this time, *this* time—" He turned and looked at me. "I was in my cups. So was he. It was wanting little more than that and a bonny lass." He shrugged lopsidedly. "Liam bred true; our tastes are much the same when it comes to bedding the lasses."

"But this time it went too far." I refused to look at the weapon.

"Too far," he agreed, turning it in his hands. "No blades, but we needed none—we are effective enough without."

Aye, so they would be, if Sean shared his brother's size. And Aileen's description of the Prince of Erinn led me to believe he was in every way a match for his bastard brother.

To myself, I shook my head, seeing it too well: two young bulls fighting with the heifer there to watch, and too much liquor in them. "Fools, both of you."

He looked from the knife to me. The blade glinted in his hands, such large, strong hands. "Fools," he echoed, "aye. And now I have paid the price."

Unexpectedly, it stung. "*Have* you?" I asked. "Have you, then, you and your men, living now in Homana . . . while your murdered prince—and kinsman—is walking the halls of the *cileann?*"

It was his turn to gape. I had succeeded at last in drawing his attention from the knife. "What do you know of the oldfolk?" he asked. "A Homanan lass like you, with no ken of Erinnish magic!"

Not of Erinnish, perhaps, but my own share of Cheysuli. Yet I could say nothing of that to him. "A little," I answered evenly. "I have heard the Princess of Homana speak of the *cileann,* as well as the Mujhar's *meijha.*"

He frowned. " 'Tis a strange word, that. And not Homanan, I'm thinking."

I cursed myself for the slip. But among those of us who share blood, it is how we referred to Deirdre. It connotes honor, since she holds no Homanan rank. "Old Tongue," I told him truthfully. "Are you forgetting the House of Homana is Cheysuli?"

He grimaced. "Shapechangers."

"Better than murderers."

His hand gripped my knife. "Aye, so they are." He walked the three steps, gave the knife back to me with nary a word of the device. "Well, lass, I'm thinking I'm remiss in my manners, having left most of them behind. Will you stay the night with us? Share our supper with us? The liquor you've already tasted." He grinned. "Or it's tasted *you,* by the black look of your eyes."

I closed a fist over the telltale hilt. "Why Homana?" I asked. "Why not Atvia or Solinde?"

"Atvia is our enemy."

"Was," I said plainly. "Alaric has been dead two years. Corin rules now."

He shrugged. "But a lad, is Corin, and unschooled yet in ruling. 'Twill take time, and he may not have it . . . not with the Ihlini witch on his doorstep and Mad Gisella in his castle."

It made me angry that he could so easily discount my brother. "He is the rightful lord of Atvia—"

"Right has nothing to do with it," he snapped. " 'Twill be who is strongest that holds the throne . . . oh, aye, Corin means well, of that I'm having no doubt, but 'tis early yet to predict who will win. Might be Lillith yet, and Strahan with her . . . no, no, Liam makes no judgments, nor Sean—" He broke it off, as if recalling Sean might never again make judgments.

"Then what of Solinde?" I asked. "Solinde and Erinn

have never been enemies—that portion has been Homana's—
so why not go there? It is closer to your homes."

His tone was elaborately even, but his eyes gave it away.
"We have no homes, lass. As for Homana?" He shrugged.
"No particular reason, I'm thinking, only—" But he
stopped short. "No, lass, 'tis a liar I am. There was a reason, aye . . . but I lack the courage to do what I intended,
what I *hoped*—" He sighed, giving it up. "What Sean asked
me to do, once, if anything befell him."

I swallowed painfully. "Which was?"

He was backlit by firelight. It set a nimbus around his
head, at the edges of his beard. Quietly, he said, "To go
myself to the lady and beg her forgiveness and understanding."

I stared. "Beg—? Why? What need is there of forgiveness *or* understanding?"

"For leaving her a widow."

Sluggishly, I shook my head. "But—how can she be a
widow if they were never married?"

He frowned. "In Erinn, a betrothal is much like a wedding, and as binding. In Erinnish eyes, the lass would be
Sean's widow even without the wedding." He shrugged.
" 'Tis customary, lass, especially in royal houses when the
heirs are but wee bairns, to make certain the betrothals
hold."

It did make sense, though in Homana it is different.
Kings barter children in exchange for all manner of treaties
and accords; without the betrothal holding weight, the same
child could be offered again and again, at the king's
convenience.

But I did not like the practice. Widowed before the wedding? Married without the vows? I found the latter most
disturbing; it consigned me to the buyer without a trace of
courtesy, nor respect for Cheysuli customs.

Between my teeth, I said, "I am sure she would give her
forgiveness, if not her understanding."

He looked at my knife, hilt still clasped in my fist. And
then he took it back before I could speak, replacing it with
his own. "We'll be hearth-friends, then."

In shock, I stared after my knife. "What?"

"An Erinnish custom for wayfarers in need of a fire and
a place to sleep. Strangers are welcomed in to sup before

the hearth, to sleep in the host's own bed." Teeth glinted as he grinned. "No, lass, I promise—the bed is empty of host."

I was not afraid of him or his dishonored men. Mostly, I was exhausted, stiff with crusting rope burns and bruised from the awkward landing. *Lir*-shape, I knew, was futile; even if I gained it, the shape would not last. What I needed was food and rest.

I refused to glance at my knife or say anything of it, for fear of making him curious. With effort, I looked into his shadowed face. "King's man," I said, "have you a real name?"

He hesitated a moment, as if he feared to tell me; as if I could give him away. "Rory," he said at last. "But also known as Redbeard."

"Rory Redbeard," I muttered, "remember I have a knife."

" 'Tis *my* knife, lass . . . and remember, I have yours."

I looked again at the blade in his hand, aglint with royal rubies. Shut my mouth on an answer and went slowly to the fire.

Seven

One might think the Cheysuli, a race so steeped in honor, are blind to dishonor in others, to deception and subterfuge, believing all men are as they themselves are. Once, perhaps, but no longer, nor has it been so for time out of mind. Contact with the Ihlini, who share some of the Firstborn's power but nothing of their wisdom, has educated the Cheysuli to what unchecked avarice and ambition, augmented by twisted sorcery, can do to a race.

As had Shaine's *qu'mahlin*, the war of annihilation leveled against us by my kinsman, my great-great-grandsire on the Homanan side, nearly a hundred years ago.

So no longer do we trust, nor blind ourselves to betrayal, deception, and subterfuge. We have learned to judge, to weigh, to measure, knowing very well that to a people reluctant to show strong emotions to those who are unblessed, the feelings and convictions of other races are often ludicrously transparent.

Men are easy to read. Even Erinnish exiles.

Rory Redbeard was kind in his own rough way, and solicitous of my well-being. In the morning he fed me journeybread and venison stew spiced with thyme and wild onions, eating what all of them ate, and poured me a cup of water. I ate, drank, felt better, but wished I had my knife.

"Lass," he said quietly, "will ye not let me tend your scrapes?"

"No time," I said briefly, chewing the last tough bite of bread. "I must get back to Homana-Mujhar."

His tone was idly kind. "Surely you can wait *that* long, lass . . . I see how they're hurting you."

Well, they were. Abraded flesh had seeped fluid and watery blood, then crusted as I slept. Movement had broken

open the beginnings of fragile, puckered scabs. I could
barely turn my head and forbore to use my right arm.

"I must get back," I repeated, thinking of Aileen. But I
quailed from it, afraid; quailed also from the acknowledgment I would have to tell Brennan *something*. I had lost
his prize colt; how, by the gods, could I tell him?

And how would I get back? *Lir*-shape was out of the
question. As a bird, I would lack a wing. As anything else,
I would lack a foreleg, much limited in speed.

Walking would be faster.

"I have a horse," Rory said, and I looked at him so
sharply it cracked a knot in my neck. I winced.

A glint crept into his eyes. By daylight he was a different
man: younger in face—what I could see of it above and
beneath the beard—though weathered by Erinn's sea-clime;
in clothing and accoutrements more obviously a man denied his homeland, as well as the trappings of normal life.
Like the others, he was travel-stained and shabby, though
knives and swords were well tended.

Aye, they would be. For by knives and swords—and
cunning—new lives would have to be forged.

I drew in a deep breath. "My father—" Stricken, I cut
it off, then rapidly reshaped it. "My father, the Mujhar's
arms-master, would give you no welcome, nor would his
master, if they knew."

Rory Redbeard laughed. It was but a short bark of
sound, underscored with the knowledge of ironic futility.
"Would he not? And *why* not, I'm wondering? In killing
Sean—if I have—I've stolen a husband from his lass. 'Tis
a serious thing, that, and worth contemplation by men who
are merely fathers in addition to Mujhars." Absently he
stroked ruddy mustaches into neatness, though all of him
wanted washing. "Niall and Liam are friends as well as
allies . . . your father's master will have no more love for
me than Liam, should news come that Sean is dead."

My father's master . . . with effort, I made the adjust-
ment. I wanted nothing more than to throw off my own
subterfuge so I could speak freely again. Never in my life
have I *lied* to anyone regarding my heritage; there has been
no need for it.

"If the Mujhar learned you were here—"

"But he won't be learning, will he?" He paused significantly. "Unless you're for telling him." A friendly man, was Rory, on the outside of his skin, but willing enough to show steel around the edges when he felt it required of him.

It irritated me. "What would you *have* me tell him?"

Rory shrugged. "Don't lie, lass, save for telling my heritage . . . tell him the truth of everything but that, as you can. Tell him, if you like, there are brigands in Homana—I doubt 'tis anything he doesn't know already, judging by the men who chased you to my fire." He rose, turning away on some errand, then abruptly swung back to face me. His expression was, yet again, masked. "Tell him what you will, lass . . . for when the Mujhar sends men to find us, we'll be in another place." Then, casually cruel, "D'ye think I'm so daft as to trust you?"

It stung. But I gave him a glimpse of my teeth in return. "Nor I to trust *you*."

Rory smiled, then laughed. "Agreed, then! Come, lass, we'll be saddling my horse. 'Tis a long ride, I'm told, to Mujhara . . . we'd best be setting about it."

I stood, gritting my teeth against the aches and stiffness, and followed him from the fire into a thicket. "How would *you* know how far it is to Mujhara?"

He laughed explosively. "We're here for a reason, lass: the road. I'm told it goes from Mujhara clear to Ellas."

Frowning, I nodded.

"Then so does trade, my lass . . . as well as wealthy merchants."

I stopped. "A *thief!*"

He paused, half-turning, putting out a hand to screening foliage, but hesitated to draw it aside. "Become one," he agreed. "Can I be presenting myself to the Mujhar, asking for a place in his service?" His tone was cool. "I'm thinking not, lass . . . not with Aileen there, who knows me. I'm thinking the best way for me to feed myself and what's left of my command is to acquire a bit of the wealth others have in plenty."

"A thief," I said again, thinking of the others; of the man whose knee I had bent—or broken—and the companions who had chased me, intending revenge and rape.

"Aye," he said evenly, and drew aside the foliage.

I started. "Brennan's *colt!*"

Blond brows arched. "Yours, then; I was thinking so,

when they brought him to me last night after you fell asleep." His mouth hooked down in a wry smile. "I'm for keeping him, lass."

"But—no . . . not *him*." I pushed past Rory, threading my way through foliage, and went to the chestnut colt. Tied up short, he could barely turn his head. "Not him," I said again, cupping chin and muzzle, thinking of my brother. "He belongs to the Prince of Homana."

"He belongs to Rory Redbeard."

I turned on him angrily. "What right have you to *steal*? This colt belongs—"

"—to me." Rory moved to the colt, deftly shunting me aside. " 'Tis what thievery *is*, lass . . . and that 'right' you speak of is right of conquest, or requirements." He saddled the chestnut easily, tightening girth, snugging buckles. "I'm thinking the Prince of Homana has more than this bright lad in his stable."

"Aye, of course—but—"

"Then he'll do as well without him. 'Twill give him time to ride the others." He turned the colt, swung up, reached down to clasp my hand. "Will ye be coming, lass?"

"You were a *king's* man, once—"

"Once," he said quietly. "Now I may be the cause of my brother's death . . . d'ye think stealing matters to me? Or who I steal *from*?"

It silenced me easily, as he intended it to. I wanted nothing more than to denounce him, but there was nothing left to say. Nothing left to *do*; I clasped his hand, let him pull me up, settled a careful leg on the colt's sleek rump and slid slowly into place.

Thinking violent thoughts.

By the time we reached the outskirts of Mujhara, I was near to tumbling off Brennan's mettlesome colt. That we had arrived at all was nothing short of a god-gift; the colt was bred for speed, not for carrying a man the size of Rory nor the additional weight of a second rider. It had taken all of Rory's strength and skill—and my determination not to be thrown—to tip the colt out of rebellion into a grudging surrender. He had brought us to Mujhara, but not precisely unscathed. Rory complained the saddle was too small—for him, it was—and the long ride had set my head and neck to aching again, as well as breaking open once more the thin crusts on throat and arm.

We were nearly to the gates when I roused from my half-stupor with a stifled curse. "No!" I said sharply. Then, more quietly, "Stop here, Erinnish. No need in going farther."

No indeed, no need: the guards on the city gates knew me too well. I was less willing than ever to admit my true identity, because of Rory Redbeard's link to the House of Eagles. He was in no position now, in exile, to do anything about it, but should Sean prove to be alive rather than dead, I wanted no brother—bastard or no—telling tales of me to the man who intended to name me his wife before we were even wed.

"Stop *here,*" I said plainly, bracing to slide off it Rory did nothing to halt the colt.

But he did halt him, all of twenty paces from the Eastern gate with its archivolted barbican. The walls themselves are gray, penning up the city proper in a huge, soft-cornered rectangle. But Mujhara has grown, as cities do; too fast, too far, without regard to the future. Now there was a second city clustered outside the walls, though built of less permanent materials than stone—mostly haphazard, flimsy wooden structures, or soiled canvas tents bearing no resemblance to the jewel-dyed and *lir*-painted pavilions of Clankeep.

Inside, warded by a webwork of narrow, twisting streets and a curtain wall thick as three men lying head to toe, nestles Homana-Mujhar herself, breasting above baileys and sentry-walks, wearing banners for her gown and torchlight for her jewelry. Rose-red in the light of day, bloodied-gray by night. The place I knew as home.

Twenty paces is not too far for a keen-eyed gate guard to see a person clearly, even at night, so long as he has torchlight. But my leathers were badly soiled, and one sleeve of my quilted undertunic shredded nearly into nonexistence. My hair, free of cap or braid, was a mass of tangles sculpted by dirt and tree sap; I doubted sincerely anyone would recognize *me*.

But they might recognize the colt.

I slid off painfully, ignoring Rory's hand. The landing was awkward and jarred my head; I gritted teeth and turned to look up at the Erinnish brigand, putting my back to the gate. The street, unpaved and thick with dust, was thronged with people going this way and that, even now, after sundown. It was possible, if not probable, a passerby might recognize me if I did not act soon to detach myself from Rory Redbeard.

"My thanks for the food and drink," I told him. "My thanks for your aid against the thieves—" I paused "—the *other* thieves—" I ignored the glint in his eyes, "—but I will not give you my gratitude for stealing Brennan's horse."

He pursed lips—and beard—thoughtfully. Thick brows drew down, met, knitted, then slanted back up again as he tilted his head to one side. "Is that the way of it, lass?"

"What?" I frowned. "Is *what* the way of it? What are you talking about?"

"Brennan," he said, "and you."

Dumbfounded, all I could do was blink.

Slowly, distinctly, he nodded. "Aye, I thought so—always Brennan this, Brennan that . . . never the Prince of Homana. Never 'my lord,' though you'd be having it from me, and for my own brother." He shrugged a little. "Well, I'm not judging ye, lass . . . I'm born myself of a bedding between a prince and a bonny lass—"

I was astounded. "Are you saying you think Brennan and *I*—"

"No shame in it, lass . . . at least, not so much as to ruin your prospects." He grinned. "He'll leave you wealthy, being a prince . . . you could do worse than the heir to the throne of Homana." The glint was more pronounced. "Once he's cast you off, *I* might even consider—"

I smiled up at him insincerely. "Take your stolen horse and go, before I bring the guard down on you."

Laughing, he reined the colt around. "Or your Cheysuli prince?" And laughed more loudly as I mustered elaborate curses. "Lass, lass . . . you'll be getting no censure from *me*—d'ye think I'm so daft as to throw mud at my own reflection?"

I swallowed laughter, not wishing to show my amusement to Rory Redbeard, and put shielding fingers across my lips. With great effort I managed a frown. "Just go," I choked.

Rory nodded, but his share of amusement faded. He worked his mouth thoughtfully, absently soothing the colt with a gentle hand on his neck.

"Lass," he said finally, "there's a thing I must ask you to do."

Wary, I frowned. "Me?"

"Aye." His face was pensive. "Say nothing of it to Deirdre or Aileen, this thing of Sean and me. We're neither of us knowing if he's alive or dead—I'm thinking it might be better left to Liam to give them the truth of the matter." Uneasily, he eyed me. "Lass, will you promise? 'Tis a thing of the House of Eagles—I may be only a bastard, but still kinborn . . . 'twould be better, I'm thinking, not to tell them a thing that might not be true, giving them a grief they may not need to suffer."

"Or may," I said quietly.

He looked over my head at the barbican gate, thinking private thoughts. "Aye," he said finally, "or may."

I owed him nothing . . . except, perhaps, my life. Certainly my virtue.

In pensive silence, I nodded. That much I would give him.

Rory Redbeard leaned down out of the saddle and set a hand to the top of my head, tousling filthy hair. "*There's* my good lass," he said.

And rode away, laughing, before I could summon an answer.

Eight

I went at once to Aileen's apartments, to her bedchamber. The heavy door was shut. I put out my hand to push it open, knowing she would give me welcome no matter what my state—and stayed the hand even as splayed fingers tensed to push.

I could not face it, could *not;* would not chance walking into a room scented by death and extremity, knowing myself a coward for not returning at once from Clankeep, for staying away to hide from possibilities, from the responsibilities of a *cheysula*.

Oh, gods, how can I deal with this?

I swung back abruptly, rolling shoulders against the corridor wall, to lean there, teeth gritted, eyes shut tight, skull pressed into stone. Helplessness and futility altered fear into something more, into a wealth of tangled emotions unfamiliar and therefore treacherous, because if I could not name the emotions, neither could I control them.

Under my breath I swore, stringing together every epithet I could apply to myself, for being such a failure as companion, kin, *kinspirit*—

"Keely."

I snapped upright at once, turning stiffly toward him, petitioning the gods to let it be someone else, *anyone* else, so long as it was not my father, who would doubtless take me to task for betraying Aileen when she most needed me, for fleeing responsibilities—knowing if he said none of those things, what he *would* say was that Aileen was dead.

But he said none of those things, because it was *su'fali* in place of *jehan*. Uncle in place of father.

"*Leijhana tu'sai,*" I breathed, and relaxed as Ian approached.

"What has *happened*—Keely, are you ill? Are you injured?" His concern was manifest, intensifying my guilt; Aileen was more important. "Keely—"

I shoved back tangled hair. "Aileen," was all I said.

It shut his mouth, but only for a moment. I looked for signs of grief: saw none, only concern and acknowledgment. But then he is not a man for giving things away, my *su'fali,* having suffered grievously for giving away something he treasured more than anything: honor, self-control; for a while, even sanity.

He gave nothing away now, even to me. To no one, I thought, again. Lillith of the Ihlini had taken far too much.

"Alive," he said quietly, wasting no time. "Niall brought her through with the earth magic, *leijhana tu'sai,* though it was much too soon for the babies. But at least Aileen is well." Briefly he sketched a quick gesture I know so well, *too* well: cupped hand turning palm-up, fingers spread.

It was so powerful a relief I could afford to be caustic. I chided my father's brother. "Aileen is not Cheysuli, therefore she has no *tahlmorra.*" But my right hand twitched as if it, too, wanted to make the gesture denoting fate and the gods.

Ian's expression did not alter. "She has Brennan. I think it is enough."

Aye, of course: *Brennan.* Truly she was blessed.

And then I thought of the colt lost to Rory Redbeard, and shifted uneasily. "She will recover, then? Fully? She will still be Aileen?"

He frowned. "Of course; what *would* you have her be?"

"Anything but a broodmare." Wearily, I shoved a rebellious lock of hair from my face again. "*Su'fali,* if she goes through this again . . . if she is forced to bear a child—or *two*—simply because Brennan—"

"Keely." He took my arm—the left one, thank the gods—in a firm grasp, turned me away from the door and guided me down the corridor even as I tried to protest. "No—not now, Keely . . . Aileen is resting. Later." He continued to lead me. "You need not worry she will be required to go through this again . . . the physicians say it is unlikely she will ever bear another child." His fingers remained firmly entrenched in my arm. "Now, as to being *forced*—"

I resented being guided, but was too tired, too worn, to

do much more than test his grip. "She *was*. She nearly died with Aidan, and yet within a year of his birth she is required to try again, simply to shore up Brennan's claim on the Lion—"

Ian muttered something in Old Tongue under his breath, escorted me ungently to the closest door and pushed it open, pushing *me* in behind it. Then, closing the door by kicking it shut, he guided me over to a chair and plopped me down in it. Only then did he release my arm.

Without preliminaries, my uncle called me a fool, in both languages, to make certain I understood, which I did twice over. And a blind one, as well, twice over again; which did not, particularly, sit well with me.

I stood up. A firm hand on one shoulder pushed me down again. "You *will* listen," he said mildly.

I opened my mouth to protest, shut it to think a moment, glanced around to delay. And frowned. We were in Ian's quarters, which I found unusual; he is very private, my uncle, and keeps parts of himself closed to others, even kinfolk. I had not been in his personal chambers for years, not since I was a child begging him to teach me how to shoot a Cheysuli warbow. No one else would.

Immensely comfortable chambers, filled with Cheysuli things. In recent years our people have begun reclaiming some of the crafts *qu'mahlin* and exile denied, for the threat of extermination leaves little time for things other than defense. Ian had collected stoneware sculptures of different *lir,* foremost among them Tasha, but also his brother's wolf, in addition to the nubby, round-framed weavings many of the women do. Across one ironwood table spilled a river of prophecy bones, but made of silver instead of ivory; a gift from Hart, I knew, who intended it for wagering. Our uncle used it instead merely to help him think, idly throwing patterns.

Something squalled. I glanced around sharply at the huge bed, draperies hooked up on the bedposts, and saw Tasha sprawled there with her cubs, all tangled amidst the bedclothes like knots in Deirdre's yarn basket. Three young mountain cats, all rich tawny bronze.

I smiled in delight. *Lovely*, I sent through the link. *They will make magnificent* lir, *should the gods give them the honor.*

Amber-eyed Tasha wasted no time in agreeing, but before I could say anything else Ian cut me off.

"Not now," he said distinctly. "At this particular moment I want to make very certain you understand something clearly."

"Su'fali—"

"No," he said firmly. "You are here to listen, Keely, which is something you should practice more often—certainly more often than the sword with Griffon. *That* you may have mastered; listening you have not."

The meal I had shared with Rory and his men curdled in my belly. Anger and astonishment evaporated; what I felt was humiliation. Hot-faced, I stared back at him, wanting to look at the floor but denying myself the refuge.

He sighed, folding arms across his chest. He is not much like my father, being thoroughly Cheysuli in coloring as well as habits, though the black hair is frosting silver. And nothing at all like the Mujhar in temperament, either, being considerably more relaxed and less prone to worry about things. It is sometimes hard to believe they are brothers, although only half; Ian is bastard-born, the son of Donal, my grandsire, and his half-Homanan *meijha*.

"Keely," he said quietly. Too quietly; I know his methods. "Has it never occurred to you that perhaps Brennan and Aileen are content with one another?"

It was the closest *he* would ever come to speaking of love, being so Cheysuli, and therefore characteristically reticent to discuss such things with others, even kin. I have no such qualms; it must be the Homanan in me, which speaks oftener than it should.

"Content." I thrust myself against the back of the chair. "You mean, in their bedding."

"I mean in everything."

I recalled Brennan's behavior, his *eyes*, when I had told of Aileen's condition. Clearly, he was "content." But I also recalled how it had been between them when Aileen had first come to Homana. "But—*Corin*—"

Ian's tone was steady; he knew how I felt about my *rujholli*. "Corin is gone, *has* been gone, for nearly two years."

I shrugged. "What does time matter? You know as well as I Aileen wanted to marry Corin instead of Brennan . . . it was only because of the betrothal to Brennan—*and the* prophecy—that she had to give up Corin. Do you think she would have otherwise? Do you think Corin would have let her?" I sat upright in the chair. "Brennan cares, aye—I have seen it—but what of Aileen? She was forced, *su'fali,* no matter what you say. Forced in marriage, forced in bed . . . forced to bear heirs for Homana." My hands clenched on the chair arms. "Just as *I* will be, one day, if for Erinn instead."

"We are not speaking about you just yet," he said gently. "We are speaking of Brennan and Aileen, who have had a difficult time reconciling old feelings *and* new ones, with no help from their sharp-tongued *rujholla.*"

I disliked intensely being trapped in the chair. It made me want to squirm, like a child; it made me want to jump up and stride around the room, taking solace in activity. But I refused to squirm, and I knew better than to jump up. Ian would only push me down again.

"Aileen and I have talked, it is true," I admitted, "but she has her own mind, *su'fali.* You know that. She is Erinnish. Those born in the House of Eagles know very well how to fly."

"Unless someone puts jesses on them and locks them in the mews."

I stared. "You think *I*—"

"I know." He rose, walked idly around behind me, paused, rested hands on my shoulders. "Keely, you are not a vindictive person, nor one who wishes ill of kinfolk. But you are so strong in your convictions, so *pronounced* in your biases, that you overwhelm other people. Aye, Aileen has her own mind—she is Liam's daughter in that, as Niall says, and Deirdre—but how often do you listen and weigh what she has to say? Have you ever asked her how she feels about Brennan?"

No. Because I knew how she felt about Corin.

Ian's hands tightened. "I do not ask you to betray your loyalty to Corin. He is your twin-born *rujholli*—that is a link no one of a single birth can share, can even *comprehend* . . . but neither should you continue to defend a relationship that ended nearly two years ago."

"How do you know—"

He overrode me easily. "Because *you* prefer not to marry does not mean you should expect every other unwed

woman to feel the same, nor a married one to feel guilty
if she is content." He paused, squeezing aching shoulders
very gently. "Nor should you ridicule them if they do not
feel as you do. Their beliefs are as important as your own,
and they have as much right to them."

Anger boiled up. "*You* say. *You* say: a man." I sat rigidly
in the chair. "What would you know of being forced against
your will into a liaison you do not want?"

The hands dug painfully into my shoulders. I thought he
did it purposely, to punish me—until I realized what I had
asked, and of whom I had asked it.

"Oh, *su'fali*—oh, gods, I *swear*—" I wanted to jump up
and turn; to face him, to apologize, but he held me firmly
in place, denying me any chance to take back the cruel
question. To assuage my guilt, his pain.

"Oh, I know," he said quietly. "I know very well, *harana*.
I know what it is to be chattel, to be needed only for the
servicing, like a stallion brought to the mare. I know very
well what it is to be valued only because of my seed, of
the child I can sire . . . and *did*." He sighed wearily. "Not
so different, I think, from what many women face. But it
need not be what Aileen faces, nor you. She has a chance
to be happy with Brennan, as do you with Sean, *if* you will
allow it. As for me, well . . . that is a thing I have learned
to deal with, after so many years."

I swallowed painfully, clearing the tightness in my throat.
"Have you, *su'fali?*"

"Oh, aye—of course."

His tone was too light, his hands too heavy. Slowly I
slipped out from beneath those hands, rising, and turned
to face him squarely. To look into haunted eyes; so yellow,
so *Cheysuli,* beneath the silver forelock.

"Is that why you practice *i'toshaa-ni* every year on the
same day, trying to bleed your soul clean of her?" I steadied my voice with effort. "Is that why you never speak of
Rhiannon, the daughter you sired on her?" I drew in a
breath. "Is that why you take no woman as *meijha* or
cheysula—because she soiled you?"

"I am not celibate," he said tightly, "nor do I lie
with men."

I made a gesture with my hand. "No, no, of course not—
but even with a woman in it, your bed is often empty." I

felt uncomfortable speaking of such things with him, but I would not stop now. "I heard Deirdre once, with *jehan*—she was saying she thought you were much too hard on yourself for something you could not help. And *jehan* said—" I stopped, seeing the look in his eyes.

Softly, he asked, "What did Niall say?"

I drew in a deep breath, blew it out. "That you believed yourself disgraced. Dishonored. That a dishonored warrior asks clan-rights of no woman."

"No," he said only.

"But, *su'fali*—" I sucked in another breath. "She held your *lir*, your *life* . . . what else was there to do?"

"Then: nothing. Afterward—" He shrugged. "There are ways of expiating dishonor. There is *i'toshaa-ni*—"

"Not *every* year."

"—and there is self-exile from the clans—"

"Not for such as *that!*"

"—and there is the death-ritual."

I stared. "You would *not!*"

Slowly, he shook his head. "I am liege man to the Mujhar."

Words tumbled out. "Is that why—is that the *only*—? Oh, *su'fali*, no—say you would not . . . say *no*—tell me it is a only a jest—a *very* poor jest—"

"Keely, stop. Enough." Ian is older than my father by five years. At this moment, I would have said twenty. "I swear, I have no intention of *kin-wrecking* myself or giving myself over to the death-ritual; it is far too late for either. And as for why I ask clan-rights of no woman—well, that is my concern, not yours—"

"But *any* woman would have you!"

At last, my uncle smiled. "Would she?" he asked.

"Oh, *aye*, of course! You should hear what they say of you, *su'fali*." I grinned. "Even before Brennan married, or Corin and Hart left, it was *you*—"

At last, my uncle laughed, putting up his hands. "Enough, *enough* . . . all right, Keely, you may suspend your staunch avowals of my appeal." He grinned and glanced at Tasha, whose affectionate amusement ran through the *lir*-link to us both. "Now, as to the *original* reason for this discussion—"

"Aye, aye, I know." I waved off the rest with my hands.

"I am too quick to tell others how to conduct themselves, disregarding their own opinions. I know. But sometimes—" I cut myself off. "No. No more; I will try to lock up my tongue."

"But do not choke on it."

I turned resolutely toward the door. Then swung sharply back. "She *is* all right?" I asked.

"Aileen is, aye . . . but now, as for *you*—"

"No," I said, "no. I must order a bath." And took myself out of the chamber before he could start on me.

I soaked in a half-cask until the water was nearly cold, then dragged myself out with effort. The heat had dissipated some of the pain, but nearly all of my energy. Shakily I took up the drying cloth left for me by the cask and wrapped it tightly around my body, stepping out with care. I have never been one to enjoy body-servants hovering, patting me dry and toweling my hair, and so I had dismissed them before stripping out of my filthy clothing. Now, alone as I preferred, I discovered an inclination in myself to simply lie down on the floor. It was too far to walk into the bedchamber, too hard to climb into the bed.

Irresolute, I stood on the damp floor and lost myself in contemplation of my state. Of mind as well as body; there was thinking I had to do, about missing colts and Cheysuli long-knives, and the Erinnish brigand who had them.

Somehow, I will have to get them back, both of them. I cannot let him keep them, either one—

"Keely?" A figure swam into my unfocused gaze, coming through the doorway between bed-and antechamber. *"Keely,"* she cried sharply. "Oh, gods, Ian said you looked bad—" Deirdre caught my left hand and tugged me through the doorway. "Come with me, my lass, before you fall down where you stand. I'm thinking it might be painful."

The Erinnish lilt, in Deirdre, was far less pronounced than in Aileen, only two years out of Erinn, and certainly less than in Rory Redbeard, so newly arrived. But the "my lass" rocked me; it summoned up his bearded face, his voice, and the tale he had told, of murdered princes and bastard brothers.

As well as reminding me of the promise I had made him.

Sluggishly, I stirred as Deirdre led me into my bedchamber. "No—no, I am well enough . . . only tired."

"And have you looked at your face? Have you heard your voice?" Deirdre pointed to a chair. "There, Keely—and no protests. Here—put this on." Deftly she plucked a folded nightrail from my bed and tossed it to me.

There is no arguing with Deirdre when she sets her mind on a thing. So obligingly I swathed myself in the nightrail, now cloaked in wet hair. I twisted it all into one thick rope, then asked Deirdre for a comb.

She brought it from a table, but as I reached to take it she jerked it out of my grasp. "Keely—what has *happened?*" Carefully she peeled the collar of the nightrail back from my throat. "Oh, *gods*—this needs salve. I'll send . . ." And went to the door to set a servant to the task, then came back with the much-needed comb. "What else?" she asked evenly. "Be telling no lies, now—I know you, Keely—what else have you done to yourself?"

I sighed, pushing up loose linen sleeve, "Here." I bared my arm. "No worse than the neck."

Deirdre, frowning, inspected it, hissing a little in empathy. "You said nothing of this to Ian . . . you gave him no chance to *ask.*"

I shrugged, cocking my right hand up behind my neck so the underside of my upper arm was clearly exposed. Stretched skin stung. "Someone strung a rope across the track. The horse was running; it scraped me off."

Deirdre started to say something more, but a quiet knock at the door forestalled it. She answered it, returned with a stoppered pot and soft linen cloths. " 'Twill sting a little," she warned, "but will help the flesh loosen."

Aye, it stung, and more than a little. I gritted my teeth and sat very still as she worked the salve into the crusty burns on neck and arm. Under her breath she muttered broken sentences in Erinnish, as she did in times of stress or anger. I had even heard her use the whip of her eloquent tongue on my father a time or two; they are surpassing fond of each other, but they do quarrel. Very like playful cats: all noise and flying fur, but claws sheathed for the duration. And always brief, with them.

Twenty-two years together, though neither of them show it, in habits or appearance. Deirdre's hair is still bright blonde, her green eyes direct as ever, her body slim and straight.

So *many* years in Homana . . . and before that—before Atvia and my mother had intervened, however briefly—a year in Erinn, in the Aerie, learning each other's hearts.

Vaguely, I wondered: *Could it be so for me?*

Until I recalled that, very likely, it could not; possibly Sean was dead.

I tensed as Deirdre finished my neck and moved ministrations to my arm. Ground my teeth as the consequence of such a death became more obvious.

If Sean is dead, jehan *will find another . . . he will open the bidding again, to every prince he can think of.* I shook my head a little. *Not many realms left, or princes . . . too many* rujholli *inhabiting foreign thrones . . . he will have to look to Ellas, or Caledon, even Falia—* I frowned. *But never to The Steppes. We have no trade with them, no reason for an alliance—*

"Keely." From the tone of Deirdre's voice, she had said something to me that required comment or answer, and I had given her neither. "Keely, did you see Maeve?"

Maeve. Oh, gods, my half-witted sister, going again into Teirnan's bed. "Aye," I said briefly.

"Did she say aught about coming home?"

Aye, she had. She had said "tomorrow," which now was today. Unless she had changed her mind, which I knew was possible. She was so afraid to hurt our father, whom she loved above all things.

I shrugged slightly, lifting my left shoulder as Maeve's mother worked salve into my arm. "We did not talk about much."

Deirdre sighed, lines settling between her brows. "I worry about her . . . ever since Teirnan showed his true colors and renounced everything the Cheysuli stand for—"

"She will do well enough." I spoke more harshly than I meant to, but Maeve was not a child. She was the oldest of us all, even if, I felt, the most foolish.

Something flickered in Deirdre's green eyes. I had stung her with my curtness. "One day," she said tightly, "you also will be having a child to worry about. Perhaps even a daughter. *Then* you might understand." She eased my arm from its awkward position, smoothed the linen sleeve back over it. "There. 'Twill require more in the morning, but should be better by midday. As for the hoarseness—"

"It will fade." I put out my hand for the comb.

"No, I'll be doing it . . . just sit here and be silent; give your poor throat a rest." She set the pot and soiled cloth on a table, came to stand beside me, sectioned off my hair and began to work on wet tangles. "You were in the way of being lucky, my lass—had you not put up your arm to block it, the rope might have broken your neck."

"Aye," I said absently, thinking of Rory again. There were things I wanted to ask of him, but did not know how without breaking the promise I had made. I could hardly tell Deirdre he was here in Homana without a proper explanation. She would want to know why, and was persistent enough to work it out of me one way or another. "Deirdre—?"

"Aye?" Deftly, she coaxed hair into neatness again.

I thought rapidly a moment, then drew in a breath. Blandly, I said: "I spoke to *su'fali* earlier."

"Aye, I know—he said you wanted to see Aileen."

"He told me she was resting, and took me away to talk." I chewed my lip a moment. "He never speaks of Rhiannon."

Deirdre paused only a moment, then resumed her combing. "No. 'Tis not something he wishes to recall, that time in Atvia with Lillith and the outcome of it."

"No, but she *is* his daughter . . . and in the clans, bastardy bears no stigma. He could acknowledge her."

" 'Tisn't because she's bastard-born that he won't acknowledge her. 'Tis her mother: Rhiannon's *blood*." Deirdre sighed a little. "Bloodkin to the Ihlini, to Strahan himself—even to Tynstar. A powerful blend, Keely, and treacherous as well. You know what she did to Brennan, much as her mother did to Ian."

Aye, I did know. Which led me to another line of inquiry. "By now *that* child is nearly two," I said idly. "Yet another Cheysuli-Ihlini bastard. And yet another unacknowledged child." I winced as she hit a snarl. "Brennan, like our *su'fali*, says nothing of his child."

"For much the same reason."

"Not bastardy."

"No, of course not. D'ye think bastardy matters to the

father who loves his child?" Gently, she tamed the snarl.
"You have only to look at your father to see how it happens. He loves Maeve every bit as much as he loves the
children of his marriage."

I sighed. "Kings and princes and bastards." I waited a
patient moment. "Is it so with every lord?"

Deirdre's tone was dryly amused. "If this is your way of
asking if Sean has any bastards, how am *I* to know? I left
Erinn when he was four—much too young to sire children,
legitimate or no." Now she laughed. "The eagles may be
lusty, but not so potent as *that!*"

I grunted a little. "Sons are often like the father—what
of Liam's habits?"

She was silent a very long moment, absently putting my
hair to rights. "Aye, well . . . Liam is *mostly* faithful to
Ierne—"

"But not always." It was all I could do not to turn and
look her in the eye. But to do so would give me away,
would underscore the intensity of my interest.

Deirdre sounded troubled. "No, not always . . . Keely,
there are times when men turn to other women . . . in
sickness, sometimes, or while she carries a child—"

"I know," I said quietly, "I am not questioning his morals." Although I would have liked to, since, by all accounts,
Liam loved his wife. "I was only curious. I *do* have reason,
Deirdre . . . there is Sean to think about." I would use it
as I had to, though not with any pleasure. "As I have said,
in the clans bastardy bears no stigma—I would sooner see a
bastard acknowledged, as *jehan* acknowledged Maeve, then
relegated to oblivion."

"Sean would not be so cruel," she said, "any more
than Liam."

Expectantly, I waited.

After a moment, she sighed. "Aye, he has a few. All
girls, save for one . . . a boy he named Rory, born thirteen
months before Sean."

So. He had not lied.

Oh, gods, if Sean is *dead*—

Nine

With an excess of civility—and more than a trace of reluctance—three of Aileen's ladies turned me away from her bedchamber door in the morning, saying the Princess of Homana still slept, requiring uninterrupted rest. I knew all of the ladies well enough—they had come with her from Erinn—and they knew *me;* clearly, they were afraid I would show them the edge of my tongue.

Which meant, I thought, someone had ordered them to keep me out.

"Then let me see Brennan," I said flatly, neglecting his title and not particularly bothered by it. "He *is* here, is he not?—with Aileen?"

They exchanged glances, the three of them, showing me dismay, regret, hesitation. And, at last, denial.

"Lady, no," one of them—Duana—said. "He has given orders not to be disturbed by anyone."

"*He* has, or has someone else?"

Again the furtive glances. And again, Duana shook her head. "Lady, all we can say is that you will be welcomed another time."

Something akin to desperation welled up inside, stripping diplomacy from my tongue. "By the gods, she is my *kinswoman!* Have you gone mad? What right have you to turn me away?"

"Such rights as they are accustomed to, being in service to the Princess—and therefore the Prince—of Homana." It was Brennan, of course, pulling the door more widely open and dismissing the ladies with a nod. Then he turned to face me squarely, one hand on the edge of the door. "Aye, it is true—I *did* tell them you were not to be admitted. You in particular."

It robbed me of breath. *"Why?"*

"Because Aileen needs time to rest, to recover, without listening to your babble about being forced this way and that, molded into a broodmare for my convenience." There were deep-etched shadows beneath his eyes. The rims themselves were red; clearly, he had sat up with Aileen all night, forgoing sleep entirely. Weariness and worry undermined the customary courtesy in his tone, leaving it raw in sound as well as words. "I know what you will do, Keely—you will come in here with words of sympathy on your tongue, and then it will alter itself into a sword and *cut* her, whether you mean it to or not."

"Oh, *Brennan*—"

He signed to me for silence, though the gesture was mostly half-hearted. "She needs time to understand that her place is secure with me even if there *are* no more children . . . and she will not get it with you jabbering in her ear about her loss of freedom, her lack of *value*—" He broke it off, shut his eyes briefly, threaded splayed fingers through limp black hair and scraped it back from his face. He looked so weary, so *worn*. "Gods, Keely, forgive me for my bluntness—but you know it is true."

I drew in a deep breath. "If it were not for me you would not have known she was in danger. I came to fetch you—"

"*Leijhana tu'sai,*" he said evenly. "But not *now*, Keely—another time." He started to close the door, then pulled it open again. As an afterthought, he said, "You did bring the colt?"

Gods, the colt. "In his stall," I lied.

He nodded vaguely and shut the door, leaving me staring blindly at studded wood nearly black with age and oil.

I wanted to strike it. I wanted to *kick* it, to cry out that no one, *no one at all*, even Brennan, knew what I thought, what I *felt* . . . but I did none of those things, being too angry, too hurt in spirit to dare, for fear I would waken Aileen, or even injure myself more than the fall from the colt had.

Brennan's colt. *Gods*, I was beginning to hate him!

But I went after him nonetheless, and at once, seeking physical diversion. Brennan had made me angry, aye, but he was still my brother, and needed whatever respite from worry I could give him. The gods knew he had more than his share with Aileen.

*   *   *

This time I took bow as well as knife, and full complement of arrows, hanging in a quiver at my saddle. The bow
I wore hooked over a shoulder, Cheysuli-fashion. The knife
at my belt was Rory's and would be again, once I had
forced a trade. I did not dare leave him my Cheysuli long-
knife, nor did I want to. It had been a gift from Ian on my
twentieth birthday and I wanted it back badly, as much for
sentiment as anything else.

The horse I rode was a gelding, one of my own; a long-
legged, blaze-faced bay who looked particularly good under
a saddle. I thought to give tack and horse to Rory in exchange for Brennan's chestnut, though, when it came down
to it, the difference in quality was obvious. But the bay was
a good horse, big of heart and willing of spirit. Rory would
not lose by him; *I* would. But I had lost Brennan's colt, so
it was up to me to sacrifice whatever I was required to in
order to get him back.

Now the task at hand was to find the Erinnish brigand.
Rory had said he and his men would be gone from where
I had found them before, out of concern I might lead
guardsmen back to the clearing. I had not bothered to tell
him it would be no difficulty for me to find him—in the
guise of a bird, a search is ridiculously easy—since to do
so would give away my race. But because of the gelding I
was limited to normal means, unless I left him tied temporarily along the way while I searched in bird-form, and I
had no wish to risk losing yet another royal mount to
thieves. So I rode like an unblessed Homanan, hoping for
good fortune.

They would be, I knew, somewhere along the road, lying
in wait for unwary travelers. I did not look much like a
merchant, wealthy or otherwise, nor did I look much like
a princess, dressed in Homanan-style hunting leathers, but
his men knew me by sight, and I thought perhaps it would
not be so hard to flush Rory from cover. He was a man who
enjoyed a good jest, and "surprising" me might be one.

Out of meadow into trees, and into the deeper forest.
From here to Ellas ran the wood, thick in some places,
sparse in others, but always present, shutting out the world
while quietly creating another.

It was here in the wood the Cheysuli had settled once

Shaine's *qu'mahlin* and resulting exile was over, building the first Keep in thirty years. In time, it had become Clankeep, the largest of them all, and home to so many of us. My own grandsire, Donal, had been born in Clankeep, and raised; it was there he had sired Ian and Isolde on his *meijha* before marrying Aislinn, Carillon's daughter, my Homanan granddame. Where Isolde had died of plague, leaving Teirnan with only a father.

I grimaced in disgust. My warped, embittered cousin, subtly shaped by his father's ambitions. It would have been best if the Mujhar had brought his nephew into Homana-Mujhar after Isolde died, to be raised alongside three princes, but Ceinn still lived, and it is a Cheysuli custom that children, regardless of sex, remain with their parents. There is no fosterage among the clans—except where children are orphaned—as there is in many royal houses. And so Teir had been brought up by an ambitious, avaricious father, bent on putting a son of *his* on the Lion Throne instead of one of Niall's.

Teirnan was no *kinspirit* of mine, being enemy to my House. But he was still bloodkin, my own cousin, and *of* that House, which meant he therefore had a legitimate claim to the Lion—but only if Niall and all his sons were dead.

And so I wondered again, as I had often enough in the past, if Teirnan had seduced Maeve merely because of her link to the Mujhar. How better to irritate your enemy than by taking that enemy's most cherished possession—or child—and making it your own?

He had not succeeded, if he had tried, in reshaping Maeve's opinions to suit his own. He had, however, succeeded in separating her from her beloved father, something Teir in particular would find pleasing. In the time since he had voluntarily renounced the prophecy, his clanrights, and privileges, thereby renouncing his very soul, he had done his best to fracture the clans themselves. By pitting those Cheysuli more dedicated to the old ways against a more liberal faction, he had managed to divide Clan Council more than once, as well as win warriors to his cause. And by stirring up old Cheysuli quarrels—or starting new ones—he quietly diverted Niall's attention from Homana to the Cheysuli. In the Homanan Council there were already mutters of the Mujhar's inattention to matters almost strictly Homanan in nature. Homana's need, they said, was greater; to them, it is not a Cheysuli nation but Homanan, no matter that the gods put us here first.

At that, I laughed aloud. So easily I dismiss the Homanan portion of my heritage, as Aileen had remarked, *and* the Atvian, because it suits me to consider myself almost solely Cheysuli. And more so than most, if the truth be told; I am of the Old Blood, the *oldest* blood. Halfling I may be, or worse, but I still have more power than others. Even *a'saii* like Teirnan.

It was something. And perhaps it was time I used it, to put him in his place.

The gelding snorted, twitching ears forward as he turned his head to intently eye the left side of the track, all aquiver with trepidation. I unhooked the bow, plucked an arrow out of the quiver, nocked it and waited as the gelding halted.

Oddly, I felt relaxed. The odds were different now; Hart would wager on *me*.

The wood was silent. *Too* silent. If they thought they were fooling me—

I laughed aloud, drawing as I raised the bow, and chose my target. Suggesting, in gutter Erinnish, the man give himself up; what would it do to his pride to be pinned to a tree by a woman?

Too much damage, apparently; he slid out of a shadowed copse of elm to stand quietly some ten paces from my gelding, who snorted in noisy alarm but held his ground, thank the gods.

"Aye," I told the man, "you. But then it was not you I was aiming at, but the other man over *there*—" I loosed, sent the arrow thwacking into a trunk, plucked, and nocked a second. "Now, as for *him*—"

It did not take long at all, this time. The second man came around the tree, eyed the arrow askance, grinned, shrugged; pulled it free, unbroken, and brought it to me, presenting it with a flourish as a man might present a woman a long-stemmed flower.

"Leijhana tu'sai." I accepted it, slid it home in the quiver and waited, second arrow still nocked.

They exchanged glances of amusement mingled with rueful consternation.

"Redbeard," I said quietly.

And so they led me to him.

Liam's bastard son sat with his rump on a tree stump, repairing a broken bridle. Deftly he wove leather thong through knife-punched holes, joining the broken halves of a cheek-strap so it was whole again. Beneath fallen blond forelock he frowned; his mouth twisted sideways into his beard as he knotted off the thong, taking care to see it would hold. In his teeth he clenched a piece of leather, working it absently.

Around him others gathered, though none so close as to touch him. Eight men in all, exiled from their homeland. They had the closed-faced look of men who hid a secret, disdaining to show their pain. One man tended a tiny fire, adding wood to the handful of smoking tinder. Another tended his sword, polishing the blade. A third drowsed idly, leaning against a downed log. Yet a fourth threw prophecy bones, or an Erinnish variation.

Rory glanced up from his task as I led the bay into the clearing, with a man on either side. I had put away arrow and bow, since my point was already made, and greeted him empty-handed.

He stopped working the piece of leather in his mouth. Grinned around it, baring teeth, then took it out of his mouth. "Ye see, lass, how we live—reduced to eating leather in place of meat." Sighing dramatically, he shook his head. "Once, there was a time—"

"—when you supped at the lord's own table." I shrugged, unimpressed by his avowal. "And could again, could you not—if Sean survives his broken head?"

He looked at the gnawed piece of leather as if fascinated by it. "I'm doubting it, lass."

"Why? You are Liam's son, and freely acknowledged . . . if all you did was give Sean a headache, no matter how fierce, I hardly think he would want to execute you. He might even take you back."

Rory glanced at his companions. "So we're hoping," he said, "but how are we to know? 'Tis Homana we're in, not Erinn; how many folk here care a whit for the House of Eagles?"

"That, *I* can tell you." And then quickly explained myself. "I mean, I live in Homana-Mujhar. I hear things. If Sean is dead, word will come from Liam. I can pass it to you."

Brows lanced down. "Why would you be doing that? What are we to you?"

"Exiles," I answered quietly. "For twenty-five years the Cheysuli were exiled from Homana, in order to save their own lives during Shaine the Mujhar's purge. I have heard the stories, being privy to many of them within the walls of Homana-Mujhar." I shrugged, glancing briefly at the others, hoping the explanation sound enough. "I know what exile did to the Cheysuli, so long banished from Homana; I would sooner see *you* go home again, than live out your lives here."

Rory gazed at me steadily for a long, uncomfortable moment, scrutinizing my manner. And then he shifted the focus of his stare, looking again at the chewed piece of thong. "We'd be in the way of thanking you, lass, if you could find the truth of the matter."

I pushed the gelding's intrusive muzzle away from my ear. "If Sean is dead, word will come soon enough. The Mujhar will have to be told—"

"—as well as Keely herself." Rory nodded. "No doubt Niall will be looking elsewhere for a husband in order to make an alliance."

"Aye, although he needs Erinnish blood badly—" I broke it off, not wanting to say more than the armsmaster's daughter should know. Although I *could* afford to speak of things other people could not; Rory himself had lived in the shadow of royalty and would understand how such things come to be known to anyone living within palace walls.

Rory checked knots again. "Erinnish blood, is it? Aye, well, he has it in Aileen, and the son she bore the Prince of Homana. 'Tisn't so necessary that Keely and Sean wed . . . 'twill be little more than redundancy, I'm thinking."

I thought of Aileen, sequestered in her bedchamber with Brennan as her watchdog; of Aidan, their sickly son, who might not live to see another year. And no more sons to come after.

Hollowly I said, "One son is not enough."

" 'Twas all *Liam* had . . . excepting me, of course." Rory shrugged. "But then I'm not in line for the throne, even if Sean should die."

I frowned, listening for the sound of Teirnan's ambition, for an inflection of thwarted desire. "And it does not matter to you?"

To do him credit, he thought about it. Then slowly shook his head. "I am what the gods have made me."

"And you have no ambition? Not one hint of curiosity about what it would be like to rule?"

He looked at me intently. "Would *you* want to rule, lass?"

But I will, I answered silently. Aloud, I said, "Depending."

Eyebrows shot up. "On what?"

"On expectations, anticipations . . . what people want from me." I pushed the gelding away from me again. "For a woman, things are—different. Difficult. No woman rules by her own right, not in Homana, nor even Solinde; in no land that I know of." I shook my head. "It is not fair, that a woman—princess or queen—be required to marry in order to govern the realm she was born to. A man is not. A man is free to do as he will."

"But a man—prince or king—is required to marry in order to get sons, *legitimate* sons, to inherit after him." Rory sighed, stroking mustaches. "Not so different, I'm thinking, when he'd rather do his own choosing, of time *and* woman." Brown eyes glinted a little. "Sean had no choice, did he? He was told he would marry Keely."

"Aye," I agreed sourly, "they were pledged before she was born."

Rory grinned, then laughed. "Well now, lass, d'ye see? 'Tis not so bad being who we are after all, is it? We're free to wed or not, as we choose, and *who* . . . no one binds our wills by royal whim or prophecy." More quietly, he said, "We're free people, my lass, bound by nothing but ourselves."

For all of our lives Corin and I had held conversations concerning the privileges of rank, of race, of heritage, so certain of our own. We had discussed the requirements of that rank, the dictates of our *tahlmorras*, what we could offer to the world because of our heritage. We had been insular, arrogant, too certain of our power, believing no one other than a Cheysuli could understand what we felt, because they were *lir*less and therefore unblessed, trapped in a lifespan lacking the magic of the *lir*-gifts, the power of our heritage.

Now, listening to Rory, I realized it had nothing to do with race. Men are born with eyes and ears; few of them know how to use them.

I drew in a breath, changing the subject. "I have come to make a trade."

Rory grunted, chewing idly at one of his mustaches. "That brown castrated lad in exchange for my fleet-footed boyo? I'm not such a fool as that."

"He is a fine horse—"

"No doubt," he agreed, "but I'm liking the one I have."

I chewed my bottom lip. "And your knife for mine."

He glanced at the knife snugged in the sheath at my belt, then back to my face. "No, I'm thinking not."

I bit back frustration. "And this warbow."

That put the light of interest into his eyes. "Let me see it, lass."

I unhooked and handed it over as he rose. Rory took it, examined it, felt the silk of the wood, the power, the promise of accuracy. Then waggled fingers in crude request for an arrow.

That, too, I handed over. He glanced around quickly, spied a likely target, nocked, pulled, aimed, loosed. The arrow sang its flight and thunked home in the trunk of a beech.

Rory nodded, though mostly to himself. He nodded, caressed the wood, turned back to me. "I've not seen its like before. We have bows in Erinn, but none so compact as this."

"A Cheysuli warbow," I said. "Designed for ease of hunting, perverted by Shaine's *qu'mahlin*." I drew in a calming breath. "For the colt and my knife, I give you the gelding and warbow."

He looked at the bow, the gelding, pursing lips thoughtfully. Lines formed between his brows. Then he shook his head.

"Why *not?*" I cried "By the gods, Erinnish, no man other than a Cheysuli has ever claimed an Cheysuli bow as his own, except for—" I stopped.

Slowly, Rory grinned. "Except?"

I plowed doggedly ahead; it was too late to turn back. "Carillon," I told him. "The man who ended Shaine's purge."

Rory's expression was momentarily blank. Then, vaguely, he nodded. "Oh, aye, I recall the name, I'm thinking . . . Homanan history is not my own." He looked at the bow again. " 'Tis sorry I am, lass, but why should I trouble myself to trade when I can easily take?"

"Take—"

"Both horses," he said, *"and* the warbow, lass—are you forgetting I'm a thief?" And he gestured to the man closest me, on the other side of the gelding.

He put out his hand to take the reins, but did not. The Erinnish knife I now carried was sharp as any other; the brigand learned precisely *how* sharp.

I turned, swung up into the saddle, reined the horse into a pivot to send the two closest men dodging, then reined him around again so I could face Rory. He was grinning at me broadly, idly cursing the man I had cut. "Once was enough," I told him, "I learn my lessons quickly. This one stays with me."

And crashed back through to the track, leaving them all behind.

I did not go far. Only far enough to mislead them into believing I really *was* gone. Then I slowed the gelding, turned off the track once again, rode through trees and foliage to a close-grown copse of brushy fir. I jumped off, tied the gelding securely, started back toward Rory's encampment. On foot, this time, with no intention of warning them, or of giving myself away. I would locate them, wait patiently for my chance, slip in and free the colt, stealing Brennan's horse back from thieves—

An arm locked around my throat. A hand plucked my knife free of sheath. Quietly, a familiar voice said, "I want to talk with you."

Ten

I froze in disbelief. "Teir?"

The arm did not relax, forcing up my chin so the back of my skull rested against my shoulders. The rope burn on my neck stung, protesting the pressure. I knew better than to struggle, or to attempt to assume *lir*-shape. He could choke me down too easily, before I could make the change.

"To *talk*," he stressed, "no more. You are my cousin, Keely—do you think I want to harm you?"

My voice was strained from the weight of his arm against my throat. "You may not *want* to harm me, but you would, and quickly enough, if you thought it would aid your cause."

His breath tickled my ear. Teir's tone was dry. "I am not so desperate as that."

I hated my helplessness. Another man I might try, but Teirnan was unpredictable, while easily able to predict *me*. "What do you want, Teir?"

"To talk," he repeated. "I told you so before; I do so again. But this time I have brought allies, so you understand I am serious. This is not a game, Keely . . . it is the survival of our race."

Staying trapped as I was would do no good. I gave him my acquiescence.

Teirnan released me at once and stepped aside. I swung around, saw how many were with him, did not move again. But inwardly, I grieved.

So many a'saii, *so many* kin-wrecked *Cheysuli*—

I did not bother to count them. I knew the number was higher yet, for women and children had gone with them, and none of them were here, only warriors and their *lir*. In nearly two years Teirnan had collected a clan of his own,

lured away from others, dividing the Cheysuli over an issue
that touched us all.

Striking first was required, or Teir would win the moment. "Is it worth the loss of the afterworld?"

It was what none of them expected, even Teir. Argument, anger, even name-calling. But not a simple question.
Not one such as that.

Teirnan stirred. I struck again. "I know you believe what
you do is right. But think what it will cost you."

Fifty or sixty of them, and *lir*, melding with the trees. So
still, so silent, so calm, gathering in the shadows. In Homanan parlance, perhaps not so very many. But a warrior with
his *lir* is worth several of any Homanan; Teirnan had gathered an army.

"Sit," my cousin said, "and I will tell you precisely *what*
it shall cost us—if we serve the prophecy."

"Teirnan—"

"*Sit*, Keely. Please."

I sat. Put my back against a tree. Let my kinsman talk.

He was quiet, for Teir. Also distinctly sincere. I had expected dramatics or fanaticism; what he gave me was belief.
A pronounced, abiding conviction that his way was the
right one; that if we ignored it, we would die.

At first he paced in front of me, working out his words.
Clearly he felt how he spoke was as important as what he
said, forgoing his usual manner. He was a different man.
Oddly, it frightened me.

He stopped pacing, turned to me, knelt down to look
into my face. "I have done none of this out of whim," he
said. "I have done none of this out of idle envy or jealousy.
I am ambitious, aye, to a fault . . . I think I am more suited
than Brennan—" he leaned forward intently, "—but I
swear, Keely, *I swear*—there is much more to it than that."

Slowly I shook my head. "How can there be, Teir? You
have always wanted the Lion. Ceinn made certain of that."

Teirnan nodded intent agreement. "Aye, aye, of *course*
he did—do you blame him? His *cheysula* was *rujholla* to
the Mujhar, and Ceinn himself is of a purer line of descent
than even the House of Homana. The Lion is *Cheysuli*,
not Homanan—who better to claim it than a warrior of
Ceinn's descent?"

I started to speak, but he cut me off with a raised hand.

"And now you have turned me from the track . . . Keely, you must hear me and understand me. There is much more at stake now than the Lion, *far* more—"

"How can there be?" I snapped. "Holding the Lion Throne is part of the prophecy."

Teirnan's eyes caught fire. "Aye, *aye*—and it is wrong. The prophecy itself is wrong; you serve a perverted relic." I had heard this nonsense before. I tried to tell him so, but he easily overrode me. "Keely, you have stronger gifts than any woman of the clans since Alix, our great-granddame. You know what it is to have the freedom, the *power* of *lir*-shape—what it is to fly the skies—what it is to go in cat-shape, or any form you desire—" Again he shifted forward, eyes fixed on my own. "You know better than anyone else *can* what it is to converse with the *lir*, to share in private thoughts, to have the earth magic at your beck—"

I was growing impatient. "Aye, Teir, I *know*—"

His tone hushed itself. "But what if you did not? What if you *could* not—if the power was stripped from you?"

I shook my head. "Not possible, Teir. The *lir*-gifts are gods-given—"

He was close to laughing in frustration at what he perceived as my ignorance. "And what if the *gods* did it? What if they took those gifts away and made you as all the others? An unblessed Homanan woman, with less freedom than ever before."

"Teir, you are a fool—"

He slid forward on his knees, caught my hands, held them against his chest. "I swear by all that I am, I think they *will* do it. When the prophecy is completed, the First-born will rule again, uniting four realms and two races, with nothing left over for us." He gripped my hands tightly. "*I swear by my* lir, Keely, this is not a trick. I mean what I say: the gods will take back the gifts and give them to the Firstborn."

It was suddenly painful to swallow. "What *need*, Teir? Why should they do such a thing?"

"Think," he said earnestly, "recall all the lessons, the histories the *shar tahls* taught us when we were growing up. Think of the prophecy itself, and the story of how it was shaped for us."

"Teir—"

"*Think*, Keely! Think back, remember, recall the focus of what we are taught: the Firstborn had all the gifts, men and women alike . . . but they grew too inbred, diluting the blood and the magic. And so the gods formed two races out of one, portioning out the gifts; some to the Cheysuli, some to the Ihlini." He paused, jaw set very tight. "In hopes that someday Cheysuli would breed with Ihlini and fix the gifts once more."

"Why would the gods want their children to fight?" I asked. "We are enemies, Teir—"

"Again, I ask you to think." His intensity died away, replaced with quiet appeal. "We are enemies now, aye, but was it always so? Were we *born* enemies, or did something happen to cause a rift, a schism—a bloodfeud that holds even now?" He raised a silencing hand. "Think of the Ihlini and what we have learned of them; what even the Mujhar claims: not all are engaged against us. Not all serve Asar-Suti, but the old Solindish gods not so different from our own." He smiled. "Perhaps the gods are one and the same, just as Ihlini and Cheysuli."

I pulled my hands free of his, dumbfounded by his claims. "You are saying—"

"—that it took an outside influence to plunge Ihlini and Cheysuli into interracial war. That perhaps a few ambitious Ihlini—possibly only one—decided the natural gifts were not enough. To rule he needed more, and turned to the Seker." Teirnan spread his hands. "Thus spawning a *third* race: Strahan and others like him, with power distinctly augmented by the god of the netherworld."

I licked dry lips. "Then, according to you, the prophecy is more than the unification of races and realms, but a joining of power as well."

Slowly Teirnan nodded. "And once that power is unified, dilution is undesirable. Why not take it all and put it into one vessel? It is concentrated, *augmented*—there is no need for dilution. Dilution is undesirable; so are those who dilute."

I stroked hair from my eyes. "But why, if the Firstborn grew so inbred in the first place, do the gods desire to create them again?"

"Because now there is other blood thrown into the cook-pot." Teir's eyes were bright. "Foreign spices, Keely, to make the stew taste better . . . to strengthen the heart of it."

"Gods," I said. "If it is true—if all this added blood does *indeed* strengthen the Firstborn—what will they become?"

"Children of the gods."

"But that is what—"

"—Cheysuli means, aye." Teir nodded. "We came first, Keely: *we* were the Firstborn, until they split us apart. Until they created the Ihlini." He sat back on his heels. "What need will there be for us? What need for the Ihlini? We are both of us sentenced to death."

It shook me. "Gods, Teir, you sound like *Strahan*—"

"—because he is not so wrong."

It was blasphemy. I shuddered once, shook my head vehemently. "He wants all of us *dead!*"

"He wants the prophecy broken." Teirnan sighed. "His methods are violent, aye, and deadly for those of our House, but I understand his reasons. How else do you break the prophecy than by destroying those it involves—"

"And if it *is*—"

"Then we will be free of destruction, Keely . . . free to be *free* again!"

His conviction was overwhelming. "You cannot be saying you wish to serve Strahan or the Seker—"

Teir was adamant. "No, only *myself*. Not Strahan, his god; not even *our* gods, Keely . . . only to serve myself. To have free will again, not bound by any *tahlmorra;* to be free of such burdensome rituals made to protect our fragile honor—"

"Teirnan, *no!*" I cried. "You are free to renounce your honor as you wish, but I am not so quick."

"No, nor was I." For a moment pain undermined his conviction, muting the fire in him. "It was not—easy. In no way. What we are, each of us—what we become—is shaped from birth to fit prescribed behavior patterns, all bound up in honor codes and rituals, in the name of Cheysuli gods. It becomes a sacred duty, cloaked in the mystery of faith—but as a way of enforcement, a means of *manipulation* . . . because if we were given absolute freedom of choice, would we choose to complete the prophecy? Or turn our backs on it, leaving the gods without the First-born?" He was solemn now, clearly cognizant of what he said, and of what he advocated. "Even the afterworld—is there really an afterworld?—is something we are promised since birth." Teirnan shook his head. "But how do we *know*, Keely? How can we be certain? All we know is what we are told, being taught by other Cheysuli who were taught identical things. Is there room for honesty? Or only for superstition?"

"But you renounced *everything*."

"Because I felt I had to." Teir inhaled deeply, as if requiring strength. "Keely—if Strahan came to you one day and demanded all your *lir*-gifts, would you give them up without a fight? Would you make something holy of it?"

All I could do was deny it, knowing full well the ramifications of what he asked, what he implied; knowing also it made sense. A certain symmetry.

I looked beyond him, to the others. I looked at warriors and *lir*, gathered in the shadows, and wondered how anyone could have foreseen this. It was not in the prophecy. So many things are, though many only fragments like overheard conversations distorted by distance and interruption. And so many things are not, almost as if the gods—or the Firstborn, who wrote the prophecy—had wanted no one to know the full truth. Because, if Teir was right, to know it gave us the freedom to deny it; now, we only served, with unthinking obedience.

I shut my eyes tightly, resting my head on drawn-up knees. *Oh, gods, if Teir is right—*

"What is the difference?" he asked. "Ihlini, Cheysuli, god. They will strip us of our gifts in order to give them to someone else."

I raised my head and looked into the face of certitude, the eyes of a Cheysuli. And knew, looking at him, he had not forfeited his honor. He was as dedicated to the preservation of his race as anyone else I knew.

But Teirnan risked more; in that, he was alone.

I knew what he wanted. And how badly he needed it. "The difference—" I swallowed. "The difference *is*, you want too much."

"A little thing, Keely."

"The destruction of the prophecy is not a little thing."

"But you will never see it." He was very calm now.

"Such things take time, certainly longer than you and I have."

My chest felt tight. "Teir—"

Quietly, he said, "What I ask is what you want."

I stared in disbelief.

Teirnan's tone was gentle. "Refuse the Erinnish prince. Bear him no children, Keely. It will be more than enough."

Oh, gods—

Gods?

Eleven

I sat locked in silence for a long time after Teir and the
other *a'saii* faded back into the wood. Alone with my
thoughts, my conscience, clutching drawn-up knees and
staring at nothing, I pondered the enormity of what Teirnan
had told me, considering ramifications. And realized I could
not deal with them.

My belly twisted. I felt *dirty* somehow, as if Teir had
drawn me into a web of deceit, when all he had done was
to tell me what he thought, and why, and how it might
affect us. How it might affect me.

Might. He was not—could not *be*—certain; how could
he? All he could be was committed to the cause of the
a'saii: in his new world he was clanleader, *shar tahl*,
prophet; heretic, traitor, *kin-wrecked* in the old one. Heavy
words, each of them; heavier implications.

I shut my eyes, driving fingernails into knees. *If what he
says is true . . . if the* lir *do leave us*—

I had no specific *lir*, but the loss of the bond between
the *lir* and the Cheysuli as a race was enough to strip me
and everyone else of the magic we tapped so unthinkingly.
And to consider myself unblessed, like the Homanans,
empty of magic, of flight, of *freedom*—

Gods, it was impossible.

Or was it possible Teir was right?

I swore, thrust myself up from the ground, threaded my
way back to my gelding, whom Rory would not have in
place of Brennan's colt. Well, time for that later. I had no
more taste for sneaking into the Erinnish camp and stealing
back the chestnut; Teir's words had stripped me of everything save the desire to go home to Homana-Mujhar, where
I could think about what he had said.

What he had *suggested*, knowing it might not be my

choice after all. That I might aid his cause even against my will. *Because I could not marry a dead man.*

I untied the gelding, swung up, turned him back to the track. Went home at a pace Brennan would decry, not knowing the circumstances, the turmoil in my belly.

Brennan could not even comprehend there existed a choice.

Fleetingly, I thought, *It must be easy for him, knowing his path so well . . . being so certain of his* tahlmorra.

And wishing, not for the first time, that I could be so certain.

This time when I knocked on Aileen's door, I was admitted at once. Brennan was gone; the chamber was full of Erinnish and Homanan ladies. At Aileen's quiet request, they departed, leaving the two of us alone.

She was ensconced in the huge drapery-bedecked bed, weighed down by coverlets. The brilliant red hair was unbound, spilling down either side of her face to form ropes across the silk. There were smudges beneath green eyes, but otherwise her color was not so bad. Clearly, she would survive.

Guilt churned in my belly. I ignored it, retreating into inanities. "Where is Brennan?"

Aileen smiled a little. "I sent him away to sleep. He refused, of course, but I told him his face was enough to be giving me bad dreams. So, in the end, he went."

I nodded, looking at anything but Aileen. Slowly I wandered around the chamber, picking up trinkets and putting them down, rearranging things, drifting eventually to a casement. Outside it was nearly evening. Inside the candles were glowing.

"Keely." Her tone was gentle. " 'Twasn't your fault."

I made no answer, staring blindly out the casement.

"It had begun before, earlier; I was afraid to be telling them. I meant to tell *you*—" But she broke it off.

I swung to face her. "Aye, you meant to tell me, but I refused to listen." Guilt pinched again. "As Ian has pointed out, it is a habit of mine."

"I value your honesty more than I can say, Keely . . . betimes I think there's far too little in the world." She shifted a little in the bed, rearranging bedclothes. "If anyone is for blaming you, send him straight to me. No matter who it is."

"Well then, I am here." I waved her protest away. "No, no, enough of that—how do you fare, Aileen? That is more important."

"How do I fare?" The green eyes dimmed a little. "Well enough in body—the Mujhar has seen to that—but not so well in spirit."

I looked for a stool, found one, hooked it over and sat down. Quietly I suggested, "Perhaps it was for the best."

Her tone was inflexible. "Losing bairns is never for the best, Keely. How could it be?"

I bit back the passion I longed to release, knowing now was not the time. "At least you were not lost as well."

Aileen grimaced. "Aye, so Brennan said . . . but I can't be helping it, Keely. I'm thinking of my poor sickly Aidan. I'm thinking of Homana. I'm thinking of a barren woman who one day will be queen."

I tried to make my tone light. "It is nothing new to Homana; you are hardly the first. Our House is built on fragile foundations. Shaine himself could get no heirs, even on a second *cheysula*. Carillon sired only a daughter—" Abruptly, I thought of Caro, the deaf-mute bastard who lived in Solinde, "—at least, on Electra." I shrugged. "Donal provided two sons, but only one was legitimate." I smiled crookedly. "Until my *jehan* and his brood, the Lion was poor in sons."

"And now, more than ever, the Lion is needing them." Aileen's expression was pensive. "I'm not meaning to sound sorry for myself, nor to blame the gods for taking the bairns away—" she sighed, "—but I've been here long enough to know how important the prophecy is to the Cheysuli. Corin told me much of it in Erinn—" Aileen broke that off almost at once, reflexively, flicking a betraying glance at me. Then continued in a newer, firmer tone. "Brennan, too, has told me, and the Mujhar himself, how important it is for this House to hold the Lion. They'd neither of them claim me a failure, but this must be of concern. One son for the Prince of Homana? And he a sickly boy?" Aileen shook her head. "I know how Niall must fret, though he will say naught of it. And I know how Brennan feels, though he tries to hide it away." She grimaced. "He is such a stalwart defender of the prophecy, of the Cheysuli, of the *tahlmorra* so binding on all of you."

"What about *you?*" I asked. "How does Aileen feel?"

Her voice was very quiet. "I grieve for the bairns; both boys, they said. And I grieve for my barrenness, knowing no more will be born. But—I'm thinking I also grieve for you."

"Me!" I stared. "Why?"

Aileen's eyes locked on my own. "Because now it falls to you. Now more than ever, they'll be needing you wed to Sean. And soon, I'd wager. They'll be wanting children of you in haste, in case Aidan should die. To protect the bloodlines, Keely . . . to fulfill the prophecy."

I stared blankly at Aileen.

Her tone was infinitely gentle. " 'Tis sorry I am," she said. "I know how you feel, Keely. But I'll be promising you again, as I have so many times: Sean is a man worth having."

And if he is dead? I wondered. *Of what worth is he then?*

Or if he lived, and I refused to marry him for fear of losing the *lir* and all the magic of the Cheysuli. Was any man worth that?

I rose. "Rest you well, Aileen. And know that your lost bairns are in the halls of the *cileann*."

For the merest moment she smiled, and then the tears spilled over. I went out the door and closed it, leaving her to her grief.

I ate supper in my chambers, being disinclined to talk with others of my family, and wasted most of the early evening lost in thought, pacing the floor like a caged beast. I weighed Teir's words against those I had been taught by the *shar tahls* as a child, knowing Teir had been taught them as well. It was a wheel turning and turning, raised for repair and going nowhere; spinning, spinning, spinning, made of useless motion, wasted effort, profitless thought.

Again and again I came back to the beginning. If I refused Sean, as Teir desired—as *I* desired—only one child would carry the Erinnish bloodline so necessary to the prophecy. The last bloodline required; we had all of the others, save Ihlini. And even Ihlini, at that, if you counted Brennan's bastard on Rhiannon, or counted Rhiannon herself.

Aidan. The sole offspring of the coupling between a Homanan-Atvian-Solindish-Cheysuli prince, and an Erinnish-Atvian princess. The necessary link. And possibly enough, if he survived to wed and sire children of his own.

But if he did not, it left the Lion without the proper blood. It left the link broken, the prophecy incomplete . . . unless I married Sean and provided the children Aileen and my *rujho* could not.

The wheel turned once more, and came around again to me.

I stopped dead in the center of my chamber. And then went swiftly out of it to visit my brother's son.

The nursery was empty save for Aidan. Ordinarily he was attended night and day, but his woman had, for the moment, slipped out. The room was made of shadows, heavy and deep, born of a single candle. Light crept into the massive cradle and glinted off silver thread, caressed the creamy richness of aged ivory, glistened faintly from smooth-skinned oak.

The cradle was very old. It had housed infants born to the House of Homana for many, many years. The bedding was fine, soft linen, the coverlets of blue-gray silk with the royal lion crest sewn on in silver thread. Altogether too ostentatious for a baby, I thought, but then it was not my place to judge.

Beneath the silk of the coverlet was flesh too pale, thin hair burnished red in the wan candleglow. Blue-veined lids hid yellow eyes; awake, Aidan showed both sides of his heritage. Asleep, he showed only Aileen.

He was small for a baby nearly ten months old. He cried easily, tired quickly, was fractious most of the time. No one knew what ailed him, suggesting only that his protracted birth had somehow affected his health. He caught chills easily even in temperate weather, and seemed unable to fight off the little indispositions that childhood often brings.

I shook my head slightly. Such a little lump beneath the covers. Such a large one in the prophecy; one day he would rule Homana.

Locking hands on the ivory edges of the cradle, I leaned down a little, to make certain he heard me. In his dreams, if nowhere else; it was important that he know. "It comes to you," I told him. "Not to me; to *you*. The Lion will be yours."

Aidan's answer was silence, save for the sound of uneven breathing.

"You are the son of Brennan, Prince of Homana . . . the grandson of Niall the Mujhar . . . great-grandson of Donal, who was the son of Duncan himself." My hands tightened on ancient ivory. "And of your *jehana* you are born of the House of Eagles from the Aerie in Erinn, perched upon the cliffs of Kilore. Liam is in you, and Shea, and all the other lords." I drew in a constricted breath. "So much heritage, little fox . . . so much power in your blood—"

"—and so much weakness in his body?"

I twitched, caught my breath, stared hard into the darkness of a deep, unlighted corner. It was Brennan, of course; I should have known he would be present.

I drew in a calming breath, feeling my heartbeats slow. "Aileen said you were sleeping."

"Earlier, aye—for a little." I could see nothing of his face save its shape, but his tone made it unnecessary. He was worn to the bone, my brother, and in need of more than sleep. "But I dreamed my boy was dead, and the Lion in deadly peril."

In view of the situation, the revelation did not surprise me. "May I light another candle?"

"If you like."

I liked. I lit a second candle, set it into its cup, looked more closely at my brother. The light was not good, but better than before. Now I could see his face. Now I could see his eyes.

I caught my breath up short. Then slowly let it out. "You cannot know," I told him.

"That he will die?" Slumped deeply in a chair, Brennan shrugged raggedly. "No, of course not—but I can fear it. I think every parent does. But I have more cause than most; you have only to look at him, to *hold* him—" He broke it off, pressing fingers against his temples. "—gods—I am tired. Forgive my bad company."

"Rujho—"

As always, he did not shirk the truth, nor seek to hide it from me. "There will be no more, Keely. The physicians have confirmed it."

It took me a moment to answer. "I know. Aileen told me."

He pulled his hands away from his head. "Aidan is all there is—all there can *ever* be, now; what happens if he dies?"

I had not expected such bluntness from him, especially in this place, nor at this moment. But he had brought it up, and I was free to say what I would.

Or ask what I could ask.

I turned from the cradle to face him. "What *does* happen, Brennan? There must be a Prince of Homana. There must be an heir to the Lion."

He looked older than twenty-three. More like *forty*-three. "There are—alternatives."

I opened my mouth to ask him what they were, not being versed in all the responsibilities of kingcraft, then shut it again sharply. I knew. Looking at him, I knew. Nothing else would hurt him so. "Such as setting aside a barren *cheysula* and taking another woman."

His tone was flat and empty. "It is the only provision in Homanan law for setting aside a wife."

Carefully, I observed, "Men have done it before. Princes, too; kings in particular, when sons are needed for thrones."

He did not flinch, being Brennan, who faces truths with equal honesty. "Aye, they have," he agreed, "but *this* prince—or king—will not do any such thing."

So. There it was: Brennan's commitment was made. I had expected no other answer, but it is always worth the asking. One can never be certain.

I looked at Aidan again, stirring in his sleep. Delicate, fragile Aidan, meant for too heavy a burden. It might be the killing of him. Steadfastly, I stared at Aidan, refusing to look at Brennan. Not wanting to see the pain. "If he dies, you have no heir. None of your body."

He answered easily. "No. And unlikely to get another." Now I did look at him. "Next after you is Hart."

Brennan shook his head. "Not now. *Jehan* has made it clear: on the day of his death, Solinde and Atvia no longer owe fealty to Homana. They become autonomous, subject only to their own lords. Hart will have Solinde to rule as he will, just as Corin will have Atvia. I can hardly strip Solinde of her king simply to give Homana a prince." He shook his head slowly. "*Jehan* is right to make it so, but it muddles the line of succession."

"Only because a man must be Mujhar." I lifted a single shoulder as well as single eyebrow. "*I* am left, after all. But Council would never approve."

Brennan sighed wearily: he had heard my tone before. "There is a reason, Keely, that the Lion requires a man—"

"*What* reason?" I asked. "A woman is more likely to keep a land at peace instead of war."

"Possibly," he conceded, "but there is another reason. A more compelling reason—"

"Tradition," I said in derision.

"Childbirth," he countered succinctly.

Frowning, I stared at him. "What?"

Slowly Brennan rose, pushing himself out of his chair. He crossed the room to the cradle, smoothed the coverlet over Aidan, lingered to caress the silk of his hair. "Childbirth," he repeated. "A ruler must beget heirs. As many as possible, to insure the line of succession."

"Aye," I agreed, thinking it obvious; we had been discussing it in depth.

"A woman risks her life each time she bears a child. A woman ruler would risk more than her life . . . she would also risk her realm." His tone was gentle. "I know you are strong, Keely, and you would make a fine Mujhar . . . but bearing a child every year is no way to rule Homana."

No, it was not. "And yet you willingly pack me off to Erinn so I may give *Sean* his heirs."

"More than that, perhaps." His fingers stroked red hair. "If Aidan dies, there is only you. From your union with Sean will come the next link in the prophecy. Perhaps the final one."

I thought of Rory and Teir. One perhaps a murderer, the other in fact a traitor. And caught between them was Sean, one way or another.

Folding my arms, I turned away. Took three paces, hugging myself; swung back, facing Brennan. "Men die," I said tautly. "What happens if Sean dies?"

Brennan frowned. "I hardly think—"

"Men *die*," I said again. "He is young, aye, and healthy, but men do die. Of illness, injury . . . murder." I drew in a deep breath. "What happens if Sean *dies?*"

Brennan stared back at me. At first I thought he would not answer, and then I saw he would. But he hated it. He *hated* it, did Brennan; I saw it in eyes and posture, in the tautness of his mouth.

He answered it with questions. "Who after me is left? What warrior of our blood? What warrior of our *House?*"

Only rarely is Brennan bitter. But I thought he had just cause.

"Teirnan," I said. "Oh—*gods*—"

PART II

One

Lio closed one pale eye as he screwed up his face in ferocious contemplation. It was a good face, young and boldly mobile, and without doubt better served by another expression (or so a few of Aileen's Erinnish ladies had told me once or twice), but he paid little mind to the effect. I had made a request—no, extended an *invitation*—and he was considering.

At length, he sighed and shook his head. "Lady, I should not. The Mujhar himself has forbidden it."

Progress. Lio had said should not, not *can*not. I favored him with an eloquent—and pronounced—assessment, then shook my head in resignation. "One way of protecting your pride, I suppose . . . ah, well, it might have been worth a wager or two." I shrugged, smiling warmly. "Perhaps another time."

Pale eyebrows lanced down. Lio is very blond and faircomplected, with eyes the color of water. Homanan-born and bred, but some say there is Solindish blood in him somewhere, going by his color; Carillon's Solindish wife, Electra, had identical hair and eyes, and Hart's Ilsa is as fair. As far as Lio or anyone else knows he is pure Homanan; but the jest is repeated often merely to ruffle his feathers.

"Protecting my pride?" he asked sharply. "What do you mean?"

I lifted an eloquent shoulder. "Just that one way of making certain you do not lose to me—a *woman*—is not to try at all."

He scowled, chewing bottom lip. Lio and I are much alike in pride and temperament, which means I know the tricks to winning acquiescence even when he has no wish to give it. At the moment he did not, and for good reason;

the Mujhar *had* forbidden it. But I had no intention of letting that stop me.

Now all I had to do was convince Lio not to let it stop *him*.

He sighed, shaking his head. "It would be no true contest," he told me. "I am taller, heavier, stronger—and I have won the Lady's favor two years in a row at Summerfair."

I nodded grave acknowledgment. Deirdre's favor consisted of a length of gold-freighted silk dyed bright Erinnish green; it bought him supper at the High Table in Homana-Mujhar each night for a week during Summerfair, which is a boon all young men in the Mujharan Guard pray for. It is a way of catching the Mujhar's personal interest, so that advancement through the ranks may consequently be hastened.

Lio had indeed won the favor twice, and my father's interest was subsequently piqued. Clearly, Lio had no wish to risk losing royal favor by going against the Mujhar's orders; neither did he wish to lose *my* favor. Because, after all, I too could pique the Mujhar's personal interest. Certainly more often than once a year during Summerfair.

Sometimes entirely *too* often.

I lifted my hands briefly, let them slap down at my sides. "So, we will never know who is better with a blade . . . and you will spend your nights wondering." I grinned, arching brows. "Unless, of course, we contest to see if battle *can* be joined."

Lio frowned. "What do you mean?"

I glanced around the bailey. Mostly empty of people, it nonetheless was filled with possibilities. I swung back to Lio. "A race," I suggested. "To the wall and back." I tapped knuckles lightly against the guardroom door. "Whosoever touches this door first, wins. If it is you, your duty to the Mujhar is satisfied. But if *I* win, you meet me with your sword."

Lio looked at the distant wall. Back to the door. Considered it.

"A simple race," I told him. "Nothing more than to the wall and back."

He stared at me a long assessive moment, then unbuckled his belt and stripped out of his leather doublet, dropping it and the belt to the bench by the door. Off-duty, he had left off the crimson tabard with the black rampant lion sewn onto the left breast. Now he faced me in linen undertunic, leather trews, boots. And determination.

We lined up with right legs extended, left heels against the door. "Knock," I suggested. "When it opens, we run."

Lio knocked. After a moment it opened, and we were gone.

The bailey is cobbled. No such surface can be perfectly level, and the bailey is hardly that. Centuries of summer rains and winter snows, boots and iron-shod hooves have worn pockets in the cobbles, crumbled the edges, even cracked a stone or two. But we ignored it all, and ran.

He beat me to the wall, as I expected. And, as I expected, he thrust off and was four strides ahead of me by the time I slapped and spun. But the lead meant nothing to me. In the end, I would win.

Lio was halfway back to the door. Laughing. Wasting his breath. Secure in the knowledge he would not forfeit his duty to the Mujhar to the Mujhar's daughter.

Any of my brothers would have known better. We had played this game before. Hart had invented it.

Five strides off the wall, I traded flesh for feathers. And beat him easily to the door.

Lio slapped wood as I completed the change back into human form. I folded my arms and leaned against the door. Grinning. "Fetch your sword, soldier."

He was only a little out of breath, and mostly from the shock. "You—you said—" He paused and tried again. "You said a *race*, lady!"

"It was. To the wall and back." I raised disingenuous brows. "No one required it to be on foot."

He sucked in wind to protest again, thought back over what we had said, realized I had caught him. No indeed, no one had specified a *foot*race. Merely a race.

Lio sighed, knowing defeat when it spat in his eye. "I will fetch my sword." And went inside the guardroom.

My own blade, sheathed, lay on the bench beside the door, covered by Lio's doublet. I unearthed it, unsheathed it, admired the clean sleek line of blade in the sunlight. It had been made for me specifically, not ground down from a man's blade, which meant the balance was perfect.

Such a magnificent thing, the sword. I wondered, as I had countless other times, why the Cheysuli disdained it so, refusing to learn its use. Tradition, again; clan-born warriors felt men should fight face to face, and very close, instead of at the greater distance a sword provided. It had something to do with pride and skill; the belief that a man should taste the strength of his opponent, and his blood, in order to make the fight truly honorable. For the same reason the bow had originated for hunting, not battle, but Shaine's *qu'mahlin* had perverted its use.

Yet tradition changed, if slowly. Now Cheysuli born to the House of Homana learned the sword, and had ever since my grandsire, Donal, inherited Carillon's broadsword with its massive pommel ruby. Even though my own father had given the sword to the Womb of the Earth on Donal's death, the legacy survived. My father and my brothers had learned the art of the sword, and its strength. Certainly its beauty. So had I.

And would go on learning it, regardless of my father.

Lio returned with his sword. He saw me with mine, sighed, shut one eye again. "If he learns of this, I will be stripped of my rank."

"You have no rank," I pointed out.

My words put color in his face and prickles in his tone. "If I win the favor again *this* year, the Mujhar must make me an officer. It is well known. The Mujhar rewards excellence—in duty *and* swordskill."

I eyed him sourly. "Then consider this bout practice for Summerfair."

"At Summerfair, we fight *men*." Lio grinned as I muttered imprecations against his parentage. "Now we are even, lady."

I pointed away from the door. "There."

We struck stances, tapped blades, prepared. But before we could properly begin, Lio broke off, staring past my shoulder. He went red, then white, then shut his eyes and muttered something beneath his breath. His blade was no longer at the ready; clearly, someone was approaching. Someone whose mere presence was enough to stop the bout before it even began.

Oh, gods—not jehan—

I turned. No, not *jehan*. But just as bad: Brennan.

He calmly crossed the bailey at a pace eloquent in its idleness. Sunlight struck slashes of light from the heavy *lir*-bands on bare arms. He wore Cheysuli leathers dyed black, as he often did; Brennan says he merely prefers unremarkable colors, but *I* think he knows perfectly well the color, on him, is dramatic: black leathers, black hair, dark skin, yellow eyes. He is not Homanan handsome, as Corin is or our father had been before Strahan's hawk had taken an eye, but all Cheysuli, with classic Cheysuli looks.

Some might call such looks too bold, too fierce, too arrogant. Too *feral* for their tastes.

Others might recall the magnificence of a mountain cat in motion; the stoop of a hawk after prey. And know better.

Brennan smiled. I frowned.

"Disobeying *jehan's* orders?" he asked cheerfully. "Aye, well, you would hardly be Keely if you did not."

Lio muttered again. Crossly, I told him to go back inside the guardroom if he could not bear to face the Prince of Homana, who was not precisely his liege lord; not *yet*, and in no imminent danger of becoming so, since the Mujhar was in significantly excellent health . . . which meant, I pointed out, Brennan could hardly censure Lio for transgressions not yet committed, and likely *not* to be committed, now, since Lio was sheathing his sword.

Muttering.

I scowled at Brennan. "*Jehan* sent you."

He smiled. "No."

He was blatantly unconcerned with what our father might think of my behavior, which was unlike him. Brennan had been the dutiful heir for as long as I could recall, even as a child aware of the responsibilities attendant upon his title. Although he had faced, as we all did, parental—and royal—disfavor in younger years, such disfavor for Brennan was rare, and usually the result of actions taken on behalf of Hart or Corin. While not a talebearer, Brennan was hardly reluctant to point out failings in comportment if he thought it warranted.

Lio had not gone inside the guardroom. Probably because Brennan had not given him leave to, although none was required; Lio was ambitious. Also genuinely apprehensive.

"My lord." He inclined his head to Brennan, who smiled at him vaguely and reached out to take my sword from me.

"May I?" Brennan asked.

I gave the sword into his keeping, waiting suspiciously.

Brennan tested the weight, the balance, examined the blade itself Nodded thoughtfully, then glanced past me to Lio. And gave my sword to him. "Would you sheathe it and tend it for the lady? We are going riding, and have no need of swords."

"Riding! Brennan, wait—"

"*Leijhana tu'sai,*" Brennan said easily as Lio quickly did as asked. Then he put a hand on my arm, turned me away from the guardroom, guided me across the bailey. "Aileen is feeling much better, thank the gods. I am taking her to Joyenne for the summer."

It surprised me. "You will stay away from Mujhara that long?"

He shook his head. "Not I, perhaps—*jehan* will have things for me to do—but I think Aileen will enjoy the time away from the city. Away from—reminders."

I glanced at him sidelong. With Aileen's continued recovery his own spirits revived, but he was still not entirely himself. Not yet. Perhaps the time at Joyenne would do him as much good as Aileen.

"Then you will be leaving Aidan here?"

"For a while . . . he is not at the moment strong enough to travel. Aileen will fret, of course, until he can join us, but Deirdre will tend him, and *jehan*, and all the nurses. I think he will do well enough." Brennan rested a hand on my shoulder. "I thought perhaps you might come with us for a while, to give Aileen company when I am called back to Homana-Mujhar."

"Aye, of course . . . I enjoy Joyenne—" I stopped walking. "Is *that* why you halted the match with Lio? To ask me this?" I sighed, biting back a stronger retort. "It might have waited, Brennan . . . or did you do it in lieu of *jehan?*" Pointedly, I paused. "As you do so often."

He started me walking again. "I did not stop it because *jehan* has forbidden it. Such things as your behavior are your concern, not mine." My brother smiled blandly. "I came to ask you for your company, at Joyenne and now. I thought we could match my colt against the new gray filly."

Alarums rang. "Colt," I echoed. "*Which* colt?"

"The chestnut." He shrugged. "It has been days since you brought him back, and I have yet to ride him. He will need the work."

Oh, gods, not the colt— I stopped dead in my tracks. "Brennan—" But I broke it off, unable to tell him. Not so baldly. Not after so much time. I had lied. Now it had caught up to me, and I found I could not admit it.

His brows rose. "Aye?"

I opened my mouth. Shut it. Then shook my head. "No— I think another time. Not now. I—" I paused. "There is something else I must do. Another time, *rujho*."

"Now." One hand locked around my arm, held me in place, and he smiled all the while. "Keely, I have been to the stables. The colt is missing." His tone was calm, *too* calm. "The grooms say you came back from Clankeep without him."

Oh, gods. And without inflection, "Aye."

Brennan released my arm. His expression was carefully noncommittal, which made it all the worse. "You lied to me when I asked about him, Keely . . . and now, when I give you a chance to explain what has happened, freely and without prejudice, you ignore the opportunity and create an empty excuse to leave." His tone hardened, as did his expression. "I want to know why. What have you done, Keely? What have you done *now*?"

Oh, gods, I hate *this*— I drew in a deep breath and told him the truth. "Because I was ashamed."

Brennan was astonished. "Ashamed! Why? What happened?"

My belly twisted. I felt no better about the loss of the colt now than I had then. "I was tricked," I told him curtly, though my displeasure was for me, not for Brennan, who had a right to know. "Like a fool, I fell into a trap—first thieves who wanted my coin, then outlaws who—" I stopped short. I wanted to say nothing of Rory Redbeard and his Erinnish companions. Not yet. Not with things unresolved.

"Outlaws?" Brennan prodded. "Outlaws *and* thieves? Are they not one and the same?"

I shook my head. "I tried to get him back, Brennan. I did. I went back for him the next day, but Teir—"

"Teir!" Brennan caught my arm again. "You saw Teirnan? Spoke with him? Where? Where is he, Keely? What did he say to you?"

I saw no profit in keeping my meeting with Teirnan secret, since I had sworn no promises, nor had he asked any. And so I told Brennan freely. He listened intently as I recounted a little of my meeting with Teirnan, but not all. To Brennan, I could not; he would not understand. He had no doubts of his heritage, his duty, his *tahlmorra*. He would not tolerate any in me. Certainly he would not understand how I could even consider that our *a'saii* kinsman might have a valid point . . . or two, or even three.

Which brought us back to the chestnut colt.

"What thieves?" he asked. "If you went back for him, you know where they are."

"Where they *were*," I countered. "I doubt they will be there now."

He shook his head, urging me toward the stables again. "Take me there anyway . . . we may find a trace— something to tell us where they went."

"Brennan—no." I twisted my arm free. "No. Leave it be. I want nothing to do with those men."

"If you are afraid, we can go in *lir*-shape . . . they will never even know—"

"No," I told him curtly. "I have coin put away—I will buy you another horse."

Brennan's short bark of laughter lacked all humor. "Are you mad? That colt was the last get of a stallion who died the day after the mare was bred—there can *be* no more, Keely! And even if there could be, you would not have the coin to buy him. *I* nearly did not—"

My temper deserted me. "A *horse!*" I shouted. "Not a woman, a child, a *lir* . . . gods, Brennan, you drive me mad—can you think of nothing else save your horses? What about Aileen? What about Aidan? What about *me?*"

"You," he agreed. "Aye, let me think about you; about why you stand here so afraid of showing me where outlaws tried to steal your coin, and perhaps your virtue—" It brought him up short. He stared, going gray around the mouth. "Gods, Keely—they did *not*—"

"No," I said shortly. "No, they did not—do you think I

would let them? I had a knife, *rujho* . . . and the Erinnish—"

"*Erinnish!*" Brennan nearly gaped. "They were Erinnish? Keely—"

My hands were fists. "Gods, Brennan, enough! *Enough!* I tried to get the colt back—I did try—but I could not. Does it matter who stole him? He is gone, *gone*—" I clamped hands against my head. "I swear, you will drive me mad—always asking questions!" I swung on my heel and walked away.

"Keely. Keely!"

I ignored him.

Brennan said something very rude in Old Tongue. I swung around, snapped back at him, tried to turn, but he had my arm yet again. "Keely, *wait*—"

But I did not. I twisted free, tapped the earth magic, felt air beneath my wings—

—and the paw that slapped me down.

I lay sprawled on my back on hard cobbles, human again, staring blurrily up at the tawny mountain cat who stood over me, one paw on either side of my neck. He is large, is Brennan, in *lir*-shape, and worthy of attention.

The tail twitched. Lashed. Then whipped down to smack my shin. I gritted teeth as the cat reached out one paw, extended one precise claw, and patted my left cheek. Like a man goading another to fight.

Or a brother warning a sister.

"Get off!" I shouted at him, rolling my head away from the paw. "Or would you have us settle this as cats, and let the tale make the rounds of Mujhara, where some still call us demons?"

The tail thwacked my leg again, and then the cat was moving, changing, flowing aside to alter fur into the flesh of a man. But the eyes were the same, and the anger.

"Aye," he agreed coldly, "let us consider the Homanans. Let us settle it as they do." He reached down, caught a wrist, jerked me to my feet. Took me to the guardroom and banged on the door.

Lio answered it. "My lord?"

"Swords," Brennan said curtly. "Hers, and one for me. Yours will do."

I drew a breath. "*Rujho*—"

"Now," he told Lio, who found my sword and his own with admirable haste, and gave them both to Brennan, who thrust mine into my arms and pointed. "There. Let us see precisely how good you are." He paused. "Or are not."

"Brennan—"

He jerked Lio's blade free and threw the sheath to the bench. "*Now*, Keely. Not ten years from now—if your tongue and temper have not gotten you killed by then. Or, for that matter, by tomorrow."

"*Ku'reshtin,*" I said calmly, and stripped my sword naked.

Two

Perversely, I was content. The anger melted away into determination, a cold, quiet calm that lent me the focus I needed. Brennan is not a truly gifted swordsman—I doubt any Cheysuli can be, lacking proper dedication—but he is strong and quick and solidly grounded in technique. I was no less so, since he had taught me what he knew, but it had been nearly two years since we had faced one another and I had improved tremendously.

Over the blade, I grinned. "Well met, *rujho*—"

But Brennan wasted nothing, not even his breath on me. He engaged before I could blink.

Sparring only, but with an element of genuine risk. Blades clashed and hissed, filling the bailey with song. I grunted, caught my breath, expelled it noisily, bit my lip, spat blood, gritted teeth until they ached.

He beat me across the cobbles to the wall Lio and I had slapped. And then turned me, working me back toward the guardroom.

I stopped him, held him, pushed him back three steps. Then he came on again.

I was dimly aware of people gathering in the bailey. Guardsmen, grooms, horse-boys, even passing servants. I heard mutters, comments, wagers being made. Not on me, I hoped; Brennan was clearly winning.

It made me angry. I had expected him to hold back because of my gender. It was not what I *wanted* from an opponent, but I had come to expect it. Come to depend on it; an advantage I enjoyed. But this time, *this* time, Brennan gave me none. He had a point to make, and he was using his to do it.

We were nearly to the guardroom. I caught a heel, went down on my back, dropped my blade, tried to snatch it up

again, but Brennan trapped it with the tip of his own and
slung it away from me. It rattled and rang on the cobbles.

I rolled onto belly, trying to stretch and catch the hilt,
but Brennan's sword tip was at my reaching hand, stinging
flesh. I snatched it back, cursing, tried again with the other,
suffered another sting. And then the tip was at my throat,
pressing me onto my back, guiding me gently down upon
the cobbles. I sprawled there, hot-faced and humiliated, and
impugned his ability with every epithet I could think of.

Brennan listened, and laughed. He lifted his blade,
paused, brought it slashing down.

And stopped it, precisely as he intended, with the edge
caressing my throat. Tipped my head back easily with only
a single nudge. "So," he said, "now you know."

That I could lose, aye. I had not expected to win. I had
expected only to prove I was good enough; instead I had
failed. As before, I sprawled on cobbles, with Brennan over
me. This time in human form, but the degradation was the
same. With claw or with sword, he had forced his will
upon me.

But he was brother, not enemy. We did not fight in truth,
only to settle a point.

Another time, I told myself. *There will be another time.*

I shut my eyes. Willed the anger to go. In a moment, so
did the sword.

Brennan tapped my boot-toe with his own. "Keely, come
up. Here—take my hand."

I took it. He snapped me up, released me, bent and
scooped up my sword. I accepted it with a muttered, *"Leijhana tu'sai."*

Brennan assessed my temper. Then slowly grinned. "You
were better than I expected."

My mouth hooked wryly. "So were you, *rujho.*"

He laughed. Slapped a hand against my back to brush
away the dust and nearly knocked me down. "Now," he
said lightly, "will you tell me about the outlaws? Erinnish,
I think you said?"

I looked past him, focusing abruptly. I did not answer
him, being unable. All I could do was stare.

Ian. Deirdre. *Jehan.* Along with all the others.

Frowning, Brennan turned to follow my gaze. And stiffened, even as I had, though he had less cause, being Bren-

nan, who *always* has less cause. Which meant I was the one who would bear the brunt of our father's displeasure.

Well, it had happened before.

I sighed, glanced at Brennan, strode across the cobbles to halt before the Mujhar. "I started it."

Gravely, he nodded. "So I assumed, when Lio came to tell me my son and daughter were fighting."

I scowled. Lio again; I would speak to him later. As for now, from my father, there was no sign of anger. No sign of impending punishment. I waited a moment for something more; when he did not appear prepared to say anything else, I frowned a little. Glanced around at the crowd who had gathered to watch the Mujhar's son and daughter match strong blades and stronger wills, and realized he would do or say nothing in front of so many people.

A quick glance at Deirdre showed me apprehension melting away into relief. A look at Ian showed me a man openly amused and not in the least afraid to display it even before his royal brother. He nodded a little and grinned at me, which made me feel better.

"But I lost," I told him.

My father glanced swiftly at Ian to see what had prompted my comment. And frowned, but only a little; he had learned the value of giving nothing away in public.

Brennan came up beside me. "She is not due all the blame," he said. "I suggested the match, *jehan* . . . I thought it was time she learned what it is for a woman to fight a man. Particularly a man unimpressed by her gender, and more than willing to overlook it while wielding a sword against her."

"*Leijhana tu'sai,*" I said sourly.

Brennan laughed and touched my shoulder briefly. "You did well enough," he said. "Griffon has improved you."

"But not enough. Not *near* enough; how many times did you break through my guard?" I asked. "How many times did you—"

Our father broke in at that. "*Enough,*" he said. "Quite enough, from both of you." His single eye was stern, though his tone was mild in deference to those watching. "I am quite certain you have impressed everyone with your prowess, Keely, and certainly your courage, which means your point has been made. Which means you can put away the sword and think of other things."

I grinned at him, unperturbed; Ian was my ally. And I *had* proved something, though not as well as I might have liked. "Other things, *jehan?* Such as weddings and having babies?"

My father sighed. "It would be best, aye . . . but I know better than to expect it."

I nodded. "Good. I would prefer not to be predictable; it makes a person boring." I glanced again at Ian and saw the laughter in his eyes. It made me grin back, failure diminished, and then I turned to Brennan. "Another time, *rujho.*"

"No," our father declared.

Brennan made no answer, which did not in the least surprise me. I also kept my silence, which our father accepted as assent, and watched as he took Deirdre's arm and escorted her back toward the palace entrance.

I looked at Brennan. "Promise me, *rujho.*"

He sighed noisily. "Keely, you heard what he said."

"Aye, I heard. But promise me, Brennan. Once more only. Win or lose, I will be content. Only give me one more chance."

"What will it hurt?" Ian asked.

Brennan stared at him in surprise. "You support this madness?"

Ian shrugged. "What is madness, *harani?* She is refused the chance merely because of her sex. If Keely were a man, Niall would not say no. It is only because he thinks Sean may not want a sword-wielding *cheysula* that he refuses to let her learn. He is afraid to risk the union."

Brennan's tone was flat. "Because if Aidan dies, he needs the blood from other sources."

"Aye," Ian agreed, sparing Brennan nothing. "You should understand what it is to put so much value on a union that other feelings no longer matter. Not even the feelings of your children; you simply do what must be done. And so, because there is risk to the prophecy if Aidan dies, Keely's life becomes all the more precious." His eyes were on me. "The union is necessary. So is the Mujhar's caution."

I frowned. "But *you* advocate that we fight again."

"Because you will let it gnaw your belly to pieces if you do not, just as Niall did when he was told not to do a thing he wanted to do badly. I remember, even if he does not." Ian, smiling, shrugged. "Once more, you said. I think it will do no harm."

Brennan sighed again and waved a hand to indicate resigned surrender. "Once more, then. When?"

I shook my head. "Not yet. Later. When I have learned a little more. I will tell you when." And then, thinking again of Erinnish brigands and a curious older brother, I made haste to go away. Taking my sword with me.

It was to Ian I went later, rather than to my father. I knew what the Mujhar would say, bound up by paternal duties. But Ian had none of those burdens, which took away the barriers and allowed me to speak freely.

He opened his door at my knock. Arched eyebrows as he saw me, but stood aside to let me enter. Shut the door behind me, then waited quietly as I glanced blindly around the chambers, wondering if I should go even though I wanted to stay.

"You may sit," he said. "Or pace, if you prefer."

I looked at him sharply. "You know me too well, *su'fali*—do you know why I have come?"

He smiled and sat down in an X-legged chair. "No. But I know you are Cheysuli, even without the color . . . and I know how these walls can chafe us. How they bind our souls too taut."

"*Is* it the walls?" I asked. "Or the prison of our duty?"

Ian's smile died. "Both," he told me quietly. "Have you only just come to know it?"

I stared at him. "Do you mean—*you*—? You, *su'fali?* But—I thought—"

"That as liege man to the Mujhar, I could only relish the duty?" He shook his head. "No, Keely . . . I am as troubled as you by the burdens of honor-bound oaths, by the demands of the prophecy."

"Is that why you supported my bid for another sword fight?"

He stroked his bottom lip with a negligent finger. "Oh, partly. And partly because you deserve a second chance."

He gestured to a second chair. "Why not sit, Keely? Pacing wears down the knees."

I sat. Stretched out my legs, knees intact, and frowned at him pensively. *"Su'fali—"*

Quietly, he overrode the beginnings of my question. "Keely, what I told you outside was the truth. The union is necessary, which makes Niall's caution understandable. He has no wish to curb your spirit, but he must. You are too impulsive at times, inviting accident." He gestured a little. "Today, as an example; you might have been hurt. You might have been killed."

I shook my head. "Not with Brennan, *su'fali*. Nor with any of Mujhara; they all know who I am. And besides, I know how to fight."

Ian sighed. "Arrogance born of ignorance . . . aye, well, Niall was as guilty of it when he was young. It is why I do not approve of the royal fledglings being kept so close to the mews." He smiled a little and shifted. "Keep-raised children know better; they have learned to trust no one at all, until that trust is earned. 'Solde and I grew up in Clankeep, but Niall did not. It left him unprepared for the world."

I stared at him in shock. "My *jehan?* But he went by himself to Valgaard and faced Strahan alone."

Ian shrugged a little. "Well, he went with me, but I fell ill . . . aye, in the end, he did face Strahan alone. And that is what shaped him, Keely . . . Strahan, Lillith, the plague, the loss of a *jehan*, also a war with Solinde." He looked at me intently. "It was much the same with your *rujholli*. Before they came back from Valgaard, none of them were men. Warriors only in name, even with the training. Because until they faced the demands of their *tahlmorras*, they were nothing but lumps of clay. Strahan fired each of them in the kiln of Asar-Suti."

I felt oddly cold, disliking intensely the prickling of my scalp. "Are you saying I, too, must face Strahan?"

"By the gods, I *hope* not!" He thrust himself upright in the chair. "I would wish Strahan on no one, and never on one of our House; do you think I am a fool?"

His intensity took me aback. "But—you just said—"

Ian sighed and slumped back again. "It was an example, Keely. I was pointing out how loss and hardship can shape a soul. Carry a boy from childhood to manhood." He waved off the beginnings of my question. "I mean only that you too readily assume no danger can befall you. You are Keely of Homana, Cheysuli, and daughter to the Mujhar. Your power is greater than most, which intensifies your belief that nothing can ever harm you." He touched a finger to his head. "In here, or without—" The finger moved to his heart, "—and certainly never here. Where it can hurt the most."

I drew in a deep breath, then expelled it slowly. In its place fear crept in. "I am afraid, *su'fali.*"

"Something I well understand." There was distance in his eyes that spoke of private things. Things he would not divulge in words, but revealed all the same in posture and eloquent eyes.

"But you dealt with it," I told him.

"Did I? *Do* I? Or do I simply ignore it?" He shook his head slowly. "I sired a child on Lillith. An Ihlini-Cheysuli child, who serves Asar-Suti. *Abomination*, Keely; she should not be allowed to live. I should have hunted her down. Should have made sure of her death. But I did not, ignoring it; believing, somehow, that such a course would alter her aim . . . gods, I was a fool—" he sighed, "—and Brennan paid the price. Now *another* such child, bred for Strahan's amusement, for Strahan's purposes." For a long moment he was silent, then shook his head again. "The Wheel of Life keeps turning, too often repeating itself."

I looked at him without blinking, transfixed by his eyes. "I could stop it," I told him. "I could stop the Wheel."

"How?" my uncle asked, when he saw I did not jest.

"By not marrying Sean of Erinn."

He frowned. "Oh, I hardly think—"

"*I* do. If Aidan dies, and he might, it all comes down to me. And what if I refused?"

He sat like a stone in the chair, not even so much as blinking. And then he blinked, and smiled. "You will not," he said gently. "You are not that selfish."

Am I not? I wondered. *Oh, but I think I am . . . gods, but I think I could be.*

Given reason enough.

But for now, I was not selfish, looking at my uncle. "*Su'fali,*" I said, "is there nothing to bring you peace?"

After a moment, he nodded. "Her death," he said, "or mine."

"Rhiannon is your daughter."

"She is a servant of the Seker."

"Blood of your blood, *su'fali*."

The flesh of his face was taut. "I think not, Keely. I think it has been replaced with the excrement of the Seker."

Relentlessly, I went on. "And when Rhiannon came here, clad in the garments of subterfuge, you welcomed her. I recall it clearly, *su'fali*. I was in the room."

"Unknowing, I welcomed her. Ignorant of the truth."

"And had she come to you begging for mercy? Asking for your protection? Throwing off her *jehana's* designs?" I paused, sensing his pain; the anguish of grief denied. "Would you have felt the same?"

His tone belied the pain. "What do you want, Keely? Why do you ask these things?"

"Blood," I told him simply. "We hold it in such esteem, this blood of our ancestors. And yet when it comes to Ihlini blood mixed with our own—*the blood of our ancestors*—you say it should be spilled."

"And so it should," he answered, "when the Ihlini try to spill ours."

"But not all Ihlini," I said. "There are those who desire peace as much as we do, turning their backs on Asar-Suti. Does it make them enemy?"

"Keely—"

"There are those of the Cheysuli who no longer serve the prophecy. Does it make them enemy? Does it make them servants of Strahan, or merely of themselves?"

Ian shut his eyes and slumped. Wearily, he said, "Teir has been at you, then."

"Not *at* me . . . he spoke to me, aye, and explained how he feels . . . how the *a'saii* feel, who fear to lose their *lir*."

Ian's eyes snapped open. "Is that what he told you? Is that the lever he used?"

I felt the flare of resentment, waited until it abated. "He came to me and told me why they feel the way they do. Why it is impossible for them to work toward an end that will be the end of *us*."

"And he suggested you not marry Sean." The intensity of his anger was as startling as it was sudden. "By the gods, girl, I gave you more credit for sense . . . how can you be so blind? How can you be such a lackwit?" He rose and stood before me, no more the tolerant kinsman but liege man to the Mujhar, and an angry Cheysuli warrior. "Teirnan wants the Lion. Teirnan has *always* wanted the Lion . . . and this is how he gets it. Because if Aidan dies, it does come to you—as you yourself have said." He drew in a steadying breath. "If you refuse to marry Sean, there will be no proper heir . . . there will be no proper blood—"

"I know," I said. "I know very well what it means: Teir will inherit the Lion."

"Then if you *know*—"

I stood and faced him squarely, strung so tight I nearly trembled. "What if he is right? What if the *lir* do go? What does it leave us, *su'fali*? What does it make the Cheysuli?"

"Teirnan is an ambitious, avaricious fool."

"I know all that!" I shouted. "But *what if he is right?*"

Ian looked at Tasha, sprawled in his bed with her cubs. She stared fixedly back at him, but the link was conspicuously empty of conversation, empty of what she felt.

Blankly, he said, "I asked her once before—asked her if it were true—if the *lir* were meant to leave us—"

Fear stirred sluggishly. "What did she say?"

"Nothing," he said, "as now. Tasha holds her silence. Tasha keeps her secrets."

Something inside me broke. "Oh, gods, *su'fali*—oh, *gods*—what happens if Sean is dead?"

His head snapped around. *"What?"*

"What happens if Sean is dead? Does it end? Is it over? Does Teir win after all? Or do the Ihlini win?"

Frowning, he shook his head. "Keely, there is no reason to believe—"

"Oh, there is," I said hollowly. "Sean may indeed be dead."

He said nothing at all, asking no questions at once, demanding nothing of me. He merely put his hands on my shoulders, guided me into the chair, sat me down again. Then knelt in front of me quietly, holding my hands in his. "I think you had better tell me."

I told him all I knew. Of stolen colts and knives; of Liam's bastard son. Knowing now, better, the weight of possibilities; the promise of things undone.

I *could* stop the Wheel. If Rory had not himself.

Three

Ian released my hands and stood up, staring hard into distances though he looked directly at me. "Niall must be told."

"No!" I said sharply. Then, more quietly, "Promise me, *su'fali* . . . say nothing to *jehan*."

He shook his head. "This concerns him, Keely. This concerns us all."

I drew in a deep breath and tried to remain calm, knowing too much emotion would tip him away from me. "But we cannot be certain Sean is dead. It is only a possibility." I sat very upright on the edge of the chair, hoping the reasonable tone of voice was enough to keep him bound, if only for the moment. I needed time to think. "If you tell *jehan* that Sean is dead, murdered in a tavern brawl by his bastard *rujholli*, you may well set in motion events that could cause us harm."

He said nothing, patently unimpressed. Watching me and other things, distant things. Things I could not see.

I needed something more. Another reason, a *better* reason—and then it came to me. The reason Rory himself had used to win the promise from me. "How would Aileen feel? Or Deirdre, hearing news that may or may not be true, and not knowing which to believe?" I shook my head. "It would cause Aileen much grief, and she needs none of it just now. What she needs is her ignorance, until the truth is known."

Now he was frowning, dearly perturbed. "Keely, we have no time to waste. If we sit here waiting for news from Erinn that may or may not come—"

"But we must," I insisted quietly. "If Sean is dead, it will come. And then you know what *jehan* will do." I grimaced and pushed myself back in the chair. "Open the bidding again."

Gone was the wry amusement. He was deadly serious now. "There is far more to this than your likes and dislikes."

Guilt flickered briefly. "Aye," I agreed. "But if you tell him, and he, in his Mujharish wisdom, sees fit to betroth me to someone else without knowing the truth of the matter, what happens if Sean is *alive?*" I spread my hands in a questioning gesture. "I am then promised to two men. And you know as well as I what broken betrothals can cause."

In view of our history, it was a telling blow. Had it not been for Homanan Lindir's repudiation of Ellic of Solinde in favor of a Cheysuli, there would have been no *qu'mahlin*. And the threads of prophecy would have been knotted that much sooner, leaving Teirnan with nothing to use as a means to rebel.

Ian, thinking deeply, turned away from me and paced absently to a table. He paused, gathered up the silver prophecy bones, began to pour them, chiming, from one hand to the other. "Time," he said softly. "That is the key to the truth."

I drew in a deep breath. *"Su'fali—"*

He swung around once more, cutting me off intently. "How long has Rory Redbeard been in Homana?"

I shook my head. "He did not say. Not long, I think—" I shrugged. "I could not say, either."

"And did he tell you when this tavern brawl occurred? Three months ago? A sixth-month?"

Again, I shook my head. *"Su'fali—"*

"Time," he repeated, pouring the bones again, back and forth, back and forth. "The first thing Liam would do is send word to Niall, as well as to Aileen and Deirdre. That means if this tavern brawl occurred a sixth-month ago, the likelihood is that Sean is alive. We would know by now if he had been killed."

Numbly I said, "Messages go astray."

Bones chimed. "Aye, so they do. Which means it might be wise for us to send to Liam ourselves."

Tension knotted my belly. "Then you *will* tell *jehan—*"

Ian shook his head, still frowning a little. "No. Not yet. I think it might be better if we kept this between us, at least until the truth can be discovered." He watched the bones a moment, then looked at me. "You should have told me sooner, but I understand your apprehension. No, I will say nothing for the moment. It seems likely if something befell Sean just before this Redbeard sailed, we should hear very soon. If not, we must assume Sean survived."

Wearily, I sighed. "I would prefer to know."

"It is necessary to know, for the safety of Homana." His expression was unyielding. "Do you know where he is?"

I shrugged. "In the wood. But he is not a stupid man; he moves his camp about."

"Could you find him?"

"I did before. In *lir*-shape, it should be a simple task." I looked at him sharply. "But I am to go to Joyenne with Brennan and Aileen, and you have no recourse to *lir*-shape while Tasha has her cubs."

His decision was quickly made. "Go to Joyenne," he said quietly. "I will send a message there, asking you to come back on one pretext or another. It will content Brennan, who might question it if you decided to go on your own. Niall will believe you are at Joyenne, Brennan that you are here. No one will question your absence from either place. It will give you an opportunity to find the Erinnish outlaw."

An honorable man, my *su'fali*, oathbound to his brother. And yet now he served another, forsaking the other he owed. I drew in a deep breath. "You would do this for me?"

The smile was slight, but present, hooking down at one corner. "For you, Keely? Perhaps. But also for Homana—"

"—and for the fate of the prophecy." I smiled back, matching his irony. "Oh, aye, of course."

"Find him," Ian said. "Be certain of what he says; it will give us the answer we need." He paused a moment, significantly. "And then you will take that answer immediately to the Mujhar and tell him, in detail, everything you know. Everything you *think*."

His price, plain and simple. All I could do was nod.

Joyenne ordinarily is only half a day's ride from Mujhara, less than that in *lir*-shape. But Erinnish Aileen was hardly strong enough to ride so far, and the bulky horse-borne litter used to transport her in comfort made the journey twice as long. I went with her, lolling languidly on bolsters, forgoing a mount to give her closer company.

Brennan rode Bane, his black stallion, accompanied by Lio and a small detachment of the Mujharan Guard. We expected no trouble between Mujhara and Joyenne, but the escort lent us as much prestige as protection. Before us all rode the young man with the banner of the Prince of Homana: black rampant lion on a field of scarlet, very similar in nature to our father's device, but smaller, and lacking the crown signifying the Mujhar's royal personage. I had thought blazons and banners ostentatious and altogether unnecessary, until Brennan pointed out such things were little different from the *lir*-bands and earring each warrior wore so proudly. The Homanans, he said pointedly, were no less hesitant about displaying their pride in heritage as we were; the banner was thus carried about the countryside whenever the Mujhar or his heir went anywhere officially. This visit to Joyenne was not precisely official, but Brennan wanted to give Aileen as much honor as possible, in hopes of shoring up her confidence.

Riding with her in the litter, warded from road dust by gauzy hangings, I thought it unlikely a royal banner would accomplish much toward buttressing her confidence. For one, I thought her confidence unshaken; Aileen is strong and stubborn and plain-spoken, needing nothing of ceremony to convince her of her worth. She was understandably depressed by the loss of the babies, but in no danger, I felt, of falling prey to a permanent affliction of her spirits.

We spent most of the journey engaged in idle conversation. The motion of the litter was relentlessly monotonous, lulling even me toward drowsiness in the late afternoon sun. I yawned, stretched, resettled myself against the cushions and contemplated the vision beyond the loose-woven fabric. Lazily, I smiled, liking what I saw.

Late spring, almost summer: thick grass was vividly lush, providing a carpet for scattered skeins of brilliant flowers, while distant trees formed a smudgy hedge of greenery against the blinding blue of the sky. All around us was meadowland cradled by undulating hills. Hedgerows formed the warp and weft of crofter holdings. Here and there, nestled within a fold of hill, was a gray stone croft with thatched roof, or a cluster of two or three whitewashed with lime. Low rock walls flowed across the land, meeting and dividing, forming boundaries. Moss carpeted the unmortared stones, binding each in place. Ivy and other vegetation took root in cracks and crevices. Some bloomed, scattering loose gemstones against the green velvet gown.

Aileen's tone was slow and soft, reflective. " 'Tis beautiful, Homana. Far more gentle than Erinn, so buffeted by the sea . . . the colors here are brighter, more vivid, like cloth newly dyed. In Erinn colors are muted, softened by mist and fog . . . everything is salty, like the sea—it soaks our wood, our sheep, our wool . . . and the wind has teeth in it, sharp teeth, biting the land, the folk . . ." She sighed, stroking back a strand of hair. "But there is power in the wind, and magic in the soul of the land . . . 'tis what gives us our strength, our pride—" Then she broke off, laughing. "Gods, but I sound like a widow grieving over a new-dead husband!"

I shook my head. "You sound like a woman who misses her home."

Aileen sighed. "Aye, well, I do, though there's no sense in it. Homana is my home now."

"There is sense in missing what you prefer," I said. "You are of the House of Eagles, Aileen, born to the Aerie of Erinn. Daughter of Liam, of Ierne, shaped by wind and sea and the soul of a wild land." I paused. "And we have clipped your wings."

"Ye *skilfin*," she said crossly, "you've done nothing of the sort. 'Tis only you're so bound up in your Cheysuliness and your own desires you can't see what others are wanting."

"I know what you want." I kept my tone inoffensive. "You want Corin."

Though she sat perfectly still, too still, something moved in her eyes. "No."

I nearly laughed. "No?"

Aileen shook her head. "I miss him, aye. I think of him often. I wonder how he fares in Atvia, trying to replace Lillith's influence with his own, dealing daily with the madwoman who is his—and your—mother . . . but no, I'm not *wanting* him. Not as I did." Her tone was oddly compassionate, as if I was the one who required comforting. "Things have changed, Keely. I took vows, made promises.

'Tis another man I'm wed to—and I've borne that man a child."

I frowned. "Does a child make that much difference?"

Aileen's eyes widened. "Oh, *aye*, Keely! Every difference there can be." Clearly, I had surprised her; she struggled to explain in terms I, childless and unmarried, could understand. 'Tis one thing to lie down with a man—'tis no burden at all when you give one another pleasure . . . but another thing entirely when you bear that man a child. When you *know*, looking at that man, that he's given you his seed, and that seed has taken root—" She broke off, frowning, and shook her head. " 'Tis hard, Keely . . . all I can say is aye, it makes that much difference. 'Tis the Wheel of Life, turning; the promise of things to come." Finally, she said, " 'Tis *magic*, Keely . . . a sacred, perfect power far greater than any other."

Something deep inside twisted. "You might have borne Corin a child."

After a moment, she nodded. "Aye. I wanted it. I wanted to be everything to him a woman should be: wife, bedmate, mother." Briefly, she smiled. "In the Old Tongue, I've been told, the words are *cheysula, meijha, jehana.*" Aileen shrugged thoughtfully. "But 'twasn't to be, Keely. I was intended for Brennan, and Brennan it was I wed."

"You might have said no."

"I did." Aileen laughed at my expression. "Keely, you're not the first woman promised to a man she isn't wanting. And hardly the first to be saying no when it comes to making the vows." Absently she touched the neckline of her russet gown. Beneath the fabric lay the *lir*-torque Brennan had, Cheysuli-fashion, given her as a token of their marriage. "But when I said no, Corin said aye; he refused to steal his brother's betrothed."

Once, he might have. But Corin had changed. He had gone away to Erinn on the way to Atvia, where he had met his brother's betrothed, whom he wanted for himself as much as he wanted the Lion. And then he had gone to Valgaard and met himself, his *true* self, at the Gate of Asar-Suti. The Corin of old was banished.

The Corin I knew was gone; the boy replaced by a man. Quietly, I said, "He would be worth more now."

"Aye. But so am I. I am *cheysula, meijha, jehana*—and I'd be changing nothing."

Impulsively I asked it, knowing I should not. "Do you love Brennan?"

"No," she answered steadily. "Not as I should."

Unexpectedly, it hurt. "But he cares deeply for you. I know it, now—I have seen it."

After a moment, she nodded. " 'Tis what grieves me most."

"But you yourself said it: you bore him a child!"

"And would again, if I could." Aileen shut her eyes, slumping against her cushions. "What do you want me to say? That I hate him? No. That I dislike him? *No*—Brennan is dear to me in many different ways. But—there is a difference. I don't love him the way I should. Not as much as I'm wanting to—" She stopped. Opened her eyes and met mine. They were hard and bright and piercing, allowing me no escape. "Not as much as you're wanting—no, I think, *needing*—to love my brother."

It shocked me utterly. *"What?"*

"You are afraid," she said gently. "Afraid to give up that part of yourself no one else has known. More than merely virginity, which is all too often a burden—" Aileen's smile was wry, "—but much, much more. No man can understand. No man can ever comprehend that a woman, bedded the first time, surrenders more than virginity. She also surrenders *self*."

Struck dumb, I merely stared.

Aileen smiled sadly. "How can I know, you're thinking. Well, we're not so different as that."

"But we are," I said numbly. "You accepted what you were given, regardless of your reasons. While I continue to fight against what they want to give me."

"Aye. You're very like Corin in that; he hated living up to expectations, although now he's far surpassed them." She smiled, bright of eyes. " 'Tis not so bad as you might think, Keely . . . there's no question that in marriage you lose a part of yourself, but so does the man. And if you're wise, you work together toward making a new life, one born of both."

Grimly, I shook my head. "I have yet to meet a man willing to let me be me . . . except, perhaps, for Ian, and he may give me my freedom merely because he is in no position to take it away."

Aileen smoothed the coverlet over her knees. Her tone was quiet, but with an underlying note of compassion. "I know how it's been for you, Keely. You've spent your life fighting one battle or another. You win, you lose, you compromise, dealing with each as it comes. But with a man, you're thinking there's no way you can win. That he'll *take*, not give. That he'll be stripping you of the Keely you've fought so hard to make."

Gods, how can she know—? And yet it seemed she did. She had reached in very gently and touched me in my soul, in the deepest part of my fear.

I drew up my knees and rested my forehead against them. "Aileen, I am so tired . . . of losing, of winning, of compromise—of having to fight at all."

"I know," she said gently. "I understand, Keely. I know why you have to love him, and why you think you can't."

I raised my head. "How can you?"

The light was gentle on her face. Sunlight muted by gauze softened the angles of her face, dulling the vividness of her hair. "You have no reason to believe there is room for love in an arranged marriage, and why should you? You've never seen it. Not in Niall and Gisella, not in Brennan and me. There is Deirdre, aye, but she is mistress, not wife . . . to you, a wife exists only to bear children, to pass on the proper blood. She is therefore unworthy of the man's love, being nothing more than a broodmare, as you've so often said."

Mutely, I nodded.

Aileen's voice was quiet. "To you, a wife is taken out of one mold and put into another, shaped to the hand of the man." Her eyes were tranquil once again, and full of empathy. "You are a proud, strong woman who's wanting nothing from that man, because whatever he can do for you, you can do for yourself."

I stared blindly at her face. "But no one will let me do it."

"And there is more, Keely. The last of all, I think, but by far the most important." She reached out and touched my hand. "For you, lacking love, lacking desire, lying with a man will be nothing more than rape."

It was not the answer I wanted. It was the only one she gave.

Four

For two days I waited at Joyenne, growing more and more restive and distracted, until at last the messenger came. I was summoned back to Homana-Mujhar, though no reason was given. Brennan thought it odd, but did nothing more than remark upon it; Aileen regretted aloud the need for me to go. I felt guilty at that, but could hardly tell her the summons was false, contrived only to learn the truth of her brother's welfare.

I made my good-byes to Aileen, then Brennan walked me out into the bailey, squinting against the noon sun. Joyenne, built of ocher-colored stone, was awash in the sunlight, a warm, welcoming patina of rich old gold. In Shaine's time it had belonged to Fergus, his brother, passing on Fergus' death to Carillon, to become the country dwelling of the Prince of Homana. Since then it had remained so, although Carillon had had little time to live in it, or Donal, or my father. Now it passed to Brennan, but he also was kept close in Homana-Mujhar. Joyenne was often empty, save for the servants keeping it in trust for absent landlords.

Brennan offered me a horse, but I declined, saying I preferred the swift freedom of *lir*-shape. My things he would send later, though I had brought little enough. I chafed to be gone, but reined in my impatience so as not to make Brennan suspicious.

"Odd," he said lightly, "but perhaps it has to do with Sean."

I glanced at him sharply, feeling the knot tie itself in my belly.

But Brennan shrugged one shoulder only, as if his curiosity was merely idle. "Liam may have sent at last, saying it is past time you and his son were wed."

"Perhaps," I agreed evenly. "Or perhaps it is Corin, saying he plans to visit."

Black brows arched up. "I would expect the message to include me as well, if that were true."

Resentment flickered briefly, then died. Lightly, I said, "Corin is *my* twin, not yours."

Brennan, understanding, merely rocked on his heels a moment, smiling wryly, locking thumbs into his belt. "Oh, aye, of course . . . but we shared something, he and I, in Valgaard, fighting Strahan. We are not the enemies we once were."

Again the resentment flickered. Corin had always been mine, in a manner of speaking, linked by birth and temperament. He and Brennan had never been close because Corin had long wanted the Homanan title and the promise of the Lion; later, he had even wanted Brennan's bride. Brennan had always claimed Hart as a boon companion, twin-born even as Corin and I were, which left the Mujhar's legitimate children evenly divided by habit as well as birth.

But Brennan spoke the truth: in Valgaard, battling Strahan, he and Corin had indeed shared something. Out of resentment and jealousy a new respect had been born.

I waited a moment, seemingly idle, then shrugged. "Aye, well, perhaps it is something entirely different . . . it may have something to do with Sean, or not. The best way to discover it is to go."

He put a hand on my shoulder, holding me back. "Keely—" He broke it off, frowning, then sighed and went ahead as I waited. "You and I have shared nearly as many misunderstandings as Corin and I . . . and I regret them. Too many times we argue for the sake of argument, trying by force of will to alter opinions, convictions, ideas . . . I think we would do better if we simply agreed to disagree, and let each of us do as he—or she—will."

I laughed at him. "I see Aileen has been at you."

He smiled, but there remained a trace of solemnity in his eyes. "She has said a thing or two, aye, but that is not what prompts me to speak now. We are very different, you and I, in temperament as well as desires and ambitions, but it does not mean we must be wrong, either of us." He sighed, shaking his head. "I think you are less selfish than I so often believe when you make noise about women being forced this way and that. I begin to think your concerns are legitimate, some of them, and that indeed women *are* made to do this or that, even against their own wishes."

I was astonished to hear such things from him, but said nothing at all for fear he would withdraw them, and his understanding. Instead, I waited in silence for him to finish, wondering how much of his new belief came from proximity to Aileen.

Brennan touched his left ear, absently fingering the remains of his lobe. Once, it had borne an earring of solid gold, shaped to mirror Sleeta, as his *lir*-bands did. But he had lost the earring and lobe to a Solindishman masquerading as Homanan, in service to the Ihlini. Not so much, I thought; he had nearly lost his life.

"It is not a Cheysuli way to make decisions for our women," he said intently, "and yet all too often I see those decisions being made for you. It is unfair; Maeve is free to do as she pleases, to wed whomever she desires to wed—though the gods know I pray those desires no longer include Teirnan—and yet you are made to wed into Erinn merely to satisfy a prophecy that *some* Cheysuli no longer believe or serve."

"Birth," I told him flatly. "Do you think for one moment that if Maeve were legitimate, she would be allowed that freedom?" I shook my head. "No indeed . . . and I would be willing to wager *she* would be wed to Sean in my place, leaving me to be whatever I desired to be."

"And so now you will resent her for that as well." Brennan's tone was clipped and cool, betraying his favoritism. Save for Hart he was closest to Maeve of us all, sharing her confidences—and yet I wondered how much she was willing to share after all, even with him; it was *me* she had told of the child. Teirnan's bastard halfling.

"No," I answered quietly. "Maeve has her own *tahlmorra*, even if of her own making."

Brennan sighed in weary exasperation, making a placatory gesture that swept away our brief contentiousness. "Aye, well, let us recall our agreement, Keely."

"To disagree?" I grinned, making light of it. "Is this your way of avoiding another sword fight, Brennan? Tell the woman what she wants to hear, so she will go away?" Smiling, I shook my head. "Oh, no, *rujho*, I hold you to it."

"Aye," he said absently. "Of course, Keely—I promised."

Clearly he was troubled. And though he said many of the things I had tried to make him hear from me for years, I found myself defending the practices if only to make him feel better. "Well, it has always been so in royal Houses . . . it is hardly a new thing, wedding sons and daughters into foreign lands." I shrugged. "As for the Cheysuli, we hold the Lion now. Sacrifices must be made. It is not always the women who suffer, though usually it is so—there is another side to it, as well." I smiled at him. "It is easy for me to look at Aileen and see a woman forced to marry you. But the same was required of you, *rujho* . . . and what if you had wanted another woman?"

Brennan said nothing. My question was innocent enough, but between us rose the specter of Rhiannon, daughter of Ian and Lillith, and *meijha* to the Prince of Homana. She had made her presence felt in Homana-Mujhar, and in Brennan's bed. He had not, I knew, loved her, but there was more to it than simple lust.

Something stirred inside me. Something of fear and unease. *Ensorcellment. That only. Brennan could never truly care for an Ihlini.*

"The child—" he began, and stopped.

"Aye," I agreed. "There is a child, *rujho*. Somewhere. Probably in Valgaard, with Strahan, at the Gate of Asar-Suti." I drew in a deep breath. "What if it is a boy? All this talk of Aidan's fragility, the need for me to marry Sean so as to insure the proper bloodline . . . what if the child you sired on Rhiannon is a boy? Ihlini, illegitimate—but still the son of the Prince of Homana, and grandson to the Mujhar. The gods know the Homanan rebels tried hard enough to put forth Carillon's bastard for the Lion, and some even say Caro had more right than our *jehan* . . . according to Homanan law, a son of your loins could petition for a hearing on the legitimacy of his claim. Even a son gotten on an Ihlini woman."

His jaw was hard as stone. "Such a petition would never be granted."

"No, of course not—but the claim could be made. Look at the turmoil when Elek put forth Caro's name . . . it nearly divided the Homanan Council. It could have cost our *jehan* the throne."

"Teir is bad enough," he said tightly. "Gods, he is a fool—but I would sooner deal with him than deal with Rhiannon."

"Ian would deal with her." I looked away from him to the sun again, lifting a hand to shield my eyes. "You know as well as I that Strahan is not finished. He will find a way to trouble us, to destroy our House's claim to the Lion. He will use the child, Brennan . . . he will use whatever—and *who*ever—he can."

"Gods," Brennan muttered, "I curse that Ihlini witch."

"Ihlini and Cheysuli." I glanced at him in concern, disliking the look in his eyes. Not knowing what to say. "I must go, *rujho*. Tend Aileen well. She is worth the care."

I left him then, before he could answer. Into the earth I went, sliding through all the layers, to tap the power that lies so unquietly in the depths of Homana's soul, waiting for release, answering instantly with an upsurging welcome that nearly hurled me free again, bereft of the wings I wanted.

—up—up—

—unfurling feathers, stretching wings, screaming triumph to the skies—

—free—

Below me, so far below, my brother stood caged in ocher stone, staring upward, shielding human eyes. Watching the falcon mount the skies and fly, reaching toward the sun. And I knew a moment's pleasure, sharp and intense, that he was not as I. Cheysuli, aye, and therefore blessed. Capable of sloughing off human flesh for the fur of a mountain cat, to run on four legs in the deep-shadowed woods. But still he could not *fly*.

An earthbound soul, my brother's.

Mine knew no limitations.

I flew straight to the wood near Clankeep and then searched it diligently, drifting here, there, soaring and circling, until at last I found them. Such small men, little more than awkward shapes, until I banked closer, closer yet, drifting down toward the treetops. Arms and legs became more than sticks, faces more distinct, words distinguishable.

They shouted, did the Erinnish, calling encouragement and insults to the two men who fought.

Rory was one; from here I could see the brilliance of his beard, afire in the sunlight. They gathered in a clearing unscreened by limbs and leaves: eight king's men and their captain, exiles all, two of them matching strength and speed and skill. In their hands were swords.

Lower still, until I settled on a low-grown bough on a tree near the tiny clearing. I heard the clangor of steel, the grunts of effort expended; smelled the tang of sweat-stained flesh and damp leather. And laughed within my falcon shape to watch without them knowing.

It is hardly a new trick. As children, Brennan, Hart, and Corin had vied with one another often over who would get a *lir* first, and what that shape would be. It had been no wager in the end; Brennan and Hart, twin-born, firstborn, had fallen *lir*-sick within an hour of one another, and each, at thirteen, had gone into the woods to seek a *lir*. Brennan had come home with Sleeta, Hart with his hawk, Rael.

Corin had not been so fortunate. It had been three more years before he linked with the vixen, Kiri, and until that time Brennan and Hart had often teased him by sneaking up on him in *lir*-shape, catching him unaware. It had not been fair, adding substantially to Corin's resentment of Brennan in particular, but it was a trick every newly-linked Cheysuli child played on those who still lacked a *lir*.

It was a game *I* had played, and often, when I had come into my own gifts. I had made Hart and Brennan pay for the tricks played on Corin. And now it seemed I could play the game again, this time with Rory Redbeard as the victim.

He was very good with the sword. Soon enough I lost my private amusement and watched out of interest in technique, marking his moves, his patterns, the positioning of his feet, the distribution of his weight. I watched the opponent as well, judging him for the quality of his defense, and knew he gave Rory a good match. The man did not hold back, but neither did he get through.

But they stopped too soon for me. Neither won; they stopped. Because, Rory said; the light was dying away. It would be dangerous to continue, for fear of missing a block, or turning a feint into a genuine blow. And so they stopped, calling one another names, slapping each other's shoulder, trading friendly insults. They were close to me, very close. All I needed to do was let go and drop, to shock them into silence.

Inwardly, I laughed. Time for truths, I thought, and pushed myself off the bough.

Midway down, I changed. Traded wings for arms, feathers for flesh, talons for booted feet. I heard curses, caught breaths, muttered petitions to the gods of Erinn. By then I was on the ground, standing squarely in front of Rory. Laughing at them all, but mostly at his expression.

"Try *me* with a blade," I challenged. "Sundown means nothing to me; I can see in the dark."

Hands were on swords, on knives, but no man drew a blade. Instead they stared, mouthing things beneath their breaths, stealing glances at one another to judge the degree of shock each expressed. As for Rory, he did none of it, standing quietly before me.

Then he scratched his beard. "Lass," he said lightly, " 'tis a poor way of stealing a horse to come in so boldly as this."

I grinned. "Aye, if I wanted the horse. And if I did, I would have taken him easily; do you think a Cheysuli knows nothing of stealth?"

He arched one eyebrow beneath a tangle of brass-bright hair. "I'm hardly the one to be asking a thing about the Cheysuli. I've never met one, lass . . . unless, of course, this bit of trickery is more than an illusion."

"Oh, aye," I agreed, affecting his lilt, "a wee bit more than illusion. Would you care to see it again?" I spread my hands. "Name your animal, Redbeard . . . I can be them all."

The light was behind him, blinding me to his expression. But his tone was eloquent: disapproval, disappointment. A reassessment of me. "Lass, you lied to me."

It was not what I expected. In no way. Not from a man such as he.

I stared at him. Amusement died away. Something twisted in my belly. "There was need."

"Was there?" He sheathed his sword with a hiss and click. "*Was* there?"

I felt empty inside. "Aye. Great need."

Rory made no answer. He strode past me out of the

clearing, moving into the trees. Eight men followed him, leaving me alone.

I turned. Stared hard at his back before it disappeared. And then he swung back. "Come to the fire," he said. " 'Twill be worth a drink or two, the truth. If you'll be telling it to me this time."

Part of me was angry that he, a man of no honor, of exile, could take me to task for lying. Part of me was angry. Part of me was ashamed.

I went with him to the fire.

He perched himself upon a tree stump, unearthed a wine-skin, unplugged it, and drank deeply, even as his men found places and did much the same. And then he replugged the skin and slung it at me. I caught it awkwardly, clutching it to my belly, and felt the heat in my face.

"Drink," he advised. " 'Tis easier to explain away a lie when the tongue is properly loosened."

Pursing my lips, I nodded. "And was it easier for you to fight Sean over a wine-girl because your tongue was properly loosened?"

Brown eyes narrowed. Lids shuttered them a moment. "Aye, well, you'd be knowing nothing of that." He gestured. "Sit. Drink. Say what you've come to say."

"Ask what I've come to ask." I glanced around, saw nothing worth sitting on, settled down on the leaf-cushioned ground. And because he had challenged me, I drank the Erinnish liquor.

Rory sat with legs spread, at ease on the stump. The sun was gone and firelight took its place, painting his bush of a beard with glorious red-bronze color, flowing together with blond hair tangling freely on wide shoulders. A true brigand, the Redbeard, with a quiet compelling strength that shouted of competence. King's man, aye, and clearly a royal hatchling as much as my brothers were, or Deirdre and Aileen. A bold-faced, bright-eyed eaglet, born of Erinn's Aerie even if out of the mews.

Is Sean dead? I asked. *Did you murder your brother, Rory?*

But I asked it of myself, afraid to hear the truth.

"Ask it, then," he said curtly.

For a moment, only a moment, I did not understand. And then I recalled why I had come. "How long?" I asked.

"We need to know how long it was before you sailed, so we can judge if Liam has sent—or *will* send—a message bearing word of Sean's death." I saw the widening of his eyes, then the downward lancing of his brows, the interlocking of them. "Do you see?" I asked. "If you have been here long enough—if you sailed from Erinn at once, and have been here long enough—chances are good Sean recovered. Liam would send word at once of his death—" I shrugged, "—to the Mujhar, to Deirdre, to Aileen—"

"—and to you?" Eyes narrowed, Rory nodded. "Aye, I know you, lass, *now*—'tis not so difficult to realize you're no arms-master's daughter, not coming here with such words in your mouth." He sighed, frowned blackly at the ground, picked at a tear in his leggings. "A matter of timing, is it? To decide if 'tis time to cast a net for another fish?" His head came up slowly. His eyes were black with anger. "So soon you bury Sean and look for a new husband?"

I nearly dropped the wineskin. *"No!"*

"Well, I'll have none of it." He jerked his head in a westerly direction. "Send to Liam yourself, girl . . . see what *he* has to say. I'll give you no word of when we left or how long we've been in Homana if you'll be using it to replace my brother in your halfwitted shapechanger prophecy."

Astonished, I nearly gaped. And then I laughed aloud, disregarding the look in his eyes, the set of jaw beneath the beard. *"You* are the one who murdered him. You are the one who makes these questions necessary." I slung the wineskin back at him. "You are a fool, Erinnish, to think that is why I am here; to make certain of his death so I may seek out another husband." Slowly, I shook my head. "You know nothing about me, nothing at all . . . or surely you would know that is the very last thing I would do."

Rory unstoppered the skin and drank, then nodded idly. "Aye, lass, I know little enough . . . only that you lied."

Bitterness and arrogance warred for my tongue. Both won. "You fool," I said scathingly, "do you think it would be so easy to replace him? Are you forgetting the demands of the prophecy?"

Rory spat to the side. "Are *you* forgetting I know next to nothing about it? D'ye think I care?" He rose, still holding the wineskin. "Come with me. There's a thing I have to show you."

Suspicious, I stayed where I was. "I am not a fool."

"No, only stubborn." Rory bent, caught a wrist, pulled me to my feet. "Come with me, lass. I'm thinking you might want to see the bright boyo, to know he's well looked after."

He led me through leaves, branches, foliage, walking as one with the shadows. And showed me Brennan's colt, who snorted and sidestepped as we appeared, then settled as Rory put a soothing hand on his shoulder, whispering meaningless words of reassurance. In Erinnish, of course; the tongue was made for horses.

I moved to the colt, cupped the soft muzzle, felt hot breath on palm and fingers, heard the nicker deep in his throat. "Brennan wants him back."

"Aye, so would I if I'd lost him." Rory grinned. "But I'll be keeping him, lass."

I grunted. "Unless Brennan comes for him."

"Let him. I've fought better men than the Prince of Homana." And then his tone altered from challenge to memory. "I've fought the Prince of Erinn."

I ducked under the colt's silken neck and stood on the far side, using him as a barrier. It made the words easier. "How long?" I asked again. "We must know, Rory. It has nothing to do with casting nets for a new fish . . ." I shook my head, stroking the chestnut back. "If Sean is dead, there is no one left for me. No one at all. It is Sean or no man: we need the Erinnish blood."

"Aileen is wed to Brennan. They already have a son." His mouth jerked briefly sideways. "Liam held a feast in honor of his first grandchild's birth. I beat Sean for the right to be the bairn's champion in a sword match."

"Who won the match?"

"I did."

I stared hard at the chestnut shoulder, not knowing how better to say it. "Aidan is sickly. He may not live to adulthood."

Rory said nothing immediately. And then he sighed, muttered something briefly in Erinnish, spoke wearily. "Aye, well, if the gods want him, he'll be walking the halls of the *cileann* . . ." He drew in a breath. "Aileen is young and of healthy stock—the House of Eagles breeds true . . . there will be more children. Another heir for Brennan."

"No."

Across the colt's back, he stilled.

"No," I repeated. "Aileen miscarried of twins less than a month ago. There will be no more."

"Aileen," he said sharply, and I recalled they knew one another. Aileen herself had said so.

"Well," I answered at once. "Recovering in the country; I promise, she is well. But there will be no more children. If Aidan dies, there is no heir for Homana."

Rory's tone was taut. "Men set aside barren wives."

"Brennan has said he would not."

The flesh under his eyes twitched. "It does him credit, that."

I said nothing of Homanan law forbidding it. For one, Brennan would have refused even if it were allowed. He had made it plain.

"So," I said, expelling a breath, "you see how it is with me. We need the Erinnish blood. If Aidan dies, it leaves us with none in the House of Homana." I looked away at once, to stare at nothing, seeing his expression. "You must understand, Rory—it is more than simple lack. It could be destruction."

Doubt was plain. "How?"

I ran my hands, one by one, down the colt's spine, smoothing silken hair. It gave me something to do as I tried to explain the binding service Teirnan, and too many others, no longer were able to honor. "The prophecy says one day a man of all blood shall unite, in peace, four warring realms and two magic races. The Firstborn shall come again, a man born of all the power, all the gifts, to take precedence in the world." I shrugged, twisting my mouth. "You may believe it or not, as you wish, but it is what the Cheysuli live for. It is our sacred duty."

"Duty," he echoed. "Aye, I know something of that." His face was mostly shadowed. "And without that duty the Cheysuli are as nothing?"

"So we are taught from birth." I stroked hair out of my face and tucked it behind an ear. "Beginning, ending, continuation . . . how can I say, Erinnish? I only know that if Aidan dies, the blood is denied to us."

"Until you bear children to Sean."

I met his unyielding eyes across the colt's sleek back. "It is difficult to bear children to a dead man."

Something altered in his gaze. Something *recoiled*. With a jerk, he turned away.

And swung back, shaking his head, fighting something within himself. "Lass," he said, "lass—" He shook his head again, lips pressed together. "We sailed at once," he said, "before the blood on the floor was dry. If he died, if he did die, you'll be knowing soon."

"But not yet," I said numbly.

"Soon," he repeated. "Today, tonight, tomorrow. Or perhaps a month from now, depending on the weather." His face was stark in the moonlight. "If Sean is dead, what will you do? What is left to you?"

"Prayer," I said succinctly. "A petition to the gods that Aidan survives to sire a son."

He judged my temper a moment, then smiled a little. "Not a daughter, then?"

Sourly, I said, "The Lion requires a male."

Rory Redbeard laughed. "Only because he's not met *you*."

I hardly knew the man, and yet I felt I could trust him. There are times when strangers give better advice than friends, than kin, who seek only to give pleasure, to say what the other wants to hear, hiding honesty behind diplomacy. Rory Redbeard, I thought, would say precisely what he thought no matter what the cost. No matter who the hearer.

I told the truth to a stranger, in hopes he would understand. In hopes I might learn to myself. "I want nothing at all of Sean; of wedding, of bedding, of children."

Between us, the colt moved, stomping, stretching his neck to sample the leaves on a tree limb. Rory stood very still, saying nothing, doing nothing, hidden in shifting shadows.

"I would never wish him *dead*," I told him, meaning it, "not even to save myself. But I have no desire to marry. I want nothing to do with children."

Considering it, Rory unplugged the wineskin. "Have a drink, my lass. I'm thinking this will take time; why do it without good liquor?"

I ducked under the colt's neck, accepted the skin, watched in silence as Rory sat himself down on the ground and rested his spine against a tree. Now I could hardly see him, but I knew he was there.

Gods—how do I start?

I stared blankly down at the wineskin clutched against my belly. "Can you understand?"

"I'm not needing to, lass. 'Tis *you* requiring it."

So, I was transparent. I drank, swallowed convulsively, nearly choked, plugged the skin again. "I have three brothers," I told him. "And each of them has, in different ways, showed me what men think women are for." I saw the reflexive squint of skepticism. "Even *you*," I pointed out, "fought Sean over a wine-girl, to decide who would take her to bed."

Rory sighed, nodding. "Aye. Aye, we did . . . but lass, there are women and there are *women*—"

I silenced him with a gesture. "Women *are* women. Men should not distinguish us dependent upon the bedding."

Rory chewed his lip, which also included his mustache. "I'll not be saying you're wrong, lass . . . but you've never been a man. You're not knowing how it is."

I smiled wryly. "As I said, I have three brothers. One of them is my twin; Corin and I have always been frank in matters of men and women."

Rory shook his head. "Unless you've *been* a man, you can't know how it is. How much a woman is *needed*."

"No," I agreed, "no more than an unblessed man can know what it is to shapechange." I sighed, crossed to him, handed down the skin. "Aileen said it best. She said when a woman gives up her virginity she also relinquishes *self*. She has her thoughts, aye, and her feelings, and can keep all locked away—but she can never be whole again. Never be *new* again. She can never be the woman she was before the man." I gestured emptily. "You have only to hear the jests regarding a woman whose maidenhead is unbroken . . . the ridicule, the insults . . . and yet when a man means to marry, he demands virginity. Certainly a king does . . . or the heir who will be king."

"Sean," he said heavily.

I kicked at the ground, toeing out a stone. "There was a man some time ago, an Erinnish sea captain, who claimed

Sean a lusty man, and hot for his shapechanger princess. Sean would, he said, have her wedded and bedded and bearing an heir, all within a year." I stopped kicking abruptly. "It has stayed with me all this time. I know he meant nothing more than crude flattery—Sean is no wilted flower, he said—but think what it was to me. A promise of *usage*, Rory. A woman duly bedded, to be shown her proper place and to do the proper service by bearing her lord an heir."

Rory stared into darkness. "Words are not enough, lass—words are never enough. They say things we're not meaning to say, and twist the truth about." He did not look at me. "Too often, I'm thinking, we say what we're expected to say, to prop up fragile pride, and hide the feelings beneath."

It stabbed deeper than expected. "You should be Cheysuli."

Rory sounded puzzled. "What are you saying, lass?"

"That for us, it is harder." I shook my head. "It is tradition within the clans that true feelings, deep feelings, never be displayed. Not in public. Not where people can see, where enemies might use them. We dare not show weaknesses, and strong emotion is one of them."

Rory's disgust was plain. "And that includes affection?"

"Cheysuli say nothing of love . . . at least, those who practice the old ways." I shrugged, knowing how it sounded. "Not all of us are so strict, certainly not my House. My father keeps it no secret that he loves his Erinnish *meijha*. Things are different, now, but the old ways are hard to change."

"Lass," Rory said, "why d'ye not want bairns?"

I turned away stiffly, gritting my teeth against the sudden wrench of regret. How to tell a man? How to explain that childbed is dangerous? Surely he knew it. I had said it of Aileen.

And then the words flowed easily. I turned to face him squarely. "Babies make me uncomfortable. There is no mothering in me. I would sooner do without."

"You're not the first who's thought so, lass—"

"—but of course I will change my mind? Once I have borne a child?" I sighed wearily. "So glibly said, Rory . . . and in such ignorance."

"Is it?" He pushed himself to his feet and handed me the wineskin. "I'm thinking not, lass. I'm thinking you're only afraid."

Gods—how can he know—?

"Afraid," he repeated. "Of everything, I'm thinking . . . of wedding, of bedding, of bairns . . . of facing what women face when they leave girlhood behind." His eyes were kind in the moonlight. His truth less so. "Not so different from men, my lass. Not so different from me."

"But you are a *man*," I said.

Rory shook his head. "No man is unafraid. The one who says so is a liar."

I hugged the wineskin to me, seeking answers, peace, security. A way to be unafraid.

"Come to the fire," he said. " 'Tis time for supper, I'm thinking. My belly's clamoring."

My belly was tied in knots. *Gods, I* am *afraid.*

I wondered if Sean was also.

Five

I was panting, laughing, too winded to speak, which suited him well enough; it gave him time to insult me, which he did with great skill and pleasure in his lilting Erinnish tongue. Grinning, he eyed me, nodding to himself. He was not so winded as I, but then he had more experience, more reason to feel at ease.

"Gods—" I said, "—you are good . . . at least as good as Griffon, and certainly better than Brennan." I paused, sucking air, then blew out a gusty sigh of satisfaction. "Aye, it ought to do—I will give him a better match."

Rory pushed back hair from the tangle near his eyes. "Will you tell me a thing, then?"

I nodded absently, scratching a bite on my forearm.

His eyes were perfectly steady. "I'd like to know what it is from someone who ought to know, instead of trusting to tales."

We stood facing one another in the clearing near the camp, where I had found him a handful of days before, near sundown. With swords in our hands, too; Rory had, reluctantly, agreed to show me a trick or two, but now the reluctance was gone. He enjoyed it as much as I. The sword I used was borrowed, too heavy for me and unbalanced, but it was enough for now.

Sweat ran down my face. I wiped it away with a leather-wrapped wrist, exhaling heavily. The match, for now, was done, and Rory had won again. "What *what* is?"

"What it is to shapechange."

I said nothing at all, meeting his too-steady eyes, then turned from him abruptly, walked into the trees, found the sheath for the sword. Its owner took it from me as I thanked him grimly, then returned to the camp. Hard-faced, secretive men, saying little to me other than what they had to say. But not, I thought, my enemies, merely respectful of my rank. I was their lord's betrothed.

If their lord is still alive.

Rory was behind me, sheathing his own sword. I swung back to face him. "You had best know what you are asking."

He was taken aback by my attitude. "Why, lass? 'Tis not a thing, I'm thinking, no one has asked before."

No, it was not. But no one had ever asked *me*.

I told myself it was a perfectly natural question, particularly from a foreigner who had no firsthand knowledge. But I found myself strangely defensive about my *lir*-gifts, oddly reluctant to readily admit to him just how different I was. Always before I had known nothing but pride in my blood, but now I felt something else. Something very much like foreboding.

If I tell him the truth, no matter how much he protests, he will believe me unnatural . . . even if he says no, he will think I am born of beasts. The unblessed always do, no matter what they say . . . I have seen it in their eyes, in the masks they wear as faces—

I broke it off with effort. The realization hurt. It hurt much worse than expected, because I had not cared before.

Accordingly, I was brusque. "I doubt you could understand, Erinnish. Take no offense—but you are an unblessed man."

"Unblessed! Unblessed?" He shook his head. "Lass, I *am* Erinnish, born of the House of Eagles . . . 'tis more in the way of blessing than many things I know."

"No, no—that is not what I meant." Irritably I kicked a stone away, aiming it toward the clearing. "Aye, you have the right of it: people have asked before. People will always ask, being horrified by the truth while fascinated by the horror."

"Lass," he said patiently, "I'm not a man to take fright. I'm not a man to scoff. Aileen married a mountain cat, Deirdre lives with a wolf . . . and I have seen *you* change."

I looked at him levelly. "No one can understand. They hear stories, trade tales, foster untruths, all the while making ward-signs against us." I shook my head grimly. "Not all, of course, but more than enough. There are still those who prefer to hear the darker side of the magic because it makes a better tale."

"Darker side," he echoed.

I stared hard into the clearing, not looking at him. "There is a story, a tale of a man who lost control . . . a warrior who lost himself. There is always the risk, of course; *lir*-shape is seductive." I glanced at him intently. "He stayed too long and lost himself, forsaking his human form. Caught in *lir*-shape forever, but now was something in between. He lost the sense of either side, becoming a little of both."

Rory frowned. "I thought you told me there was this thing of the death-ritual."

"He was no longer human, no longer truly Cheysuli. Such things only bind those who are willing to be bound. He was not. He was beast, abomination . . . man and wolf in one."

"Wolf," he said involuntarily, recalling traditional fear.

I nodded. "But not bound by a wolf's behavior, nor by a man's humanity. He was a thing of nightmare." I shook my head, twitching shoulders to dismiss prickling flesh. "I cannot say if the tale is true, only that it exists. Only that Homanans used it—*use* it—to frighten naughty children."

Slowly, he nodded. "And yet, it might be true. Is that what you're telling me?"

I drew in a breath. "Aye, it might be true. There is such a thing as losing balance. As I have said, *lir*-shape is seductive."

All his humor was banished, replaced by solemnity. "Tell me," he said. "Let it be truth from one who knows."

I shook my head decisively. "Words are not enough. *Lir*-shape is born of magic, shaped of power . . . there are no words for that. Only the knowledge of *feeling*."

"Tell me," he repeated. "Make me feel it, lass . . . if only for a moment."

He was deadly serious, and therefore deserving of truth no matter how discomfiting. No matter how alien.

Then let him have the whole of it. "Sit," I suggested.

Rory sat, placing the sheathed sword beside him on the ground. As always, he used a tree for a back rest.

I knelt down before him, tucking heels beneath my buttocks. "Close your eyes," I told him.

"Lass," he said doubtfully.

"Close your eyes, Erinnish. Unblessed eyes are blind."

After a moment, he closed them. "Be gentle with me, lass. I only asked a question."

"And I will answer it." I drew in a deep breath. "Think of nothing," I said. "Think of *nothingness;* lose yourself in emptiness, in the utter absence of self. Banish Rory entirely; live only for the *being*."

Slowly the flesh of his eyes loosened. The line in his brow went away. His breathing was deep and even.

"There is power," I said, "much power. And if you know how, you can tap it . . . if you are Cheysuli. If you have the blood. If the power acknowledges you." I reached out, touched his hands, took them into my own. *"Sul'harai,"* I told him, "the union of man and woman. The binding of warrior to earth—or, in my case, a woman; once, it was always so."

Sweat ran down his face. Rory said nothing at all.

"Power," I repeated, "unlike any you have known. And at your call, it answers, binding flesh, blood, bone: giving back other things. Flesh. Blood. Bone. But of a different shape."

Rory's mouth slackened.

"There is a moment," I said, "when you are neither being. Neither man nor animal, nothing more than formlessness, waiting for the shape. But it comes, it always comes, and you are free, *freed*, to be what you must be, dictated by the gods. Mountain cat, fox, hawk; wolf, owl, bear. Whatever you must be, dictated by the blood." I tightened my fingers on his. *"You* are an eagle, Rory—a bright, bold eagle born of Erinn's Aerie, above the cliffs of Kilore. Below you the Dragon's Tail, smashing against the shoreline . . . below you the fishing boats, coming home on the tide . . . below you the House of Eagles, perched atop white chalk cliffs . . . below, forever below—*you are the lord of the air*, the sovereign of the skies . . . there is magic in your blood and power in your bones . . . the hard, bright knowledge that you are different from men, that you are *better* than men: higher than they can go, freer than they can be, able to ride the wind even as they are bound to the earth, to ships, to legs, to horses—" I gripped his hands in my own. "So much freedom, Rory—so many fetters broken—so much power loosed to fill your wings with wind . . . and you fly, *you fly*, where no one else can go . . . being what no one else can be: born of the earth but not bound to it, because it lives in your soul, your heart, your flesh, locked inside your bones. Burning in your blood." I drew in a trembling breath, as lost in the moment as he was. "*Sul'harai*, Rory: a perfect and binding union." I paused. "And like all of them, it ends."

He did not speak at once. When he could, his voice was hoarse. "*Why* must it end?"

"There always must be an ending, or your true shape can be lost. The thing that makes you human."

"And if I found I preferred the other?"

I let go of his hands. "You would be beast: abomination. A thing of ancient nightmares, like the tale I told you of the warrior who lost his soul to his other form . . . or whatever was left of it."

Rory opened his eyes. He was lost also, swallowed by distances, by things he had never known. Of things he could never share, even as I had shared them; he was an unblessed man.

I had lent him a piece of my soul. Now I wanted it back.

"Lass—"

I drew in a very deep breath and gave him my innermost truth. The thing that made me different from any other woman, from any other Cheysuli, because with my gifts came a sacrifice I had acknowledged long ago. "Do you see now," I said clearly, "why I have no need of a man?"

His eyes sharpened at once. Plainly, he understood. "Oh—gods—*lass*—"

"What man can give me that? What man would even *try?*"

"I would," he told me fiercely. "Why d'ye think I asked?"

—oh, gods—oh, no—

Unsteadily, I rose. "You are a fool," I said tightly, "and I a fool for staying. It is time I went back to Mujhara."

He gathered his sword and stood. "Will you be taking this with you, then?"

I thought he meant the sword. Then I saw the knife. My silver Cheysuli long-knife, aglint with royal rubies. "But—you said . . . I thought—"

"Hearth-friends, aye," he agreed, "and knives to mark the bond. But there is more to us now, I'm thinking . . . whether you know it or not."

Helplessness welled up. *"Ku'reshtin,"* I muttered.

"And other things, I'm thinking. So are you, my lass."

Grimly I accepted my knife and gave him back his own. "And the colt, as well?"

Rory Redbeard laughed. "I'm thinking not, my lass . . . the bright lad stays with me."

I shoved my knife home in its sheath and took to the air as an eagle. To show him what it was. To show him what he missed.

But I knew no triumph in it. Only emptiness.

I lost *lir*-shape near Mujhara. Abruptly, unexpectedly. Full of shock and outrage I tumbled toward the ground, using wings to break my fall even as the eagle-form turned itself inside out.

Wait—oh, gods—wait . . . what is happening—how can *it happen—?*

There was no answer, only a cessation of the *lir*-shape. Like a ewer of water used up, the magic was gone from me.

How—?

It simply happened. One moment I was an eagle, the next something in between. And finally a woman, possessed of arms instead of wings.

I was fully human as I landed, and though it was unpleasant and painful, it was not so hard, thank the gods, as to hurt me seriously, since the wings had lasted long enough to bear me close to the track. Mostly it bruised my pride. Sprawled awkwardly and undecorously—thank the gods I wore leggings in place of skirts!—I stared hot-faced at the man on the horse and mouthed angry, embarrassed curses.

For someone who, one moment, had been riding unconcernedly down the road leading into Mujhara and the next nearly struck by a falling eagle busily resolving itself into a woman, he was remarkably unperturbed. The horse was more upset. Absently, he soothed it, speaking words in a foreign tongue.

The knowledge was sudden and ugly. I thrust myself to my feet, reaching for my knife. "Ihlini," I challenged furiously. "What else could bring me down?"

I expected some manner of reaction, some expression of his feelings, even if only in posture. Instead, he inclined his head politely in a courtesy that rankled. "My apologies," he said quietly, still soothing the spotted horse. "When the gods created their children, they might have thought of this. It is a bit disconcerting."

It was not at all what I expected. Angrily, I began, "The gods—" but let it go, thinking of other things. "Why are you here?" I asked. "Why do you come to Homana?"

"To see the Mujhar," he told me. "I have an invitation."

"*No* Ihlini—" I stopped. Looked more closely at him: white-haired, blue-eyed, exceedingly fair of face. Ancient in the eyes, young in his demeanor. Anger spilled away, replaced with realization. "You are Taliesin." Heat crept into my face as shame stung my breasts. "Oh, gods, of course you are . . . they told me what you were like. Brennan, Hart, Corin . . . even our *jehan*." Distractedly, I took my hand from the knife hilt. "I am Keely, Niall's daughter . . . I apologize for my rudeness."

"I know very well who you are, regardless of your *lir*-shape—though that, I agree, is eloquent proof of identity." Taliesin smiled. "You are very much like Corin in ways other than coloring . . . he has a tongue in his mouth, and wit enough to wag it. You, I see, do also, if in a prettier mouth."

I twisted my pretty mouth. "Harper born and bred, regardless of race . . . your own tongue is much too glib."

He laughed. Once the harper of Tynstar himself, until he chose otherwise. Until Strahan ruined his hands. "Aye, well, there is little occasion for me to flatter a woman, meaning it or not. In your case, I mean it; you have a reputation." His eyes were amused, though his tone inoffensive. "As for this thing of rudeness, I think it is certainly pardonable in view of the circumstances. The fall might have killed you. For that, *I* apologize."

I disavowed it quickly with a dismissive wave of my hand. "You are welcome among us," I told him, echoing the ritual greeting of a clan-leader. "*Jehan* will be glad to see you. He has always wished you could come." I grinned. "Ihlini or no, you have done our House many services. Even the Lion is grateful."

Memories crowded close; I could see it in his eyes. So

many services, for so many of my House. First my father,
who had lost an eye to Strahan's hawk . . . then to Brennan,
Hart, Corin, as they escaped from Valgaard. Fleeing Strahan himself, and his noxious god. Asar-Suti, Ihlini call him:
the god of the netherworld. The Seker, who made and
dwells in darkness.

I swallowed painfully, recalling how each of my brothers
had come home from that god, and what had been done
to change them from the boys I knew into men. Especially
Corin, who had left the woman he loved to go back to
Atvia. I had not seen him again.

Taliesin sighed. "The Lion," he said obscurely, "knows
me as well as you." And then he was smiling, if sadly,
stroking a wisp of hair from his eyes with a twisted, knotted
hand. "I know Hart and Corin are gone, but I will be glad
to see Brennan. The news I have concerns him as well as
Niall. And you as well as them; all of the House of
Homana."

A chill slid down my spine. "Why are you come?" I
asked. "Not for pleasure, then—it is far more serious." I
wet my lips as he nodded. "What news, Taliesin, that brings
you down from Solinde? That brings you down alone, without Caro to be your hands?" I took a step closer to the
horse, catching one of the reins to hold him in place; realization turned my spine's chill to ice. "You are *alone*,
Taliesin . . . but you are never alone. What has become
of Caro?"

"Caro is dead," he said. "Strahan is loose on the land."

Six

My father is not an emotional man. Perhaps he was once, in his youth—Ian had said as much—but he had changed. For as long as I have known him, he has hidden much of what he thinks. Out of habit, if not inclination; a Mujhar can say little without putting much thought to it, or suffer the consequences. I was beginning to learn that even kings are bound by expectations, as much as the folk who serve them.

When I brought Taliesin to my father in Deirdre's sunny solar, I expected some measure of joy. Some reflection of happiness. But he knew. He knew at once. And quietly bade Taliesin to give him the whole of it.

The Ihlini harper stood quietly in the solar, refusing the wine Deirdre offered, the chair Ian did. His crippled hands he thrust within the sleeves of his belted blue robe, putting them out of sight. And yet the words he said banished hiding places.

"I was wrong," he said. "I thought he would not look so hard for us, nor so close; we have been safe in the cottage for years. Under his very nose . . ." Taliesin sighed, dismissing it consciously. "He came, with others, to our cottage. He said he had grown weary of my interference, of my service to the House of Homana in place of the House of Darkness." Something twisted his face briefly. "That is what he called it: the House of Darkness. Ruled by Asar-Suti, with Strahan as his regent."

"Or his heir?" My father rubbed the flesh of his brow beneath the leather strap. "My sons believe Strahan fully expects to trade humanity for godhood. That he serves not so much out of a genuine conviction, but out of greed, out of ambition . . . out of perverse intent to assume a place of his own in the pantheon of the Seker."

Taliesin stared at him. Slowly the color drained from his ageless face. "He—would not . . . he *could* not, unless—" He stopped.

Ian turned from a deep-silled casement. "Unless?"

Unsteadily, Taliesin sought a chair, the chair he had declined, and sat down, hunching forward, hugging hands to chest. "If he did—if he did—" Slowly he shook his head.

Standing so close to him, I had only to put out my hand to touch Taliesin's shoulder. "Please be plain with us. You have come all this way to tell us."

"Not *that*," he said. "It was not what his father wanted. Tynstar wanted Homana. He said it was his birthplace, but denied him by the gods who cast the Ihlini out into another land, while saving Homana for the Cheysuli." His eyes were stark. "Do you see? Tynstar wanted revenge. Power, aye— how else to effect revenge? but mostly he wanted Homana. To spit at the gods themselves."

My father's voice was steady. "But Tynstar's son wants it all. Strahan wants everything. How better to spit at the gods than to make himself one of them?"

"Reward," Taliesin said. "His reward for destroying the prophecy, for keeping the Firstborn from power."

"Godhood?" Deirdre drew in a breath. "How can it be done? A man made into a *god?*"

"Power," the harper explained. "There are two kinds, lady: the power of a king—a strictly temporal thing—and the power of the earth. Power absolute, tapped by those who know how. The Cheysuli know, a little . . . so do the Ihlini. But Strahan knows more than most, being liege man to the Seker." Frowning, he shook his head. "A two-fold threat to us all, I think—if Strahan destroys the prophecy, his reward will be godhood . . . but in order *to* destroy it, he may need godhood now." Taliesin closed his eyes. "Who can say what will happen? Who can say what *can?*"

"But you are saying it could." My father sat very still, as if movement would shatter the truth and show us additional possibilities none of us wanted to face. "You are telling us now there is a way to become a god."

Taliesin looked at his hands. "I am a harper," he said slowly, "and harpers know these things. Harpers hear these things; old ones hear everything." Now his hands were trembling. "The lord I served was Tynstar in the halls of

Valgaard itself; how could I not hear things? How could I drink the blood of the god without comprehending what I did, and what was left to do?" He steadied his voice with effort. "Like Corin, I overcame it. Like Corin, I suffered for it. But I never thought it would come so far; that Strahan could want so *much*."

My father's eyes did not waver. "Can it be done, Taliesin? Or is this a harper's tale, made of style instead of substance?"

The ageless face was old. "Anything can be done with the blessing of the Seker. Am I not proof of that?" He sighed. "Nearly two hundred years old."

My father rose. He walked away from us to one of the casements and stared out into the bailey. What he saw I could not say. "How did Caro die?"

"Strahan put his hand upon him."

The Mujhar swung around. "He did no more than that?"

"Nothing more was required. A man grows old, and he dies."

My father was taken aback. "Aye, over a span of *years*."

Taliesin shrugged. "With Strahan's hand upon him, a moment was all it took."

I shivered in the sunlight. *Strahan did that to him—what could he do to us?*

Ian shifted from his casual stance against one wall. "There are stories that Tynstar stole twenty years from Carillon by putting his hand upon him."

Taliesin nodded. "It is one of the darker gifts."

"And yet he gave no such gift to you." My father's tone was resolute. "Forgive me, but it seems odd he would kill Caro and yet leave you alive. You are the one he wanted, surely; Caro was innocent."

"Jehan!" I said sharply. "You cannot believe after all he has done that *Taliesin—*"

"No," my father said. "Not willingly; never. But Strahan is powerful. No man can stand against him."

"Three men did," I said. "Four, counting yourself."

The flesh near his ruined eye twitched. "The asking was required."

Taliesin nodded. "Your father is right, Keely—no man comes away from Strahan's presence unscathed, unless

Strahan intends him to. None of your brothers did, nor did your father. So, you see, he is right to question my loyalty."

"Not that," my father said quickly. "Never, from you—you know that. After what you have done for me and my sons?" He shook his head slowly, recalling private things, private feelings, showing only the edges to us. "No. I only question Strahan's purpose."

"In leaving me alive?" The Ihlini harper sighed. "With death the punishment ends . . . he left me alive to suffer." He raised twisted, dessicated, trembling hands. "He did not kill me when he might have, all those years ago—instead he gave me *these* . . . and all the days of forever to suffer the destruction of my soul. Not my talent, no—music still lives in me—but my true gift was the harp, and that he took from me."

No one said a word. No one dared to breathe.

The harper's voice was unsteady. "Now, again, he takes, if only to punish me for the services I have done you. Killing is too easy, too transient for me . . . he wants me to live forever, knowing myself alone." With effort, he stilled his hands. "He killed Caro," he said. "He killed the man I loved."

It was Deirdre who went to him. Deirdre who bent to him; who held him against her so his anguish was seen by no one. In Erinnish words she soothed him, and put me in mind of Rory. It put me in mind of Sean, for whom I should but could not grieve, not knowing if he were dead.

Not knowing if I cared.

Ian made a sound. Startled, I glanced at him, thinking him unsettled by Taliesin and the truth of his preferences, which are unknown within the clans. But he did not look at the harper. He was looking out the casement into the bailey beyond.

"Niall," he said, "is it? By the gods, I think it is!"

"Is what?" I frowned, went to Ian's casement, stared out. Commotion raged below: horses, litters, bodies, shouting. "Who—?"

And then I saw the face upturned to my own, showing white teeth in a grin. A dark face framed by raven hair, with gold glinting from one ear.

"*Hart,*" my father said disbelievingly. "By the gods, it *is!*"

Deirdre looked at him over her shoulder. "Were you expecting him?"

"No. No message ever arrived."

"By the gods," I said crossly, "does he require an invitation?"

And then I was gone from the solar, running down the hallway. *Gods—I wish it was Corin—*

But Hart would do well enough.

I met him on the steps before he could come inside, and fetched him a hard buffet on his bare right arm above the *lir*-band. *"Ku'reshtin,"* I cried, grinning, "have you spent your allowance so soon that you must come and beg for more?"

He rubbed his arm, of course, and said something about my strength being greater than his own, then patted me on the head. It was a habit I had abhorred for all of my life; now I welcomed it.

"No, no," he demurred, "I have not come seeking coin, not from the Homanan treasury." His grin was warm and wide, self-mocking as well as winsome; he could charm the maidenhead from an oath-bound virgin, and she not regret it. "Why should I? I have the Solindish treasury now, and the jewel of Solinde as well."

"Well, no doubt you will wager it." I grinned again, intensely pleased, and shook my head at him. "Have you wagered away your title?"

"I am reformed," he explained solemnly, but the glint in his eyes was pronounced. Sky-eyed, silk-tongued Hart, born but moments after Brennan and yet so very different. "Now I only wager the allowance Ilsa gives me, which is little enough, I fear." He sighed. "She is a termagant."

"Am I?" the lady asked. "I thought I was something else; the jewel of Solinde, you said?"

Hart, smiling, turned automatically, moving just enough to leave my view unobstructed. I saw Ilsa getting out of a cloth-swathed litter, settling lavender skirts over the tops of white-dyed slippers. And again, as had happened more than a year before, I was struck by the magnificence of her. Ice-eyed, pale-haired Ilsa, whose beauty was legendary. A manifest incandescence.

We are not twins, Hart and I, as he and Brennan are,

but we are closely linked by blood, and as closely bound by emotions. I looked from Ilsa to him, sensing instinctively he was no longer the man I had known. It had nothing to do with rank or race—he was the Prince of Solinde, now in fact as well as title—nor to do with the realization all over again that he lacked his left hand. No. It was a consuming and focused intensity directed solely in Ilsa's direction.

He had married her for Solinde. He had gotten considerably more. Much more, I think, than he knew; certainly more than expected.

Hart? I asked inwardly. *Has the world turned upside down?*

And Rael was in my head with his liquid, golden tone. *Right side up,* the hawk said. *What you sense is happiness, and the elation of satisfaction with what has become of his life.*

I looked into the sky, squinting against the sun, and saw the lazy spiral as he drifted toward the bailey. He was pleased to be home again; I could sense it in the link.

The hawk's comment surprised me. Hart's life before had not been so bad, though filled with the inconstancies of wagering and a clearly defined reluctance to assume personal responsibility for anything else at all, least of all his title. Hart had always been supremely good-natured, untouched by Brennan's solemnity or Corin's moodiness. He had been, I had believed, the most satisfied of us all even when he had very little.

Now, in eminent clarity, he had more than any of us.

Ilsa smiled at us both, then turned back to the litter and took from someone inside a linen-wrapped bundle. From the folds emerged a wail.

"Wet," she said succinctly, "and too long a time in the heat. But at least she has Hart's coloring . . . with mine, she would be sunburned."

For a distinct, startled moment, all I could do was stare. And then I turned on Hart. "You sent no word of a *baby!*"

Black brows arched in feigned innocence. "Did I not? I thought I did . . ." He shrugged it away easily, seemingly unperturbed, and then the grin came back. "I wanted to surprise *jehan.*"

"*Jehan,* me, everyone else," I agreed dryly. "I suppose

it is natural enough, but I think even you will admit you make an unlikely father."

Ilsa laughed, resettling the fabric-swathed infant. "He is a fool for the girl, worse than I am myself. You would think *he* had borne her, the way he mothers her."

Her Homanan was still accented, but less so than before. Because of Hart, I thought, and wondered about his Solindish. Bedtalk, I had heard, was good for improving language. His Homanan—and Erinnish—had always been superb.

"Is Brennan—?" he started to ask, but then *jehan* and the rest arrived, laughing, exclaiming, asking questions, and I was no longer consulted. Hart had others to talk with.

"Keely." It was Ilsa, climbing the stairs to stand beside me. "I have brought the baby's wet-nurse—is there a place we might be private?"

"Hart's old rooms, perhaps . . . ?" And I laughed, marking the bloom in her cheeks. "Aye, of course—the nursery. There is room for more than Aidan."

I led her there, Ilsa and her retinue, through halls and winding staircases, conscious of change, of *difference;* of the turning of the Wheel. But two years before, Homana-Mujhar had been full of the Mujhar's children, each of us concerned with the passage of time in a detached sort of way. Our lives had been the same for so long it was impossible to imagine anything changing them, even though we knew it would come. And it had, unexpectedly, when an accident caused by the Mujhar's sons had resulted in the deaths of thirty-two people.

Punishment had been swift: Hart was sent to Solinde, Corin to Atvia. Aileen was summoned from Erinn so that she and Brennan could marry.

And then Strahan had intervened. He had stolen each of my brothers and practiced his arts upon them. That any of them had come out of the captivity with mind and soul intact was solely due to Corin, who had come of age in Strahan's fortress.

They had changed, each of them, or had been forced to change in ways none of them ever mentioned. Some were obvious: Hart had lost a hand. But Hart had also gained Ilsa and the baby she held in her arms.

*Not so different from Brennan . . . and yet nothing is
the same.*

"Here." I pushed open the door to the nursery and let
all the Solindish in. That, too, had changed; once they were
enemy, usurping Homana-Mujhar.

The chamber filled with women. Aidan's wet-nurse, his
attendants, Ilsa and all of her ladies. I found myself standing close to the door, recoiling from all the noise, the chatter of women's concerns. Baby this, baby that; who wanted
changing and feeding? It was nothing I had heard before,
having avoided Aidan's routine. Aileen had known better
than to speak of such things to me, since my interests lay
most distinctly in other directions.

They stripped the girl bare and cleaned her, disposing of
soiled wrappings. Then swaddled her again, but not before
I had seen her. Not before I had seen tiny feet and tiny
hands, the taut, rounded belly. Such pink, soft helplessness,
unaccustomed to reality. Hostage to the world.

The wet-nurse bared a breast. I saw engorged flesh, swollen nipple, blue ropes beneath fair skin. But I also saw the
woman's face as she put the baby to her breast.

*Gods—how can she like it—how can she shackle herself
to such binding, consuming service—?*

But there was peace in her face, not resentment. An
abiding satisfaction.

The baby is Ilsa's, not hers—how can she be so content?

Aidan also had a wet-nurse, but I had never watched
him feed. I had never asked anything of it, being disposed
to avoid such things.

Ilsa looked at me. "Keely—are you all right?"

The gods know what my face showed. "Aye . . . aye,
of course."

She smiled, setting the chamber alight. "When she is
done, would you care to hold her?"

The immediate response was instinctive. "Have you
gone mad?"

Ilsa laughed. "If you fear you will drop her, be certain
you will not. It is a fear all of us have. You should have
seen Hart the first time I put her into his arms."

I shook my head. "I have no desire to hold her. It has
nothing to do with fear."

Ilsa said nothing at once, being more concerned with the

baby. She tucked in a fallen fold of linen, then traced the fuzzy black hair as the baby sucked greedily. The wet-nurse murmured something in Solindish, crooning to the child.

"Did you want her?" I asked abruptly, heedless of the others.

Ilsa looked at me in shock. "Did I—? Of course I wanted her! How could I not?"

"Did you *want* her?" I repeated. "Not because you hoped for an heir—no need to speak of that to me—but because you desired a baby . . . for yourself as well as for Hart, the throne, the title . . . were you willing to let your body be used so simply to bring a child into the world?"

Ilsa stood very still. Then she turned to the wet-nurse, said something in Solindish and took the sated baby from her. In silence, she crossed the chamber to me.

"You will hold this child," she commanded. "You will hold this tiny girl who is the flesh and bones and spirit of all our ancestors, and then you will tell me there is no room in your heart for compassion, for love, for empathy, for awe and tenderness . . . even, I know, for fear, because fear is what every woman feels." She thrust the baby into my arms. "You will hold her," she said fiercely, "and I promise, you will *know*."

I recoiled as far as I dared. "Ilsa—I beg you—"

"*Hold* her," she said. "Do you think you are the only woman in the world who believes she cannot want a child?"

I shivered, chilled to the bone. I had not thought it so obvious.

Desperation welled. "But it is true," I told her rigidly, feeling the baby squirm. "Take her back . . . take her *back*—"

Ilsa turned from me and looked at the others in the room. She said a single word. As one, all of them left. All. Even Ilsa. Leaving me clutching Hart's tiny daughter.

And *knowing,* as she had promised.

All of it, and more.

Seven

Alone, in the darkness, I went to see the Lion. To see the mythical beast shaped in wood to form a throne, and to ask him for the answers. Surely he had *one.*

I lighted a torch, thrust it into a bracket. It was hardly enough to fill the Great Hall with light, but sufficient for what I required. I left it near the silver doors and made my way toward the dais.

Out of gilded, ancient eyes it watched me as I walked. Such a huge, gape-mouthed beast, rearing up from the marble dais on bunched, wooden legs. No one knew who had made it, or even how old it was. For century upon century it had crouched in Homana-Mujhar, holding sovereignty in the Great Hall as the Mujhar held Homana. Cheysuli-made, I thought, like the rest of my father's palace.

I stopped short of the dais. The flame far down the hall danced on its pitch-soaked wick, distorting light into darkness; darkness into light. The Lion seemed to yawn, displaying ivory teeth. Giltwork gleamed, lending depth to the woodcarver's skill.. Lending the Lion life.

"You," I said quietly, "are a selfish, demanding beast, requiring too much of us. Stealing our freedom from us, denying us free will . . . warping us to *your* will in the name of a vanished race."

Silence from the mouth. From the eyes, emptiness.

A wave of frustration rose to lap at my accusations, driving them shoreward toward the Lion. "For how many decades—how many *centuries*—have you sat here on the dais, secure in your power and pride, your absolute *arrogance,* knowing us faithful, dutiful children too honor-bound to even consider turning our backs on your demands? To reconsider our place in the tapestry of selfish gods, weaving us this way and that?"

Yet again, no answer. Nor did I expect it; it was only a beast of wood. Nothing more than a symbol, yet binding a race regardless. Locking shackles around our souls.

I climbed the marble steps. Faced the Lion squarely. Then, without thought, swung around and sat myself down on the cushion. Settled hands over the paw-shaped wooden armrests and thrust myself back, back, into the depths of the Lion Throne, feeling the head looming over my own, sensing the weight of years, of strength, of *power*. Acknowledging what it was even against my will.

Ambience. The trappings of heritage, shaping my heart, my will, my beliefs. I could deny it no more than myself.

And I wondered: *Is this what Teir has done? Denied himself in his quest to free our race from gods-made iron?*

Far down the hall silver flashed. The hinges were oiled so the door made no sound as it was opened, but the glint of torchlight on hammered silver gave the visitor away.

For a moment, it was Brennan. The height, the weight, the posture . . . everything was Brennan, except for the missing hand. And then he let the door fall closed and stepped into the guttering torchlight, and I saw clearly it was Hart.

Wrapped in the Lion, I waited. He came, slowly, as if in audience to our father, and paused, smiling a little, knowing what I did; possibly even why. Before the dais he halted, and inclined his black-haired head.

"It suits you," he said, "the Lion."

I grunted briefly; eloquent skepticism.

He grinned. "But it does. You have the pride for it—" lightly, "—and the arrogance."

I sighed, propping an elbow against the arm and resting my jaw in a hand. "Aye, aye, I know . . . others of my kin have labored to tell me much the same." I shifted, trying to find a comfortable position. "But I find the beast too demanding; I would prefer my freedom."

Hart turned from me in seeming idleness: head tipped, lips pursed, brows arched, appraising the Great Hall. It had been very nearly two years since he had been in it. Life for him had changed utterly.

His back was to me, which pitched his comment toward the firepit instead of at me. Which was, I realized, precisely what he wanted, to make his approach of the topic easier. "Ilsa told me what happened earlier today, with Blythe."

Blythe. I had not even asked. "She should not have done it, Hart. What if something had happened?"

He shrugged, still looking around the hall. "She felt it necessary. Ilsa is—intuitive. And also immensely compassionate." He swung back almost abruptly, reassessment duly completed. "Are you forgetting one of the foremost tenets of the clans?" he asked intently. "Something you, of all people, should know: *'If one is afraid, one can only become unafraid by facing that which causes the fear.'*"

I tensed against the Lion. "And you think I am afraid of a *baby?*"

"I know you are. I know you, Keely: you are terrified."

I drew in a slow breath, to keep my tone light. He wanted me to lose my temper, so he could play the part of peacemaker, of compassionate older brother. "If I had dropped her—"

A flick of his only hand dismissed the beginnings of my retort. "Not of dropping her; that is natural. No. You are afraid of the baby itself, *your* baby, and what it represents." He climbed the bottom step of the dais and stopped, arms tucked behind his back. So casual, my middle brother; so nonchalantly intent. "You are afraid to leave the womb, Keely . . . afraid to set free your emotions for fear of losing yourself."

Denial snapped me upright. "I hardly think a *baby*—"

"I *do*. You forget: I was the most irresponsible of us all, the least likely to be trapped by the demands of my *tahlmorra*." He climbed another step. "I was the middle son, the *wastrel* son, whose only concern was how to win the game, how to take a chance and win; to risk myself, my *lir*, my title, all on the fall of a rune-stick." His twisted grimace was self-mocking. "Aye, what I did made no difference at all, I *thought*, which left me free to conduct myself as I chose. And I chose to wager away Solinde, Ilsa . . . my hand."

Instantly, I denied it. "Oh, Hart—"

His tone was perfectly steady. "I wagered it, Keely. And it was easy, *easy*—" he thrust his left arm out in front of his body, between himself and me, "—so easy, Keely, because I thought I did not matter. Because I thought I could *win*." He took the third and final step. Now he stood on the dais, level with the Lion, and held me with his eyes, his posture; with the intensity of his being. "I have been afraid of many things, and I have been afraid of nothing. Neither is comfortable, though ignorance makes a better bedmate." He shook his head; the earring glinted. "Your fear is not misplaced, but it can be overcome. The gods know you have the strength and courage for it, Keely . . . I know it, too. We all do—" he grinned, "—which is why you drive us half mad with the violence of your passions."

I swore without heat or intent, slumping back in the wooden embrace. "You are a fool," I said wearily, "all of you. You undervalue my convictions, thinking my opinions are born out of female contrariness—"

"Not at all," he said flatly. "Gods, Keely, do you forget the power in your blood? We do not; we *cannot*. You are more gifted than any of us, and such power carries a price. I know what *I* feel in *lir*-shape . . . I know the overwhelming allure, the draw and danger of the link. And that is with only one *lir*, Keely—do you think none of us knows how difficult it is for you, with recourse to *any* shape? How strong you have to be to maintain your balance while lured by so many possibilities?" He shook his head slowly, sympathetically. "You are afraid, *rujholla*; that I promise you. You are afraid you will lose the 'Keely' the power has shaped. Wed to Sean, you are *cheysula*. With a child you are *jehana*." He paused, speaking still more quietly, more gently. "But what becomes of Keely? What becomes of the avatar of our race?"

I stared blindly into the darkness, shrouded by the Lion. "She is buried," I whispered thickly. "Swallowed by the expectations, the hopes—the *needs*—of all the others, *so many* others." I swallowed painfully. "Kin, clan, husband." My mouth was dry. "Child."

"Who could well embody more of what we were than you." Hart smiled as, startled, I snapped my head up to stare at him. "Aye. Have you not thought of that? Your child, your *children*, may be forged of stronger iron than even the *jehana*. And they, too, will be required to find the proper path. No matter how difficult." He was close to me now, so close. He put out his hand, his only hand, and touched my head, smoothing tangled hair. "You are not alone, Keely . . . not while any of us live. Not while your children live."

I shut my eyes tightly. "I am tired," I said, "so tired."

"I know, Keely. Nothing for us is easy, least of all for you." He sighed. "So much—*too* much—is at stake."

I thought of Teirnan again. Of Maeve and the child in her belly.

"Hostages," I told him. "Every single one."

Hart frowned. "Who?"

"The children. Born, unborn . . . does it matter? Hostages to the gods. Prisoners of tradition." I pulled myself out of the Lion. "She is a lovely girl, *rujho* . . . a lovely little Cheysuli. I hope the gods are kind to her."

Ian caught me as I went down the corridor to my chambers. In the hall we met one another, knowing things no one else did, and came face to face with reality.

"Well?" he asked.

"I found him," I said grimly. "I asked him. He sailed from Erinn immediately after the brawl in the tavern, and did not stay to discover if Sean survived or not."

Ian's face was solemn. "How long ago?"

I drew in a breath. "He said we should hear, as he put it, today, tonight or tomorrow . . . or perhaps a month from now." I shrugged. "We remain in ignorance, *su'fali*, and no way of knowing. All we can do is wait."

"And tell Niall, which is what you agreed to do."

I stiffened. "Now? At this moment? But—"

"No, not at this moment; he is closeted with Taliesin. Tomorrow, I think . . . or perhaps the day after." He shook his head. "There is Strahan to think about, and now that Hart is come—"

"—he will want nothing to do with questions of Sean's health." I nodded. "We have waited this long . . . a little longer will not hurt."

"A little longer, and you will be an old woman." He smiled, brows arched, as I glared. "Well? You are nearly twenty-three, are you not? Niall had five children by this age."

"And you, *su'fali*?" I asked sweetly. "You are—forty-five? Forty-six? And there is frost in your hair . . ." I grinned, turning toward my chamber. "I think you had best go look in the polished plate before we speak of age."

Eight

Hart set the bowl on the table and poured into it a collection of flattened, bone-white stones. Frowning, I saw nearly every one was marked with some sort of symbol. I picked one up, studied it, saw the etched design.

"A scythe?"

Hart nodded. "It portrays a generous harvest. A good stone, in Bezat." He showed me a handful of others. "Each carries its weight in meaning, but when drawn in conjunction with others, it can alter everything. Except, of course, for this one." He showed me both sides: blank. "The death-stone," he said. "Bezat. Draw this and the game is over."

I grunted. "I can see why you would like a game like this, Hart . . . the risk is greater than in the fortune-game."

The late afternoon sun slanted through the casements, cutting the chamber into a lattice of shadow and light. We sat in Deirdre's solar, hunching over a low table on which rested a flagon of wine, a cluster of cups, the Solindish game. Ilsa and Deirdre worked together on the massive tapestry of lions I had grown sick of seeing, talking quietly of things such as childbearing, the preservation of certain foods, the need for new dyes to freshen wardrobes grown outdated. I was, as usual, uninterested, and therefore ignored them completely.

Ian, my father, and Taliesin were still meeting with the Homanan Council, discussing Strahan and the need to send forces to the northern borders in order to reinforce them against any incursions the Ihlini might make into Homana. The harper reported loss of life near the border, though as yet on the Solindish side, across the Molon Pass; nonetheless, it underscored our need to keep close guard on the borders. If Strahan was killing Solindish he considered disloyal, I doubted little would stop him from crossing the border to kill Homanans or Cheysuli, who were more traditional enemies.

I wondered why Hart was not in the meeting, said so, and was told by the Prince of Solinde that he had already dispatched patrols to the far north. Valgaard, he explained, was in a pocket of Solinde that was and had always been steadfastly loyal to Strahan, as it had been loyal to Tynstar before him. While ostensibly part of Hart's holdings, Strahan held the real power. And until Hart had won the loyalty of the Solindish who still preferred Solindish rule, he could hardly expect the entire realm to rise up against the Ihlini, who did, he said dryly, have more right to the realm than we, Solinde being the home of the Ihlini. And not all of them were as Strahan.

And so Hart, having discharged his duty, sat with me at the table, rattling runestones and urging me to wager all the coin I had, even to my last copper penny.

"Why?" I asked suspiciously. "Is it that you *have* wagered away your allowance? Now you want mine?"

His smile was slow and sweet, his eyes, guileless; gods, but he was good! "Without risk, there is no point to playing."

"Without risk, there is no loss." I smiled back at him with equal sweetness; I am, after all, his sister. "I thought Ilsa had reformed you."

The lady herself laughed. "Only to the point of keeping him home to wager on small games such as this one."

Hart chewed on his thumb, the only one he could. "Will you play?"

"Only if *I* name the stakes." I thought it over. "I think—"

But what I thought remained unsaid, because Hart was paying no attention to me at all. "Brennan," he said intently. "Aye, it *is*—"

And so it was, coming through the door, but Hart had said it before he was in sight, and Rael, in the link, was silent. Hart had simply *known*.

Their grins were identical, though set in different faces. Black-haired and dark-skinned, both of them, with very similar bones, but more than the eyes were different. Their thoughts worked differently; although, at this moment, what they thought was the same, and there for everyone to see.

Hart was standing now. Sleeta, flowing through the door next to her *lir,* went immediately to Hart and threaded herself around his legs, butting his knees with her head. Through the link I felt her contentment, her greeting, though Hart heard nothing at all except the purr that was nearly a growl. To him, she was merely giving him catlike welcome. To me, and to Brennan, she was giving him honor as well.

Brennan took two long steps and stopped. Appraised Hart solemnly. Opened his mouth to speak.

But Hart, doing much the same, beat him to it. "You have grown fat," he announced.

"You *ku'reshtin*, I am nothing of the sort!"

"Soft," Hart added, nodding. "Fat and soft. Lazy, too, no doubt . . . domesticity ruins a man such as you."

Brennan's eyes narrowed. "Then I suggest we find ourselves a friendly tavern and discuss my domesticity—and various other shortcomings—over a jug of wine."

"Usca," Hart said promptly. "And a fortune-game."

Ilsa's head came up. Smoothly, I stepped between her husband and his brother. "I will come as well, to keep you both from trouble. I recall what it was like the last time you went drinking and gaming in Mujhara."

Clearly, so did they. Just as clearly, they preferred to go without me. But they said nothing of the sort, perhaps Hart out of deference to Ilsa; Brennan, I thought, because he knew better than to argue. If they did not take me with them, I would follow on my own.

Corin had taught me that.

The tavern was called The Rampant Lion. Its walls were whitewashed, its lion-shaped sign freshly painted. Lighted lanterns hung from posts. Altogether it was an attractive place, but instead of going in we stood outside in the street, looking at it.

"Well," Hart said finally, "I imagine they have replaced the benches and tables we broke."

"Undoubtedly," Brennan agreed, "and undoubtedly they have replaced the owner and wine-girl as well." He touched his lobeless ear, then took his hand away with effort. "Let us go in."

Hart and I followed as Brennan shouldered open the door. The interior was as clean as the exterior, well-lighted, with hardwood floor. Hart sat himself down at the first open table and called for *usca*. I joined him, but Brennan, looking around, did not at once sit. He seemed to be searching for something, and when the girl came with the jug of *usca* and cups he looked at her closely. She was young, blonde, blue-eyed; he relaxed almost at once, and paid her. Then pressed a gratuity into her hand.

"A silver royal?" I was astonished. "That is enough to buy us ten meals and all the *usca* we want, *rujho*—and you give it to a wine-girl?"

"My choice," he said quietly, and sat down next to me.

Hart's expression was uncharacteristically blank. "There is *i'toshaa-ni*," he remarked with carefully measured neutrality. "If it will give you peace again—"

Brennan cut him off with a raised finger. "I know that, Hart. But I do not notice it has done our *su'fali* any good."

"Ah," I said, "Rhiannon. Aye, it was here, was it not, that you met her?" Like Hart, I kept my tone empty of challenge; Brennan is a fair man, and even-handed, but he is all Cheysuli beneath the Homanan manners, with prickly Cheysuli pride. "And was it not here that you two and Corin fought that pompous fool, Reynald of Caledon?" I grinned. "You near destroyed his escort, as well as the tavern itself—"

"Aye." Brennan's tone was severe. "Keely, we did not come here to speak of old times."

"No?" I made my surprise elaborate. "Then why come here at all? Another tavern would do as well."

Brennan poured a mug full of *usca* and pushed it across to me. "Drink," he said succinctly. "You have come to drink, so drink . . . my business is my own, and I would rather spend the time talking with Hart than with you."

Hart's gaze on me was briefly sympathetic—he had been the subject of Brennan's irritation more often than I, and knew how it felt—then he turned to call for a fortune-game. I marked how he had adapted to using his right hand for everything, keeping the cuffed left stump away from the edge of the table. I wondered if it still hurt, as our father's empty eye-socket did when he was tired or worried. I wondered how he felt recalling how he had lost it in Solinde, to Dar, Ilsa's Solindish suitor, who served Strahan for personal gain.

And who had, I knew, been executed for it. But it did not bring back Hart's hand, which he had himself thrown into the Gate of Asar-Suti to keep Strahan from buying his service with the only thing that might: his reinstatement within the clans as a full-fledged Cheysuli warrior.

Kin-wrecked. An old custom, but still in force. Brennan had tried to have it changed, but there was as yet opposition in the clans. Already we lost traditions, the old ones said, including the *shar tahls,* because our assumption of the Lion was making us into Homanans. If we severed all ties with the old ways we would no longer be Cheysuli. A Cheysuli warrior needed *all* his limbs to be whole—otherwise how could he defend his clan?

So, for now, the custom was retained. And Hart, regardless of his title, was cut off from his clan, enjoying none of the things rightfully his by birth, by blood, by the *lir*-link with Rael.

Feckless, irresponsible Hart, who seemed the least likely of us all to care about the loss of clan-rights, since it did not affect the *lir*-gifts, nor his taste for gambling. But who, oddly enough, seemed to feel the loss the most.

Aye, Strahan had changed him. Strahan had changed them all.

We drank, played, talked. Mostly *they* talked, my brothers, renewing the link of shared birth, reconfirming the strength of their special bond.

It was different from the *lir*-link. And in many ways, more powerful. I shared my own with Corin, so I understood . . . but he was far away. Much too far away, leaving me with no one.

I drank *usca,* cursing the need for responsibility. It was, I thought, a curse Hart himself must have sworn, and often, being what he was; and yet he had changed. He had learned. He had done what was required, in the end, to maintain the delicate balance.

Even Corin, so slow to let grudges die; my angry, rebellious *rujholli,* who had resented Brennan for nearly everything, overlooking what he himself had in abundance. Even

Corin had succumbed to the call of his *tahlmorra*. Now he lived in Atvia, putting his House to rights. Ridding himself of Lillith, I hoped, and dealing firmly with our mother, Mad Gisella, who would hag-ride him to his death, if he let her.

I shivered briefly. I had no memory of our mother, who had been sent in exile to Atvia before I was six months old. But I heard the tales, the whispers, the comments. I sensed the unease in our father whenever her name was spoken, because she was truly Queen of Homana, his wife by Homanan law, *cheysula* by Cheysuli; if she came back to Homana, she would have to be properly received before he sent her away again. She had borne him sons. She had given him the means to hold the Lion, the means to further the prophecy, merely by bearing boys.

Deirdre was our mother in everything but name. But Deirdre, some said, was a whore, regardless of her blood.

If Gisella ever came back to Homana to petition for permanent residence, Deirdre would have to go. There were proprieties, customs, manners . . . she would go, be *sent*, and leave our father bereft of happiness.

It was all I had known in him, happiness, in childhood and adulthood. Because of Deirdre. Because they were content with one another.

I sucked down gulps of fiery *usca*, letting it burn out my temper. Letting it let *me* admit to possibilities.

If it could be that way with jehan *and Deirdre after so many*—twenty-two!—*years . . . if it can be that way with Hart and Ilsa*—I gritted my teeth and swallowed liquor—*then why not with Sean and I?*

It was not impossible. If I opened my eyes, I could see it. If I could shake off my stubbornness, suppress my pride, my frustration, renounce my hostility. . . .

If.

It was not impossible. But only if Sean were alive.

And then what would become of Rory?

—*oh, gods, what am I thinking*—?

Nine

"Keely."

It took a very long time for me to make sense of the word. Or what it portended. Or might.

"Keely."

Aye, of course: my name. But who—? Oh, aye, Brennan; of course, Brennan, who else? It was always Brennan hag-riding me to death . . . no, no, it was Corin who would be hag-ridden—

"Keely!"

No . . . not Brennan after all, at least, not this time . . . perhaps it had been the first time, or the second, or the first time *and* the second . . . but who now—? Oh, gods, *Hart*—of course, I had forgotten. Hart was here from Solinde, with Ilsa . . . Ilsa and a baby.

I looked first at Brennan, then at Hart, and sighed. "Both of you: babies . . . babies and *cheysulas* . . . gods, I think I will be sick—you make me *sick*—"

"If you are sick," Brennan observed, "it has nothing to do with us. You are too far gone in your cups, Keely . . . and *usca* is powerful."

"Everyone having babies." I shook my head in despair. "You, Hart, Maeve—gods, it will be Corin next, or *me*—"

Brennan went very still. "What do you mean, 'Maeve'?"

"—such a fool, such a *lack*wit! You would think she had learned her lesson after what Teirnan did . . . but *no*, he claps his hands and she runs to him, like a dog—like a *bitch*, offering herself to the hound—"

Brennan's hand came down on mine, pinning it to the table. "Keely, that is enough. It is the *usca* talking, not you—but you are, it seems, the one with all the secrets. What is this of Maeve and Teirnan—and a *baby?*"

"She went to him," I said plainly, over the *usca*-blur in

my head. "She went to him, lay with him, and now she will bear his child."

Brennan's eyes were startled. "Is *that* why—"

I overrode him rudely. "Aye, of course it is—why do you think?" I scowled at him blackly. "That is why she keeps herself to Clankeep. She is ashamed. Afraid. She thinks *jehan* will be angry."

Hart, frowning, poured the stones into the bowl and began to stir them around. "Is Teir still with the *a'saii?*"

I grunted. "With them, of them, leading them . . . he has founded a new clan, and he is the clan-leader." I sat more upright on my stool. The *usca*-haze remained, mixing with candlelight to fuddle my eyes, but I knew what I was saying. "And I am not entirely certain what he claims is false."

Brennan made a sound of disgust and shoved the jug at me. "Have more *usca*, Keely . . . it improves your imagination."

"Is it my imagination that we risk losing the *lir?*" Aye, that got their attention. "Teir has pointed out that if the Firstborn come again, there will be little need for us. Or even the Ihlini. Both will be redundant. And since the Firstborn shall have all the power, why not let them have all the *lir?*"

"Because it makes no sense," Brennan retorted. "We have always had the *lir*—why would we lose them? What reason for the gods to take them from us?"

I leaned forward intently. "Because the Firstborn are their favorites. *You* should understand that, being favored yourself—" I smiled without amusement "—and generally reaping the rewards, you and Maeve both—" But I cut it off with a chop of my hand. "It does not matter, none of it, only that I wonder again if Teirnan has the right of it . . . he said the Ihlini fight us the way they do because they understand what it means . . . they understand that if the prophecy comes to fruition, they will be destroyed." I swallowed heavily, tasting sour liquor. "Perhaps we will suffer the same fate, being discarded like soiled wrappings . . ." I put my hands over my eyes. "Gods, it is too bright in here—I swear, I will go *blind*—"

"We should take her home," Hart said uneasily. "She will be sick right here at the table."

Brennan sighed. "Better to let her be sick outside." I

heard stools scraping. "Well enough, Keely, we will take you home. Where, I daresay, someone will be delegated to put you to bed, since I doubt you are able to do it yourself."

Hands were under my arms, lifting me. The common room reeled. "Agh—*gods*—" But I bit my lip and let them escort me out of the tavern into darkness; was it evening, then? Already?

"Just as well we walked," Hart remarked in dry amusement. "I doubt she could sit a horse."

"I doubt she can *keep* a horse." Brennan's tone was bitter. "I entrusted her with my fleetest colt, and she lost him—she *lost* him . . . she let thieves take him from her, and then was too frightened to lead me to where they stole him. I did not require her to come *with* me, only to tell me where—"

I stopped dead and jerked my arms from their grasps. "*I* know where," I told him. "I *know* where, and who, and how to go about it . . . and I am *not afraid!* Not of him. Not of Rory. He would never harm me." I swung my head from side to side. "Not Rory Redbeard."

"*Who?*" came in unison.

Then, from Brennan, pointedly, "You said the outlaws were Erinnish. But you did not say you *knew* them."

I was hot. Sweating. "Gods—" I gasped. "—oh, *rujho*—"

Hart's voice was urgent. "In the alley—*there* . . ."

"Let her go." Brennan's tone was less friendly. Most distinctly lacking compassion. "She drank all of it without our assistance . . . let her be quit of it that way, too."

An alley . . . I caught a wall, tried to hang on, felt it spill out from under me. On my knees I paid homage to the darkness, as well as to all the *usca.*

It was Hart, eventually, who helped me up and held me, making certain I could stand. Brennan was a shadow in the darkness, silhouetted against lantern light, muttering something beneath his breath. I saw gold on his arms and in his eyes; in Hart's I saw compassion. But his were blue, after all . . . not fierce Cheysuli yellow.

I drew in a gut-deep breath. "I am sorry, *rujho* . . . I have shamed you, shamed myself—"

"Hush," Hart said gently. "No more, Keely—not now.

Now is the time for you to be still, be silent . . . *usca* is not always a boon companion.''

I looked past him. "Neither is *he*."

Hart smiled a little. "Aye, well, you and Brennan have always played grinding wheel to the other's steel." He sighed, smoothing tangled hair from my face. "One day, perhaps, the grinding wheel will stop turning and allow the steel to be put away."

I looked down at his other hand; no, at the stump. Carefully I reached out and caught his forearm, making certain I did not touch the wrist or the leather cuff. I brought it up into the light and stared at the emptiness. At the absence of a hand.

"They are fools," I told him, "all of them. Blind old fools, keeping to customs no longer needed." I looked at his rigid face, at the recoiling in his eyes. "*Fools*, Hart . . . each and every one—" I stopped, fighting back tears. "And I never said—I never told you . . . I was sorry."

"I know," he said. "I knew."

"I never *told* you."

He hooked the handless arm around my neck and pulled me close. "I knew, *rujha* . . . I always knew. You wear everything on your face."

A sob caught on a laugh. "Aye. Like now?" I touched my cheek. "No doubt there is more on my face than I would care to admit."

"Aye, well . . ." He grinned. "We shall go home and wash it off."

I drew in a deep breath. "Gods—I wish Corin were here."

"I know," he said, "so do I."

"But you have Ilsa—and now the baby, too."

"Aye, and I love them both. But there is still room in my heart for others . . . for everyone else I might want. Brennan, my *lir*, you . . . did you think the space predetermined?"

"Corin," I said again, as Brennan came into the alley. "Corin—and a *jehana*."

Brennan, annoyed, sighed. "Oh, Keely—"

But Hart cut him off. "She is sick," he said. "Drunk and sick and unhappy. Have you been none of those?"

Something moved in Brennan's face. "All of them," he

answered at last. "All of them, and worse." And then he came to me, to step in beside me and curve one arm around my back as Hart did much the same.

A brother on either side. But neither of them was Corin.

It was Deirdre who told me. I sat bolt upright in bed and instantly wished I had not.

"Oh, *Keely*," she said.

I stared at her in mounting alarm, then hastily bent over the edge of the bed. Deirdre pushed the empty chamber pot into my groping hands and I promptly rid myself of more *usca;* the last of it, I hoped.

I was hot, shivering, humiliated, belly-down on the bed. Lank hair, still in its braid but coming loose, dangled over the edge. My spirit, I discovered, was as flaccid as my belly.

"Gods," I muttered, "what a *fool*."

Deirdre shook her head. "They did not say it was *this* bad." She sighed, moving to help me clean my face with a damp linen cloth. "I will send for hot broth, something to settle your belly."

"No." I pushed myself up again, waved her away and did my very best to ignore the thumping in my head as well as the aftertaste in my mouth. "You said they went *where?*"

Dutifully, she repeated it. "To find Brennan's colt."

"Gods—they *cannot*—" I threw back the bedclothes, checked, swallowed back bile. "I think—I think I had better go—"

Deirdre shook her head. "You'll be going nowhere in such a state. Have you lost your wits as well as your belly?"

I balanced myself carefully on the edge of the bed, squinting against the morning light. "How long ago did they leave?"

"Not long." She shrugged, not really caring. "But you'll not be catching them—oh, lass, don't. You'd do better staying in bed."

The "lass" only firmed my resolve. "I have to go, Deirdre. Another time, I will explain." I stood up, began to dress carefully in the leathers I had worn the night before, since they were at hand, and I lacked the strength or inclination to look for fresh ones. "Did they go in *lir*-shape?" If they had, I needed to hurry.

"No." She was frowning, plainly troubled. "No, not with

Hart lacking a hand—he says it makes flying distances too difficult. They rode."

"Better," I said, nodding, "I can beat them in the air."

Deirdre shook her head. "You're too ill to hold *lir*-shape. But if you *must* try, at least keep to the ground. I'd not be wanting you to fall."

Thinking of Taliesin—and my embarrassing landing—I answered her truthfully. "I have done it before."

She said nothing as I pulled on my boots, cursing, buckled on my belt with its sheathed Cheysuli long-knife, and rinsed my mouth with water from the pitcher on my dressing table. She said nothing as I paused long enough before the polished silver to mutter over the state of my hair, the death's-head look of my face; neither did *I* say a word. I simply headed toward the door.

"Keely," she said as I reached it, "why did you say nothing of Rory Redbeard?"

I stopped short of the door and turned. "You *know*?"

"Brennan said you mentioned the name." Deirdre's tone was intent. "Is it truly Rory Redbeard, or a stranger using the name?"

"He is Erinnish," I answered, "and he named himself Liam's bastard."

Blankly, she shook her head. "Why is he here?" she asked. "Without Sean? In secret? Stealing Brennan's *horse*?"

"I have to go," I muttered, pulling open the door.

"Why is he *here*, Keely?"

"I have to go," I repeated, and went out of the chamber as swiftly as my aching head would let me.

Neither Brennan nor Hart knew where Rory was hiding, which would slow them down. Hart would send Rael to seek the Erinnish brigand out, but it would take time. Going horseback slowed them further; I knew I had a chance.

Outside, I paused on the marble steps and gave myself to the magic, to the shapechange, to the power that made me different, as Hart had pointed out. Except this time the power was sluggish, and left me feeling drained.

I drew in two breaths and began again, trying to ignore my headache, my belly, the shakiness of my limbs. And again, the shapechange failed; I lacked the concentration.

"Lady . . . are you all right?"

I opened my eyes, squinting. Lio. Pale-haired, pale-eyed Lio, wearing my father's too-bright crimson livery and staring at me in alarm.

"No," I told him truthfully.

"Is—can I help?" Such an earnest tone and face.

I scowled at him, disliking him for his health, his lack of sour spirits. "Unless you can tap the earth magic for me and feed it into my bones, I think not." I rubbed at gritty eyes. "Can you do that, Lio?"

"No. I could try, if you want me to."

It earned him a wry smile, which was more than I had expected to give. "No, no—*leijhana tu'sai* for offering . . . no, I will have to manage alone." I sighed. "Why do people drink so much when it makes the next day so bad?"

"*Ah.*" He understood instantly. "It takes practice, lady— I think you are too new at it."

"And so I shall remain." I squinted past him to the gates. "Perhaps I should give up trying to fly, which takes more effort, and go on four feet instead."

Lio, obviously uncomfortable, shrugged awkwardly. Plainly he could not conceive of changing shapes to suit purposes. "Aye, well . . . you could."

I shut my eyes again, tried to relax, to let the discomfort ebb away.

I need you, I told the power. *I need you now, today, this moment . . . I cannot account for the actions of my rujholli, and the Erinnish is deserving of my aid. He helped me, once . . . it is the least I can do, to repay him. Good manners, if nothing else.*

Something paused, listened, answered.

I smiled, feeling immeasurably better. Certainly stronger. *Leijhana tu'sai*—

My mind cleared. I thought of flowing along the track effortlessly . . . of giving myself to the day . . . of striking an endless singing rhythm within the sinews of my body . . . my fleet, magnificent body—

"*Lady*—" Lio said, and I knew the change complete.

As a cat, I left the bailey. As a cat I was lord of the world.

Rory, I said, *here I am*—

Ten

Rory was, as I arrived, preparing to mount the colt in question. One foot was in the stirrup, the other in mid-swing; the tableau abruptly altered as I arrived because I was still in cat-shape, and the sudden appearance of a large mountain cat leaping through the woodlands, yowling loudly, is enough to upset any horse, even one accustomed to Sleeta.

Thus upset, the chestnut deposited an equally startled Rory Redbeard unceremoniously on the ground.

His roar brought everyone running, except the colt, who retreated with alacrity. I found myself surrounded by eight men more than a little shocked to discover their prey feline rather than human, but who nonetheless exhibited a perfect willingness to show Erinnish steel.

Overhead came the cry of a hunting hawk.

I shed my assumed shape and faced him as Keely again, ignoring the uneasy comments and oaths from Rory's men as they rubbed eyes and winced against the unsettling disorientation of my transformation. I wasted no time on them, but peered upward through the screening of tight-knit limbs. "Rael," I said briefly. "It means they are very close."

Rory's brows, which had been knit in a black-faced scowl, disappeared high beneath his hair. "Who, lass?"

"Hart and Brennan—"

And then they, too, were crashing through the brush, if on horseback, to join us, and Rory's men spread out to include two more Cheysuli in their thinning net of steel.

Eight men—nine, counting Rory—and two warriors with *lir*. Not enough, I knew, not *nearly* enough.

It made me proud; it made me uneasy. It made me frustrated.

"No," I told my brothers.

I had, I knew, succeeded in astonishing them as well as
Rory and his men, which amused me—or would have, had
I the time—but all it got me was a reassessment of
circumstances.

And then Brennan was glaring at me, much as Rory had.
"What are you doing here?"

"More right than you," I retorted. "I know this man;
do you?"

Brennan's glare was replaced by a certain familiar grimness. "Aye," he said, "I do. He is a thief. He is the man
who stole my horse. That is enough, I think; the situation
hardly warrants an introduction."

In the shadows, Sleeta growled. The sound climbed from
deep in her throat, rising in pitch and promise. There is
nothing, even to me, quite so unsettling as a mountain cat
expressing hostile intentions. I saw Rory's men come to an
abrupt and unhappy realization that what they faced required something more than they had assumed. Men are
one thing, even Cheysuli; a mountain cat is another.

Rael shrieked overhead and came smashing down
through branches to settle on Hart's outstretched arm. Not
a stoop, but close enough; enough to startle them all.
Enough to make them realize, yet again, what manner of
men they faced.

The white hawk bated, stretching wide black-etched
wings, then lifted and flew through the clearing to settle in
a tree very near a still-recumbent Rory.

Are you quite finished? I asked sourly.

Rael said he was.

Hart glanced at me, eyes amused, but swallowed the
crooked smile. He was trying to look very fierce; laughing
would not help.

"No," I said again.

"No, *what?*" Brennan was irritated. "No, this is not the
man; no, this is not the horse; no, these are not bandits?"
He shook his head. "Decide on one, Keely, or we will be
here all day."

Hart's tone was less annoyed, being more intrigued than
anything else. "How are you here?" he asked. "I thought
you would be abed most of the day, after all that *usca* you
drank." He grinned. "Drank *and* lost."

It was not precisely what I wanted to hear—or to have

heard by others, particularly Rory—but trust Hart to say it. I shot him a disgusted glance. "I am here," I said plainly, "to make certain you do no harm to a man who gave me aid when I needed it."

"The man," Rory announced, "can speak for himself, lass." He got to his feet, ignoring Sleeta's accompanying rumble, and brushed his leathers free of clinging leaves and debris as he fixed his gaze on Brennan. "Your colt, is it, then? The fine bright lad?" He pursed lips as Brennan nodded. "So, then, I am addressing the Prince of Homana?"

Brennan, as always, was precise. "As well as the Prince of Solinde."

"*Two* princes!" Rory showed irreverent teeth through the bush of his beard. "Then I'll be thanking the gods for this day, and telling my children about it."

I gritted my teeth. "Rory."

"What, lass? Am I to bow down to them? Am I to kneel here in the dirt and leaves? Am I to swear fealty?" He laughed aloud, patently unimpressed by the exalted presence of my brothers. "Lass, lass . . . they're only men! *Men!* D'ye expect me to give them a respect they haven't earned?" He shook his head. "No, I'm thinking not. I'm thinking my lord Brennan has more horses than a single man can ride, and me with none at all—except, of course, the bright boyo."

I glared. "You at least owe them *courtesy!* Have you no manners at all?"

He grinned. "Oh, aye, lass, I do . . . but I'm for showing them only to those who are deserving. This man called me a thief."

"You are," Brennan said coolly.

Rory's brows slid up. "Am I? Am I, then? And I was thinking I got him in payment for saving the lass' life."

Hart frowned. "What do you mean?" His attention was now on me. "What is he saying, Keely?"

I was heartily sick of the subject. "Nothing," I said impatiently. "He did me a service, aye . . . some thieves—*other* thieves . . ." I scowled at Brennan. "I told *you* this already."

"A little," he agreed. And then he looked past Rory to the colt, who had recovered himself enough to wander back into the clearing. "But—did you really give him in payment?" His tone sounded uncharacteristically forlorn.

Hart snorted inelegantly. "If she did, *rujho*, surely she is worth the price."

Brennan's mouth hooked down. "Perhaps. Sometimes. Not today." He looked at me pointedly. "Nor last night." Then his attention focused itself on Rory again. "My thanks for aiding Keely—*leijhana tu'sai*, in the Old Tongue—but I will make the payment in coin."

Hart, oddly, was watching me instead of his brother. "Let him go, *rujho*."

Brennan shot him an unappreciative scowl. "Who—the colt or the thief?"

Hart's gaze was unwavering. "Both, I think."

I was hot, suddenly, and strangely unsettled. Lighthearted, good-natured Hart was more perceptive than I appreciated.

Brennan glanced at me briefly, sensing something in Hart's studied lightness, but apparently learned nothing from my red-faced expression. He shook his head, swung a leg across his saddle and jumped down. "No. I came to fetch home my colt, and so I shall."

Behind me, Rory shifted.

I thought of Brennan in Sean's place, dead of a broken skull. And also I thought of Rory, dead of a shredded throat. Swiftly I moved between them.

In the Old Tongue, Brennan told me to get out of his way. He also called me a fool and a dithering female, which I did not particularly care for, and suggested I might do better to differentiate between my possessions and his, before I was so generous with their disposition.

Equally glib, I called him a pompous, humorless *ku'reshtin* and suggested he give his *cheysula* a large portion of the respect and affection he reserved for his precious horses . . . which was not fair and did little to soothe his temper, but made me feel better nonetheless, if only briefly. Then I felt guilty.

Brennan is a fair man, and even-tempered most of the time, and does not react rashly to the provocations others, and I, give him. Usually. But he is Cheysuli, and none of us are made of stone; he had, upon occasion, lost his temper entirely, and people suffered for it.

Certainly Rory might.

Brennan put his hands on my shoulders. I pulled out of his grasp, spun, jerked my knife free of the sheath and pressed the hilt into Rory's hands.

"Lass—"

"Take it!" I hissed, and swung back to face Brennan.

Hart, I saw, was nodding, surprised by none of it. But Brennan clearly was.

He looked at Rory, who cradled the long-knife in his hands. He looked at the knife itself, as if he needed to assure himself it was what he thought it was. And then, white-faced, he looked at me.

I said nothing at all, knowing there was no need. Not for Brennan's benefit; who was Cheysuli, and knew.

He swallowed tightly, reining in the shock, the dull anger, the sudden hostility. The latter puzzled me until he spoke. "Keep your mouth from Maeve."

I was, suddenly, hot, so hot I was wet with it. I wanted to tell him he was wrong, *wrong*, but to do so revoked the gesture, diluting its purpose entirely. Destroying the meaning altogether, and therefore the protection.

Maeve, who was his favorite of the Mujhar's daughters. Whom I baited to her face and ridiculed behind her back, even before the brother who most loved her of us all.

"Aye," I agreed hoarsely.

Brennan turned back to Bane, his fidgety black stallion. He swung up, gathered reins, stared hard at me down the blade of his aristocratic nose. "Sean," he said tightly, "may be a bit discommoded."

Hart let Brennan go, holding his own bay gelding back. He looked at Rory, looked at me. "Or not," he said clearly, and swung the bay to follow his brother.

I watched Sleeta, mute, melt back into the shadows, making no sound with her passing. I watched Rael, also silent, lift from the branch and go. And Rory's men, saying nothing, disappeared into the trees.

Rory put the knife back into my sheath. "Lass," he said, "you smell."

It took effort to close my mouth.

"And your hair wants combing," he noted.

Aye, well, it did. But now, so did my temper.

Rory merely grinned, crinkling the flesh by his eyes.

"Come to the fire," he said. "What you're needing *most* is a mug of Erinnish liquor."

I put my hand to my mouth. "None of that," I told him unevenly, speaking through muffling fingers.

"Aye." His hand was turning me, guiding me, pushing me through the vines and branches. "Aye, lass, you do . . . 'tis the only thing 'twill help the thumping in your head and the ocean chop in your belly."

His words made it worse. "Rory—I have to go back."

"Aye. After." He plopped me down on his favorite tree stump, then retrieved a wineskin and poured a pewter mug full. "Here, lass. Drink it all. 'Tis better than anything a leech might give you."

I clutched the mug, staring blankly over its rim. The pungent smell evoked The Rampant Lion. Candlelight, smoke, the aroma of fresh-carved meat. Shadows. Laughter and curses and shouts of victory; the rattle of rune-sticks and dice.

Brennan: searching for Rhiannon in the face of the Homanan wine-girl. *Hart:* rolling stones, explaining about Bezat. And me; of course, *me:* drinking cup after cup of *usca* for no reason at all I could think of except a need to escape.

"Sean," I said, remembering, and then I looked at Rory.

He sat down close by, arranging his bulk comfortably. Across the ash-filled fire cairn his men with averted faces quietly played an Erinnish wagering game, giving us the only privacy they could short of leaving the tiny camp.

Rory drank liquor straight out of the skin. His eyes were very calm, mostly shielded beneath lowered lashes. A strong, tough, proud man, made for better than outlawry. Made for a throne, I thought, as much as Brennan or Hart or Corin.

But he is bastard-born. Even if Sean were dead—

The liquor stilled my belly. It also cleared my head and gave me an odd, bright courage. "Why not you?" I asked. "You said Liam had acknowledged you—that your paternity was no secret from anyone in Erinn . . ." I drew in a deep breath. "Why not *you?*"

Rory's lashes lifted, showing me hard bright eyes. "Me, lass . . . for what?"

"The throne," I said clearly. "I am the last to wish harm

to Sean—I promise you that, Rory—but I am also the first, here, at this moment, to be completely practical in things such as successions . . . I am, perhaps, more my *jehan's* daughter than I thought." I shrugged a little, gripping the cool pewter, pressing it hard against my breastbone. "If Sean *is* dead, Liam will need an heir."

Lowered lids once again shuttered his eyes. He hid thoughts behind thick lashes.

I wet drying lips. "When kings have no sons, no heirs, they make shift where they can."

His tone was oddly flat. "I said much the same to you of Brennan and Aileen."

"Aye, and I told you what Brennan would—or would not—do." I paused, wishing I could be delicate; knowing it was not a particular gift of mine. "Do you mean Liam would turn from Ierne and wed another woman in hopes of getting a new son—an infant—rather than make legitimate a full-grown, proven man?"

Rory sucked down wine, squeezing the skin more firmly than was required. It sent a broad, tight stream shooting into his mouth to splash against teeth. Droplets jeweled his beard.

I became aware of silence across the way. Eight men watched him, watched me, waiting. Mute. Unmoving. Waiting.

They would serve him . . . by the gods, they would serve him, as prince, as king, as bastard . . . to them it does not matter. It is the man they honor, not the coincidence of birth.

I looked at Rory again. He had less right, perhaps, than Teirnan to a throne, being born out of the line of succession, and yet I believed him far more worthy. And far more dangerous, if he set his mind to have it.

Liam could have him killed—

Kings had done it before.

Rory looked straight at me. "D'ye think I'm fit for it?"

"Aye." I did not hesitate.

"You hardly know me, lass."

"Enough," I said. "Enough."

The line of his mouth hardened. "Do you, now, I'm wondering . . . *and* I'm wondering how."

I shrugged, frowning, scowling into the pewter mug. "I know," I said. "I can tell. I can *feel* it—" I shook my head, avoiding his eyes for fear of what I would see. "I grew up with brothers, Rory . . . boys who were raised to be kings. They are all of them fit, I think . . . and you no less than them."

Rory's gaze was unwavering. "If I'm fit for a throne, lass, am I also fit for you?"

I nearly dropped the mug. "What?"

Deliberately, he said, "The heir to the House of Eagles is betrothed to Keely of Homana."

Something stirred sluggishly within me. Not anger. Not fear. Something like—*anticipation.*

I was curiously light-headed. "So he is," I said.

Rory's eyes changed. "No," he said abruptly, and I felt the tension snap.

"What?" I asked. "What?"

"I'll take nothing not offered, lass . . . neither a woman nor a throne."

A blurt of bittersweet laughter scraped my throat. "In Brennan's eyes, I am."

"What d'ye—?" And then, comprehending, "Oh, lass, *no.*"

"Cheysuli custom," I explained. "The gift of a knife from woman to man is similar to your custom of hearth-friends, but with a substantial difference. In the clan, the guest *does* share the host's bed."

Rory's eyes were steady. "Only if invited. And the other, I think, knew better . . . he said something of the sort."

I lifted one heavy shoulder. "*Brennan* thinks you were. By giving you my knife I was extending Cheysuli protection to you." I swallowed tightly. "I was offering you my clan-rights."

I could not judge if he comprehended the nuances of what I had told him. The language, to me, was well known, but to a foreigner the words had different meanings, different intentions. Yet I did not know how else to say it without stripping myself naked, without baring my true feelings.

Rory smiled faintly. "You did it to keep us from fighting."

"Aye."

"To keep him from getting hurt."

"*And* you," I retorted. "Do you think Brennan would be so easy?"

He chewed his lip, considering. "Depending," he decided, "on whether he was cat or man."

I scowled blackly. "*You* are sure of yourself."

Rory's smile was benign. "I'm Erinnish, lass . . . born of the House of Eagles."

And so we returned to the beginning. In my mind's eye I placed him on the Lion, because it was the only throne I knew. And then flinched away from it, retreating onto ground that gave me comfort.

"What you are," I told him, "is an arrogant, puffed-up fool." I set down the mug and rose.

Rory caught a wrist as I turned, holding me back. "Will you stay for meat, lass? And more of the liquor you're in need of?"

Gods, I am so weary— I rubbed gritty eyes. "What I am in need of is a bed."

The bearded grin was broad. "I've that as well, my lass."

"*Ku'reshtin,*" I said half-heartedly, catching the skin as he tossed it to me.

Eleven

In the morning, Rory brought Brennan's colt to me. "Take him, lass," he said. "I'll not be responsible for setting you and your brother at odds."

I made a face. "Oh, Brennan is just—*Brennan*."

Rory shrugged, putting the reins into my hands. "Take him anyway. I stole him from you, lass. 'Tis time he went home again."

"But—what you said to Brennan—" I frowned. "I thought you meant to keep him."

What I could see of his mouth was pulled down into a wry curl. "Aye, well, 'tisn't always a woman saying one thing and meaning another . . ." He grinned. "Take him, lass. He's a bright, fine lad, deserving of better care and stables than I can give him, I'm thinking."

"And yourself?" I asked.

For a moment he was baffled. And then the brows unknitted, the frown disappeared, the lashes briefly veiled his eyes. When he looked at me again, he wore the mask I had seen before. On him and on the others.

"Go home," I suggested quietly. "You are no good to your House here."

Rory jeered at me. "Neither are you to yours. You're supposed to be in Erinn, wed to my royal brother and whelping him lad after lad." He paused in silent consideration. "And perchance a few lasses . . . one or two might do, to wed into other Houses."

"Blathering fool," I said sweetly, and swung up into the saddle. "My thanks for the meat and drink, *and* the empty bed." I grinned at his sour expression. "*Leijhana tu'sai*, Erinnish—and may the next horse you steal belong to an Ihlini."

Rory slapped the chestnut rump. With effort I hung on, and was gone much too quickly to even say good-bye.

This time, I felt him. I sensed his presence obscuring the link as I approached Homana-Mujhar. It was hardly noticeable, but so close to the palace I was also close to *lir* such as Sleeta, Rael, Tasha, and Serri. It did not matter that I reached for none of them. They were always present, and I was always aware of them. It was my task to screen them out, so as not to lose my mind.

But now the link was warped, and growing worse. Weakening. A warning of Ihlini; thank the gods it was Taliesin.

He came into the outer bailey as I rode through the big gate, turning toward the stable. He smiled, gave me good welcome, added news of my brothers. "Hart has won his wager."

I pulled the chestnut to a halt, ignoring his pleas to go on. He knew he was nearly home. "I should have known," I sighed. "Do you know what it was?"

The harper laughed and nodded. "He believed you would stay the night. Brennan said no, that your pride would prevent you."

I scowled at the colt's bright mane. "My pride has nothing to do with it." And then I looked sharply at Taliesin. "Do the others know?"

"That you spent the night with Erinnish outlaws?" Taliesin nodded. "The wager was made before witnesses, including myself. Also the Mujhar."

"Also the M—" I cut off the incredulous echo. "By the gods, I swear they have no sense. Either of them. Hart is no surprise, but *Brennan* . . ." I shook my head in disbelief. "He must be very angry with me, to traffic in such dealings."

The harper's voice was dry. "He suggested the wager."

It snapped my head up. "Brennan—?" But I nodded almost at once. "Oh, aye, of course . . . his way of telling *jehan* without actually bearing the tale." I sighed heavily and picked at a knot in the colt's mane. "So, everyone knows of Rory. But then, Deirdre already did, after The Rampant Lion; it comes as no surprise." I flicked him a glance. "Was *jehan* very angry?"

Taliesin considered it. "He said it was behavior most unlike you in some ways, and very like you in others."

I brightened. "But you are sure he was not angry?"

He tucked hands inside his sleeves. "I think he wanted to be. But Hart said there was no cause. That he knows you better than Brennan, who sees only what you show him."

Absently I unhooked a foot from the stirrup, swung the leg over, slithered down the colt's firm side until I stood on cobbles. "I gave him my knife," I said slowly. "There was more to it than merely staying the night—they are accustomed to me spending time away from Mujhara, when I visit Clankeep." I avoided the harper's eyes, looking instead at the chestnut's hooves. "I gave the man my knife."

Clearly, he knew what it meant. "You must make your own integrity," he said gently. "And then you may keep it or discard it, depending on your desires."

I turned, clutching reins, ignoring the colt's nose planted in my spine even as he nudged. "You are saying no one could—or *should*—do it for me."

Taliesin's eyes were oddly serene. "You must not allow them to, if you are to know true freedom."

There came a clatter of hooves behind us. I glanced over, saw a rider come into the bailey from the city, looked again at Taliesin. "No matter who you are?"

"Perhaps because of it." He put out a twisted hand, and I saw what he waited for. Not me, but for the horse-boy who brought his spotted gelding and provisions for a journey.

It startled me. "Are you going?"

Taliesin accepted the horse, thanked the boy, hooked the reins through twisted hands. "Aye. I have given Niall my news. I did not intend to stay."

The rider clattered by us, bound for the inner bailey. He was a stranger to me, wearing livery I did not know.

I looked back at Taliesin. "I wish you would stay," I told him. "You have only just come, and you yourself said Strahan destroyed your cottage."

Taliesin smiled. "Then it is time I built a new one."

Beyond the white-haired harper, the rider was stopped at the gate to the inner bailey. Lio had the duty, asking the rider's business. When he had his answer, he gestured the man to pass. And then, seeing me, checked the rider abruptly by catching his horse's rein.

I frowned. Lio was pointing to me, or perhaps to Taliesin. I saw the rider bend down to hear better, then he looked at us, nodded, rode back the way he had come.

Reaching us, he reined in. He was brown-haired, brown-eyed, dressed in road-stained green wool, dark leather. The braided messenger's baldric stretched diagonally across his chest. Its shoulder boss was massive silver, shaped like a leaping hound.

He had the courtesy of a trained messenger, but the undertone was startled. "The Princess Royal of Homana?"

Taliesin and I exchanged an amused glance. "Aye," I agreed, knowing precisely what he saw.

He jumped down from his horse at once and presented me with a flat sealed packet he took from inside his doublet. "Lady," he said, "from my lord. He's wishing you good health, and hopes to join you soon."

The accent was unmistakable. "Erinn," I said numbly.

The young man grinned. "Aye, from Kilore. Prince's man, lady, come to serve you as well as my lord."

Alive, alive . . . he is alive after all . . . Rory, you did not kill him, you did not break his head.

Oh, gods. Rory.

The packet was heavy in slack fingers. "Serve me—?" I echoed dully.

Brown eyes were shrewdly judgmental, but what he thought I could not tell, not being disposed to try. "I'll be taking your message back to Hondarth, where my lord waits at The Red Stag Inn." He paused delicately. "If you'll be sending one, lady."

I stared hard at the silver hound on his baldric. Then at the identical impression made in green wax sealing the packet closed. "How is his health?" I asked.

The messenger was dearly startled. "Of good health, he is, lady . . . and of great good spirits, now that he's to wed." His smile was slight and private; he was, I thought, altogether too discerning for my taste. "Will you be sending a message?"

I signed for him to wait, then broke open the seal and unfolded the parchment. A blunt, inelegant message, in a blunt, inelegant hand; had he no clerk to write it for him?

It lacked salutation or honorific, beginning simply:

> *Keely—*
> *Past time the marriage was made, so we may get the heirs*
> *needed for Erinn. I am my father's only son, and Erinn*
> *must be secured. Enough tine has passed, I think, why*
> *waste any more? We are both of us more than old enough,*
> *and the betrothal long made. Let us wed as soon as possi-*
> *ble, so the bairns may be begun.*

Even Rory, I thought, had more eloquence than this. I
read the message again, noting the signature in its bold,
black hand. And yet a third time, aware now of rising anger
and a cold hostility.

With great care I folded the parchment. Clearly the messenger knew what his lord had written; I could see it in his
eyes. "A message?" I said. "Aye, indeed I have one . . .
but I will give it to him myself."

It startled him. "Lady?"

"Are you deaf?" I asked coolly, aware of my rudeness
and, in an odd, clear detachment, not caring in the least.
"I said I will give it to him myself." I gestured briefly.
"You may take yourself to the kitchens, where you will be
given food and wine. Stay the night, if you wish; I require
nothing from you save your immediate absence."

His face was white, but he said nothing more. Simply
bowed stiffly, turned his horse, walked smartly toward the
gate to the inner bailey.

Taliesin's disapproval was manifest, though little of it
showed in his expression. Saying nothing, I handed the
parchment to him and bade him read it.

When he had finished, I saw comprehension in his eyes.
"Sean," he said delicately, "is prince, not diplomat."

"Even princes learn better," I said curtly. "Are there no
tutors in Erinn? Has he no one to write a better hand, *and*
with better words?"

The harper folded the parchment again, though the task
was awkward for him. "Are you angry because of what
he has written, and how—or because your freedom is at
an end?"

"All of it," I said flatly. "By the gods, who does he think

he is? To write me such things when he has never written before!"

"Perhaps this is why." Taliesin's tone was gentle. "Instead of dwelling on his crudeness, think instead that he wrote it himself. He did not delegate it to a clerk, who indeed would choose softer words, but wrote it in his own hand, speaking of private things to the woman he must marry. Some men find it difficult, much more so than women do. Perhaps he felt hideously awkward, and took no time about it." His smile was empathetic. "He wrote in Homanan, after all, which is hardly his firstborn language. Think of the man in place of the message. Judge Sean when you have met him."

The note *had* been in Homanan, not in Erinnish, though I could read it well enough after years spent with Deirdre. It showed he had taken the time to put it in my own tongue. It was something, I supposed . . . but I could wish— and *did* wish—he had spent his care on the content instead of on the tongue.

I looked at Taliesin, seeing Rory's face before me. Bluntspoken, forthright Rory, yet a man nearer my own heart than the prince more concerned with heirs.

His father's only son? No, I think not. What I think, my Erinnish eaglet, is you had better count again.

Perversely, Taliesin's last words came back to me: *Judge Sean when you have met him.* "Aye," I agreed, "so I shall. I am going at once to do so."

"To Hondarth?" Taliesin, like the messenger, showed his surprise openly. "Why not send word he is welcome here, instead? Have him come to you." He made a simple placatory gesture. "It is, after all, what he must intend . . . he would not expect you to come to him."

I smiled slowly, savoring the moment, anticipating what was to come. "Then he will learn, and soon, that I never do what is expected, by him or by anyone else." I took the parchment back from Taliesin, crushed it in trembling hands. "I have to do this thing. Sean must know what I am."

"Do *you?*" the harper asked.

I stared blindly at the crumpled parchment. "Not any more."

After a moment, he nodded. "Then I will come with you."

In shock, I stared at him. "To Hondarth? But—you said you meant to go north . . . to rebuild your cottage."

He shrugged. "That can wait. If you truly mean to go, I will accompany you."

I would welcome him ordinarily, but his presence now would interfere. "I meant to go in *lir*-shape. A horse will slow me down, and with you I cannot fly."

"Fly, and have Sean think you too eager?" Taliesin smiled. "If you must go, Keely, do it with a measure of decorum. Or you will surely have him thinking you are hot to share his bed."

I smiled grimly. "That, I assure you, is the last thing I am—and I will see he knows it."

Taliesin watched in growing alarm as I prepared to mount Brennan's colt. "Do you mean to go now? As you are? Without telling Niall or the others?"

I swung up on the colt. "I have coin," I told him, "and you a few provisions. We can buy more on the road, and in Hondarth we can bathe. I am not entirely blind to the appearance I present; I will take pains to change it, though not as much, perhaps, as Deirdre would have me do." I grinned, envisioning her expression; also envisioning Sean's. "As for telling the others, let the Prince of Erinn's royal messenger spread the word. They will know what I have done." I gathered reins. "And, probably, why."

Twelve

Very slowly, with infinite care—much more than is my custom, which is dictated by impatience—I braided heavy waist-length hair into a single tawny rope plaited more loosely than usual. Not because I particularly desired to make myself beautiful for Sean, but because it gave me time.

My silent curse was self-mocking. Beautiful. Oh, *aye.*

I stopped short, swearing, and ripped out half the braid. Started over, forcing treble sections into a twisted rope, weaving it smooth and sleek, taming the stubborn wave of my hair into something controllable.

And will Sean try the same with me? Yet again I stopped, fingers clutching hair. *Gods, what am I doing?*

I was going to Sean.

The tap on the door was soft. Taliesin, I knew; he had come to escort me to The Red Stag Inn. It was but one street over, close by the sea. We had stopped at another inn to rest the night and to buy a bath, so I would not offend a princely nose with the stink of a two-week journey.

"Come." Quickly I finished braiding my hair, tying it off with leather.

He entered and shut the door, then paused with his back to it. His blue robe was freshly brushed, his white hair newly combed, silver harper's circlet in place. He was, as always, elegant, with a quiet, uncluttered grace. The only movement he had not mastered was the awkwardness of his hands.

Taliesin smiled. "I thought you might refuse the skirt, even after you bought it."

I scowled at him darkly. "Aye, well, I was wrong to think I might wear it. It was a waste of coin." I rose from the edge of the cot, bent to pull on boots. "I refuse to be what I am not; Sean must take me as I am."

"In leggings, jerkin, long-knife." His voice was quietly amused. "It will do, Keely . . . I promise, it will do."

I tugged on the second boot, settled my foot as I straightened. "I am not Ilsa," I snapped. "I am not a beautiful woman."

"No," he agreed.

Hands went to hips. Elbows stuck out from my sides, "You might have *disagreed,* if only for courtesy's sake."

"Why? You value honesty above all else, do you not? And, not being a vain woman, you have no patience for empty flattery." His tone, as always, was polite and inoffensive, while stripping bare the truth more eloquently than a blade. "Beautiful women rely on their beauty; you rely on *you.*"

I sat myself down again, lacking the Ihlini's grace. But then I had never had it; grace or beauty. "Gods, I am *afraid—*"

"Of course you are," he agreed. "But as for your appearance, there is nothing to be ashamed of. You are not beautiful, no, not as I have seen women beautiful, women such as Ilsa, but there is a wondrous strength and courage in your face, in your carriage, in the set of your head, the way you unerringly seek out the truth in a man's soul." He smiled warmly. "Your spirit was bred in your bones."

"Another way of saying I am plain." I sighed, clapping a hand to either side of my face. "Why am I saying these things? I never cared before. I sound like *Maeve,* now, staring into her polished plate!"

Taliesin crossed the tiny room to me and pulled my hands away. His candor, as always, was couched in courtesy, but lacked no point for all of that. "Your nose is too straight," he said, "your cheekbones high and too sharply cut, lending the set of your eyes a slant. Your jaw is masculine rather than feminine, and your mouth too wide and bold for the accepted style in employing feminine wiles." He saw my expression and laughed. "You use your eyes for seeing, not for luring men, and your tongue you use as a sword, not for promises." Gently, he cradled my chin in warped, knotted fingers. "You are not a great beauty, no,

but most definitely a Cheysuli . . . with pride and power
intact."

"But not the color," I said hollowly. "Blonde hair in
place of black, blue eyes in place of yellow. And my skin
is much too fair."

"Does it matter so very much?"

"Aye." I stared down at my boots as he took his hand
away. "Aye, indeed it does. You have only to look at Brennan to see what I should be . . . to see what I am not."

"What I see," he said plainly, "is a frightened, unhappy
woman. I thought I came with Keely."

Something pinched my belly. I stared back at him
bleakly, silenced, and then drew in a belly-deep breath that
filled my head with light. "Aye, so you did." I rose, pulled
my jerkin straight, resettled belt and buckle. "Shall we go,
then? Shall we amaze the Prince of Erinn?"

Taliesin smiled. "Indeed, I think we shall."

I am accustomed to being stared at when I walk into a
tavern or the common room of an inn, because women
rarely enter either, being content to go to tamer places for
food and drink and company. But I have never been one
for avoiding a hospitable place, regardless of the behavior
of its patrons and the thoughts they might care to think.

What the men in The Red Stag Inn thought, I could not
say. They said nothing to me, none of them, being disposed
only to watch, and with a quiet courtesy I had no reason
to question. The common room was mostly empty save for
a handful of strangers, and they kept to themselves in a
private corner. They ate, drank, wagered, but did it nearly
in silence, clearly knowing each other so well they had no
need of words.

Much like Rory's men—

I broke it off at once. I was here for Sean, not Rory; it
would do none of us any good if I set one brother against
the other, even inside my head. Out of it was more dangerous; they had already proved themselves more than willing
to fight over a wine-girl. What of the Mujhar's daughter?

"Here." Taliesin indicated a table near the wooden stairway. "We will send word through the tapster, and take our
time over wine."

I hooked out a stool and sat down. "More delay for the sake of decorum?"

"There is no need to *run*." He seated himself, signaled the tapster, smiled at me kindly. "I know it is your way to rush headlong at things you wish to confront, but in this case it may be wisest to wait. You are to *marry*, Keely, and live your lives together . . . give yourselves time to learn how the other thinks, before accusing one another of being blind to needs and desires."

"*My* needs—" But I cut it off voluntarily as the tapster hastened over.

Taliesin ordered wine and cheese and then quietly, so very quietly, suggested the tapster take word to his royal guest that someone was here to see him. He said nothing at all of names, knowing there was no need; the tapster would describe both of us in detail, and Sean would know at once.

I sensed attentiveness from the other side of the common room as the tapster hastened away. I thought it more than likely they were Sean's royal escort, being clothed in Erinnish green and bearing hound-shaped bosses on leather tabards, much as the messenger had. I cast them a sidelong glance, saw them talking among themselves, and then one of them rose.

Not Sean. I knew it. Aileen had described him—blond, brown-eyed, big—and this man did not fit.

He paused at our table. His smile was tentative, but not his courtesy. "Forgive me," he said, "but would you be the Princess Royal of Homana?"

"Why?" I asked bluntly.

His grin widened. He had a good face, and green eyes glinted. "Because my lord sent a message somewhat lacking in diplomacy, and we wagered you might come if only to set him to rights." Sandy brows arched up. "You *would* be her, would ye not? Come to set him to rights?"

I exchanged glances with Taliesin. "If I were not," I said, "would you still be so free telling your lord's business to a stranger?"

"Oh, aye. He's not a man much troubled by appearances, being made for other things." He touched two fingers to the wolfhound brooch. "Lady, have you come? Will I win my wager?"

I sighed, disliking intensely that I was so predictable, especially to a man—*and* men—I had not met. "You wagered I would come?"

His eyes brightened, acknowledging my concession. "Aye, lady, I did . . . only a few of us did not. Your reputation—" But he checked instantly, turning red, knowing he had transgressed. "Lady . . . oh, *lady*—"

I shook my head. "It makes no difference. I know what I am; so, it appears, do you. Well, it will save me time making myself clear to your lord." I looked past him to the tapster. "No doubt he knows by now."

The tapster took that for permission to come forward, and did so. "Lady, the Prince of Erinn knows. But he sends to tell you he is in his bath. Will you wait?"

Dryly, I answered, "Rather than walking in on his nakedness? Aye, I will wait. There will be time for that later."

It amused the young Erinnishman, who told me his name was Galen and ordered The Red Stag's best wine for his lord's lady. Taliesin he all but ignored, though his manner was above reproach. He was simply more taken with me, since I would become his mistress once the vows were made and was therefore worth more attention.

Taliesin was unperturbed, but equally amused. He said nothing as the Erinnish slowly came over one by one, to pay me their respects in nearly inaudible Homanan. Homanan, not Erinnish; their accents were quite bad. I answered them in their own tongue and saw subtle glances exchanged, silent secrets passed, just like Rory's men. Were all Erinnish so?

When the wine came, Galen poured it and proposed a toast to the Princess Royal of Homana, wishing her perfect health. Again, in bad Homanan, making an effort to please me. I answered again in Erinnish and saw them, one by one, drink the wine left in their cups even as I drank my own.

And then I was poured a second, this time drinking to Sean. I thought it only polite to do so, since I had already been honored. They were pleasant men, and courteous, lacking the slyness I had seen in the messenger's eyes, knowing what he carried. It seemed they all knew, but none was amused by it at my expense. Plainly, they had thought

Sean's words less than tactful, even in Homanan, which was why most had wagered on me.

As bad as Hart, all of them—

"Lady." It was the tapster at my side. "Lady, will you come up? The prince has sent to ask it."

Oh, gods. I swallowed down more wine, trying not to gulp. Over the tankard I looked at Taliesin, beseeching him with my eyes.

He gave me nothing back save grave courtesy. He would not come, I knew; it was for me to do. He had come this far with me, but Sean was my *tahlmorra*. Taliesin had his own.

I set down the tankard with careful precision. The others melted away, leaving only Galen with his green Erinnish eyes, waiting silently to escort me to his lord.

A litany ran in my head. *Tell Sean the truth. Tell him how you feel. You told Rory the whole of it—well, nearly the whole of it—now you must tell Sean. He is Aileen's brother—he cannot be so bad.*

Galen escorted me to a room, opened the door, stepped aside to let me through. I swung back in surprise. "No one is here."

He shook his head. "No, lady . . . 'tis Sheehan's room, not the prince's. He'll be with him now, helping him to dress . . . shall I send Sheehan to you, or would you prefer I stay?"

A third voice intruded. "No need," it said. "I am here now. You may go, Galen."

Galen melted away at once, going back down the stairs as the other came into the room. For a moment only I thought it might be Sean, but I knew at once it was not. Sheehan, then. Whose room I was in.

He smiled, closed the door, spread his hands as he leaned against it. His expression was rueful. "Lady, I must apologize. We've not been completely truthful with you concerning my lord's condition."

"Condition?" I echoed. "I thought he was taking a bath."

"So he is," Sheehan agreed, "but only because we put him in it to settle his wine-soaked head. And, I fear, his wits. He drank too much last night."

"*Did* he?"

"Aye." He attempted to mask his amusement, but the rueful smile crept out. "I'm afraid 'twas your fault."

"*My* fault!"

"Aye. It was in your honor, lady . . . he was drinking to good fortune, good health, strong sons and daughters . . ." He spread his hands again. "He was singing your praises, lady—and making up whatever he could of those he doesn't know."

I slanted Sheehan a glance of wry disgust. "Oh, aye . . . did he drink to a wine-girl, too? Did he drink to his banished brother?"

Sheehan pushed himself off the door and paced slowly away from it, showing me his back. He was tall, inherently graceful, lacking Rory's bulk but none of Rory's presence.

He turned. "My lord says nothing of his brother."

"Perhaps it is time he did." Sheehan, I thought, would be worth cultivating. He had the look of a man accustomed to learning the truth, even though he divulged none of it until it suited his—or his lord's—purposes. "Is he often in his cups?"

Sheehan's mouth was taut. "Since his brother left."

So, it meant something. That I could respect. "He could ask him back."

He frowned minutely. "You know his brother?"

"Rory?" I grinned. "Aye, I know the Redbeard. He came here in his exile. I had occasion to meet him."

Sheehan gestured to the tiny table by the window. "Wine? Sean should not be long . . . we've set four men to making him presentable. 'Tis why so few were downstairs to pay you honor. You'll forgive them, I hope?"

I smiled, thinking of my own experience with too much liquor. "Better you should ask if I will forgive *him*."

He turned from pouring wine. "But why? Sean is a man, lady . . . he does as he pleases. If it includes drinking overmuch, 'tis his choice. And it *was* in your honor."

"Aye, of course, that excuses it." I took the cup he offered, sipped out of courtesy, found the wine to my taste. "I will wed no drunkard, Sheehan. No matter who he is."

"You might reform him, lady." He smiled, drank, gestured toward a stool. "Will you sit? 'Tis but a poor room, but my lord was in no mood to go farther. We took what we could find in the way of accommodations."

I sat down, sipped wine, contemplated Sean's man across the rim of the pewter mug. "What are you to the prince? Not a soldier, I think . . . you have not the manner for it." I studied him more closely. "Nor much of an accent, either, for a man born in Erinn."

Sheehan smiled. "What accent I have is due to my circumstances. Erinnish-born I may be, but I grew up in Falia."

"Falia!" It astonished me. "How did you come to be *there?* We have trade with Falia, but little more than that. I have met no one who lives there."

He did not sit, being disposed to pace the room idly, indolent as a cat. He sipped wine, thought private thoughts, turned at last to me. "My father is Falian. A merchant. He came to Erinn for trade, and there he met and lay with my mother. He went back to Falia before I was born." He shrugged a little, as if dismissing the pain he must have felt once. "When I was eight my mother sent me to him, to Bortall, the High King's city, where he had his business. He knew I was his by looking at me. He accepted me, acknowledged me; I grew up there, and came back to Erinn twelve years later. I have been here—*there*—ever since." He smiled. "A poor tale, I fear—my life has been uneventful."

"But you serve a prince now."

"Sean is a good master. I could ask for no better." He stood at the table again, and again he did not sit. His voice was very soft. "You say nothing of my eye."

I smiled. "My father lacks an eye. I am accustomed to seeing a patch."

He raised dark brows, one mostly obscured by the strap that held the patch in place over the left eye. "That would explain, of course. You have tact, lady . . . a wondrous sense of discretion."

I laughed at him. "I? Oh, no, Sheehan, that I do not have. Anyone can tell you. Anyone *will*."

He smiled warmly. A handsome man, Sheehan, even lacking an eye. He was black-haired, bearded, showing good white teeth. Thick hair was cropped to his shoulders, where it curled against the drape of a soft leather doublet dyed blue. The color matched his eye.

"What else are you?" he asked. "If lacking in tact, in discretion, what do you *have?*"

He was due the truth, asking such of me. "Power," I told him succinctly. "Magic in my blood."

"Aye, of course: the shapechange." His beard was trimmed short and neat, unlike Rory's bush. I could see his mouth clearly as it moved into a smile. A polite, skeptical smile, telling me what he thought. "I have heard the tales."

"More," I said, "much more. Is there no magic in Falia? I know there is much in Erinn. How can you disbelieve?"

"Show me," he said lightly.

Over the cup, I stared at him. And then I set the cup down. "I think it is time you saw to your lord, Sheehan. I am content to wait alone."

"Show me." More intently.

Sluggish anger rose. "I am not a trained dog, performing at your whim. What I am is—"

"*Show* me," he hissed. "Or is it all a lie?"

I stood up. "Do you think—" I caught myself against the table, trying to blink sudden weakness away. "Sheehan—"

"No," he said plainly. "*Stra*han." And stripped the patch from his perfect brown eye.

The wine . . . of course, *the wine*—

I turned to run, but fell. Nothing was right any more. The floor had become the roof—the roof was beneath my feet—the walls were closing in—

"Keely," he said gently, "running will not help. By now you can barely crawl."

His Erinnish accent was banished. Now he spoke fluent Homanan with a faint Solindish undertone, precisely as Strahan would. As my brothers said he did.

I pulled the table over, spilling wine as the jug broke. Shards littered the floor; wine stained my hands, my face, my leathers. I picked up the cup and threw it.

It did not so much as go near him. He guided it aside with a subtle gesture from a single negligent finger.

—numb—

Strahan came to me, knelt down, caught me in both hands. I tried to spit in his face but could not raise the saliva.

"Much too late," he said. "Do you think me a foolish man? I prepared well for this . . . it took me all of two years." Hands tightened against my bare arms. "Ever since I lost your brothers."

Taliesin. If I could reach the door somehow, or shout his name, or summon the magic to me—

"Try," he suggested. "*Try*. It will please me to see you fail. It will please me to see you cry."

—gods—so numb—too *numb*—

"Come up with me," he whispered. "Come up with me from the floor . . . we are both of us due better. It does not become you, Keely. Cheysuli never kneel. Cheysuli never grovel—"

He dragged me up from the floor, set me on my feet, laughed when I would have fallen. Only his hands kept me up.

"Where is the magic?" he asked. "Where is the power now? Where is your Old Blood, Keely . . . your legacy from Alix?" His face was so close, *too*, *too* close. "What has become of your spirit? Your famous sword-sharp tongue? Your vaunted warrior prowess?"

I tipped back my head and screamed, but nothing came out of my throat.

"Too late," he said sadly. "Much too late, Keely. Taliesin, too, I have taken, and this time I will keep him. This time I will kill him."

Bodily, Strahan turned me. Pressed my back against the wall. I hung there in his arms. My bones had turned to water.

"You *need* me," he said, and stepped away from me.

I fell. Down the wall to the floor, legs tangling with my arms. My head thumped against the wood.

He left me lying there, helpless in my own flesh. "I need *you*," he told me, "to bear the Firstborn children. I have begun already, with Rhiannon, with Sidra, but I require the proper blood, the proper body. Yours will do, I think."

I twitched. Rolled my head. It was the only protest I could make.

Strahan knelt once more. His hands were gentle on my wrists as he pulled me upright from the floor. He leaned me against the wall, legs sprawled in two directions, and made shift to put them right, as if to give me back some decorum.

Decorum, when he had stolen my dignity.

Spasms set arms and legs to twitching. In his hands, I shuddered.

"I know," Strahan said gently. "The first effects are unpleasant, but I promise you it will get better. This will not last long."

I was hot.

I was cold.

Cramps bound up my belly.

Strahan gripped my wrists. "Let it take you," he said. "There is nothing you can do. Let it change the blood in your veins, and then you will feel no pain."

—my *blood*—?

I writhed away from him.

"Here," he said, "I will show you."

Strahan took my knife. Turned over one of my arms to bare my wrist. And cut deeply into the flesh.

There was nothing. Nothing at all. No rush of bright red blood. No spillage across my flesh. Just a deep, clean cut, enough to kill me if left untended.

But I did not *bleed.*

Fingers were locked on my wrist. "There," he said. "There."

And so it was. There. Sluggish, but *there.* Welling slowly out of the wound to creep across my flesh.

At last I made a sound. Not much more than a whimper. Black. My blood was *black.*

Strahan's eyes were intent. "Not forever," he promised. "For only as long as I need you. But I need you without your *lir*-gifts, and this is the only way."

The room was too bright. I shut my eyes against the light; against the mismatched eyes. One blue. One brown. In a face of incredible beauty, if muted by the beard.

He had cut his hair. Grown a beard. Worn a patch over one telltale eye. He had set and baited the trap, and I had put myself in it.

I felt his hand sliding my knife back home in its sheath. Aye, and why not? I could do nothing against him. I could not open my eyes.

Tenderly, he stroked a strand of hair out of my lashes. "I will get a child on you, and I will use it against your kin. Your father, your uncle, your sister, your brothers . . .

I will destroy the House of Homana, and all with the aid of our child."

Not mine. Not his. *Ours.*

His voice was very gentle. "Do not fret, I beg. It will bring no pain to you. I am not a cruel man, Keely, to cause pain for pleasure's sake. I am a simple, devout man, no different from any other, save I am sworn to serve my god, even as the Cheysuli are sworn to theirs. What I do is *required,* not a perverted whim. So I will make it easy for you."

I forced my eyes open and stared.

Strahan's smile was sweet. "There will be no dishonor in it, no besmirching of your race. By morning, Keely, I promise, you will have forgotten you were ever Cheysuli."

PART III

One

Her memories began coming back in bits and pieces, slowly. Carefully she hoarded each one like the rarest of gems, gathering them one by one to her breast until she could judge each stone for flaws; finding none, she named it good and put it into safekeeping.

Slowly her hoard grew until she had a double handful of bright stones. Looking at them all she saw the colors of the rainbow. The colors of the world so long, too long, denied her.

Looking at them all she saw a reflection of herself. And knew herself again, after a timeless, endless space and place where she had known nothing at all. Nothing, nothing at all, except the man who used her body.

The open casement in her room was high and narrow, but by pulling over a bench she could see what lay beyond. Heathered hills and tangled forests; beaches blushed silver by moonlight, blinding white by the light of day; slate-gray ocean and endless skies. Sea-spray and mist hung over the island like a veil: the breath of the gods themselves; thick by morning, thicker by night, burning bronze in afternoons.

A faint breeze blown in from the sea caught tawny hair. She wore it unbound now, unbraided, falling freely to her waist. Because Strahan preferred it so.

She stood on the bench and hugged the stone sill, pressing cold cheek against colder stone. Staring past beaches, past mists, trying to see Homana.

"A caged bird," said his quiet, vibrant voice. "A linnet, I think, or a sparrow . . . certainly not the fleet falcon, who would never condone it, nor the fierce Homanan hawk, who knows how to avoid the hunter."

She did not turn. She remained on the bench, at the case-

ment, driving fingers into stone with such force her nails splintered.

And his hands were on her, lifting her down, turning her to face him, to look on his remarkable face. Bearded now, but beautiful, in the way of perfect sculpture. "You must not grieve." A tender, beguiling sympathy. "Women who grieve do not suit the men who want them." His tone softened yet again. "And I want you, Keely."

She closed her eyes as his hand slid between the folds of her loose robe to caress her breasts. His touch, as always, raised her flesh into prickles.

He smiled with infinite tenderness, with contentment, sharing with her his pleasure, his satisfaction at her response. He was pleased by the reaction, as if to kindle any response in her at all, even revulsion, was enough to arouse him.

He withdrew his hand and wove spread fingers into the loosened hair, dragging it forward over her shoulders to be gathered and caressed, pressed possessively against his mouth. "I will keep you as long as it takes," he whispered into her hair. "If you begin to age before me, I will keep you young, until the child is conceived. Until the child is born. And still after, perhaps, if you please me."

She refused to look into the eerie eyes that had a power of their own; to do so admitted defeat. She had learned not to fight him when he took her to bed because to fight gave him reason to use sorcery on her, and that she hated worse than his intimacy.

Her hair was freed at last. "Keely," he said quietly, "I have brought someone to you."

She did not answer. When she eventually opened her eyes she saw only the white-haired harper, whom she had not seen for—

—how long?

Now, at last, she could cry.

He rocked me in his arms, as if I were a child. He sang me a lullaby, as if I were a child. And I feared perhaps I had gone much too far to come all the way back to myself.

"So long," I whispered. "How long has it been?"

He did not answer at once. And so I asked him again.

Taliesin sighed. "Three months, Keely. We are on the Crystal Isle."

I pulled away unsteadily, turning again to the casement. The mists were heavy beyond, but at least they were gone from my head.

"How do you fare?" he asked.

I stared out blindly. Shivered. When I could, I told him. "I have food and drink and excellent health. He makes certain of that."

Taliesin came up next to me. For a moment, only a moment, I recoiled out of habit. And then bit my lip in shame.

He took my hand in his twisted ones and sat me down on the bench even as he sat himself. He said nothing at all to me, knowing, perhaps instinctively, I needed the time to adjust. *Three months,* he had said; three months with only Strahan. His mouth, his hands, his manhood.

Bile rose into my throat. I swallowed it back with effort, and bit my lip again.

"What of you?" I asked. "What has he done to you?"

"Fed me, as he has you. Given me wine to drink. Left me quite alone. But he has also taken my lifestone." The harper smiled wearily. "So many times before, I thought he would do it. He has threatened, certainly, but only to trouble me, to *tease* me. Now, at last, he has, and I find, to my surprise, I am very afraid to die."

"Lifestone," I echoed blankly.

He put his hands away into his sleeves. "Those of us who choose to serve Asar-Suti are initiated through ritual. Corin himself began it, though he escaped before he could be taken by the god. As for me, there was a time I served Tynstar, and a time I served the Seker." His tone was oddly brittle. "It was Tynstar who required the ritual of me so I would live forever, and witness what he had wrought. I did what I was made to do, and so death as you know it is denied me."

My voice did not sound natural, though I labored to make it so. "Strahan told me he meant to kill you."

"Oh, he can. I am not immortal. I can be *killed,* certainly, but I cannot die of sickness or old age. Much like a *lir,* who lives far past a normal lifespan until the warrior dies, or until the *lir* is killed." He sighed. "The lifestone is the physical embodiment of an Ihlini's oath to the Seker and the ritual he performs, much as the *lir* are the physical embodiment of a Cheysuli's service to his gods. It is heart, soul, *power*. Without it, we die. Even those sworn to the Seker."

Prickles rose on my flesh. "He can kill you through the lifestone?"

Taliesin looked back at me squarely, avoiding nothing, not even the truth. "Strahan need only destroy it. And this time, I think he will."

The pain was sudden and absolute. "Oh, gods—*gods*— it was me he wanted, not you . . . you should not even *be* here!"

He caught my hands in his own. "Keely, I swear—I would sooner be here with you than have you bear this alone. That I promise you. I do not regret my presence, only my inability to stop him." Twisted hands tightened. "To keep him from you. To get us *free* of him."

"Free," I echoed scornfully, trying to swallow the pain. And then I asked him for the buckle of his belt.

After a moment he complied, stripping it free of leather. A simple round bronze buckle with a prong to keep it in place, hooked through a loop of leather. It was the prong I wanted.

I shut my right hand around the buckle. Gripped it tightly, feeling the flesh protest. Turned my left arm over, baring my wrist, and showed him the delicate tracery of scars in pale, translucent flesh. Taliesin was plainly baffled, staring at my wrist, until I thrust the prong deeply into the flesh.

He cried out, grabbing my hand to tear the clasp from me. I let him have it, saying nothing, and watched the blood, too slowly, begin to flow at last.

It welled gradually out of the gash and crept down my arm, leaving a track of glistening blackness like the slime- trail of a slug. The excrescence of the god.

Quietly, I asked, "Have you seen its like before?"

Taliesin was trembling. He closed both hands around my wrist, shutting off the blood.

"Have you seen its like before?"

"Aye," he answered harshly. "In my own veins."

Slowly, I nodded. "He calls it the blood of the god. He says it replaces my own, until my own is strong again, and only then will I be free."

His face was very pale. He knew more than he was saying, knowing Strahan better than I.

I smiled, but only a little, and none too steadily. "I have done this before, as you see, though when he learned of it he took everything from me that could be used to cut." I stared hard at the blackened blood. It bore only a tinge of red.

"Keely—"

"I am tainted," I said. *"Unclean."*

"Oh, Keely, *no*—"

I overrode his protest, his attempt to silence me. For my sake as much as his own; he wanted me to forget, so I could live with myself. "Each night he takes me to bed. Spills his seed into me. And promises me the child I bear will bring down the House of Homana."

He stared blindly at my arm, then took his hands away. Aye, he knew. Being once Seker-sworn, he knew. The gash was already closing, sealed by blackened blood. The god looks after his own.

"If he knows *I* know," I told him, "he will make me forget again. Say nothing, Taliesin, when I play my part too well."

His voice was nearly shut off. "You should play no part—you should be required to play no part—" He shook his head, trembling. "Not *you*, so blessed, born of ancient blood—"

"I think it is why," I said. "Clearly Strahan does not expect it. He thinks I am still ensorcelled."

"Then *why*—"

"Because I have conceived."

I saw him age before me, though it was impossible.

"He will take it from me," I told him. "He will pervert it. He will make it a reflection of himself. He will use it to pull down the Lion." Firmly, I shook my head. "If I tell him, he will have won. I will not let him win."

"Keely." He took himself in hand. "Keely, if you tell him, if you admit you have conceived, you will save yourself from his bed. He will not trouble you now, not expecting a child. He wants it too badly."

Fiercely, I promised, *"I will not let him win."*

Taliesin shook his head. "You cannot hide it forever. He will know very soon."

Strahan's voice intruded. "Sooner than you may wish."

I recoiled violently. Usually he uses the door. This time he did not. Out of lilac smoke he appeared, to smile benignly at us both.

"Leijhana tu'sai, harper, as the Cheysuli would say. You have served your purpose. I have the truth out of her."

I pressed myself into the wall, knowing all my secrets laid bare. The child, my memory . . . gods, he would steal them both!

Strahan smiled at me. "Linen must be washed. Did you think you could keep it from me?"

"Then why—" I broke it off, sinking teeth into my lip. *Say nothing—nothing at all, to him show him no fear, no weakness—let him think you are strong—*

"Because I wanted to hear you say it. To Taliesin, you would. To me, you would not . . . and so now you see the result." His hands were eloquent. "Less than six months, I believe . . . and then I shall have the child."

"Take it now!" I shouted. "Do you think I will let it live? Do you think I will bear an abomination? An Ihlini-Cheysuli halfling?"

"Rhiannon did," he said. "So has Sidra, though it lacks the Cheysuli blood. And so, I think, will you. You have no choice in the matter." Strahan smiled serenely. "No more than bitch or mare."

I still held Taliesin's buckle. Such a poor little thing, meant only to clasp a belt. But I held it, and I used it, thrusting it toward his face.

—an eye—take an eye—his hawk took one of jehan's—

But I was stopped. Simply. Eloquently. He put out a hand and held me.

It was not a hand made of flesh.

Strahan stood very still in the place from which he had issued out of air. He smiled. Flesh crinkled by his eyes. Teeth split his beard, and he laughed. He *laughed,* as the hand caught my wrist.

Not his. Something made of nothingness, conjured out of ice.

Hands. One stripped the buckle from me and threw it down, where it rang against the stone. Another touched my breasts and pushed me back and back again, until I stood pressed against the wall.

"Strahan!" the harper cried. "By the gods, let her be!"

"Why?" he asked coolly. "Because she is a woman? No. No, indeed . . . I respect her too much for that. Keely would never countenance special treatment because of her sex. She has made it very clear." The Ihlini's smile was serene. "I give her what she wants. I give her equality."

He did not touch me, Strahan. He had sorcery to serve him.

The hands were in my hair, stroking it back from my face. Insinuating themselves in strands, in waves, in tangles, loosening all the knots. Combing it into silk.

"So much," Strahan said, "and yet so very little. Would you like more? I can conjure for your pleasure much more than hands, Keely. Mouth. Tongue. *More.*"

I pressed my hand against my mouth to keep myself from vomiting. I would not give him the pleasure.

One of the hands stripped mine away.

Strahan looked at Taliesin. "Shall I make you watch?"

There was nothing he could do with twisted, ruined hands. And Strahan held his lifestone.

"*Go—*" I cried. "Oh, *go*—he will do as he pleases—he always does as he pleases—but it will be worse if you are here." And cursed myself as I said it, for I had given Strahan a weapon. A means to make me beg.

"Then watch," Strahan said, and replaced conjured hands with his own.

Taliesin sought his escape the only way he had left, shutting his eyes, losing himself, giving me what little privacy he could summon. Little enough, but much. He had his own share of magic.

As Strahan took me there on the stones, the harper began to sing.

Two

I sat on the floor near the casement, huddled against the wall. Light spilled into the chamber, but I saw none of it. Blind, deaf, and dumb, focused solely on the child. On the abomination Strahan had put in my womb.

I spread hands across my belly, showing nothing of the child. Still flat. Still firm. Still mine. Still hiding its treacherous secret. It housed the seed of the Ihlini, the downfall of my race.

I dug fingers into my flesh. "You will get no kindness from me."

It was the first time I had spoken to it, aloud. The first time I had acknowledged it as a living being. Boy, girl, it hardly mattered; what mattered was that if I allowed it to live, it would destroy its heritage.

"*No* kindness," I repeated.

Cheysuli, and so much more. Solindish, Atvian, Homanan. Also Ihlini. So close to the Firstborn, but made to serve another. Begotten of an Ihlini to serve Asar-Suti.

"You will die, first," I told it. "I will do what I can to kill you."

I thought of Ian, who had sired abomination on an Ihlini woman. Of Brennan, who had done the same. But they were men, both of them. This was different. This was not the same. They had spilled their seed into the womb, no more; *I* was left to bear it. To harvest Strahan's crop.

This is so very different.

I thought of Aileen, nearly dying in the effort, who truly regretted she could not try again. Of Ilsa, glorious Ilsa, who risked beauty and life, and would again, to give my brother a son to inherit the throne of Solinde.

Of women through the ages, bearing and burying children. Accepting what the gods gave them, while I cursed them for what they gave me.

"You have to die," I told it. "There is no place in the world for you. No place in my heart for you."

I drew up my legs and hugged them, staring at my cell. A fine room, large and airy, filled with bright bronze light. A huge draperied bed. Tables. Chairs. Fireplace. Worthy of my station, worthy of my name. Certainly worthy of my blood: it was Cheysuli-built. This was the Crystal Isle, birthplace of my people.

But now it was Strahan's lair.

I hugged my legs tightly and put my head down on my knees. "I have to kill you," I whispered. "There is no place for you here."

The shutters were snatched from the casement and slammed against the wall, banging, breaking, falling. The storm swept into my room.

I sat bolt upright in my bed and stared blindly into the blackness. It was dark, so *dark*—had the gods stolen the moon? Had Strahan perverted the light?

Wind roared into the chamber and stripped my hair from my face. With it came rain and leaves, scattered across my bed. It dampened the linen of my nightshift and made it a second skin, clinging like funeral wrappings and smelling of the grave.

I was wet, cold and wet, and astonished by the storm. It filled my chamber with fury, hammering at the palace, hammering at my ears. Lightning lit up the casement and invited the thunder in.

I flinched from the sound, and then knew it was more than thunder. It was the crash of wood on stone; the dull ring of iron unbolted.

Taliesin stood in my room. "Keely," he said, *"come."*

I went, and at once, dragging the weight of clinging linen up around my knees. "Where is he?" I asked as we shut the door behind us. "Where has he gone? He cannot be *here*—he would know."

Taliesin bolted the door so it looked the same as before. "The violence of the storm has drawn their attention, interfering with a rite of obeisance to the Seker. Strahan has set all the guards to searching for damage. My own, so abruptly summoned, forgot to set a watch-ward; it was easy for me to unlock my door with a bit of the old magic." Wryly, he smiled. "I had put away such things because of how it has been perverted by Strahan and others like him. I was not certain I could summon it, but a little of it came. Enough to get me free."

"*And* me."

"And you. There was a watch-ward on your lock, but it was easy enough to break. Strahan expected no trouble from an Ihlini; it was set against Cheysuli." Frowning, he stretched out a gnarled hand. "I shall have to make one myself, so no one knows you have gone. Step back, Keely . . . your nearness may warp the power."

Aye, so it might. We were too close to one another, our magic neutralized. I had no recourse to *lir*-shape or any of the gifts, he could barely summon the *godfire* to make his crude little rune.

I moved away, scraping along the wall. The wind had torn open all the shutters and come in uninvited, blowing out candles, lamps, torches. It filled the palace with darkness. It filled me with trepidation: Strahan could be near.

"Hurry," I whispered urgently, as he summoned his share of *godfire*.

I saw light, tiny light, dancing on fingernails. Such fragile, twisted hands conjuring fragile, twisted light. It glowed purple in the darkness and set his eyes aglitter.

He knitted the individual flames together into one, forming a knotted rune. Its brilliance made me squint and then it began to gutter.

The strain was plain in his face. His flesh was damp with it. "Farther," he urged. "Only a little, Keely . . . you are still too close to me. It is a watch-ward against Cheysuli— if it senses you, it can kill you, or at least bring Strahan to us."

I might be too close even outside the walls. And even then, it might not matter; this was the Crystal Isle. As sacred to the Cheysuli as Valgaard to the Ihlini.

"Farther," he whispered urgently, as the rune intensified.

It leaned toward me, like a hunting hound catching a scent. And it *knew* me, just as Taliesin had promised. It tasted Cheysuli in my blood.

Taliesin whispered something to it, soothing as father to

child. I did not know the words, having learned no Ihlini. But clearly the rune understood. It bathed his face with light, then bowed in the palm of his hand.

The harper turned. He placed his forefinger against the lock, shut his eyes, sent the fire from flesh to iron. I saw it begin to glow.

"Weak," he muttered, "too weak . . . but it will have to do."

He turned, saw me waiting, came away down the corridor. Took my hand, squeezed it, led me down a winding stairway to a low, arched door. Beyond howled the storm.

"There is a bailey," he said, "and gates. He will have set watch-wards there as well, to keep us in—if I can, I will break them. If not, we shall have to find another way."

Taliesin pushed open the door and let the storm inside the palace. It soaked us both at once, pasting the linen to me and flattening hair against scalp and shoulders.

We waited for the lightning, huddling in the doorway. And then, when it came, he pointed a twisted finger. "There," he said, "the gate." It was just visible through the rain, blackness tarnished silver by a necklace of lightning clinging to the sky.

I ran, squinting and mouthing curses, clutching sodden linen now heavy and cumbersome. I was barefoot and cold, nearly knocked down by the force of the wind. Now I cursed aloud; Strahan would never hear me. Only the roar of the storm.

Wet cobbles were slick and treacherous under my feet. Moss softened as did mud, turning the bailey into a morass. The palace had been too long unattended, and the lack of care showed. It made the place dangerous.

"Here—" Taliesin caught my arm, pulled me close. We had reached the massive gate and huddled at its foot.

"Watch-wards." A trace of Ihlini *godfire* clung to iron crossbars. "Can you break them?"

"If not, we are trapped. This is the only way out." He stood in the wind and the rain, trembling from the effort it took to stand upright against the storm. "Stay down," he said, "stay down. This will take time, and I fear we have little left. Strahan is not stupid."

I hunched down at the foot of the gate, craning my head

to watch. Rain filled my eyes again and again even against an upraised hand.

How he labored, Taliesin, drawing on self-exiled power, on his tremendous strength of will. I stared fixedly at his face and saw the tension there, the enormous effort expended, and all on my behalf. An Ihlini serving Cheysuli, risking his life to do it.

His alien, Ihlini face, so very much like my own. It is the color that makes us different. They are so often black-haired, even as we are, but there the sameness in color ends. Fair-skinned, the Ihlini; we are, for the most part, dark. And they lack yellow eyes. But the pride is the same, and the arrogance, the single-minded determination. You have only to look at the faces, at the shapes of distinctive bones and the fit of the flesh over them.

For too long we have been blind. For too long we have not looked, afraid to admit the truth.

Strahan was kin, I knew, in spirit as well as blood. He was Teirnan in different flesh, striving for different goals, but serving the same dark end. The end of the prophecy.

I stared blindly across the bailey, lashes beat down by the rain. *Why do we have to be one? Why not leave us divided? Sharing power equally, not fighting for all of it . . . not risking* lir *and lifestones. Both children of the gods—*

"Keely," Taliesin gasped, "I cannot. I am too long out of practice . . . the wards are too strong for me—" He bent over, coughing, and I saw how he cradled his hands. The tips of his fingers were burned. "Strahan holds my lifestone at this very moment . . . I can sense it, I can *feel* it. Keely— Strahan *knows*—"

I stood back from the gate and stared up. "If I could only take *lir*-shape—" But I cut it off at once. There is no sense in wishing aloud for what you cannot have. "We will climb," I said firmly. "There is no other choice."

He interlaced ruined fingers to form a step. "Then allow me to be your servant. It is you he wants, not me . . . you must go first, Keely. Promise me you will."

I reached out to catch a shoulder. "Taliesin—"

His tone, for him, was curt. "Say *'leijhana tu'sai'* later."

I kilted up linen as best I could, lacking a belt, and lifted a wet, bare foot. Taliesin set his hands beneath it, braced himself, thrust me upward toward the gate. Higher, higher, stretching to lift me as high as he could, pushing me toward the top.

I reached, stretched, caught the top hinge of the massive right leaf. Hung there, gritting teeth, hating the wind and the rain. Scraped toes across wet wood, colder iron, caught the crossbar with my left foot. Hooked my toes as best I could, using the brackets to balance.

Something touched my foot. Cold, lethal fire, spilling out to embrace my flesh.

—gods, it is the watch-ward—

"Keely," he cried, "hold on!"

Taliesin no longer held me. My weight hung from my arms. My right foot I hooked in the niche between gate and wall, jamming my ankle to brace myself, sprawling very nearly spread-eagle across the gate leaf.

I tried to tear my left foot free of the crossbeam, but the *godfire* held me too tightly. It crept from toes to heel to ankle, seeping through flesh into muscle and blood.

"Climb!" Taliesin cried.

Rain beat into my head and ran continually into my eyes. The thin fabric of my nightshift snagged on splintered wood, tore, gaped open. The gate scraped my breasts, chafing tender nipples.

"Taliesin—the watch-ward—"

I saw him look. He saw then how the *godfire* had spilled from iron onto flesh, trapping me easily. It ran uphill to shin and to knee, crisping the tattered hem of rain-soaked, muddy nightshift.

He put out his hands and touched the iron. I saw the *godfire* waver, reassert itself, then abruptly flow out of my flesh into iron again, and then into Tahesin. He was afire in the darkness, burning unabated in wind and rain.

"Climb!"

"Up—" I whispered. "—*up*—"

The wood was studded. Clinging carefully, I toed out from the crossbar and felt for the iron nails. Aye, here and there, in regimental lines. If I could find one not so flush, having worked itself out of the wood . . . just enough to provide me purchase—

There. My toes caught, curled, clung. Carefully I worked my right foot out of the niche, freeing my aching ankle, then lunged upward toward the top. Leaving the hinge behind, with only the lip above me.

—caught it. Used my momentum to pull myself up, *up*—

—gasping, wheezing, swearing, flogging myself with words—

oh—gods—up— Is it so much to ask?

The wood was wet with rain. Flesh could find no purchase.

"—gods—" I grunted, *"—up—"*

I jammed my right foot into the slot again, bracing myself unsteadily. Then I used it, shoving upward, chinning myself on the top.

—almost—almost—

I jerked, lifted, hooked an elbow over the top. Swung my left leg up as high as I could, felt the heel catch briefly on the iron-bound lip. Swung it again, grunting, felt it catch, and hold.

—up—

My right ankle came out of the slot, leaving skin on hinge and wall.

—hold on—

I was up, up . . . balancing so precariously, one leg hooked over the lip. Clinging with rain-slick hands and praying with rain-slick mouth.

I looked down at Taliesin, face upturned to mine. He was smiling against the rain, hiding his pain from me. Luminous in the darkness, ablaze like a funeral pyre. But alive, so *alive,* repudiating the man who had so carelessly repudiated the gods-given gift of the harpsong.

O gods, I thank you for Taliesin . . . leijhana tu'sai *for this harper . . .*

I grinned back and called out his name—

—and saw him changed into dust.

Taliesin?

I clung to the gate and stared.

Taliesin?

Water washed dust away. There was nothing of Taliesin.

Oh, gods, not Taliesin—

Rain beat me into wood.

I sang him a keening funeral song on an anguished, muted wail, not believing what I had seen. Not believing I saw nothing in the place of a living man.

Never *Taliesin*.

"Strahan," I said aloud, though it was lost in a crash of thunder.

Escape was what he had died for. Failure would dishonor the death.

I scraped myself over the lip of the gate and dropped.

Three

I scraped elbows, chin, breasts, and knees. Bruised feet when I landed, and more yet when, overbalanced, I fell backward awkwardly to plant buttocks solidly on hard, cold cobblestones.

Instinctively, one hand spread itself across my belly. *Are you dead yet, abomination? Has this killed you yet?*

As if an answer, *godfire* crept through cracks in the massive gates and set the darkness alight.

I was up at once, and running, snatching wet linen from ankles and knees, cursing my lack of boots. The cobbles were slick, cracked, unsteady, turning from under my feet. And then it was earth, not stone; mud and slime and water. A rope of soggy vine fell out of the trees to snare me.

I tore it from me, cursing, beating away the net. It was gods-made, not human, but serving Strahan in ignorance. I was off the path through the forest, fleeing more deeply into the wood, with nothing to cut my way.

I tripped, fell, lunged up, tripped, and fell again. The light was bad, but better; each time lightning netted the sky I could judge the way to go, even with no marked path. I could not help but think of Brennan with his superior night vision. It was the animal in him; I lack the yellow eyes.

Foliage crowded my way. I shredded it and ran on.

—*far enough, no farther far enough from Strahan, and* lir-*shape will defeat him*—

An exposed root tripped me. I fell hard, gasping, feeling blood spill out of my lip. It tasted of salt and copper.

Behind me, Strahan laughed.

I lunged forward on hands and knees, thrust myself up, turned with my back against a tree. Hung there, panting noisily, conscious of pain in my chest, in bone, in flesh. I wanted badly to spit at him but had no strength with which to do it.

He wore a circlet on his brow, rune-wrought, glinting silver, alive with alien shapes. And a blood-red, *true*-red robe, belted with silver bosses. The folds of the robe washed purple.

Strahan smiled his seductive smile within the shadow of his beard. *Godfire* flickered in eyes, in mouth, in nostrils, setting fingertips ablaze. "You," he said serenely, "are most direly in need of a bath."

Now I did spit.

Strahan's smile widened. Teeth parted the clipped beard. "A bedraggled, cast-off kitten thrown down a well to drown, then pulled out unexpectedly by a very thirsty man." He paused for effect, lifting winged brows. Wrought silver gleamed on his brow. A painter, transfixed by beauty, would make Strahan a king. The Seker would make him a god. "Shall I drink you, then?"

I told him what he could do in succinct, explicit Old Tongue.

Clearly he understood. *"Reshta-ni,"* he answered, equally at home in the Old Tongue as he was in Homanan. He held his ground even as I did, making no effort to move in my direction. Ten long paces lay between us. "You may run," Strahan said quietly, linking hands behind him, "for as long and as far as you like. I will not move to stop you, only to recover you when you fail. This is an *island,* Keely . . . there is no place you can go. *Lir*-shape is denied you, even with your Old Blood . . . and I am stronger now than ever before, less subject to the bindings other gods have put upon us."

Rain ran down my face, washing the blood from my chin. "This is the Crystal Isle, the birthplace of the Firstborn. We hold dominance here, even as Ihlini do in Valgaard."

"Once, aye, with me, and over others, still. But things have changed, Keely . . . even as *I* have changed."

I bared my teeth. "Are you a godling, now? Has the Seker taken your manhood and given you back divinity?"

Strahan raised one brow. "As to the state of my manhood, surely you can tell me. You have reason to know if I am made castrate by greater power, giving up one for the other."

My belly clenched within me. "Is it the only reason?" I cried. "For godhood, for reward, you try to tear down Homana?" I braced against the tree and drew in a gulping breath. "You have always claimed before to do it because of your race. Salvation, you have said—salvation out of destruction."

"It is precisely that," he agreed, "and indeed, I do it for my race."

"Strahan—"

He overrode me. "What I have said before is true: the completion of the prophecy will destroy Ihlini *and* Cheysuli. Stopping that completion will void the extermination of my race, which is what we all face. You. I. All of us." He shrugged, frowning a little, then banished it with a wry twist of his mouth. "You name me demon, I know, and the servant of even worse . . . well, I will not stop you; you may call me whatever you like. No doubt there is some truth in it, when viewed through Cheysuli eyes." Strahan no longer smiled. "But the blade is two-edged, Keely. You and the rest of your House are doing everything you can to harm my race. To stop it, I must harm yours." He grinned slowly, disarmingly, astounding me with humanity: man in place of demon. "It was, after all, what I was bred to do, being born to Tynstar and Electra. I was reared in Valgaard, not Homana-Mujhar. The Seker is my lord, not the pantheon you serve." The mismatched eyes were eerie, reflecting self-made *godfire.* "I honored my *jehan* and *jehana* as much as you honor Niall. Are we so very different?"

Beguilement was part of his magic. I shook my head firmly. "But you want more. Much more even than Tynstar."

Strahan considered it, and nodded. "I want more."

"Why?" I cried. "Why make yourself into a god? Is this not enough?" I flung out my hands. "You are Ihlini, and powerful . . . you have more magic than any man I know. Why trade it for something else?"

Winged brows rose to touch silver, as if he considered the question ludicrous. "Because I want to," he answered. "What I want, I get. What I want, I take. And occasionally, if I must, what I want I *make.*"

My hands clutched my belly. "You made this child. Against my will, you made it . . . you made abomination."

He shook his head. "Not against your will . . . you *had* no will. Now, of course, you do—I shall have to do something about that. If I cage you up with your mind intact, you will beat your wings against the bars until you burst your heart. And that I cannot allow. A dead woman bears no children."

I turned into the darkness and ran.

Yet again, I ran from him. As long and as far as I could. *You will get no children from me, Ihlini . . . this one or any other.*

In the deepwood, I was sheltered from much of the storm. Close-grown trees and self-woven boughs set a ceiling over my head, shunting water and wind to other places. Lightning still laced the sky, but the storm was dying away.

Run as far and as long as I like, he says—well, so I shall, godling . . . I will run all the way to Homana, regardless of the sea—

I ran. I *ran*. But I did not reach Homana. What I reached was something, some*where* older. A place of ancient and binding power, though lost to long disuse.

It loomed before me, made of stones atumble one against the other; a small, private place, shining wetly in the lightning, washed black and silver by rain. Old, ancient stones, set in a crumbling circle. Time had toppled them, spread them, knocked their heads together like drunken soldiers in a tavern, while their bodies slid slowly apart.

The light of the storm was fading. In its place was darkness, the deep, heavy darkness of a spent storm only sluggishly giving back the world the moon and the stars it has stolen.

Light came up from behind me. A cold, spectral, purplish light, cast in the form of nightfog rolling low against the ground. I had seen its like before. I knew it all too well.

Five steps only, and I was inside the tumbled chapel. It smelled of mold, of age, wet stone, mud. But more: it smelled of *power*.

I swung back and faced the fog. "Well, then, will you come?"

It came. It flowed like Sleeta, hunting; like Brennan running with her; like me, in sleek strong cat-shape, flowing smoothly under the sun. It came now hunting *me*, throwing itself forward to enter the chapel, but found it could not do so. I stood back and laughed as it tried, splashing against an old and abiding magic it had no power to break.

Splashed and fell back, like waves against a shoreline. It hovered just before the crooked doorway, stirring sluggishly at the threshhold. Then flowed to either side, encircling the ruined chapel with an ankle-deep mire of *godfire.*

The roof of the chapel was gone. I could see traces of old beamwork, though most was tumbled against the ground inside the chapel walls. Timbers leaned haphazardly against broken stone. Part of the interior was still sheltered by a woodfall of ancient beams, but most lay open to the elements.

Wet walls gleamed. I looked up, up past the broken beams, and saw the moon scudding out from behind the clouds. And stars, heralding it. The storm at last was gone, giving me light to see by.

A shaft of new moonlight lay upon the remains of an altar. It tilted precariously sideways, pedestal plinth shattered, propped up by another stone. It was choked with vines and lichen, but beneath them I saw runes.

I crept forward slowly and knelt down before the altar in wet, leaf-strewn earth. I put out a scraped, muddy hand and tore away the lace of ivy, the soft cloak of bronze-green moss. Beneath my fingers were runes, grown smooth over the years, but depressions nonetheless. I let my fingertips linger, following the shapes. Old Tongue, and very formal. The form only infrequently used in the clans, and then mostly by the *shar tahls.* We have grown too far away from the old language, and the years have altered our tongue into a mixture of Cheysuli and Homanan. This language humbled me. This made me feel unworthy.

This language put me in *awe.*

I traced out the runes I could reach, then pushed more foliage out of the way. Shadows shifted, sliding aside, showing me deeper secrets. Someone had been here before me. Someone who knew the ritual forms for asking *lir*-grace of the gods, and sacred, binding blessings for a warrior gone out of life and entering into death, in honor, on his way to the afterworld.

The step was loud behind me. "Petitioning for salvation?"

It brought me upright, swinging around to face him. The altar was at my back. He was at the doorway.

At it, not in it. Much like the glowing *godfire* that clung to his booted feet, so close to the rune-warded entrance.

He wore no knife, no sword. He needed neither of them. Strahan was power incarnate.

But here, I thought, my own might do.

"Still bedraggled," he sighed. "Still in need of a bath."

I raised my chin and smiled. "Come in and give me it *here*."

He laughed. But he lingered. It was enough to tell me the truth. "If you lose the child through this night's folly, be assured there will be another. You are young and strong and healthy; a child a year, I think, will be a good beginning."

I touched my still-flat belly. "Then make another *now*. Surely this one will not mind. And I am twin-born, Strahan—perhaps there will even be two."

He said nothing in answer at once, being disposed only to reassess me. I had been too long benumbed, and he had never truly known me. Only my father, my brothers. Never had he known *me*.

Strahan reassessed me. Light glittered in his eyes and sparked off rune-wrought silver.

"What if I die?" I asked. "Women do, bearing children. Or what if, in losing it, I become barren? Women do, Strahan. And our House is full of it . . . how is your own, I wonder? There is you, and Lillith . . . Rhiannon? How many of you are left? How many Ihlini like you inhabit the House of Darkness?" I paused. "There are others, Strahan . . . others like Taliesin. Your House is a minority—how many of you are there?" Again I waited a beat, altering emphasis. "How *few* of you are there, Strahan, beloved of Asar-Suti?"

His tone was very quiet. "If you think to stay, to thwart me, remember you must eat."

It was confirmation: he could not enter the chapel. But neither could I go out. It was, I thought, annoyed, a bitter-sweet victory.

Until Strahan drew a five-pointed star and stepped through it into the chapel.

My back slammed hard into stone as I lurched away from

him. The altar shifted, slid, toppled, taking my balance with it. I fell awkwardly and painfully, sprawled across the remains of the pedestal.

I pressed hands into damp earth to steady myself, to find purchase, to scrabble away, and felt metal bite my fingers. Something sharp. Dangerous. Something I could use.

I clutched it and came up, twisting from the ground. The litany ran in my head: *When in danger use any weapon at hand, even that which is not a weapon.*

But this one *was* a weapon. This one was a *knife.*

I thrust it home in his heart, clean to the twisted gold hilt.

Four

I sat in the ruined chapel with Strahan's blood on my hands. Black, viscid blood, stinking of the Seker.

I sat in the midst of stormwrack and looked on my handiwork.

The knife stood up in his chest. Moonlight gilded the hilt, setting the gold to glowing. Setting the rubies to blazing as if they might banish the *godfire*. Thus banished, it flowed away, tearing like tomb-rotted linen.

I stared fixedly at the knife. Not mine, but very like it, hilted in gold and rubies, with the face of a snarling lion swelling out of the satiny grip. The Lion of Homana. I had seen its like before, carved into the marble of royal sarcophogi deep in the vaults of Homana-Mujhar.

And now Strahan's body profaned it.

At last I could move. And I moved, lunging forward, kneeling close to the body, settling both hands around the hilt and jerking the blade from the cage of Strahan's ribs. It stuck, held firm, came free. Blood fouled the blade.

"No," I said aloud, and caught a corner of crimson robe, now free of clinging *godfire,* to swab the blood from the blade.

Clean, good steel, burning brightly in the moonlight. I cradled it to my breast. *"Tu'sai, leijhana tu'sai—"* And then abruptly I broke off, recalling the more recent runes carved into the ancient altar.

I turned to it, creeping forward, and knelt again before it. It was chipped, cracked, blemished. Many of the runes were destroyed. But I saw the newer ones, the ones I had meant to read before, denied by Strahan's arrival. Now I had the time. Now I had the chance.

I traced them out carefully, reading them aloud. It was a Cheysuli birthline, naming the generations, the lineage of

the warrior gone ahead to the afterworld. The names were
all familiar, being of my clan. Being also of my House; he
had been brother to my great-grandsire.

I sat very still for a long time. And then I reached beneath the broken altar, scrubbed away the debris of decades, brought out the armbands and earring.

Metal chimed. I saw in the bands, now dulled by dirt,
the shape of a wolf running. In motion in the metal. Nose
to tail, nose to tail, sweeping around the curves.

Homanan knife. Cheysuli *lir*-gold. Only one man with
both.

"Gods—" I said in wonder, and then I began to laugh.
"Gods—" I said again, this time through the tears, and
clutched the gold to my breasts: knife, armbands, earring.
Only one man with all. *"Leijhana tu'sai,* Finn. Your murderer is dead!"

I knew better than to tarry. Strahan was dead, but there
were still Ihlini on the island. If I did not leave now they
would catch me and they would keep me, to bear a dead
man's child.

Carefully I set down the knife and the *lir*-gold, laying
all aside until I could tend them again. Then, with great
determination and even greater distaste, I went to Strahan's
body and caught handfuls of heavy wet wool, refusing to
touch his flesh. Slowly, muttering charms against the taint,
I dragged him from the chapel.

It would have been easier to leave him. But the chapel
was Cheysuli, built to honor gods, not pretenders; I wanted
no profanation. Neither did I desire to trespass upon Finn's
spirit, which surely watched from somewhere.

The body was slack and heavy, utterly graceless in death.
It was, I thought, an obscene parody of what he had been
in life. I paused, hunching beside him, looking on his face.
Wasting a moment to look, because he commanded it. Even
in death, there was beauty.

He had died in shock, in disbelief. It showed in the set
of his mouth, in the staring of his eyes. One blue. One
brown. Set obliquely above the cheekbones so very like a
Cheysuli's, if housed in fairer flesh.

Bile rose in my throat. It was all I could do to swallow
it back. "So," I said aloud, "you win after all. No prince

of a royal House will take to wife a despoiled woman. Even *without* the child . . . virginity is a necessity, and I no longer suit."

Strahan made no answer. If he could, he would have laughed.

I looked down at myself, at scraped and muddy arms, at torn and soiled nightshift. I could hardly go to Hondarth in such a disreputable state, or I would be rudely received, dismissed as a beggar-girl, or worse. I had no coin, nor a pouch to carry it in. All I had was the *lir*-gold, and that I would not spend.

I looked again at the body, sprawled outside the chapel. And in the end, ironically, it was Strahan who served me. He wore no belt-purse, providing me with no coin, but he did wear silver on brow and hips and a soft wool robe over leathers, even wet and muddy. It was better than what I had.

I looked grimly at the body, *"Leijhana tu'sai,"* I muttered, and bent to strip the robe from him.

It took all my strength, all my control to make myself touch him, to touch the body that had, in living flesh, stolen mind and will and *self*. I worked in haste, unfastening the belt, bending arms still flexible. And then I touched a hand and felt the last vestige of warmth in his flesh.

Fear stung tender breasts. *Is he alive after all?* I bit my lip to keep from vomiting, from surrendering my purpose. If I did not complete the task he would have a final victory, even after death.

Like a nightmare, it faded slowly: *No, of course he is not.* And I tugged the belt free at last.

With Finn's knife I cut the hem shorter and also the belt, tying the extra silver bosses into a corner of the robe. The touch of his clothing swaddling my body wracked me briefly with revulsion, but I set it all aside to think of escape instead. Now I was clothed enough to go into the city. Now I had enough silver to buy me food, drink, rest, and herbs to loosen the child.

But even for its value, I could not touch the rune-wrought circlet. It rested against his brow, tangled in fallen hair; a crown for the Seker's heir. I wanted none of it. His minions could have it back; or the skeleton itself.

In the chapel again, I knelt briefly at the altar. Not in the name of gods, but in the name of my long-dead kinsman. I held the knife and *lir*-gold to my breast, cradling deliverance, and in Old Tongue and Homanan thanked him for intercession.

"Kinsman, I honor you for your care. But Carillon gave you this knife when you swore yourself to his service, and I will not take it from you. Not after all these years."

Next, the *lir*-gold, glinting dully in thin moonlight.

I passed my thumb over the image of the wolf, smiling a little. "I am a woman, and therefore have no *lir*. But I honor yours, knowing who he was, and give him back to you. Storr's name will be remembered."

I tucked the earring and armbands into shadow beside the knife, pressing all into the mud. Scraped debris over the glint, then packed it down to form a seal. It was not my place to determine if the weapon and *lir*-gold should ever be found again, or used. My place only to return it, to let Finn make the decision for another Cheysuli in need.

I turned to go, but halted. Knelt there still on leaves and mold and mud, staring at my hands. At the scrapes and cuts and grime.

Strahan's blood was gone; I had wiped it from my body. But my own remained, a little, in a cut, a scrape, a welt. Red, watery blood, no longer thick and black. Red as the robe I wore, and without the sorcerer's taint.

For a long moment all I could do was stare blindly at my arms. And then I recalled my lip, my swollen, bitten lip, and bit into it again.

Blood welled. I tasted the salt-copper tang. Rolled it across my tongue and then lifted the back of my hand to my mouth. Pressed it against my lip and stared at the result.

"Red," I said intently, and then laughed out loud for the joy of it, to know myself set free.

At once I reached for *lir*-shape, summoning the magic. It came instantly, and powerfully, spilling into my weakness and making me strong again. It stripped away the exhaustion, the grief, the lassitude of long imprisonment, and gave me back my life again, replenishing me with my magic.

Strahan's power was banished. In its place was my own. "A hawk," I said intently, "not a linnet or a sparrow. A fierce Homanan hunting hawk, whose freedom is the skies."

It came with a rush, like a river in full spate. It washed

over me, sucked me down, tumbled me against rocks. There was no kindness in it, no soft welcome or gentle comfort. Power knows nothing of flesh, only the blood that summons it.

—*drowning*—

I gasped, sucked air, tried to breathe again. Felt the shift in muscle and viscera, the shrinking of my flesh, then the twisting of the bones. Power was sucking me down, taking me back, wrenching my shape from me. I had offered and it had accepted; no longer was I wholly Keely, but neither was I a hawk.

—*such pain*—

Power rearranged me. Took the *"me"* from me and made me something else.

—*too strong*—

The shape of the world was different, and all the colors in it.

"—gods—" I croaked, "you will kill me with your kindness—"

Something heard, and listened. Power receded a little. Enough to give me respite.

I lifted twisted limbs. Saw them ripple, twitch, then blur. Flesh melted into feathers.

The shape of the world was different, and all the colors in it; as different as I myself, and viewed from altered eyes.

Screaming of joy, of victory, I hurled myself into the sky.

—*surely this is the best form of all, superior to any other— surely every warrior must long for flight, all of those men with earthbound souls, earthbound lir; the women with nothing at all . . . oh, gods, I thank you*—leijhana tu'sai *for this gift!*—*gods, there is nothing like it, nothing to touch the exhilaration, the joyousness of flight . . . surely nothing can fill mind or body with such a perfect satisfaction—oh, gods, Rory, I wish you knew how to fly*—

And then, abruptly, I fell.

—*down*—

—*down*—

—*DOWN*—

Thinking, as I fell, —*but a hawk knows nothing of swimming*—

Five

Strahan's robe. Wet wool is heavy; wool in water, worse. Strahan's robe would drown me.

I fought the weight, the water, trying to reach the surface. But I had no breath, no breath at all, having come back to myself too late. Sinking even now.

Gods, am I to drown? Is this how the child dies?

I had meant to kill it, but not myself as well.

Kicking, kicking and sinking . . . I tried to unhook the belt of bosses to free myself of the robe, but my fingers were swollen and sore, too clumsy to undo the hooks.

Inwardly, I laughed. *Is this how he takes his revenge?*

Something snagged my hair. Was I so near the bottom already?

Snagged, caught, held. Dragging me toward the surface.

I let it take me, praying for air, petitioning for a rescue—

—and broke into air, choking, with an arm around my neck.

The forearm was under my chin, forcing my face out of the water. "A rope!" my rescuer cried, and I blessed him for his Homanan.

Something came down and struck my face, scratching mouth and cheek. It slapped water, was dragged down and looped around my ribs, then knotted beneath my breasts.

"Up!" the voice shouted, and I felt the rope snap taut.

Rough hemp bit through wool and linen, chafing skin already tender. The knot rolled beneath my breasts, pinching; I clutched it with both hands as I fell upward into darkness.

A boat. More than that: a ship. Well, Hondarth was a seaport; I was a fool to be surprised. I clung to the rope with all my strength and used my feet to steady my ascent.

I was pulled up and over the taffrail, lifted by many

hands: large hands, toughened hands, the hands of sailors and soldiers. None of them kind or gentle, but infinitely welcome. They lay me upon the deck and took the rope from me, throwing it over the rail again to pull up my rescuer.

Men talking, shouting, laughing, calling comments to the one coming up the side. The rest knelt around me. Then one put his hands on the belt, as if he meant to strip me.

Power had left me before. Now it came rushing back.

—cat—

Claws unsheathed, I slashed, and cut somebody's hand. Blood welled, dripping; fear-scent fill my nose. I screamed and slashed again, giving rein to the magic in me.

They fell back from me at once, offering no threat. But they were men, all of them men, and one had put his hands upon me.

Acrouch upon the deck, I held my ground and snarled, showing them my teeth. I smelled blood and fear and shock, all mingled together with man-smell, the musk of an animal equally deadly as myself. Hands were on knives, on swords, but none of them drew steel. Instead, all they did was stare.

I saw the man, my rescuer, climb over the rail and drop to the deck. Wet wool stuck to his body and hair to his face. Water pooled on wood, running down to taint my paws. He flung back head and hair and showed me eyes I knew. Eyes as blue as my own, in a face, except for the beard, almost too familiar.

In shock, I banished *lir*-shape, still crouching on the deck. "*Rujho*," I blurted hoarsely, "when did you learn to swim?"

And then I sat down all at once, legs asprawl, one hand over my mouth. My belly expelled seawater with abrupt efficiency.

He came forward at once, saying something in shock, but I heard none of it. I retched and brought up seawater, retched and did again. Wondering if the baby would try to climb out as well.

He touched me. I lurched back, then cursed myself for my folly. It was Corin, *Corin*, not Strahan. But the body, at first, was blind, reacting only to what it remembered; what it needed to forget.

The spasms died. The cramping passed. I looked at him through ropes of hair and saw the tears in his eyes.

"Keely," he said softly. This time I suffered his touch.

"Get it off," I said thickly, "get it *off*—" I clawed at the belt, at the robe, trying to tear it from my body. "Corin— get it *off*—throw it into the sea . . . better yet, *burn* it, so the taint is gone from the world . . . gods, oh, *gods*, take it—take it *off* me, Corin—"

"Keely. Keely, stop."

"Corin—Corin *do* it—do it *now* . . ." I saw the men staring, eyes shining in the moonlight. "Do you think I care?" I cried. "Do you think I care about them? Let them see, let them *see* . . . after Strahan does it matter? Do you think I care anymore? Do you think modesty worth the trouble when I have been in Strahan's bed—?"

"Keely, *stop*—"

His hands were on my wrists, holding them tightly, like shackles; trapping human claws. The robe hung awry from my shoulders, baring the remains of linen nightshift shredded nearly to nothingness. Blood showed through the rents: I had scratched myself in my frenzy, and reopened other scrapes won in my escape. Sea-salt and wind were corrosive.

Beyond him, I saw the others, clustered at the railing. Strangers all, to me, staring with watchful eyes. The gods knew I had given them cause.

I recalled what I had said for everyone to hear. Recalled what had been done, and whose child lived in my body.

I looked from them to Corin. "You should have let me drown."

His eyes were full of questions but he asked none of them, which was a change from the old Corin, the one I had known so well. This Corin simply ignored the things I mumbled, too exhausted now to make sense, and pulled me up from the deck into his arms, to carry me below.

It was the new Corin who, taking me into a private cabin, stripped the hated belt and robe from my body, and also the shredded nightshift, then made me sit on the edge of a bunk while he washed me, cleansing salt residue from cuts and scrapes, and all done in comforting silence.

At first I protested, wanting him to see none of me. But we had been children together, and though during the difficult years of adolescence we had been modest, it had passed with adulthood. I had seen him naked and he had seen me more times than I could count; I would have thought nothing of it had it not been for Strahan's intimacy and the results in breasts and belly.

Then he put me in a nightshirt, wrapped a soft blanket around me and held a cup of wine to my mouth. "Only a little," he said, "and beware your lip as you drink."

I sipped carefully, only dimly noticing the sting of it in my cut lip. My hands shook on the cup, but his steadied me. I drank half, then shook my head, and he set the cup aside.

He asked nothing of me, which I was prepared to give. In silence we sat on the bunk, side by side, sharing nothing of what we thought and felt because it was not necessary. Born of the same labor, we often require no words.

I shivered with a sudden chill and he put an arm around me, pulling me close against his side. And then as the shivers deepened into convulsive shuddering, he wrapped me up in both arms and pressed my head against his shoulder, rocking me back and forth.

"Shansu," he said, *"shansu.* I am here for you. I promise, unless you ask it, you will not be left alone."

All I could do was shake.

"Shansu," he said, *"shansu.* There is no dishonor in tears. Drown me if you like; I think I will survive. I have learned how to swim."

It did not matter to me that he was wet, or that his hair dripped into my own. It did not matter that his beard dampened my face, or that the power of his embrace set bruised flesh to aching. All that mattered was who he was: Corin, my twin-born *rujho,* who knew me better than any.

But there was something I could not tell him, no matter who he was.

"Shansu," he said yet again, with a manifest gentleness I had never heard in Corin, so often given to intolerance born of a powerful impatience. Atvia had changed him. She had taken my brother from me and given me back a different man.

After a while he stopped rocking. I shut my eyes and slept.

Warmth. Incredible warmth. It crept throughout my body and undid the knots in all my muscles, leeched the worst of the soreness from my flesh. I burrowed toward the warmth, wanting more of it, and felt the damp nose press itself against my neck.

Startled, I opened my eyes. Kiri gazed back at me, so close as to make me cross-eyed.

I drew back my head a little, blinking, smiling, reaching out to touch the warm, plush fur. Corin's russet vixen was snugged up against my body. It was her warmth I felt, and an abiding empathy.

Awake, she said, *at last. They thought you might sleep forever, but none cared to disturb you. My* lir *has been most solicitous; he will be relieved to know you are better.*

Am I? I asked. *Is the child gone, then? Or do I carry it still?*

Kiri hesitated. *Still,* she told me at last. *You were ill, but not from that. The child has taken root and will not be easily dislodged, certainly not without risk.*

Her tone was eloquent. I gritted my teeth against it. *You think I should not take that risk.*

You will do what you will do; it is your perpetual habit. But you should consider carefully what the attempt might do to you.

Kill me, do you mean? Or make me barren, like Aileen? I sighed; the warmth was receding as I came farther out of sleep. *What does it matter, Kiri? No man will have me now, so barrenness makes no difference; it might even prove a blessing, in view of my preferences. And while I have no desire to die, I have even less to bear this abomination. I think the risk is worth it.*

So everyone thinks of everything until the risk is faced. Kiri pressed her nose against me again. *You are not a lackwit,* liren, *but too often a headstrong fool. Human desires, even Cheysuli, are often shaped out of ignorance, out of needs too often too small. Do what you must do, but consider it carefully, first.*

"Aye," I agreed wearily, and felt her withdrawal from me in the link. It meant she wanted privacy; all *lir* can close themselves to me, just as I can close myself to them. I knew she was talking to Corin.

He came, as expected, almost immediately, ducking to enter the tiny cabin. He smiled when he saw me watching

him, turned briefly to say something to someone outside
the door, then shut and latched it, coming over to the bunk.

How he has changed, my rujho . . . *the others will be
amazed.*

It was more than just the beard, which I had forgotten
he wore. He was taller, broader, harder, more significantly
a man. There was no boy left in him, and I found I missed
my Corin.

He grinned at me, reading my expression. Teeth split the
beard, reminding me of Rory. Equally tall, equally broad,
equally thick of hair, though his was darker than Rory's
and the beard blond in place of red.

Corin perched himself on the edge as I sat up and made
room for him. Kiri took herself to the end of the bunk and
curled against one of his legs. "Hungry?" he asked. "I have
sent for food and ale."

I nodded, reaching out to touch his hand. Briefly our
fingers locked, squeezed, then fell away again. We would
say nothing of it again, though what had been said was
in silence.

He pushed back a lock of my tangled hair, then put a
comb into my hand. "Here. And there is clothing for you
as well; we are anchored just off Hondarth, and I bought
them for you."

"Clothes?" I waited as he rose, fetched them, brought
them over to me. "Smallclothes," I said dryly, "and a tunic
and a *skirt?*"

Corin grinned. "I could hardly buy you Cheysuli leggings
and jerkin. You will have to wait until we are home again
for that."

I examined the tunic and skirt, holding each up. Nubby,
soft-combed wool, summerweight; the weave was russet and
cream. Also a belt, and thin leather slippers. "No boots,
then?"

His tone was firm. "These will do."

"Aye, so I suppose." I dropped everything into my lap.
"I had best begin on my hair. The clothing, I think, can
wait."

Corin pulled a small stool from under the bunk and
perched himself upon it, watching idly as I began working
on the worst of the knots in my hair. But his tone was far

from idle, being clipped and tightly reined in. "How did Strahan catch you?"

"With cunning, guile, and patience." I picked at a stubborn tangle, looking at it instead of at him. "He was clever, *rujho,* and much too knowledgeable of me . . . he knew what inducements to use. He knew what would bring me running all the way to Hondarth."

"Strahan has always been clever . . ." His tone was reminiscent; he was recalling, I knew, his own entrapment in Atvia, and the inducements Strahan had used to lure him from lifelong beliefs. It had very nearly worked.

"He came out of Valgaard," I explained, "first. And then, with seeming intent, he began killing those who did not serve him. Ihlini, only Ihlini, but creeping closer to Homana." I drew in a breath, took up another section of hair. "He killed Caro, but not Taliesin, because he knew what the harper would do: go straight to the Mujhar." I tightened sore lips, then wished I had not. "Because, of course, it would draw *jehan's* attention all the way north, leaving the south to Strahan." I tore mats out of my hair with more violence than was needed. "And it worked. *Jehan* sent patrols across the Bluetooth. Hart sent Solindish troops. All of us thought of the northern borders, not of Hondarth, or of the Crystal Isle, though he has used it before."

"Decoy," he murmured.

"He knew me too well, *rujho* . . . he knew how to bait the trap." That, most of all, cut deeply. I shredded more hair, starting a pile in my lap. "He lured me to Hondarth, caught me, took me to the Crystal Isle. *South,* not north; if anyone looked for me, it was in the wrong direction." I thought bitterly back to the messenger: Solindish, not Erinnish; Strahan had planned well. Undoubtedly the "Erinnishman" had told no one my direction. Or, if he said anything, he told them the wrong one. "Taliesin came with me. Strahan caught us both."

I had, I hoped, kept my tone free of inflection. But Corin heard something regardless. "Where is he?" he asked intently, but I think he knew the answer.

—on the gate again, rain beating into my face—in wind and rain and despair, staring down on the crystallized dust—

I clutched the comb in my hand. "Strahan had Taliesin's lifestone. He destroyed it when we escaped."

Corin stared hard at the floor. Beneath tawny hair his brow was deeply furrowed, reflecting the grief he fought so hard to keep from showing. "Again," he muttered, "*again!* How many lives does he take? How many more will he—"

"None," I said flatly. "I have always said, if given no choice, I could kill a man."

Corin's mouth opened. "*Strahan* is dead?"

"In the chapel," I told him, "though I pulled him out of it."

His eyes were full of blindness, glazed with the realization of deliverance and the disbelief it could happen. "*Strahan,*" he said.

I had thought to rejoice. Surely there was relief, curling deep in my belly, but not a trace of satisfaction. Strahan was dead, but his child lived on in me. And there was also Sidra's, somewhere in the world.

"Dead," I agreed.

"Do you know what you have *done?*" He was up from his tiny stool, standing rigidly before me. "Do you *know* what you have done?"

His intensity amused me. "I have some idea."

He paced back and forth, rubbing upper arms as if he was cold. "Keely—oh, gods, *Keely*—do you know? Do you have *any* idea—" He broke off, staring at me. "No more Strahan . . . no more proxy for the Seker . . . gods, I think we are *free!*"

Amusement disappeared. "The House of Darkness still stands."

It stopped him with a jerk. "What?"

"The House of Darkness," I repeated. "There is Lillith, and Rhiannon, and Brennan's bastard on her." I drew in a steadying breath. "Also a child by Sidra, who bears Strahan's blood." I shook my head. "Tynstar left us Strahan as his heir. Strahan left one as well."

"Unless it died." Corin shrugged as I looked sharply at him. "It could have. Babies die. Women die in childbed. It is possible Strahan has no heir at all, in which case we are free."

I thought of the child in my belly. *Are we, then?*

Corin frowned, still considering. "There is Lillith, aye—

and Rhiannon . . . but they have been followers, not lead-
ers. With Strahan dead, we may be free of them both."

"Perhaps." *Perhaps not.* It would take hours to untangle
my hair, and I preferred another subject. "How long will
you be staying? Is it for pleasure, or for business?" I
glanced up abruptly. "Is it *jehana?* Had Mad Gisella driven
her son out of Atvia?"

"No," he said curtly, then, sighing, sat down on the stool
again. "No, not *jehana* . . . she lacks the wits to try."

I might have asked more, but something else intruded.
"Is Lillith still there?"

"I sent her away. I assume she went home to Solinde.
There has been no word of her in Atvia." He shook his
head. "No, Keely, I am not here for myself. I came for
you."

"Me?" I gaped. "There was not time to get you word of
my disappearance and have you be here by now—"

He shook his head again. "No, no, of course not . . . it
had nothing to do with that." He chewed his lip a moment,
purposely delaying. His eyes avoided mine. "It has to do
with Sean."

"Sean," I echoed blankly. *So, Rory, here is the truth at
last.* I knotted my fingers together. "Is he dead, then? Are
you bringing word from Liam?"

Corin's brows ran up beneath his hair. "Dead? Sean?
No." He frowned. "Why would you think he is dead?"

I opened my mouth to tell him, but shut it almost at
once. Not now. In silence I began to comb my hair again,
simply for something to do. "Then he is alive."

"Aye, of course. Very much so. This is his ship we
are on."

The comb snagged a tangle. "*Sean's* ship? This ship?
Sean is on this ship?"

Corin nodded his head.

Oh, gods. Oh, *gods.* "Sean is on this ship?"

"Come to pay suit to his bride."

I clutched the comb in one hand. The other was full of
hair. "Was he on the deck? When you rescued me—was
he on the deck?"

"It was Sean who pulled you up."

I remembered little of it, merely hands and faces, all

jumbled together, nothing of one man. Only noise and pain and hands.

"Then he knows," I said dully. "He *knows,* and all his men. How could he not? I shrieked it at everybody." I looked straight at Corin. "Tell him to go home."

"Keely—"

—*and the cat, crouched on the deck, showing them teeth and claws, screaming her rage and fear—*

Humiliation set me afire. "Tell him to go *home.*"

Six

Rory grinned down at me. "You're a daft lass," he said, "to be loving the sword so much. But I'll not take you to task for it; I'm fond of the blade myself."

I grinned back, content; I had learned a new trick. "Show me again, Rory. I will need it against Brennan."

Heavy brows arched up behind the bright forelock of curling hair. "'Tis the only reason, then? You want to beat your brother?"

I shrugged, still grinning. "That, and more. I have to prove myself. I have to prove my sex."

The Erinnish brigand laughed. "That's not needing proof, my lass . . . I have eyes in my head, I'm thinking."

"Now," I said succinctly, and preceded him into the clearing.

"Now," I said aloud, and then realized I was awake.

Oh, gods: awake. It meant I had only dreamed him.

I lay swaddled in blankets, alone at last; not even Kiri was near. It was the first time since my rescue, and I had requested it.

The ship swayed gently, bobbing against her anchor rope. I heard creaks and groans and thumping, though none of it was human. The ship was singing her song.

"No more," I said aloud, and got out of the bunk to dress.

It did not take me long. Smallclothes, skirt, tunic and belt; lastly, detested slippers. I combed and braided my hair, then went out onto the deck.

She was, I thought, deserted, left behind while her men went ashore. Even Kiri was gone, accompanying Corin. I did not mind the solitude; it was better than meeting their eyes, their looks, their murmuring, the ward-signs against the shapechange.

We lay anchored just off Hondarth, too big to tie up dockside. Wind blew off the ocean, beating wavelets shoreward and causing the ship to bow and curtsy. The city shone in sunlight, all limewashed white with bleached gray thatching, and heather all over the hills. But the trees were beginning to turn and I smelled autumn in the air. Strahan had kept me through summer. I had missed a whole season.

I heard a sound and turned sharply, wishing I had my knife. A single step some distance behind me, not so close as to offer threat. A tall, quiet man, unperturbed by my awkward stiffness. He hitched one hip against the rail and leaned there, waiting in silence.

It angered me intensely, that I should be so frightened; that I should show it so readily. I said nothing at first, clenching the rail, willing the fear to go.

And, at last, it did, giving me leave to speak. "Aye," I said, "of course. Who else would stay behind?"

Wind ruffled his hair. Blond, as I expected, though lighter than Deirdre's or Rory's. Aileen had said there was red in his hair, though only a tinge of it, but the voyage had bleached it fair. It curled, too, as she had said, tangling against wide shoulders and falling into his eyes, brown eyes; Rory's, too, his eyes, and long-lashed like a woman's.

He wore no beard at all, which bared a strong, firm jaw too prominent for beauty. Big of bone and squarely built, with power in his posture. The House of Eagles is very strong; her men are often giants.

In shock, I looked away, thinking: *You are more like him than I thought.*

He said nothing at all. I made myself look back. "Do you like what you see, my lord? Am I better or worse than expected?"

Still he leaned against the rail, idly hipshot, riding the ship easily. The breeze combed hair from his face. "Lass," he said finally, "there's no secret to what became of you, so I'm not blaming you for the hostility . . . but what have *I* done to you save come out to share the day?"

Even the voices were similar, though his a trifle deeper. He did not have quite the same air of casual negligence, or Rory's quickness of laughter; although, as he had pointed out, I had given him little reason to laugh.

I drew breath so deep as to make me light-headed and

turned to face him squarely, planting feet on wooden planking. "Our business is finished, I think. The sooner I leave, the better, so you may go back to Erinn."

"And court another lass?" He folded heavy forearms, bared by the length of his tunic sleeves, dark green, which barely touched his elbows. He wore thick copper armlets twined like snakes around his wrists, and a matching torque at his throat, shining in the sun. Sean was, I thought, more bear than man, though lacking the hair, bigger of bone than the men of my race. We have the height, but not the weight. Aileen had warned me he was large, but this was unexpected. "You're quick to settle my future, lass, when you're supposed to be part of it."

"But you *know*—"

He nodded once. "And better than you think." He displayed the back of his hand; I saw the scratch across it.

"You," I said bleakly. "Oh, gods, for that I am sorry. I meant to hurt no one, but . . . but—" I checked. There was nothing left to say, to him or to anyone else.

"I know," he said quietly. "Lass, there's no need for explaining. I have eyes; I saw what happened. I have ears; I heard what you said. And I also have understanding: Strahan took you captive. Should I be blaming you for that, when you had no choice in it?"

"Men would," I said bitterly. "Why not you?"

He spat over the rail. "I'm not much like other men, being born to the Aerie of Erinn."

And cognizant of it, too. "So much for humbleness."

He narrowed long-lashed eyes. "Is that what you're wanting, then? Humbleness, from me? Lass, I'm thinking you're daft, or blind . . . you're hardly humble yourself, being an animal when you choose. With such power, how could you?"

"Are you afraid of it?"

He spat again over the rail. "You were a frightened, half-drowned pup of a girl, bruised and scratched and bloody. What was there to fear?"

His arrogance was astonishing. "I was a *mountain cat*," I said pointedly. "Did that mean nothing to you?"

He grinned, tugging an ear. There was copper in it as well, and shining on his belt. "It meant something, aye: it earned me a new sort of battle scar, *and* the sort, I'm thinking, few other men can claim."

I stood very stiffly, holding onto the rail. "And does it mean nothing that I can be a wolf? A hawk? A bear? Or anything I choose?"

He put on a face of false amazement. "*Can* you, lass? Anything at all?"

Through my teeth, I promised, "Anything at all."

He considered it. Fingered his lip. Gravely, he nodded. "Then I'll be watching my place with you, or be naught but a scratching tree."

"You *ku'reshtin*," I said scornfully, "you are as bad as *he* is."

Blond brows arched up. "He? He who? Have I a rival already?"

Something twisted deep in my belly. I thought it was the child, then recognized it as a new and increasing despair. We had spoken so often of Sean, of death and life and the past, that we had ignored the future, and now it stood before me.

Sean, Prince of Erinn, whom I was supposed to marry. And wanting no part of it.

"Rory," I said blankly.

He stood off the rail at once, solidly braced against wind and sea. His thighs were hidden in trews, the calves in drooping boots, but neither wool nor leather hid anything of the size. "Rory," he echoed. "Rory Redbeard is *here?*"

"He was afraid he had killed you."

Sean stared past me, toward the shore, brown eyes oddly transfixed. His hand rose to his head, pushed back hair from his face, fingered the hairline. "No," he said distantly, "all I did was bleed. And not enough to be dying; he didn't break my head."

"He thought so. He feared it. And he feared Liam's retribution."

He swung toward the rail slowly, ponderously, gripping it with both hands. It creaked beneath his weight. "Liam loves us both. There'd have been no retribution."

I shrugged. "Obviously he believed otherwise, or he never would have come."

"More like he feared he'd be named in my place, if my head proved broken." His smile was a trifle twisted. "Rory

Redbeard is not a man who cherishes the throne, being content with what he has."

"A captaincy in the prince's royal guard?"

He heard the irony in my tone and swung abruptly to face me again. "Aye. Bastards have known worse. 'Tis enough for Rory. He's *said* so, lass."

I nodded. "So, there *was* a chance he might have been named heir if you died . . . he said there was not."

He shrugged, folding his arms, setting his weight on the rail again. I waited for it to snap. "I've no doubt Liam expected to have more boys. He got me, and Aileen—nothing more. Rory, so far as we're knowing, is his only bastard son, which makes it likely, I'm thinking, he'd stand to take my place. If there was a need." His expression was oddly masked. "Why, lass? Is it what you wished? Rory in my place?"

I opened my mouth to say no, of course not; how could he ask such a thing? But nothing at all came out.

Sean's eyes narrowed. "Has he stolen away your affection? *Your* affection, lass? I thought 'twas nigh impossible; 'tis said you cannot love."

"*Who* says that?"

"Stories. Tales. Rumors." He shrugged. "Enough to make a man wonder."

"Lies," I said bitterly. "But what else?—I am Cheysuli."

"Has nothing to do with that, my girl. Has to do with what's in here." Briefly, he touched his chest.

I might have laughed, once. Or I might have shouted at him, or coldly denounced the stories. But now I did none of those things, being disposed only to stare at the face so much like another man's.

"So," he said at last, "I'm seeing they were lies."

I shrugged. "Some of them, aye. Perhaps not all."

"So," he said again, "you're thinking it's done between us, that no marriage can made. Because of Strahan, then . . . or is it because of Rory?"

"After what has happened, even Rory would not take me."

"D'ye want to be taken, lass? I'd heard you wanted no man."

"No man," I agreed. "Needed, or necessary."

He sighed heavily, stripping hair out of his eyes with

large, blunt fingers. "Lass, I'm no woman, and I can't be knowing what you feel, but I'm thinking we're not so many of us much like the Ihlini."

"Corin told you who—and what—he was. Strahan."

"A little, aye . . . I'd heard the name before, him being brother to Lillith, Alaric of Atvia's leman. But Corin has since chased her off, so we'll hear no more of her." He watched me with quiet sympathy. "Aye, I know a little, and a little is all that's needed. A man like that should be butchered."

"Oh, I killed him. But a clean, straight thrust. Like any man would do." I turned to face him squarely. "*That* is why, my lord. Not because I was stolen, or made to be his *meijha*. But because I am myself, and have no need at all for a man to tell me otherwise."

Sean tried not to smile, but the skin at his eyes crinkled, and then the grin broke out. "Any man who tried is more than half a fool."

"You?" I smiled back, not meaning it. "How much of a fool are you?"

"Half, I think," he said. "But no more than half, I'm thinking . . . because I'm too wise to try."

"You bold, arrogant *ku'reshtin.*"

He grinned. "No different from Rory, lass."

It was all too true. "He said you were boon companions, with similar tastes in many things, including women."

"Including lasses, aye." He sighed. "Has been trouble for us both. And always the willful lasses, never the quiet ones." His tone was purposely idle. "Deirdre was willful, too, taking to bed the Prince of Homana . . . and then going to Homana-Mujhar to be naught but a leman to him, no woman of rank there." He pursed his lips thoughtfully, leaning again against the taffrail. "And then there was Aileen, in love with the wrong prince, and knowing better, too. Oh, aye, I'm much accustomed to willful women . . . in the House of Eagles, how not?" He paused significantly. "D'ye know what I'm saying, lass?"

My mouth was dry. "Aye."

"I'd not ask you to change your ways. I'd not ask you to be milk-mouthed. I'd not ask you to be what you're not."

"No?"

"Why would I, then? 'Tis not how a marriage is made."

But so many of them were.

I drew in a long breath and spilled it out between us. "Strahan took me to bed. Again and again and again, for three very long months." I paused. "Need I be any plainer?"

The humor ran out of his eyes. Slowly he shook his head. "No, lass, no plainer. I'm thinking you've said enough."

Seven

Corin did not like the idea of taking me ashore even after I swore I felt well enough. Even after I explained, with exceptional clarity, that while it was quite true I was bruised and stiff from my escape, I had suffered much worse falling off various horses.

He sat slumped on his bunk with Kiri beside him and gnawed at a thumb. "You always say you are well, even when you are not."

"But I am," I insisted. "Do you think I *want* to fall down in a swoon in the middle of the street? Do you think I would even risk it?"

"A good reason for staying aboard."

"Corin." I glared, hands on hips. "Have you gone deaf and dumb? Are you blind? Do I look likely to swoon to you?"

He studied me a moment. "You look weary," he said at last, removing his thumb. "Your color is too pale."

I spoke very slowly. "Because I have been locked up for three months, you fool. What do you expect?"

He sighed, slanting Kiri a glance of weary disgust. "If there is something you need, I can fetch it for you."

"I prefer to go myself. I need to see an apothecary."

Corin sat upright. "I thought you said—"

"—that I am well. I *am*." With studied carelessness, I shrugged. "I am having trouble sleeping."

He blinked. "That is all?"

"That is all. I mean to ask for a medicinal tea."

"Sean has wine aboard, and a strong Erinnish liquor—"

"I have no desire to drink myself into a stupor merely to sleep," I said dryly. "I would feel worse the next day for being in my cups than I already do with no sleep." I said it feelingly, recalling how poorly I had felt after drinking *usca* with Hart and Brennan.

Corin smiled and slumped back again. "Tell me what you want and I can send someone to fetch it for you."

"Oh, gods—I swear, you will coddle me to *death*. Are you forgetting that we cannot sail to Mujhara, but must spend two weeks on the road? If I am strong enough for that, I am strong enough for this!"

He shrugged, avoiding my eyes. "I had thought of a litter for you—"

"A *litter!*" I stared at him. "I will ride, or I will fly. I want nothing to do with a litter."

"Keely—"

"No." I unlatched the door. "I go with you, or without you. It is one and the same to me."

Corin knew better. He got off the bunk scowling and preceded me out the door.

It had been two years since I had been in Hondarth, and with Corin. Clearly, he recalled it as well as I. Newly banished, in punishment, from his homeland for a year, he had come down full of fear and anger, resenting Brennan as always for having what he could not. I had joined him halfway, intending to go with him, but he was bound for Erinn first, and the thought of seeing Sean that much sooner turned me back again. And so I had watched Corin sail away, hating myself for my cowardice, for failing my twin-born brother, who had never failed me.

He frowned even as I did, walking the streets of Hondarth. Much had happened since then, to both of us, and it had altered us forever. Now he was Prince of Atvia in fact as well as title, and Sean had come for me since I would not go to him.

Corin asked directions of a passerby to the nearest apothecary. The streets were narrow and winding, turning back on one another and climbing hills up from the ocean. I felt awkward in my skirts, longing for familiar leathers.

The silence between us was heavy. And at last I asked what I had wanted to ask all along. "Do you miss her?"

Corin's smile was empty. "For you, that is tact. Why not ask what you mean to ask?"

Now there was no need; he had answered without meaning to. "Is that why you never came back?"

"Aye."

"And yet you come now."

He stared at the street as we walked, gone somewhere away from me. And then came back, quietly, but with an underlying passion that belied the casualness of his tone. "I cannot hide from it—or her—forever. Though we had never met, Sean sent word he was sailing to fetch you, and asked if I wanted to go. I thought it was time I did."

Sailing to *fetch* me, like a wandering cow. But I set it aside quickly enough, thinking of Corin instead. "They have a son."

"I know."

There has never been much need between us to speak in words. There was no need now. I sensed his pain, his awkwardness, his longing to know the truth of Aileen while fearing it as well. It would hurt him beyond bearing if I told him Aileen loved Brennan, but to do so would be a lie. I was not required to.

"And she lost twins," I said. "Now there will be no more. Aidan is the only heir, and like to ever be."

Corin caught my arm and steadied me over a fall of stone, which was unnecessary as well as unlike him; I thought it was the skirts. "Aye, so *jehan* said in his last letter. And since Aidan is sickly . . ." He shook his head. "It will make things precarious, until his health is secured." And then he laughed a little, in startled realization, and tightened his hand on my arm. "Except that Strahan is *dead* . . . which means a sickly heir to the Lion need not be so worrisome anymore. The gods grant the boy's health improves, but if not, it makes the burden lighter." He laughed exultantly. "Gods, Keely—what you have done by ridding us of the Ihlini!"

"Only one," I muttered.

"The only one who matters." He paused. "Here is the shop. Shall I come in with you?"

I kept my voice lightly inflected, knowing, with him, I needed to be on my guard. Or he would come in with me, and I would be left with no chance. "No, no need. It should not take me long."

I turned to go in, but Corin caught my arm again and

held me back. His eyes were very steady. "I meant to come," he said. "I swear, I did, for you. Gods, Keely, I missed you—but I was afraid to come . . . afraid to see her again, knowing there was still so much between us, and no hope for either of us . . ." He sighed and shook his head, letting go of my arm. "Brennan is better for her. He can give her more."

"That depends on what she wants." I touched his shoulder briefly. "*Leijhana tu'sai,* for coming. Especially now, with Sean."

Corin shrugged, leaning back against the stone wall of the little shop. "I remember what you told me here two years ago, when I had booked passage to Erinn." He paused. "Do you remember? In the tavern, in the rented room . . . you told me you were afraid, and that you needed more time." He smiled a little, seeing my expression. "But I know you, Keely . . . two years is not enough. And so I came with Sean, hoping you would still need me, so I would have someone to tend while Aileen was near, and Brennan."

"Well," I said, "you do. Tend me as much as you like, if it will make you feel better." I grinned. "As for me, I will feel better if I can sleep." And went past him into the shop.

It was a tiny, musty place, awash with herbal effluvia. The commingled stench was so powerful I nearly went out again. But I thought of Corin, so trusting; I thought of Strahan's child.

There was a single man in the shop, tending a mortar and pestle while seated on a bench. It was to him I went.

He was not old, not young, but lingering halfway in between. He had thin, flaxen hair, and pale blue eyes. His skin was of the sort that reddens easily from drink, high temper, or sun. He pursed his lips as he worked, scraping his powders together.

"Aye?" he asked. "Forgive me, but the order is wanted at once. Tell me what you need, and when I'm finished here I'll fetch it straight away."

I opened my mouth, and lied. "My mistress has sent me."

He nodded patiently. "Aye?"

Oh, gods, how do I say it? I drew in another breath.

"She has conceived an unwanted child, and desires an herb to be rid of it."

He nodded, watching his work. "Betrayed her husband, did she? And now carries a bastard? Aye, well, it happens, to the high as well as the low." He did not look at me. "Tell your mistress no."

I was willing to overlook his high-handed assumption regarding my nonexistent mistress' habits, but his outright refusal surprised me. "No?"

"Aye. Tell her no."

"But—" I broke it off, began again. "But this is a shop—you *sell* such things—"

"I do," he agreed. "But to heal, not to kill. You tell your mistress that if she had not been so loose with her favors she'd not be in such a way . . . she may be naught but a whore, but the child deserves a life. You tell her that, now . . . I'll not be party to murder."

Frowning, I shook my head. "But if the child is not wanted—"

"Doesn't matter," he interrupted. "Unwanted or no, it should live."

I thought of the child, my child, most distinctly unwanted. I thought of what it could be if given leave to live. To come into its father's powers. "And if there is a danger?"

"No child is born without it."

His serene stubbornness amazed me. "And if it is ill-formed?"

"The will of the gods, girl . . . tell your lady to pray."

Now it was a challenge. "And if it is unloved? What then? Should the child suffer an unhappy life?"

"The will of the gods, I say . . . there is always fosterage. If the lady or her husband cannot bear to keep the child, there are men and women who will."

I felt anger replace amazement. "You fool," I said curtly, "do you have all the answers? You, who are a man, and cannot know the choice?"

"There are women who feel as I do. Good women all—" Abruptly, he stopped working. Color filled his face. "It's you," he said thickly. "It's *you*, then—" And he was up, forgetting his order, putting hands on my arms. "Girl, girl—think. *Think* what you do. There is life inside of you—"

"There is *death* inside of me." I was shaking with rage,

fighting to keep my voice down so as not to alarm Corin
and bring him into the shop. "What right have you to dic-
tate my life? What right have you to tell me how to conduct
myself? What right have you to usurp my freedom of
choice when it does not even affect you?" I stripped his
hands from my arms. "Will *you* carry this child? Will *you*
bear this child? Will you feed it and raise it? Will you bury
it if it dies? Bury me if *I* die? Keep it from killing others?"
I drew in a noisy breath, nearly hissing in my anger. "Will
you do *anything at all* except tell me what to do?"

He was nearly as angry. "A woman is *meant* to bear
children . . . it's what the gods intended when they gave
her the means to conceive!"

"What of a child born of rape?"

His color waned. He averted his eyes.

"It happens," I said, "oh, it happens."

He moistened his lips. "The child is not to blame."

I shook my head. "Not every woman has the patience,
the willingness, or the strength."

"A child will cause her to learn it."

Gods, he was driving me mad! "And what of a child
whose mouth is so ill-formed it cannot even eat? Will you
eat *for* it?"

"The gods—"

I did not let him finish. "What of a child," I said silkily,
"who is begotten of a demon? Should we suffer *it* to live?"

And I recalled, even as I asked it, how I had challenged
my own uncle to give me good reason for desiring to kill
Rhiannon. Now this Homanan gave me much the same
challenge, and I finally understood the shame, the anguish,
the humiliation Ian felt for having sired Rhiannon.

I looked hard at the Homanan, understanding him better,
but more angry than ever. He had no answer for me, gazing
at me in startled silence out of watery blue eyes.

I could not hide my contempt. "So many answers," I
gibed, "and born of such arrogant ignorance. The next time
you petition them, ask the gods for better instruction. They
have more compassion than you." Blinded by anger, by
tears, I walked out of the shop into Corin.

Except he was not Corin.

"You," I said in surprise.

Solemnly, Sean nodded. He leaned against the wall even

as Corin had, big arms folded casually and displaying all
their copper.

I frowned. "What are you doing here?"

"I came looking for Corin, whose direction I'd been
given. I meant to invite him to a tavern . . . he said you
were here, and I said I'd bide my time while he went on
ahead to the one just down the road." His hand was on
my arm, guiding me away from the shop. " 'Tis near time
for food, and I could stand a dram. What of you, lass?"

I ignored his question, asking one of my own. "How
much did you hear?"

"Babble," he said succinctly, "but you sounded angry,
lass."

"He was a fool." I dismissed the red-faced man and his
well-intentioned stupidity. "I will buy from someone else."
But who? I wondered uneasily. *And I have so little time.*

"If you're having trouble sleeping, I could sing you a
song or two." He shrugged. "Some night."

I nearly stopped dead in the street. "Sing?"

Sean grinned down at me, guiding me with elaborate consideration around a puddle of urine left by a passing horse.
"You've heard nothing at all till you've heard the Prince
of Erinn singing a lass to sleep."

I lifted brows. "And do you do it often?"

"I've not been celibate, lass. Nor will I lie about it." And
then he laughed ruefully, pulling at an ear. "But you already know that, since Rory's told you the tale of how he
near broke my head."

"And how many bastards do *you* have?"

He nearly missed a step. "D'ye dislike bastards, lass?
D'ye think they're less than men?"

"Or women?" I laughed at his expression. "No, of course
not . . . in the clans bastardy bears no stigma. For too
long my race was very near extinction. Babies, regardless
of parentage, were always warmly welcomed."

"Ah. Then you'll not be minding—"

"Oh, I might . . . if any come *after* the wedding."

Sean threw back his head and laughed aloud. "Put in my
place," he said ruefully. But his long-lashed eyes were
alight. "Still, I think 'twas worth it . . . you've said there
will *be* a wedding. 'Tis more than you've said before."

So it was. Much more. And it made my flesh go cold. *Oh, gods, how can I? After what Strahan has done?*

"Lass," he said, "we're here. Will you allow me to buy you a cup?"

A kind man, I thought. A warm, kind man, more compassionate than I had expected, in view of my stubbornness.

"Bastards," I muttered, thinking of my own.

Sean's face closed up. " 'Tis Rory, then, after all."

I looked at him in shock.

" 'Tis Rory, then," he repeated.

"Sean—"

"I love him," he said, "he's my brother. But there are things I cannot share."

His face was masked to me, but I saw something in his eyes. Something that spoke of self-denial and constraint, of a self-control so stringent it made his voice too harsh for the throat that housed it.

He was clearly unhappy, though his manner remained almost indifferent. I had expected anger, resentment, a possessiveness typical of men who feel themselves threatened by another man; they are so often like male dogs, fighting for territory. But Sean was not, though I had given him cause. Sean loved his brother, bastard-born or not.

I owed him something, Sean. And so I gave him the truth, albeit with difficulty. "Do you think, my lord of Erinn, that after what Strahan has done, I could ever lie down with a man?"

Realization altered his eyes.

"Bastard or trueborn, do you think it really matters?"

Sean said nothing at all.

I pushed open the tavern door. "What prince wants that sort of wife?"

He pulled it closed again. "I might, lass."

Oddly, it made me angry. "How can you? You are the Prince of Erinn, Liam's heir—any man in your position must take to wife a woman beyond reproach. A woman whose virginity is intact."

" 'Twasn't your choice that yours was lost, was it, lass?"

My face burned. "Of course not."

"Then how can I blame you?"

I stared at him, mouth agape. "Do you mean to say that you will take me regardless?"

Sean sighed heavily. " 'Tisn't my decision."

"No? Whose, then? Mine? Well, *I* say—"

"Nor yours, lass. 'Twas a thing of our fathers. 'Tis for them to say yea or nay."

I stared up at him. Such a tall, strong man, powerful in spirit. I could not believe he would so meekly turn his back on independence. "Do you mean to say you will do whatever Liam tells you to do, even if you disagree?"

Sean rubbed the bridge of his nose. "Liam and I disagree on a great number of things. Sometimes I win the argument, sometimes I lose . . . but this one, lass, *this* one—" He sighed and shook his head. " 'Twas done between Liam and Niall for the good of both our lands."

"And therefore it makes no difference what either of *us* may want?"

He shrugged. "It only makes a difference if I'm opposed to the match."

It came out dully, in shock. "And—you are not."

Sean smiled a little. "Sure as I'm standing here, I'd be a fool to tell you the truth . . . or so it's said of a woman. Never tell her the truth, they say, or she'll make it into a weapon."

I gritted teeth. "Then I will say again what I said before: after what Strahan did, do you think I could ever lie down with a man?"

Sean did not even hesitate. "Aye," he said, "you will. I'm not excusing what that beastie did, and I'm not saying 'tis a thing a woman forgets . . . but aye, you'll lie down with a man, because you're too much a woman not to."

It startled me. "Too *much*—?"

Sean pulled me aside from the door as someone stepped between us to enter the tavern. The door banged closed. "Too much," Sean repeated. "Oh, I know, men have told you you're too much a *man*, I don't doubt, because you've a liking for men's things. And no doubt they say 'tis what you'd rather be: a man in place of a woman." His mouth hooked wryly. "But I'm not a fool, Keely . . . I'm not a man for judging a woman's mettle by her liking for swords or if she favors trews over skirts. You're a braw, strong lass, full of spirit and pride and temper, and a need to be free of things such as duties required by rank." His hands were on my shoulders. "A bright and shining lass, gods-made for a man like me—" his hands tightened painfully, "—*and* for a man like him."

After a moment, I shook my head. "What if I said neither?"

He did not even hesitate. "I'm thinking both of us would lose."

Gods, what a fool. I pushed open the door and went in.

Eight

The child was a boy, born on a night with no moon. A healthy, whole child, strong of limbs and lungs. He screamed in outrage at the woman who dared expel him from his safe, dark place, and thrashed in the midwife's hands.

She cleaned him, wrapped him, put him into my arms. "Strahan's get," she said. "You have only to look at his eyes."

Tangled in blankets, I cried out, fighting to get free. I sat up, tearing at wrappings, and then hands were on me, kind hands, holding me in place.

"Keely. Keely, no." The hands tightened. "It was a dream, Keely—nothing more. A *dream*."

I blinked into darkness, knowing the hands, the voice, the kindness. Corin. Aye, of course: *Corin*. Not Strahan. And no midwives, bringing forth the Ihlini's child. I had dreamed all of it.

I sagged, let him guide me back down into my blankets, all disarranged by my violence. And then sat up again, pushing his hands away, muttering something about being all right, being fine, being well enough, *leijhana tu'sai;* would he please leave me alone?

And so he did, saying nothing; going back to his own bedding where Kiri waited, leaving me to sit with my blankets pulled around me like grave-wrappings, staring blindly into the coals of the nearby fire ring.

We had left Hondarth the morning after my aborted efforts to get herbs to rid myself of the child, leaving me with no time to seek out another apothecary. I knew women who had purposely miscarried bastards and unwanted children, and those who waited too long died, or came near to it. I was not interested in dying, or in bringing myself close to it; I wanted the child gone, but not at the risk of my life.

Hear me? I asked it. *Hear me, abomination? I want you gone. I want you dead. I want you unborn, so there is no risk to the world because of the power that, gods know, will live in your bones. I refuse to be the woman who brought forth destruction.*

There was, as I expected, no answer. It was too soon, the child too small; yet nearly too late, the child too large, for me to rid myself of it without risk.

Unbidden came the thought: *But what if, left to live, it turns its back on the dark side of its heritage? What if, reared by Cheysuli, it pays no homage to Asar-Suti or to its father's memory?*

But what if it *did?*

I sat with elbows on blanketed knees, leaning my face into my hands. What if, what if, what if.

What if I married Sean and went to live in Erinn?

What if I refused on the grounds of banished virginity, couching the refusal in polite references to my dishonor, which I had no wish to share with Sean?

What if Aidan died and there were no heirs for Homana?

What if Aidan died, and there was no Erinnish issue from me?

No link, no blood, no prophecy.

Strahan would win. Teirnan would win.

And the *lir* would stay with us.

With a muffled groan I lay down again, yanking blankets up around my ears as I turned onto my left side. All around the fire ring were lumpy bundles of men rolled up in blankets, save for the watch Sean had set. His Erinnishmen were much like Rory's, which did not surprise me; they were the remains of Sean's personal guard, the ones who had stayed behind while Rory and the others sailed. They had grown more accustomed to me once on the road, apparently deciding I was unlikely to take *lir*-shape unless threatened. Corin they treated more familiarly, having grown used to him on the voyage, but to me they gave honor and impeccable manners. I was their lord's betrothed.

Vestiges of the dream stayed with me. It would always, I thought, until the child was gone. I tucked a hand down beneath my blankets and touched my belly, following the curve of flesh beneath skirt and tunic. Three months and more, nearly four: to me, it had become obvious.

Do you hear? I asked. *I have no choice. I cannot risk so much.*

I shut my eyes, squeezing tightly. Bit deeply into my lip. Wished myself a child again, safe in Homana-Mujhar, safe in my huge cloth-draped bed, warm beneath the covers, with all the *lir* within reach, and my father present. My strong, tall *jehan,* who could chase away the demons who preyed on his daughter's dreams.

Chase away this one, I begged. Jehan, *please . . . chase away this demon.*

But I was not in Homana-Mujhar. And even if I were, and *jehan* was present, this was a demon I would have to conquer myself.

I scrubbed away hated tears. In the darkness, from the watch, came a voice I knew. Deep, warm, soft, singing something in Erinnish. A song of peace and comfort.

The Prince of Erinn, as promised, was singing me to sleep.

We clattered through the massive gates of Homana-Mujhar near sundown two weeks out of Hondarth. The Mujharan Guard saluted Corin, grinning; welcomed me more moderately, but with obvious relief; paid appropriate honor to Sean and his contingent once identified. But none of us lingered, wanting to go straight into the palace. And yet at least two of us dreaded it: Corin, knowing he would see Aileen; me, knowing I would have to speak aloud of the bastard in my body.

I found myself next to Sean as we rode toward the inner bailey. Thick blond brows meshed over his bold nose as he frowned, looking around; I saw he judged the fortifications, the architecture, the width of the heavy walls, the guard manning sentry-walks and towers. In the setting sun walls glowed rosy-gold. Torchlight glittered off glass and ran, like water, across marble steps and archivolted entranceways.

" 'Tis grander," he muttered. "Kilore is a fortress, an aerie on rocky cliffs . . . this is more. This is—different."

This was home. I could judge it by no other.

"Gods," Corin muttered.

I saw his face, all strained and tight; his eyes, black in

the dying light. Felt the tension so close to breaking. And knew I had to say something, *do* something, so he would not shame himself with the intensity of his emotions.

"When I left, she was not here," I told him. "Brennan took her to Joyenne. She may still be there."

Sean looked at me sharply. "D'ye mean Aileen? Are you saying she isn't here?"

I was glad I was not required to look at Corin for the moment, though I meant my words for him. "After she lost the twins, Brennan thought it would do her good to spend the summer away from the city." I shrugged. "She *may* be back, but she may have stayed on. How can I say?"

"No need," Corin said harshly. "It has been two years, and there is a child between them . . . I would be a fool to expect her to feel the same."

I could not help it. "*You* do."

"I am not married to someone else." He drew up his mount in the inner bailey as horse-boys ran out from the stables, calling out startled greetings. "I should have come before; there is no sense in hiding from old demons."

Sean swung down from his horse, moved a step to mine, reached up to help me even as I told him, pointedly, I could manage on my own. But at once I regretted quick tongue and quicker temper; there was no need to give him bad manners in return for his courtesy.

"Lass," he said calmly, unperturbed, "I've no doubt you'd do well enough in leggings. But skirts are cumbersome—should I leave you to fall on your head?"

"Occasionally," Corin suggested, and grinned as I scowled at him. But the grin faded too quickly; he was staring at the entrance to Homana-Mujhar. Someone had come out in answer to the clatter and loud welcome of our arrival.

Swiftly I looked, expecting the worst. "Deirdre!" And was running across the cobbles with skirts dragged up to my knees, folds flopping as I ran.

She was laughing and crying and speaking unintelligible Erinnish mixed with Homanan as I mounted the steps, nearly tripping over my skirts, and then caught me in a hug that told me, with an eloquence unmatched by words, how very much she had missed me. How very much she cared.

I am not one for hugging women, or even men, preferring to keep deeper emotions private. But Deirdre was Deirdre, *jehana* in everything but name, and I loved her. More deeply than I had believed I could love anyone, save *jehan* and Corin.

"Oh, Keely—oh, gods—Keely . . . oh, we feared you dead . . . we thought he would kill you—"

"No. No. I am well, I promise, I *swear*—"

She was crying unabashedly. "The messenger said you had ridden out with Taliesin, to accompany him back home . . . oh *gods*, Keely—Niall was near mad with grief and rage when he realized it was a trap."

"How *did* he realize it?"

"None of the *lir* could find you. Not even when Hart sent Rael out for leagues. And we knew then it was Strahan, it *had* to be—and then no one could find a trace of you even when they went north—"

"I was south," I told her. "On the Crystal Isle." I drew back as she released me. "Is *jehan* here?"

Deirdre shook her head. "No. He and the others are still searching. Each report of your presence sends them in a new direction . . . lately they have gone south, but obviously they missed you." She swallowed heavily, fighting back more tears. "Oh, Keely, they have searched half of Homana, from here to all the way to the Solindish border, so close to Valgaard—" And abruptly she stopped, staring past me. "By the gods—Corin? And—no, not *Liam*—"

"Sean," I said dryly. "Come to fetch his reluctant bride."

Deirdre was in shock, staring at the man she had last seen more than twenty years ago. Then he had been four. Now he was—twenty-six?—and no more the small boy. Not even a small man.

"Liam," she said again, still stunned. "The height, the bone, the hair—gods, he even has Liam's mouth!"

"And uses it right well." I sighed, pushing loosened hair out of my face. "I will leave you to your greetings. There is something I must do."

She might have remonstrated; I expected it. I expected her to insist on putting me to bed, or sending me to the kitchens, or banishing me to a bath. But she did none of those things, being too distracted by the presence of her nephew, and so I left her quietly, saying nothing more.

Corin, next to Sean, mounted the steps into Deirdre's arms as I went into the palace.

I wasted no time. I climbed directly to my chambers, absently greeting startled servants, and stripped out of tunic, skirt, slippers. Out of everything. And replaced it all with soft Cheysuli leather: leggings, jerkin, boots. Lastly, my favorite belt. Except that when I tried to set the buckle prong into the proper hole, I found it three inches too small.

Oh, gods.

I stared blindly at the hole, now inadequate to its purpose. I am long in the waist and narrow-hipped; on another woman, a wider woman, a child so small would not show, would not interfere so soon with her clothing. But I am too much a Cheysuli: long of bone, in muscle, carrying no excess flesh.

Now carrying excess baby.

Oh, gods—

I broke it off angrily. Found a knife, though not the one Strahan had taken; that one was gone forever. Grimly, I sat down to cut a new hole.

"Keely?" Someone thumped my door: Maeve. *Maeve?* "Keely?" she called again. "Deirdre said you are home . . . Keely, are you here?"

I told her I was, and also to come in. She did so as I worked the tip of my knife through the leather, frowning at the bluntness of the steel. It needed honing. It needed tending. It would have to take the place of the other, and I did not like the idea at all.

Maeve shut the door. "What are you doing?" There was a startled note in her voice, and something that spoke of concern.

I did not bother to look at her. "Cutting a hole in my belt."

"After nearly four months of captivity, this is the first thing you do?" She came forward. "Did you think it more important to put on leathers than to greet Ilsa and me, who have been so worried about you?"

Sighing, I glanced up to tell Maeve I had not even thought she might be present—she had been gone when I left but I stopped in midsentence. Stopped dead, open-mouthed, and stared.

Gods. I had forgotten. Forgotten her child entirely, in the knowledge of my own.

She smoothed a hand across her belly, so much larger than my own. "Two months left," she answered, seeing the question in my eyes.

All I could do, transfixed, was stare. At the loose tunic, the skirts, the swelling of her breasts. The way her posture had altered. The texture of her skin.

In one hand hung my belt. The other clutched a knife. The hole was barely cut. "You decided to have the child."

"Aye. Teirnan knows nothing of it; the child shall be *mine*, not his." She smiled. "I will make certain it is a loyal, steadfast Cheysuli, untouched by its father's folly."

I felt so odd, so distant. "You said once that the seed was sown, but the harvest not begun . . . and asked if you should make the child proxy for Teirnan's sins."

"Did I?" Maeve shrugged. "I do not recall . . . we said many things to one another the last time we met, and most of them worth forgetting." She came closer yet, one hand resting on the bulge of her swollen belly. "You might have come to us first, Keely, before this. Ilsa and I have been worried."

I heard the faint undertone of reprimand in her voice. Too often Maeve honored me with such, playing the wiser, older sister, but this time it did not matter. This time nothing mattered.

I stared at the belt. "I had to cut a new hole."

Maeve laughed once, in disbelief. "Keely, are you mad? Do you think the fit of your clothing—" And she cut it off. Instantly. The silence was absolute.

I set down the belt, the knife, and placed my hands over my belly. When I looked up at her I saw comprehension in her eyes, and, oddly, tears. "I have less courage than you," I told her. "I cannot bear this child."

Maeve swallowed heavily. After a moment she came to the bed and sat down next to me very close, but making no effort to touch me, to soothe me, to offer meaningless comfort. I knew better than to expect it; she knew better than to try.

"How long has it been since you knew?"

I shrugged. "I knew at once. Within a week of my capture. At first I hoped it was shock, the drug he gave me . . . but when I did not bleed the second month, I knew the truth of the matter." I sighed, crushing leather jerkin in my hands. "Four months, I think. Perhaps a week less."

Maeve tensed beside me, meaning to speak at once, but forced herself to relax. To speak quietly, so as not to stir my temper. "You know it is too late. There is too much risk attached."

Patiently, I told her, "I will not bear this child."

"Keely—" But again she fought back her emotions. "It is too late. The physicians will tell you, the midwives . . . Keely, promise me—"

"No."

Her hands, as she clasped them, shook. "Do you want so badly to die?"

I laughed, though it had a brittle sound. "I would much prefer to live. No, Maeve, I promise you, this is not an attempt at suicide . . . but I cannot bear this child. Strahan is dead—he can sire no more—and I will not give him the pleasure, even in death, of leaving this one to assume the father's place."

Her teeth clenched tightly. "If you think I will allow you to do this to yourself—"

I stood up abruptly and turned to face her. "You had better! This is none of your concern, Maeve . . . this is *my* task to do. *My* child to lose. Keep your own if you like, but I will not do the same with this one. I cannot risk the chance it will follow Strahan's path."

Maeve clutched the bedclothes in impotent anger, clearly wanting to rise, to challenge me, but knowing better. Her condition would defeat the attempt. "Do you think any child of yours could even be tempted to? Gods, Keely, there is so much blind loyalty in you that you cannot even see yourself! *Your* child, a traitor? *Your* child, a servant of the Seker?" She shook her head violently, blonde hair shining. "A child born to you, shaped by your hands, could *never* be like Strahan. Not even if it tried."

I appreciated her unlooked-for sisterly loyalty and confidence, even if I did not share it. "I cannot risk it, Maeve. His child could bring us down."

"So could your death," she snapped. "Have you forgotten Aidan?"

Fear stabbed deeply. "Is he dead? Has he died? Oh, gods—"

"No. No, he lives. He is at Joyenne with Aileen." With

effort, Maeve controlled her voice. "But if he dies, it leaves only you. And if *you* are dead because of this selfishness, what happens to us then?"

"How do you know Sean will even have me?" I demanded. "How do you know there will ever be a child of that union, since there may never *be* a union?" I tapped my chest, leaning forward. "I have been Strahan's whore, Maeve, sharing his bed nightly. I carry an Ihlini bastard. Am I worthy to be Sean's wife? To give him the heirs he needs, while sparing one for Homana?"

She rose slowly, steadying herself against my bed. "If you try to rid yourself of this child, and die in the effort, how will you ever know?"

"Maeve, I *have* to—"

"No," she said bitterly. "No. You will do it because you *want* to; 'tis how you live, Keely. 'Tis how you have always lived, so certain of your path." She drew in an unsteady breath. "I have hated you, and loved you . . . with neither winning the throw. But always, *always* I have envied you: your freedom, your strength, your courage." Her green eyes were bright with tears of anger. "But now, seeing this, knowing what you will do, all I feel is pity. Later, perhaps, I will grieve, when we put you in the ground."

I turned from her rigidly and walked across the chamber to a casement. It was shuttered; I threw it open to darkness. And then I swung back, facing her, and told her, with exquisite precision, what else I feared so much.

"She is mad," I said flatly. "She has been mad since her birth, they tell us, even *jehan,* who wed her. Mad Gisella, they call her, speaking in whispers of her behavior, of the bizarre things she has said. Of the treachery she has *done.*" I drew in a painful breath, trying to keep my tone uninflected. "She meant to give her children—her sons—to Strahan. To serve Asar-Suti. There is no sanity in her . . . should I risk a mad child as well?"

In shock, Maeve said nothing.

I wiped sweaty hands on the leather of my jerkin, trying to still their shaking. "This child already has Strahan for a father . . . do I risk mixing the blood of the Ihlini and the blood of a madwoman? Abomination, Maeve—how can this child be normal?"

"But Keely, you can't *know*—"

"Only that there is a chance. There has always been a chance."

"Oh, *gods*," she said softly, " 'tis *this*, isn't it? The reason you've never wanted a child . . . the answer to all the questions . . ." She pressed hands against her cheeks. "*All these years, Keely . . . this? This? This* is why!"

"She is mad," I said again.

"Keely—"

"How can you know?" I asked. "How can you even suggest you understand? Your mother is sane. There is nothing for you to fear." I could not stop the shaking. "You know what madness means to the Cheysuli . . . to a *lir*less warrior . . . he must *leave*, Maeve! He sacrifices clan, kin, *life* . . . do you think I could live with that? Knowing that my child, in addition to being an Ihlini halfling, might also be *mad*—" I closed my mouth with both hands, then spoke through them. "Madness is anathema to anyone of the clans. You know that. You *know* that—"

Maeve's face was white. "All this time—"

"I have to be rid of this child!"

Shock faded quickly. Maeve was angry again. "You are a fool!" she cried. "A headstrong, stubborn fool. I should go straight to Deirdre—*she* would set you straight."

I took a single step toward her. "Say nothing," I said tightly. "Say *nothing*. This is mine to do!"

Maeve turned from me and walked heavily to the door. There she paused and swung back. Clearly she was angry, very angry; now, I thought, mostly at herself. "When I came home from Clankeep, I thought surely *jehan* would know about Teirnan's child. That you had told him." She laughed a little, self-mockingly. "But you had not. You said nothing, leaving me to my own decision."

I shrugged a little. "It was not my place."

Impatiently she scrubbed tears away. "And for that, I give you my silence, much as I hate myself for it. But it is the last debt I will owe you; we are quit of anything else, regardless of our blood."

I stood mute in the center of my chamber as Maeve left the room. Then, as the door thumped closed, I went back to my bed and picked up knife and belt, meaning to finish cutting the hole.

But I did not. There would be no need for it. Once the child was gone, the belt would fit again.

Nine

The solar was full of women: Deirdre, Ilsa, Maeve, and assorted Erinnish and Solindish ladies, all helping the Mujhar's *meijha* with her massive tapestry. Uninterested, I paid scant attention to it, mostly concerned with Deirdre's reaction.

It was what I expected. "How can you?" she cried. "You've only just come home—how can you think to leave again?"

"A week, no more," I promised.

Astonishment faded quickly enough, replaced with firmness; Deirdre is accustomed to dealing with my whims. "Corin has only this morning sent Kiri out to link with Serri and the other *lir*. They will be home very soon. You would do better to stay here, until they are back."

I hung onto my patience, speaking very quietly. "I need to go, Deirdre. Only a week, and to Clankeep. Not so far this time, nor for so long. I promise."

Maeve refused to look at me, staring grimly at the tawny yarn clutched in her hands. Her face was tight and color flushed her cheeks, giving away her thoughts, but no one, thank the gods, looked at her. All stared at me.

The morning sun slanting through open casements set the whitewashed room alight. Pale-eyed Ilsa, all in white, fair hair braided and netted back from her flawless face, was an ice-witch with blood to elbows; the yarn piled in her lap was red. "Keely," she said quietly, in her accented Homanan, "I think you would do well to be aware of how worried everyone has been, and what such worry does to people: griping bellies, stealing sleep, haunting dreams." She smiled a little, though her eyes were grave. "Give them time. You will have your freedom again, I know, but for now let them feel safe again, with you here where they can see you."

I stared hard at Deirdre's ladies, at Ilsa's, and then looked at my sister, at Hart's wife, at my foster-mother, knowing I would hurt them with my cruelty; knowing also it was required, or they would never let me go.

"You are none of you Cheysuli," I said harshly. "None of you, save Maeve, but even she will tell you she has no magic in her blood." I drew in a deep breath, trying not to shout; nor to cry. "None of you," I repeated, "and therefore you cannot know what it is to be stripped of honor, of worth, of *self*—" I cut it off with a sharp Cheysuli gesture, meant more for myself than for them. "I will go, because I must. There is *i'toshaa-ni* to attend to, and other, private things. If you worry for what my *jehan* will say, and my *rujholli,* and my *su'fali,* and all the *lir,* tell them I have gone to cleanse myself. They will understand. They will. I promise you they will; all of them are Cheysuli."

But Deirdre was not vanquished. "What of Sean?" she asked calmly. "Will he understand? Or will he know only that you have run from him again, as you have for so many years?"

Dull anger flickered, died. "I know him better than you." I watched the knife go home. "Sean will make shift for himself, regardless of what I do."

"Keely!" Maeve was furious. "If you think I will let you come here and speak such words to our mother—"

"No," Deirdre said quietly. "No, that will come next, will it not?" She was looking at me, not at her daughter. "You are using all your weapons, I see . . . well, why do you wait? Maeve has said the words—now *you* are to say that no, Deirdre is not your mother, but your father's light woman. *Meijha,* in your tongue." Her brows rose. "Well, why do you wait? Why not say the words, Keely, so you may cut yourself free of us all?"

Tears welled up before I could stop them. *Gods, I am grown so weak because of this thing in my belly—crying all the time—* "No," I said tightly, "I will say no such thing. I will *do* no such thing . . . all I want is a week to myself at Clankeep, for *i'toshaa-ni*—" I stared hard at a blurred Deirdre, swallowing painfully. "How can you think I would say such a thing? To you? How could I? Even in anger, I would not—oh, *gods,* Deirdre, do you think me so cruel as that? Do you think I am Strahan, preying on weaknesses—"

She rose, dropped forgotten yarn, came to me at once. Closed her arms around me as tightly as she had the evening before, if for a different reason.

"Shansu," she said in Cheysuli, having learned her share of the tongue in twenty-two years with my father. "Oh, Keely, forgive us . . . we have been so worried, all of us— and now that you are back, we're not wanting to lose you again, even for so brief a time as a week." She smoothed her hand against the crown of my head, whispering quiet words first in Erinnish, then in Homanan. "It has been so difficult for all of us, over the long years . . . Gisella in Atvia, Niall's light woman here in her place . . . you never had a mother, not as I had; as Maeve has, and others. Only me in her place, and no one able to admit it for fear of damaging proprieties, foolish Homanan proprieties, reserving a place for a banished queen and never letting you or your brothers forget it—"

I held onto to her very tightly. "She was never my mother. Never. Always, it was you."

Deirdre clung to me. *"Leijhana tu'sai,"* she whispered, and then stood back from me. "Go. Go. Take what time you need."

For Deirdre, I wanted to stay. But Deirdre had set me free.

I went mutely out of the solar, unable to say what I felt. Hoping she knew it anyway; Deirdre knows so very much.

I went to Clankeep, spoke to the *shar tahl,* set about my ritual. I fasted; built a small, lopsided shelter of saplings, twigs, and vines in the center of a clearing swept free of all save sand; sweated impurities from my flesh. Lost myself in memories, in imaginings, in things too private to tell. Bathed in smoke, water, and sand; cleansed soul, self, mind; within and without, according to the ritual my uncle still observed.

Three days. On the fourth, I would eat. On the fifth, return to Clankeep and request aid in losing the child

But on the fifth, Teirnan came.

I crawled out of the tiny shelter, burning stick in hand,

and stared at him, struck dumb. Amazed at his transgression; at the audacity of his appearance.

He was alone, save for his *lir,* the small-eyed boar named Vaii. It has been said before that often the *lir* reflects the personality of the warrior; in Teir's case, I agreed. Small-minded, selfish man, equally unpredictable and dangerous when trapped.

Teirnan smiled. "Finish."

The stick in my hand smoked. "You should not be here. This is private. Personal. You should go at once."

"Before I profane your atonement?" Teir shrugged, dismissing it with an eloquent wave of one hand. "Too late, Keely . . . Strahan has already profaned you more than *i'toshaa-ni* can cleanse."

I wanted nothing more than to thrust the burning stick into his face. But he would slap it aside, and I would have betrayed my instability, which would please him. Instead, I turned calmly and set my shelter afire. It smoked, crisped, caught; I threw the stick inside.

"So." I turned back to my cousin. "What do you want from me?"

"The answer to my question. Or, better, the answer to my proposal."

Behind me the heat increased as greenwood was slowly consumed. "What proposal, Teir? What business is there between us?"

He gazed past me, watched the fire, then reached out and caught my wrist, pulling me forward. "If you remain where you are you will burn. Keely—" But he broke it off, pulling me farther yet from the fire, then let go and squatted on his haunches. He made a gesture, and after a moment I sat down. "We feel the same way," he said. "I know we do, we *must* . . . you know what I told you is true, that we stand to lose the *lir*—"

"Not everyone believes that. Very few, in fact."

His eyes were very steady. "Are you going to marry the Prince of Erinn?"

Months trickled away. Once again I faced Teir, but in another time and place, with *a'saii* gathered around, flanked by all their *lir*. He had told me to refuse Sean, to bear Sean no children, to bring down the prophecy by denying it the blood so necessary for completion.

Then, there had been no reason, other than my own intransigence, yet I knew better. It was not enough; more would be required. And so I was given it, by Strahan. Now I had sound reason: a bastard in my belly. Heir to Strahan's power. More than enough reason to refuse the marriage, and no one could name me wrong.

But Teir did not know it.

I pushed myself up from the ground. Standing, I stared down at him, aware of rising apprehension; the comprehension of his intentions, and his dedication to them. "How far?" I asked. "How far are you willing to go?"

Teirnan spread his hands, as if to promote innocence. "A thing worth doing is worth doing well. So we are taught in the clans."

"How far?" I repeated. "If I refuse to wed Sean, it guarantees nothing. There is still Aidan. The Lion has an heir."

His eyes were shuttered by lids. Then he looked up again. "He is a sickly child."

"But *alive* . . . unless you take pains to kill him."

He is good, very good. But I have learned from Strahan to judge by things other than what a man says, or even by his silence.

"So," I said quietly, "first you come to me. To persuade me, with guile and skill, not to marry Sean. And so I do not. Part of the prophecy dies." I smiled my tribute. "And then there is Aidan—small, sickly Aidan. He may die any day . . . he may be *helped* to die, and so only Brennan is left. Brennan, heir to the Lion . . . the only one in your way."

So very cool, is Teirnan. I almost believed him. "I am not interested in the Lion. This is a far greater service."

"Destroying the prophecy?" I shook my head. "First me, then Aidan, then Brennan. And, perhaps, the Mujhar? Hart is Prince of Solinde; he inherits the kingship on *jehan's* death, and will have no time for Homana. Corin inherits Atvia; the same applies to him." To mock, I inclined my head. "Leaving the Lion with no heir, and only one man close enough to lay claim in his own name. Son of the Mujhar's dead sister, your claim is quickly granted."

Teirnan's voice was very quiet. He did not look at me, but at his loose-linked hands. "If Aidan lives to wed and sire a son, completion is nearly accomplished. If he dies, and Brennan lives to marry another Erinnish girl and get a son on *her,* completion is nearly accomplished. And if you wed Sean and bear a son to take dead Aidan's place, completion is nearly accomplished." Now he looked up from his hands. His eyes were intensely feral, consumed by dedication. It is the bedmate of obsession and often pleasurable, but this, I knew, was not. "To destroy the prophecy, I must stop all of you."

I looked at the strength of his face, the determination so valued by someone who required it; so feared by someone who knew what it could mean. Teirnan had passed the point of reasoning. His commitment was commendable for its exactitude, but the results of it would destroy my family.

And yet I dared not show him the edge of my tongue. He had needed me before; now he did not, and I was expendable as anyone else unwilling to serve his purposes.

Behind me the sticks which were my shelter snapped and blazed. Quietly, I said, "Brennan will never set Aileen aside."

Teirnan pursed lips. "So he says. But men have said things before, and have had their intentions changed. Why should he be different? If anything, he is all the more dangerous because of his loyalty—he will do what he has to do to preserve the dynasty."

"Are you forgetting Corin?" I asked. "He is unwed . . . he could well take to wife an Erinnish girl, and all your plans laid waste."

Teirnan smiled. "Corin is in love with Aileen. He will wed no other. And if Brennan is prevailed upon to set her aside, as is possible, Corin will marry her. Barren, she is no threat. No, Keely . . . Corin is no danger. Nor is he *in* danger."

"But the rest of us are." I kept my voice steady with effort. "If I say no to you—if I say I will wed Sean—what do you do then? Kill me?"

Teirnan rose in silence. "No need," he answered quietly. "I have other means."

Once, I might have—*would* have—laughed, taunted, denied, but I knew better now. Strahan had showed me very well how dangerous is arrogance; how deadly is misplaced pride.

"Teir," I said quietly, reaching for patience and, to my

surprise, finding it in abundance, "we are not enemies in this. What you have said regarding the loss of the *lir* frightens me, and badly, because I begin to think you may be right. And so you are right to question it, to bring the topic before Clan Council and all the *shar tahls*—"

"Keely, it is too late."

I tried again. "You know very well that if you try to bring down those close to the Lion by violent means—"

"There need be no violence."

I hated him for his quietude. "Teirnan, think of Maeve—"

"I have. And of you, and Niall, and even Brennan, whom neither of us has much cause to love—though I have, I think, less cause than any of us." He smiled. "Keely, you know as well as I you have come to terms with your *tahlmorra* . . . you know as well as I you will do what you feel is required to keep the prophecy whole. Lying now alters nothing. So why not simply allow me to do what must be done—"

I reached for the magic, intending to flee, but nothing came in answer.

Teirnan smiled a little. "I have an ally, Keely. Someone who needs to destroy the prophecy as much as the *a'saii.*"

Behind me, the shelter collapsed. From the ruin came Rhiannon.

No time to waste—

I spun back. In two strides I braced Teirnan, lifting my knee to thrust it home where it would do the most damage. But Vaii knew my intentions nearly as quickly as I did, charging to rake tusk through boot leather into the ankle beneath.

Teirnan caught both wrists and held them firmly, unperturbed by my struggles, by the curses I heaped on him. My ankle bled and burned.

"Let me see her," Rhiannon said.

Teirnan turned me forcibly, twisting my arms behind me. I was weak from the fasting and my ankle was afire. I could not believe Vaii had attacked me. A *lir* attacking a Cheysuli?

But Vaii was Teirnan's *lir,* equally committed to treachery.

I had not seen Rhiannon for more than two years. Then,

she had been Brennan's *meijha,* masquerading as a sweet-mouthed Homanan girl madly in love with the Prince of Homana. I knew better, now; she had given herself away on the day she stole Brennan for Strahan. Ian's Ihlini daughter, born of Strahan's sister, Lillith.

Black-haired, black-eyed, as so many Ihlini are, but with skin fair as Ilsa's. A lovely, striking woman, now more so than ever, who had borne my brother a child to be matched with Strahan's own, bred on his *meijha,* Sidra. Such a twisted, tangled birthline, now firmly entwined with mine.

She wore leathers, which shocked me. And gold at her throat, dangling from her ears, hooking her belt in place. Slim, deadly Rhiannon, half Cheysuli, half Ihlini, with no *lir* but all the power.

She held up a silver chain, displaying it. From it depended a ring: sapphire set in silver. It was, I knew, a trinket Brennan had once given her; she had kept it well since then, using it to augment her spells. Because it had been Brennan's, she could use it as a shield. It was why I had not known of her presence. It was why my magic was useless.

She tucked the ring and chain away. "Call me *a'saii,*" she said, "it will do as well as another."

"Strahan is dead," I told her, hoping it would hurt.

Rhiannon merely nodded. "Some of us die younger than others. He is a great loss, aye, and we grieve for his absence, but there are things to do. Life must continue, and so must the duty, until our task is finished."

She had known. That much was clear. And since she was here, aiding Teirnan, I knew very well Corin's hopes for waning Ihlini influence would not come true.

"You and Lillith," I said.

"Lillith, me, the children." Rhiannon smiled slowly. "And yours as well, Keely. Did you think we did not know?"

Teirnan's hands tightened. I felt his breath against my hair. "Are you saying he got her with child?"

"A potent man, my uncle . . . in his children, his name lives on." Behind her the shelter burned low; little was left but smoke and ash. "Have her kneel, Teirnan . . . ah, better, aye. Hold her. *Hold* her. She is weak from fasting, and angry, and the child affects her power. Hold her so,

Teirnan—aye, better . . . it will not be so awkward after all."

Shoulders burned from the tension of their entrapment. Teirnan stood behind me, knees pressed into my back. My own were on the ground, much as I longed to stand.

"Teir . . . she is *Ihlini*."

"I know what she is," he said, "and I know also that we want the same thing: destruction of the prophecy."

"She will destroy more than that—" I broke off as he twisted my arms.

"No more noise," he said. "For once in your life, *listen*."

Rhiannon stood before me. "Listen," she echoed softly, "and I will tell you a tale. Of a proud Cheysuli woman with Old Blood in her veins, and the thing she had to do."

I hissed as Teirnan twisted my arms, denying me escape.

"—the thing she had to do—"

Oh, gods, stop her . . . she is coming inside my head.

"*—the thing she had to do—*"

Deep inside, something broke. Gave way before her power.

First Strahan, now Rhiannon. First body invaded, now mind.

Gods. Which is worse?

"A little thing," she said, "and well within your means."

Deep inside, the child moved. As if it knew who she was.

Rhiannon's hands were in my hair, holding my head still. Her face was close to mine. "First you will do this thing, and then you will bear the baby. A strong, healthy baby, worthy of Strahan's name. Of the blessings of the Seker."

No, I will *not*—

But the world I knew winked out. In its place was Rhiannon.

And the thing I had to do.

Ten

They were back, all of them. I could hear the low rumble of male voices, lighter-pitched female ones, laughter, the dry tones of jests once played on one another, now repeated for the entertainment of others. And such a sense of well-being and joy flooded through me that I ran up the last few steps, grateful for leggings instead of cumbersome skirts. The door to Deirdre's solar was ajar; I pushed it two-handed and grinned as it slammed against the wall, serving to silence them all.

I set one shoulder against the door and leaned, folding my arms. "Aye," I observed dryly, "I can tell you were worried. Such long faces, furrowed brows, tears of grief and anguish." I grinned at staring faces trapped in myriad expressions of astonishment. "Aye, well, I am back, and none the worse for wear. You may celebrate; I intend to, myself."

I strode into the room, caught the cup of wine from Corin's hand, drank it down. Then gave it back, laughing, as his surprise shapechanged to a scowl.

They were scattered about the solar like a handful of prophecy bones: *lir* here and there, sprawled on rugs—Rael perched on a chair; Hart with Ilsa beside him, tiny Blythe snugged into his chest; Deirdre with *jehan,* perched on the arm of his chair; Corin nearest the door, feet propped up on a stool; Brennan by a casement, but looking at me instead; Ian slouching in the sill of another; Maeve sitting with yarn in her hands and Sean holding a cup of wine.

Sean.

Oh, gods, *Sean.*

"When did you get back?" I asked into the silence.

"This morning," my father answered. "Quite early, just at dawn . . . we came in *lir*-shape through the night, once

Kiri passed the message." With quiet deliberation he rose. "Keely—"

I thrust my arms out from my side, as if a seamstress worked to fit my gown, and displayed myself. "I am well. Well, *jehan*—I promise. See?" I turned. "No need to fret. He left me both eyes, both hands—no scars to remember him by. He had no interest in harming me." I let my arms flop down. "Instead, I harmed him." I smiled. "He is dead, *jehan* . . . or did Corin already tell you?"

My father's face was stark. "He told me."

"Good. No need for me to repeat it, then . . . old stories bore me." I went to the low table nearest my father, found a cup amidst the jumble of yarns, poured myself what wine remained in the jug. "So, what do you think of Sean, Liam's son? Is he so much like his father? Will he be a fitting prince? A fitting husband for your daughter?"

"Keely," my father said.

I saw his face. Stood very still a moment, then with an awkward rush set down the cup and went into his arms. "Hold me," I whispered. "*Hold* me."

He said nothing, merely holding. It was all I needed from him. And all, I think, *he* needed, holding me so hard.

"I am well," I told him, "I promise."

"I never learn," he murmured. "So many times Strahan has lured my children into captivity—"

"No," I said firmly. "Enough. He is dead; we need never concern ourselves with him again." I stepped out of his arms, picked up my cup yet again, and drank. Then smiled at them all, but my face felt brittle. "So much silence! I would sooner have you trading jests—even at my expense— than gaping at me like motley-fools at a Summerfair!" I raised my cup. "Drink. Celebrate my homecoming, and Corin's, and give good welcome to Sean, Prince of Erinn, come to collect his wayward bride."

"Oh?" Sean's thick brows rose. "And is the wayward lass willing to be a bride at last, after so many years?"

I shrugged. "It matters less at this point what she is willing to do . . . more if you will have her, after what has happened. And more yet what the Mujhar says. So *you* said, aboard your ship."

Sean frowned, baffled. "Lass—"

I turned abruptly to face my father, though I swept a

glance around the solar. "You are all of you kin, by blood and marriage . . . there is no sense in hiding the truth. We all know why Strahan wanted me, why he took me, and what he did while he had me: Keely, Princess Royal of Homana, is no longer the virgin she was." I clutched the cup in both hands, seeing the withdrawal in their eyes; the pain, the grief, the empathy. "Well, I can live with that, and I will—what choice have I . . . but what of Sean? Should he be expected to? Should my dishonor be his?" I looked at him briefly, then at the Mujhar. "Should the Prince of Erinn be expected to take a ravished woman to wife? To hear the gibes, the jests, the comments . . . the suggestions that the new-made Princess of Erinn is not a *maid* at all, but a whore who lay down with an Ihlini? Because they *will* say so. Just as they call Deirdre whore here in Homana, and Maeve bastard, so they will call me and the first child I bear in Erinn, if it be born any time within a year of my last day with Strahan." I drew in a steadying breath. "Tell me, *jehan*. Do I become a bride? Or do we give Sean his freedom, you and I, so he may wed a woman worthy of him? Worthy of giving him heirs?"

"Lass, you're worthy of anyone." Sean drank more wine, then lowered his cup and looked at the Mujhar. "My lord, she and I did speak of this aboard my ship. What she says has merit—there will be questions asked, and comments made—but I'm not a man to be troubled by the maunderings of others. She's a braw, bright lass, and I'd be a fool to look for another." He smiled at me crookedly, brown eyes alight. "But there's someone else to ask, I'm thinking. Someone other than your father."

"Someone *else?* Who?"

"Rory," he said evenly. "Hie yourself to the Redbeard, lass, and hear what he'll be saying."

It took most of my breath away, as well as stunning the others. I felt the stares but managed to ask, weakly, "Why should I? What has he to do with this?"

Sean sighed, rubbing the bridge of his nose ruefully. "More than I'd like to admit. No man likes to say the lass he fancies is in love with another man."

"Gods," Brennan said, "I think he means the horse thief!"

Hart smiled a little. "I never thought you a blind man,

rujho." The smile stretched to a grin as I turned to glare at him. "Oh, aye, I saw it then, Keely—save your thunder for someone else."

"He is a *horse thief,*" Brennan repeated.

"Well," Sean said lightly, "once he was something more. A bit more, lad, being bastard brother to a prince." He laughed easily, seeing Brennan's reaction. "Have ye none of your own?"

It was a most telling question. Brennan opened his mouth, shut it, looked at me instead. "So," he said, "him. And where does that leave Sean?"

"Here," Sean replied, before I could think of an answer. "Go to Rory, lass. Hear what he'll be saying. He's a head on his shoulders, when it isn't full of liquor, and he'll be saying what he feels."

"And if he does?" I said. "What then?"

"Depends on what he says, lass . . . but I'm thinking I have an idea."

Belligerence overcame tact. "How?"

"We've the same taste in lasses, my girl . . . 'twas why he near broke my head."

Brennan shook his head. "Sean, you are mad. You must be. My stubborn *rujholla* has fought against this marriage for as long as she has had the words—and fists—to do it, and now you give her a weapon. You put it into her hands and show her how to use it." He laughed a little, in sheer disbelief. "All she has to do is come back and say Rory will have her in your place, and then when you are gone she will calmly change her mind. And she will get what *she* wants, as she has so many times, leaving the rest of us to patch together the remains of the prophecy."

Sean's face was oddly serene. "I'll not be taking a lass who loves another man. 'Tis more in *your* line, I'm thinking; how fares Aileen?"

Deirdre clearly was shocked. "Sean! 'Tis enough!"

He was unperturbed by the reprimand. "Deirdre, my lass, you're my aunt, not my mother. I'll say what there is to be said. My father taught me so."

"There are times," she said grimly, "Liam is a fool."

"And I his son, lady." Still Sean smiled.

Corin stirred, dropping his hand over the chair arm to

touch Kiri's head. "Sean," he said wearily, "Aileen is not the issue."

"No. No, she is not. 'Tis Keely, I'm thinking . . . and also my brother, whom I love, trust, and value as much as you do your own, all of you, even my lord Mujhar." Now he looked at my father. "You married Gisella of Atvia, but you sleep with Deirdre of Erinn. Surely you understand, my lord, what it is to be loving someone other than your mate."

"Indeed," my father said, and sat down in his chair again. Like Corin, he touched his *lir;* Serri lay sprawled at his feet. "Well, I see this has gone far beyond the simple agreement Liam and I made so long ago, binding our Houses through marriage. Brennan for Aileen, Keely for Sean." He sighed, rubbing at scars. "Clearly, we were wrong. We should have done it another way."

"But it *was* done, and for good reason," Brennan said irritably. "Aidan may die. Aileen is barren. The marriage between Keely and Sean may be the only alternative we have to get the blood for the prophecy."

Sean merely shrugged. "Rory is Erinnish. Rory is Liam's son. 'Tis the proper blood, I'm thinking, if got from another man."

Brennan's eyes narrowed. "Why are you so eager to be rid of my *rujholla?* Is it that you *are* shamed by what Strahan did, and think to cast her off on some byblow of Liam's so you may go home and seek another?"

I had not thought of it. Now I did, as all the others did, and I stared even as they did, as one, and hard, at Sean, who had the grace to color.

"'Tis not that at all, ye *skilfin!* I'm thinking of the lass. I'm thinking of my brother. *And* I'm thinking of me." He took a stride forward. "If you like, I'll wed her tomorrow." A hand was thrust toward the door, wrist aglint with copper. "Have the priest called; I'll not shirk the chance. But if you have any decency in you, you'll let her see Rory. She can't be told what to do, or turned this way and that. She'll make up her own mind, my lad, or she'll go to her grave unhappy. D'ye think I want an unwilling wife? D'ye think I'm wanting a cold bed, where she dreams of someone else?"

Brennan's face was ashen. I have seen that look before

on him, when he is terribly angry or terribly shaken. If Sean had tried harder, he could not have found a more deadly weapon. "I think," he said quietly, "we should settle this argument elsewhere."

Hart scooped up Blythe and handed her to Ilsa, rising so rapidly he upset Rael, who bated on the chairback. "Brennan."

Brennan simply ignored him, looking only at Sean. "Are you any good with a sword?"

Sean grinned broadly. "I'm thinking better than you."

Deirdre looked at my father. "Stop them."

He shook his head. "They are men, not boys, *meijha*. This will be settled between themselves."

Now Maeve was standing awkwardly, hands spread over her belly. "Brennan, no! What do you care what Keely does, or whom she marries? *She* doesn't. She doesn't care if she lives or—"

"Enough," I said sharply.

Sean grinned at Brennan. "A bit of sparring, then, to see which one is better? Shall we name the stakes?"

Brennan glanced at me. "If I win, she stays here. If you win, she goes to the horse thief."

"Wait—" I began, but Sean's agreement overrode my protest.

Ian slid off the casement sill, stepping over now-cubless Tasha. "A bright day," he said lightly. "Shall we go outside?"

Outside, it was very bright. The Mujhar and assorted kinfolk went into the bailey, where Brennan and I had sparred before. He carried a sword, as did Sean, given one from Griffon, who came to arbitrate. It was a match, no more, but the forms must be followed.

It did not take long for word to spread. Within moments others gathered. Sean, seeing how many, grinned. Brennan's face was masked, hiding what he felt, though I had a good idea.

Sean stripped out of green velvet doublet and tossed it aside. It left him in linen shirtsleeves, with the ties undone at throat and wrists, baring copper necklet and broad, furred chest clear to his belt. He rolled up sleeves to elbows, flexed muscled forearms, considered stripping off wristlets. But did not, smiling a little, seeing Brennan and his gold.

I grinned at him, then stepped up as if to wish him good fortune. Instead, I took his sword. "First, there is something else to be done." I turned, ignoring his blurt of surprise, and crossed the cobbles to Brennan. "Months ago, you made a promise. Now I hold you to it. *Su'fali* served as witness; you promised a match to me. I say now."

"Not *now*," he protested. "This is for Sean and me."

"You promised." I glanced at Ian. "Did he not, *su'fali?*"

Ian's expression was rueful. "Aye. He did. But—"

I turned back to Brennan. "Well? You will beat me, of course . . . it should not take long, nor much of your strength, and you will be able to turn to Sean once you are done with me."

Brennan looked past me to our father. *"Jehan—"*

"Did you promise?"

"Aye, but—" Brennan shrugged, frustrated.

He was not happy, our father, but would not allow his heir to renege on a promise, even to his sister, of whom he was not overly fond. "Then fulfill it."

I laughed at my brother. "Your chance, *rujho,* to show me up before the others. Surely you will enjoy it."

He waved a hand. "Then go. Move away. Let this be done properly."

"Oh. Aye, of course." I turned and took a single pace away, then swung back, still in range of his blade, and he in range of mine. "Far enough, *rujho?*"

Brennan scowled. "Gods, Keely, must you overplay this? It is a travesty, no more . . . why do you want to do this?"

I grinned. "Because you promised. Because I want to. Because I have learned a trick or two since the last time we met."

"From whom? Not Griffon."

"Not Griffon, no. A little from the horse thief, who has a way with steel."

Brennan's mouth tightened. He cast a glare at Sean, who merely laughed, showing teeth.

I grinned and waved the sword under my oldest brother's aristocratic nose. The blade was one of Griffon's, not mine, and was therefore too heavy for me, but I knew it would do. I would not need it for long.

"Keely!" Brennan ducked aside. "Gods, Keely, take care—do you wish to slice off my nose?"

"It might improve your looks." I smiled sweetly. "Why are you waiting, *rujho?* Are you afraid to begin?"

"We are still too close," he said curtly, and turned to move away.

I let him go a pace, then ran my blade through his back.

Eleven

It was Corin who smashed me down, face down, grinding me into the cobbles. The sword lay beneath me, trapped in my hands. I felt the steel cut. I felt the blood flow. I heard the people screaming.

It hurt. I was hurt. I was *bleeding*—

Everyone was shouting.

I squirmed, thrashed, trying to pull away, to drag myself from beneath him. His weight was crushing me, pushing the breath from me, jamming my hands against sharp steel.

Why is he hurting me?

Why are people shouting?

I kicked, and caught a boot. "Let me go—" I gasped. "Let me *go*—"

He dragged me up from the cobbles, pulling me to my knees. The sword clanged out of my hands, rolled, rang against the cobbles. I saw blood on the blade. Blood on the stones. Blood on *me*—

"Leave her to me!" he shouted as bodies crowded around. "Gods—leave her to *me*—"

"—bleeding," I said raggedly. "Corin—all the *blood*—"

Maeve was in my face, sobbing aloud and shouting. Over the bulge of her belly she bent, then smashed her hand across my cheek and mouth. My lip split on teeth.

Someone pulled her away. Ian. Ian, pulling Maeve away, guiding her toward the palace.

Sleeta's keening wail carried throughout the bailey.

I spat blood. Stared at my hands. Blood *everywhere*.

Someone was on the cobbles. Not me; Corin held me. Someone else on the cobbles, sprawled across the stone. One arm was twisted beneath him, legs sprawled obscenely . . . it was all I could see. Too many other people, gathered around. So many *people*.

Deirdre was crying.

"What is it?" I asked. "What is it?"

So much noise and confusion.

Corin held me up. He bundled me like a bedroll; only my hands were free.

They moved the man on the ground. Turned him over onto his back, and then I saw his face.

"Brennan!" I cried. "Not *Brennan*—"

Corin's tone was choked. "Keely, hush. Say nothing. You will make it worse."

"But *Brennan*—"

"Keely, I beg you—"

"Let me *go,* Corin! By the gods, are you blind? Why are you holding me? Why not let me go to him?"

They were strangers all around me, though their faces were familiar. "Take her inside," someone said. "Lock her up if you must . . . we will need everyone for the healing."

"Lock me up? Lock me up? Why are you locking me up?"

"Keely, *hush,*" Corin begged.

"Take her inside!" someone shouted.

Corin dragged me to my feet. "Come. No, no—Keely, I beg you, save your struggles—"

"Brennan is hurt," I told him. "Let me go—let me see—Corin, *let me go*—"

He dragged me toward the palace.

"Corin, *please*—"

Up the steps, through the open doors, past staring, white-faced servants.

"Corin, where are you taking me? Why are you locking me up? Why are you hurting me?"

Down stairs, around and around, into a shadowed corridor.

"Corin—Brennan is *hurt*—"

He held me up as I tripped. Then pulled me to a halt in front of a door, slammed it open, pushed me bodily into the chamber.

"Corin—Corin, *no*—"

He shut the door in my face. I heard the bolt go home. Locked in.

"Corin!"

No answer.

"Is it Brennan? Is it Brennan? Has someone killed Brennan?"

He was gone.

I sagged against the door, leaving bloody handprints. "Have I done something wrong?"

A cold, dark room, stinking of disuse. No window. Only a door, and locked.

I stared at the walls. Tasted blood in my mouth. Spat it out, and looked at the cuts in my hands. Spread fingers and saw the cuts pull apart; blood sprang up afresh.

Confusion.

Who has hurt me? Who has cut me?

Oh, gods, is Brennan dead?

I sat down on the ground, hard. Crossed my arms at the wrists, palm up, warding hands against further pain.

And waited, wrapped in silence, seeing Brennan's battered, bloodied face as they turned him onto his back.

Gods, what did I *do?*

Three of them came, and I knew them: Ian, Hart, Corin. They bent, knelt, squatted. Pushed hair out of my face, cleaned the blood from my lip, offered me water. I wanted none of it.

"Keely, drink," Corin said.

I drank. Hart touched a hand; I hissed.

"She is cut," he said. "Both hands—see?"

Corin shut his eyes. "She still held the sword when I took her down. It was beneath her . . . I should have kicked it away."

Ian shook his head. "You had more than enough to do." He touched my head again, smoothing fingers across my brow. "No lumps. I thought she might have struck her head . . . but this is more, I think. Much more . . . well, we will do what we can to set her to rights. Keely—"

"Is he dead?" I asked intently. "Did I kill Brennan?"

It silenced all of them.

Ian's tone was quiet. "Do you remember everything?"

"Is Brennan dead?"

He shook his head. "I promise."

"But nearly."

"Nearly. Without so many of us there to tap the earth magic, he would have died."

I stared at my hands. "I am mad, then. Like my *jehana*. Like Mad Gisella. The tainted blood runs true."

Corin's voice was strained. "Keely, *jehana's* madness has nothing to do with blood—"

Hart shook his head. "Leave it. Tell her later. For now, we should take her to her own room—"

"No," I told him. "Leave me here. Lock me up."

"—gods," Corin choked.

Ian's voice was quiet and infinitely soothing. "Corin, she is confused—and, I am sure, tampered with. Here, let me move in." I looked into yellow eyes. "Keely," he said gently, "you went to Clankeep for *i'toshaa-ni*. What happened?"

"I completed the ritual."

"Then what did you do?"

"I completed the ritual. But Teir came—Teir was there—Teir profaned the cleansing—" I lurched up into hands. "Teir—Teir—Teir . . . it was Teirnan and *Rhiannon*—"

"Trap-link," Corin blurted. "Oh, gods, Rhiannon—"

Hart swore softly. "Strahan may be dead, but there are others in the world who will assume his place. Lillith. Now Rhiannon?"

Ian gave me more water. "Keely, can you remember? Can you remember what she told you?"

I mopped my chin with the back of a hand, careful of the lip Maeve's blow had cut open. "That—there was something I had to do. A task. A thing I had to do." I shivered and shut up my hands, then hissed from the pain of salt and dirt in the cuts. "I was—I was to *kill* him . . . I was to kill *Brennan* . . . and then Aidan would die—there would be no one for the Lion." I frowned, remembering. "Hart in Solinde. Corin in Atvia. No one left for the Lion—"

Hart's face was taut. "Except Teir. Of course."

"I was to kill Brennan, and then—" But I shut it off. I could not tell them that; not about the child. "I was to kill Brennan."

Ian nodded. "All right. All right, Keely . . . time to leave this place. We will stand you up—aye, *harana*, stand—and we will take you up from the dungeons—aye, *harana*, I know you are unsteady; lean against me—and put you in your room, in your bed, and let you sleep the night through. In the morning you will be rested, and so will all of us. We can deal with the trap-link then. Aye, Keely—come. Through the door and up the stairs—aye, *aye*—see? Not so very hard."

"It hurts," I said intently.

"Aye, Keely, I know."

"It *hurts*," I said again.

"Shansu," Ian whispered. "Not so far—a few more stairs—"

I began to laugh. "—bleeding," I gasped raggedly. "Oh, *leijhana tu'sai—*"

"Keely—" Corin began.

Warmth flooded my thighs. *"Su'fali,* wait—oh wait . . . gods—the child is *coming* . . . no more abomination—" I sagged, unable to stand, to climb, to do anything but grind my teeth together, trying to bite back a moan.

Ian scooped me up. My leggings were wet with blood.

"Corin," I said through the pain, "is Brennan really alive?"

"Aye, Keely—I promise." And then, on a rising note of fear: "What is wrong with her?"

"Miscarriage," Ian said grimly. "Strahan got her with child."

Spasmodic pains wracked my belly. "—gods—put me *down*—"

Ian lunged up the stairs.

No more abomination . . . but—oh gods—it *hurts—*

It gives me a perverse satisfaction to miscarry Strahan's get. Child of rape, of sorcery, bred to be our downfall. The destruction of Homana.

Now, it dies so easily, spilled out onto the sheets. Gender unknown, or untold; they will spare me what they can. Knowing, as they spare me, that in the dying of the child the fragility of my own precarious hold on life increases.

—so easy to die—

"Keely . . . Keely fight it—"

And I laugh, knowing myself caught at last. Trapped by tahlmorra, by gender, by self. Acknowledging the capriciousness of the gods; the vulnerability of the prophecy, only as strong as those who serve it. Until now, this moment, here, incredibly strong, served by sons and daughters of the

Lion, who lived and died in the names of ancient oaths and older gods, in bondage to themselves.

"Fight the pain, Keely . . . you are much too strong for it."

Teir has the right of it; we are deaf and dumb and blind. Bound by the swaddling clothes of honor, the grave soil of tradition. We are a dead race living, cloaking our lack of self-purpose in the trappings of prophecy, depending on gods to give us direction, to show us the proper road. And always a single road, when so many lie before us. The world is full of roads—but we choose only one. Always. Forever. Until the end is reached, stripping us of purpose, of ambition; even of our lir.

Will the gods even bother to thank us?

Or will they pat us on the head and send us off to bed?

Turning to smile paternally on the ancient cradle called Homana, holding the Firstborn child. The child of true and abiding power; of Ihlini and Cheysuli, and all the other bloodlines.

Will they call him Mujhar?

Or will they call him god?

"Promise me, Keely, you will not give in to this."

Jehan? Are you there?

"You are the daughter of the Lion, who relishes a fight. A braw, bright lass, as Sean himself has said . . . oh, gods, Keely, do not give up now."

—dying is not so easy . . . too many things undone—too many fates unknown—

Knowing, if I die, Strahan may win after all.

Twelve

Someone sat next to my bed. I heard shallow breathing, the slight alteration of posture, the scrape of leather against wood. Someone sat in a chair beside me, smelling of leather and gold; the musk of a mountain cat.

I mouthed it. *Su'fali.* Then opened my eyes to see him; saw Brennan instead.

Oh, gods.

Not Brennan.

I shut my eyes again.

"Keely."

Humiliation bathed me. "Go away," I told him.

"Keely, this is nonsense. I am alive. I am well. Weak, aye, and sore, but all of that will pass. Keely—I am *alive*."

"And, being Brennan, full of forgiveness for me."

His tone was odd. "Let us say, full of comprehension. I understand what happened."

I opened eyes. "Then you are *not* going to forgive me?"

Brennan's smile was slight. "You would hate me if I did. What you want from me is accusation and disapproval, so you can get angry. Anger is always your best defense; it allows you the chance to climb up on the highest of your horses. But if I forgive you for running four feet of steel through my body—and I am told a foot of it came out the other side—I take away the anger, the guilt, your sense of humiliation, leaving you only with resentment. The gods know there has been that and more between us, for a variety of reasons—good *and* bad—and I am weary of it. So no, I do not forgive you . . . you nearly killed me, Keely."

"Ku'reshtin," I said weakly. "You always have the answers."

"Is that enough reason to kill a man?"

I was aware of weakness, of lassitude; of a strange apathy. No more pain, but discomfort. My belly felt oddly empty. "They told you about the baby."

"Aye. Teirnan, Rhiannon, the trap-link . . . also the baby, Keely. But why—" He broke it off. "No. Now is not the time, nor is it my place—"

I answered him anyway. "Because I could tell no one. Only Maeve, and she guessed. I meant to tell no one at all. I meant only to rid myself of it." I grimaced. "It rid itself of me."

He shifted again in the chair, settling his back carefully. For a man who had been run through with, as he had said, four feet of steel, he looked surprisingly hale, if pale of face and bruised. But it was earth magic, not normal healing, and such power takes its toll. Of the healed as well as the healers. "Keely—"

"Go to bed," I told him. "I see indeed you have survived, but there is no more need for you to sit here beside me and taunt me with such magnanimous empathy. It is what I expect of you, being you; go to bed, rest . . . and tell me you forgive me when I am best able to mount my highest of horses." I smiled weakly. "*Leijhana tu'sai, rujho* . . . as you say, disliking you for having all the answers is not reason enough to kill you. I shall have to find one better."

He smiled. His color had worsened, which made the bruises down the left side of his face all the more ugly, and he rose with a wince he tried but failed to suppress. "I sent for Aileen. She will be delayed—Aidan has a fever—but she should be back within a five-day. I think perhaps there are things you two may share that no one else can understand."

"And surely I more than most am in grave need of understanding." I grinned briefly as he opened his mouth to respond, and waved him away with a limp hand. "Go. Go. Before Deirdre comes to fetch you and tuck you into bed, or Maeve—most likely Maeve!—and strips you of all your dignity."

He rubbed his midriff tentatively. "The gods know they stripped me of everything else, for the healing—" He grinned. "Rest you well, *rujholla*. When you are strong again—when *both* of us are strong again—we shall have to meet a final time to decide which of us is better with a blade."

I waited until he was at the open door. "You would risk that?"

Brennan shrugged, then winced. "Why not? The trap-link is gone, banished days ago by *su'fali*, who has some knowledge of them . . . I think there is no danger."

"No . . . I meant would you risk *losing* in front of so many people?"

Brennan laughed in genuine amusement, which did not particularly please me, and took himself out of my chamber before I could respond.

They came in couples, in trios, alone, wishing me well, asking after my health, apologizing for harsh words and the roughness with which they had treated me. Maeve cried prettily over the blow she had fetched my face, but I knew she would not hesitate to repeat it, or worse, if I ever again threatened her beloved Brennan. Well, I did not expect her to do otherwise; it was the same with Corin and me.

And yet Corin was the worst, apologizing for throwing me to the cobbles and for locking me away; he was convinced his roughness had caused the loss of the baby. Perhaps it had, or perhaps ill-wishing it had, or perhaps the gods themselves had intervened. I did not care and told him so; also that I had intended to be rid of it one way or another, and he had saved me some trouble.

He was unconvinced, so I cursed him crossly and sent him away, telling him to leave me alone until he could bear to see me without apologizing.

Corin went away. Into his place came Ian.

He was uncomfortable. I saw it at once, and was astonished. I had never seen him so ill at ease.

And then I thought I knew.

"No," I said flatly, before he could open his mouth. "I will not have it. Do you think for one moment I will blame you?"

"She is my daughter. If I had not lain with Lillith in Atvia, regardless of the sorcery, Rhiannon would not exist." His face was very stiff. "She would not have come to Homana, to seduce Brennan and bear his child, who even now grows up with the tending of Ihlini . . . and she would not have been able to set a trap-link to murder him, using you as her weapon."

"Teirnan's as much as hers." I shook my head at him. "How many times have you told me we must not live in the past, but look forward to the future? Rhiannon exists; short of killing her, we cannot change it. The child exists; nor can we kill *it*, not knowing where—or who—it is. But mine does not survive, for which I thank the gods . . . Strahan will have no heir of *me*."

He made a slight banishing gesture with his hand, and I knew the topic closed. "I came also to get honesty from you. Will you give it?"

Plainly, he wanted no jest. I nodded.

"Strahan forced you," he said, "much as Lillith forced me. I know what that does to a soul."

"And you want to know how I feel."

"I know how you feel, Keely. Dirty. Soiled. Besmirched. Entirely worthless as a person, as a Cheysuli . . . as part of the House of Homana."

Painfully, I swallowed. "I fulfilled *i'toshaa-ni.*"

His eyes were oddly intense. "And was it enough for you?"

I opened my mouth to say aye, of course it was; it was a cleansing ritual, and I was now purified . . . but I said nothing. I bit into my lip to keep from crying and slowly shook my head.

Ian smiled, though it was an odd, bittersweet smile. And then he put his hand on my head, cupping my skull with his fingers. "You and I," he said. "You and I, *harana* . . . together, we will defeat it."

Quietly, he went away, leaving me gazing at his absence.

I slept. And then awakened, aware of a presence, and saw another man in my room, his face grown old before me.

"Jehan?" I pushed myself upright against piled bolsters.

He made a staying gesture. "Keely—no. Stay as you are." And he sat down in the empty chair, reaching out to catch my hand. "Listen to me. Say nothing, Keely: *listen.*"

After a moment, I nodded.

He closed my hand in both of his, gripping it very firmly. "She is mad, Keely, not because of anything in the blood . . . not because of anything gotten from ancestors— but because *her* mother fell while carrying her; the fall injured Gisella, who was born immediately after. She is mad because of that—and *only* because of that; you cannot inherit it. You cannot pass it on. You are sane and will always be sane . . . and so will all your children."

My hand clenched spasmodically.

"I promise you, Keely. I swear on the life on my *lir*."

Through my tears, I smiled. "It took you too long to get him."

He nodded gravely, though his single eye was bright. "Which serves, I think, to make the oath all the more impressive."

I held onto his fingers. "All my life I have been afraid."

"For *nothing*."

"All my life, once I was old enough to understand, I feared I might go mad; that my children might be born mad."

"Keely, we have never hidden the truth from you. You know the story of how Bronwyn in raven-shape was shot out of the sky. She died of her injuries just after Gisella was born."

I stared blindly at the coverlet. "She tried to give her sons to Strahan."

"She was made to do that. What do you expect of a woman reared by an Ihlini? Lillith was foster-mother, and Alaric—her true father—turned a blind eye. Gisella was mad already. She would have done anything and believed it expected of her." He sat back in the chair, releasing my hand; the memories, for him, were still painful. "She gave me four fine children; for that I am very grateful."

I looked up into his face. "But you will not have her here."

He shook his head. "There is no place for her here. She is better off in Atvia."

"Where Corin must deal with her, while Deirdre warms your bed." I caught my breath. "Ah, *jehan*, I am sorry. I have no right to say such things."

His tone was oddly calm. "The day Gisella dies, Deirdre will be my *cheysula*."

A long time to wait. I sighed. "I wish it might be tomorrow. Then Maeve becomes legitimate *and* the oldest daughter of the Mujhar of Homana. Let *her* be marriage bait; I am weary of it."

The Mujhar of Homana laughed. "So are we all, Keely. You are hardly the first." He rose, leaned down to kiss my head. "Nor will you be the last."

"*Jehan*—what will you do about Teir?"

His face aged before me. "Find him, somehow. And when we do, he will be brought before Clan Council to answer for what he has done."

"What will Council do?"

After a moment he shook his head. "No warrior has ever done as he has. Not even Ceinn, his father, who raised his son on rebellion. We are not a treacherous race, nor one in need of punishment . . . but what Teir has done is reprehensible."

"Because he believes differently? Are you so sure he is wrong?"

"Keely—"

"He could be right, *jehan* . . . we may lose the *lir*."

He rubbed again at scars. "If that is so, we must deal with it as it comes. But as for Teir—" He sighed; Teirnan was his dead sister's son. "He will have to be punished."

Mutely, I nodded.

At the door he paused. "*Leijhana tu'sai*, Keely."

I blinked at him, baffled. "Why? What have I done besides try to kill Brennan?"

His face tautened a moment as memory came back. But he banished the expression and smiled a crooked smile. "Aye, you did . . . just as I once tried to kill Deirdre, her brother, and her father—if more indirectly. You used a sword. I, fire . . . a beacon-fire blazing atop the dragon's skull, setting assassins to work." He sighed and resettled his patch. "But that is done. I say thank you for killing Strahan."

In startled silence, I watched him go, wondering uneasily why he said nothing of Sean; why he said nothing of Rory. Nothing of marrying either, though surely he could have. Surely he had *meant* to, being father; Mujhar; Cheysuli. Faithful servant of the prophecy.

Or had he?

I considered it carefully, then scowled blackly at the door. "But we *need* the Erinnish blood."

And knew Teirnan had lost.

But neither had I won. Sean himself had said it: "*Rory is Erinnish. Rory is Liam's son.*"

Making it all the harder.

Swearing, I got out of bed. Slowly, carefully, with infinite delicacy. I unearthed fresh leathers from a deep trunk—my belt fit now—and eased myself into them. Eased my feet into soft house boots, grunting against the effort, shutting teeth against one another in response to residual aches and weariness.

Swiftly I braided hair, ignoring my need for a comb. "You are soft, my lass . . . *soft*. What would Rory say?"

Anguish blossomed. I took myself out of my room—cursing the need for deliberation—and went to find Sean.

Thirteen

The Prince of Erinn, when he saw me, did little more than raise eyebrows. And then smiled, bright-eyed, and said he had never seen even a newborn foal as wobbly as the Princess Royal of Homana.

It was, I thought, most unflattering, but at least better than the solicitude the others plagued me with. I hung onto the wall, smiled back sweetly, called him something less than the legitimate son of a woman who sold her favors to any man with coin. Or without, depending on how she felt.

He thought about it, said it would do, then caught me under both arms and plopped me, none-too-gently, in a chair. "Wine?" he asked politely.

Too many stairs— I slumped sideways, hooking an elbow over the chair arm, and let loose a breathy sigh. *Gods—I am weaker than I thought.*

"Lass—will ye do?"

Would I do? Depending. What did he want me to do?

"Stay alive," he answered succinctly, and threatened to call brothers, uncle, and father to hie me back to my bed.

"No, no." I waved a limp hand. "I will 'do,' Sean—give me time. I have been in bed for—five days?"

"Six."

"Then I *should* be weary—bed-rest wears down a body." I sighed again and pushed myself upright. "Aye, I will have wine. Unless you have *usca*; that will put me to rights."

" 'Tis *my* room, lass . . . what I have is Erinnish."

I waved again; he interpreted it as assent, and poured me a cup. I drank, choked, nodded. It was familiar fire; Rory had given it to me.

Rory.

I took the cup from my mouth. "Do you know why I am here?"

"Not to share my bed; you're a bit weak for that." He grinned, sat down in a chair that creaked beneath his weight. "D'ye make a practice of going alone into a man's bedchamber?"

"This is your *ante*chamber, not bedchamber . . . and why should it matter? We are betrothed, and I have been dishonored. What more harm can befall my name?"

The brightness faded from his eyes. "Bitterness doesn't become you."

I drank again, trying to hide my weakness. I had eaten little but broth for five—no, *six*—days, and drunk only water; the liquor warmed my belly and set my head to spinning. "I came to ask a service of you."

Something flickered briefly in his eyes. He shuttered it with lowered lids, hidden behind long lashes, and then looked at me again. " 'Tis Rory, then."

"Will you fetch him? I can hardly go myself, and this must be settled."

Sean pressed hands against chair arms and abruptly thrust himself upright in one powerful movement. He walked away from me, offering his back, and stared out the nearest casement. It was midday; sun flooded the chamber with light.

A broad, hard back. Stiff the length of the spine. And then he swung to face me. "D'ye know what you're asking?"

"You to fetch Rory."

"Here, lass. *Here.* In the household of your father. A bastard-born exile, who nearly killed his lord."

"His brother," I said calmly. "So did I, my lord."

It stopped him only a moment. "Have you decided, then?"

"No. But you were the one who said I should see him."

He swore. "Aye, I did, that. And aye, so you should. But you're a fine, strong lass, and I'd hate to be losing you."

I arched unsubtle brows. "I did not know you *had* me."

He scowled. "You know what I'm saying, lass."

"And you know which of you stands a better chance. You are the Prince of Erinn. He a bastard-born exile."

He tilted his head to one side. "I'd be taking him back with me, lass. My head's not broken, so there's no need for him to stay."

I had not thought of it. I had thought only of Rory in Homana, and me—with Sean—in Erinn.

One way or another, I will have to leave Homana.

I held the cup too tightly. "Will you do me the service?"

"If you'll be doing *me* one."

"Aye," I agreed, "of course."

"Go to bed, my lass . . . you're needing it, I'm thinking."

I was too tired to nod. "You can call one of the servants, or one of my brothers—" I dropped the cup abruptly.

Sean plucked me out of the chair. "I'm thinking I'll do it myself."

When he came, he glittered with mail. I stared at him in surprise. "Are you going to war?"

His scowl was much like Sean's: brow bumping brow, hair hanging low, brown eyes nearly black. "From what my brother's been saying, I'm thinking I may have to."

"Why are you wearing *mail?*"

Injured pride was manifest. " 'Tis all I've got worthy of you."

"Worthy of *me!*" I laughed in disbelief. "By the gods, Rory, what a man wears is not what he is!"

"No?" His scowl had not abated; if anything, it deepened. "He said you were a lass mightily impressed by what a man wore, and the title before his name."

I smothered my laughter, seeing the bleakness in his eyes. "He lied," I told him gently. "I have been in your camp, Erinnish . . . I have spent a few nights with you, albeit not in your bed. You should know very well what it is I judge people by."

Behind the beard, he muttered, "I'll be breaking the *skilfin's* head."

"You tried it once, Rory . . . next time you may succeed, and where would you be then? Exiled somewhere else, and crying into your wine because the beloved brother is dead."

He smiled, then laughed, then nodded. Then glanced around the room. "Where is this, lass?"

"Deirdre's solar. I like it for its sunlight, and the comfort of its chairs." I paused. "Would you care to sit in one, or pace the room like a bear?"

"Pace," he answered succinctly, and suited action to words.

I made myself more comfortable in one of the comfortable chairs. Sean had gone, as requested, and fetched his brother to the palace. It had taken three days even with my explicit directions; now, seeing Rory, I thought the delay was to purchase assorted finery. He wore winter-weight quilted wool tunic beneath the shirt of mail—Erinnish green, of course, or as near to as could be found in raven-and-red Mujhara—edged with silver-gilt braid. The trews were new as well, though the boots as I remembered: drooping, stained, nearly out in the toes; boots must be made, not bought, if they are to fit at all.

The curly hair was combed, but too long; the beard required trimming so as to prove the face beneath it. But he was clean and smelled of bathing, which was more than was offered before.

He stopped short and swung toward me. "Are ye well, lass? He said you'd been near to dying."

"Do I look near to dying?"

"Halfway near," he said seriously. "You've none of the color I recall, and there's blue beneath your eyes."

I put a hand to my face, drew it away at once. "Aye, well—did he tell you why?" No more need to avoid it.

He turned away again, stood still, then spun back and came to my chair. "'Twas a child, he said. Strahan's Ihlini bastard."

I listened to the nuances of his tone. There was genuine concern. Anger on my behalf. Frustrated helplessness, that he had done nothing to aid me. But also an odd, almost strangled note of something I could not name.

"I miscarried it," I told him. "Does it make a difference to you? Do you think me soiled, now?"

He opened his mouth, then clamped it closed. Something glittered in his eyes. Tears, I thought in surprise, but not of anger, of shame, of futility. What he gave me was anguish, and an empathy almost palpable. "Lass," he said, "oh, *lass*—"

"Sit down," I told him plainly.

He stared hard at me, looming like a tree. And then sat down, as I had suggested, but on the pelt at my feet rather than in a chair. He spread both hands over my knees, as if in holding them prisoner he also held me. "I near went mad," he swore. "They came to me, your brothers, saying all manner of things not to my liking. They asked if I'd had the stealing of you—as if I would!—and did I care to feel their wrath? The wrath of a Cheysuli?" Rory nearly spat, but refrained out of respect for Deirdre's solar. "After they'd done with their talking, and I was done with mine, 'twas decided I'd seen none of you; that Strahan had done the taking."

"He had."

"I offered to ride with them. For free, I said, and no stealing along the way. But they refused, saying the search would be done in *lir*-shape, and I had naught of the magic." His eyes glittered angrily. "I told them no, 'twas true, but I knew a little of it because of you . . . and they laughed, as if my ignorance lessened me . . . as if my lack of magic made me less than a man! Unblessed, they called me . . . *gods*, I wanted to break their heads and teach them manners, to tear down that arrogance . . . how *dare* they show it to me! I am their equal in everything!"

"You just agreed you cannot shapechange."

It quieted him a moment. Then he showed me teeth through the blaze of his beard. "Aye, well, no . . . but the *arrogance* of them, lass!"

I sighed a little. "I have my own share. A common trait, in this House . . . *lir*-shape is mostly a blessing, but others might disagree."

"You've spirit, lass, and pride. There's a difference to those when compared with arrogance."

I laughed. "Only sometimes—Rory, you are crushing my knees."

He crushed them all the harder. "How can you ask it, lass? How can you ask it of me?"

I peeled back his fingers. "Ask you what?—Rory, let go."

"If I could think you soiled?"

I let go of his fingers. "Am I not?"

"I'll break the head of the man who says so, *and* the woman, lass!"

So *fierce*; I laughed. "Leave the heads intact."

He took his hands from me. "D'ye want my brother, then?"

I drew a breath. "Rory—"

"Do you *want* him, lass? In place of me?"

Oh, gods. "Rory—"

"Because he has a title? Because he's not a bastard? Because his sweet, lying mouth has done far more than it should have?"

"Rory!" At last, it shut his mouth. "Is railing at a woman the way you think to win her?"

"No," he answered quietly.

"Then why are you doing it?"

"To make you pay me mind, my girl . . . to make you hear what I'm saying."

"What have you said?"

"This." He rose to his feet, looming yet again and all aglitter with mail. "That I'm not caring about the baby. That I'm not caring about what the Ihlini did, other than wanting to break more than his head—though I heard you finished him yourself with no need for a man to do it." Very briefly, he smiled, but it faded almost instantly, replaced by intensity. "What I'm caring about is *you*, lass. Just you. Not what you are, but *who*. Not the blood you have, but simply that you have it, rich and warm and red." His smile, beard-clouded, was crooked. "And if you're not wanting bairns, I'll not insist upon it."

"Bairns often follow the bedding," I answered vaguely, thinking of Aileen. "Your sister is coming home."

Rory froze. *"Who?"*

"Aileen. Your sister. You may be bastard-born, but Liam's daughter is still your sister."

He stared at me hard a moment, then sighed and rubbed both hands over his face, ruffling beard and tangling forelock. "Agh, gods—sister and brother . . . where'd a man be without them? One will be Queen of Homana, the other—agh, *gods!*" He pulled his hands away. "Lass, there's so much I'm wanting to say. So much I'm *needing* to—"

"No." I cut him off curtly, rising. "No, say nothing more. You need to say nothing more." I laughed once, painfully. "You and Sean, both of you, should never have come to Homana. Because you and your royal brother have put me in such a coil I think I shall never unwind myself."

"Lass—"

"Aidan is sickly," I told him. "The blood must be preserved. Aileen is barren, which leaves only me . . . and the

Erinnishman I marry. The blood *does* matter . . . more than you can know."

Rory jerked his knife free of its sheath and placed the blade against the underside of his wrist. "Shall I show you the color, then? Rich, red, and *Erinnish?* What more d'ye need; lass? I'm an eagle of the Aerie! No more, no less: *Erinnish!*"

Aye, so he was. As much as Sean himself.

Oh—gods—Sean.

I turned my back on Rory. Shut my eyes. Pressed both hands against my mouth.

And abruptly, spun back to face him. It was all I could do not to shake. "Do you know the Mujhar?"

Rory stared. "No."

"He looks very like Corin—no, Corin looks very like him; I must put the order right."

"Lass—"

"Go to the Mujhar."

"What?"

"Go to the Mujhar and tell him to fetch a priest to the Great Hall."

"Lass—"

"Tell him to gather the House of the Lion together—as well as *both* the eagles of the Aerie—and wait for me in the Great Hall." I drew in a breath. "With the priest, if you please."

"Keely—"

"And ask Deirdre to fetch me something to wear."

"Lass! I can't just take myself down to the Mujhar and his lady and tell them—"

"Why not?" I interrupted. "Open your mouth, Erinnish—the words will take care of themselves."

"But—"

"Go, Rory! Were you not taught never to keep a lady waiting?"

Swearing in Erinnish—which I understood too well—he took himself out of the solar. I buried my face in my hands.

Oh, gods, I am mad . . . mad as my mother is, to forswear myself so easily for the sake of Liam's son. What if Teir is right? What if we lose the lir?

But I am nothing if not loyal; the Lion requires an heir.

* * *

Deirdre arrived in my chambers just after I myself did. Her face was pink from running. "Keely—"

"Did you bring a gown?"

Her hands were empty. "No—"

"Good; I have decided to wear leathers." I dug more deeply into one of my clothing trunks. "Is the priest in the Great Hall?"

"No. Niall—he . . . *Keely*—"

"Is he having one fetched?"

"And everyone else as well." Her shock was fading quickly, replaced with comprehension. "Is this truly what you want?"

"No. It has never been what I wanted. But I have no choice, have I, if I am to be as good a Cheysuli as all three of my *rujholli*, as well as *jehan* and *su'fali*—it is a family tradition." I straightened, shaking out a soft, sleeveless jerkin dyed a deep, rich black. "I have leggings for this as well . . . Deirdre, will you look in my caskets and see if I have any rubies?"

"Rubies?"

I nodded intently. "Red ones."

Deirdre fought a smile and went to do as asked, pouring trinkets across my table.

I found my leggings and quickly stripped out of what I wore, replacing brown with black. And black boots, nearly new, but creased in all the right places, and with red tassels hanging from them.

Deirdre came with wristlets: hammered gold set with rubies. "And this," she said.

My lion's-head belt. I had forgotten it, since I so rarely dressed with any degree of elaboration. I smiled and took it from her, hearing the chime of heavy gold. Dozens of lion's-head bosses the size of a woman's fist, glaring out of gold, linked together into a rope to go around my hips. The largest was the clasp; its eyes were blood-red rubies.

"Homanan colors: black and red." I put it and the wristlets on. "Enough," I said, laughing. "More would blind them all."

"Turn," Deirdre ordered.

I swung to give her my back. She stripped leather tie from my hair and shook out the braid. "Loose," she said firmly, catching up a comb. "That much I'll have of you, if you'll not be wearing skirts."

"It will fall in my face. It always does."

"I'll make certain he sees your face."

I stood very still as she combed, suddenly afraid. "Do you know which one I will take?"

"No. But neither do you."

It hurt worse than expected. "I should have Hart throw dice!"

"It would do as well as anything else." She sectioned off more hair. "What is there to choose from, Keely? Two men. Both tall, both strong, both battle-proved. Both young, but not too young. Both Erinnish, to which I am partial—save for Niall, of course—and both of them Liam's sons. Eagles of the Aerie, bred of the *cileann* and blessed at birth on the sacred tor . . . what is there to choose from, Keely? Wealth? Health? Love? Or will the title make the difference?"

"Blood," I said numbly.

Deirdre came to stand in front of me. She caught both hands and turned them over, palm-up. "When you cut yourself on the sword, did one bleed red? The other green?" She shook her head calmly. "No. Exactly the same, from either hand; *it made no difference, Keely.*"

"No difference?"

"None."

I wish I had her innocence— I closed my hands on hers. "Ask Maeve if that is true. Ask your bastard-born daughter if the blood *does not* matter."

Deirdre's face went white. I turned to go, but she reached out and caught my arm. "Keely! Keely—wait."

She scooped something up from the table, then put it into my hands. A slender gold circlet, twisted upon itself to form a slow, sinuous coil, them hammered nearly flat. "To keep your hair from your face."

Slowly, I put it on. It was cool against my brow, but warmed quickly to my flesh.

I swung from her abruptly. "They have waited long enough."

The hammered silver doors to the Great Hall were heavier than I remembered; or I weaker. I decided on the latter, grunting, and scraped one of them open even as Deirdre tried to help.

Brennan, Hart, Corin. Maeve and Ilsa, tiny Blythe. Ian. And *jehan.* And Liam's two tall sons, born of the Aerie of Erinn.

Also one priest, bewildered as everyone else.

"Oh, gods," I muttered, and strode the length of the hall to the marble dais, where the Lion of Homana crouched in mute, maleficent glory.

"Keely—" my father began.

I looked him straight in the eye. "You wanted me wed, *jehan.* So. I will wed. Have the priest take his place."

Rory was scowling at me. "Which of us is it, lass?"

I stood before the dais, the pit, the Lion; before them all, who stood in clusters, but none of them by the throne. I pointed at Rory, then at the place next to me, on my left. "You," I said firmly. And then, before he could speak, I motioned Sean to take the place at my right. "You." I then turned politely to the priest, who stood up one step but not on a level with the Lion, which was only for the Mujhar. "Will you recite the vows? And when you ask for the name of the man I am marrying, I will tell you which one."

"Keely!" My father was astounded. "If you intend this as a jest—"

"No," I told him coolly. "When the priest is done, I promise, your daughter will be wed."

Sean sounded alarmed. "Which one of us *is* it, lass? D'ye think this is fair?"

I glared back. "Is it fair to ask me to choose?"

His face was very white. He looked past me to Rory. "*I* think—"

One of the doors scraped open. Each of us turned to look, for all of us were present. All save Aileen, who came walking down the hall with Aidan in her arms.

I looked at once to Corin. His face was still and white, but he did not turn away.

She saw him. Color rose, fell. And crept back again, slowly, setting her eyes alight even as she smiled. A small, bittersweet smile meant for neither of those who loved her, but only for herself.

Aileen looked at Brennan. Then directly at Rory, frowning, until her expression cleared. "*Sean,*" she said, laughing, "when did you dye your beard red?"

Fourteen

My kinfolk deserted me, they and the man I had known as Rory. They left me alone in the hall with only the Lion for company.

The Lion and Liam's eaglet.

Mail glittered as he moved. The red beard—*dyed*—was burnished by sunlight. A tall, strong man, nearly as large as the other. Alike and unalike, both bred in the Aerie's mews.

He stood very close, too close, looking down on me. And then, with no change of expression, he drew his knife and cut into his hand, tipping blood across his palm.

"Rory—" I checked. "*Sean.*"

He put his hand in front of my face, allowing the blood to run free. It rolled to his wrist, stained the cuff of his tunic, hid itself beneath mail. "Red," he said, "Erinnish. Will that do for you?"

I stretched out a single arm, bare of everything save Mujharan rubies and hammered, clan-worked gold, and pointed to the throne but three steps away from us both. "Ask that."

Blood ran from his hand. "I said something to you earlier. I'll be saying it again: *'I'm not caring what you are, but who.'*" Blood dripped onto stone. "I don't want the beastie, lass. What I want is you."

Slowly I shook my head. "With me, you get the 'beastie.' What do I get with you?"

He turned from me then, sheathing the knife, and mounted the dais steps: one, two, three. Stood beside the Lion, then put his hand upon it. Blood glistened dully; was taken into wood.

Sean sat down in the throne. I opened my mouth to protest, closed it almost at once. His House was as old as

my own; I thought the Lion of Homana would not be-
grudge the eagle of Erinn his moment.

" 'Twas not a jest," he said. "I never meant it to hurt."

Until the last, it had not. They had fooled me utterly.

" 'Twas well known, lass, what manner of woman you
were. A high-tempered, sharp-tongued lass not in mind to
lie down with the lads . . . not even the Prince of Erinn."
He paused. "*Especially* the Prince of Erinn."

I swept the circlet from my brow. Hair fell over
shoulders.

He shifted in the Lion. "Never in my life have I had to
beg a lass. We are both of us, Rory and I, accustomed to
filling our beds with naught but a flick of an eyelash." He
did not say it to boast; he spoke frankly and evenly, com-
manding more with quiet candor than anything else could
do. "I was four," he said softly, "and you yet unborn. Our
fathers linked us, lass, without considering what we might
feel . . . without considering what we might *do.*"

I clutched the circlet in both hands, but looked at him
instead.

"I knew what I felt, lass, when it came time to think of
wedding. And not being blind to women—no lass, I'm
not—I knew what *you'd* be thinking; you with such glorious
freedom and no one to understand . . . not even, I'm thinking, your brothers."

I recalled the day he had asked it: *"Make me feel it,
lass."* And recalled how I had answered, showing him how
to fly.

The quiet voice continued. "I thought of sending for you.
I thought of coming myself: I, the Prince of Erinn. But
neither would do, I knew . . . 'twould lose you rather than
win you." He sighed, chewing his lip. "And so I went to
Rory, who shares with me so very many of my feelings . . .
between us, thinking of you, we conjured the tale we hoped
might win a Cheysuli princess."

"A thief."

"I robbed no one; the coin I spent was my own, come
all the way from Erinn."

"You stole Brennan's horse."

"And gave him back, lass."

So I could lose him in Hondarth. "They were your guard,
those men."

He smiled. "To keep me alive in a foreign land where shapechangers are more than myth."

"You told me you murdered your brother."

Sean's mouth hooked wryly. "I told you I *thought* I had, or might have, was more likely. I near broke his head, aye, 'twas true . . . but I made it sound worse than it was, to make the tale better. And it wasn't much of a lie, lass . . . it was the Redbeard who suffered the hurt, not me—not the Prince of Erinn. We only twisted it a bit, or traded places, in all the tales we told."

With effort, I kept myself calm. "How long was it to last?"

His mouth altered into grimness. "Not so long, lass. Rory was to come sooner, but Liam kept him back. I meant it to go on only long enough for you to be certain . . . for you to *want* the marriage—or, I hoped, want *me*—and then I'd tell the truth."

"What part had Rory to play in this?"

He smiled. "None of what I told you is a lie. He is indeed my brother, though bastard-born, and he is indeed Liam's son, freely acknowledged, a captain in my guard. The words I was saying in his place are things he's said to me . . . I used as much truth as I could, lass."

"And the two of you fought each other over a 'bonny lass.' "

"Aye, that we did." He shifted in the Lion. "We're very alike, Rory and I . . . and either of us would be killing the man who meant one or the other harm."

"So. Rory was to come as Sean and emphasize, oh so subtly, that I had an option other than marrying the man I believed I *had* to."

"It *was* subtle, lass. If you agreed to marry the Prince of Erinn, there I was. If you agreed to wed Rory Redbeard instead, exchanging duty for what you wanted, there I was." He shrugged. "It was to be a clean choice, I promise, and made soon after Rory's arrival."

"But then Strahan intervened." I drew in a very deep breath. "You know what he did. You know the result of it."

"Lass—"

"I am not fit for the Prince of Erinn, or even a royal bastard who has every right to inherit if his brother gets no sons."

His eyes were nearly black. "I'll be taking the lass who stands here before me, regardless of the Ihlini. She's a braw, bright lass, and I'd be a fool to want another."

The laughter was painful. "Rory told you that."

Sean fingered his mustache. "We're much alike, lass . . . 'tis why this was dangerous. He's a man for the lasses, my brother . . . he might have won you for himself."

"And very nearly did. That was a *priest*, Sean! What would you have done?"

"Oh, I'd have stopped it. 'Twas what Rory was asking, just before Aileen came. He knew then what we'd done, and how unfair it was." A smile crept out of the beard. "But then we're not certain which of us you meant to name."

And still was not, I knew, which suited me very well. I tossed hair out of my face. "You carried out this mummery to make certain I took the man I wanted. Not because of what he was, but who . . . and now I ask *you*, how do you know I will not wed him? Bastard-born or not, you have proved it does not matter."

Sean held up his hand. "This." Blood stained his palm.

I laughed out loud at him. "You are both of you Liam's sons."

The color drained out of his face, what of it I could see above the beard. "*Which*, then, lass? Which of us do you take?"

I placed the circlet back on my brow. "The Prince of Erinn, my lord."

Sean smiled, grinned, then laughed in triumph, thrusting himself to his feet. And then checked, staring. "To you, that is *Rory!*"

"So it is," I agreed. "I think you had better go."

He was shaking; mail glittered. He had taken himself to the edge, and I had pushed him off.

I waited. He walked stiffly to the end of the hall, all the way to the silver doors, and then swung to face me, shouting, to reach me at the Lion. A powerful, angry shout, full of unexpected anguish. "D'ye want me to fetch him, then? D'ye want me to fetch my brother the way he once fetched me?"

Satisfaction died; I did not want to hurt him. "I want you to fetch us *swords*, my lord . . . swords—and a priest!

If I'm to be Princess of Erinn, it will be done the Erinnish way, after the fashion of the *cileann*."

His voice was clearly startled. "How d'ye know about that?"

"Aileen told me, ye *skilfin* . . . how else would I be knowing?"

Sean began to grin. I could see it clear to the Lion, creeping through the beard. Blond, I thought; it would dye easier.

I sighed. "Were you not taught never to keep a lady waiting?"

He went immediately out of the door, filling the hall with silence.

I watched the doors swing shut, silver glinting in the distance. Then turned slowly to face the Lion.

Fixed in wood, it glared. I glared back. "You have won," I told it, "but then, you always do."

Mute, it made no reply. But no longer did I need one; the question had been answered.

I sat down on the dais, doubling up knees and arms, perching rump on hard smooth marble. Thoughtfully, I said, "He's a braw, bright boyo, the eagle from Liam's mews . . . I think he might just do." I chewed idly on a thumbnail. "If he lets me have a sword."

Appendix I

GLOSSARY

CHEYSULI/OLD TONGUE GLOSSARY
(with pronunciation guide)

a'saii (uh-SIGH)—Cheysuli zealots dedicated to pure line of descent.

bu'lasa (boo-LAH-suh)—grandson

bu'sala (boo-SAH-luh)—foster-son

cheysu (chay-SOO)—man/woman; neuter; used within phrases.

cheysul (chay-SOOL)—husband

cheysula (chay-SOO-luh)—wife

cheysuli (chay-SOO-lee)—*(literal translation)*: children of the gods.

Cheysuli i'halla shansu (chay-SOO-lee i-HALLA shan-SOO)—*(lit.)*: May there be Cheysuli peace upon you.

godfire (god-fire)—common manifestation of Ihlini power; cold, lurid flame; purple tones.

harana (huh-RAH-na)—niece

harani (huh-RAH-nee)—nephew

homana (ho-MAH-na)—*(literal translation)*: of all blood.

i'halla (ih-HALL-uh)—upon you: used within phrases.

i'toshaa-ni (ih-tosha-NEE)—Cheysuli cleansing ceremony; atonement ritual.

ja'hai ([French *j*] zshuh-HIGH)—accept

ja'hai-na (zshuh-HIGH-nuh)—accepted

jehan (zsheh-HAHN)—father

jehana (zsheh-HAH-na)—mother

ku'reshtin (koo-RESH-tin)—epithet; name-calling

leijhana tu'sai (lay-HAHN-uh too-SIGH)—*(lit.)*: thank you very much.

lir (leer)—magical animal(s) linked to individual Cheysuli; title used indiscriminately between *lir* and warriors.

meijha (MEE-hah)—Cheysuli: light woman; *(lit.)*: mistress.

meijhana (mee-HAH-na)—slang: pretty one

Mujhar (moo-HAR)—king

qu'mahlin (koo-MAH-lin)—purge; extermination

Resh'ta-ni (resh-tah-NEE)—(*lit.*): As you would have it.

rujho (ROO-ho)—slang: brother (diminutive)

rujholla (roo-HALL-uh)—sister (formal)

rujholli (roo-HALL-ee)—brother (formal)

ru'maii (roo-MY-ee)—(*lit.*): in the name of

Ru'shalla-tu (roo-SHAWL-uh TOO)—(*lit.*) May it be so.

Seker (Sek-AIR)—formal title: god of the netherworld.

shansu (shan-SOO)—peace

shar tahl (shar TAHL)—priest-historian; keeper of the prophecy.

shu'maii (shoo-MY-ee)—sponsor

su'fala (soo-FALL-uh)—aunt

su'fali (soo-FALL-ee)—uncle

sul'harai (sool-hah-RYE)—moment of greatest satisfaction in union of man and woman; describes shapechange.

tahlmorra (tall-MORE-uh)—fate; destiny; kismet.

Tahlmorra lujhala mei wiccan, cheysu (tall-MORE-uh loo-HALLA may WICK-un, chay-SOO)—(*lit.*): The fate of a man rests always within the hands of the gods.

tetsu (tet-SOO)—poisonous root given to allay great pain; addictive, eventually fatal.

tu'alla dei (too-HALLA day-EE)—(*lit.*): Lord to liege man.

usca (OOIS-kuh)—powerful liquor from the Steppes.

y'ja'hai (EE-zshuh-HIGH)—(*lit.*): I accept.

Appendix II

GENOLOGICAL TABLE

THE HOUSE OF HOMANA

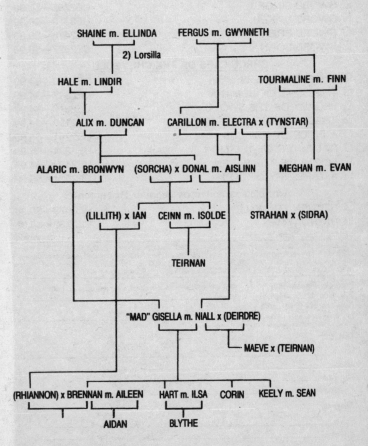

Jennifer Roberson

THE NOVELS OF TIGER AND DEL

☐ SWORD-DANCER	UE2376—$6.99
☐ SWORD-SINGER	UE2295—$6.99
☐ SWORD-MAKER	UE2379—$6.99
☐ SWORD-BREAKER	UE2476—$6.99
☐ SWORD-BORN	UE2827—$6.99

CHRONICLES OF THE CHEYSULI

☐ SHAPECHANGERS	UE2140—$4.99
☐ THE SONG OF HOMANA	UE2317—$4.99
☐ LEGACY OF THE SWORD	UE2316—$4.99
☐ TRACK OF THE WHITE WOLF	UE2193—$4.99
☐ A PRIDE OF PRINCES	UE2261—$5.99
☐ DAUGHTER OF THE LION	UE2324—$4.99
☐ FLIGHT OF THE RAVEN	UE2422—$4.99
☐ A TAPESTRY OF LIONS	UE2524—$5.99

Anthologies edited by Jennifer Roberson

☐ RETURN TO AVALON	UE2679—$5.99
☐ HIGHWAYMEN	UE2732—$5.99

DAW:200

Prices slightly higher in Canada

Payable in U.S. funds only. No cash/COD accepted. Postage & handling: U.S./CAN. $2.75 for one book, $1.00 for each additional, not to exceed $6.75; Int'l $5.00 for one book, $1.00 each additional. We accept Visa, Amex, MC ($10.00 min.), checks ($15.00 fee for returned checks) and money orders. Call 800-788-6262 or 201-933-9292, fax 201-896-8569; refer to ad #200.

Penguin Putnam Inc.
P.O. Box 12289, Dept. B
Newark, NJ 07101-5289

Bill my: ☐Visa ☐MasterCard ☐Amex_____ (expires)
Card#_____

Please allow 4-6 weeks for delivery.
Foreign and Canadian delivery 6-8 weeks.

Signature_____

Bill to:

Name_____

Address_____ City_____

State/ZIP_____

Daytime Phone #_____

Ship to:

Name_____	Book Total $_____
Address_____	Applicable Sales Tax $_____
City_____	Postage & Handling $_____
State/Zip_____	Total Amount Due $_____

This offer subject to change without notice.

ALSO AVAILABLE FROM THE AUTHO[R]
THE GOLDEN KEY

MELANIE RAWN

EXILES

☐ THE RUINS OF AMBRAI: Book 1	UE?
☐ THE MAGEBORN TRAITOR: Book 2	UE?

JENNIFER ROBERSON

THE NOVELS OF TIGER AND DEL

☐ SWORD-DANCER	UE?
☐ SWORD-SINGER	UE?
☐ SWORD-MAKER	UE?
☐ SWORD-BREAKER	UE?
☐ SWORD-BORN	UE?

KATE ELLIOTT

CROWN OF STARS

☐ KING'S DRAGON	UE?
☐ PRINCE OF DOGS	UE?
☐ THE BURNING STONE	UE?

Prices slightly higher in Canada

Payable in U.S. funds only. No cash/COD accepted. Postage & handling: U.S. book, $1.00 for each additional, not to exceed $6.75; Int'l $5.00 for one book, $ We accept Visa, Amex, MC ($10.00 min.), checks ($15.00 fee for returned orders. Call 800-788-6262 or 201-933-9292, fax 201-896-8569; refer to ad #1

Penguin Putnam Inc.
P.O. Box 12289, Dept. B
Newark, NJ 07101-5289

Bill my: ☐Visa ☐MasterCard ☐Amex_____
Card#_____

Please allow 4-6 weeks for delivery.
Foreign and Canadian delivery 6-8 weeks.

Signature_____

Bill to:

Name_____

Address_____ City_____

State/ZIP_____

Daytime Phone #_____

Ship to:

Name_____	Book Total
Address_____	Applicable Sales
City_____	Postage & Handli
State/Zip_____	Total Amount Du

This offer subject to change without noti

In a
sw[ ]
sup[ ]
des[ ]
a y[ ]
tor[ ]
sur[ ]

☐ K[ ]
☐ F[ ]
☐ T[ ]
☐ C[ ]

Price[ ]

Payabl[ ]
book, [ ]
We ac[ ]
orders[ ]

Pengu[ ]
P.O. B[ ]
Newar[ ]

Please all[ ]
Foreign a[ ]

Bill to[ ]

Name_[ ]
Address[ ]
State/ZI[ ]
Daytime[ ]

Ship to[ ]

Name_[ ]
Address[ ]
City_[ ]
State/Zip.[ ]

THE HOUSE OF HOMANA

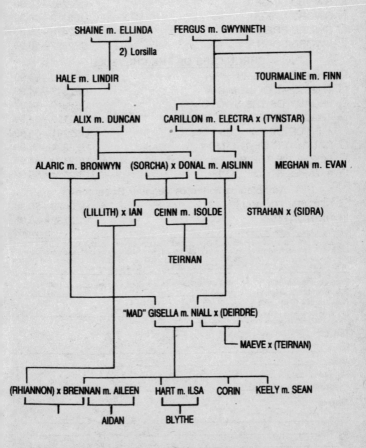

KATE ELLIOTT

CROWN OF STARS

''An entirely captivating affair''—*Publishers Weekly*

In a world where bloody conflicts rage and sorcery holds sway both human and other-than-human forces vie for supremacy. In this land, Alain, a young man seeking the destiny promised him by the Lady of Battles, and Liath, a young woman gifted with a power that can alter history, are swept up in a world-shaking conflict for the survival of humanity.

☐ **KING'S DRAGON**   0-88677-771-2—$6.99
☐ **PRINCE OF DOGS**   0-88677-816-6—$6.99
☐ **THE BURNING STONE**   0-88677-815-8—$6.99
☐ **CHILD OF FLAME**   0-88677-892-1—$24.95